Also by J. L. Larson

- Book I: The Raid at Lake Minnewaska

- Book II: The Disappearance of Henry Hanson

- The Assumption

- The Accident at Sanborn Corners... and
  Other Minnesota Short Stories

'The Choices of Adam Bailey'

Book III:
A Minnesota Lake Series Novel

J. L. Larson

Library of Congress Control Number: 2021924773

HARDBACK: 978-1-956803-95-2
PAPERBACK: 978-1-956803-94-5
EBOOK: 978-1-956803-96-9

Ordering Information:

For orders and inquiries, please contact:
1-888-404-1388
www.goldtouchpress.com
book.orders@goldtouchpress.com

Printed in the United States of America

In the first novel of the Minnesota Lake Series, 'The Raid at Lake Minnewaska', it was Saturday, June 6, 1931, during the huge ten-day opening summer celebration in Glenwood that the happenstance took place. At one of the finale events…a charity golf tournament…five people's lives crossed paths that would prove to have dramatic impact on their futures.

It was a fluke how they even met at the secluded Chippewa Lodge golf course located five miles south of the town. Two of the five were law school buddies, James Lawton and Charlie Davis. They never intended to be in the town that weekend. Two others, a father and son, John and Adam Bailey, lived on a struggling, barely productive farm on a bluff overlooking the grandiose and beautiful Lake Minnewaska. The final member of what would become an accidental alliance was Lindy MacPherson, an inexperienced investigative attorney from the Minneapolis branch of the U.S. Attorney's office. She was assigned to go undercover and find any evidence of a rumored gambling operation, an alleged shelter for wanted criminals and a possible booze running operation transporting alcoholic products from Canada where Prohibition wasn't against the law. The assignment was not supposed to be a particularly hazardous task.

All five of them became aware of a major illegal enterprise secretly run out of that lake resort by members of the Chicago mob. That venue would include an array of 'guests' composed of wanted criminals, escapees, felons, hoodlums wanted for questioning and various members of Chicago crime families. It was obvious a state police and federal officer raid on the Lodge would result in an incredible number of arrests and close down the entire unlawful operation. The problem MacPherson encountered was discovering who was running the whole show. Without that arrest, the raid would be incomplete and not be the law enforcement achievement that it could have been.

With time running out to schedule the raid, she was able to enlist the help of the four males she'd met to find the needed evidence against this king pin. The limited window of opportunity to find that culprit had to happen before the charity golf tournament had concluded Sunday afternoon. At that time players, guests and visitors would be promptly leaving the resort property.

The five of them decided to go ahead with a high risk deception that eventually brought the key gangster out into the open. Their success brought down the Lodge's illicit house of cards including the arrest of the ring maker, a Chicago gangster, Loni D'Annelli. The story could have ended there, however, it was only beginning.

The results of their deceptive actions brought some unexpected consequences. The mob members present at that golf event were irate at being targets of a surprise raid at a place they considered a safe haven. Very soon they began seeking revenge against those who'd caused the intrusion.

It became immediately apparent to the five collaborators their secretive efforts had to be kept in the strictest of confidence to avoid mob reprisals. MacPherson, Lawton, Davis, and the two Baileys pledged confidentiality. Literally their lives would depend on that trust. What would develop was a relationship among them so deep and dependable that they would become like family from that point on.

Unfortunately, the repercussions from their actions against the mob did not end just because of their code of trust and confidentiality. There would be reoccurring instances where each one faced challenges keeping their involvement in that raid at Lake Minnewaska concealed. And, when one of them did run into difficulties, whether a nosy newspaper reporter or a Chicago mobster investigating and getting close to the real story, the other four would promptly come forward to help deal with the threat.

Originally, the private understanding amongst the five of them would simply be that MacPherson stumbled upon the proof that Chippewa Lodge was the base for a number of illegally run businesses. Then she logically called in various branches of law enforcement to raid Chippewa Lodge. No mob reprisals would come toward her since she was depicted as an innocent, inexperienced federal investigator just doing her job. Further, that explanation would not implicate Lawton, Davis and John and Adam Bailey in any way, even though they were crucial in the success of finding D'Annelli and organizing the timing of the raid. Most importantly, they would be free from any mob vengeance.

If only that account of her actions would have worked out the way the five of them had visualized. Within days the mob, the press, and even members of the law enforcement community were doubtful she could have been working alone. There was a belief that the raid had run too smoothly and effectively for her to have found the proof against D'Annelli and organize the expedient timing of the raid by herself. Her unceasing response would always be that she had plenty of support and backing of the state police and the agents of the Bureau of Investigation. In truth, they didn't know anything about the planned raid and her evidence until very early that Sunday morning.

In the weeks…months…and years that followed, rumors would continue about whether Lindy MacPherson worked single-handedly. But, that hearsay would always be thwarted with the help of her counterparts. This would also mean the repercussions from the raid at the Lodge would never be out of sight. Their lives would be effected in various ways and at various times from then on….and only because of that chance meeting they had on that June weekend in 1931.

Book III: 'The Choices of Adam Bailey' now tells the incredible story of the short and long term impact from that raid on the youngest of the five…the eighteen-year old son of John Bailey. Interestingly, as those months and years followed after that incursion at Chippewa Lodge, Adam Bailey would initially have the least problem dealing with the complications caused by the press, the mob, and even law enforcement. It was his father, MacPherson, Lawton, and Davis who primarily had to ward off rumors that MacPherson, undercover for two weeks prior to the raid, had other more personal support in bringing down Loni D'Annelli and putting an end to his highly successful unlawful enterprise at the Lodge.

For the younger Bailey, the aftermath of the police raid and attempts to find anyone who might have supported MacPherson, his involvement was minimal. It required no particular effort on his part to sustain the secrecy since only months later in the fall of 1931 he would become a first-year student at the University of Minnesota. His departure to the Minneapolis campus gave him further distance from the pressures that surrounded the other four individuals. Yet, his move to Minneapolis hardly kept him from developing a closer relationship with MacPherson, Lawton and Davis. He even lived for his first three years in college at the same boathouse apartment on Lawton's Lake Johanna property that Lawton and Davis lived in seven years before during law school.

Young Bailey would enjoy almost four years of college virtually unbothered from any consequences of the Chippewa Lodge incident. At least, that was the way his life flowed as he approached his college graduation in the spring of 1935.

Then, as suddenly as a bell ending a school day, Adam Bailey was thrust into a dilemma coming face-to-face with a couple of the hoodlums who were regulars at Chippewa Lodge and participated in that 1931 charity golf event. After all, it wasn't as if he wasn't well known at the former Chippewa Lodge. During his high school summers he not only worked at the Lodge but he played golf with many of the so-called 'guests' at that lake resort. Above all those factors, he just happened to be the permanent caddy for the leader of the entire unlawful enterprise, Loni D'Annelli himself.

Suddenly that last spring of his college career, he would learn very quickly the raid at the Lodge, the deception perpetrated against those golfers and other 'guests' attending that golf tournament, and even the death one month later of D'Annelli were all very raw remembrances to those hoodlums involved at the time.

For Adam Bailey if that chance meeting with MacPherson, Lawton, and Davis was flukish, this happenstance of meeting a couple of those gangsters once again four years later would bring a second twist of fate. The situation would require him to make a number of choices that would invariably impact his immediate and long term future as he determinedly made the effort to preserve the secret pact with his other four collaborators.

Chapter 1

Milan, Italy – City Jail
Thursday, April 1, 1940

When the guard in the Milan city jail shoved Adam Bailey roughly into his cell, the young man was impassive until the guard was out of earshot. Then he let go with a volley of emotion filled invectives... of course all said under his breath. His frustration, fear, and anger had been at a constant high pitch since his surprise arrest at the Milan train station just a short time before. His captors offered no explanation why he was being detained; he was told simply he was being taken to the Milan jailhouse. What had been particularly disconcerting was how the Italian military police had literally been waiting for him when the train stopped in Milan.

While being handcuffed, he'd loudly complained, "I have bags on the train."

One of the officers grunted, "We have your bags. Please follow us."

While being transported in a noisy military truck with two husky guards sitting beside him, he'd not put up a fight but determinedly kept inquiring why he was being arrested. The only answer he got was one of the surly guards hissing at him in broken English to stay quiet and that he'd hear soon enough.

Bailey kept mulling over how he could be in these circumstances. The Italian government, although certainly no friend of the U.S. in that spring of 1940, was showing no fairness or humanity. He'd done nothing obvious against the state other than fulfilling what he considered a minor favor for a Minnesota acquaintance back in the Twin Cities...and the Italian authorities shouldn't even be aware of that act of generosity. He'd been asked to simply deliver a suitcase over the Italian border to be given to that man's relatives. He'd done the same favor in some previous trips into Italy over the past year- and-a-half with no repercussions. He'd never asked what was in the travel bag, but he wasn't naïve. It had to be money to assist the downtrodden old country family in their struggle to survive under the Fascist regime led by Benito Mussolini. Bailey felt no guilt in performing the task. In fact, he felt a sense of gratification. It neither took much effort nor caused him much inconvenience.

Arriving at the dilapidated looking city jail in handcuffs, he was forced down a dark winding staircase to the basement where a sickening number of cells were split by a long, dingy corridor. Prisoners looked up at the latest addition to their miserable surroundings. As their hollow, fearful eyes peeked up momentarily, each prisoner then quickly jerked his head down promptly to apparently avoid eye contact with his captors.

The smell and conditions in the cells as Bailey shuffled along were appalling. It caused him to show more resistance by insisting he be able to see the commandant...that what was happening was all a huge mistake. The response had been the butt of a rifle landing squarely on his left shoulder blade. The shock of the pain had left him breathless as he waited for a guard to open a heavy metal barless door. All other cell doors had bars. He was being given the most secure and isolated cell in the entire block.

As his handcuffs were removed, Bailey spoke in a more restrained voice. "Why am I here? Ask me anything. There is no reason for me not to cooperate. Just let me talk with someone."

There was again no response. The cell door was locked. Before leaving, one of the malicious guards barked through the steel door in broken English, "You'll get your chance, Senore. The commandant will see you tomorrow in his office. Until then, if you are wise, you'll remain quiet."

Alone in a semi-lit cell from a stained vertical window high up the cell wall, he sat down on a hard slab that was supposed to be a bed. A dusty blanket was thrown over to one end of the slab; his arm would be his pillow. There was little doubt he was receiving harsh treatment reserved for someone having serious charges against him.

Minutes passed into hours in the dreary cell with no sound but muffled groans from fellow prisoners down the dirty corridor. Only when the vague light diminished from the tarnished thick glass window at the top of his cell wall did Bailey have some sense that night had finally fallen.

What kept eating Bailey as he sat on the slab in semi-conscious bewilderment was how the Milan policia had become familiar with his arriving at the train terminal. How could they have known? He'd only made the decision to pass through northern Italy in the past couple days. Few others knew his destination was Lugano in southern Switzerland. His flight to Marseilles, France had left him with the choice of taking the longer route by train up to Geneva, Switzerland and then continuing across the mountainous terrain of that neutral country. But, he was an experienced traveler. He preferred the shorter route across northern Italy from Marseilles to Lugano via Genova and Milan. He'd passed into Italy so many times in the previous four years with no incident. This jaunt was not going to require an overnight stop anywhere in Italy.

Oddly, he was going to take the longer route through Switzerland until his acquaintance back in the States again asked him to drop off a suitcase for his family in Milan. With a shrug Bailey had agreed. Knowing the deteriorating circumstances in Western Europe, he also knew he'd likely have fewer other chances to help the Italian family. There was no reason not to do this one last favor. And, by taking the short cut across northern Italy he'd be saving so much time.

Finally a lone bulb was turned on in his cell and a tray was shoved under his cell door. The pungent smell of a hot liquid and a bowl of mush were being offered for his evening meal. The nauseating smell permeated his cell serving to deaden any hunger pangs. He didn't move from his cement slab bed; he had no urge to touch the sickening grub.

Minutes later a guard opened the cell to check on him. Seeing the untouched food and drink, he scoffed, "Senore, in time you will find this food quite edible."

Bailey didn't say a word.

The guard picked up the tray, slammed the cell door shut, and trudged down the long basement corridor yelling at the groans and cries within the other cells as he passed. He warned the prisoners to stay quiet or face a beating. His truculent words had their effect. The moans became barely audible as the guard slogged up the stairwell.

Returning his focus on the possible reasons for being jailed, Bailey wondered what could have put him in this situation. The guards had to have already been through his luggage as well as the suitcase of his American acquaintance. They would have found his clothing and a camera....normal things a traveler carries. They'd probably found the secret compartment where he'd hidden a revolver. That could be explained given the dangerous times in Western Europe. But, it was the contents of the suitcase he was delivering that should have caused some immediate questions. Although he'd never checked, there had to be enough currency in the parcel to catch someone's attention. How could it not be considered cash being smuggled into Italy?

He ruefully smiled. Then again, maybe those military police who arrested him had confiscated the case; the money might already have been divvied up amongst themselves. He would soon find out if the contents of that suitcase were never brought up during his interrogation the next morning by the city jail's commandant.

He lay back on the slab figuring his acquaintance's family members living in Milan had to be distraught over not receiving the parcel. They might think he'd kept the contents of the bag for himself.

Then he shook his head. That wasn't likely. He'd proven his trustworthiness as a courier. His hope now was that the family might find out about his arrest and already be fighting for his release. Moreover, he held out a further hope for assistance if his detainment went longer than a day or two. The individual he was to meet in Lugano, Switzerland should wonder where he was. Andre Pizzorno, a Swiss businessman, was waiting to meet and discuss with him some plans for a smoother entrance and exit in and out of Italy as the military and political circumstances situation in Western Europe continued to deteriorate. Certainly Pizzorno would communicate with cohorts back in the States of Bailey's disappearance.

What Bailey wasn't allowing himself to face was whether the Italian authorities would have any other reasons to suspect his true purposes for entering Italy. It was verifiable he'd been doing business representing a U.S. food and wine distributor for almost five years in Western Europe including Italy. Certainly the Italian authorities wouldn't have any idea he'd been doing what he considered minor work for the U.S. State Department since 1938. That work had developed when it was learned by one of that Department's assistant directors of his European travels and his fluency in Italian. Bailey had been asked and agreed to observe military installations and other military build-ups as he journeyed around Italy. His efforts had gone far beyond what the State Department could have expected. By the end of 1939, though not yet at war with Italy, the State Department had accurate evidence where key supply centers and war material manufacturing were located thanks to Bailey's initiative and resourcefulness.

But, for all that sub rosa work, Bailey never considered himself a true spy. He was only an international representative for his American company, Northwest Distribution, Inc. based in Minneapolis, Minnesota. However, by 1940, that rationalization ended as his business had under gone change. Conditions caused all his Italian clients to become former clients. The Fascist government had closed down all shipping channels of Italian products to the Western Hemisphere. Mussolini wanted all Italian productivity aimed at helping Italy become a respected military power, especially in the eyes of Nazi Germany.

In April 1940 Bailey was about to make his first sojourn into Italy without his usual business credentials as his cover. Prior he'd never been arrested for any of his quasi-intelligence work in Italy. That meant he'd never even been stopped and questioned as he inconspicuously took photographs of Italian military and industrial sites during any previous travels in Italy. There was no reason the Italian military police should suspect him of doing anything covert.

His puzzlement as he sat there in that dirty cell contributed to what would become a very restless night. It provided extra time for another thought....in particular, how his life since graduating from college almost five years before had seemed to intrinsically place him on a path to the very egregious situation he was now in.

There had been a series of happenings at the very crossroads of leaving college and entering the outside world that occurred in a remarkable short period of time. Those instances had caused him to make some seriously life altering decisions… including his agreement to work for the State Department. Without those choices he'd made, maybe he'd be playing golf with friends back in Minnesota instead of dealing with such life and death circumstances in an Italian jail. Maybe he'd be living a more sedate life than the extensively traveled one he pursued in the previous five years. Maybe with the world scene seeming to be falling into another major conflict, he might have chosen a military career given his father's background as an influence. Or, his life might have been dedicated to something more self-aggrandizing. What would have happened if he'd followed his original whim after college and become a professional golfer like Byron Nelson, Sam Snead or Ben Hogan? He had an impressive amateur record in the sport. Where would he be if he'd succeeded as a professional?

But, things had happened...some out of his control...that had required him to make choices that had led him along questionable trails. And, he could not ignore that one episode in his life had been the true catalyst for why he'd had to make certain decisions during college and his life since then.

He thought specifically of that summer of 1931 before he entered the University of Minnesota. The odds of him meeting three people on a June weekend back in his home town and then they having such an everlasting impact on his development and his decision-making....well, those probabilities were incalculable. He'd been introduced to imperturbable Jamie Lawton, a Twin Cities lawyer and top amateur golfer in the state by his father after Lawton had made an emergency landing of his biplane on the road next to the Bailey farm to avoid an approaching thunderstorm. Lawton's friend from law school, Charlie Davis, then came into the picture as he drove to Bailey's hometown of Glenwood, Minnesota to meet Lawton. Davis only lived up the road in Alexandria. He was a real estate attorney and had made himself into a self-made millionaire in that arena as the rest of the investment world since the Wall Street collapse in 1929 had fallen apart. With his constant joking and casual style, no one could guess Davis was becoming such a financial success.

Then there was the irrepressible Lindy MacPherson, now the wife of Lawton. She'd strode into Glenwood at the end of May as an undercover investigator assigned to find any truth to rumors of a gambling ring. She had not only authenticated the gossip, but soon discovered a major center of illegal businesses at the very isolated lake resort where Bailey worked during the summers.

How innocent he'd been not seeing what was occurring at Chippewa Lodge. Then again the same could have been said about his father, John, to say nothing of the local citizens of Glenwood.

But, the innocence had evaporated as she'd shared her evidence about the illicit businesses being run out of the Lodge....first with Lawton and Davis...and then with Adam and his father as she asked for all of their help in unmasking the man who ran the whole enterprise at the lake resort.

The result of their furtive actions had been astounding going far beyond what any of them believed could be accomplished. What they hadn't counted on was the furor they'd caused among the gangster community. Recriminations were quite real if any of them were discovered to have conspired in setting up the record number of arrests, the destruction of the lake resort illegal business operation, and the arrest of one of the slipperiest cons out of Chicago, Loni D'Annelli himself.

The threat of discovery was so real that they'd formed a pact to not only stay quiet about what they'd done, but to protect each other from any hearsay hinting that they might have been involved in the take down of the mob at Chippewa Lodge. Over that summer and from then on, the five of them became close...and stayed very close.

Bailey often marveled how the five of them were never found out by anyone... not the mob, not law enforcement, not local townsfolk, not even the press. Certainly there were dicey times while he was in college the others had to face; yet they'd kept him safe. As a college student, he'd been fortunate never to have encountered any adversity. At times he didn't even know the close calls Lawton, Davis, Lindy MacPherson, and his own father John had to divert or overcome.

Then, as if lightning struck, in just one night just a week before his University of Minnesota graduation, his good fortune simply melted.

Thinking about that time, Bailey lay back on the hard cell slab and couldn't help but smirk recalling that exact time when one choice that had seemed so inconsequential had propelled him onto a path where there had been no turns. That decision had caused a defining moment in his future influencing his life right up to that very minute as he sat in his Italian jail cell.

A piercing cry echoed down the smelly corridor between the series of basement jail cells. A fellow prisoner apparently had had enough of his hopeless plight. He wouldn't stop screaming.

Finally, the plodding steps of a guard could be heard as he trudged down the staircase toward the tormented man. Bailey couldn't see anything, but he could hear everything. A cell door was opened; there was a scuffle until the cries of the prisoner were silenced. Keys were heard locking the cell door once again and a discomforting quiet returned to the dark, musty chain of basement jail cells.

Bailey closed his eyes tightly to try to erase the probable scene in that cell. He forced his mind away from his surroundings to visualize that time in May, 1935. He hadn't seen his former roommate for a couple years, but now to make the intolerable more tolerable, Bailey forced his brain to focus on the image of Dan Dykstra, one of his best college friends, and the man who'd steered him to that crucial decision five years before.

Though it seemed like a lifetime ago, Bailey was able to envision his roommate's ever present smile. He chuckled remembering how the two of them kidded each other incessantly. They had so many differences but how well the two of them had gotten along during their fourth and final year of school in their Larpenteur Avenue apartment in St. Paul.

He let out a strong sigh wondering how life would have turned out had he not surrendered to Dykstra's urgent request that one Friday just a week before graduation. There was not a doubt in Bailey's mind his previous five years would have been entirely different had he simply said 'No' to his imploring roommate.

He tried to remember what had caused him to surrender to Dykstra's pleas? Had there been any way he could have dodged the urgent request? Bailey concentrated hard and recalled the innocent conversation with Dykstra trying to decide if he'd truly had a choice.

Chapter 2

May, 1935
St. Paul, Minnesota

"So, Adam, have you picked up your cap and gown yet, or are you going to wait for the last minute like normal?" It was his college roommate, Dan Dykstra, in a kidding mood and feeling pretty cocky following some encouraging interviews that morning with a major banking institution in downtown Minneapolis. At least for that day, he felt he had the world by the tail.

Adam Bailey was shuffling through his casual shirts and not paying attention to the flippant comment. He yelled out from another room, "Dan, you going to join Charlie, Jamie, and me for a round over at Midland Hills this afternoon, or is it your preference to wait for the telephone to ring from that damned bank?"

After knowing each other throughout college and living together for the last year, the two of them were hardly sensitive to each other's comments, snide or otherwise. While Bailey laughed, Dykstra ignored the playful dig. "Nah, I'd like to play, but I have other things on my plate. For one, I've got to drive over to Wisconsin and help my father finish inventory at his store. I promised him I'd be there. I'll be back tonight for that bash at Carol's apartment. She'd kill me if I stood her up."

It was a Friday noon at their apartment off Larpenteur Avenue in St. Paul near the new University of Minnesota golf links. Bailey hadn't been concentrating on finding full-time employment as diligently as Dykstra. In fact, he'd not interviewed with any company. Upon graduation his only plan was to continue his part-time jobs for the summer while practicing and competing in some national or highly notable amateur golf tournaments around the U.S. He figured to make some further decisions about his career ambitions based on how he achieved in golf during the next few months.

That afternoon he was looking forward to playing golf with his two very close friends and mentors, Charlie Davis and Jamie Lawton at their private golf course. Midland Hills Country Club was located just a few blocks away. Davis and Lawton were twelve years his senior, but more like brothers to him in the four years he'd known them.

He'd often thought how lucky he'd been when those two fellows showed up for a charity golf tournament at the Lake Minnewaska lake resort he worked at during his high school summers. And then that June weekend happened shortly after his high school graduation in 1931. The result was, among other things, a dramatic change in the pattern of his father's and his life after that incredible weekend thanks to Lawton and Davis....as well as Lawton's wife, the former Lindy MacPherson.

Of course he'd known his future was going to go through a vast transformation anyway with his first year of college coming up that fall at the University of Minnesota, but meeting those three people helped create a college life made more enjoyable and productive. He recalled how he was the only kid in his high school class who had applied and been accepted at the large, respected school. His classmates were doubtful. They kept saying he'd get lost in such a large university. In the four years as a student he'd proved them wrong.

The two Lawtons and Charlie Davis had a dramatic effect on John Bailey as well. When that weekend was completed Charlie Davis and Jamie Lawton had agreed on a deal that helped John rid himself of the unprofitable family farm and do so for a more than fair price. Adam was amazed how his father's entire outlook on his future changed during his son's first year in college. Among other things, John lived his winters along the Gulf coast in Florida and Mississippi. In the warmer months he'd return to Minnesota having gotten involved in some business matters with Charlie Davis. His father now lived along the east shore of Lake Minnewaska two miles south of Glenwood...and then leave the cold area for parts south when the snow began to fall each November.

For Adam the alteration of his father's life was something he never thought possible. The two of them had been dealt a tremendous blow with the death of his mother and sister back in 1925 in a car accident. While they both had to live with the burden of the tragedy, his father had never truly recovered. The extra weight of the failing farm had also contributed to his father's ongoing downheartedness.

Then his father and he met Lawton and Davis. Those who knew the Baileys before that June weekend and then meet them four years later at Adam's college graduation would hardly recognize the father and son for the vicissitudes made in each of their lives.

Now Adam was getting ready to move on from academics and his college life to what promised to be a more nomadic existence with his upcoming summer of golf tournaments. He was looking forward to the challenge.

Finding the right shirt and slacks to wear for golf, Bailey stayed quiet as he gazed over and watched his friend finishing up yet another job application. Dykstra was a serious-minded guy from just over the border in River Falls, Wisconsin. He was hoping to get into law school by the fall, but needed a job in the interim. Then it would be juggling the job with the law school classes and study time. But, Bailey had no doubt his friend would meet and exceed his own challenges. Dykstra was focused. There was no doubt the guy would be successful.

However, his roommate had one other task in his life that Bailey was pleased he didn't have to face. Along with everything else, Dykstra had to make time with his girlfriend, Carol Jamison, a junior at the local private girl's college in St. Paul, St. Catherine's College. Bailey simply didn't have that kind of time...or at least he didn't want to make that kind of time. Or, maybe it was just that Bailey hadn't met any female who intoxicated him like Carol did to Dan.

Bailey knew her as a nice Catholic girl from an apparently well to do family living along the bluff on Summit Avenue overlooking downtown St. Paul. Dykstra had been entranced with her since he met her a year before. He liked that she was down-to-earth and didn't strut her family's good fortune.

As much as Bailey respected his roommate, he watched Dykstra constantly juggle his time. It just wasn't worth it. Bailey dated enough to sense the time investment and got cold feet usually after just two dates. Dykstra took notice and kidded how any female likely wouldn't invest their own time in a third date with Bailey anyway.

But, Bailey definitely had the edge in teasing Dykstra, especially with his roommate always rushing to hurry Carol back to her private college to avoid curfew problems. That factor alone wiped out any thought in Bailey's mind of dating any of Carol's friends at St Catherine's College.

Dykstra was quick with the silver lining. He'd claim the curfew gave him more study time. It was a feeble comeback and both knew it. Nevertheless, with Dykstra about to graduate with honors, that point became more valid. Getting into a law school that fall was a forgone conclusion; his roommate was just trying to find the right school with some kind of scholarship inducement.

Bailey, on the other hand, had been a decent but unmotivated student. He studied well enough to maintain his solid 'B' average despite being chided constantly by Lawton and Davis for what they considered second rate grades for a valedictorian of his high school class. It took Jamie's wife, Lindy, to remind the two men that Bailey's grade point average was on par with theirs when they were in school. Lawton, and especially Davis, argued that because they weren't valedictorians, that whatever they achieved academically in college was, in fact, over-achievement.

His father, John, just smiled when he saw the grades each quarter and told his son how proud he was of him. That was the only voice that truly mattered to Adam Bailey.

Bailey had another feather in his cap that made his grade point average a bit more acceptable. Being captain and a leading scorer on the University golf team, he'd gotten plenty of exposure in meeting people around the Twin Cities. Even at Midland Hills, he had various members advising him to make a career out of professional golf. That life had risen in respect and public attention thanks to various nationally known golfers like Gene Sarazen, Horton Smith, Walter Hagen, and the up and coming Texans, Byron Nelson and Ben Hogan.

Bailey had the game and the confidence to actually consider golf as a career. He just wasn't certain if he'd like the nomadic life and the uncertain pay checks. By the middle of May, just two weeks from graduation, he'd made plans to explore whether he could make a living out of golf. He'd registered to play in several national amateur and received two professional golf tournament invitations in the coming summer. June through August would be his testing ground for evaluating his resolve and skill. With enough money saved to finance six months of travel and living expenses, he was excited by the adventure. Trying to qualify for the U.S. Open in Chicago just a week after graduation would be his first stop. The possibility that he wouldn't succeed never entered his mind.

During May when he wasn't studying for finals, he practiced and played every day...rain or shine. He was blowing his competition off the golf course. Jamie Lawton was even insisting on handicap strokes when they wagered. Bailey of course knew better. Whatever the kibitzing, both knew when they teed it up, their match would be head-to-head even up.

As for betting on a match with Charlie Davis, the negotiation was far more challenging but very necessary given Davis' inconsistent play on the golf course. Both Lawton and Bailey knew Davis' skill level varied like the weather, so there were more side bets during the round to balance whether he was having a good or bad day on the links.

Bailey had always appealed to the Alexandria lawyer's sympathy about being a penniless college student. It was untrue, but with Charlie Davis, Bailey said whatever needed to be said to negotiate a more advantageous wager. Seeing Davis reach in his pocket to pay off losing bets was a particular joy for both Bailey and Lawton.

It was that Friday of the third week of May; however, that Bailey detected some unnatural awkwardness from Dykstra just minutes before he was to leave for his golf match. His roommate was half-heartedly working on another job application, eyeing Bailey, and obviously having a hard time broaching a subject that might involve begging.

Gathering his keys and wallet before walking out the door, he looked curiously at Dykstra and finally snickered, "What, for Christ's sake? Will you just spit it out?"

Dykstra snorted not realizing he was being so obvious. Almost sheepishly he asked, "When are you going to be done golfing with Charlie and Jamie?"

Bailey shrugged, "Maybe 5:00 and then we'll probably have something to eat at the club. Why do you ask?"

Dykstra then put on that desperate look that only a good friend could get away with...and let his problem flow as if a dam had broken. "Carol's got this friend at St. Catherine's College who lives down the hall in the same building.

She's also from St. Paul and broke up with her boyfriend about a month ago. Carol's trying to help her come back from the dead. Can you help us out and be this girl's date tonight? It's a spring social at the college. These things happen rarely at that school so it's a big deal to the girls at her school. It'll only be from 8:00 to about 10:30 so we're not talking a huge time investment. Besides, from what I hear, the girl isn't half bad."

Bailey rolled his eyes and looked at his roommate like he was nuts. "I hope you're kidding. Thanks, but no thanks. I do not want to spend a Friday evening at a nunnery sipping tea and eating stale cookies with some girl who is described by my good friend and roommate as a girl who 'isn't half bad'! That means she's only half good."

Another importunate look followed. "It's not tea and cookies. It's actually a lively time. I attended a similar event last autumn and ate myself sick. Those folks at St. Kates will do anything to bribe a bunch of males. They'll load you up with food. They even allowed some music outside down by the pond for a dance. It's great. It's a girl's school, so for once you'll get stared at instead of the other way around. Come on Adam, it's only for a couple hours. I told Carol yesterday I'd find her friend a date. I had you in mind when I made the offer. You've got to say yes."

Bailey truly had nothing else on his agenda, so he could do the favor. He just couldn't come up with a good enough reason to say, 'no'. Knowing better, he finally caved in figuring every now and then a guy should do a favor for a friend. Two and a half hours with free food wasn't going to kill him.

But, he didn't say 'yes' so easily. He countered, "Dykstra, you owe me. I'll do it just because I like you owing me. At least tell me her name so I can practice saying it. Do I have to call her 'Sister' before I say her name?"

Dykstra again ignored his friend's sarcasm. "Her name is Ellen or Ellie or Esther something like that. Edna…that's it…it's Edna!"

Bailey said no more and continued walking out the door with his golf clubs over his shoulder. Dykstra sensed the commitment was too tenuous and ran after Bailey shouting, "Adam, I really appreciate this. Now, for God's sake, don't forget. Let's leave here about 7:30 and go over to St. Catherine's together. I'll drive since your car looks like hell. Also, it might be nice if you take time to talk with your date for a few minutes before you start filling your mouth with food at this spring social. By the way her name is Edwina……or maybe Wendy. God dammit…I can't remember. Anyway, I'll find out before we leave."

Bailey shook his head. His roommate really made him want to meet this girl of a thousand names. The evening promised to be a real losing proposition. At least it would end at 10:30. He knew a late night café on Snelling Avenue where he could later eat some real food….and say hello to a waitress he'd taken out a few months back.

The golf with Charlie Davis and Jamie Lawton was competitive and fun like always. Ending the eighteen-hole match about 5:30, they stayed at the club bar snacking and having a couple beers. Despite Davis being the least skillful golfer amongst the three of them, he'd negotiated far too many strokes and yanked $5 from each of his opponents. Lawton was not pleased, especially with Davis' gloating at the bar. He kept reminding Davis the payoff was only a loan. The next time they played...which was the next day...he fully expected to fleece Davis of the five dollars...and another ten to boot. Despite the banter amongst them, Bailey sensed Lawton and Davis had some other things on their mind...just like Dykstra had earlier that day. They'd been trying to talk him into law school; maybe they were again going to attempt to persuade him to apply. Yet, for the summer he was glad they supported his desire to try the vagabond life of a traveling golfer... at least until he grew tired of it, found it too expensive, or judged his game not to be strong enough to compete. Besides, playing some national golf tournaments wouldn't keep him from checking out some law schools.

As they talked Bailey found their conversation actually drifting away from the law. They had a more deep-seeded concern regarding his trip down to Chicago for the U.S. Open qualification. From four years before there were plenty of gangsters from that city who played in Loni D'Annelli's final charity golf event back at Bailey's hometown. It was very possible he could run into some of those hoods from Bailey's Chippewa Lodge days where he'd worked every summer during his high school years. He'd even become if not friends, then on friendly terms with many of them.

Their worry was not so much if he played poorly. Lawton and Davis surmised he'd be just another face in the crowd of players who didn't make the cut. The unease was if he played well and qualified.

As Lawton stated succinctly, "Adam, your game is good enough that you are highly capable of qualifying. Your name would be in the newspapers. A good number of D'Annelli's former friends living in the Chicago area would recognize your name in the *Chicago Tribune* sports page. They would remember you as a real favorite of that Chicago con, D'Annelli, and that you caddied for him during the summers while you were in high school. It would be natural they might come out to watch you play on the second day of qualifying just for old time sake. After play was completed, it would be normal for any of these guys to invite you out to dinner, even put you up for the night so you could relive old times with them and maybe play a round of gold the next day at their club. It wouldn't be that any of those hucksters would suspect you of any wrongdoing at Chippewa Lodge, but they certainly might want to hear your perspective on the whole Loni D'Annelli affair.

Adam, you should know that their efforts to get you talking would relate more to the rumors still flying around that after the police raid there was still some D'Annelli money stored in other places in Glenwood besides the money found in the basement of Henry Hanson's Feed & Grain Mill. Stirring up their attention on this possibility would not be in the best interest of any of us...and we can now include Henry in that concern as well. And, let's face the primary concern. Many involved in that whole D'Annelli affair, including the gangsters, the townsfolk and even the press still have a hard time believing that one person.... Lindy....found the evidence which set up the police raid timed just right for him to be caught red-handed at the mill with his illegal contraband and profits.

Your father, Lindy, Charlie, Henry and I still have to douse the flame of controversy whenever something raises interest about what really happened that Sunday, June 7, at the Lodge. Adam, the bottom line is that we just don't want you accidentally putting yourself or us in jeopardy. You've got to be very careful if you see any of D'Annelli's old gang."

Bailey responded with a bit of bravado. "Jamie, we can't be hiding forever from the those gangsters staying at the resort. There's been a lot of water over the dam. What could cause them to suspect any one of us? Back then, Lindy got a free pass from mob vengeance because she made it look like she was just trying to do her secret investigation and simply stumbled over the evidence at the Lodge. Isn't it time we quit being so paranoid?"

Davis and Lawton looked at each very conscious that their young friend hadn't faced some of the backlash they'd had to overcome in the past four years. Davis, normally being the last man to be serious, cast some stern words in the young man's direction. "Adam, we're talking about something very important to all six of us. We never can take what we did four years ago lightly. It's not paranoia. It's plain good sense. All of us have to be ready for any surprises that could occur. And, when you travel into the home territory of D'Annelli's friends, you are vulnerable and by association, so are we. Retribution will always be on their mind where they think it's deserved."

Bailey didn't want to appear insensitive. He responded, "Guys, we've talked about this in the past. You've coached me again and again what to say if I ever cross paths with any of those fellows from back in the D'Annelli days. Simply said, I'll play ignorant and talk to them only as old acquaintances if the circumstances arise. As for my plans for trying to qualify in Chicago, I'm not about to go carousing the evening after the first round. I'll get up on the second day, finish the tournament, and get the hell out of the city promptly. I won't be going out to dinner with anyone. I'll be keeping a very low profile."

Lawton and Davis glanced at each other and seemed satisfied. Nothing more was said on the subject as the conversation quickly turned to the following morning when the three of them were scheduled to play with one of Lawton's clients. John Fena was not a good golfer, but he was entertaining. They called him the 'ditch-digger' for his penchant for hitting more turf than ball on his golfing excursions.

It was getting on toward 6:45 when Bailey finally departed Midland Hills. He knew his roommate would be squirming back at their apartment if he was too late and not ready for that night's blind date. Lawton and Davis had acted thrilled that he was going out that night...for their own selfish reasons. They both voiced hope Bailey would stay out all night and show up on the first tee Saturday morning looking like death.

Davis had summed it up by turning to Lawton and saying, "Jamie, if our young golf pro can make it an all-nighter, we should be eating steak tomorrow night. It should be easy money on the golf links tomorrow morning."

Then smiling at Adam, he added, "Have fun tonight. Sleep is overrated."

Dykstra was indeed waiting impatiently when Bailey finally sauntered into their apartment. He tried not to show it, but he was greatly relieved. "Christ, I thought for certain you were going to blow off this double date. Hurry up and shower. It's time to go!"

Bailey was ready in ten minutes while his roommate paced. They took off in Dykstra's 1934 American Austin Roadster. He had just purchased it when the price was dropped from $375 to $355. It was a lot of money for a new college graduate with no full-time job, but it was all part of Dykstra's strategy. He figured he had to look successful.

Arriving at the St. Catherine's College gates about 7:30, they drove straight to Cecelian Hall to pick up their dates. Bailey kept asking what his 'not half bad' date looked like and kept inquiring whether she had any teeth missing. He was holding out hope the food being served at the spring social would make up for what he expected to be a thoroughly wasted evening.

Marching into the hallowed halls of the woman's dormitory, they strutted straight up to the dorm housemother sitting at a bare table except for the book she was reading. Bailey did notice with some relief it wasn't the Bible. She had blue hair, wire glasses and carried a look that could dissolve sperm. As her eyes narrowed there was no doubt she considered them reprobates of the lowest order solely put on the earth to ruin the reputations of at least two young maidens matriculating at the private girl's school. Dykstra had faced her many times and he was still intimidated.

Bailey leaned over to his roommate and whispered, "Maybe I should hug and kiss the lady just for further shock value."

Dykstra rolled his eyes trying not to visualize that particular horror.

The housemother's nasal voice cackled with not one ounce of warmth. "You gentlemen can go down to the waiting room. The young ladies will be summoned."

Her statement made it sound like she'd call the girls when she was good and ready...and that might not be until sometime the next day.

Dykstra said 'thank you' in a voice so echoing of a sycophant Bailey couldn't help but guffaw. The blue-haired lady scowled over her wire rims. Dykstra quickly grabbed his roommate's arm and pulled him down the hall to the waiting room. He knew Bailey didn't give a damn and just might perform what he'd threatened to do with the straight-laced housemother. The kiss and hug to the stern guardian of womanhood could end Dykstra's ever being allowed through the virtuous gates again.

As they trudged back down the hallway, Dykstra whispered, "If that old bat had her way, every one of these girls would be a nun. I think her goal is to have no more male-female procreation and therefore end civilization with our generation. I'm certain this social including the dance down by the pond is a personal disappointment for her."

Bailey nodded. As far as he could see, Dykstra had the lady's purpose in life well defined.

Dutifully they waited with four other "gentlemen" in the small waiting room. This time it was Bailey who showed mock discomfort. "Dan, you don't suppose that old witch would throw a grenade in this room just to eliminate six potential fathers and thereby preserving the virtue of six of her girls."

Dykstra didn't say anything. He only nodded showing Adam's comment was definitely a possibility.

Five minutes later Carol Jamison with her friend walked into the small waiting room. Bailey was at first dumbstruck. He'd not expected his blind date to be anywhere nearly as attractive as she was. In fact he was stunned. She had long auburn hair, a very full smile...with all her teeth...and sharp green colored eyes. He was speechless and suddenly wasn't focused on the food being served that evening.

Introductions were made and the four of them walked out of the cramped waiting room to the front door of the dormitory. Bailey's date was named Anna. Dykstra's guess as to her name had not been close. Her last name was muddled in the awkward initial niceties. He was so intent on hearing her first name, it didn't matter. He figured if he liked the girl, he'd find out her last name soon enough.

"Don't be late girls!!" The piercing sound of the old blue-haired housemother echoed down the hallway. She was doing everything not to let an on-campus social taint the reputations of her wards.

As soon as they were out the door, Anna pretended to gag saying, "That old bag has caused more guys to run away from this campus than free beer someplace off campus. If one of her girls ever got knocked up, she'd only believe it was immaculate."

Bailey immediately appreciated her humor.

Then she pulled out a pack of cigarettes from her purse and offered all of them a smoke. The night was starting out with a bang. When she saw Dykstra's new Austin Roadster, Anna cried out, "Carol, marry your date or I will. I'll give you until morning to make the decision or I'm going to have his baby. Let's take a spin, Danny-boy. We've got time before we have to show up at the social."

The four of them dove into the car with Bailey and Anna sitting close in the backseat. He found himself liking how she smelled, how she looked, and couldn't imagine what was going to come out of her mouth next. She was a hoot as she prodded Dykstra to pick up more speed. She kept repeating, "Is this all the faster this machine will go, 'Danny-boy'."

They flew up Cretin Avenue toward St. Thomas College. There he took a left on Summit Avenue toward the River Road where the vehicle could be opened up even more.

As they just made it onto River Road, Anna yelled out, "Hey...we're just a couple minutes from my folk's home. Let's stop by. I want to get a sweater in case we go riding around later."

Dykstra nodded and Anna gave him directions. Within five minutes they were driving into a stately mansion with a horseshoe driveway. The hedge along both sides of the driveway was perfectly trimmed and high enough so people at street level couldn't see anyone on the property. The entire presentation of the gardens and the nursery items around the lawn and house indicated wealth.

Both Dykstra and Bailey looked at each other with widened eyes. Anna's father obviously did O.K. whatever he did for a living. They stopped by the front door. A couple men in suits and ties were standing outside as if they were coming or going to a party. However, the way they gazed sharply at the approaching car, Bailey had a strange sensation he'd seen this type of behavior before. He just couldn't place it.

One of the men standing in the shadows called out, "Hi sweetheart. You got a little date tonight, huh. You gonna go dancin?"

She smiled at him while getting out of the car. Bailey watched as she leaned towards the man in the shadows and kissed him on the cheek. He heard the man break out in a huge appreciative and guttural laugh. It was obvious Anna could do no wrong in that man's eyes.

Then she blurted out sardonically, "Uncle Tony...you betcha...we're going to kick up our heels at a social at the college. Talk about dull. But, we'll probably go driving around later, so I've got to get a sweater."

Bailey could hear his response. "That's why your daddy sent you to that college, sweetie. He wanted dullness and safety for you. But, you and I know different, don't we?"

Then the large man named Uncle Tony exploded into a raspy laugh with Anna giggling along with him. Dykstra, Carol, and Bailey just sat back in the car with the top down and chuckled unconvincingly. They wanted to appear like they knew what Uncle Tony and Anna were joking about...which of course they didn't.

Then as Uncle Tony turned and disappeared further into the shadows, Anna looked back at her three acquaintances and offered, "Hey, why don't you guys come on in. I'll just be a moment. Maybe my father is home. He'd get a kick out of meeting you."

The three shrugged and got out of the car under the focused eye of two other men who remained emotionless and straight-faced. As the four college students entered the huge house, Anna directed them to the library. "I'll be right back. My bedroom is upstairs."

Dykstra and Carol ambled around the library obviously taken in with all the beautiful paintings, statutes and the rich oak shelves teeming with old books. Bailey just stood at the entrance to the large library looking up at the twenty foot ceiling trying to imagine the cost of that one room alone. A sense of unease passed through him as he meandered slowly over to a window looking out onto the back patio and at more gardens. The whole place was elegant. He saw some men sitting around a table smoking and drinking and very involved in whatever they were discussing. Two others were playing chess. The other men just sat showing little interest in doing anything else but imbibing and taking a drag on their cigarettes.

In the next instant Anna's footsteps could be heard tapping hurriedly down the wide circular staircase. As she entered the large library, Bailey saw something that startled him. There was a portrait above the fireplace apparently showing her entire family. Anna looked much younger so the picture had some age on it. By her height, he guessed she was the oldest of the six children pictured. The mother looked very conservative and matronly. As for her father, there was something familiar about him. He wore a forced smile. Even though he was seated in the portrait, Bailey could see he was not a tall man. There was some gray hair around the temples making him look very distinguished. It was the man's eyes, though, that were the most striking feature. They displayed a confidence that literally radiated from the painting.

As Anna bounced toward the three of them, Bailey simultaneously saw some envelopes on the desk. For a moment he lost his breath. They were addressed to a Mr. William LaCurso.

He felt a cloud suddenly encapsulate his body followed immediately by a jolt as if lightning had hit him squarely between his eyes. He was in the house of Willie LaCurso, a well-known businessman in the Twin Cities area…and a purported racketeer. In fact, Bailey knew there was nothing 'purported' about it. LaCurso and his people controlled much of the sales and distribution of grain in and around the five-state area. More frightening was this man, this father of Anna, was also the same Willie LaCurso who played golf for so many years up at Lake Minnewaska with his good friend, Loni D'Annelli. Bailey had caddied for D'Annelli too many times to count when LaCurso was in the same foursome. The gangster never talked with Bailey, but he had to have noticed the kid growing up each summer through Bailey's high school years.

There was no question in Bailey's mind if he happened to meet LaCurso, the man would soon recognize him…maybe even right away. Bailey had filled out some but hadn't changed that much in four years.

He couldn't believe not two hours before he'd had been talking to Lawton and Davis at Midland Hills Country Club about being careful never to put himself in a situation where he had to converse with individuals participating at that last charity golf event at Chippewa Lodge in 1931. Now here he was at the home of one of D'Annelli's best friends in crime. His blind date was none other than Anna LaCurso, the oldest daughter of Willie and Sarah LaCurso.

His mind began spinning. He edged toward the front door hoping Dykstra and Carol might follow. But, they were pointing at some rare books and didn't seem in any hurry. To her credit, Anna was ready to leave. It had dawned on her that seeing her father might put some restrictions on her evening.

All Bailey could think about was his unbelievable bad luck. If he ran into Willie on the street, it would be a different story. The older man wouldn't know him at all. But, in this setting Willie would be focused on the young man taking his daughter out on a date...like any father would.

Bailey's heart beat faster and more impatiently seeing his roommate and Carol were causing the delay. They even sat down at the piano and Carol began playing something classical. He found himself shouting, "Let's get back to St. Catherine's. We'll be late for the social."

Dykstra gave him an irritated look. All previous times Bailey had been speaking of the occasion with comical dread.

Bailey finally grabbed Anna's hand and began retreating out the front door. She seemed to like his forward action and began staring at him with a new kind of interest. The two of them had known each other thirty minutes, but something was clicking. She normally took control when dating...something that didn't square well with most men. With Adam Bailey she liked his self-assuredness. She thought he was a bit thin, but he was a half a foot taller than her, so she figured he was just another starving college student. She wondered what it would be like to make out with this blind date in the back seat of 'Danny-boy's' new car.

Bailey was interested in her as well, but at that moment any romantic thoughts were not gelling. He just wanted to leave.

Finally Dykstra and Carol came out the front door as Adam and Anna jumped into the backseat. That was when Bailey heard a voice that was peculiarly familiar only lighter and more affectionate in its tone.

The voice called out, "Anna, honey, is that you? Come give your old man a hug and kiss. I haven't seen you for a week."

Anna smiled and slipped out of the car towards her father. She whispered to Bailey, "I'll be just a moment. Let me say hi to Daddy."

In the next moment Willie LaCurso was standing out the front door of the rock framed entry. To Bailey's surprise the slight man hadn't changed much in four years. He did, however, appear more relaxed as his daughter gave him a big hug and kiss and whispered something endearing into his ear. She knew how to charm because he melted. She was obviously very much loved by her father. From what he could see, the feeling was mutual.

As Bailey leaned back hoping not to be seen in the backseat, Anna returned with her arm around her father. She piped up, "Daddy wants to meet all of you. I guess he can't believe I actually go out on dates."

She rolled her eyes playfully making her dad laugh. Getting out of the car, Bailey kept his head down and tried to stand to the rear of his roommate and Carol. With the sunlight disappearing and the couple blocking him from being viewed, he hoped not to be recognized. That whimsical wish disappeared in the next few seconds.

The introductions ensued with Bailey being last. She simply referred to her father as Willie. She kidded, "Everybody calls my Dad 'Willie'...except for his children of course,"

Willie shook hands with Carol, then Dan, and then with Bailey. There seemed to be no acknowledgment of past times on LaCurso's part with only first names being said. Bailey's relief was palpable. He moved back toward the car not wanting any more time to be spent on this ordeal than necessary.

It was Carol who wouldn't stop talking. "Willie, you have such a beautiful grand piano. I couldn't help but play something on it. I hope I didn't bother you or your guests."

Willie smiled very graciously. "No, I'm glad you played. It was the only way I knew someone was in the house. Tony hadn't had the chance to tell me Anna was home."

Bailey's heart was practically in his mouth. The last thing he wanted was some chit-chat with one of the... if not the...top gangsters in the Twin Cities. Unfortunately, Willie was also in the mood to talk. Having not seen Anna for a week, he wanted to catch up on her life. He said to the group, "So, tell me where do you young men go to school?"

That trite little question made Bailey's blood freeze. Dan chimed in. "Well, Adam and I go to the University. We're both about to graduate. I've been dating Carol for a long time. I invited my roommate along tonight to be Anna's escort for the St. Catherine's social tonight."

That statement seemed innocent enough. Yet, like any father, Willie took a renewed look at the tall college student standing in the shadows who was his daughter's date. He came closer to Bailey as Anna pulled him out of the shadow. Bailey now felt as naked as a newly sheered sheep.

Willie studied the face and his forehead creased. Within seconds he asked, "So, your name is Adam, is it. I wonder...have we met before?"

Anna, Carol, and Dykstra looked surprised. Bailey wanted to crawl into a hole. After four years of not once coming into contact with any individuals who played golf at Chippewa Lodge, he was suddenly being placed directly into the sights of one of the key players at the D'Annelli charity golf tournament.

He had no choice. He had to play it straight. Responding with factitious youthful energy, Bailey brightly responded, "Of course we have Willie. You probably can't recognize me because I've grown a bit. I'm Adam Bailey...from Glenwood, Minnesota. I caddied for Loni D'Annelli at his Chippewa Lodge charity golf tournaments and saw you often when you played in that event. That last time we saw each other was the summer before I started college."

Then Bailey sadly added, "I know you and Loni were great friends. And, I guess you know that Loni was like an uncle to me through all those summers when I worked out at the Lodge golf course. I remember being crushed when I heard of his death in Chicago."

He watched LaCurso carefully as he spoke. He was laying his story on thick hoping the older man would be convinced Bailey only cared about what had happened to Loni D'Annelli and not about the conman's background. As closely as he examined Willie, no indication was forthcoming. Their gazes at each other were equally riveted.

The silence between the two began to border on discomfort until LaCurso finally blinked. His eyes brightened and he responded, "Of course, Adam. I certainly remember you. You've grown so much since you caddied for Loni all those years. He spoke so highly of you. You're right. We all thought you were related to him somehow."

Bailey nodded sensing no more was needed to be said.

The older man then escorted the four young people back to the Austin Roadster, glancing constantly toward Bailey as he spoke to all of them. "Well, you kids have fun tonight, but not too much fun."

His laugh had an edge to it. Dykstra, Carol, and Anna laughed and nodded obediently. Bailey nodded unsmilingly.

As Anna and Bailey scrunched into the back seat, Willie still wasn't done. He leaned toward the car as he stared at Bailey. "So Adam, you must be about through with school if it's been four years?"

Bailey nodded, "Yes sir. I graduate from the University a week from Saturday."

He hoped that repeated statement would end their conversation....but it didn't. Willie replied, "So....what are your plans then?"

Wishing his roommate would just accelerate the car forward, Bailey was being forced now to share more conversation. Still appearing friendly, he proceeded very carefully. "Well, I've got some irons in the fire and I play on the college golf team so I plan to test my skills in a couple national tournaments coming up over the summer."

LaCurso brightened. "Well, Adam, if there is anything I can do to help you, feel free to call me. After all, I have some history on you. I know you were a good kid and something like that doesn't change. I guess my daughter wouldn't be going out with you if you weren't a decent fellow. Anna obviously has my phone number."

Bailey patiently smiled and thanked the man for his thoughtful gesture. His actual thoughts were that it would be a cold day in hell before he sought help from a notorious gangster at the level of a Willie LaCurso. He then turned his attention to Anna, Carol, and Dykstra and more animatedly said, "I guess we'd better go. The social won't begin until we show up."

Everyone dutifully laughed and Dykstra finally pulled away toward the front gate of the LaCurso mansion. The car completed the horseshoe driveway and entered onto River Road. Bailey looked back and saw LaCurso waving and leaning over to say some words to the men standing outside. He knew he was the topic of their conversation.

As they drove on, Anna, Carol, and Dykstra were laughing at something. Bailey was a million miles away but smiled widely so the other three wouldn't suspect anything might be wrong.

Chapter 3

The St. Catherine's College social was actually far better than Adam Bailey could have guessed. The four of them were enjoying each other's company and relishing the tasty food items. Compared to the cuisine the two young men generally prepared at their apartment, this was a banquet.

Nonetheless, Bailey kept looking at his watch waiting for 10:30 to roll around. Anna was absolutely a fun date, but he'd determined that as the young princess of a very wealthy underworld figure, she could have her way with most everyone and everything. She could drop him like a piece of dirt the moment she might get bored with him. He figured this would be another first and last date.

Then, as the evening progressed, he was getting quite the opposite reading from her. She sat a bit too close to him. She touched his arms and shoulders a lot when talking to him. When he got her some lemonade she referred to him as 'such a dear'. If that was all that was required for him to be a 'dear', he acknowledged that the evening was certainly going in the right direction. When the dancing started, she was practically attached to him. Normally he would have loved the intimacy, but this situation was altogether different. He felt as if he was walking a tightrope. He was not turned off by Anna, just by her father. The thought of seeing her father again put chills down his spine. He was determinedly trying not to show too much interest in Anna. His attempt at distancing himself from her seemed only to make her more determined...as if she was not used to a male not giving her absolute attention.

As the evening social closed in on 10:30, his attempts to show Anna her feminine charms were being wasted on him weren't working. He'd already decided that as soon as this date was completed, he was going to return to the University and marry the first girl he saw on campus on Monday just to end any subsequent interest Anna might have in him.

After the last dance, Dykstra came up to his roommate and whispered, "So, she's not half bad, is she? In fact, by the way she's been carrying on with you, I don't know if you'll get away with your supposed virtue still intact."

Bailey only nodded. "No, she's not bad,"

Dykstra rolled his eyes. "Adam, the way she dances with you, you two could be in a family way nine months from now."

They both chuckled over Dykstra's low level humor until Bailey showed his true feelings. "Well, Dan, I guess we'd better get the girls back to that blue-haired bat at their dormitory before she sends out an infantry division."

Dykstra patiently smiled and shook his head. "Roomie, sometimes you're deaf, dumb, and blind. Just so you know, both girls signed out for the night and told the housemother they would be staying at Anna's house for the night. Adam, wake up to opportunity. They have no curfew. My boy, this night could get memorable...yes sir, very memorable indeed."

Bailey for once had no interest in what Dykstra was implying. Any relationship with a daughter of a notorious Twin Cities crime figure wasn't going to happen...as beautiful and interesting as Anna LaCurso was.

In no uncertain terms he declared to his roommate, "Dan, I've got to meet Jamie, Charlie, and one of Jamie's clients tomorrow morning for breakfast and then we're going to play some golf. They told me not to be late. I've got to be able to function tomorrow."

Dykstra looked exasperated. "Who cares about functioning tomorrow morning? You're young. I've seen you rebound quickly. It's tonight that you want to function!"

Bailey knew he was on weak ground. Dykstra was right. Late hours had never been a problem for either of them. Besides he'd lied. The golf match was at a reasonable hour...10:00 AM.

Then thinking of Anna and her obvious affectionate intent, he abruptly changed his mind. "O.K., my friend, how about we take the girls over to the St. Paul Club. We'll dance a bit and then drop them off at Anna's house around midnight. Will that work?"

His roommate looked at him disappointedly and shrugged his shoulders. "I'll see if they're up for the Club."

Bailey could see a problem arising when the two young ladies nodded enthusiastically to Dykstra's question about the St. Paul Club. They were definitely game. Bailey doubted his roommate hadn't mentioned anything about midnight. Unfortunately, this night had all the markings of seeing a morning sunrise.

The four of them took off from the campus party and sped down Randolph Street to 7th Street on their way to downtown St. Paul. None of them noticed the dark-colored 1933 Aston Martin Le Mans that was following them once they left the pearly gates of St. Catherine's College.

Fifteen minutes later they were walking in the front door of the St. Paul Club. Thanks to Jamie Lawton, Bailey had a membership number to the former speakeasy establishments both in St. Paul and Minneapolis. Moments later they had drinks in hand and had found a convenient table close to the dance floor.

Anna popped her drink down like she'd done with a glass of lemonade just an hour before at the social. "Wow," she screamed above the noise of the small orchestra on stage, "a couple more of those bourbons and that should break down the sugar content of that damned lemonade. Come on, Adam. Let's dance."

Dykstra gave Bailey a smirk as if suggesting he'd better hang on to the saddle because he was in for a long ride. Bailey shook his head knowing what his roommate was thinking. He was still in control. He let Anna drag him out onto the floor. In his mind she was better off dancing than drinking. They danced non-stop for the next hour and a half. The couple even lost track of Dykstra and Carol.

About midnight as Anna went to the lady's room, Bailey went looking around the large dance hall for his roommate. It was time to leave. Ten minutes later Dykstra and his date were still nowhere in sight. He walked out to the parking lot to look for Dan's roadster. He couldn't believe it, but the vehicle was gone.

His temper flared as he wondered what could have possessed his roommate to leave Anna and him high and dry. Something had to have happened. It wasn't like Dykstra to leave Bailey in the lurch.

Returning to the dance floor Anna was three sheets to the wind and dancing by herself. He grabbed her arm and motioned her to a table where he informed her they were going to be taking a cab back to her parent's house. She didn't seem to care. It was going to cost him a few bucks, but at that point he just wanted the night to end."

As they left the Club, she kept asking where they were going to sleep that night. She was hammered. Bailey practically picked her up as he asked the doorman to hail them a cab. As he did so, the 1933 Aston Martin Le Mans drove up. The back door opened and a gruff voice said, "Get in! We'll take you two back to the house."

Bailey looked in the backseat and there was Anna's Uncle Tony. Bailey recognized the huge man right away as someone he'd seen back during the D'Annelli era at Chippewa Lodge. The large man appeared neither pleased nor agitated. He was just taking care of business. Assisting Anna into the backseat of the vehicle, Bailey closed the door thinking his part was done.

The gravelly voice called out, "Come on kid. We'll take you home too."

The offer came out more as an order. He got in the back seat with Anna between Uncle Tony and him. Too tipsy to understand what she was saying, she leaned toward Tony and said, "On hi, Uncle Tony. Are you out carousing tonight too?"

Then she giggled, leaned against his shoulder and fell asleep. Bailey felt like he was guilty of something but couldn't define the offense. Tony just sat staring out the window not saying a word. Bailey decided to share his silence.

Fifteen minutes later they were driving into the horseshoe driveway at the LaCurso home. Her father met them at the door. Anna awoke the moment the automobile stopped. It was as if she had been conscious all night. She looked around gaining her equilibrium and then started jabbering as her father opened the door of the Le Mans.

She seemed pleased to see him and chortled a little too loudly, "Oh Daddy, we had a great time at the social. You should have been there."

She walked toward the house under her own power as if she'd never taken a drink at the club. Turning at the door, she dramatically kissed her own hand and blew the remnants of the gesture toward Bailey as he huddled in the vehicle. He meekly waved and sat back in the seat envisioning how he was going to kill Dykstra.

When Anna was in the house and up the stairs, Tony nudged Bailey. "Let's go in the house. The boss wants to talk."

Again there was no choice.

As Bailey was ushered into the library, it was a place he hoped he'd never see again. The night seemed full of unwanted happenings. With the Willie LaCurso family portrait looming overhead, the patriarch finally walked in.

Bailey began uttering sounds of apology for the lateness of the hour, but Willie cut him off. "Adam, I know where the four of you went from the time you left the house earlier this evening. We didn't expect you to go to the St. Catherine's social, but you all surprised us and did. Then we fully expected the four of you to go someplace else. It was only 10:30 after all, so there's no need to apologize. Tony says you were showing my daughter a good time and were looking out for her. When it got closer to midnight, Tony told your friends to take off and that he'd make certain you two got home safely. So, don't be mad at your friends."

Then without missing a beat he continued, "Anna has been quite broken up over a former boyfriend moving away. She'd been sullen, careless, and prone to drink a bit too much wine of late. I've had to watch out for her. Being my daughter she has to be careful."

He paused to see Bailey's reaction. The young man furrowed his brow slightly to exhibit concern, but that's as theatrical as he got. Bailey knew damn well what LaCurso meant. His daughter could be an obvious target for any of Willie's adversaries...at least those enemies still alive.

Bailey began looking at his watch hoping LaCurso would take the hint. Unfortunately, the older man seemed to have other things on his mind. The night was turning into shear torture. He'd have to prime himself to deal with Willie's questions relating to the last time they'd seen each other four years before. He took a deep breath and waited.

Noticing Bailey was on edge, Willie tried to ease the young man's angst with an attempt at humor. "Like I said, Adam, your friends are fine. They probably needed an excuse to ditch you and Anna anyway. How else were they going to get some of their frustrations out in the back seat of their car?"

He laughed at his own joke.

Bailey smiled thinking back to the crass humor so prevalent when D'Annelli and LaCurso's group of friends were playing golf together at Chippewa Lodge.

Beyond the attempt at comedy, Bailey knew there was more than an element of truth to the comment.

Willie pointed to a leather chair. "Adam, please sit. I appreciate so much you taking my daughter out this evening. You proved again what a fine young man you are. We haven't seen each other for a while. I've added a few more gray hairs. You would too with three daughters. I see you have transformed into a very strong looking and mature young gentleman. Tell me about yourself and how your father is doing."

Bailey realized he was being set up but was still gratified that this gangster could remember Adam and his father were alone. The crease in Willie's brow indicated he could be very emotional when it came to family.

He still responded about his father very cautiously. Untruthful or deceptive in any way and Willie might spot a facial tic or body language indicating a lie.

"Well, Willie, my dad sold the farm where I grew up once I came down to the Twin Cities. He also luckily found and married a very wonderful and attractive woman. They've been married for two years."

Willie's smile was genuine in hearing the story. He leaned forward as if he wanted to hear more. Bailey, though, was done.

The older man was unperturbed. He asked more questions centered on Bailey's college years.

Bailey felt safer conversing about his classes and his University of Minnesota golf team experiences. Being a golfer himself, Willie reacted very positively when Bailey told him of some of his more memorable matches. He listened intently and nodded with enjoyment.

Then with hardly a break in sequence, Willie suddenly switched to the topics on his mind. "Adam, what do you remember about the last days of Loni's golf tournament at Lake Minnewaska? As his caddy you were around him constantly. Did you hear or see anything that was strange. Could he have somehow prevented all those arrests and problems he had to deal with...that is, until his untimely death?"

Bailey was impressed how LaCurso had lulled him into conversation about Chippewa Lodge. The man made D'Annelli's illegal gambling scheme and his equally spurious charity golf tournament sound like an innocent vacation among good friends and businessmen.

His head began to ache from the strain of weighing every word, phrase, or sentence. He felt perspiration dripping from his armpit to the waistline of his trousers tickling the side of his body. He had to say something preferably poignant and brief.

He sat back and spoke very slowly. "You know, Willie, I was just a kid trying to make a buck as a caddy. I earned some good money from Loni, so I really only paid attention to him. That's why we became like uncle and nephew. We cared about each other. As I grew up I could see he was proud of the way I behaved and certainly the way I could compete in golf. The summer before my junior year of high school, he and I often teamed up against a lot of his buddies. It was a great time in my life....and I can't remember ever losing."

He hadn't answered Willie's question, but he'd given a response that showed his affection towards D'Annelli...and it was the truth. He really had felt pain when he'd heard Loni had been gunned down in Chicago.

Willie nodded silently as if not expecting the young man's heartfelt but not very helpful response. He tried again. "I understand. I felt the same sadness. But, tell me, did you know much about Loni when he wasn't in Glenwood?

Concentrating hard, Bailey again shaped his answer by dodging the real intent of the question. "No... not much. I learned that he stored a lot of his business profits in the basement of the Glenwood Feed & Grain Mill. I thought it made sense since both banks in town were struggling to keep their doors open."

Willie remained patient doing everything to keep the conversation flowing. "Well, given the number of times I traveled up to Lake Minnewaska, you could probably tell Loni was a friend of mine. We went back a long way. He was involved in the construction business in Chicago. There were a lot of jealous people who wished they could get the same contracts with the city of Chicago and with the Cook County Building Commission like Loni was able to obtain. As a result, he had some enemies. In fact, there were some opponents who even played in his charity golf tournament each summer. You might have heard some comments about him that weren't very nice."

Willie was serious, but Bailey turned it into a joke. "Yeh, Willie, I heard them all the time! When he was playing various guys for some big money on the golf course, I heard every threat in the book against Loni. All he did was laugh and collect his wagers. He had a very competitive game."

Then for theatrics, Bailey leaned forward towards LaCurso and lied through his teeth. "Seriously, Willie, I heard nothing that had any serious intent. In fact, I heard quite the opposite. In town the man was beloved. He contributed to the churches and civic projects. Everyone in Glenwood who knew him was quite taken with his friendliness and his generosity."

It was still not the kind of responses Willie had hoped to hear. He changed his direction and kept asking. "How about that MacPherson woman...the one from the U.S. Attorney's office...did you know her very well?"

Bailey answered deceptively. "Yes. She was in town for a couple weeks. Like my dad and a lot of citizens, we all thought she was a writer for a travel magazine. We all were surprised when we found out she was undercover just innocently checking out a rumor of a gambling ring in the area. From what I heard she basically stumbled onto some questionable things going on at Chippewa Lodge. I guess she recognized a couple guys staying there who were wanted by the law. Then she just did what would be expected of someone in her line of work. Being way over her head, she called in the state patrol. When they realized there were more than a few...ah...law breakers...at the resort, they decided to raid the place."

Willie shook his head showing his doubts. "Yes, I heard the same story. But, it has always seemed peculiar how a young, inexperienced female could have stumbled onto Chippewa Lodge. Then D'Annelli gets arrested because he kept a lot of his profits from his Chicago businesses at that feed and grain mill basement rather than some unstable banks. You should know Loni had little to do with the stuff the authorities discovered at that lake resort. There was a gambling operation...and some booze running...and maybe a few cons were holding out there...but it was some other guys who were guilty, not my friend, Loni. I just know that he liked the community and was able to relax at Lake Minnewaska and play golf or fish with a lot of his friends who followed him up there."

That was the first time Willie LaCurso had blatantly lied. Bailey did everything in his power to keep a straight face. Willie's rendition was playing on the young man's apparent ignorance. Then again, that was the image Bailey wanted the older man to believe.

There was a prolonged, uncomfortable silence before LaCurso lit up a slim cigar and showed that he was done trying to squeeze information out of someone who didn't have any to give. He then re-directed the conversation back toward his guest. "So Adam, you said you haven't decided the direction you wish to take after graduation. With the economy the way it is, finding a job anywhere has to be a difficult task."

Then he gazed at Bailey. "Maybe you should consider working for one of my enterprises. Depending what you want to do, I own some grain mills, some restaurants and nightclubs, and a trucking firm. There might be some worthwhile positions available for a sharp, young college graduate."

Given the friendly nature of the dialogue, it would have been senseless for Bailey to say what he wanted to say. He held back from shouting, "Hell no!" Instead he remained polite and said what any young man in his position might say. "Willie, I actually do have some irons in the fire. That's very generous of you to make that suggestion. Thank you."

Willie stood up indicating their late night conversation was finally over. He reached across his desk to shake Bailey's hand. It seemed a legitimate show of respect and Bailey grabbed the hand firmly.

Willie added, "Again, I appreciate you taking good care of my daughter. It was nice to see her so full of life again. Her former young man left the area without saying good-by to her. He apparently decided to take a job in California. She's not smiled like she did tonight for almost two months."

Bailey saw through that deception with little problem. Willie hadn't approve of the fellow and likely paid him off to leave the state. Anna was not the type of girl a guy would leave hanging."

Another car came up to the front door as Bailey and LaCurso walked outside. No longer was his ride going to be in the 1933 Aston Martin Le Mans. It was a basic Ford V-8 Sport Cabriolet assigned to transport him home.

He gulped for a moment seeing only one man in the car. Bailey glanced in the back seat trusting that there was not some guy sitting there with a rope to strangle him.

Willie again shook Bailey's hand and said they'd be talking again soon. He didn't say maybe. It was more an absolute. He then disappeared into the house.

Bailey's sigh was almost audible. His preference was quite the opposite...like never hearing from the gangster again. As he sat quietly in the passenger seat while some guy named Eddie drove him back to his apartment, Bailey's mind was racing. He pondered whether he should bring this coincidental meeting with Willie LaCurso up to Lawton and Davis...or even to his father. Nothing of real concern had been discussed. They'd only worry.

Back at his apartment it was past 1:00 AM and Dykstra was nowhere to be seen. There was a part of him still agitated with his roommate. The absence also made him uneasy. Anytime underworld figures were involved in the equation, anything could happen.

He slept intermittently that night and got up the next morning before his alarm began blaring. Dykstra's bed had not been slept in. That could mean anything including he'd driven out to River Falls to stay at his folk's place for the weekend. On the other hand, Bailey ruefully smiled allowing his depraved mind to think of another alternative.

By 8:30 he'd made his way over to Midland Hills Country Club for breakfast. Lawton and Davis were already there. They looked like they hadn't left the club since the previous evening, except they had a change of clothes.

They greeted him with typical humor. Davis smirked, "Well, Adam, you look like you didn't do too many things wrong last night. I've certainly seen you in worse condition. It must have really been a lackluster night."

Bailey chuckled and only nodded.

Lawton then told him more about the man who was going to round out their foursome that morning. John Fena, a respected general manager of a local international food distributorship called North American Distribution, Inc., was to be their golfing companion. His company was a national dispenser of specialty foods, spices and wines. He was originally from the Iron Range area around Hibbing and Eveleth. Bailey had met Fena one time and remembered the guy being a real character...in the good sort of way. He had curly black hair and wore thick glasses. He always had a smile on his face. He talked with a laugh and very fast. It was hard not to like the man.

Lawton repeated the description of Fena's golf game as grave digging... meaning the man rarely hit the ball squarely and invariably took a lot of turf with each swing. Lawton had worked with him on his game enough in the past year that Fena could participate in some worthwhile wagering and have some fun on the golf course.

Golf that morning turned out to be great escape for Bailey helping him put aside some of this thoughts of the previous night. He played well and took a few bucks off Lawton and got eight dollars off Davis. But, beating Lawton was the mark whether the round was truly successful. Lawton also beat Davis so the morning was not a complete loss. Lawton kept lightly jabbing Davis in the arm playfully insisting he wanted the same bills he had lost to Davis the previous afternoon. He claimed a desire to take the bills home and wash them. He said the currency did not deserve to spend another day in Charlie's unlaundered golf pants. Davis in turn threatened to pay the lost bet off in change. It was the typical banter between the two friends.

Afterwards the four of them sat down for lunch at the club. Arriving shortly thereafter was Lindy with the Lawton's young son, Matt. Lindy was also pregnant with child number two. She always looked radiant with her beautiful eyes and flowing auburn hair. The luncheon became a real family affair with the young kid sitting in a high chair playing with his food and getting it all over his face. Bailey was used to the sight and automatically wiped the young man's face and placed more bread or pieces of meat on the tray for Matt to make another attempt at eating. Adam was a real favorite of the child.

Lindy had her own game going with Charlie Davis. She was merciless pointing out the sloppiness of his tattered clothing. "Charlie, this is a country club, not a boy's gymnasium.'

Then minutes later she followed up with another barb. "You've worn that shirt after polishing your car with it. You know you could wear that Christmas present I got for you last year? What are you saving it for...to wear at your funeral?"

Davis was used to the jibing. He played like he was hurt, but there was a glitter in his eye as he countered, "Lindy, why get that shirt you gave me dirty. It's only for special occasions....and playing golf with the likes of these three goons does not constitute anything special."

The reactions from the other three men were loud and full of playful derision. It was a while before the good-natured ribbing subsided and when it did, Adam saw his three playing companions looking at each other as if to decide who should bring up the subject that was obviously on their minds.

Finally, Davis began asking John Fena how his business was going. It was awkward but it got the discussion started. "So, John, what's happening with your hopes of increasing some of your international business? A couple months ago you said you were hoping to gain more contacts in Western Europe, particularly France, The Netherlands, Italy, and Switzerland. How's that going?"

Fena scrunched his nose. "It's tough. I have contacts overseas, but no contracts. I could go overseas, but I don't have the time. I have to run the damn business. I just don't have local people with knowledge or skills to build business in Europe. And, of course, language is a barrier for most people or they don't want to be away from their families for extended periods of time. There also could be risks given the tenuous political situations in some countries bordering Germany with their Nazi movement. I guess I've just accepted there's business I have to leave on the table for now. It's unfortunate. The opportunities are there waiting to be picked up. The added challenge is that I'd also need the person I hired to continue going overseas and take care of our new clients.

Bailey swore he saw a momentary glance from Jamie and Lindy. If they thought Fena had just outlined a business opportunity for him, they had a lot more confidence than he had. Bailey couldn't imagine taking on such a responsibility...maybe in another ten years with some appropriate business experience, but not at present.

Nonetheless, he couldn't help but ask Fena, "Does the person you're looking for really have to speak all those languages? That's impossible. And, how much time overseas would be required?"

Fena looked at Bailey with some curiosity before responding. "Frankly, Adam, the people over there speak adequate English. There might be places in Germany, France and Italy where there would be a language barrier, but nothing serious. As for the amount of travel, I would expect the person to be gone for one month to six weeks initially...less when some of that talk about transatlantic flights from New York becomes more than just talk. But, there's no question. There would be quite an investment of travel time in foreign countries.

Fena then reciprocated with a question. "So, Adam, you're graduating. Jamie tells me you want to try your luck in the world of professional golf. I'm no expert, but from what I saw today on the golf course, you certainly have the game for it. I guess in that line of work you'd be traveling just as much as the representative I'm looking to hire."

His comment brought a nod from Bailey.

Fena then added, "You know, if you decide to stay an amateur, we should talk. I have to be honest. When Charlie told me you were fluent in Italian, I told him I wanted to talk to you. And, Jamie tells me one of your strengths is that you are not easily daunted. You'll talk with anyone. Dealing with all kinds of people is a real asset no matter what kind of business you might pursue.

Bailey gazed at the three men at the table. Lindy seemed to know what was going on as well. Bailey was being interviewed. Everything he'd done that morning including the way he handled himself on the golf course, his manner of communication, the way he joked...all this was being scrutinized by Fena.

Fena then asked, "How did you learn Italian so well having not been over in that country."

The question brought sharp looks from the Lawtons and Davis.

Bailey responded with a shrug. I seemed to have an ear for that language. I spent a fair amount of time with some Italians when I was growing up in my hometown."

The answer was good enough for Fena. The Lawtons and Davis sat back and smiled. The response was good enough for them as well.

Fena then leaned back and took a huge drag of his cigarette. "Adam, no doubt you're probably too young, but you might just be able to handle this type of work if we give you some worthwhile training and help you understand the international food business. You've put in a lot of practice time to be a good golfer. I have a feeling you'd do the same thing for us.

He paused pondering his next comment before saying it. "Yeh...it's a good idea. Give the golf a chance. If you change your mind, you and I might have something to discuss.

The talk had gone a bit fast. To slow things down, Bailey joked, "John, if we talk again, you may have second thoughts."

Fena chuckled. "Maybe...but I doubt it. Call me later this week. Let's have lunch. Let me show you the business and meet a couple people at our headquarters in Minneapolis. At least you'll have an idea what North American Distribution, Inc. is all about."

Fena then got up winking at Lawton and Davis. All three sensed the pre-planned lunch had gone well. They all shook hands with Fena and he left.

Bailey sat back down and just stared at his friends. They were grinning.

Leering at them, his eyes softened. "It's nice to have friends like the three of you. Obviously this lunch was a set up for me....the golf was secondary to your real plan. Anyway, I'll talk more with Fena but I think he's crazy to consider me. He needs more business experience than what I've got

Lindy took some of the pressure off. "Adam, it's nice to have some other opportunities to consider. It might even help you relax when you play in the qualifier for the U. S. Open golf tournament if you know you have some other avenues to consider. But, do understand something. His interest won't just stick around forever. He's got a job that needs to be filled."

Arriving back at his apartment, he was somewhat relieved to see his roommate calmly studying for a Monday final. Dykstra seemed completely unbothered by the previous night's surprising departure. His greeting was low key. "So, how did last night go? You and Anna kind of disappeared."

Bailey gawked at him. "You and Carol were the ones who disappeared. Where the hell did you two go? You left me with an inebriated blind date at the St. Paul Club?

Dykstra looked startled. "What do you mean? That guy Tony we saw at Anna's house came up to Carol and me while you and Anna were dancing. He said he was taking you two back to Anna's place and that Carol and I could leave by ourselves when we wished. I wasn't about to argue with the guy. He looked like he could break my neck with one hand. He made that suggestion sound more like there was no other choice. Carol and I started going over to you to say farewell, when that big fellow grumbled at me saying, 'Take off, kid, it's all been arranged. Have some fun with your girl. I'll say good night to your friends for you.' Honest to God, Adam, that Tony guy was scary. We left right away."

Cooled off, Bailey apologized. "Dan, you're right. There was nothing else for you to do. I know Big Tony from my summer days back home at the golf course where I worked. Nobody argues with that fellow."

Nodding, Dan added, "Well, just so everyone is all right. The rest of my night was interesting. I didn't get Carol to her parent's house until after 3:00 last night. Then since I was closer to River Falls than the apartment, I drove to my folk's place and snuck in the back door an hour later. I was half-dead when they woke me up for breakfast this morning at 7:00."

Bailey marveled at his roommate's innocence. He was totally oblivious to LaCurso's profession and the real reason Big Tony was at the St. Paul Club, that is, to protect Willie's daughter.

With the discussion of the previous night no longer important, Bailey threw his friend a beer from their small icebox. Dykstra put aside his studies and they talked about Bailey's golf that morning and the meeting with John Fena. His roommate immediately picked up on the predicament created by Fena's possible interest in hiring Bailey and Adam's preference to follow the more undefined adventure of professional golf.

Dykstra finally shrugged and resolved the problem as a typical college age young man might respond. "Well, it's not as if your entire life is hinged on this one career decision. In three years you could be teaching school, finishing law school, in the military, or driving to your next professional golf tournament. We've got time to make good and bad decisions that likely won't mark us for life."

To that statement, Bailey nodded but didn't mention the interest one of the top gangsters in the Twin Cities had shown towards him the night before. Dykstra would have thought it was fantastic...until Willie LaCurso's real livelihood was mentioned.

There was also something else he didn't tell his roommate. Bailey found himself intrigued by Anna LaCurso. He'd thought about her too many times while playing golf that morning. He now knew the reason she got so inebriated the night before. She was dealing with demons from a past relationship. He sensed she enjoyed herself the previous evening and he'd obviously helped her get rid of the memories of the imbecile would split town.

From Bailey's standpoint, he honestly liked her spontaneous, free-wheeling nature, her sense of humor, and her high energy. The fact that she was beautiful and she had a very interested look when she stared at him didn't hurt either.

As the day continued, he calculated his chances of seeing her again were probably minimal...and it was better that way. 'Besides,' he rationalized, 'she probably wouldn't remember anything about him after a couple days anyway.'

Chapter 4

It had been almost a week since the St. Catherine's College social where Bailey had met Anna LaCurso. Despite the busy week before college graduation on the coming Saturday, he'd found himself thinking about her...and wishing he wasn't. On Wednesday with finals completed and nothing more to do but wait for the ceremonies, he drove over to her college hoping her term had finished and she'd no longer be at her woman's dormitory. He could then justify to himself that he'd tried to see her, but had failed. Once she was back at her home, Bailey figured it would be a cold day in hell before he called on her there. His interest could then wane and he could concentrate on his plans for the summer.

Stopping in front of Cecelian Hall around 6:00, he walked slowly up the steps to the entry and then even slower as he shuffled down the hallway to the house mother's desk. There sitting menacingly at her nest was the same blue-haired crotchety lady at the bottom of the three flights of stairs going up to the virtuous co-eds who were in her charge.

Her eyes cast a disapproving look as he asked to see Anna. She looked at her roster and disappointedly announced, "Well, she hasn't signed out. I'll see if she wants to see you."

The old bat made it sound as if there was little chance of that happening.

Calling to the third floor where there was one phone for the all the girls living on that level, Bailey heard a shriek that echoed down the three story spiral staircase. With some delay the disappointed house mother said in a testy voice, "She'll be right down. Please go to the end of the hall and wait for her. I doubt she'll have much time for you. The girls are packing and leaving for the summer break."

Bailey tried hard not to be sarcastic. "Thanks for your help." He wasn't certain if his voice had been sincere or not.

He'd been sitting for less than a minute when the long haired beauty glided into the waiting room. He'd been thinking what to say to her, but that turned out to be unnecessary. He loved her self-confidence as she unhesitantly kidded him. "So, Mr. Adam Bailey, what took you so long to contact me? There are telephones you know. But, I guess you coming here personally will make up for your oversight. So, what are we going to do... go eat or do you plan on taking me someplace to make out for a couple hours?"

Bailey just shook his head and laughed. He couldn't help it. She was way ahead of him. He responded as if they'd known each for years. "For God sakes, Anna, we already did that after the social last week. I'm a bit disappointed you don't remember. Of course, I'd have to guess at least some of last Friday night might not be entirely clear to you."

She was embarrassed for only a second before countering, "You got me drunk and were going to take advantage of an innocent Catholic girl. Thank goodness my virtue was saved by Uncle Tony when he drove us back to my place."

Again Bailey laughed hard. Between their two brains, he wondered who was wittier...as if the answer really mattered. She was casually dressed with no apparent plans for the night...and she was as attractive as he remembered. He wasted no time as he continued his flirting. "Anyway, I'm here for our date."

She looked at him in mock horror. "What date?"

He responded just as quickly. "The date you told me we were going on tonight. I didn't even ask. You told me we were going out."

For once she was momentarily baffled...until she saw his eyes begin to sparkle. Then she went along with the gag. "Well, you're late. I thought you'd forgotten. I was about to call you and tell you what a louse you are for standing me up."

She was a pistol...no doubt about it. Smiling, he held out his hands as if wondering why the delay. "Well, go get a jacket. We're going out to eat. I'll wait here."

She tried to show some indifference, but it didn't work. She flew back down the hallway and was back in five minutes. She had transformed herself with some make up, combed hair, and a clean outfit. Bailey liked that she could be ready so quickly. It was another plus.

They were out late that night and the next night as well. Along the way there was non-stop conversation as they stopped by a number of cafes and bars. There was also an abundance of making out. Not once did either of them take notice that a black LeMans was following them. Uncle Tony was doing his job.

The two of them planned on continuing what they thought was their secret liaison Saturday evening after Bailey's congratulatory dinner with his family and friends. They even planned ahead for a Sunday night date as well. She'd been done with finals after her junior year for a week but had chosen to remain in her dormitory until the last hour in order to enjoy more freedom from her home life. While Bailey was at his graduation ceremonies, she was moving her personal items only two miles away back to her LaCurso River Road location. To keep their dates for Saturday and Sunday evenings private, they agreed to meet at a Ford Parkway restaurant in Highland Park.

At the Saturday afternoon ceremony, Dykstra and Bailey sat together with hundreds of other graduates at Memorial Auditorium. It had been a great day. His father, John, had flown in from Washington D.C. along with Catherine. They were sitting next to Jamie and Lindy with their small son, Matt, on Charlie

Davis' lap. Davis had tears in his eyes. For a man with a cool business head, he was a shambles when it came to special family occasions.

John Bailey and Dykstra's father and mother met for the first time. John was bursting with pride, although difficult to recognize with his low-key nature. A constant smile was not his custom. As for his wife, Catherine, she made up for her husband's quietness. She and Lindy knew each other well and were in constant chatter. At the end of the formalities all of them had that congratulatory dinner at Midland Hills Country Club.

Unbeknownst to Bailey or anyone among his family and friends, there were two other individuals attending the graduation specifically to see Adam Bailey receive his college degree. Willie LaCurso and his right hand man, Tony Bando, were peering at the spectacle from the back of the huge auditorium. They had other interests besides seeing young Bailey receive his diploma, although that moment even brought satisfied smiles and applause from them as well. They couldn't help it. They'd both known Adam since he was in the eighth grade.

LaCurso and Big Tony did gain what they wanted to see....maybe even more so when they saw the people surrounding Adam. There was Lindy MacPherson, now married with a child in her arms...and another on the way. And there was the young man, whose name Willie didn't even know, who played in Loni D'Annelli's foursome and basically won the first day's Calcutta for his team back in 1931. With his arm around MacPherson, LaCurso immediately understood the golfer and MacPherson had hooked up sometime after that final D'Annelli charity golf tournament four years before.

Then LaCurso recognized the taller, larger fellow who'd been cheering D'Annelli's team onto victory back then. He was loudly applauding and wiping the tears openly from his eyes as Bailey crossed the stage to receive his diploma. And, there also was Bailey's father who Willie recognized from years before. The father was always there at Chippewa Lodge at the end of the day to pick up his son...as if he didn't want his son, Adam, to be influenced too much by the wild bunch who were guests at Chippewa Lodge. LaCurso always had a respect for the Glenwood area farmer after hearing from D'Annelli that the man's wife and daughter had perished in a freak car accident some years before. In Willie's mind, the farmer had done a masterful job of bringing up his son.

What was pleasing to LaCurso was how each of those individuals surrounding Adam looked so happy. Adam's father especially looked healthier and more energetic from Willie's memory of him as a very quiet, downtrodden farmer. He also took note how well the older Bailey got along with MacPherson and the two men at her side. It was as if they were all from the same family. As the two underworld figures departed the graduation ceremonies, they both agreed another conversation with Adam Bailey might be in order...just to clarify how this close knit relationship had developed.

The days after his graduation and those late night dates with Anna LaCurso, Adam practiced long and hard at Midland Hills Country Club for the U.S. Open qualifier in Chicago the following Monday and Tuesday. In the evenings he continued to sneak out if only for dinner with Willie LaCurso's daughter. He had no idea where the relationship with Anna might go. He just really liked being with her. However, in no way did he want to interface with her father...or above all things, become friendly with the man. He was satisfied just to live day to day having a good time with Anna. There was the stage act at the Orpheum Theatre in downtown St. Paul, a party at a golf teammate's home at Lake Minnetonka, and another night just a movie and dinner in Highland Park. Bailey knew he was playing with fire, but it seemed worth it. He kept rationalizing that he was going out with a fantastic girl...not LaCurso's daughter.

As for Anna, she enjoyed the freedom. She was used to her father giving any boy she'd ever dated the third degree. She didn't know exactly why, but for some reason Adam Bailey was trusted. Her father seemed to accept without questions that she was going out with her girlfriends each night even though she had a good idea she was being followed for her own safety. At least Uncle Tony was respectfully keeping a certain distance behind in the Aston Martin Le Mans. Bailey never suspected they were being followed. Each evening he just let her off at her friend's home after midnight. She either slept there or Tony picked her up. He of course reported everything to the boss except how long Bailey and Anna were sparking in the car.

It was the Thursday before he was to travel down to Chicago for the U.S. Open qualifier that they met in downtown St. Paul. They were already talking about where they would meet when he returned to the Twin Cities.

Bailey knew the story she was telling her folks about being with her friends. The tale was getting a bit worn and he was getting a bit nervous. For all the things he liked about her, he also knew she could be reckless. He actually wondered sometimes if they were being tailed, but she seemed unconcerned. As her father's favorite and growing up in relative luxury, her father likely had warned her repeatedly that she could easily become a kidnap victim. That gave Willie the excuse to always have her guarded. Even then, it had been her personal challenge to evade Tony or any other driver who might be assigned to follow her on a date.

She told Bailey after a few dates that her past elusive tactics irritated her father yet made him smile as well. Her recalcitrance was straight from Willie's bloodline. In one of their conversations she told Adam how her father often called her 'Alice

Roosevelt' in deference to the free-spirited daughter of former President Teddy Roosevelt. Anna didn't fully get the comparison until Bailey quoted Roosevelt's famous line, 'I can be the President of the United States or the father to Alice, but I can't be both!' Then she got it.

Bailey sensed no matter what trouble she might create, she never would have a real problem with her father. Like a lot of fathers, she had Willie wrapped around her fingers. Her only real concern was his tendency to squelch too many of her potential boyfriends...at times even before they rang the doorbell for the first time. If a beau should last through a second date, he might find himself under too much scrutiny. This would cause most of those suitors to take themselves out of the game.

She intimated to Bailey how she acquiesced to her father's preference for the private Catholic girl's college located ten minutes away from home. She did this hoping her father might relax a bit. It never really happened.

Anna also let Bailey know about her recent break up with a fellow she'd been dating for two months. It wasn't so much the guy was from an alcoholic family living in the Iron Range, it was when her hockey player boyfriend and she were discovered in the swimming pool storage shed with nothing on but towels after skinny dipping in the family pool very late at night. Her father thought her virtue had been tampered.

The next day some of Willie's boys visited the kid. He had no idea Anna's father could have him ground up in a South St. Paul meat factory with a snap of his fingers. The suggestion was made to the young man that he return to his home in the Iron Range. The kid dissented. LaCurso's boys rolled their eyes knowing this kid was so blessedly ignorant it was almost charming the way he stood his ground.

The young man finally accepted an expense paid trip to California with a job waiting for him in turn that he promise not to be seen in Minnesota for at least two years. It cost Willie some money but his daughter was safe...or so he hoped. What he hadn't planned on was the effect on his daughter. As she said to Bailey, "I have become even more determined to get out of the clutches of my father."

On that Thursday night date, Anna seemed unusually nervous...as if what she had to say might cause some problems between the two of them. She finally sullenly admitted, "Adam, my father somehow has found out about us. He wanted to know where I actually stayed overnight last night. I told him the truth....that you dropped me off at Carol's home. I didn't tell him what time, but at least I didn't lie."

He was angrier than I've ever seen him. He was not annoyed with you. He's used to me playing games with the guards that follow me. He was just disappointed that I would put myself in harm's way by ignoring the protection he'd set up for me. I know he's involved in some big business deals, but I confronted him as to why I had to be under so much security."

She paused....and then added, "Adam, he looked at me as if he was surprised I'd question him. I've complained to him before, but lately the protection has just been relentless."

Bailey didn't say a word fully understanding Willie's motives. He was surprised how she had no concept the kind of world her father was involved. What he didn't know was the number of attempts on Willie's life including some threats to his family members including Anna. With Willie's underworld successes there bred hatred against him on both sides of the law.

One of the more serious situations was following a Saturday night dinner ten years before in downtown Minneapolis shortly after a Calvin Coolidge inauguration party in early 1925. In LaCurso's Republican crowd there was general satisfaction that the somnambulant and lackluster President wouldn't do anything to upset business as usual.

Willie had been sought out at that party. His potential assassin was mowed down before he could get a shot off. The assassin's death was not the only death that weekend. By the next night, Willie's people had uncovered who the plotters were. Within a month these three individuals and a number of their family members were gunned down as they left their respective places of employment.

A more serious attempt directed at Willie's family was after mass in Highland Park during Anna's senior year of high school just three years before. This time a shot was fired at Willie. It missed and hit his wife in her left arm. She recovered. The wound left her mentally traumatized. She became pathological about the safety of her children. It was shortly after that incident that Willie had a series of bodyguards protecting each of his children, especially Anna as she got ready to attend college.

She finally got to her main point. "Adam, my father seems to be preoccupied with a kidnapping scare. I've been hearing that fear since grade school. I'd like to ease his mind and have us talk to him. It helps that he knows your background. He trusts you. No matter what we say to him, though, he'll still want Uncle Tony to follow us. I just don't want him to follow us too closely.

Then her coquettish eyes flashed at Bailey. "...and, I know you know what I mean."

Bailey did.

In some ways he was relieved that the two of them had been discovered. Anna and her clandestine maneuvers against her protection had to end sometime. His growing relationship with her required that he figure some way to deal with her father and hopefully from a distance as much as possible. What helped was Anna's zest for freedom from her father's clutches. He knew it might take a long time to convince Willie to put down the heavy safety net, but Bailey was willing to be patient.

Later that Thursday evening, the two of them decided to enjoy a ride out to the airfield on the other side of the Mississippi River before he would drop her off a friend's house as had been their routine. Finishing a light dinner at what had become their favorite café in Highland Park, Bailey eased his vehicle onto the River Road towards the bridge to Ft. Snelling. That was when Bailey noticed the distinctive LeMans following them. He couldn't believe he hadn't notice the automobile in earlier evenings out with Anna. It irritated him he'd been so smitten talking with Anna he hadn't paid much attention to anything or anyone else.

Anna was already lighting up a cigarette and sharing it with Bailey as they decided to have some fun and lose Tony. With the top down on his old 1931 Chevrolet roadster he'd owned all through college, her hair blew in the breeze. Her eyes were dancing as Adam sped along with his tires squealing on a couple sharp turns. Turning toward the bridge that crossed the Mississippi River and then onto the airfield along the bluffs, they both were laughing as Aston Martin LeMans could not be seen. Bailey took another turn at Fort Snelling after crossing the bridge just to make certain the LeMans would not find them.

Now they were free. Slowing the car, they drove on a side road along a runway of the airfield and watched a transport plane land on the newly lighted runway. As he was scheduled to leave for Chicago the next day, they had to cut the night short. It was 11:15 when Bailey turned his car around and back towards St. Paul. In their conversation they agreed upon his returned from Chicago the next week, they'd talk with Willie and be more straight-forward about their budding relationship.

When they passed back over the Mississippi River bridge, Bailey turned off on the River Road and again hit the accelerator towards Town & Country Golf Course where Anna's friend lived. They laughed and howled as they passed other vehicles. Bailey didn't even notice the dark ominous looking Ford V-8 Sport Coupe moving up behind them. The last thing on either of their minds was that in the next minute Anna LaCurso would be living the last minute of her life... and Adam Bailey would begin an entirely new journey in his own life.

As the sport coupe began moving up too closely on the right side, he could see three men in the trailing car as it passed. They were hunched over as if ready to pounce. Then, like a bad dream, as the car passed one of the men leaned out the side window of the coupe and began firing a repeating rifle. The shells exploded through the right front windshield. The Sport Coupe then sped on. In the turmoil of broken glass and trying to maintain control of his car, his mind was jolted by the sight of blood flowing from Anna's neck and shoulder. He yelled her name but got no response.

Bailey braked and scrunched down in the front seat. Anna's body had been thrown forward onto the dashboard. That horrible image would be displayed too often in his future thoughts.

The gunmen apparently had deduced they'd finished off both driver and passenger and driven on. Bailey reached over to shake Anna's now lifeless body; he wondered when the pain of his own injuries would finally reach his brain.

Not feeling anything, he moved his arms and legs. He felt his head. Miraculously he felt no pain. Unbelievably, he'd not been hit. It was clear he had not been a target. The shots were entirely directed at LaCurso's daughter.

Within minutes, Bailey was in a fog as people surrounded his shot up roadster either trying to help or just scrutinizing the horror. The distant sirens of the police and an ambulance could be heard...but unneeded. Anna was gone and except for the shock, Bailey was sitting at the curb unscathed not believing what had just happened. He had just seen the world of Willie LaCurso and how human beings could be so cruel and violent.

Unfortunately, the death scene would also remind him of the emotional and tragic memories of his mother's and sister's deaths from a highway accident outside of Glenwood ten years before. His mind went into a kind of despair as he wondered if all females who he felt a close connection were destined to die so horrifically.

He hardly remembered the next hour. It was as if his mind was completely separated from the present biosphere. He tried to make sense of what had happened. He kept thinking how Willie LaCurso lived in a violent world....and by relationship, his family did too. And now, though innocent of wrongdoing, she had died cruelly. It sickened Bailey how she had fought to get away from the pathological dominance of her father. Now it was proven in no uncertain terms that Willie LaCurso had been absolutely correct to have a guard on his family and himself at all times. That the LaCurso family had been spared from early death was a testament to how aware he was of the dangers that faced his family. People were out to get Willie LaCurso. When they couldn't get Willie, they went after his family. They had finally succeeded.

Bailey rode with Anna's body to the hospital. He sat in the lobby alone with his head in his hands oblivious to everything and everyone around him. Was he to blame? While Anna either didn't know or didn't care what her father did for a living, Bailey did know. He just didn't take it serious enough that LaCurso's family was so vulnerable. Escaping Uncle Tony's surveillance had been a game. Anna and he had won the game that night and the prize was her death...all because they wanted some momentary freedom.

The next few hours were a nightmare. Bailey watched the ashen face of Anna's father walk into the hospital to see his daughter one last time. Her mother was in convulsions in the back of the family's Imperial Sedan. Uncle Tony's eyes were swollen. Both men saw Adam sitting alone in the hospital lobby but were not yet willing or able to talk with him. There was a look in both men's eyes as if he'd been somewhat at fault for Anna's demise. The look was neither forgiving nor did it show understanding. In fact, Bailey knew by their gaze he would always be associated with her death, likely making him some kind of pariah to the entire LaCurso family.

Having nothing else to do and not feeling like calling anyone, Bailey stayed in that hospital lounge area feeling empty. He wondered if he was simply waiting for some kind of human response from the LaCurso family. By their discomfort in seeing him, he finally realized they were not ready to offer any sympathy towards him.

Finally, Willie LaCurso stood in front of Bailey. Tony stood twenty feet away not able to look at the young man. LaCurso's voice was listless as he tersely said, "Tell me how it happened."

Haltingly, Bailey gathered a breath. "Anna and I were driving down the River Road. We were just laughing when we realized Tony's Le Mans had long since lost us. We thought we were completely free of being watched. I felt she was safe with me at all times. I just didn't know……I just didn't know." His voice just trailed off.

Tony and Willie nodded their heads. It's something they had heard many times before. Anna always liked to outrun Uncle Tony. Often her dates made the attempt. Uncle Tony had put up with the game because he loved Anna like a niece. Very few times did she ever get away. This night he had completely lost Bailey's car....and lost her as a deadly result.

They could see Bailey was devastated over the ghastly shooting. Willie then leaned down by Bailey's ear and said something that made the young man's blood curdle. The older man whispered, "Why is it that whenever I'm around you, eventually someone dear to me loses their life? I don't blame you, but I don't like how this happens. Please understand that I never want to see you again. The vision of you will only tear my heart out and remind me of my beautiful daughter. Do I make myself clear?"

Those would be words etched into Bailey's brain forever. LaCurso did not have to repeat himself. Bailey understood the statement was said from emotion rather than logic. Nonetheless, the young man nodded his head. Any other response was not needed.

A law officer then came up to Bailey requesting time for questions to help their investigation. He silently got up.

Not expecting another word from either LaCurso or Tony, he suddenly felt the huge right hand of Big Tony clasping his upper right arm. Pulling Bailey's ear close to his mouth, he whispered in his gravelly and broken tone, "Kid, do not say anything to the police. Willie will take care of things."

It was as menacing of a statement as Bailey had ever heard. He left with the cop as LaCurso and Tony stared at him ominously. They had a strong confidence he wouldn't say much if for no other reason than mentally he was so distraught.

The police questioned him and Bailey really didn't have much to say. His silence was expected by the authorities given the shooting was nothing more than a gangland murder. The detective took Bailey's name and address saying he'd get back to him at another time. He never did.

The LaCurso family had gone with their daughter's body to the funeral home. Bailey sat there alone at the hospital just hoping he'd find the energy to call the Lawton household. It wasn't happening. He just kept sensing he was living another life. Everything prior to that evening was no longer pertinent to his future. He was experiencing either feelings of immortality or that he was starting all over...as if reborn. Anna's assassins could have killed him, but they hadn't. Maybe they figured he'd just die in the hail of bullets. If that were the case, it was purely divine providence that his life had been spared.

Eventually Bailey would call the Lawtons but it took him until 3:00 in the morning to dial the telephone. Jamie Lawton's voice changed from light-hearted to solemn as Bailey numbly opened the call saying Anna LaCurso had been shot and killed. Lawton knew nothing about the young lady but put two and two together very fast. Adam had not mentioned word one about any young lady to him or Lindy. They knew there was something that happened, however, since he hadn't been stopping by their home after golf at Midland Hills.

When Lawton heard Adam say the LaCurso name, however, it cued Lawton that something drastic had happened. He didn't hesitate. "Adam, where are you? Are you O.K.?"

"Yes. I'm at the hospital. They just took her body to the morgue."

Lawton continued without emotion. "Adam...listen carefully. Leave the hospital now. Grab a cab. Get yourself to the front gates of St. Thomas College on Summit Avenue. I'll be there to pick you up. If anyone is following you, I want to be there to see it."

Bailey mumbled, "Yeh...cab...to St. Thomas. Then his voice got even hoarser. He whispered into the phone, "Jamie, I need your help. You'll be there, right?"

Lawton could tell Bailey was in shock. The young man was not thinking straight. He repeated the location where he'd meet Bailey.

Bailey only responded vaguely. "Yeh...St. Thomas College."

Adam Bailey slumped on the couch at the Lawton's lake home. The brandy offered him sat on the table untouched. When he'd arrived at the Lawton's home he was still ashen-faced. As cadaverous as he looked, he was in no mood to sleep... or talk. Lindy and Jamie Lawton just sat with him in their living room hoping he would eventually let them know what happened.

As the morning haze brightened the night, he finally said a few words. As sympathetic as they were, they had known nothing about his short tryst with Anna LaCurso. Understandably they were particularly curious about Adam's apparent contact and continued communication with one of the key hoodlums in the Twin Cities.

Bailey haltingly spoke of the chance blind date with LaCurso's daughter whose last name he didn't know until she had brought him into her home.

Knowing they'd be concerned, he was more specific as he repeated what got said when he crossed paths with Willie LaCurso himself. The Lawtons were spellbound. That June weekend four years before had again been brought back into their lives. Damage control was likely going to be needed.

When Adam pleaded exhaustion and fell asleep around 5:30 AM on the Lawton couch, Jamie phoned Charlie Davis in Alexandria, Minnesota and summarized what Adam had said. Davis was on the road to the Twin Cities within an hour of the telephone call and three hours later he arrived at the Lawton's Lake Johanna residence. The two Lawtons were having coffee on their patio while Adam remained out cold on the sofa in their living room. He would sleep until noon.

Needless to say, Bailey did not go to Chicago that next day to prepare for the U.S. Open qualification. For the following two days he walked around in a daze at the Lawton house. While he answered every question from Lawton and Davis, he did little else but fish off the dock or sleep.

The consensus was that Adam hadn't had that much interaction with Willie except that first night of the blind date with Anna. There was general satisfaction how Bailey had cautiously maneuvered around LaCurso's friendly but pointed interrogation regarding that June weekend four years before.

Anna's funeral was at St. Catherine's College on Tuesday. Bailey attended and sat alone in the back of the church. No one from the LaCurso family spoke to him or acknowledged his presence. He was treated as if he didn't exist.

The complete disregard for him by Willie and his family did have two effects. There was no question Anna's father and family would always associate Bailey with her death. Secondly, Anna had become a target whether she had been with Bailey or not. Her free-wheeling nature was going to be her downfall and it happened. The fact that Bailey wasn't killed in the crossfire was a miracle.

He left the funeral service with deep sadness for Anna and the potential for happiness they might have had. He also drove away from St. Catherine's College with a new appreciation for his life.

It would be the next day on Wednesday that Bailey again appreciated his close relationship with the Lawtons. His Chevy Roadster miraculously was repaired and sitting in the Lawton driveway.

It was the shot of energy he needed and that day he returned to his apartment. Dykstra was out of town checking out two law schools. On Bailey's agenda now that he'd missed the Chicago U.S. Open qualification was getting prepared for a huge amateur tournament in St. Louis, Missouri. As big as that event was, he was struggling to get motivated. He decided to forfeit his invitation. He still had his part-time jobs at both Midland Hills Country Club and the Lawton law firm that would keep him busy.

Even then he worked the hours listlessly and had to force himself to practice golf in the evenings. The trauma of Anna's death and almost losing his own life was causing him to go through the daily motions of both jobs like a machine.

A week after the tragedy Bailey went over to the Lawton home for dinner. He was early and wandered out to the dock to just stare at Lake Johanna. He wondered how long it would take to get his competitive fervor back.

Lindy joined him on the dock with some lemonade and sat down next to him. She was the closest female friend he had in his life. Her words were soothing as she talked about so many things he'd done in his short life and how bright the world was in front of him. She even put a positive spin on his relationships in his high school years with a bunch of rowdy but fun fellows who just happened to be gangsters and how he'd put that strange experience behind him as he carved out a strong college career at the University. .

Jamie arrived home soon thereafter and joined them. He got more to the heart of the matter very quickly. "Adam, we're truly sorry you've had to go through this horror. From what you've said about her, Anna was the kind of girl so many people would like….but especially one who you'd be attracted. You've told us she was beautiful, fun-loving, intelligent, and how you'd come to really enjoy being with her. I know for a fact that's someone hard to find. I could say a lot of things to try to ease the pain, but nothing but time will eventually allow you…not to forget about her…but to heal. She'll always be special."

He was looking at Lindy as he was speaking and continued, "Adam, you can imagine Lindy, Charlie and I have been talking about you. We can empathize with your melancholy, but you've know the three of us for over four years. We look for ways not necessarily to put difficult times completely out of our minds, but to learn, if we can, and move forward. When you are ready and able, we believe it's better to have some kind of path ready for you to follow. You'll have a better chance to re-energize and let your normal instincts take over. Of course, there are no guarantees where this path might take you, but it's a hell of lot better than being unfocused and depressed.

He smiled and paused, "So….in that light…the three of us have a few suggestions if you're interested?"

Adam knew he needed something to spur him forward. What better way than to listen to those individuals who sincerely had his best interests at heart. He nodded, "How could I not want to consider anything you say?"

Lindy began first. "We're proposing you hold off with your travel and your professional golf aspirations for now. Your mind is about 60% ready to face the challenges of travel, faring for yourself, and trying to put up some decent golf scores on the board. 60% is not enough concentration. You'll fail."

Bailey nodded blankly. She was right.

Lindy continued, "We're going to make a recommendation and it has to do with working for John Fena's company. His willingness to bring you on board is still on the table. At the very least you should assess the company and the offer he might make you. After all, it's not like you're going to be in that same job even five years from now...or if you are, it'll likely be quite a different one than when you first started. And, if you find the work doesn't suit you, it'll likely give you the experience to more confidently move on to other opportunities...even competing in national golf tournaments as a professional or amateur. What you should recognize about the job John Fena outlined was the number of qualifications or requirements that actually fit your skills and abilities. You are completely free to travel. You are reasonably fluent in Italian. And, he's willing to take you forward with him and learn the international business his company is involved."

Having succinctly made her point, the three of them sat on the dock each measuring what just got suggested. Bailey naturally pondered those factors why their recommendation might not work out. The more he thought about it, though, there was nothing contrary he could bring forth.

He finally replied, "Lindy, Jamie, of course you're absolutely right. A change in direction might be very helpful. I've made my life and your lives more difficult with a couple choices I've made....in particular, bringing Willie LaCurso back into our lives being the worst. My actions these last couple weeks could easily have caused problems for all of us including my father and Henry. The overseas marketing job with Fena's company will put me on a more purposeful path that at the very least will pay off in business experience."

He paused for only a moment as if digesting the words he'd just said. Then, with his eyes staring out at the lake, he added, "In the morning I'll call John Fena and see if he's still interested in discussing that job with me."

The Lawtons only nodded. They already knew the answer. They'd talked with Fena the day before.

———

The call to John Fena just eight days after the death of Anna LaCurso was warm and reassuring. Fena expressed his sincere sorrow for the loss of Bailey's girlfriend and relieved that Adam had come out of the ordeal without any physical impairments. Bailey wondered for a moment where Fena had gotten the information about Anna LaCurso being his girlfriend. There had been no mention of that fact in the newspaper reports...only that the young lady and a friend, Adam Bailey, were out pleasure driving when the tragic shooting took place.

But, Bailey's question got lost almost immediately as Fena got right down to business...just as the Lawtons had suggested he do. "Adam, I think you have the tools to take this job and make something of it sooner than you might think. You can learn this business. That's not a big problem. I can make certain you get trained properly. I'll take it in steps at the start. If you like the sound of what we're discussing, I suggest you come into my office tomorrow. I'll give you an overview of the business and what we'll need you to do in Europe to build our business. There're some basic attributes you bring to the table that should give you the satisfaction of making progress real soon. With your availability to travel, your ability to communicate in Italian, and your character, I believe in a relative short time you could influence our international business revenue in a very profitable way.

He slowed his cadence not hearing any objections from his potential new hire. "So, Adam, by the end of the day tomorrow, if you walk out of my office excited and seriously interested, then get ready for quite a ride. You'll be getting a crash course in the world of international business and how North American Distribution, Inc. plays in that domain. However, you have to promise me if your interest ever wanes, don't hesitate to tell me. Neither of us should waste any further time on the project."

Bailey assured him he'd be straight-forward. After he hung up the telephone, he was completely impressed with John Fena. The guy was a grave digger on the golf course, but in business Fena was confident and inspiring. His attitude and energy were like a breath of fresh air. Bailey sensed something exciting could happen if he put forth his normal effort. He didn't sleep much that night.

He spent four hours with John Fena on Saturday and walked out of the company headquarters even more primed. He called Fena later that afternoon and asked to start the indoctrination with North American Distribution, Inc. the next day.

Fena's response was equally positive but he replied drolly, "Adam, that's good news, but for Christ's sake I'd like to go to church with my family if you can keep your shirt and pants on until Monday."

Laughing, Bailey hadn't allowed his mind to consider what day it was. He sheepishly acknowledged that he could patiently wait until Monday morning.

Back at his apartment later that Saturday afternoon he got calls from the Lawtons, Charlie Davis, and his father congratulating him on his decision. He hadn't said a word to them. It was evident the four of them not only were good friends with John Fena, but they were hoping Adam might recognize the depth of the opportunity.

What didn't get said was how the job would further help in taking Adam away from Willie LaCurso. While it seemed that factor had been said in no uncertain terms by LaCurso, it was a relief to have another reason for the Twin City gangster never to darken Adam Bailey's life again.

Chapter 5

In 1931, Willie LaCurso had been as close of a personal friend to Loni D'Annelli as two mobsters could be. It likely helped that D'Annelli and LaCurso lived in two different cities and made their underhanded money without tripping over each other's playground.

The two of them were both first generation American citizens of Italian descent. LaCurso had landed in New York as an eight year old in 1895. His father had been forced to immigrate to American with his seven children because he was no longer allowed to be in the family business in Naples. That wasn't the entire truth. Willie learned later that his father had killed someone and had to leave the country immediately in order to ward off reprisals. The family didn't leave immediately. Willie's father had to establish a job. That happened relatively quickly when he found a job with an Italian business owner in Chicago, Illinois.

Willie would recall often his being appalled by the fear on people's faces sitting at a place called Ellis Island within shouting range of New York City. He despised the border patrol given the power to decide whether or not a person would be admitted to the United States. He watched as destitute people from overseas were turned away before they were allowed to take steps onto the streets of New York.

Willie's sister, Ella, had been ill on the trip overseas from Naples. Her illness threatened to keep her from gaining admittance. Willie's father saw to it that certain people got paid and the problem ended. Ella was allowed to enter the U.S. That proved one key point to the young Willie. America was the land of opportunity just like in Italy........if you had enough money. He determined that he was not going to be poor in America.

When he finally made it to the family's final destination in Chicago, he was underwhelmed. He wondered why this city was his father's choice. The sheer size of the city astounded him. The never-ending uncleanliness and smell of the city disappointed him. Naples could take no prize for being an all-world city, but the steel mills of south Chicago made the air in the lowest point of Lake Michigan difficult to inhale. Everyone living on the south side seemed to be coughing. And, when the cold season set in, Willie had never felt cold like he felt in America's second largest city with the wind and snow coming off the large lake.

Willie's father had been in a family business in Naples. Now, he was working for another family. His job was to protect the man's business. At least that's how his father explained it to his son. When Willie was seventeen years old, he had quit school a year before and had been working as a trucker in that same family business. The patriarch of that family, Antonio Cantorio, was involved in distributing booze and food items to restaurants and clubs on the south side. Willie's father was responsible for ten trucks to daily deliver these items no matter conditions of the streets or the weather inconveniences. The blame fell on Willie's father if anything wasn't delivered. It was a low grade job and Willie hated that his father didn't have near the status he'd had back in Naples. But, it was a job that paid well enough for a family of nine to survive.

Once he was one of the truckers, Willie had to witness too often his father being degraded or being treated as a minion by the business owner or some middle supervisors. His anger reached a boiling point each time he saw the maltreatment aimed at his father. His impression of the Cantorio business was not very favorable either. It was disorganized compared to the LaCurso family businesses back in Italy. But, his father still felt lucky he had the job. Overtime, though, Willie promised one day soon he'd do something about Cantorio or his right hand men demeaning their employees.

It was during the autumn in 1912 when it happened. Willie witnessed Cantorio belittling his father in front of other workers. The disrespect was too much. LaCurso could not see himself investing another day working for such a man. And, if his father felt obligated to keep the job because finding other jobs was difficult at his age, then Willie was at least going to meet with Cantorio to see if there was a different job for his father in the organization. The only time to do that would be in the evening hours after work. He figured to catch Senore Cantorio at the man's home.

Once the discussion about better work for his father was done, Willie had plans to catch a train to Minneapolis, Minnesota. He had friend there who used to live in Chicago. His name was Loni D'Annelli and they had been discussing some business ideas in letters to each other. In one recent letter from D'Annelli, his friend kept repeating the many opportunities there were in the Twin Cities for the two of them. D'Annelli's perspective was that with their initiative, hard work, and luck, working together they had a better chance of success.

First he had to have that discussion with Cantorio. It was a Sunday night when he chose to walk the mile over to Cantorio's house. He was nervous, but not about being mugged. He always carried a weapon when out at night. No, he was uncomfortable about talking with the boss...and he hated that feeling in his stomach more than anything. He didn't like having another man causing him so much anxiety. Cantorio might tell him to get lost or refuse even to see him. After all it was also Sunday night. Cantorio might understandably want to be with his family.

Willie was getting madder and madder as he pawed the revolver in his coat pocket. Just the thought of what the cantankerous and disrespectful Cantorio might say caused Willie's furor to molten. By the time he arrived at the Cantorio house he was thinking of a few different things he'd prefer to do with Cantorio than sit down and talk with him.

More than an hour went by as Willie stood in the shadows of two homes across the street. There was a guard at the front door, but he didn't seem especially concerned about any break-ins or assaults. He was mostly standing by a front gate talking with a few people who were out for an evening stroll.

From his location Willie saw Cantorio wander from the kitchen to the living room to his study on the first level. Through the large window, the man sat down at his desk, pulled out some files from his desk, and then pulled the curtains.

Those were the circumstances Willie hoped for. Walking to the rear of the house, he jimmied the lock of the back door and gained entry. His effort had changed somewhat. Cantorio would not be given a choice to talk with him. The pistol in his coat pocket would ensure a worthwhile discussion and guarantee his father would be put in a better position.

Without knocking Willie opened the door of the study and sat down in a leather chair across from where Cantorio was sitting imperiously at his desk. The entry made no sense to the older man. He was startled but showed no fear…only anger. He sneered, "What the hell are you doing in my house? How did you get in? Get out of here before I call the police. I don't see anyone on the night of the Sabbath!"

Willie wondered if Cantorio even knew who he was. But, what rankled him most was the man's incessant tone of superior disrespect. It had become simply unacceptable.

Willie didn't move. He just sat there feeling a sense of power with the gun in his pocket. He felt amazingly calm as his words flowed. "Senore Cantorio, I am here to tell you that I am quitting your employment because you are a bastard."

Cantorio's gave him a supercilious glare and replied, "Young man, you don't quit Cantorio's operation. I decide if you work for me or not. But, you can be sure I'm firing you as of this moment. Now, get out of my house!"

Everything the boss man said and how he said it grated Willie. He kept his composure. "Senore Cantorio, my family was highly respected back in Naples, yet you treat us like the worst Irishmen begging for a meal. Before I leave we need to discuss how you treat my father. I insist that you not only treat him better but he should be given a job that better represents his work experience from the old country and the admiration he enjoyed there."

Willie then stopped. He had succinctly stated his purpose. His requests were very reasonable, at least in Willie's mind.

Cantorio sat back with a mocking stare as if not believing what he was hearing. He finally exploded, "Who are you, you little shit, telling me what you want for your father as if I should comply without so much as a blink? I'll tell you what, not only will I not give your father anything, but you can tell him he no longer works for me either!"

That was the burning point that ended Willie's coolness. As Cantorio grabbed his telephone to call the guard posted outside by the gate, Willie pulled out his gun. He got up from the chair, leaned over the desk and placed the barrel of the pistol in Cantorio's ear. The older man got flushed and practically stopped breathing on the spot.

Willie regained his composure and quietly murmured. "Senore, you would be wise to put the telephone down."

Cantorio realized immediately he was not dealing with a normal person. He put down the telephone and spoke slowly. "This is not wise, young man. I know you are a LaCurso. If there is any trouble tonight, you will be hunted down like a dog. Your family will suffer. I would be very careful what you do next."

Cantorio's voice was not as strong as it had been. Willie always admired the power gained from having the upper hand...and at that moment he had the advantage. He loved the feeling.

Maintaining his composure, he leaned closer to the now very uncomfortable Cantorio and whispered, "Senore Cantorio, let me tell you why you will comply with my request. I have two very good friends. We have been watching your family for the past month. We know your schedule, your wife's schedule, your three daughter's schedules and your two young sons' times when they go to and from school. You will have a choice before I leave here tonight. You will obey my request or one by one your wife and your children will die. You will be the last to go. You no longer will strut around like European royalty and treat people so shamelessly. Do you hear me?"

Cantorio's face was red with rage. He nodded his head saying nothing.

Then Willie saw the fear in the man's eyes and realized he had the powerful Cantorio totally under his control. It was like a drug. He wanted to hear more concessions and feel more power over the daunted boss man. Willie was enjoying his new found power. He hissed right into Cantorio's face, "You know what...I'm struggling to even allow you to live. And, if your children are going to be like their father, then they don't deserve to live either."

Willie noticed there was some perspiration beginning to drip from the forehead of the pompous Senore. The older man's formidable stature was crumbling away like cheap concrete.

With the loaded gun stuck in his ear, he said haltingly, "You cannot get away with this. My people will hunt you down!!"

Willie laughed scornfully, "We've covered that, Senore. You'll be dead. A dead man can't give orders."

The Senore finally began nodding. "O.K....O.K,"

With exasperation he cried out, "I will give your father a raise. Now, will that make you happy? Can you now please leave my house?"

Willie liked what he'd heard but the response was too easy...too artificial. He shook his head. "No, Senore. Your word means nothing. I don't think you have one thought of carrying out my request."

Intoxicated with his newly discovered clout, he blustered, "Your attitude is sad. My friends will be disappointed when I tell them of your unwillingness to help my father. Oh, the problems they will cause for your family. It will be tragic when your family members one after another begin to fall whether getting maimed or suddenly dying...and only because of your stubbornness and disregard for my father. But, this should come as no surprise to you. You certainly have caused so much difficulty to other families. Why shouldn't the same thing happen to your family?"

Making up the horrors as he went along, Willie asked, "Tell me, Senore, when we start with your wife, will life be difficult for you and your family without her? Or, will you simply bring in one of your other lady friends to take over the household?

Willie cackled inside. His wickedness was having an amazing impact.

Sweating profusely, Cantorio's eyes were bulging. He gasped, "You wouldn't dare, you animal. How can you talk like this?"

Willie ignored Cantorio's cries. "Within a few days if my father is not being treated properly and paid more money, one of my friends will gun down your wife as she goes to the market. You're eldest daughter will be next."

Willie's cold cadence describing assault and death was too much. The Senore was becoming completely undone. The gun lodged in his ear added to his agony. The stress of hearing heartless descriptions of his family's pending deaths made his face turn red and his breathing became uneven.

Rubbing his chest he gasped, "My heart pills...I need them. They're in my coat pocket slung over the chair. Please let me have them."

Willie watched the desperate man plead and felt only great satisfaction...and no sympathy. He found himself loathing Cantorio even more. Once the older man was dislodged from his high pedestal, he was just a fragile, miserable human being.

Willie kept on the pressure. He growled, "Senore, you are an evil man. It makes me wonder why you should live through the night. Maybe without your pills you will put all of us out of our misery. We'd not have to look at your ugly face ever again. I want you to die this very night. A heart attack would be ideal. A bullet won't have to be wasted. I will stay right here and tell your men and the medical people that you took ill while you and I were discussing a new job for me. I will be a hero for trying to save you."

The Senore was apoplectic. He panted, "How can I convince you. I need my pills! I will comply with your wishes!"

Willie removed the pistol from the man's ear and backed away only slightly while observing Cantorio's deteriorating condition. He kept his weapon inches from the older man's temple.

As the Senore grabbed his handkerchief to mop his brow, Willie responded to the man's desperate question. "Senore, now that you mention it, I will also want a loan from you this evening. I will be taking on a new business venture and I will need some start-up money. I believe $25,000 will be an adequate amount for the loan."

The Senore turned and gazed at the gun barrel now pointed at his forehead. Slumped back in his chair, Cantorio tried a completely different tack while breathing very unevenly. "You know my young friend, I like the resolve you show...and you're attention to detail. All this talk of death and killing; we needn't continue in that vein. Let us think more creatively...something more advantageous for both of us. My organization needs people like you who can take charge. What would you say to that?"

The pomposity of the man sickened Willie. It was all he could do to hold back pulling the trigger. Instead, he found himself more gripped by the command he had over the horrible man.

Willie moved closer and put the gun barrel directly between the eyes of Cantorio. The words he spoke were as cold as any he'd ever voiced. "Senore, do you think me an idiot. I would not stoop to work for you or your organization. You are an imbecile consumed in your own self-importance."

Whether an act or real, the Senore then stood up and began holding his chest pleading, "I need my heart pills. Please! I must have them...my coat pocket... please. I must have them or I will die!!"

Holding the pistol on the blubbering older man, Willie grabbed the coat from the chair and found the small container of pills in the pocket. There was also a key. It looked like a safe key. The power he felt at that moment was all-consuming.

Willie put a pen and paper in front of the Senore. "Cantorio, you write down that you want my father given a new position in your company as a manager of all the deliveries on the south side down to Hammond, Indiana. Also, raise my father's salary to $15,000 plus 5% of the profits. Then I will let you have your pills."

Cantorio was now turning slightly gray. He wrote furiously and then signed the letter before throwing it at Willie. Willie slowly read the letter word for word while the older man lay back in his chair moaning.

Satisfied, Willie took the letter and placed it on the desk of Cantorio's study still holding the pill container in his hand. Then he dropped the pill bottle into his own pocket. The Senore's eyes grew even larger. He'd been had. The young man had no intention of opening the pill bottle. He was going to win this night.

In a final effort to save himself, Cantorio got up from his chair to attack Willie. But, his legs wouldn't support him. He fell clutching his chest as he sprawled across the rug in front of the fireplace. Willie watched emotionless as the older man made several attempts to suck in one more breath. Lying on his back, his eyes dimly focused on the young man. He began shaking his head as if not wanting to admit this adversary would be the last challenge he would ever face. And then, a slight smile appeared on the older man's dying face as if remembering back during his own youth when he displayed the same coldness and guts in winning his own battles.

The last thing Senore Cantorio remembered before the room closed into darkness was the young man pouring himself a drink. He was tossing the bottle of pills up in the air and catching the bottle as it descended. The young man's eyes were impassive as he serenely sat on the leather sofa watching Cantorio breathe his last.

When the older man fell into unconsciousness, LaCurso didn't even check if the man was still alive. Instead, holding the key he hurriedly began inspecting the office for the safe's location. He had no doubt there would be both important papers and money in that vault.

In less than five minutes the safe was found in the most likely place... above the fireplace and behind a picture of a Tuscany landscape. A minute later and the picture with heavy frame was carelessly laid atop the corpse on the floor. The key opened the vault and Willie began pulling out the contents.

The papers meant nothing; however, the cash he found in envelopes was quite meaningful. He just kept stuffing his shirt and coat pockets until he looked twenty pounds heavier. Carefully placing the papers back in the safe, he closed the vault and placed the large picture frame back on the wall. He had no idea how much he had just relieved from the Cantorio family estate, but he was certain his life had just changed for the better.

Before leaving Cantorio's library, LaCurso inspected the body one last time. The death stare and flaccid facial color confirmed the Senore would not be a future problem. LaCurso then took the pill container and placed it in the dead man's hand. He'd told Cantorio he would give the man his pills. That statement after an unfortunate...or fortunate...delay was being fulfilled...just a little late to do any good.

Making certain the Senore's handwritten letter was visible and on the desk, LaCurso slipped through the kitchen and outside the back door. The night had turned very chilly, but the contraband stuffed in his coat and shirt provided special warmth.

He'd never felt more exhilarated than the long walk back to his home. The overweight pompous man had died so cooperatively without LaCurso having to lay a hand on him. He finally admitted to himself the true purposes of entering Cantorio's study; he had wanted the man dead. Reasoning with such a haughty person was not possible. Now he'd gotten away with murder without pulling a trigger. The night couldn't have worked out better.

It was almost midnight when Willie arrived at his darkened family home. The wind had picked up on the crisp, clear night. About to enter the house he faced a problem he hadn't foreseen. With so many family members sleeping in the cramped quarters, where was he going to hide his bounty?

He sat down on the porch and by the light of the moon and the glow of the street light, he began shedding himself of the money he'd stuffed in his clothing. He counted slowly and carefully. In one thick envelope there was $17,000. In another there was $12,000 and in smaller bills. He kept stacking and counting as he cautiously looked up every other second to make certain he was not being observed. In a half hour of counting and recounting, Willie had tallied over $80,000 and still had a couple envelopes inside his tee shirt.

Hearing a noise from within the house, he scrambled to re-stuff the envelopes back into his coat. As one of his relatives went out the back door to relieve himself, Willie hunkered down in the corner of the porch. When his cousin came back to the house and walked right by him, that was the only time all night LaCurso sweated.

By the time he went in the house he had just over $105,000 in cold hard cash pressed against his body inside his clothing. He slept in his clothes that night…..that is, when he could relax enough to sleep. His chief thought had yet to be resolved…where to store the unexpected bounty. While lying down with his relatives around him, he'd occasionally break up laughing not believing his unprecedented heist and the convenience of his victim expiring of natural causes. Never once did he consider himself a killer or dishonest…only opportunistic.

He'd also taken note of the many things he'd learned that night. He had the ability to truly intimidate with his evil intonations and wicked words. Admittedly, having a loaded weapon in his victim's ear also helped.

Before daybreak he quietly placed the envelopes under his mattress. It would only be a temporary accommodation.

At sunrise he accompanied his father on the routine trip to the Cantorio residence where orders would be given for the week. Willie had to keep from smiling seeing many more vehicles than normal out in front of the house including an ambulance and three police cars.

Parking the car across the street, his father's face showed concern and shock as he witnessed his boss' body being taken out of the house on a stretcher. As they slowly walked to the house, the younger LaCurso stayed in the background while observing his father dealing with the spectacle. With Cantorio neighbors and associates milling around the front of the house, a medical person could be heard saying it was a heart attack that had taken the Senore.

Immediately, Willie could see his father becoming distraught…not so much about the death, but more about his job and pay check.

One of Cantorio's men who seemed to be shaken in the same way as Willie's father then came outside and walked straight up to the older LaCurso saying, "Senore, please come in. A letter was left from the boss. It affects you."

Willie wished he could watch the discussion going on inside Cantorio's house. He waited anxiously for his father to reappear.

Twenty minutes later the older LaCurso exited the house. His face looked more puzzled than sad.

As the two of them drove away, Willie became slightly concerned. He asked, "Papa, what's wrong?"

Perplexed, his father replied, "Willie, as you heard, the Senore died last evening of a heart attack. What's surprising is that he was in the midst of finalizing some business decisions...one that included me. He had written down and signed a paper order to put me in charge of transporting products along the lake front down to Hammond. It's a very lucrative area. He wrote that he wanted my salary tripled."

The astonishment on his father's face was a moment Willie would never forget. He'd done something for his father that the older man would never know.

His father kept on talking, almost blabbering incoherently. "I can't believe it. I thought the Senore hated me. He must have just been testing me all this time. It had been a position open for about a month ever since the shooting death of his cousin, Satori. I never thought he would even consider me for that job."

Then it was quiet in the car as they continued to the lake shore storage building where Willie's father's was now in charge. The older LaCurso tried to be sad about his boss' death, but the sudden news of his promotion and a better life for the family caused a small smile that simply wouldn't go away.

Willie had to look away from his father to hide his even wider grin. He'd just experienced the most important victory in his young life. His father's renewed confidence was worth more to the son than the money he'd hidden temporarily under his mattress in the house. He would find, however, that the cash would bring him other pleasures and advantages in the months and years ahead.

Within two days everything on the letter came to pass. The lawyer for Cantorio's family called the older LaCurso into his Dearborn Street office verifying that the job and salary increase were valid. The lawyer sensed this final Cantorio decision was going to be a good one. Standing in front of him was a very confident looking man with a new suit of clothes. The attorney wondered why Cantorio hadn't put this man into a higher position before.

Willie then broke the news to his father and the rest of the family that he was going into business with a friend up in Minneapolis. His father was saddened but understood. The fact remained the older LaCurso worked for another family's business. For his son to distinguish himself he had to get out from the shackles of the Cantorio family. He respected his son's initiative and resourcefulness. He even offered to give Willie some money to get started and was surprised his son respectfully declined the offered capital.

It was during that early winter of 1912-13 that Willie traveled by train to Minneapolis. He was young, strong-minded, and brimming with confidence after the coup he pulled off in Chicago. His friend, Loni D'Annelli, was to meet him at the St. Paul train station. Willie had $45,000 in envelopes taped to his body. He also had over $60,000 stashed in his two suitcases. The suitcases never left his sight throughout the train ride.

On his way up to the capital city of Minnesota, Willie deposited $20,000 in three different Wisconsin banks. He had to remain patient as each bank president at first tried to redirect the young man to one of his vice presidents. LaCurso wouldn't accept the lower status. Within minutes, the young man was one of that bank's finest clients. Willie had one prerequisite for all three banks. There would have to be absolute confidentiality or the bank president would lose the deposit as fast as a train ride back from St. Paul.

The bank presidents in Eau Claire, Menominee, and River Falls, Wisconsin were happy to keep their mouths shut. Besides the remaining $45000 attached to his body, LaCurso had $5000 remaining in his money belt for fast cash and seed money.

In the next few weeks D'Annelli and LaCurso got reacquainted and would discuss various partnership ideas. Both were brash and self-assured that they had the street smarts to make anything work. D'Annelli had some action already brewing in the local trade union. Stealing meat from the South St. Paul stockyards and selling it on the side to some large food markets and restaurants had been working well.

Willie paid heed to some business advice from his friend...that is, never get too closely involved in any heist...and therefore making oneself too visible. Always be the secret money behind the action and let others perform the work.

The two business partners did well together for almost six years in the Twin Cities. With Prohibition conveniently becoming law in 1913, opportunity sprang forward. Delivering booze was their most dependable business. They also opened some restaurants and financed a couple men's haberdasheries. Business was good enough that both men were making extraordinary money for two men turning thirty years of age.

If competition threatened, either man was capable of taking care of the matter. The two men became the kingpins of under the table booze running in both Minneapolis and St. Paul.

In 1919 they found it necessary to split up when Loni D'Annelli's father passed away in Chicago and his family business needed someone to take over. D'Annelli's father was in charge of one of the construction unions and had provided the family a very comfortable living. Loni saw ways to make that opportunity into a bonanza. Willie bought out Loni's share of their Twin City businesses. It was a fair and amicable split that both of them didn't really want to see happen. Unsaid was luckily how smoothly that transaction had sustained their friendship. Their relationship would remain deep and absolutely loyal until the day Loni D'Annelli was gunned down in the streets of Chicago in July 1931. It was the saddest day of LaCurso's life.

When D'Annelli and LaCurson, both men went at their autonomy with a new ferocity. If triggered properly, either one of them could well have been an industrial magnate or a top government official. Instead, they became leaders and successes in less reputable underworld activities.

There was one well defined difference between the two men. D'Annelli had been part of a growing family enterprise in the U.S. LaCurso still had a lot of family and friends in the old country. He basically was the first one in his family in America to create an ongoing family business. His success was appreciated by his father and mother while they were alive in Chicago. Also, word of his attainment filtered back to the LaCurso clan in the old country. By the late 1920's Willie had become a kind of hero to his heritage. On trips to Italy with his wife and young family during the early and mid- 1920's, he was welcomed like a king. He also offered jobs to a few of the younger male family members who wanted to immigrate to the U.S.

The LaCurso name was well-known for both good and bad in Italy. The family was surviving reasonably well despite some dour economic conditions following the First World War. Their breaches of Italian law regarding shipments of food, booze, and armaments had largely been overlooked by the Italian leaders. Government officials and wartime generals were desperate to reap any benefits for Italy or themselves resulting from the country supposedly being on the winning side in the 'Big War'. The government's preoccupation with gaining the spoils of war made it more possible for families like the LaCurso clan to continue their lawless pursuits of profit.

When a new man and his Fascist political party began their rise in power in 1923, the circumstances for the LaCursos gradually became more difficult. The egoist, Benito Mussolini, as the Fascist leader, was winning over the hearts and minds of poor Italians suffering much in the years after the war. While Willie's family in the old country re-established itself as a prominent transporter and shipper, the overbearing and crippling tax structure imparted on various large private businesses began to leave its mark on the family's profits. The LaCursos became convinced the Mussolini regime was out to get them and take over as many of the family operations as possible.

By 1930, many of the LaCurso businesses had to be sold to friends of Il Duce if any value at all was to be gleaned. The price was less than a quarter of what the businesses were worth. Not surprisingly the businesses improved after they were sold and reincarnated with less tax burdens.

Willie observed these economic atrocities perpetrated against his family with fierce distaste. His hatred toward Mussolini became pathological as members of his family were being gunned down by Fascist military police for setting up new businesses contrary to government regulations.

By the mid to late 1930's LaCurso visited his Italian family once, sometimes twice a year, to bring financial aid. He and his younger brother, Roberto became especially close as they discussed more and more the possibilities of eliminating this madman who had taken over Italy. They went so far as agreeing that if Roberto could put together a confidential team of assassins, Willie would finance the effort. From the very beginning, however, both men were highly conscious of keeping the LaCurso name entirely confidential from any scheme designed to assassinate Mussolini.

Roberto's part of the bargain was especially challenging. At first he tried hiring hitmen...a common practice within the family. However, for these professional killers to make it through the labyrinth of security and Mussolini's constantly changing plans was making each mission impossible to complete. None of these hitmen hired by Roberto and funded by Willie ever got close enough to Il Duce to even take a shot.

After another meeting between the two brothers in late 1937, it was decided that a more organized plan would have to take shape. It would be up to Roberto to find a trusted individual to take charge of an assassination team. The group's mandate would be to get inside information on Mussolini's schedule and choose a number of dates and sites where it would be best to take out the Italian leader. Additionally, more attention was placed on establishing an escape mechanism for the lone assassin or the group of assassins...anything to lessen the chance for capture and keep any line from being drawn back to the LaCursos. The whole idea would take more money, but the result seemed worth the investment.

The brothers didn't get a break until the spring of 1938. Roberto had been partnering with a Swiss entrepreneur on some illegal contraband shipments from Switzerland into Italy. The man, Andre Pizzorno, hated Mussolini with as much passion as the entire LaCurso family. Italy had gone from a major market for the goods and equipment he was illegally shipping to a country where under the table costs were crippling his profits. Once he began doing business with Roberto LaCurso's organization, getting around border patrols and untrustworthy government scavengers, Pizzorno's operating costs decreased....at least up to the end of 1937. With more absolute power by Mussolini and the Fascists, however, even the LaCurso connections were not guaranteeing the deliveries of either the LaCurso or the Pizzorno shipments.

Roberto, keeping his brother's name out of the conversation, discussed the assassination team concept including the absolute necessity of keeping his Italian family name out of the scheme. The only thing the LaCursos would be responsible for was the financing.

Pizzorno volunteered to take charge. In his favor was that he was Swiss and didn't have a family to protect.

With the confidence having already been secured in their relationship, Roberto became the middleman open to supplying more money and weaponry where needed. The time table was six months, if not sooner, for Andre Pizzorno to hire his team and carry out the assassination.

That handshake agreement occurred in the late summer of 1938. What was hoped to be a quicker result turned into a rash of misfortunes that caused constant delays and missed opportunities...most notably because of hiring the wrong people or dealing with Mussolini's constantly changing travel and business schedule. More financing from Willie LaCurso became necessary.

Adding to these problems was actually making certain Willie's cash sent from America was safely crossing the border. Not only was there increased scrutiny by the Italian border guards and not knowing how many needed to be paid off, there was the problem of the actual delivery process. One suitcase full of money had simply disappeared with the entrusted courier. If a deliveryman disappeared with the cash, that was bad enough. However, the possibility of Willie's money being confiscated and ending up in the troughs of the Mussolini regime was entirely unacceptable.

Delays in money transfer proved intolerable. These hired assassins were often unstable and undependable. With inaction and no pay, these professional hitmen would simply vanish with little or no communication. Then it became a perceived problem of keeping their mouths closed. Those individuals deserting the assassination team could subject the remaining hitmen group to blackmail.

In early 1939 Pizzorno's efforts were put on hold until Roberto LaCurso could hire some hits on those former Pizzorno team members...something the LaCursos never considered. While this unseen challenge was eventually solved... with added expense... Willie and Roberto had to come up with a dependable conduit...a reliable person who could bring the money overseas and personally be trusted to get the valuable suitcase into Roberto's hands. One person had come to Willie's mind...an experienced Western European traveler who lived right there in the Twin Cities. Moreover, this business nomad was absolutely trustworthy. Willie had known this individual since the kid was in high school. His name was Adam Bailey.

Chapter 6

Beginning Monday, June 20, 1935, Adam Bailey began a crash course covering North American Distribution, Inc. and its business practices. John Fena took the young man under his wing involving him in every aspect of the trade. Fena appreciated very quickly he may have found a diamond in the rough. Each day as he dealt with the young man proved why he was so highly recommended by the Lawtons and Charlie Davis...as well as the private owner of the company...a man named Henry Granville. Fena didn't know Granville well, but Fena himself had been recommended for his general manager job by his two friends, Lawton and Davis.

Within a month Bailey was traveling to California and Florida calling on some of the company's domestic business clients. He faced the typical client questions and objections while representing the company's capabilities. Business actually increased with those clients after meeting Bailey, something Fena had not expected.

By late September, only four months since Bailey graduated from college, John Fena and his protégé were outlining his first trip overseas. Bailey was to concentrate on bringing aboard key wine producers and specialty food makers in Western Europe, particularly France, Belgium, Holland, Switzerland, and Italy. The latter country was of major interest to Fena as he had many letters from that country who wanted their products marketed in the U.S. Now he had a willing employee reasonably fluent in Italian who might close some of that business potential.

Fena estimated if Bailey brought just three foreign producers on board in that first overseas business trip, the investment would be profitable for the company. Yet, there would be continuing factors that went with the job. Bailey had to be willing and able to continue his journeys, establish trust with the new clients, and find his ways to other vineyards and towns where prospects could be contacted. All the exploratory calls would take time and more expense.

Bailey's first trip was by ocean liner landing in Le Havre, France on October 28. From that port city he wasted no time and took the night train down through Paris and didn't stop until he got to Dijon. From there he traveled in the direction of Lyon and eventually all the way to Marseilles in the south of France making contact with wine producers and potential food specialists along the way. Only a few of these French vineyard owners had made contact with North American Distribution, Inc. by letter. Whether they'd heard of the American distribution company or not, they were surprised to see a young man literally knock on their door to introduce them to the advantages of marketing their products into the American market. With the U.S. being a relatively untapped market, most were open to the possibility of a new potential revenue stream.

Most of these businessmen were complimented that a representative from an American distribution company chose to see them. They were generally open-minded to his ideas for growing their business, but one concern did repeatedly get voiced, especially as he traveled to various vineyards in Italy. There was an apprehension that the revenues could be short-lived given the deteriorating political and military conditions in Western Europe.

It was an objection Bailey was prepared to handle. He suggested it was wise to establish a viable working relationship now. If military or political interruptions caused a shutdown then so be it. The affiliation could more easily be reconstituted when the time arrived that business could be normalized. He stressed in the meantime why not glean what new revenue they could from exporting their products to America. It was a concept that left some of his prospects dumbfounded as they were used to giving in to more futilitarian talk. Here was a young man in a friendly, trustworthy, and business-like manner opening their minds to something actually hopeful. The notion was refreshing to a lot of the French and Italian vineyard owners and specialty food producers. And, in 1935 and early in 1936 with no knowledge or understanding as to the destruction and horrors that were to come, Bailey's idea took root.

Where Bailey at twenty-three years of age had wondered if his relative youth might be a deterrent, both the reputation of North American Distribution, Inc. and his boundless energy and basic knowledge of marketing wine and food specialty items from his three months of training and sales work in Florida and California.helped him gain credibility. Fena expected him to be overseas for as long as six weeks. Bailey didn't return for two months.

In the first two weeks in France, the language barrier was only a slight problem, especially once the French wine or food producer admitted knowing some English. But, there were other factors that worked to Bailey's advantage. His agricultural background helped him. He even participated in harvesting some grapes at two vineyards. Folks found the young man highly likeable.

Orders were written during that two-week period amounting to seven new clients. Bailey sent the results of his campaign in France via telegraph back to John Fena in the States. Fena was stunned....and of course very pleased.

By the time Bailey crossed the border into Italy, he had gained tremendous self-assurance in what he was representing. And, with his workable Italian, he figured he'd be able to carry on more entertaining and fruitful conversations with his prospects.

As his night train to Florence was arriving at dawn, all those reasons Fena hired him made sense. His very character seemed to fit the job. The people he met were friendly and took pleasure in showing the 'American farm boy' their establishment. Being able to converse and joke more in Italy, his prospective clients were won over with his obvious affection toward them. Bailey became quite comfortable in a country he'd only visited in travel magazines.

In the following three weeks he signed up fifteen new clients in Italy where North American Distribution, Inc. would handle the dispersal and delivery of their products to the Midwestern states once they were received in the harbors of New York City, Boston, or Charleston, South Carolina. Bailey was already looking forward to his next trip to France and Italy. He would be experiencing even more popularity with his new clients as they would begin to be receiving the new revenue from American.

When Bailey finally made it back to the States and then to Minneapolis, it was the middle of December still in 1935. John Fena was elated with Bailey's results and gave him a raise that almost doubled his salary. It had been an amazing year for a young man who had only finished his college degree the previous spring.

Fena and Bailey wasted no time in January, 1936. They sat down and planned out extended trips overseas to Switzerland, Belgium, and Holland besides return visits to new clients in France and Italy. Fena left it open how long his protégé should stay overseas, but suggested each trip should last no more than two months. As Fena remarked, "I'm not trying to make a European out of you, just an international businessman."

For the next two years Adam Bailey enjoyed resounding results even as the European military and political conditions were deteriorating. Bailey became known amongst his international clients as a purveyor of the American phrase, 'make hay while the sun shines'. While Fena agreed with Bailey's reasoning about establishing a U.S. business connection with as many overseas vineyard owners and specialty food producers as possible, he too had to face the loss of revenue if or when the political and military situation might end this tremendous added source of revenue for his company. The hope on both sides of the ocean of course was that there would be no interruption; that another great war could be avoided.

During those two years, Bailey made three or four extended trips overseas each year. He became at ease with the geography of France and Switzerland. It was Italy that he became most familiar. With John Fena's confidence in him, Bailey was able to work independently and generally solve most shipping problems. His real advantage was his willingness to immerse himself into each country's culture building further trust among his clientele. He rarely ate dinners alone.

And, it was not all work. In Italy he became close friends with two different vineyard owners who had U.S. connections. During harvest seasons he helped out at both family vineyards...one located a hundred kilometers south of Milan, Italy...and another nearer Pisa. Still other families invited him to family outings in their mountain villas. He even went sailing with a customer on the Ligurean Sea near Corsica.

He eventually became aware that a few clients liked him enough that they had a hidden agenda...that of introducing him to their marriage eligible daughter or niece. At large family dinners he would be seated at the head table next to the young lady with hundreds of eyes exhibiting hopeful signs of mutual interest.

After a few too many of these invitations for dinner, he created a story that he had a girl back home in the States...and added that she 'was a nice Italian girl as well.' When asked more about her, he found himself describing Anna LaCurso. While a convenient lie, the deceit would unfortunately bring back her memory. That bit of inventiveness did take the pressure off considerably, but brought with it some melancholy. With each return trip to Italy he would still get questions about his status and question why the delay in his marriage.

Disappointingly, he found the females he met in Europe and the few dates he had back in the U.S. just never measured up to Anna. At times he wished he hadn't met her. She'd placed the bar so high for the kind of girl he preferred. And, when he thought of her, he no longer thought of her father, a man he hadn't seen in over two years.

As for his interest in professional golf, that desire faded with each trip to Europe. He still had the game to play as a top amateur in plenty of local and some national tournaments, but the priority wasn't as high as it was in college. The experience he was gaining and the respect he was earning from his overseas business endeavors far outweighed any alternatives.

Bailey's client base would hit its peak in Italy, France, and Switzerland at the end of 1937. He wanted to add more customers in other countries, particularly in Spain and Portugal but the threats of war looming in Western Europe plus the Civil War in Spain caused him to face the realities. Regarding Spain, the economy was paralyzed; worse yet with the 40% of the younger male population dying in that horrible conflict, he had to wonder if any prospects would be alive to discuss any business. Besides, there was no reason to put himself in harm's way by getting caught in the crossfire.

As for adding more clients in Holland, Belgium, and even the Scandinavian countries, it was evident his efforts would be wasted with Germany becoming even more of a daily threat to those populations. Trade with the U.S. for the foreseeable future would not be possible if Germany dominated those countries. That factor became more real at the start of 1938 in his three key countries of France, Switzerland, and Italy. He could see a time as early as 1939 when his overseas travel might not be cost justifiable. The most crushing loss of business would be in Italy. He was already experiencing some talk whereby Mussolini and his Fascist government were beginning to pressure exporters to no longer do any commerce with the U.S.

And that time came sooner than he'd expected. As encouraging and positive as the previous years had been, 1938 would see half his client base in Italy evaporate.

In discussions with John Fena, Bailey estimated he could lose the other half by the end of 1939. Fena and Bailey began talking about pointing his international business experience more in the direction of countries in South America. Fena had no contacts on this unfamiliar continent. It was a vast untouched and available market. Bailey looked forward to the challenge and visiting Chile and Argentina. Mentally he began gearing up to focus his attention on developing business opportunities in those two countries by the middle of 1939.

At least, that was his plan until something seemingly out of the blue would happen that would thwart those visions in South America. Adam Bailey would receive a letter at his North American Distribution office from the State Department in Washington D.C. In fact it was hand-delivered to him by courier. At first, he was concerned he'd done something wrong with regards to his travels in Western Europe.

In fact it was a letter of introduction from a man named David O'Brien. The salutation gave no hint as to the title of the man....just that he was going to be in the Twin Cities the following week visiting his parents in Mendota Heights. The note was concise and direct. O'Brien said he'd like to meet for lunch. For an official type of delivery on formal U.S. Government stationary, the invitation seemed quite casual.

With the courier waiting for a reply, Bailey re-read the note and felt complimented...like a warm wave was passing over him. He wrote a quick response accepting the invitation and handed the note back to the messenger. While flattered he also felt puzzled over the invitation...and he would remain that way right up through actually meeting the man from Washington D.C.

The luncheon meeting with David O'Brien of the State Department was only a week and a half before Bailey's last planned trip to Europe for the months of November and December, 1938. A few days before, Bailey received another communication...this time a telegram. It was from O'Brien. The wire said to call his Washington office collect to set up the time and place for their lunch.

Bailey thought it strange. Why didn't the man just call himself? Was he really that busy? Or, maybe having lunch with some hick from Minnesota wasn't high on this guy's priority list.'

Later that afternoon, Bailey followed the directions in the telegram and called O'Brien's number reversing the charges as directed. The secretary acted as if she expected the call saying, "Yes, Mr. Bailey. Mr. O'Brien would like to meet you at Murray's on 7th Street in Minneapolis on Thursday, October 20 at 1:00... if that would be convenient.

Bailey was impressed with her efficiency, but even more fascinated that O'Brien knew about the popular restaurant in downtown Minneapolis. Clearing his throat he replied as formally as he was able, "Yes, ma'am...1:00 will work on my schedule."

She responded with the same strong voice, "Thank you, Mr. Bailey. He'll see you then." Then she curtly hung up.

Bailey stared at the dead receiver. Apparently the State Department required brevity in their communication. On that basis he wondered if the lunch would last more than ten minutes.

The following Thursday David O'Brien was at Murray's waiting for Bailey ten minutes before their appointed time. He was dressed in business attire despite claiming to be taking a few days off to visit his folks. As they shook hands, Bailey couldn't help but feel comfortable with the man. He didn't stare and look disappointed because of Bailey's obvious youth. Instead he loosened his tie and ordered a beer. Bailey stayed with coffee.

With the introductions out of the way, O'Brien immediately took charge. He reached in his lapel pocket and pulled out an envelope saying, "Adam, this note might explain why we're sitting here today. It's from your father to you."

He then joked, "Your Dad wanted to save a stamp and asked me to deliver this letter personally. Why don't you read it and then we'll talk."

Bailey nodded and began reading the very recognizable script. It turned out O'Brien was very good friends with Catherine and his father. After some personal niceties, the letter went on to add:

> David O'Brien happens to be head of a 'division' in the State Department focused on the on-going European military and political state of affairs. He'll likely go into further detail during your lunch. I should tell you after I expounded on your overseas business career over the past three years, especially in Italy, he seemed to take great interest. When I told him of your heavy travel in that country and your fluency in the language, he said that he wanted to meet you. I told him your age and that didn't seem to deter him.
>
> I don't know what he's got up his sleeve. I think you'll find he's a real interesting fellow....and, I might add, a former Minnesotan, so he can't be all bad.
>
> I'll be calling you this Sunday night like normal and certainly looking forward to seeing you when you return from your upcoming trip overseas.
>
> As always, travel safely.
>
> Love,
> Dad

Putting the letter down, they talked lightly about O'Brien's connection to Minnesota and that his parents actually did live locally in the Mendota Heights area across the Mississippi River from Wold-Chamberlain Airfield. Ten minutes would go by and O'Brien hadn't said one word about the real purpose of their lunch.

Gradually and without Bailey realizing it, O'Brien turned the conversation around to the political and military circumstances facing the world. When the talk covered Western Europe, Bailey found himself already aware of O'Brien's overview. Still, he was impressed how well-informed the man from Washington actually was.

Then he began asking Bailey some questions about his business in Italy. The inquiries caused Bailey to scoff. "David, with the advent of that pact called the Rome-Berlin Axis, it's just a question of time before Italy joins the Germans in their quest to probably take over Europe. As far as my business is concerned, my Italian clients are disappearing. Too many of them are fearful of continuing any exports to the U.S. and facing reprisals from the Fascists. As for my customer base in France and Switzerland, the way the European conflict is going, I'll likely lose that business soon as well. It's tough for me to swallow. I worked hard traveling around those three countries. Now all that business is evaporating like melting ice."

O'Brien nodded. With each comment Bailey made, the man from Washington realized he was sitting with a person very knowledgeable on the economics and the political situations in Western Europe. He asked more questions to check Bailey's geographic familiarity. The young man knew the location of every city often adding what each area was known for producing. His pronunciations of the Italian cities and names of people and areas proved his effectiveness in the language.

Bailey tried to hold back his disappointment, but his frustration about his loss of clients was obvious. He also expressed distress in seeing some manufacturing plants in Italy being restructured to become armament factories in support of Italy's war efforts and in some cases to provide supplies for Francisco Franco in Spain. When Bailey mentioned three converted factories south of Milan producing uniforms and war supplies, O'Brien actually took some notes.

What started out as a friendly conversation had soon turned into an energized discussion on the entire European scene. It took well into their conversation before Bailey woke up to what might be happening. It was not hard to figure out. O'Brien was seriously considering if Bailey could be of some help to the State Department.

Peering at Bailey, O'Brien hesitated for only a moment before carefully phrasing his idea. "You know, Adam, with your business connections even at your relative young age and your knowledge of the countries we've been discussing, you are a very unique person. You should know I've talked with more than your father and Catherine about you. John Fena and I have had a short conversation.... and another individual who knows you but shall remain nameless right now. These people are very high on your capabilities. They confirm that you are fluent in Italian and can get by in French if those Frenchmen can put up with your accent. They also say you work very independently and your perseverance is unquestionable. They also describe you as rather non-compliant. You're willing to take certain risks and you're a quick study. Those attributes would interest almost anyone. But, right now they mostly interest me."

After hearing the word 'risk', he interrupted O'Brien. "David, you're buying me lunch for a reason. What do you hope to gain from our meeting together?"

O'Brien chuckled, "Oh, I didn't know I was picking up the check. I thought you were the big international businessman with an unlimited travel budget."

It was a relaxed laughter from both of them until O'Brien became serious once again. "Adam I believe you know which way the world in Western Europe is heading. I also believe you already have a sense where this conversation is going. Other than being too young and having no experience for the work I do with the State Department, a person would have to be deaf, dumb, and blind not to realize you could really help my department and frankly this country. I don't mean to sound so melodramatic, but we need constant details about the political, military, economic, and social statuses in Italy."

Bailey stared at O'Brien feeling his throat getting dry. He was stunned where the direction of their conversation was going. For absolute clarification, his voice lowered automatically, "David, I was not born last night. Are you suggesting I become some sort of spy?"

O'Brien cleared his own throat and momentarily looked around the restaurant to check out how many ears were close to their conversation. Much quieter he murmured, "Adam, I'd appreciate it if you would recognize we might be talking about something quite sensitive. Hold that trombone of a voice down for me, will you please?

Then smiling patiently, he retorted, "Let's not get too sensational just yet. What I want to talk to you about is only helping us...as an observer...while you're traveling around Italy and Switzerland. While roving around on your business travels, you might just pay a bit more attention to certain military operations.... like armament manufacturing, war material production, and even where training and testing is taking place. Our interest is more Italy, but even Switzerland, though neutral, carries our interest. Germany is locating some of its military training and manufacturing to that country.

Now, I'll be very straight forward. I know about and have great regard for your father's World War I record. I asked his permission to even talk to you about this endeavor. Understand I am not talking about you becoming some sort of international spy. I see this role as being just what I said...only an observer while you're carrying out your normal responsibilities for North American Distribution, Inc. Certainly I'd like to suggest places in Italy I'd like you to 'observe' if you can safely do so. Yet, it's important you explore other locations you deem active in Italy's military build-up. In no way, though, do I intend for you to put yourself in danger."

As O'Brien was talking, Bailey was a bit taken aback. He now realized he was talking with a rather high level man from the State Department. No matter how unpremeditated O'Brien was communicating his needs for information in Italy, Bailey was very aware being in harm's way was quite probable. If spotted loitering near an arms manufacturing plant or taking pictures of a military training center, his health could get rather perilous.

O'Brien excused himself to make a telephone call and Bailey sat at the restaurant table dumbfounded. He recalled he'd dined in that very restaurant with Anna LaCurso years before. He remembered them laughing and talking hardly noticing what was on their plates. Now he was again not eating much on his plate for entirely different reasons.

As O'Brien made his way back to the table, Bailey smirked as he thought, 'Is this really how a person gets involved in the world of espionage? It starts with a simple little lunch at a restaurant and in no time one could be taking secret pictures of Il Duce in the shower with his favorite mistress?'

O'Brien took a swig of his beer and appeared preoccupied although still picking up where he'd left off. "So, Adam, I'm curious if you'd consider helping us. Naturally, if you don't feel comfortable in carrying out a task like I described, you shouldn't do it. But, based on your record and what people have said about you, you've got some basic tools and abilities to take on an endeavor like this one. You've already got a built in cover with your business travel and language skills. All I'm suggesting is that you pay a bit more attention to the things you've already spoken about in your travels in Italy. Then I'd just like a report on what you observed. When you return from your trip in late December, I'd likely meet you in New York. There'd be no reason for us communicating until then, so don't romanticize that I'm asking you to be some kind of clandestine agent complete with revolver, trench coat, and code name. I just want you to observe."

Bailey gazed at the former Minnesotan. O'Brien certainly made it sound like it wasn't so much a mission as it was just being more attentive. The task was not intimidating in the least. In fact, it sounded rather rudimentary given he knew the regions of Italy so well.

Without giving any response of "yay" or "nay", Bailey replied, "So, David, where do we go from here? Do you want my answer now?"

O'Brien chuckled, "Of course not. Think about it. As you know, I'm seeing my folks in Mendota Heights. Here's their number. You call me at any time with questions. I'm available here for two more days and then I'm taking a military transport plane back to Washington D.C. I'm aware you leave for Europe in a few days. It would be helpful if I had some idea of your interest by then."

Lunch ended abruptly. O'Brien picked up the tab. Bailey went back to his apartment somewhat dazed. It made sense the State Department would have interest in him. He really did have some potentially useful advantages for gathering intelligence. Besides, the task was only as big as he wanted to make it.

But, there was another more prideful factor. He'd been recommended by his own father. That meant something. It was his father who'd gone far beyond just serving his country. Bailey didn't know the full story, but enough to understand that John Bailey was a war hero from World War I. His father had come home with war medals from both France and the U.S. proving he'd faced danger... and likely quite often. He'd taken chances. He'd risked his life on another continent....and he gotten results while saving many French and American lives in the process. Bailey wondered if his father's actions and mentality ran in the bloodline. Then again, Bailey had to keep coming back to reality. What he was being asked to do was nowhere near what his father had accomplished on the fighting fields during the Big War.

Only hours after the lunch Bailey was already re-structuring his upcoming trip into Italy to cover more of the country by rail. There was no doubt he was going to take on the assignment. He did, however, have to face another cold hard fact... his cover as a representative for North American Distribution, Inc. had a time limit. Italy was not on good terms with the U.S. and his client base was receding fast. His free pass into Italy was likely to come to an end very soon as would his value to the State Department. But, until his cover was no longer useable in Italy, he wanted to contribute. By noontime the next day he'd called O'Brien in Mendota Heights to share his altered agenda for his Italian travels.

His response to O'Brien was blunt and urgent. "I can help. Let's meet."

They had lunch once more at a small eatery along University Avenue near the campus a few hours later. O'Brien repeatedly stressed to Bailey not to put himself in any danger. Bailey dismissed that statement but did speak again of his depreciating clientele in Italy. He also fudged a bit by assuring the State Department official that he should maintain some clients well through 1939 unless the European mess declined even more rapidly.

The question of his youth and inexperience in gathering intelligence never came up. It was as if O'Brien wasn't certain how valuable young Bailey might be. The upcoming trip into Italy would be a test case. O'Brien only asked that Bailey pay closer attention to all factories in and around Torino, Genova, and Milan. That was the primary manufacturing area and of most concern to the State Department.

They again shook hands with O'Brien saying he'd be in touch before Bailey sailed overseas. That salutation left Bailey feeling important...like his efforts might be considered potentially worthwhile.

Chapter 7

There was something else that happened between the time Adam Bailey met with David O'Brien and when he caught a Saturday, October 29 morning flight to New York to catch his transatlantic boat the next day for France. His thoughts were entirely on the Italy portion of his upcoming trip. For someone who was supposed to be observant, he hadn't noticed a car trailing him to and from his office one day and then doing the same the next day.

It was Tuesday and he was one of the last to leave the office. It was cold and rainy...a typical Minnesota introduction that winter was around the corner. He was trudging out onto the parking lot of North American Distribution, Inc. His head was down trying to stay protected from the chilly northwest wind. He was thinking about O'Brien and how respectful he was toward John Fena willing to have his European 'employee' use corporate travel money for the good of the State Department as well. Then again Bailey wondered how in depth that conversation had been between Fena and O'Brien. No doubt he'd stressed to Fena the absolute need for confidentiality. While he'd not brought up the subject once with Bailey, Fena had to have mulled over the similar question Bailey had. How long could Bailey be of any service to the State Department with the declining number of foreign clients, especially in Italy? It would not be long before Bailey's cover would dissolve. His junkets to Europe would end.

Lost in that thought, Bailey strode to his new 1936 Ford Roadster Street Rod not fully noticing a late model Cadillac looming out on the lonely street waiting for him. When he arrived at his apartment, he saw the Cadillac pass by slowly and then speed up and cruise on down the street. It was a maneuver meant for him to take notice.

The next morning, there it was again....a 1937 black Cadillac Series 70 that gleamed in the sunshine. Again he was supposed to see the car. For what reason, he had no idea. The classy car just pulled away as Bailey arrived at the North American Distribution, Inc. parking lot.

The next day was a repeat other than he left earlier to meet some friends for dinner. But, there it was...the black Cadillac...waiting at the far end of the parking lot. When the vehicle followed him home and then onto the restaurant, Bailey sensed who might be interested in his activities. Who else but Willie LaCurso would have him followed? The reasons were unclear but the method of making contact was predictable.

He'd recently read in the *Minneapolis Star* about a mysterious death with one of the leaders of the local grain millers union. To him that had Willie LaCurso's name written all over it. Willie was the president of the union. If someone didn't comply with his wishes, that someone would pay in some way. In this case the victim had paid the ultimate price.

Seeing the black Cadillac the following morning only made him reminisce about Anna once again. As much as he liked thinking of her, he hated the idea that he was back on her father's popularity list. Why after three years would LaCurso be checking up on him?

He began to steel himself for the inevitable 'invitation'. It was the last thing he wanted. He didn't fear the contact with the notorious hoodlum as much as he just didn't want to put up with the bother. The gangster Willie LaCurso wanted something from him. Bailey could only hope the reason had nothing to do with the Loni D'Annelli affair...a subject that made him highly discomfited. He now wished his upcoming trip overseas had already occurred so he wouldn't have to be subjected to LaCurso's predictable demand that they get together.

It took until that Thursday evening two days before he was to leave for New York that the recognizable Cadillac shimmied up behind him as he was walking to his car after leaving the office. It was dark. The street in front of the building had no traffic. Most people would be apprehensive with a car slowly moving towards them. Bailey just shook his head and rolled his eyes knowing the game that was being played. He was frankly relieved to get the tailing process done and get on with the impending summons from Willie LaCurso.

Bailey lit a cigarette while leaning against his Ford Roadster. He purposely showed absolute unconcern. He wanted to disappoint the driver of the Cadillac and not show any fear.

He stared coolly at the windshield of the imposing black car as it pulled up beside him. When it finally stopped, Bailey looked away emphasizing his indifference.

The driver's side window finally opened up and there was Uncle Tony complete with a sneer that looked rather natural. The right hand man to Willie LaCurso spoke as if his throat was drowned in mucous. His words were succinct and filled with the accent Bailey had forgotten the man had. "Hey, kid. Looks like you landed yourself a pretty good job....a sweet car you're now driving."

Bailey didn't respond. There was a brief pause before the gravelly voice continued. "Willie wants to talk to you. Why don't you follow me over to the house?"

It was the kind of question that required no response or dissent. Bailey wanted to show his irritation that Tony or Willie had no respect for what he might have planned for the evening...even though he had nothing going on. But, any complaint would be wasted effort. He shrugged. They had nothing on him. If they had wanted to kill him for being in the same car with Anna the night she was murdered, he would have been dead years before.

Finally Bailey said casually, "What took you so damn long, Tony. You wasted a lot of gas and time following me."

Then not waiting for a response he added, "O.K....I'll follow you. Let's take the River Road and get there fast. If you go too slowly, I'll be waiting for you at the front gates. I've got some other plans for tonight."

Tony didn't get a chance to say another word. Bailey got in his car and started the engine. Tony accepted Bailey's plan and peeled off.

Bailey's mind swirled as he followed the Cadillac too closely. They went at high speed down the roadway toward St. Paul atop the bluff overlooking the Mississippi River. His demeanor on the outside was unruffled. His gurgling insides spoke to nervousness and disgust. Even though he was going to see the top gangster in the Twin Cities, he knew the man well enough not to be intimidated. For certain he was going to let Willie know he didn't appreciate being followed for no good reason. He knew Willie would likely respect him for showing his irritability.

As the two cars approached the impressive mansion just down the street from Town & Country Golf Club, Bailey felt some perspiration on his forehead despite the night being so cold. He drove into the horseshoe driveway behind Tony. The big man got out of his automobile and didn't even wait for Bailey. He just expected the young man to follow. As much as he wanted to say something smart and acerbic to Tony, he knew Willie's right hand man was impervious to back talk. Uncle Tony, as Anna had always called him, was just doing his job and making a delivery. Bailey kept his show of confidence and hardly looked at Tony as he was ushered into the grand foyer of the LaCurso home where his coat was taken by a butler.

As Bailey walked in, Willie was smoking a cigar in his library and talking on the telephone. There was no joy in his eyes as he motioned for his guest to sit down.

Bailey took his time doing so. He instead stood and gazed at the pictures on the wall and some of the art pieces on a series of shelves. He hoped his audacity would not go unnoticed.

Taking another minute to finish his phone call, Willie began talking to Bailey before he'd hung up the telephone. There was no welcoming handshake. The words echoed in the huge empty house as he got up to close the library door. "Well, Tony tells me you've found a pretty good job over at North American Distribution, Inc." They've been a pretty solid small company for a number of years. In fact, they seem to be putting a lot of faith in such a young, inexperienced kid out of college. They have you going overseas and making contact with some fairly substantial food and wine producers. My...My...that's very heavy work for one so young. It's amazing you got the job with your limited background, but they seem pleased with your results."

None of what LaCurso was saying showed any respect. The older man had suddenly just gone into making judgments on Bailey's worth to his company. The younger man found his dander increasing and with that last little dig, he moved towards the wiry thin man until he was two feet away. He towered over the gangster. He so wanted to say a few choice words of how he really felt about the bastard...like if LaCurso wasn't such an underhanded, evil crook maybe Anna would still be alive...but he held his tongue from being that vicious.

Instead he stood tall, stared down at the evil eyes of LaCurso and snarled, "Willie, first thank you for such a nice greeting. We haven't seen each other for a couple years and you choose to cast aspersions on either the company I work for or me...I couldn't tell which was your target. Tell me, do you do that type of welcome to all your guests? Secondly, I want to know what in the God damned hell I ever did for you to think you could treat me this way."

Willie blinked, but Bailey wasn't done. His words were spoken with no nervousness and verbalized very clearly. "Let me tell you something before you continue defaming me or my company. I think of Anna every blessed day. She was special. I'm very sorry her life ended the way it did. But, God dammit I didn't pull the trigger. If anything, I wished I could have been in the way of those bullets to save her life. She and I were just developing our relationship. And, for the love of God, you've known me since I was thirteen years old...and deep down you know I was the kind of guy you would have wanted for your daughter. But, for reasons far beyond my control, it didn't happen. So we both lost.

And now, for some unknown reason you want to see me. You don't politely invite me out to lunch or over to your house; you have Tony follow me for a couple days apparently to intimidate...which is a big God damn waste of time.... and then you expect me to come to your house on your whim with no regard for my schedule. I should have told Tony and you both to go to hell. So I come here anyway only to have you in the first minute tell me you know what I do and offer your opinion that I'm not qualified to handle my responsibilities. Well, Jesus Christ!! Willie, what the hell do you say to people you don't like?

So, if you're point was to make me feel badly, you've completed your task. If you're going to treat me like trash, then before I walk out of here, why don't you get your final disparaging comments off your chest? Then I can move on to something I'd prefer to do this evening.

Bailey turned away from the older man and began heading for the library door. He knew he'd said words to LaCurso that the man's ears had rarely, if ever, heard. He was playing on their long-term knowledge of each other and gambling he could get away with his terse diatribe.

He continued to play out his hand by opening the library door. Then he stopped and looked back at LaCurso saying loudly with angered voice, "Last chance, Willie, what else you want to say to make this day even more miserable for me than it has become already?"

He stared from the door directly into the eyes of a man who could arrange his death in the next minute if he was so motivated. But, Bailey knew he had scored. LaCurso's eyes burned only slightly hotter. He sensed the older man was almost proud of him for going into the tirade. In fact, he guessed the man even enjoyed his comment about what Willie said to people he didn't like.

The conman's voice now became calm as he walked towards Bailey offering his hand. "Adam, my boy, I'm so sorry if I got your feathers ruffled. Please sit back down. I just finished an important phone call and my mind was on something else. Accept my apology. I'm certain your boss, John Fena, would not be investing in you if you weren't showing a lot of promise and getting results. Now, again, please sit. Let me get you some wine. I was just curious how things have been going for you. We haven't talked for a long, long time."

Bailey shook the hand but returned only a half-hearted smile. He wasn't convinced in the least LaCurso was being sincere. But, he was certain the gangster had invited him to his house for a reason beyond just summarizing his life since last they saw each other. The conversation would lead to something. No doubt he'd first ask questions to Bailey of which Willie likely already knew...like where he'd traveled in Europe, where he ate three days ago, and even the name of the girl Bailey had taken out to dinner the previous weekend.

Knowing what to expect from Willie put Bailey in a better comfort zone than others who wouldn't know the gangster as well. He maintained his confident posture but was still a bit hot. His voice was still hostile as he said, "O.K., Willie, you asked me how things are going. Let me tell you. They're going damn fine.... about as fine as things can go if you consider that the girl I was so fond of and was beginning to know was shot and killed while driving with me. A part of me was taken that day with her. I doubt they'll be a day in the future that I won't think about her and that horrible end! Now, why did you really want to see me?"

Bailey's continued outburst caused LaCurso's shoulders to slightly stoop. He really hadn't considered the impact on the young man of his daughter's shooting death. He'd always known Bailey not to be shy, but he also saw that Bailey was no longer a naïve kid. Maturity and a few more years had made the young man more self-assured. Willie no longer could take for granted the innocence of the kid as he still envisioned him being. He also couldn't take offense to Bailey's eruption. Those were words of a person hurt deeply by Anna's death. The wounds had not healed for either man.

LaCurso came down from his perch. Bailey saw a much older man than the intense competitor on the golf course when Loni D'Annelli was still alive...even noticeably looking older than the last time he'd seen Willie after Anna's death a couple years before.

Though moved by Bailey's strong words, the older man had to stay somewhat in character and remain stalwart in his approach to his guest. There indeed was another purpose for Bailey being invited to the River Road mansion.

LaCurso sat back in his leather chair and took a long inhalation on his cigar. Then nodding as if appreciating what the young man had just expressed, he said, "Adam, let's not fight. I'm too tired tonight. Let's just talk about how you're doing and how your business is being affected by the conflicts in Europe. Your boss... and you...probably already figure the new business you brought in from overseas is temporary. It's only a matter of time before that imbecilic leader of Italy will completely shut down shipments to North America. He'll proclaim everything produced in his country should be for the betterment of Italy...or, what he really means is for the growth of the Italian military. Your travels to Italy will become less profitable and unfortunately the same can be said for the other countries in Europe with whom you're doing business.

Switzerland and France have their own unique problems. Switzerland will be neutral, but you can just as well call it a German state. Food and wine exports will suffer. France will probably be at war with that renegade Hitler in another year. When that happens, it'll be interesting what help they might request and receive from the U.S. Anyway, as we approach 1939, it doesn't look good for a lot of businesses...and I don't mean just yours. I'm being affected as well. As you might guess, I have extensive family in Italy. Their businesses are suffering and I pray for their health and safety every day. As you can guess, my family and I are no fan of Benito Mussolini."

Bailey held back a smug grin. The LaCurso family businesses in Italy were no doubt anything but legal. Nonetheless, Mussolini and his regime had to be a major obstacle whether difficult government regulations or officials constantly having to be paid off. Watching LaCurso drift from irritability to calm to acidic in describing the ills caused by the Italian dictator, Bailey took note how alarming the man's hair trigger personality could change. When he was composed he exhibited an intelligent world view noting military and political themes and consequences that seemed quite accurate and even thought provoking. When his dander increased, he became more impulsive and truculent.

As their conversation continued in the LaCurso library, Bailey found himself often times agreeing with LaCurso's opinions and added some of his own views. For not seeing each other for a couple years, he found it surprising they were having such an affable interchange. In their first half hour conversation, he could see Willie was impressed how much he knew about Italy in general....and that Bailey had a similar strong dislike for Benito Mussolini. The older man kept repeating the constant struggle his younger brother Roberto was having as the de facto leader of the family in Italy. Willie admitted trying to send money over to his brother to support the family, but he was at times uncertain if the cash contributions were reaching Roberto's hands in Milan.

It took until a blustery wind outdoors knocked a branch against the library picture window for both men to chuckle and realize how nonstop they'd been conversing. Still, Bailey knew very well their discussion was only leading up to something else. Willie was only warming him up. The real subject would soon be introduced.

Willie paused to pour his guest some more wine, but Bailey put his hand silently over his glass. He wanted his host to know he intended to remain sober and aware.

The older man stared at him, smiled, and then withdrew the bottle only to fill his own glass. Then as if the previous thirty minutes of international business and political talk had not happened, LaCurso abruptly altered the direction of their talk.

With no attempt at a smooth transition, his face and voice became more serious. "Adam, we talked once about that weekend back in 1931 when the police raided Chippewa Lodge and arrested our friend, Loni D'Annelli. All of us have read various accounts of how all that happened and conjectured what might be true or what was not. With his death just a month after the raid, it doesn't matter anymore to what degree he may or may not have been involved in that operation. What I didn't like was how his supposed friends in Chicago, Milwaukee, and even among some here in the Twin Cities assumed that counterfeit money issue was his to bear. There were many other businessmen at Chippewa Lodge who could have been involved. And, if Loni truly had anything to do with the gambling operation, he'd never pay off wagers to his friends with funny money. The man had more brains than to do that type of thing."

Bailey had a hard time not rolling his eyes as Willie tried to paint an ambiguous picture of who was really in charge of the illegal activities at the Lodge. LaCurso had over seven years since 1931 to create his own story. What he'd apparently forgotten was that Bailey was right there at Chippewa Lodge. All evidence had pointed conclusively that Loni D'Annelli was the king pin of the entire enterprise.

Willie continued, "I hated what happened to him, but there was little I could do. He should have been given a better chance to explain himself. I still think that fake money was planted in the basement of that feed and grain mill. Loni was simply storing a few personal items and some of his profits from his businesses."

Bailey wasn't certain why he was an audience to LaCurso's sudden bizarre and highly inaccurate defense of his deceased friend. He kept his mouth quiet and his head not moving. There was no point responding one way or the other to Willie's poppycock. Besides, Bailey sensed the older man had still not gotten to the real reason for their meeting.

He was not done. LaCurso took a long drink of his wine and finally exclaimed, "Adam, you must wonder why I'm bringing this subject up with you after all these years. Well, let me share something with you I've told only few other people. When the authorities clamped down on my friend, they confiscated every last dollar bill that was being secretly kept in the basement of the mill whether counterfeit or real.

He paused and placed a sharp eye on his guest. "Adam, you were living in Glenwood at the time. You might have heard the rumble about the local manager of that feed and grain mill having given that storage space to D'Annelli as a kind of gift from the town for all Loni had done for the community. It was an unknown location and a safer place than certainly the damned banks that were closing down faster than a Minnesota summer."

On that point about the banks, Bailey couldn't disagree. That was a verifiable fact. D'Annelli was smart to store his money in that secret basement storage area. He allowed himself to nod at Willie's comment.

The older man then murmured, "You should understand that the mill was not the only place in Glenwood Loni stored his profits."

Bailey sat forward. This was something new that likely his father, and friends, the Lawtons and Charlie Davis might not have heard.

"You should understand I had entrusted large sums with Loni. He was a special friend. I trusted him. I asked him to protect a large amount of my own money and he mentioned he'd secured some of his money and my money in two other secretive places as leverage against anyone ever discovering the Glenwood Feed & Grain Mill storage area.

I didn't think much of it. I knew he'd keep my money and his money safe. In fact, I thought it was a good idea. When he was arrested and the figures were divulged in the newspapers, the dollar amount was way low. Some of his and my money had been saved. He and I were going to meet so he could personally tell me the other locations and provide me a map and a key. Our meeting was scheduled two days after he was murdered by some of those so-called friends he had in Chicago.

So, I was left hanging. I had no information, no maps, only the assurance that my money had not been touched by the authorities. I had a couple of my men do some investigation months later after everything had calmed down in Glenwood. They came back empty.

I'll never give up on finding that money. It was a substantial sum and it's someplace in your hometown. So...that's the main reason I wanted to talk with you. Adam, you know the town, the mill, Loni and some of his right hand people. I don't mind paying a percent of the money when it's found to anyone who might be able to help. I wanted to ask if you might have any idea of where else valuables could be stored. Did Loni have other local friends besides that Henry Hanson fellow who ran the mill? I know Hanson departed the town rather suddenly that weekend and never returned. I'm concerned that he may have left Glenwood with a lot of money that wasn't his to take. However, I'm inclined to discount him. I met him. He didn't impress me as someone with that much gumption. I think he left town to avoid arrest."

Bailey almost choked. Hearing Willie's assessment of Henry Hanson was as opposite of the actual description of Henry as could be possible. Now Henry

Granville, a hotel magnate living in Charleston, South Carolina would be ecstatic if he heard LaCurso's inferior description of him. It proved again how Henry had pulled the wool over so many people's eyes since he left Minnesota back in '31' to begin a new life.

Stifling his laugh, Bailey tuned back to Willie's rant. "Adam, you can imagine in the seven years since that incident I would have liked to have found that Hanson guy, but he's disappeared for good....likely changed his name, his appearance, maybe he doesn't even live in the U.S. anymore. My boys believe the guy might be dead. Still, I really don't believe Hanson has my money. He just might have some ideas that might help me locate my lost capital. But, his help isn't going to happen. He's gone for good."

Again Bailey had to bite his tongue. He'd just seen Henry the previous summer when the man was visiting and staying at a lake resort at White Bear Lake. Henry Hanson, now going by the alias, Henry Granville, would be pleased to hear Willie's hypothesis of his being dead. It was exactly as Henry would hope.

Well aware of the tale that Henry took some money from the Mill basement before departing Glenwood, Bailey didn't believe it nor did he ever think of asking Granville. It wasn't the type of question you ask someone. What he did know was that Henry had amassed some working capital through some shrewd investments before leaving Glenwood. That money gave him the seed money and leverage to begin building his first hotel once he'd arrived in Charleston, South Carolina.

Henry had come out of hiding back in 1933 when he visited Minnesota to see some of his property investments and to visit some friends...in particular the Lawtons, Charlie Davis, and his father John. It was the first time Adam had seen Henry since before the police raid at the Chippewa Lodge. Henry was unrecognizable as a southern gentleman with Granville as his last name. Since then Bailey had learned how much Henry had been involved in bringing down Loni D'Annelli and what his role had been in silently helping end the illegal operations at the Lodge. As well, since 1933, Henry Granville had become reacquainted with Adam's father and was now very much a part of the family of co-conspirators. Adam didn't see the man often, but was aware the others saw Henry a couple times a year in South Carolina.

He tuned back into LaCurso still lamenting his lost fortune. It was strange the apparent reason he was being summoned to the gangster's home was to be queried about other possible locations where Loni D'Annelli might have stored money in Glenwood. It was odd enough that Bailey wondered if the real reason had still not been yet divulged.

With hopes of leaving, Bailey finally shrugged. "Willie, I'm sorry you took such a loss. I wish I could help. However, you have to remember I was an eighteen year old kid when everything blew up out at Chippewa Lodge. I was as surprised as anyone when all that money was found in the Glenwood Feed & Grain Mill basement. I have no thought as to where other monies could have been hidden."

LaCurso seemed only slightly disappointed as if he expected the response. The story of the lost capital then turned into a transition to a more uncomfortable topic. The spry older man gazed into Bailey's eyes and asked point blank, "Adam, I happened to have attended your college graduation and saw certain people close to you who were at the last Chippewa Lodge charity golf tournament four years before. I thought it curious, not so much your father, as were those other people hugging and kissing you in congratulations. I recognized Lindy MacPherson, the investigator, who tried to distance herself from being credited by the newspapers for her part in that police raid. I know she has constantly downplayed her role. She claims to have just stumbled upon the activity at Chippewa Lodge and recognized a few cons. In looking back, things certainly fell into place for the cops when they raided the Lodge. She had a lot of evidence that made all those arrests that day stick. And, there have always been rumors she didn't work alone."

He stopped momentarily and glimmered at Bailey obviously looking for some kind of telltale reaction. Bailey had always wondered how he'd react if he ever got cornered with a question LaCurso was inferring. He'd prepared mentally ever since that June weekend in case the conjecture was introduced. That time had just arrived.

He calmly leaned back and moved not one facial muscle as LaCurso continued, "Then I saw those other two guys sitting with your father at your graduation. I recognized one as the golfing partner on Loni's foursome team. I still don't have any idea why Loni invited that guy to play in the tournament, but he did and that fellow did quite well as I recall. I have since found out that the golfer is a lawyer here in Minneapolis and a first-rate golfer. I assumed Loni and that fellow had some mutual business interests, but it never got confirmed. Now, it no longer matters. D'Annelli's gone."

Bailey felt a bead of sweat run down his back. He determinedly remained quiet as LaCurso kept answering his own questions and seemed satisfied with his reasoning.

Willie then said, "Now, Adam, I don't expect you to remember everything about that incident or know anything about Loni's cash reserve. But, I do find that your father and your immediate friends were there that weekend strikes me as a hell of a coincidence. Doesn't it to you?"

Then he stopped talking and just stared at Bailey.

And there it was. The entire D'Annelli incident had just been exhumed and now lay naked on the table. In all the conversations with his father, with Jamie and Lindy, and with Charlie Davis, he never once figured he'd be questioned so directly. He had been coached how to respond, but he was still stunned. He prayed silently he could be believable for the sake of his father and friends. Their futures were right now in his hands.

He took a deep breath and leaned forward with a slight smirk. "Willie, I don't know what to say besides the truth. You know Loni was a special friend to me.

He treated me very well and helped make my summers growing up in Glenwood unforgettable and a lot of fun. A lot of his friends became my friends too, even though they were a lot older than me."

Willie nodded showing complete agreement, but waiting for the real response.

"You apparently are now asking if my friendships with Lindy MacPherson or those other two guys, Jamie Lawton and Charlie Davis had anything to do with what happened to my friend, Loni. Well, you know as well as I that Lawton got into the tournament with an invitation from Loni. The two of them must have known each other.

Once in the tournament, Lawton called his friend, Charlie Davis. They'd been friends since law school and Davis lived right up the road in Alexandria. Well, I didn't even meet either of them until that first day of the tournament. Lawton played in Loni's group and through the day, my father and I got to know Lawton and Davis. They were two good guys. As for Lindy MacPherson, I didn't really get to know her until after the whole episode with the police raid. It turned out that she and Lawton caught each other's eye on the golf course that weekend, exchanged numbers, and eventually began dating. By that autumn I was down living in Minneapolis going to school. Lawton invited me to play golf when Charlie Davis was in the city and the three of us became friends. I must say they truly helped out a lonely farm kid feel more comfortable in the big city.

During school I got to know Lindy, Jamie, and Charlie even better. They'd invite me over for dinner periodically, especially when Davis was in town. We frankly didn't talk much about what happened that summer of '31'at the Lodge. It didn't affect our lives other than we all met that weekend. So, our lives moved on. We had far more other important things going on than talking much about that weekend."

Bailey then shut his mouth and stared at LaCurso to see if his simplified, manufactured story was being believed. He had sugar-coated over what had actually happened very smoothly.

Willie took a slow puff from his cigar and tried once again to catch Bailey in some kind of inconsistency. "So Adam, you're asking me to believe these people only became your friends because you all happened to be together all day and got to know one another during that first day of Loni's charity golf tournament."

It was another ploy by Willie to intimidate by showing disbelief. Bailey continued his performance. Showing irritation, he raised his voice. "Willie, for Christ's sake, the answer is yes....but our friendship didn't just happen in one day. Friendships as you damn well know take time. But, we definitely had a very enjoyable day together that Saturday....and Loni was right there with us in the same foursome. I can tell you absolutely that he enjoyed that day as well. Lawton, Davis and Lindy MacPherson and even my father had a chance to build on our meeting from that day forward; Loni of course was otherwise preoccupied the rest of that Saturday night with all the players and picking up his winning bets.

Then the next day happened...and I needn't go on." Bailey put a disappointing look on his face and let his voice trail off.

Willie was coming around but still repeated, "So, you don't think those two lawyers had anything to do with Loni being set up."

"If you would have asked me after that weekend, maybe I could have seen your point. But, I've now gotten to know them. They aren't the type to stick their necks out. Besides, they'd never been to Glenwood and only drove down to Chippewa Lodge that Saturday morning. They were on the golf course all day and were exhausted after the first day of the tournament. They drove back to Davis's place that night to sleep."

On Sunday morning for that second and last day of the tournament, Lawton was getting warmed up out on the golf course when the cops arrived. Davis was with him. They made a decision to stay out on the golf course rather than face the cops. They knew nothing and were only there to play golf. I think a lot of those other players wished they'd been warming up out on the course as well.

LaCurso nodded emphatically in full agreement remembering he was one of those arrested and brought down to the Pope County jail. He'd been released with help of his St. Paul lawyer later that Sunday, but the whole episode had been embarrassing and brought with it unwanted publicity.

Bailey sensed he'd simmered the older man's concerns. "So Willie, that's what I know and how I got to know those folks. They became very good friends and kind of make up for the family I lost almost fourteen years ago."

Willie reacted somberly. He knew of Bailey's unfortunate family loss as a kid and nodded sympathetically

Bailey finished up his somewhat fabricated explanation by adding, "If you're trying to lay blame on those two guys or Lindy for what happened to Loni, I think you're swimming up the wrong stream."

LaCurso began chuckling. He pointed his cigar at the young man with only a hint of accusation. "Adam, you've got guts. I'll say that for you. You stand up for your friends and your father very well. I wish I had you on my side."

He looked forlornly outside his library window towards some of the men standing in the driveway at that late hour guarding him and his family. He lamented, "Yup...that's for damned sure...I could certainly use some of your kind of spunk in my corner."

Then he shot those sharp eyes back at Bailey and made a blatant lie. "Adam, all I care about is where Loni might have stored that other money. It was a lot of cash...I mean a lot of money. That's what I'm interested in finding. Counting Loni's profits, there could be as much as a million bucks still missing."

The amount left Bailey momentarily stunned. He'd known about the approximate $500,000 that MacPherson, Lawton, and Davis had hijacked that Saturday night for evidence from the Feed & Grain Mill basement. He'd heard there was even more loot in the basement that his three accomplices had left for the police to find. However, in no way did they hint there was anywhere near that amount of additional money Willie LaCurso was describing. That made it entirely possible D'Annelli probably did have another place to store other business profits...including LaCurso's money.

Convinced he'd effectively defended his fellow conspirators; Bailey began looking at his watch as a way of hinting he had nothing more to share. By showing his positive feelings for the departed D'Annelli and apathy towards LaCurso's lost fortune, he hoped this small meeting might be the last time he and the underworld boss would ever have to talk again.

Trying to end the torturous evening, he retorted, "Willie, I guess the whole story about Loni pretty much ended for me when they arrested him. I never saw him again. When I heard he was shot and killed in Chicago, I'll always think of that day as the end of my youth and my life in Glenwood. He meant a lot to me."

LaCurso just sat in his leather chair his eyes blinking emotionally over what the young man had just shared. Still, he stared at Bailey like a card shark waiting for him to show any sign of insincerity.

But, there was none. Bailey had seen Willie glower at people the same way out on the Chippewa Lodge golf course. He was not going to show any weakness, especially knowing the wiry man was not going to harm him. In fact, Bailey sensed the older man had gained new respect for him after that night's exchange.

Finally blinking away his menacing stare, Willie stood up indicating their conversation was done. His sudden jovial smile only made Bailey trust him less. Willie now talked as if what they'd discussed was only trivial. He exclaimed, "Adam, it was good to see again. I wish you continued luck in your job and truly hope your efforts in Italy will continue bearing fruit. Honestly, though, I think we both know Italy will likely not be an important market for you until some military action finally ends the reign of that idiot Mussolini. I guess you'll have to pull clients from other Mediterranean countries...maybe even countries from another continent...like South America."

Bailey only nodded wishing LaCurso's comments weren't true. Unfortunately, he couldn't disagree. But, given his new assignment with David O'Brien and the State Department, he wanted to hang onto those Italian clients as long as he could.

Willie then added, "You know, Adam, I have many relatives over in Italy. I wish I was going with you on your upcoming trip just to give them words of support."

He then put his hand gently on Bailey's shoulder as if they were old friends and walked the young man to the front door of the mansion. There he nodded his head, shook hands with Bailey, and with nothing more to say promptly closed the door the moment the young man was out the door.

Uncle Tony was standing outside smoking a cigarette by the black Cadillac. He looked at Bailey quizzically. "So kid, it's been a while. You two must have got reacquainted. That's nice. I didn't think you'd be done so soon."

Then he threw his cigarette onto the driveway, mashed it with his massive foot, and simply said, "See you around, kid." He then turned away and joined a conversation with the guards protecting the LaCurso mansion.

As Bailey drove slowly out of the circular driveway from the mansion, the security gates operated by the guards opened briefly then closed as he drove onto River Road. He thought about what got said in Willie's library all the way back to his apartment. He found it interesting how LaCurso not only knew the nature of his overseas job, but was aware of his upcoming travels to Italy. There had to be someone at the North American Distribution headquarters who was being paid or coerced to keep an eye on him and his schedule. As uncomfortable as that obvious fact made him feel, he knew that was the way Willie LaCurso operated.

Bailey sardonically thought he should have offered to send Willie a copy of his upcoming monthly schedule just to save the conman some money paying off a company staff person to do the same. Then, letting out some of his nervous energy, he shouted out to no one within his quiet car, "The hell with him. Let that hoodlum pay somebody to get my travel schedule at the office."

Then more sedately he mumbled to himself, "What does that man really want from me?"

As Adam Bailey was driving out of the LaCurso estate gate, Willie LaCurso from his library window watched the young man's vehicle disappear into the dark night. It had been an interesting conversation. Bailey had done a lot since graduating from the University of Minnesota in May, 1935. In the three-and-a-half years since then, the young man had gained a tremendous amount of international business experience and the increased confidence to go with it. That self-confidence was shown in how strongly he stood up for himself and his friends. However, there were still some discrepancies in Bailey's comments.

He did want to hear Bailey's interpretation of the police raid and Loni D'Annelli's arrest back in 1931...not that he cared so much about the actual incident anymore. It had been unfortunate the way D'Annelli had been gunned down on the streets of Chicago just a month after the raid at the Lodge. But, LaCurso had seen it as inevitable. There were too many mob members who believed D'Annelli had scammed them with wagers being paid with counterfeit money. D'Annelli had worked tirelessly that last month of his life trying to clear himself of that particular perception. But, he'd failed. It had cost him his life.

The only thing that lingered was the money for his family he'd entrusted to D'Annelli just in case the authorities somehow arrested him and froze his assets. He'd retrieved some of the cash...maybe a $100,000...just weeks before the cops showed up at Chippewa Lodge. But, there was still a substantial amount yet to be found. It wasn't a million dollars as he'd said to the young man. He'd just used that figure to see Bailey's reaction. Surprisingly, Bailey showed little response.

However, he knew he did have at least $500,000 hidden somewhere in the Glenwood area. D'Annelli had said the two other locations were as safe as the Feed & Grain Mill basement. After the police raid it could be argued the remaining sites were even better. Not even his men had come up with any clues as to the whereabouts of those other secluded places. Willie had hoped some kind of post-mortem note would be delivered to him after D'Annelli's premature death. That communication never happened. It showed D'Annelli never anticipated being a victim of a gangland shooting on Dearborn Street in Chicago.

LaCurso had even sent Baldy Machowitz, one of his more trusted boys, to live for the rest of the summer in Glenwood and then two years later during the summer of 1933. Masquerading as an injured former railroad worker, Machowitz got closer to the locals than anyone since the whole D'Annelli episode had exploded. Baldy had plenty of conversations with people he'd befriended in the community. When the subject of 'other D'Annelli money' being buried somewhere, the locals usually got quiet. They never talked to outsiders, especially nosey newspaper reporters, about anything related to the mob run lake resort or about all the gangsters who'd roamed freely around their community for five years leading up to the 1931 raid.

However, amongst themselves, one of the hotter topics was where might there be other D'Annelli money hidden in the town. Since the infamous raid causing Chippewa Lodge to close down, Glenwood had slid back to just another struggling town in the midst of the worst depression to ever hit the country. The citizens whispered constantly about how that extra cash could boost the town's economy....as if the person finding the cash might divide up the proceeds to each town member. Even Baldy rolled his eyes on that dream. If any local citizen discovered a large amount of cash, they'd be gone from Glenwood faster than a bank could pull its shades after a forced closing.

After both those summers and a good tan from fishing and golfing, Baldy was sadly called back to the Twin Cities from Glenwood by LaCurso. He'd checked out every lead and come up with nothing. It was back to late nights and taking direct orders from the boss. Baldy made a lot of friends during those two summers in the Glenwood area. He would look back on those tasks at Lake Minnewaska as the best times of his life.

LaCurso had also brought Bailey over to his house to evaluate the possibility of the young man doing him a favor. He needed someone trustworthy to possibly deliver a suitcase full of cash to Milan and personally hand it over to his brother, Roberto. It would be the surest way of having the money end up in the proper person's hands. His large overseas family was in need of financial support, but the money was also intended for another reason. Willie was financing through his brother, Roberto, a secretive group with the aim to topple the Fascist regime in Italy by assassinating Mussolini. Recent attempts at getting the cash across the Italian border and into his brother's hands had proved risky. There was even one suitcase containing $25,000 that never did make it to Milan. Some border guard had opened the suitcase and disappeared with the money.

The endeavor Willie was trying to finance was expensive enough without taking losses of that proportion. If it happened once, the same thing could happen quite easily again. LaCurso had become aware of Adam Bailey and his business exploits overseas. It was a small article in the business section of the *Minneapolis Star* that reported on a local distribution company doing business quite successfully in Western Europe despite the deteriorating economy over there. Much of the credit was being given to a young man who'd only been with the company just over three years named Adam Bailey.

That was the germination of LaCurso's idea and resurrected his interest in meeting the young man once again. His ill-feelings for Bailey still existed, but in business he'd learned not to let personal matters get in the way of something that had to get done. He figured to invite the young man over for a drink, talk about his career, and evaluate if Bailey's trips overseas might make him a candidate to be a courier.

What LaCurso hadn't expected were two things. His own negative emotions concerning Bailey were overwhelming when the young man walked into his home. Bailey had been the last person with his daughter before she was killed. LaCurso still considered him partially to blame for outrunning the security Willie had set up for his daughter.

He'd started the conversation with Bailey on a very highly-charged adverse tone. Bailey, to his credit, had stood his ground showing no fear. That brought out the second thing LaCurso hadn't expected. He found himself respecting the kid....even liking him. The two of them had shared some wine, talked of international business concerns, and even briefly discussed the Loni D'Annelli debacle going back to 1931.

Whether young Bailey was speaking the entire truth or not, Willie liked how the kid had matured and could talk confidently from his experience traveling in Western Europe. He could even speak Italian surprisingly well.

LaCurso hated to admit it, but if things had worked out differently, Adam Bailey was the type of fellow Willie wished his oldest daughter would have eventually married...if she'd had the chance.

That meeting with Bailey just days before the young man was to leave for Europe verified to LaCurso the kid was as honest and straight-forward as he'd always been. That evening's investment of time was well worth it. It laid the foundation for future contacts with Bailey. He envisioned this representative for North American Distribution, Inc. becoming a trustful messenger. LaCurso could make the delivery sound as if it was more a benevolent act to help Willie's oppressed family in Italy. In fact, Bailey would totally unaware he was carrying money to be invested in a group hired to murder Benito Mussolini.

Chapter 8

More important to Adam Bailey than the Thursday night get-together at Willie LaCurso's house were the continuous calls that week from David O'Brien or from some of his staff in Washington D.C. O'Brien's associates seemed very pleased...even enthusiastic...of his willingness to potentially help the State Department. Each one kept reminding him to be cautious and don't take chances when he was overseas. They also shared information, though sparse, regarding intelligence they already had and then informing him they needed more updated data on the locations and numbers of known manufacturing plants and military training facilities. Bailey was familiar with each locality they mentioned.

At times he felt like a boy among men when talking to O'Brien's people. They spoke as if the U.S. was already at war with Germany and by association with Italy as well. He rarely felt daunted but his involvement with such focused people at the State Department left him overawed. Eventually that feeling would subside when he sensed his contribution could be important.

A code was given him if there was reason to call the State Department's London office. The inference was that kind of contact shouldn't be necessary.

That first junket overseas representing his company and his government simultaneously turned out longer than his original itinerary. It would be eight weeks of constant movement through the end of 1938. Though a rough and cold Atlantic Ocean voyage, he had arrived on the northern tip of France on November 8, 1938, at the port of Cherbourg. The ship had been on the water for nine days.

Wasting no time, he took a night train deep into the French wine country southeast of Paris. His business required him to still see clients. They generally greeted him warmly and positively despite the growing concerns over Germany very real threats to Western Europe. His business in that country was not declining like in Italy, but he knew it was inevitable. Exports to the U.S. would likely be delayed if not eliminated completely.

It would be the same case in Switzerland. The viability of trade between that country and the U.S. was declining by the month. Despite the same predicament in Italy, he was determined to maintain relationships as much as he could if nothing else than to sustain legitimacy for his travels in that country.

Bailey went back and forth from Italy into France twice during his two months of travel. He used the 'safe line' connection from Vernier, France to London once and another time from Grenoble. He liked the convenience of Vernier because it was across the border from his favorite Swiss city, Geneva, Switzerland. His telephone messages were brief only alerting David O'Brien that he was trying to be of value to the State Department. His information was coded with statements like, "A lot of new businesses in northern Italy. Have photos of some beautiful vineyards south and east of the city including harvest yields. See you at year's end." His nondescript language translated that Milan was adding more war supply plants and that he had pictures, verifiable locations, and production numbers.

While Milan in Italy had become his center city for his business exploits it was Geneva, Switzerland where he preferred to spend many of his weekends. For relaxation, he skied and made time with a couple French and Swiss females who were on holiday. That was the extent of his social contacts.

During his travels through Italy he'd found even more plants and factories that had processed Italian foods or additives for export to North and South America that no longer were in that business. Too many factories had been converted to production of shell casings, ammunition, uniforms, and military vehicle parts. At times he committed the location and factory to memory. Other times he was able to photograph the installation and even learn from locals what the plant produced. At Torino and then down toward Genova he recorded even more military output. Former automobile factories were now turning out tanks, jeeps, and airplane parts.

Through all his surveillance, he dutifully stopped at wine distributors whether they were clients, former clients, or neither. While most were friendly, they were uncomfortable. Each one either subtly or blatantly communicated to him that if someone in the Fascist regime discovered they were talking with an American capitalist, their lives could be made even more unpleasant.

Bailey therefore did not stay long at any of these vineyards or factory offices. Yet, he made certain they understood his purpose for seeing them repeating that if the political situation ever allowed them to do business again, North American Distribution, Inc. would be ready. With that pretext, if he was never questioned by the Italian military police during his travels; his objectives could be supported by these contacts.

By the second trip into Italy, he no longer could commit his observations of manufacturing plants in northern Italy to memory. Adding to this challenge was what he was learning just in idle chatter at the vineyards or even in bars at the end of his work day. Talk about new installations or converted plants were everywhere.

He was forced to invent ways to document his notations. Coding them on the back sides of papers in his business files was best. The info was put into words that related to his wine and food business and not easily discernable if the Italian authorities ever rampaged through his briefcase. While he felt completely unobserved and thereby feeling free to take discreet photos of various transformed factories, his apprehension grew with that exercise as well. Carrying unprocessed film would be the most damning if he was caught.

He eventually found a place to hide these items. It was at the hotel he usually frequented while in Milan. The Hotel de Italiana had been his home away from home since 1936. He concealed the most sensitive materials…like the film rolls… in some large vases outside his first floor room near the hotel main patio. The vases were filled with large plants. Placed in a plastic bag, the film and his notes were buried in the dirt in two of those vases.

At the end of December when leaving Italy, his plan was to stay the night at the Milan hotel and recover the plastic wrapped packages. That strategy didn't work out as smoothly as he'd hoped. That one evening unfortunately had a staff Christmas party and the participants flowed out onto the patio making his access to the vases difficult. Along with that inconvenience, he was unable to stay in his normal hotel suite. Additionally, the couple using the room sat out on their small terrace imbibing while the party went on.

Bailey didn't get much sleep that night. It was 4:00 AM before he could recover the hidden intelligence. The next day he slept soundly on the train with the film and notes tucked securely in the lining of his coat as he traveled north out of Italy through Switzerland. While crossing the Swiss-Italian border by Como, it did occur to him he was vulnerable if searched. He was new at the 'spy' game. When one of the Italian border guards stared at him for what seemed like an inordinate amount of time, Bailey's heart rate actually caused him to sweat.

Finally the guard blinked and told him to move on. Bailey hoped he may have looked too innocent to be an infiltrator. Then again, he pondered what a foreign spy was supposed to look like. Nonetheless, the fear of that moment stayed with him.

From Switzerland, he crossed into France from Geneva and made his way to Antwerp, Belgium where he boarded a cruiser bound for New York. Before boarding, Bailey sent a purposeful ambiguous note through the London office about his returning home. He made no mention of his January 3, 1939, arrival time.

The ocean weather was especially fierce all the way across the ocean until the coast of Newfoundland finally appeared. A day later the ship was moving by the Statute of Liberty as it ended its journey at a New York harbor pier. Bailey had mixed feelings about the intelligence he'd gathered, that is, whether any of it was useful. He did hope the rumors and hearsay he'd overheard being voiced by Italian workers in bars after theirs shifts might add some further value to his reconnaissance.

From the Manhattan pier he expected to take the next train out of Grand Central Station down to Washington D.C. and check into a hotel. That had been at O'Brien's request. He wondered if a hotel in the District would have open rooms as he'd be arriving quite late.

That concern disappeared the moment he walked off the boat. There was David O'Brien waiting for him at the end of the gang-plank. He was smiling and quipped, "Welcome home to the international food and wine expert."

O'Brien's Minnesota accent was evident. Bailey's ears had been attuned to different languages and accents over the previous two months. The greeting was unexpected but appreciated. It was nice to have someone truly look pleased to see him again.

O'Brien shook his hand and pointed towards a taxi. "I have a private rail car ready to take us down to Washington...unless you had something else to do in New York?"

Bailey snickered at the jibe. "So, David, how did you know I'd be on this ship?"

O'Brien rolled his eyes, "For Christ's sake, Adam, give me some credit for being somewhat capable in my line of work. Finding your reservation and arrival time on this boat was a piece of cake."

They both laughed. There hadn't been a lot of humor during his trip other than the weekend escapisms he'd had with the three lovely females he'd met during a couple ski ventures outside Geneva, Switzerland.

Once on the train Bailey was relieved to hand the secretive information and film over to O'Brien. He figured the head of European affairs for the State Department could get a whiff of some of the 'intelligence' Bailey had gathered... and then send him on his way back to Minneapolis the next morning.

Seeing the multiple rolls of film Bailey pulled out of the lining of his coat, O'Brien gave him a stern look. "So Adam, I see you played it really cautious while in Italy."

Then he began paging through Bailey's copious notes.

While O'Brien read and re-read the information, Bailey just paged through some American magazines periodically nodding off. The burden of secretly carrying the reconnaissance had been unloaded. Sleep came easy.

An hour later Bailey regained consciousness and sat up wondering where he was. O'Brien was still paging through the notes. Surprisingly, the State Department man seemed pleased. Looking up and seeing Bailey awake, he mumbled, "Not bad for a tourist."

He muttered that same statement a few more times before the train reached its destination. He'd pause occasionally to inquire if pictures had been taken of certain factories as well.

To every question, Bailey nodded.

O'Brien eyed him. "It seems by the content of some of this data you were literally in some of these plants."

Bailey nodded almost casually. "Yes...at times. You have to remember some of these factories were my clients a year ago bottling wine or processing tomato sauce. I just walked in based on that premise to see some of my friends who worked there. The protection was rather lax in many of these converted plants. In the three plants I entered in northern Italy I saw nothing that resembled bottled wine or the making of sauces. I saw parts for military vehicles being made. In one factory they were producing ammunition for tanks. They camouflaged newly built tanks under a canopy apparently to test the new ammunition.

O'Brien began to look at Bailey with some astonishment.

Bailey noting the page O'Brien was studying added, "In that third plant forty kilometers west of Milan, I simply ambled into the plant without ever being stopped. I just looked like a regular Italian worker. Then I saw a good friend named Alfredo who worked there when the factory bottled wine. Alfredo was obviously surprised to see me. Turned out he was the factory manager of this new military plant. I saw rifle barrels by the hundreds.

I told him other friends had mentioned he worked at the factory and I just wanted to see him and have lunch since I was in town only a short time.

He was delighted. We went down to a small café for some bread and wine. While we talked mostly of wines, he talked of how they'd re-structured the plant to build war supplies and where he was shipping them. He was under heavy pressure to complete production goals set down by Mussolini's people.

Our lunch ended and he talked forlornly of old times which were only two years before. I wished him well and told him I looked forward to doing business with him again when he was back as a wine producer. He nodded but we both sensed that might be a long time."

Arriving in Washington O'Brien and Bailey taxied over to the historic Willard Hotel. A room was waiting for Bailey. While O'Brien continued to question him about his travels, a courier came and took the numerous rolls of film. They had dinner and went back to the room where another courier was waiting by the hotel suite with a huge envelope. The photos had been processed.

If Bailey hadn't understood the level David O'Brien had within the State Department, that day and night made it quite clear. O'Brien could get things done very efficiently and quickly.

They talked for another two hours matching photos with Bailey's notations. He finally remarked, "Adam, you got away with murder traveling around Italy like a roving vacationer. My God....your activities and gained knowledge in these industrial sectors are quite significant to us.

Almost in shock, he murmured, "You really did a hell of job. I didn't expect this quality. You went far beyond what I thought you could do for us."

Then he again got lost while reading more of Bailey's notes. Once he sighed audibly saying, "....yes, a compilation far beyond what I could have hoped."

Then, just as he did during their two lunches over two months before in Minneapolis, O'Brien had no more to say. He put down the materials and just stared at Bailey as if being forced to redefine his personal image of the young man.

He was tired as well as he yawned and said, "Adam, I need some extra days from you if you don't mind staying here at the Willard. I want you to meet some of my associates...many of which you talked with before you left the U.S. two months ago. They'll have even more questions."

Bailey shrugged. "That's fine. I'll just call my boss, John Fena and let him know my probable arrival in Minneapolis will be delayed."

O'Brien joked, "Don't be too specific. We may need you longer."

It was 2:00 AM when O'Brien left Bailey's suite. By the next evening he was having dinner at an upscale restaurant on K Street with O'Brien and two others from State Department offices. The next afternoon he was still at O'Brien's Constitution Avenue office talking with three other staff members. In both instances he recognized they were all startled by his age in combination with the depth of information he was providing. As Bailey kept responding directly to their questions, their astonishment gradually gave way to deference. They were impressed with his initiative and his fluency in Italian. Developing his own code for his intelligence was something that especially intrigued them.

When they queried him about political and economic matters in Italy, they were rapt. It wasn't just his understanding of the current situations in various European countries; it was his knowledge of the history that had brought the circumstances to root.

O'Brien did voice concern more than once about his safety. He would inquire, "Adam, did you ever feel as if you were being followed? Did you have any close encounters with the Italian military police? Was there any risk of your written intelligence being found buried in the plantings at the hotel in Milan while you continued your travels around Italy?

To those questions, Bailey simply shook his head. "David, I did what you said. I was cautious."

The response caused the three State Department officials with them at the time to silently glance at one another. They knew Adam Bailey's definition of 'cautious' was quite different from theirs. They would all leave that dinner admiring what this inexperienced 'observer' had done by instinct.

From that day on, Bailey was given total clearance to enter and leave the State Department office building. The word had spread quickly about him with other O'Brien staff. He was ushered into meetings that had anything to do with Western Europe. His initial apprehension given the credentials and experience of others in the room gave way when he realized his field perspective brought added current value.

Saturday evening, January 7, he'd been in D.C. four extra days. O'Brien took him to Washington National Airfield for his flight back to Minneapolis. As they shook hands in farewell, Bailey had a strong feeling he'd be contacted again. It was confirmed in the next minute when O'Brien exclaimed, "Adam, my colleagues were very impressed...and I don't mean with just your information. They don't want you to get away. Let's talk after you take some time for yourself back home. Be prepared to tell me when next you plan on returning to Europe?

Your built-in cover provided by North American Distribution, Inc. gives you incredible access to Italy....for now.

You should be aware with recent German military actions, in particular November's night of terror against the Jews, Germany's continued pressure on Poland, and Hitler's obvious desire to seek Italy's continued acquiescence as Germany seems to be expanding its geographic takeover in Eastern Europe, it's a matter of time before Italy is going to declare complete support to future aggressive moves by the Nazis. Soon it will become very difficult for Americans to travel freely in Italy unless they have very good reasons. To us in the State Department, it is inevitable Germany and Italy will be raising arms together. With the U.S. not exactly a neutral party, we'll be unofficially involved in the European conflict...until it becomes official. Adam, you might as well face facts. As this matter grows....and it will....whatever remaining clients in Italy and even Switzerland you may still have, they will be fearful of even speaking with you."

Bailey shook his head. "It's already happening. That's why my business will require me to invest more time in Portugal and Spain as that country tries to put itself back on its feet after their civil conflict. I have contacts in Spain, but Franco's people are so close to Germany and Italy, exporting to the U.S. from that country could still be problematic. How the political scene is going to impact my company's business in Switzerland, France and Belgium is still unclear. If this whole thing blows up in Europe, I go from making some pretty good dollars for my company to being jobless for the first time since I was in college...and no particular prospects in sight."

O'Brien drew heavily from the Camel he was smoking. "I would disagree. I believe the State Department can find a job for you tomorrow if you feel like venturing further into the field of security and surveillance. You've shown yourself to be quite naturally talented. You don't exactly have the perfect education......a farm boy from Minnesota who works for a food company.....but, sometimes it's the motivated individual with his God given attributes that can make a person more valuable. Anyway....it's something to think about."

Bailey brightened a bit. "Well, to answer your question...April is likely my next trip overseas. I suppose I could move up my plans if you believe I could be helpful. By that time, however, I'll be on thin ice to substantiate why I'm traveling around Italy as a U.S. businessman."

O'Brien nodded but showed no real concern. "Adam, when you feel your cover is no longer effective, let me know. My department is pretty good in establishing aliases for individuals. There are other ways you can enter Italy and with your prowess speaking the language and knowing the culture, I'd bet you'll be able to maintain your same free-wheeling status....at least until war breaks out completely and the U.S. officially and inevitably becomes Italy's foe. That's why your efforts are...and will be...so valuable. But, it would still be best to use your job with North American Distribution, Inc. for as long as possible."

Then so as to leave no doubt, he added, "Adam, we'd like your help even before April. We have some operatives in Italy, Switzerland, and Germany, but they don't have your access to people and the manufacturing sector. They don't have your cover or your business experience in Italy. Besides, their efforts are focused on some other........assignments."

His voice then trailed off indicating he didn't want to go into any further detail. They parted company in front of the Washington National Air Terminal while looking up the Potomac River toward the Washington Monument. Winter was in full force with the cold wind blowing off the nearby water. It was raining and chilly, it was mild compared to what Bailey would be flying into back in Minnesota.

As the airplane took off he observed the familiar historic buildings and monuments below off the right wing, he felt a satisfaction beyond what he thought possible. His business concerns seemed trite compared to the work he'd done for the government. He found himself wishing he was going back overseas the next week.

Those first weeks back in Minneapolis during January, 1939, took a turn Adam Bailey hadn't expected. John Fena and he had multiple discussions where his next business efforts should be focused. Investing more time building clients in Portugal and possibly parts of the wine country in southern Spain seemed more advisable. Opening new business ventures on the Iberian Peninsula might counter the lost revenue happening in Italy. Discussions about journeying to Chile and Argentina were also under consideration.

Simultaneous to these discussions were the frequency of telephone calls from David O'Brien. The purposes were ostensibly to clarify locations of his photos... at other times to shed more light on the notes he'd made...and always to thank Bailey for the job he'd done. It was more obvious that O'Brien just wanted to remain in close contact.

By the third week of January a personal letter from David O'Brien arrived on State Department stationary giving accolades to him in more official form. Also a check was enclosed for his services. It was unexpected and astonishingly generous. It reminded Bailey how he'd never broached the subject about pay. He'd agreed to the surveillance work because it made sense given he would be in Italy anyway. Money hadn't even crossed his mind. He'd just done the job he thought he'd been tasked to do. The letter and money verified that he accomplished the task with more vigor and detail than O'Brien and his staff could have ever imagined.

On Tuesday, January 24, he got a phone call from O'Brien checking to make certain Bailey had received the letter and the pay. Not wasting further time he voiced his true purpose. "Adam, is it really going to be April before your next business jaunt overseas?"

Bailey reacted disappointedly. "David, I'll say it again. My business travels into Italy are fast becoming a joke. I've run out of reasons to represent my company with any real purpose. Mussolini's regime has closed the door on me. Most of my clients would like to continue exporting their products to America, but they're flat out scared.

O'Brien's voice was calm. "Well, that's why I wanted to talk to you. There are other reasons for you to "visit" Italy. I'd like you to fly into Washington this coming Monday and discuss some ideas."

Bailey perked up with O'Brien's expression of interest. It brought to mind his father and his efforts twenty-two years before in the Big War. What Bailey had been asked to do at the end of 1938 paled in comparison, but it was nice hearing O'Brien implying he had value.

He responded promptly, "Of course I'll fly in Monday. How many days will you need me?"

The response was equally as terse. "How much time do you have?"

When he hung up the telephone, Bailey had the feeling he was jumping into a much deeper body of water. In no way was he overwhelmed by the task...just concerned that his cover could remain effective while in Italy.

There was no fanfare when he arrived at National Airport on Monday, January 30. As O'Brien had told him on a Friday telephone call, a State Department vehicle would be waiting out in front of the terminal with a placard saying "Minnesota" on it. The driver introduced himself to Bailey, showed him he was the legitimate driver of the car, and held the back door open. The non-descript 1937 Ford Slantback Sedan delivered Bailey to O'Brien's offices on Constitution Avenue twenty minutes later.

His meeting with O'Brien was constantly being interrupted. The staff seemed busier and a bit more harried than the few weeks before when Bailey was last in Washington D.C.

Bailey even made that observation getting an eye and a chuckle from O'Brien. "You are alert. I don't need to tell you that Western Europe is like a powder keg. As you know, just last fall officials from Britain and France met in Munich and acquiesced to the demands of Germany wanting to take part of Czechoslovakia. To the British and French, their justification was an attempt at preserving peace. Hitler had said to them it would be his last territorial demand in Europe.

We here at the State Department won't be misled by that so-called agreement. A person would have to be brain dead to believe that German megalomaniac. Now we are receiving word that Hitler is ready to break that pact by soon moving into Czechoslovakia and taking over Prague and the entire country. Whatever appeasement policy had existed before will disappear. We see Hitler's aggressive actions will not stop."

Bailey was listening to this head of intelligence for Europe in the State Department not believing he was sitting in the man's office. There was no doubt O'Brien was already considering him more than just an observer.

Passing a folder to Bailey, O'Brien mumbled, "That's a confidential file composed mostly of information you found for us and your analysis of the economic and political impact the Fascist regime is having on Italy. Relations between Italy and the U.S. are disintegrating as consistently as your business interests are in that country. We now need constant updates anyway we can get them on their military buildup. You represent one of the better resources we have....that is, when you're over there."

Reading Bailey's mind, O'Brien continued, "Adam, we've discussed your cover and really feel it's still viable. Travel in Italy by Americans is still happening. We're not at war with that country yet. As long as you continue to behave and travel in similar fashion to your previous business excursions, you should be all right. However, this time I'll make certain you have some emergency numbers in case any problem arises while you're in Italy."

Bailey didn't have the confidence O'Brien exuded, but nodded in agreement just the same. He wasn't about to indicate he was fearful...just not as assured. What he'd done the last two months of 1938 could well be more difficult to duplicate.

Again O'Brien was ahead of him. "Adam, until your next journey overseas, I'd like you here in Washington for some graduated training. We don't want you to go back to Italy as casual as you previously were. Having more access to various credentials and codes so you can pass information back to us faster would also be more helpful. We need at least two weeks with you starting now. You should know I've already talked with John Fena. He's on board and sworn to secrecy. He doesn't know the extent to which you might be involved with us. His only interest is that you'll be safe. He and the owner of your company are the only ones outside of this department who know you'll be doing some more work for us. Your company is being reimbursed for much of your travel costs...at least while they can still be your cover. Once that ends, we'll make other arrangements."

Bailey didn't have anything to add. He just nodded. O'Brien seemed always two or three steps ahead of Bailey's brain.

O'Brien then added, "We'll take care of any extra clothing needs you have until you can return to Minneapolis. Then soon thereafter, we'll need you back here for more planning sessions for your next sojourn into Italy."

Bailey replied, "David, I guess my April trip is getting moved up."

O'Brien didn't miss a beat. "Oh...I thought you said March was your original return voyage."

They both chuckled. The urgency of Bailey's next trip was obvious.

Bailey admired how smoothly O'Brien handled everything. No problem was too big. There was nothing more to say. It didn't get past him that he was gradually being sucked into the vacuum of the espionage game. How far he'd go, no one including O'Brien or himself could predict. But, Bailey felt no qualms about the direction he was heading. It was as if his previous business experience was all intended for this path. The seemingly unbridled support and assuredness of one of the top men in the State Department certainly added to his own conviction.

He thought back to the previous week's conversation with John Fena. They'd laid out an alternative plan for venturing into South America much like Bailey had done with the man before he first traveled to Western Europe. Now he realized Fena had discussed those plans as an alternative if Bailey had second thoughts about working for the State Department. While O'Brien implied that Fena didn't have a complete picture of what Bailey was being asked to do, his boss in Minneapolis was no fool. He had to believe what Bailey was doing in Italy was not play time.

O'Brien was called away and Bailey sat alone in the silence of the State Department fourth floor conference room overlooking the traffic on Constitution Avenue. One other question arose. O'Brien had mentioned he'd already talked with Fena...and to someone else he'd offhandedly mentioned was the "owner of your company". Bailey had failed to react to that statement. He'd thought all along that Fena was the owner and manager. That it could be any different had never occurred to him.

He filed that thought as two staff members entered with arms full of files. They greeted him with short smiles and a resolute look indicating much had to be covered. Except for a break the coming weekend, he would either be in training or involved in the ongoing discussions about the U.S. involvement in the inevitable war efforts and support throughout Europe, North Africa, and the Middle East.

When he finally returned to Minneapolis two weeks later and entered his apartment, he looked in the mirror and wondered if he was still the same person.

***

By the first week of March, 1939, Bailey had been back and forth from Washington D.C. twice since his two-week crash training at the State Department. He was still being considered officially an 'observer' as if the designation would somehow make him safer while traveling in Italy. His training had a heavy emphasis on survival and personal defense. Between a coat and tie at the State Department headquarters to wearing fatigues out at the marine training center in northern Virginia, he attended all strategy and update meetings regarding active military action in Western Europe.

O'Brien at times saddled up to him during a break and murmured, "Get your eyes back in your head. All this helps you better understand the depth of the intelligence we need from you."

Bailey nodded but often couldn't believe where he was.

Bailey made it back to Minneapolis on Monday, March 6, more than anything to show some visibility within the North America Distribution offices and to maintain the reality of his cover. Employees were aware his international business had declined due to the problems in Europe. Fena and he both let it be known his business travels would be in Florida and California for the coming months and then possibly in Spain and Portugal.

Before leaving for Europe, he did finalize plans for some business calls in southern France and the Iberian Peninsula to further authenticate his cover as an international businessman. His days at the Minneapolis office were relaxing and bland compared to his other life. He had dinner a couple nights during the week with the Lawtons. He went out drinking with some of his golfing buddies talking longingly of the upcoming golf season. In the four years since they all graduated, one friend was in law school, one managed a haberdashery, and another friend was teaching in high school. None of them could truly relate to the work he did for North American Distribution, Inc. Their questions related more to the women...which countries had the looser or more robustly shaped females...and whether he had been inconvenienced chasing them by the troubles in Europe.

Bailey tended to change the subject on these matters, except about their queries about the women. Then he'd let his friends know they were hopelessly incompetent and ignorant to even think about such beautiful and sophisticated females as he had gotten to know in France and Switzerland. The ensuing laughter and derisive comments about his own lack of success with women in the U.S. got the subject away from talk of his overseas travels. While they were jibing him, he smiled inside knowing how shocked they'd be if they'd ever thought of him taking secret photos of military plants or walking in ammunition factories in northern Italy.

He'd been tromping thru the dirty snow in the company parking lot at the end of the work week when he began experiencing that same restless feeling he'd had the previous October. This time there was no mystery. He was being followed again. He didn't even look up as he knew it was all a question of time before that same black Cadillac would suddenly drive up beside him. He thought he was rid of having anything to do with Willie LaCurso. He couldn't imagine why the Twin City gangster had any reason to see him again.

It was Thursday, March 9, when the car finally sidled up to him while Bailey was leaving work. It was dark. Bailey just silently shook his head and leaned against his car.

The window rolled down and Tony Bando immediately began some small talk as if they'd just seen each other the day before. The big man grumbled, "Hey kid, with all your travels, you seem to be putting on some weight."

Bailey could only laugh to himself as he lit a cigarette with difficulty in the windy parking lot. Having someone as large as Tony making a smart remark about weight gain seemed a little misguided. Bailey felt comfortable enough with the big man to lean slightly into the open window to ward off the cold wind. Feeling the heat from inside Tony's vehicle, he responded sardonically, "Tony, thank you for noticing I gained ten pounds of winter weight that won't come off until May. The fact that I'm freezing and am wearing enough clothes to sleep outside might make me look a bit chunky as well."

Tony let go with his guttural chuckle appreciating that someone so young was comfortable enough to joke with him.

Bailey paused for only a moment. "So Tony, you didn't come over here to tell me I look like hell. There must be a better reason."

Tony laughed louder. Bailey knew the large man liked him even though Bailey was not one of his kind.

He coughed a few more times and finally gasped, "Kid, Willie wants you to come over. It doesn't have to be tonight. How about you come over tomorrow night about 8:00? Willie's got some Italian wine his brother just sent over. He wants to share a bottle with you."

It was a far better, more respectable invitation than last time. Bailey nodded and made his voice sound light. "I think my schedules clean. I was hoping I had a date, but it looks like that fizzled. 8:00 sounds O.K. It'll give me time to eat something so the wine won't leave me crawling out the door. Yeh, tell him I'll be there."

Tony chuckled again. He'd known Bailey since he was a skinny caddy out at the Chippewa Lodge golf course in Glenwood. He hadn't paid much attention to the youngster then, but since Bailey had grown up, Tony had a chance to appreciate how much the young kid had matured. He didn't like many people, but he couldn't help but be fond of this kid. Bailey was smart, quick-witted and not easily daunted. In Tony's mind that was a good combination.

Before rolling up his window, Tony yelled out over the wind, "See you tomorrow, kid. Now get out of the cold before you freeze your ass off."

Tony also liked that he didn't have to strong arm the kid. Young Bailey just understood what had to be done...and then did it.

The next evening Bailey arrived five minutes after the appointed time at the front entrance of Willie LaCurso's River Road estate. His intentions were to be late. Willie seemed not to care as he greeted his guest at the door of his beautifully decorated home and ushered him directly into his study. There was small talk about the weather while Willie introduced a new burgundy to him. That the bottle was sent to him from Italy, it offered a convenient transition for Willie to talk about his brother, Roberto, and the plight of the LaCurso family over in Italy was having to face.

Willie was completely the gentleman as he spoke. "Adam, you've been on the road a lot since we last saw each other in October. It's nice to see you both safe and healthy. On such a cold night, you might prefer some brandy over this wine. What's your pleasure?"

Bailey nodded toward the wine bottle. "Yes...I favor the wine. Thank you for asking. I know most of the wine producers in northern Italy. I'm certain your burgundy will be quite good."

Willie smiled acknowledging the young man had definitely become more sophisticated. Showing Bailey the label, Adam offered some confirmation. "Yes...I know that family very well. They seem to have another daughter or niece they introduce to me every time I visit their vineyard. Their whites are always great. We won't be disappointed with this burgundy."

Willie was in a good mood. He laughed at Bailey's story. Then toasting to good health they sat and LaCurso's small talk ended abruptly. "Adam, from our last conversation you said you normally go overseas three to four times a year. Logically, that means you have plans to leave fairly soon. And, that's why I wanted to talk with you."

Bailey couldn't remember divulging to anyone but O'Brien how many times he traveled to Italy. But, it didn't matter. Willie's mole inside North American Distribution would know the dates for Bailey's forthcoming trip. What made him uncomfortable was that he knew he was being led down a path of Willie's choosing. Furthermore, his upcoming jaunt into Italy was more for the purposes of a State Department assignment than calling on clients. In fact he expected his only business calls would be in Spain and Portugal...and that would be limited.

Willie continued to drive forward his key point. "Adam, for this overseas trip, I was hoping I could ask a favor. With my family having such a difficult time with this bum Mussolini and his Fascist dogs running the country into the ground, our businesses in Italy are suffering. They have need for my support. What I ask, and I will gladly pay you for the inconvenience, is for you to take a suitcase with some gifts for my family. I will admit to you some money will be included for my brother, Roberto. It's been up to him to keep the family in one piece during this government upheaval.

For your ease I can arrange through my brother to have you pass through the border into Italy without having any of your bags checked. Roberto can make such arrangements if you can let him know a day in advance and which border entry you'll be using. Once you get to Milan, he'll arrange a pickup of the suitcase either at your usual hotel, the Hotel de Italiana, or someplace else you'd prefer. As I said, I'll certainly pay you for your troubles and any extra transportation cost. I just want to make certain the suitcase and the gifts end up in the right hands after you enter Italy. I've known you for a long time. Your father brought you up correctly. Entrusting you with this suitcase for my family in Italy would relieve me very much."

Bailey couldn't help but smirk. LaCurso even knew his preferred hotel in Milan and had a curious way of floating past the subject of his family having no problem bribing some border guards. Had it been just a business trip, he might have cancelled his plans at that moment just to rattle the gangster. However, his travels were set. He really had no choice but to take the suitcase. Denying such a simple philanthropic request would appear thoughtless. More importantly, rebuffing a favor to a high level goon like LaCurso would be ill-advised. It could spell trouble for not just him but his father, the Lawtons and Charlie Davis as well. 'No,' he thought, 'it was better just to do this courtesy one time and not make it into a big deal.'

Bailey tried to show sincerity as he agreed. "O.K., Willie, I usually carry a lot with me, but if it's just one suitcase to help your family in Italy, I'll make it work. You don't have to pay me a penny. I'll just do it. It would be helpful, though, if your brother would take charge of the suitcase and gifts as soon as possible."

LaCurso seemed pleased and kept insisting on paying. Finally Bailey just shook his head. He couldn't see the request as being that much trouble...and it included a clean entry into Italy. He was getting some benefit as well.

Holding up his empty wine glass, he emphatically said, "Willie, let me just do this for you. You don't have to reciprocate with anything. I'm going to Italy anyway and you know I'll keep close tabs on the suitcase. I'm happy to help out."

LaCurso wasn't used to that kind of genuine kindness with no expected payback. His voice was softer. "Adam, you are being very generous. I must insist you accept a small gift I got for you. You can decline all you want, but once you see it, if I know you at all, you'll keep it."

Bailey was shaking his head not really wanting anything until Willie went behind his desk and brought out a golf club. "Adam, it's one of those new Gene Sarazen putters. I almost don't want to give it to you. I've been putting on my carpet in the study for the last couple weeks and I love the feel. But, it's yours. Now, if you don't want it, my feelings won't be hurt."

The young man took the putter and made a few practice strokes. His eyes were bright, like a little kid. LaCurso's eyes were just as cheerful feeling good about finding just the right gift for someone.

Bailey laughed out loud as he very sincerely replied, "Thanks Willie...I believe I'd like to keep this gift."

Willie joined his laughter showing that no matter the backgrounds, golf crossed barriers for a lot of people. Bailey and LaCurso were enjoying one of those moments.

Bailey truly wished he didn't like the new putter the way he did. Willie had hit his hot button. The older man could be very thoughtful when he felt like it; unfortunately it always came with a price.

As it turned out Willie would ask no other favors that night. They had a couple more glasses of wine and mostly talked golf while the cold March wind blew snow flurries against Willie's library window. They both knew it was only a month before the weather might improve enough to begin hitting some golf balls outside. That made golf a more rousing topic of conversation.

Willie sat back contentedly and told stories about the guys who the young man had known back at the Chippewa Lodge golf course. These were fellows who Bailey thought of as friends, even though many were twice his high school age at the time. They were gangsters, but he didn't know it at the time. At the golf course they were just fun-loving golfers out for a good time bragging about their good shots and swearing at their poor ones.

Now years later it was both strange and enjoyable to hear their names again. Bailey visualized those hilarious times when those fellows were constantly joking with one another and serious as death over a five-foot putt for money. No matter what people said about them after the raid at the Lake Minnewaska lake resort almost a decade before, they'd been his friends during his summers of high school. He knew he'd never forget them. Now, knowing what they did for a living, the image was somewhat scarred, but not enough to keep him from chuckling as he visualized their antics back during those special summers on the golf course.

At one point while Willie told another story about playing in Loni D'Annelli's tournament in 1929, Bailey recalled the event and gave his own perspective. They both exploded in laughter.

Tony was sitting outside the study reading the newspaper and heard the noise. He just shook his head. He hadn't heard the boss laugh like that in a very long time.

However, true to Willie's character, the hilarity stopped and he changed the subject in a blink of an eye. He spoke somberly. "So, Adam, will this next trip on behalf of your company be your last transatlantic voyage to Italy. With the European theatre becoming more and more volatile, I'm surprised you have enough customers left to make your travels into Italy worthwhile. I can't help be concerned about your own health. An American traveling in Italy during these times could be questioned."

Bailey was surprised at the apparent worry. "Willie, I'll only enter the country as long as I have customers to serve. I still have other countries where my clients are still exporting to the U.S."

LaCurso only nodded. "Well, anyway, I appreciate your help. Tony will give you the suitcase as you leave here tonight. May I suggest you enter Italy this time via Monaco? Roberto has some personal friends who are border guards there and they'll expedite your crossing."

Handing over a small piece of paper, LaCurso added, "You only have to call this telephone number when you arrive in Monaco. Roberto's border guard friends will then be notified. Also, you'll be given instructions which gate to pass through. You can imagine we want to keep the contents of the suitcase confidential. Once your passport is stamped and you're escorted into Italy you can take the train to anywhere you please. As you requested, though, if you take the Milan train from the border, you'll be able to pass the suitcase off to Roberto promptly at the Hotel de Italiana. Hopefully that can be arranged.

Bailey silently chuckled. Willie had it all figured out. There was no reason to question his plan.

Bailey stood up to leave. "I'll follow your suggestion and go directly to Monaco and then Milan. I have a few clients left near that city. Your family will not have to wait long to appreciate the contents in the suitcase."

LaCurso nodded his approval...and then showed some concern. "Adam, you and I shared maybe too much wine this evening. If you need Tony to drive you home, I can have your car driven by one of my other men."

The gangster was taking every precaution.

Bailey shook his head. "I'm fine. I've driven feeling much worse."

Willie nodded and made certain Adam had his new putter and the suitcase with him before he left. They shook hands and parted ways.

As the door closed, Tony was standing outside in the cold. Seeing the huge, ominous looking right-hand man, many people would be scared. Still questioning his own sanity for enjoying the evening at a major crime figure's residence, Bailey gave the big man a farewell wave. He couldn't help but like the guy; he sensed Big Tony liked him too.

Tony came over and walked along with Bailey to his car. Quiet for only a moment, his gravelly voice was surprisingly kind as he said, "Hey kid, Willie appreciates your effort."

Bailey nodded. It was an off-handed compliment that had a double edge. He didn't like Willie feeling indebted to him.

About to close his driver's side door, Tony stared at him and growled, "Kid, don't screw it up. Just follow the directions Willie gave to you. It'll all go very smooth if you do."

Then he walked away without as much as a wave. Bailey snickered knowing that was about as emotive as Big Tony ever got.

He left the LaCurso front gates and proceeded onto River Road back toward his apartment. There was little mid-week traffic. He made it home with ease and slept very soundly that night with help of the wine. He never noticed the Cadillac that followed him until he parked his car in his apartment parking lot.

He should have known Tony would be behind him. Willie didn't leave anything to chance.

Chapter 9

On Monday, March 13, 1939, Adam Bailey left Minneapolis for New York City. From there, according to his schedule he'd left with John Fena, he was supposed to board the evening ocean liner bound for his normal landing point on the on the north coast of France at the port of Le Havre.

His actual plan was quite different. It had been altered weeks before. Bailey instead taxied to Grand Central Station and took a train down to Washington D.C. for the remainder of the week storing LaCurso's large suitcase at the train station in Manhattan.

At the State Department O'Brien and his staff went over his actual plan where Bailey would make two separate extended missions into Italy in the upcoming two months. The State Department needed reconnaissance in southern Italy including Sicily and Corsica and then more coverage in the northern sector of the country. As he saw fit, he would stop by and visit some of his former clients to give some credence to his cover.

It was not until Friday, March 17, that Bailey was delivered by airplane to La Guardia. The luggage he'd left at Grand Central Station was at the airport waiting for him. He boarded one of the new overseas Pan American World Airline flights to Paris that evening; he would be in France by noon the next day after a stop in Ireland and London. As he'd done on previous trips, he took the night train down to the Bordeaux and Toulouse regions of southern France to make some legitimate visits with business clients. That took only two days.

So the suitcase he was carrying for Willie LaCurso would not become too much of a burden he decided to make his first foray into Italy sooner than he'd originally planned. As directed, Monaco would be his entry point. With the guarantee from LaCurso that he would have no trouble crossing the French-Italian border, he'd take the train to Milan and complete the suitcase delivery. Then he'd be free to continue his true mission in Italy.

Arriving in Marseilles on Tuesday, March 21, he called the telephone number in Milan to inform LaCurso's brother, Roberto, his intention of crossing into Italy the next day at Monaco. The phone call was short. All he said was his name. A heavily accented voice replied in broken English, "Senore Bailey, we have been expecting your call. Be at the border between 11:00 and 12:00 Wednesday morning. Choose the gate on the far left of the complex no matter how long the line might be. When the border guard sees your passport, he will stamp it and then accompany you through the gate and take you directly to the train station. Please take the next train to Milan and check in at the Hotel de Italiana. We will take it from there."

The abrupt click ended the communication. There was no repeat and no chance to ask a question. No other small talk was attempted. Bailey's job as courier would be done the moment he checked the bag in the Milan hotel. He wasn't certain he was talking to Roberto LaCurso during that telephone call, but it hardly mattered.

The next morning went like clock word. He was at the French-Italian border station at the appointed time. As he stood in line at the farthest gate on the left, a border guard came up to him and quietly whispered, "Senor Bailey, please follow me."

Bailey asked no questions. He was in Italy with a stamped passport less than a minute later. Two gruff looking men helped him with his luggage and then drove him to the train station. He was handed a first class train ticket to Milan in a private compartment. By 11:45 the train was moving and his luggage was with him including the LaCurso suitcase. Only a couple hours later he was checking the suitcase with a bell hop at the Hotel de Italiana. He was suddenly free of any further responsibility for the suitcase. The ease by which the whole matter took place made him feel guilty he initially hadn't wanted to do the favor for Willie LaCurso.

He still waited in the lobby until he saw a heavier set man pick up the suitcase from the hotel porter. Some money was pressed into the bell hop's hand and the suitcase completed its journey into the right hands. Bailey thought the man, although larger, had some resemblance to Willie LaCurso, but he couldn't be certain.

Twenty minutes later the favor was out of mind. He was on another train toward Bologna in north central Italy with several stops in between. He saw no business clients that week nor would he for the next two weeks until he ventured northward and crossed the border into Switzerland. His mission as an 'observer' took his complete attention. More thorough surveillance and record keeping on new factories and converted older plants into military supply facilities had been his primary aim. He also wanted to find out where the finished goods were to be sent. During those weeks in Italy, he stayed in small rooming houses nightly where identification was not required...just payment in advance. His friendly nature and fluency in the language carried with it a confidence; no one questioned his purpose.

It was difficult not to get too casual until a military vehicle drove by with stern looking soldiers with their noses in the air a la their illustrious leader, Il Duce. By the first of April, he had enough rolls of film and accumulated data to easily get convicted of espionage. Concealing the intelligence had again become a bigger problem than he'd anticipated. He sensed the information would be of more timely significance if he could get it into the hands of the State Department as soon as possible. The U.S. Embassy in Paris had become the one office O'Brien had emphasized as Bailey's best refuge for maintaining his cover and giving what intelligence he'd gained to an Embassy employee who reported directly to O'Brien.

It was getting across the borders that created the most concern. If he was found with questionable materials at any of the borders, he'd not only lose the data and rolls of film, but likely his cover as well. Figuring he'd have a smoother crossing at the Swiss-Italian border, he headed north toward Milan and then onto Como. The four rolls of film fit in the lining of his hat. The coded notes on his business stationary from North American Distribution, Inc. offered some camouflage. However, if the border guard was particularly conscientious, there would be questions that could lead to problems.

He dressed like a common tourist making himself look even younger than he was. He waited until he could join a party of student tourists crossing the border. He moved within the group as if he were one of them. It helped that most of them were carrying folders or bags containing their own notebooks and reading materials.

Listening carefully he tried to distinguish where the group was from, but they were all very quiet, somewhat intimidated by the soldiers and guards holding rifles. When it was Bailey's turn to show his passport, the guard gave him a close stare and then even a closer look at his leather briefcase. In broken English, he asked harshly, "What is an American doing with this group from Spain? On your passport it doesn't even show that you've been to that country."

Bailey's mind whirled. He was about to go into some sham explanation when one of the students stood by him and said to the border guard in surprisingly fluid English, "You have a problem with our new American teacher? He only met us in Milan and will be traveling with us in Switzerland before we return to Barcelona. I thought Italy felt kindly towards Spain the way our Francisco Franco got so much help from your great leader, Benito Mussolini. Do you think this man is some sort of spy or something? He's just a teacher."

Bailey gulped hearing the word 'spy' and then watched as the student stared straight at the equally determined guard. There was five seconds of absolute silence. Then with the rest of the Spanish group packing up to the gate and getting antsy, the guard blinked. He said, "O.K., American, go teach the children of Spain."

He stamped the passport and Bailey moved through the gate into Switzerland.

As the remaining group of young adults had their own passports stamped, Bailey looked for the student who'd mysteriously come forward to help him. He thought he'd lost the young man until he felt the kid beside him. The Spanish lad said, "Senor, those Mussolini border guards are parasites hoping for a bribe. I hate Mussolini. Have good travels."

Then the student grinned and moved back to his group. Bailey gave him a wave and headed for the Geneva bound train that would take him across Switzerland. In the future he could not depend on some sixteen-year old student with a lot of guts providing some assistance. He'd been very lucky. It was imperative he never put himself in that vulnerable position again. He'd been too over-confident.

Taking a couple days of recuperation in his favorite city, Geneva, he hid his reports and the rolls of film temporarily under the center of his mattress in his hotel suite. While skiing and relaxing at some of his normal hang-outs in that city, he still felt nervous. Concealing the intelligence was more a headache than acquiring it.

On Wednesday, April 5, he crossed the Swiss border into France with little problem and proceeded to Paris. There he met with David O'Brien's staff person at the American Embassy. The agent hadn't heard much about Bailey's previous exploits in Italy. He didn't expect anything of consequence from an American 'observer' until he saw the amount of data, how it was coded, and the number of unprocessed rolls of film Bailey had snuck across two border crossings.

Pierre Latif was a native Frenchman but educated at New York University. His English was almost flawless with a tinge of a Brooklyn accent. The two of them privately poured over the details of the reports before they were re-coded and sent onto London. By then Latif also had the rolls of film processed. He was awestruck and had gained new respect as he perused the pictures. Upon departing, Latif showed more concern towards Bailey than even O'Brien had displayed. The agent's parting words were, "Adam, you better understand right now that you are more than an observer. What you carried with you, despite your unique coding, would put you in jail and the key thrown into a stream.... or worse! You have an amazing access to Italy through your cover, but you absolutely need to keep whatever intelligence you've gathered off your person. Your reconnaissance will be of little value if you're not alive to give it to us."

Bailey thought the words of advice were harsh, but appreciated Latif's admonition. There was enough danger without allowing his brashness to cause a slip.

While in Paris, Bailey was able to stay closer to the news. The word from Spain was that Francisco Franco, leader of the Nationalists in Spain, had marched into the capital city of Madrid the week before on March 28. He'd taken control and ended the civil strife in his country officially on April 1. It had been a tragic internal struggle that had killed a shocking number of the male population between the ages of eighteen and forty. The newspaper article implied that the future population of Spain would be fathered by a much older male or an infirm younger male who hadn't been suitably strong enough mentally or physically to fight in the heartbreaking civil war.

There was a part of Franco's victory that was clouded. His victory was another feather in the cap of Hitler and Mussolini. They had not so secretly supported Franco's group throughout the internal conflict. It meant that Franco would be allied with the Germans and Italians if another western European conflict was repeated. Mitigating that concern was that the horrible carnage over the previous three years had left Spain unwilling and even unable to participate too fully in future conflagrations.

From Paris Bailey planned to sojourn into southern Spain and Portugal to visit some wine vineyards and possibly establish some future business contacts for North American Distribution, Inc. He felt it important to continue contacting prospects to keep reestablishing his cover.

Before he left Paris on Saturday, April 8, he also read the headlines that Mussolini's troops had invaded Albania the previous day. Bailey was stunned by the completely useless act of aggression. Albania was already dependent on Italy so little could be gained. While a victory, which was imminent, might give the appearance Italy was positioning itself for greater victories in the Balkans, in particular Greece and Yugoslavia, it seemed more a need by Il Duce to respond to Germany's recent takeover of Austria and Czechoslovakia. Italy would have control of the entry into the Adriatic Sea, but the action was costly, unnecessary, and Albania had such little to give in defeat.

Italy's invasion cut short Bailey's desire to invest very much time on the Iberian Peninsula. He made the trip anyway. From western Spain near Salamanca he called on some potential wine clients before entering Portugal to do the same. Taking the train along the Atlantic coast from Porto down to Lisbon, he felt the excitement of opening up some new accounts again for his company. If the blaze of warfare wouldn't explode into another world conflict, he felt there would be some viable new business coming out of the two countries. While pleased with his business prospects, the excitement was muted because of the anticipated State Department work he was about to continue in Italy.

It was Saturday, April 15, that he took his second excursion into Italy already celebrating its triumph over Albania launched just a week before. At least Mussolini was adamantly pleased with the so-called victory.

Aboard an ocean liner from Lisbon down through the Straights of Gibraltar and out onto the Mediterranean Sea, Bailey would dock at Palermo, on the Italian island of Sicily. This time it was more challenging entering Italy compared to his uncontested ride with Roberto LaCurso's help the previous month. The intelligence and photos he'd gathered had already been passed through to the State Department with help from Pierre Latif. He had nothing in his belongings that could implicate him with the border guards. His claim of visiting clients verified by four years of time stamps on his passport finally convinced the border guards. Their eyes were unfriendly and untrusting, but they let him pass. Through the next day he strolled around Palermo checking to see if he was being followed.

Convinced he was not, he left that night on a train to Messina where he crossed the Straits to the toe of the boot of mainland Italy. Once into the country Bailey would be equally meticulous in his undercover work in Sicily and throughout southern Italy. During his almost three weeks of reconnaissance he uncovered far more military supply factories than he thought probable in that region. Not as familiar in this area of Italy, he felt more uneasy given his more noticeable accent when he spoke Italian. Nonetheless, he wasn't slowed.

By the end of April he'd gathered enough intelligence and photos to again be faced with the similar problem of transporting the sensitive materials out of the country. His documentation was particularly incriminating since he'd not stopped by any former customers as they were limited in number anyway. Now knowing what O'Brien and his staff were looking for, he sensed the importance of getting his information across the Italian border. It was vital enough that he ended his second mission earlier than he would have preferred.

Taking the train up to Rome, he found a small excursion boat that was heading for Monte Carlo. He met with little challenge smuggling his findings and film into France. However, he was certain these holes in the border patrol would be sewn shut as the relations between France and Italy continued to decline.

From Marseilles with his records and film rolls taped to his chest and back, he boarded a night train to Paris where he again met with the American agent, Pierre Latif, at the American consulate. If Latif had any doubt of Bailey's determination, thoroughness....and boldness...after the earlier meeting a few weeks before, Latif was awed by what he was reading in Bailey's coded script. He looked up periodically at the slightly haggard 'observer' marveling at the effort and nerve required to have gathered that quality of military intelligence.

Latif was aware Bailey's excursion into southern Italy had obviously carried with it a lot more risk and strain. It was a slightly different looking Adam Bailey than the one he'd seen before. The young man was more intense and less jovial. His eyes were tired as he blandly gave clarification on the coded notes.

Latif expected Bailey to be ending his travels and returning to the States as he'd already been gone for a month-and-a-half. Yet Bailey was vague on his plans for the coming weeks other than admitting he was going down to Geneva, Switzerland to relax for a couple days. Latif had no idea Bailey had already formulated a third venture into Italy given the recent Italian attack on Albania and now some likely imminent undertakings against Greece. This time he wanted to explore the eastern shore line up and down Italy along the Adriatic Sea for military build-up and manufacturing.

Bailey did take a four-day break in Geneva; however by Friday, May 5, he was traveling back into Italy via Switzerland. It was an easier passage into Italy as he claimed to be a vacationer traveling to Venice. The Italian border guard shrugged seeing the American looking like one of the many other students coming into Italy for a short educational visit. Bailey was expecting more questions and was prepared to play whatever game he had to play. Again the many stamps on his passport alluded to a person who enjoyed coming to Italy. He was fortunate to have a border guard who was not so stringent. Another guard could have been more severe. It was hit or miss how difficult or trouble-free his entry into the country might be. He knew his exit, whenever that might be, would be far more difficult.

He walked with some Venice bound students and boarded a train with them. While on the southern coast on his previous trip, he'd heard about the defense installations being built with materials produced in factories in Trieste on the far northeastern border all the way down to Bari. His plan was to follow the coast line acquiring as much intelligence as was possible. It was an aggressive plan, one that O'Brien and he had not discussed. Yet with Mussolini now feeling as if he controlled the Adriatic Sea as well as the Straits of Otranto between Italy and Greece, Bailey felt his mission would be incomplete if he didn't checkout the complete 'heel' of the southern Italy 'boot'.

Again he was challenged with having no clients within hundreds of kilometers of that area of the country as well as being approximately a thousand kilometers from his supposed destination, Venice. His excuse for travel to Taranto and Lecce could be suspect. He'd claim to be on an anthropologic study. If his film rolls or questionable notes were found on him, his claims would be weak. He was determined to be especially careful, but always was aware too much caution realized too few results.

His jaunt along the eastern coastline of Italy turned into a twelve-day trip by train with many overnights in nondescript rooming houses in small villages. Bailey blended into the populace with his Italian attire, his skill speaking Italian, and his quiet, relaxed nature.

During his travels he would hear about a pending pact that was to be signed that very month between Italy and Germany pledging support for each other in all future possible conflicts. There was now no doubt... if there ever had been... he was in enemy territory.

His ability to disguise his accent repeatedly helped him in chance conversation in local bars. From casual, alcohol induced talk, he would learn about Italy's supposed economic improvements along the coast. There was satisfaction related to the rise of employment with east coast factories. More loose talk would often reveal the types of materials or products being manufactured. He learned that agricultural productivity was measured more on how well the military was being fed and how efficiently the food was being transported to the different regions of the country. Bailey didn't leave any coastline docking area without photos outlining the ports where barges were set to deliver military goods and vehicles.

Those three missions into Italy that spring and early summer of 1939 bolstered his confidence in how to travel inconspicuously. And, that last mission along the Adriatic Sea had wrought enough coded notes and rolls of film to have him shot on sight.

On Saturday, May 27, he arrived in Rome from Bali and looked for the same excursion boat to Monte Carlo he'd taken the previous month. Things had changed just in that short period of time. That pleasure boat no longer sailed freely to any port on the French coast. He was now facing a very real dilemma of getting almost twice the intelligence out of Italy that he'd attained on his two recent travels that spring.

With no other ways to smuggle his intelligence out of Italy, he decided to employ an idea he'd considered a last straw. He'd been escorted into Italy with

Willie LaCurso's suitcase back when he first arrived overseas in late March. He still had the telephone number for Roberto LaCurso in Milan who'd expedited his entry. He sensed he might be able to utilize the same advantage in reverse. Certainly there was nothing to lose.

While in Rome he dialed the Milan telephone number. After two rings he got the same gruff voice. He didn't know if it was Roberto LaCurso or not, nor did he care. He simply stated his situation as clearly as he could and deciding to use English for more effect.

Without giving his name, he said, "Yes...I am the American who did a favor for the LaCurso family delivering a suitcase to Milan in March. I had help from this phone number getting across the French-Italian border. I am now in Italy and need the reverse help. I need to have a smooth crossing into France. I am calling to see if that is possible?

There was no sound. Bailey at first thought the person had hung up the line. Then the deep voice answered, "Call back in an hour."

Bailey called back from a pay telephone a half hour later at the Rome train terminal. "He had barely said 'hello' when the voice blandly stated, "Be at the border gate near Monaco tomorrow morning at 11:00. Get off the train at Ventimiglia and take the bus to the border. Go to the right side of the gates. You will be met and brought through into France."

The phone line was cut off. Bailey hated that he was asking a favor of the LaCurso family, but his request had been granted. It had been as simple as calling the secret number.

He'd taken the evening train from Rome and arrived near the Italian-French border town of Ventimiglia as directed. Getting a room at a small hotel, there seemed enough military police in the small seacoast village to start an army. The next morning Bailey confidently headed for the bus line to take him to the border. The coded documents and the rolls of film taped to his chest and back made him itch as the perspiration soiled the tape. There were additional rolls of film taped inside his underwear. He promised he'd never choose that area of his body to hide anything again.

Arriving at the Italian side of the border, he exited the bus with twelve other people. Almost immediately, he had a man of medium stature, heavily whiskered, and looking as evil as death standing next to him. Somewhat knowing the ways of the LaCurso family, Bailey said nothing. Roberto or Willie LaCurso had obviously done a very complete job of describing what their American courier looked like.

Bailey only met the man's stare and nodded his head. They walked together for thirty yards until they stood in a short line at the border gate. Bailey showed

no nerves and remained quiet until it was his turn to pass his luggage along to
the border guard. The guard grabbed Bailey's passport and looked very closely
and doubtfully at him...until he saw the rough-looking Italian man standing
alongside him. Then the guard's eyes got slightly bigger.

Seconds later Bailey's own suitcase was pushed through with no inspection.
When Bailey offered his briefcase for inspection, the border guard gazed at him
as if he were nuts. Stamping the passport, he pointed Bailey to the bus on the
French side saying in broken English. "The bus will take you to Monaco."

Bailey nodded and looked back to say 'thank you' to his escort. The man had
already disappeared. Bailey walked the twenty yards to the bus and felt reassured
to be back in a country friendly to his own. He stayed on the bus as it passed
through Monaco until he found a large international hotel next to the train
station. He ended his day not leaving the room, ordering only room service for
food, and allowing his mind and body to relax for the first time in weeks while
lying in the sun on his patio overlooking the sea.

He took the night train to Paris and called Pierre Latif at the train station
the next morning. Latif sounded relieved to hear Bailey's voice. His message
was simple. "Adam, you need not stop by my office. You can go straight to the
airfield. You have a first class ticket on the Pan American 'Yankee Clipper' leaving
for New York this afternoon at 2:00. David O'Brien gave me strict orders not
to let you go anywhere but the States. He'll be looking forward to seeing you in
Washington. Have a nice flight."

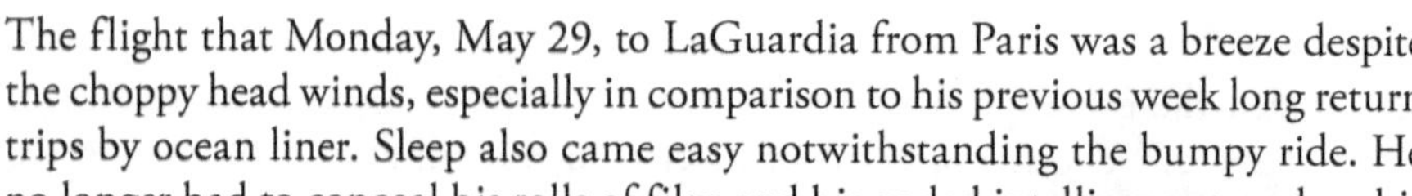

The flight that Monday, May 29, to LaGuardia from Paris was a breeze despite
the choppy head winds, especially in comparison to his previous week long return
trips by ocean liner. Sleep also came easy notwithstanding the bumpy ride. He
no longer had to conceal his rolls of film and his coded intelligence taped on his
chest and back. Everything was in his briefcase securely under his seat.

When the Pan American flight finally landed at LaGuardia, it was still
light out in New York. He had no concern with customs. O'Brien had already
cleared his passage. He'd left the city in the first cold days of spring and now
was returning to the warmer but smellier air of the airport and the city. He was
still going through the formalities of U.S. Customs when O'Brien greeted him.

It was a welcome as if he was family with a hug while shaking hands. O'Brien
seemed relieved to see Bailey back on American soil and in one piece after two
months. Bailey felt special once again. Two days before he was guided through
Italian border gates by the mafia; now he was escorted through U.S. Customs by
a high ranking U.S. government official. The contrast between the two parties
was remarkably different; the results were the same. He passed through with no
questions asked.

A minute later the two of them were in a taxi. The first thing uttered by O'Brien was how valuable the intelligence had been from Bailey's recent two ventures into Italy. He was obviously quite curious where Bailey had traveled during his third sojourn into Italy in recent weeks.

They arrived at the Waldorf-Astoria where two of O'Brien's staff people were waiting in a suite. As Bailey dumped his rolls of film and his coded files out on the table, the jaws of the three State Department officials dropped noticeably. One of the staff people disappeared with the numerous film rolls while the others began decoding the printed material. By late that evening, O'Brien was shaking his head over the glut of key intelligence...from a person who wasn't officially on his staff.

Recovering from the time zone changes, Bailey was somewhat foggy throughout the following day. He watched as O'Brien and his two staffers showed some surprise, even alarm, over the amazing build-up of arms and military resources in a country that was suffering so badly economically. The reconnaissance Bailey had gleaned along the eastern shores of Italy on the Adriatic Sea was information they hadn't expected.

In the discussions with the three State Department officials, Bailey came to appreciate how much he really knew about the western European geography along with the military and political circumstances of each country. When he spoke, O'Brien and his two staffers put down what they doing and paid close attention. They kept showing incredulity, especially when he casually offered his overview of France's situation. "David, from what I observed in my travels in France these last two months is how badly their political and economic troubles are leaving them. They are in poor shape to defend themselves if Germany decided to initiate some action to get back their losses in the Saar coalmine area and in Lorraine from the previous war. And, regarding the noteworthy reparation payments required to be paid by Germany to France from the agreement at the Treaty of Versailles, Germany's unilateral decision to end those payments has been a literal slap in the face showing disrespect and arrogance toward the French. France has no response probably because they are utterly unprepared for war. Their only hope would be limited help from Britain and possibly Russia and secretive support from the U.S."

O'Brien and his staff members only nodded their heads. Here was a person, too young and inexperienced to be expected to contribute much intelligence, and he was astounding them constantly with his reconnaissance efforts and his articulate overviews. Bailey's comments made the looming clash between Germany and France seem even closer.

Throughout that Tuesday in the hotel suit, O'Brien kept looking at the data and the photos not believing what he was seeing. That afternoon as he and his two staffers prepared to return to Washington, he poured some coffee to keep both Bailey and himself conscious. Chuckling, he said, "Adam, we'll need to talk some more. What you've done has gone far beyond just being an observer. Whether you realize it or not, you've become one of our more knowledgeable assets we have in

Italy. Calling the intelligence you've gathered simply 'observations' doesn't give your materials the credit it deserves. You completed your assignment far beyond what the intent was and what I thought was possible. It's time you go home and take some days for yourself. Make yourself visible within your company. You want to keep your international businessman cover available if needed. You can bet we'll be talking by telephone in the days ahead.

Flying back to Minneapolis the next day, Bailey found his mind spinning. Developing and maintaining wine and specialty food clients overseas paled in comparison to the intelligence work he was doing. Seeing the State Department staff react so dumbfounded and impressed with his materials and his reactions proved his efforts had value. The idea of America at war had seemed distant; now it seemed inevitable as he had learned from O'Brien how the U.S. was already supporting Britain and France.

For the next couple weeks in June Bailey rekindled his visibility at the North American Distribution, Inc. offices in Minneapolis. He took many afternoons off to play golf at Midland Hills Country Club and Fena showed a sympathetic understanding and acceptance of that need. After two months of intensive travel, a bulk of which was in a country very unfriendly with the U.S., Fena had noticed the changes in Adam Bailey. While the young man still kidded with fellow employees, he was prone to show more intensity, especially after the frequent telephone calls from David O'Brien.

He played golf with Lawton or Davis on the weekends. During the week he played several times with the caddy master at Midland Hills. Nellie Robinson was a good friend. Bailey had known the World War I veteran since his first days in Minneapolis when he was about to become a student at the University of Minnesota. That was nine years before....and to Bailey that time spread seemed like a lifetime. And, when Robinson wasn't available, he just played alone and enjoyed the contrast to the surroundings he'd been in overseas.

Back at the office there was still work to do in following up with new and prospective accounts he'd briefly met in Portugal and Spain. Both Fena and Bailey recognized it would be business slow to develop given the long recovery likely needed by Spain. Above all, the wine producers in both those countries would need more personal attention. That presented a problem. It was becoming evident Bailey was not going to be able to provide that level of support.

At times it struck him that Fena was almost too accepting of the way things had to be. He wondered how much Fena actually knew about Bailey's activities on behalf of the State Department. When Fena and he did talk about the coming trips to the Western Europe and more lately about traveling to South America, the discussion seemed more of interest to his boss....as if Fena's aim was to show Bailey he had a way out if he didn't like the direction his career was heading in David O'Brien's world.

By late June O'Brien requested that Bailey should spend more time in Washington....that his perspective was too valuable to ignore. To camouflage his actual trips to D.C. for the rest of the summer into the fall of 1939, Fena and Bailey set up bogus plans for Bailey to make business calls on various domestic accounts in California, Oregon, and Hawaii. He would return to Minneapolis every two weeks for a few days just to preserve the image he was an active employee with North American Distribution.

It was during one of those short respites back in Minneapolis in July that he received a message at his office. The receptionist thought the individual was a personal friend since he only left his first name and telephone number. Bailey winced when he saw the first name. It was 'Willie'. At least the man had the decency not to put his full name on the missive. All he needed was a rumor going around the offices that a purported high level St. Paul gangster was his friend.

He had to call back. It was that or Big Tony following him around.

Now there was the matter of Bailey having used the secret telephone number in Milan on his last exit from Italy. That would likely create some questions from LaCurso. Bailey knew he'd have to be prepared with a good lie.

The call was very cordial. Willie invited Bailey to lunch at LaCurso's private golf club in St. Paul. Somerset Country Club was an exclusive club. Only people with proven wealth were members. Expenses were divided up amongst the members each quarter.

Bailey tried to think of ways to decline the invitation, but he knew it would be futile. The mole Willie had in North American Distribution, Inc. had already told the hoodlum when Bailey was going to be back in the city from a fabricated business trip to Hawaii. Besides that, LaCurso likely had him followed when back in Minneapolis anyway. And, his routine was easily monitored. Midland Hills Country Club was practically his second home during his spare time.

In accepting the luncheon date, Bailey had no doubt the Twin City gangster had other reasons for wanting to maintain their odd relationship. It was as predictable as the coming autumn.

The lunch was light-hearted with Willie in a good mood while still sharing his concerns about his own legitimate sounding businesses. He kept referring to the cops as 'intruders'. He despised how they continually bore down on some of his 'employees' who he described as doing perfectly appropriate and law-abiding work. Bailey thought the older man's comments might even be valid...during the day. At night their activities might be a different story.

LaCurso did mention the suitcase had been picked up at the Hotel de Italiana the previous March with no problems. He said the lunch was a token of thanks for Bailey taking care of the task so conscientiously.

It had been so long ago, Bailey had forgotten the favor he'd done. Now the fog over the real purpose of the lunch began to lift as LaCurso gradually hinted another favor was needed. It never took too long for Willie to get to the point.

"So...my young friend, you have been gone a long time over the last few months. Since you returned in June, you still are traveling excessively. And, if that is so, I guess you have to be journeying to other countries than my homeland... which, as we discussed previously, is perfectly understandable. That bastard Mussolini has about cut off most if not all exports to the U.S. He's affecting both of us even though we're a long way off here in Minnesota."

Willie didn't wait for Bailey's response. Both knew he was right. Instead, just having mentioned the name, Il Duce got Willie wound up. The rant went for five minutes as LaCurso declared the sooner Mussolini could die by whatever means, the sooner Italy can get back to some kind of normalcy. He then predicted the government leader's death would certainly be soon. The prophecy caused an unexpected chill to drip down Bailey's spine. A statement like that coming from a mobster the proportions of a Willie LaCurso made the expectation sound very real.

Then, as sudden as the wisp of rain, Willie calmed down. He snapped his finger for a waiter and ordered more wine for Bailey and himself despite the young man's protestations. Willie knew Bailey had a penchant for Italian wine and played on that knowledge. He knew the two of them would always have that similar preference in wine...and golf...no matter their differences.

Taking his time as he sipped his wine, Willie lit up one of his thin Cuban cigars and inquired, "So Adam, you still have clients overseas. What do you hope to accomplish in Italy on your next undertaking?"

With LaCurso having no idea of Bailey's affiliation with the State Department, the young man ground his fingernails into the arm of the mahogany country club chair. It was a normal question. He was angry at himself for not being better prepared to respond.

Looking out the huge picture window at the vivid green fairways at Somerset Country Club, Bailey stumbled through his reply. "Willie, I can't just disappear from the face of the earth. There are few winery clients remaining, but I do have some food specialty customers who still need my help if nothing more than to find ways of getting the product out of the country. I have to play my cards out and hope whenever the military and political conflicts finally settle down, I'll also have a chance to restore my business."

Willie was nodding. Bailey's trumped up lie was working. He continued to fabricate. "In the meantime I might be investing less time in Europe and more time in South America. I'll have to see which way the winds of opportunity blow."

LaCurso slowly nodded not completely accepting that explanation. The subject was changed to golf. Willie soon invited Bailey to play his country club sometime in the weeks ahead. It was the last thing Bailey wanted. All he could think of was how he could separate himself from this Twin Cities gangster. He didn't understand why their lives had to continually cross. He wondered how this unwanted friendship could ever end.

Then Willie got to his real point. "Adam, when you next go to Europe I would hope you would let me know. I have another suitcase for my poor relatives in Italy. I can't tell you what a relief it was for me entrusting you with that damned suitcase. It took a burden off my mind. Whatever accommodation I can make for you again to enter Italy, I can make that arrangement."

Then he looked squarely in Bailey's eyes and said, "And, of course I can arrange for an equally smooth exit if you ever have need for that advantage as well."

Bailey gulped. LaCurso asked for no explanation. It was his way of sealing the deal without mentioning any obligation to do so.

While knowing he had no choice but to lug along another suitcase with enough money to buy a seat in Heaven, Bailey would also have the continued advantage of not having to go through customs entering or leaving Italy. It was a huge advantage...as long as Willie didn't ask why.

He finally shrugged, "Willie, of course I can help you out again as long as you smooth my way through the border."

Then he smirked, "I'd hate to think if I was ever questioned by the Italian border patrol about what I was carrying in the suitcase. They might think I was supplying some radical group who wanted to gun down your hated foe, Il Duce?"

There was a momentary hesitation before LaCurso got the joke and kidded in kind. "Adam, you know me well. Of course there will be shotguns, ammo, and grenades in that suitcase. Mussolini should be dead within the week of your arrival in Italy."

They both laughed....Bailey more uncomfortably.

Then more seriously Bailey thought to orchestrate a certain advantage for himself. Even with a free pass into Italy at Monaco, he was more apt to be followed coming from France. He didn't need that problem hanging over his head.

He asked, "Willie, as you know relations between France and Italy seemed to be deteriorating by the day. When I do return to Italy, I would prefer entering going south out of Lugano, Switzerland? Can that be arranged?"

He was surprised how simple LaCurso made it sound. "No problem. Just call Roberto at that same number I gave you during your spring trip and do so a day ahead so he can set up your crossing into Italy. The same plan as last time will suffice. Just bring the suitcase to the same hotel in Milan....I believe it is the Hotel de Italiana you favor. My brother's offices are right down the street. He'll pick up the suitcase at the hotel."

When they finally ended their lunch, Bailey did mention his next overseas venture would not be until September...words that were unnecessary. The gangster's mole within North American Distribution would know Bailey's schedule anyway and report it to LaCurso. Prior to his Minneapolis departure, Bailey would get a telephone call from LaCurso reminding him of the favor.

In the weeks ahead, Bailey carried out both jobs with a bulk of his time in Washington D.C. Back in the Twin Cities his life was completely different volleying his time between marketing work for the company and spending late afternoons and evenings playing golf at Midland Hills. By the middle of August he'd set his schedule for another two month overseas tour dividing his time with business in Portugal, Spain and France, but most of the time undercover in Italy.

To mask his actual itinerary from the mole at the North American Distribution offices, he set reservations for a flight from Minneapolis to New York on Wednesday, August 23, in time to board an ocean liner the next day at New York harbor to Le Havre, France. As in the spring, he would never board that boat. Instead he would again take the train from Manhattan down to Washington D.C. to discuss and finalize his surveillance efforts in Italy. To coincide with the arrival of the ocean liner at Le Havre, France, he scheduled a Pan American flight from New York to Paris on Sunday, September 3. Those plans would change with what would happen in Eastern Europe on September 1.

As for his favor to Willie LaCurso, the anticipated phone call from the gangster had occurred on Monday, August 21, reminding Bailey of the suitcase. Two mornings later there was Big Tony waiting for him with a large suitcase at the Minneapolis airfield baggage check-in.

The early Wednesday morning flight caused some factitious irritation from the large man. He grumbled, "Hey kid, what is it with you and these early morning flights? You got something against sleep? You're killing me."

To anyone else not knowing Tony's rough manner, a person might have felt the hair on the back of his neck suddenly straighten. Undaunted, Bailey kidded back, "Tony, I could leave at noon and you'd still play cards all night and be tired. So, what's the difference?"

Tony chuckled. He wasn't used to being the butt of any joke. He liked Bailey's spunk, brains, and good humor...and accepted it with great delight.

He kicked the suitcase toward Bailey and handed over a carry bag with some wrapped gifts. Sniggering he cracked, "Have a good trip, kid. Don't get in the way of any shells flying back and forth. It sounds kind of dangerous over there."

It was a weird sendoff with Tony showing some concern for Bailey's safety, especially considering the big man's vocation. Bailey was about to say the same thing to the large man about bullets flying around in the Twin Cities. He decided to remain quiet.

He waved for an air porter to take his now burdensome luggage and extra bag with some wrapped gifts. It was inconvenient, but the task served his purpose with no trouble crossing the Italian border.

The two men waved farewell which for Tony was an expression of high emotion.

After a week in Washington Bailey arrived in New York on Saturday, September 2, so there would be no glitches catching his Sunday flight to Paris. When he arrived at the Waldorf-Astoria, he had three messages to call David O'Brien.

Though it was Saturday but he wasn't surprised O'Brien was in his Constitution Avenue office. Dialing direct to O'Brien's desk, the director of Western Europe intelligence sounded harried. His greeting was mellow. "Yeh, Adam, you might as well plan to return to Washington for a few more days. We got word that Germany invaded Poland yesterday. We're not certain how Britain and France are going to react, but you may as well remain on this side of the water until we get a bit more information. How this might affect you're surveillance in Italy is unknown right now. The attack was done without Italy's knowledge or participation. The 'Pact of Steel' that Germany and Italy signed to support each other militarily in any conflicts apparently isn't worth the paper it's written on. Italy can't feel respected, but will still side with Germany. This just shows again that Italy just isn't the power they want the rest of the world to believe, in particular to their formidable friend, Germany. Italy wants to be the key 'Sphere of Influence' on the Adriatic Sea. They'll up their efforts to appear more warlike. Your assignment in Italy is now more important than ever.

Bailey did not take that flight overseas to Paris until the next Friday, September 8. In the meantime France and Britain declared war on Germany.... and therefore, Italy...on Monday, September 4. The border between France and Italy suddenly became even more perilous to cross if not closed altogether. Entering Italy via Switzerland was now Bailey's most viable choice.

The day before Bailey was to train up to New York to catch the transatlantic flight, O'Brien had taken his young recruit out for lunch and then to the FBI offices in the District. Before entering the building the two of them sidetracked to nearby Ford's Theatre. Surprisingly O'Brien directed his young protégé to enter the old theatre where President Abraham Lincoln had been assassinated seventy-four years before.

The theatre itself was small, unimpressive, and run down. There was no one around but a bored looking janitor. Bailey thought it a shame such a historical place was being allowed to crumble. But, there were reasons. The still tough economic times across America and higher priorities limited restoration budgets for places like Ford's Theatre.

O'Brien pointed to the box where Lincoln was shot and sadly said, "Booth couldn't miss from point blank range. If Lincoln had been more cautious, maybe there would have been more guards outside his theatre box...and maybe the post-war would have been different....and so on."

Then he paused. "I need only to remind you not to become complacent or incautious while in Italy. Despite your cover you'll need to be more aware than ever of being followed once you enter Italy. Our relations with Italy have automatically deteriorated in the last week given the actions of Germany. For that reason I need to make certain you have another arrow in your quill. So... follow me."

At the FBI building down the street, O'Brien brought Bailey to the shooting range in the basement of the large building. They were there for a couple hours. O'Brien was an expert on a number of firearms including a German luger. Bailey's marksmanship and comfort seemed most effective with a smaller pistol that fired a 38-caliber slug. He kept thinking this part of his on-going training seemed excessive. He'd not even thought of carrying a weapon.

The next day at the D.C. train terminal, O'Brien presented Bailey with a new briefcase. It was not as roomy as it looked. In the bottom was a secret compartment. It contained a small revolver.

His stare drilled into Bailey's eyes. "Adam, I hope to God you'll never need the weapon. You should also know why I have maintained your status as an 'observer'. You've been very helpful to us working alone as an independent businessman. For now I want you to continue to have no connection to my department, though you of course have access to our offices in Paris and London. Now that Britain and France are at war with Germany, we may have to reconstruct our contact points. I'll keep you informed, so stay in contact with me through the London office for now."

Then he chuckled, "You know, we've never discussed your compensation. We've just handled all your expenses. I guess it's time to tell you. You've been receiving pay from the government since your return to the States last May. Your pay has been going into a blind account. You have a mutual friend who is banking the money we pay you. It's another way we keep your name out of our records and maintain as much secrecy and safety for you as possible."

Bailey didn't have much to say other than to offer his thanks.

Then O'Brien added one other thing. "Adam, when your travels take you into Switzerland, there's a fellow I want you to meet...a rather well-known Swiss businessman. You may have heard of him. He lives in Lugano, Switzerland. The State Department thinks he could be an asset. He's a strong anti-Fascist and Mussolini has been nothing but trouble for this man's many business interests in Italy. His name is Andre Pizzorno and we are gambling that this international entrepreneur could be of great help to our side. Frankly, we need to check him out a bit more. Before entering Italy, I'd like you to spend a day or two with the man. I've talked to Pizzorno only yesterday and casually mentioned you're a family friend and an international representative for a wine and food distributor back in the states. He knows nothing of your activities with my department. In fact, he doesn't really know much about me other than I apparently work for the U.S. Embassy in Paris. I want any relationship you build with him to be strictly from a business perspective. I don't believe he'd suspect you'd be connected with the State Department primarily because of your age.

He did guess right away that your efforts with your European clients have to be challenging if not outright disappearing. He seemed well tuned into the economics and interruptions caused by war. My department is undecided how we might want to use this man even if his anti-Mussolini background checks out. Our concern is that he will have more focus on making money than helping us. Anything you find out about him could be helpful in deciding if we should bring this man aboard as an agent."

They shook hands knowing it would be nearly two months before they saw each other again. While Bailey left Washington not entirely feeling like he was a full-time agent, he sensed his life had just distanced itself even more from his business activities with North American Distribution, Inc.

Chapter 10

Landing in Paris on Saturday, September 9, 1939, Adam Bailey immediately detected a change in the very atmosphere of the large city. Grim faces were reflected on everyone as they hurriedly walked down the streets. The city was no longer robust and energetic. The bells chiming from Notre Dame Cathedral echoed a more melancholy tone.

He left the Paris train station that very night and traveled into the central wine country of France just to get a sense of what his clients were saying and feeling. From La Rochelle on the west coast and Bordeaux over to Lyon and Grenoble to the east, his wine and specialty food customers were understandably on edge. There was still much drinking but not much laughter.

Bailey did his best to ease their nerves about continued product shipments to the U.S., but his words sounded so empty and unimportant. Business was conducted but invariably the talk always turned to the pugilistic Germans and the possible fate of France, the Netherlands, Belgium, Spain, and even Britain.

After six days traveling in France, Bailey was ready to make his move in the direction of Italy stopping in Lugano before crossing the border. From Dijon, France he trained through the border at Geneva, Switzerland continuing the night train through Lucerne to Lugano, just north of the Swiss-Italian border. Upon arrival in the Italian influenced city, he called the number O'Brien had given him for the residence of Andre Pizzorno. There was no answer.

He stayed the night in Lugano at a hotel across from Ciani Park and enjoyed a meal overlooking the picturesque lake alongside the downtown area. It was a quaint city with mountains seemingly close enough to touch. Bailey had to give Pizzorno his due. The man had great taste where he made his home.

The next day he called twice to Pizzorno's home. Still there was no response. He sent a coded telegram to David O'Brien through the U.S. Embassy in Paris indicating the business meeting in Lugano had not been fulfilled due to 'unavailability'. He added that he'd be back in Switzerland in a couple weeks and try again.

That day he also called the number in Milan given him by Willie LaCurso to contact the gangster's brother. The inconvenience of carrying the extra bags to Roberto LaCurso would finally end once he got across the border to Milan.

The gruff voice sounded familiar. Bailey barely completed his name when the brusque voice responded, "Yes, Senore Bailey, we've been waiting for your call. Take the train to Como and then depart the train before the border. Someone will meet you and you'll be escorted across the border by car into Como. From there you'll take the next train to Milan and check into the Hotel de Italiana as is your custom. Leave the bags at check-in; someone will again pick up the suitcase and package."

Bailey barely said, "O.K." when the telephone call was cut off abruptly as had been done previously.

The trip went smoothly to the north border of Italy. He got off the train on the Swiss stop before the border. Two men eyed him and then approached. They nodded and then took over carrying the baggage.

Bailey was crunched in the back seat of a 1937 Alfa-Romeo 8C 2900B sedan and remained quiet while the two men proceeded to drive the short distance into Como. Approaching the border they drove to the far left and waited for two other vehicles being searched. When those two cars were eventually allowed into Italy, the two men then presented the border guard with an envelope. There was no search, only a nod from the paid off border guard.

The two men accompanied Bailey to the train station in Como and loaded the luggage in his private compartment on the train. He would again be going first class for the short remainder of the journey to Milan.

It was in Milan when checking into his regular hotel that he noticed for the first time...an irregularity at the Hotel de Italiana. He recalled David O'Brien exhorting him to be more cautious. He observed a few sinister looking individuals peeking from behind their newspapers. His concern mellowed as the bell captain and the desk clerk greeted him by name...gratis of being a regular guest at the hotel each business trip for the past three years. However, he still heeded O'Brien's warning and this time had the LaCurso suitcase brought up to his suite.

It was only fifteen minutes before he heard the light knock on his suite door. He called out before opening the door. "Please identify yourself."

The voice answering was almost unheard. "It is O.K., Senore Bailey. I come for the suitcase."

Opening the door there was a sinister looking fellow with slick-backed hair and a scowl. He appeared as if he could obtain what he wanted whenever he pleased. There was no smile, only a low growl in broken English. "Willie LaCurso says you have a suitcase and some gifts in a package you were to check in with the hotel porter. My colleagues and I wonder where they are."

Bailey gave him a half smile and replied in Italian. "Yes...I have them here. Are you his brother, Roberto?"

The man did not acknowledge the question. He repeated, "I am here for the suitcase and wrapped presents."

The man was obviously not interested in forming a lasting friendship, but Bailey decided to play out his hand a bit further. After all, he was the one doing a favor even if it was for a U.S. gangster. He was going to complete the task dependably.

In his fluid Italian he asked, "Senore, I do not know you. The suitcase and gifts are my responsibility to Senore LaCurso in the U.S. Can you give me some verification as to who you are?"

The man's eyes became very dark. He stared at Bailey as if deciding whether to kill him immediately or wait for another minute before completing the task.

Undeterred, Bailey stared just as menacingly back at the courier.

The man's eyes finally softened. He blinked and forced a chuckle. The mood at the suite door changed markedly. Ignoring Bailey's Italian, he spoke in better English if a bit condescendingly, "Senore Bailey, I am glad you are being so cautious. Roberto will be pleased you are taking this favor so seriously. Here is the number you called to get help in taking the luggage across the border. They will verify my identification. My name is Paulo. You will be told it is all right to give me the suitcase and packages."

Bailey took the note. On it was the same phone number he'd used the day before given him by Willie LaCurso. The brief encounter had been settled. He nodded his head and immediately retrieved the packages and suitcase. As he passed them over to the courier, he added, "I do hope the contents will help the LaCurso family. Willie seems quite concerned about the difficult times his Italian family is going through with Mussolini's regime at the helm."

Paulo was more concerned about taking the packages and replied without thinking, "Oh yes, we've been waiting for this suitcase. Roberto and Senore Pizzorno will be able to move forward more aggressively with their plans."

The name 'Pizzorno' hit him like a loud shot in an enclosed room. Bailey couldn't believe what he'd just heard. 'Pizzorno...Pizzorno!' That was the same name given him by David O'Brien. Was the name that common? The coincidence was just too odd to just let it pass by.

Accompanying the courier to the suite door, he amiably asked the Italian, "So, how is Andre. It's been a while since I've seen him? I meant to look him up when I was in Lugano."

The dull-witted man only shrugged not realizing he'd broken any confidence. More relaxed now that he had the suitcase and packages he responded, "Oh, the Senore is fine, just always traveling."

Then tapping the suitcase, he sneered, "Finally, he might get the right people."

A lot was said in those few innocent asides. Bailey began to get a queasy feeling. O'Brien had said Pizzorno's business concerns were being seriously affected by the Fascist regime. That could mean Willie LaCurso's hatred toward the Italian leader was shared by the Swiss entrepreneur. Bailey wasn't ready to believe it, but the LaCursos and Pizzorno might just be collaborating on some kind of pact to kill Mussolini. It made him wonder if the cash inside the suitcase to say nothing of the probable weapons in the gift packages were intended for something other than aid to the LaCurso family. If that was so, he could be considered part of the LaCurso coterie as an international courier.

Bailey wanted to ask more questions but the man was in a hurry. Having what he came for, Roberto's man curtly said, "Buena Notti" and then disappeared down the hotel hallway.

Bailey sat down on his bed trying to sort through what had just happened. Was Andre Pizzorno pulling the wool over the eyes of David O'Brien and the State Department? The man from Lugano was involved with the relatively wealthy LaCurso family. It was overwhelmingly possible they were working together to bring down the Fascist regime in Italy? It was definitely something of common interest.

The world seemed very small at that moment.

As he thought further, he realized his supposition could strike both ways. As a courier for the LaCursos, the Adam Bailey name might be familiar to Pizzorno. The Swiss businessman would already know the supposed innocent, young American businessman mentioned to him by David O'Brien was also connected somehow to a major crime family. Pizzorno had to wonder the veracity of O'Brien as he depicted Bailey as simply a family friend from the U.S. who did some business in Western Europe. The purpose Bailey was supposed to communicate to Pizzorno was for counsel and advice on how to sustain his rapidly deteriorating business. Pizzorno would logically have to wonder what the real reason O'Brien wanted Pizzorno to meet with the American.

The circumstances left Bailey in a quandary. There was another problem. If Pizzorno ever hinted to David O'Brien that Bailey was somehow connected with an Italian mob family, it could jeopardize his relationship with the State Department. That possibility left Bailey wanting nothing to do with Andre Pizzorno.

Then again, Bailey thought of a counter point. Pizzorno had his own issues. He had to be careful not to let an American Embassy official like David O'Brien learn he was in partnership with a prominent Italian crime family bent on taking down Mussolini.

Bailey resolved to ignore the potential problem with Pizzorno for the time being. He had more important immediate concerns....like carrying out his assignment in Italy. Later upon returning through Switzerland, he could consider whether or not any effort should be made in meeting the cagey Swiss entrepreneur.

The next few days Bailey's journeys took him to the outskirts of Milan, to Torino, and then to some rural plants north of Rome. The former food processing plants and bottle factories were churning out military gear and supplies as if they'd been doing it for years. Outside Torino the former farm equipment and car manufacturing locations continued producing tanks, jeeps, and airplane parts. In six months he took note of six more converted small factories in those cities, three of which were making guns and ammunition.

He remained in the industrial northern region for two weeks counting trains and trucks hauling products to various training grounds or other assembly plants. Booking a train south to Bari and Taranto on the Adriatic Sea, he roomed at boarding houses for the next couple weeks taking pictures and coding notes about these main dispensing areas. That area had become a more prominent and improved supply and distribution center since the Italian forces had trekked across the sea to attack defenseless Albania the previous spring. Given both cities were important shipping ports, he also observed what military products were being dispatched and where.

It was in Taranto that he attracted some military police attention. He'd gotten too sure of himself. On Monday morning, October 16, he was about to leave his hotel to taxi down to the docks when four military police jeeps came driving up to the hotel. They began asking each guest for their passports. He'd been roaming and taking pictures at the shipping port the previous day; maybe they were looking for him. He was not about to wait around and confirm it. Leaving the hotel via a side door, Bailey taxied to the train terminal. Within the hour he had embarked on a lengthy rail trip back toward Milan.

On that trip north he did make two stops at vineyards who'd been good clients the previous three years up through the beginning of 1939. Located in the Tuscany Region, both stops were quite brief. The former customers were polite and even pleased to see him but offered no courtesies beyond their welcome. He sensed how badly they felt for being so inhospitable, but he also understood why.

Showing no displeasure he claimed he was just passing through and had to be in Milan later that evening. He also reminded them that things would change and business would return to normal; it was just a question of when. It was an empty but hopeful claim. The look of despair in their eyes was palpable. Again, the only good that could come out of the visits was that he could truthfully say he was trying to maintain some contact with former clients if he was questioned by the Italian authorities.

With his cover still intact, he doggedly kept up his surveillance efforts. Hearing about Italy's attempt at building an air force he spent more time in the evenings at cafes near airplane parts manufacturing plants. He did the same at new air bases near Livorno and the Firenze area down to Terni north of Rome. Workers seeking some solace in the cafes after long hours in noisy factories hardly noticed his presence. The more inebriated some got, the more talkative they often became. Unexpected information was gleaned including productivity levels and where finished products were being shipped.

For photographs, he was especially stealthy. Dressed as a local he carried his camera in his hood flopped back over his shoulders. Holding nothing in his hands, he could freely wave to passing military vehicles and walk past policia with little apprehension.

By the first of November Bailey was facing a similar problem to his previous missions...his accumulated intelligence and rolls of film were making him too vulnerable. He was burdened with the most current overview of military related plants in the industrial north and pictures of air fields in central Italy. He knew not only the locations of these plants, but their purposes, production output, shipping methods, and numbers of employees.

Not ready to leave Italy, he journeyed the few hours to Milan to store his accumulated intelligence in potted plants along the patio of the Hotel de Italiana. It was convenient and he'd be passing through Milan on his way to Switzerland once he felt his assignment was generally completed. During the quiet of that one night stay at the hotel on Wednesday, November 1, Bailey buried his plastic encased coded notes and rolls of film in the dirt under those plants. The burden relieved, he slept late into the next morning.

Refreshed and ready to take one more excursion south into Italy, he boarded the night train on November 2 taking him along the west coast. During those weeks of November he did what had become routine from Naples all along the coast of the Tyrrhenian Sea to Sicily with photos and ample coded notations.

While in Sicily, Bailey stopped to see one particularly favorite former client just west of Catania on the eastern coast. Gerardo Giuseppe didn't seem as nervous about his visit as other former clients. Though the prospect of them doing business together was no longer possible, Giuseppe welcomed the American and insisted he stay the night at his ranch.

Over dinner it took no time for the conversation to cover the depreciating conditions all around Western Europe. Wanting to be a suitable guest, Bailey expressed hope that nothing aggressive would happen between Italy and the U.S. He'd said it before to other former business clients and the sound was always hollow. Giuseppe shook his head. "Adam, things will get worse between our two countries. Once Italy agreed to support the aggressive German military movements, Il Duce will do everything to increase manufacturing capabilities. While this effort might boost Italian stature to Germany, the cost of war for this country will cripple us.

Bailey just stayed quiet. Giuseppe carped on and on about how sickening it was to see Mussolini invest so much capital into war supplies. He railed against the trumped up 'war' in Ethiopia a few years before and the attack on Albania the previous April.

The Italian obviously trusted Bailey as he exclaimed, "Ethiopia was like two different centuries fighting. Italy didn't gain much in respect or spoils. It was supposed to provide some land for unemployed Italians to settle. I don't know too many of my fellow countrymen who've gone to that desolate place. Then the attack on ill-equipped Albania proved empty other than giving Italy some prestige as a formidable ally of Germany. At best it gives Italy a beachhead in the Balkans. And then there is Spain. Mussolini has shipped guns and war supplies to support Franco in their tragic civil war. This has been done more to prove again Italy is a willing Axis supporter. And now as Germany increases its aggressiveness outside its borders, Italy is expected to fall in behind Germany and support them anyway possible. Win or lose, my country is suffering."

Finishing his small tirade, Giuseppe apologized blaming his outburst on too much wine. Shortly thereafter, he excused himself and went to bed. Bailey just sat outside in the wine producers beautiful garden and lamented Italy's situation. It was discussions like he'd just had with his friend that gave him the depth of the frustrations so many Italians were facing...whether the common citizen, legitimate businessmen like Gerardo Giuseppe or even crime families like the LaCursos.

Bailey left early the next morning a bit fuzzy from the previous night's wine and continued his 'observations' for the U.S. State Department. Southern Italy was where Mussolini had placed significant effort to improve the agricultural output as well as some industrial production. The war materials produced in the industrial areas of Salerno and Foggia were of primary importance. Often hours from any conceivable food processing business or winery, if stopped and questioned in his travels, his claim of business calls would bring a lot of doubt.

With more unprocessed rolls of film and other damning materials and notes, he boarded a train north to Milan on Monday, November 27. In Tuscany he made one more stop at a winery to greet a former client who formerly lived in America. Family deaths in Italy had caused Louise Barbarossa to leave Chicago and return to his home country in the early 1930's to tend to the family vineyard. He had found it a far different Italy than the one he had left a decade before to go to school at the University of Chicago. While Barbarossa had been Bailey's original client in 1935, the welcome was once again more hesitant.

Seeing Barbarossa's uncertainty convinced Bailey he would stay at a hotel nearby. His friend wouldn't hear of it and insisted he stay the night. The change Bailey witnessed right away was the very atmosphere at the Barbarossa house. Usually it was riotous with parties and dinner guests. That evening's dinner was like eating at a morgue.

Later, Bailey, not feeling tired, grabbed a bottle of wine from his room and strolled out onto the Barbarossa patio. The air was crisp and carried the odors of processed grapes, fruit trees and evergreens. Settling in a lawn chair with ataman, he almost fell asleep. His constant travel and the accompanying pressure of his days had caught up to him. Physically he was somewhat tired, but mentally he was whipped.

Louise suddenly appeared with a glass of wine. He sat down on the bench seemingly more willing to be social. He sighed, "Adam, I hope your business travels in Italy are coming to an end. An American traveling in Italy is not healthy these days."

His voice seemed urgent and sincere.

Bailey chuckled, "Louise, you usually are trying to make me stay longer so I can get my hands dirty for a day or two working at your vineyards. Why the concern?"

Louise took a long drink from his wine glass. "My friend, things are changing very fast in Italy. If anything drastic happens and you're in this country, you could be held and even lost in the horrible Italian prison system. It's just too unsettled and dangerous for an American businessman or traveler to gallivant around this country...no matter what his true purpose might be."

That was the first time Bailey sensed someone was hypothesizing that he might have other reasons for his travels. He felt some perspiration forming on his forehead.

Louise talked even softer. "Adam, of course I know you have no other motives, but the perception by the Fascist regime would be that you do. My concern is for your safety. You have clients or former clients in some very diverse yet strategic areas of this country where even sightseeing might make you too visible. With so much paranoia in this country, citizens are nervous. You could be reported. Not much evidence is required for this government to verify suspicions. So, I simply suggest you get out of this country while you can."

The two of them became quiet. Then Louise got up and put his hand on Bailey's shoulder. "Adam, please do not mistake my lack of hospitality for hostility. It saddens me that I can't invite some guests over to meet you as in the past. Even my wife, Bettina, and I have to make some decisions regarding our vineyards here in Italy. Do we stay and try to persevere or do we leave. That would mean giving up our family's land and turning the whole business or the land over to the Mussolini regime. The latter might happen even if we stay."

They finished the last of the wine and bid each other a restful night. Bailey left the Barbarossa home the next morning before the sun rose. He arrived in Milan by the afternoon where he checked into the Hotel de Italiana. He figured to stay the night, recover his other accumulated rolls of film and intelligence hidden in the base of the large porcelain plant holders along the hotel patio, and go north toward Switzerland the next day.

It was 2:00 in the morning when he slipped out onto the darkened patio and groveled in the dirt of the large vase to find the plastic encased envelopes. Nothing appeared damaged by weather or maintenance people watering the plants.

The next morning with the accumulation of two months of reconnaissance notes and film, he went to the one resource he had confidence he could use. It was Wednesday, November 29, that Adam Bailey took advantage of his underworld contact with an Italian crime family. He disliked having to seek their help, but when it came down to crossing the border with no hitches, he made the telephone call.

He rationalized he was only seeking a fair exchange for delivering the suitcase and packages into Italy two months before. A return favor getting him back into neutral Switzerland would hopefully not be too much to ask.

When the gruff voice answered, Bailey succinctly stated, "My name is Adam Bailey. I'm a friend of Willie LaCurso's in the U.S. I did him a favor in early September for his family here in Italy. I now have needs to get out of Italy. As an American, I would prefer not to be searched. May I ask a return favor by helping me pass into Switzerland?"

There was a pause but only for seconds. The voice said, "Are you in Milan?
"Yes."

"Are you at the hotel you normally stay here in the city?"
"Yes."

"We will be in contact with you tomorrow. Please stay where you are."

Bailey sensed a huge problem had just been averted.

The following day he was picked up at the hotel by a 1939 Alpha Romeo 6C 2500 by two Italians who mumbled occasionally to each other but basically remained silent. After traveling in poorer quality Italian trains over the previous months, Bailey felt in relative luxury. As the vehicle moved through customs at the crossing near Como, an envelope was given to the border guard. The gate was opened and Bailey sitting in the back seat was suddenly in Switzerland having faced no consequence.

Before getting out of the car at the first train state over the border, Bailey said to the two Italians, "You have been very helpful. May I pay for something... anything... gasoline, dinner, flowers to Roberto's wife...some gift of gratitude."

The LaCurso men looked at each other as if Bailey was crazy. Finally, one of them said, "A favor for a favor. You owe us nothing."

As the black Alpha Romeo pulled away, Bailey, though relieved, kept thinking about the statement, 'a favor for a favor'. He was not exactly ridding himself of his relationship with Willie LaCurso or his Italian family. It was a problem that would have to be dealt with later. In the meantime he was safe and about to board a better quality Swiss train to venture across Switzerland to the French-Swiss border at Geneva. Crossing into France would have little problem. Not only were they a friend, but he had a coded number given him by David O'Brien. With the code, the French border guards would not search his briefcase or suitcase. And, this time he would not stop at the American Embassy to see Pierre Latif. He would go straight to the Paris airfield. The trans-Atlantic Pan American flight would have him in Washington D.C. the following day.

One obligation he hadn't forgotten was his pledge to David O'Brien that he try to meet up with Andre Pizzorno in Lugano. However, he now had a more important purpose in meeting with the Swiss businessman. The two of them knew things about each other...enough that unless they had an understanding, one could make problems for the other. They both knew of each other's association with the LaCurso crime family. They just didn't know how deep that relationship was.

Departing the train in Lugano and taking a cab to the Swiss Chalet Inn across the street from Ciani Park, he checked in and promptly called the Pizzorno residence with the hope of arranging a dinner with Senore Pizzorno yet that evening. A very dignified voice came on the line without a greeting. In Italian, he stated directly, "Who is calling please?"

Bailey chose to speak English. As soon as he identified himself, the voice warmed. "Yes, Senore Bailey, I have heard much about you. I am so sorry I missed you two months ago when you were last in Lugano. I take it you might be close given your call. May I offer you dinner whether this evening in my fine city or when it is convenient?"

Bailey smiled at the man's genteel nature. He seemed not troubled by the question that had to bother them both regarding the LaCursos.

Showing the same lack of unease, he played along and replied, "That is very kind of you, Senore Pizzorno. Yes, dinner would be very nice. As you know, a family friend in the States, David O'Brien, suggested it might be highly beneficial for us to meet. As I'm just passing through Lugano on my way to Geneva, your invitation for tonight would be very convenient."

Pizzorno's voice changed quite suddenly when Bailey mentioned O'Brien's name. "Oh yes, Senore O'Brien, a very cordial gentleman working out of your embassy in Paris. We had dinner a few months ago."

A mountain of information was given in that short response by Pizzorno. It was apparent Pizzorno's first thoughts about him related more to Bailey's connection with the LaCursos. The conversation Pizzorno had with O'Brien had almost been forgotten. The response also indicated in the last two months, O'Brien had not gone forward with bringing the Swiss businessman into the fold of the U.S. State Department as an agent. He truly did want Bailey's overview of this well-mannered businessman from Lugano. Additionally, it appeared Pizzorno had no pretense that O'Brien was anyone other than who had said he was. To Pizzorno, O'Brien was just an American representative at the U.S. Embassy in Paris.

It looked more and more that the evening's dinner likely would become a very detailed discussion about each one's connection with Willie and Roberto LaCurso. From there, a trust of silence had to be established regarding their connection to O'Brien.

More cautionary, Pizzorno then offered, "Yes, Senore Bailey, let me set up a reservation for this evening. Shall we plan dinner at the Marina de Lugano for 8:00? If I have a problem, I will call you as soon as possible. And, where are you staying?"

"The Swiss Chalet Inn."

"Ah yes...a fine hotel. I have one inconvenience that I'll need to handle, but I'll look forward to meeting you tonight. I'll get table #7 along the rail...a splendid view overlooking the water. I'll see you there."

The phone line died. Bailey felt relieved. He now had a time and place to examine how dependable this foreigner might be. He visualized a very cosmopolitan man with his Italian accented flawless English and someone who could be very sly. He planned on being very upfront; he expected the Swiss entrepreneur to have the same desire.

The conversation had been short and more one-sided than Bailey had wished. He got no sense that Pizzorno thought ill of him, but the man had to wonder what more there was to Bailey than just toting a suitcase full of money into Italy.

He wished he didn't feel so restless. He had to keep reminding himself Pizzorno and he were on the same side...the side that detested Benito Mussolini.

Arriving early at the Marina de Lugano restaurant, Bailey became immediately aware it had to be one of the finest eating establishments in the city. While everything in Lugano had an Italian influence, the specialty of this restaurant was food served fondue style.

Informing the maître de that he was to meet Senore Pizzorno at table #7, the host became immediately solicitous. The table overlooked the park and gave a breath-taking view of Lake Lugano with a background of tree laden mountains. It caused Bailey to wish he was dining with a lovely young lady rather than the Senore.

It was not five minutes before a waiter came to the table appearing slightly frazzled. "Senore...telephone please. You can take the call at the bar."

Thinking it was going to be a call from Pizzorno saying he'd be delayed, instead Bailey listened to an unrecognizable voice with a German intonation. "Senore Bailey, you are expecting Senore Pizzorno to join you for dinner...is this true?

"Yes, who is this? Where is Senore Pizzorno?"

"My name is Ernst. I work for the Senore. He has been detained. He will not be able to make dinner with you this evening. He is a thousand times sorry, but something came up and he is being forced to leave town in the next few minutes. He asks that you instead have dinner with his niece, Sophia. She is visiting and will be waiting at your table after you hang up this telephone. The dinner will be compliments of the Senore. He only asks that you would see that she gets home safely?"

Without thinking, Bailey lamely said yes. Before he could inquire if Pizzorno would be available the next day, there was a click. The man identifying himself as Ernst had given him no time to respond.

Replacing the receiver Bailey wasn't certain what was happening as he slowly strode back to his table. The disappointment of not meeting Pizzorno was irritating and frustrating. He now had to find out where Pizzorno was going or when he'd be returning to Lugano. For certain, he did not want to leave the city without having a very serious conversation with the Swiss mystery man.

Then the second request from Pizzorno's steward suddenly came into view. She was already at Bailey's table and confidently ordering a glass of wine. As stunningly beautiful as she was, Bailey was not robbed of his senses. Why would Pizzorno send his apparent niece to have dinner? If dinner had to be cancelled at the last minute, then so be it. But to send this attractive young woman as a substitute with the explicit directions of 'seeing that she got home safely' said that Pizzorno thought the young American could be bought off quite easily.

That was the telling moment Bailey truly believed something wasn't right about the Swiss businessman. The man obviously had little regard for Bailey.... and probably considered him just an American wayfarer and possibly just a puppet of the LaCursos. Nonetheless, Pizzorno had to be curious about Bailey's connections....both to David O'Brien and to the LaCursos. Sending a beautiful woman to find out this information would be better. That way Pizzorno would not have to reveal anything about his own relationship with the LaCursos.

Bailey didn't take another step toward his table. Though indeed enticing as she was, he held back being seduced by her obvious charms. She had a job to do in getting information from him that evening. He was curious what might transpire if things didn't quite go as Pizzorno and the young lady expected.

He retreated back behind a huge plant and just watched as she sipped her wine and began perusing the restaurant for the man she was to have dinner. The minutes rolled by. She began to fidget. His custom was not to make a lady wait; these were not normal times.

The young woman maintained her debonair countenance for almost ten minutes before she accepted that the young American businessman wasn't going to join her. She finally stood impatiently glancing around the restaurant one last time. Bailey hunkered down and looked the other way at the mirror behind the bar. There he could follow her every move. She finally gave a slight shrug of the shoulders and then looked across the eating area at someone as if wondering what she should do next.

Bailey looked in the same direction to observe where she was gazing until he saw a man sitting alone also nodding to her. The man was rail thin and appeared very intense. As she strolled toward her accomplice, Bailey quickly moved out of their vision behind another large plant where he couldn't be detected. Once together, they stood perplexed at the bar discussing nervously what could have gone wrong.

In the next minute the man walked toward the front entry. She then followed less than a minute later. From the restaurant window, Bailey watched as the couple chattered irritably while waiting for a taxi.

His disappearance had not been expected. Bailey felt satisfied he'd caused them so much exasperation. He had not fallen into the predictable pattern expected of any male being offered the company of a beautiful female. Still, with the addition of the lady's friend, there was something going on that made him want to find out more and how he might be affected by Pizzorno and this young man and woman.

As the couple continued to wait for the taxi, Bailey paid close attention to the male. When he finally recognized the individual, his stomach began to growl. The guy was the same fellow who'd stopped by his hotel suite to pick up the suitcase and gifts back in September when Bailey first arrived in Milan. This further confirmed the connection between the LaCursos and Andre Pizzorno.

The evening had become quite intriguing. Being more in the fox's position, he decided to follow them. He might at least get some more answers, in particular, why Pizzorno had dodged the dinner.

As soon as Sophia and her partner were in a taxi, Bailey hurried out of the restaurant and down the steps to hail another cab. He barely avoided being run over by the very taxi he was to take. The driver reacted loudly to his carelessness. "Senore....Senore...what's the hurry! If you want to die, please don't choose me as your murderer."

It was a quick-witted remark, but Bailey's mind was on following the couple. He yelled, "I will pay you double the francs if you stay up with that taxi that just left. Please hurry!"

The taxi driver spared no time. A double fare was on the line. He looked back at his passenger with his eyes mischievously dancing as he zoomed forward. "Your wish is my desire, my good man. Sit back. Louiggi will not lose your friends."

It was a short ride. The leading taxi stopped by the Monte San Salvatore tram station only a mile away. There was a four-car passenger train that was about to leave for the pinnacle of the mountain. Sophia and her friend leaped out of the taxi with no thought that they now were being followed.

Thirty seconds later Bailey paid the taxi driver the promised Swiss francs. Sneaking across the street to the station, he waited until the man and the woman were on board the tram before purchasing his own ticket. Entering the rear car, he slipped into the back seat and huddled down. They didn't know what he looked like, but there was no reason to be noticed.

As the ascent began, the Lugano city lights spread out below. A bell was rung indicating a stop for a passenger. She had shopping bags as she clumsily shuffled off the tram car and began walking toward a series of tiny homes along a street perpendicular to the tracks. The tram then continued its climb and more people exited on similarly designed little streets with quaint little cottages on each side. The tracks were literally yards away from residences and cross streets. The couple he was now following stayed in their seats and hardly murmured to one another.

Less than ten people in the four cars remained as they were two-thirds the way up the mountain. The beauty of the city lights and the blackness of the lake were entrancing. The tram halted again. Four more people exited including the couple. Just as the tram was to continue, Bailey leaped out of his seat onto the platform with the conductor rolling his eyes disgustedly that a passenger would take such a chance.

As the tram continued upward, Bailey slid over toward a shadow as the couple strode down the street not thirty yards away. When the train disappeared there was nothing but the sound of their footsteps on the street. He glanced down the track running parallel to the incline of the mountain and realized he was at a dizzying height. The track both upward and downward vanished into what looked like a black hole.

Following the echo of their footsteps, he snuck quietly to the corner of a small shop in time to see them enter a small cottage less than a block from the tracks. The entire scene was as if in miniature. It looked like the young couple didn't have enough money to enjoy such convenience and comfort....if indeed they owned the tiny habitat.

As he passed the flat where the couple had entered, he saw through the front window both removing their coats and talking feverishly. Pausing to scan whether anyone from the other cottages was watching him, he saw only darkness in each of the homes and apartments above various shops. The entire little community reminded him of a community in Minnesota with the town limit sign from both entry points on the same post. The comparison didn't die with that example. Even the street lights gave off a minor glow. It was as if the village had no pulse.

Bailey then strode quietly over to the front door of the small house and pressed his ear against the wood. He could make out some of their muffled conversation. He found his own heart rate rising with each sentence he heard.

First it was the young lady. He could hear Sophia saying, ""Luis, he could have gone anywhere. He is not a fool. Why did everyone think he would simply come back to the table and have dinner with me? He had to understand something was odd. The Senore should have gone to the dinner himself and found out whatever he wanted to know from the American."

Then the male named Luis responded, "Sophia, you are a beautiful woman. A man would be a fool not to want to have dinner with you......with hopes of some dessert to follow."

"Oh Luis, you fool." She sounded exasperated. "Not every man will blindly follow a pretty face when so many things begin to provoke him. He has to wonder what the money, the passports, and the weapons he delivers is to be used for. He's twice helped us out. He's involved in our assignment without knowing it."

Bailey's ear was practically stretched through the keyhole to hear more of the conversation. At that moment a neighbor three houses away came outside with his dog. Bailey dove to the ground to remain unseen. While doing so the noise he made caused the couple to scramble inside the cottage. Seconds later the front door opened and there stood Luis with a revolver held behind his back as his eyes carefully searched the compact area of the adjoining homes.

The dog began yapping and the neighbor tried to hush the small animal. He waved to Luis saying, "I'm sorry Senore. My puppy is jumpy this evening, but I have to let him out to do his business."

Luis relaxed and stood in his darkened doorway not six feet from where Bailey was lying down holding his breath behind a bush. Just the sight of the pistol gave further evidence this couple and Andre Pizzorno were involved in something quite serious.

The sweat now pouring down his forehead began dripping. To Bailey the dropping perspiration sounded like a golf ball bouncing on cement. Luckily Luis' hearing was not as sensitive.

The neighbor then gathered up his dog and hurried back into his cottage as Luis stared him down. Luis backed up through the front door keeping an eye tuned to any movement. Once the door closed, the voices inside were strident but imperceptible. The only thing heard after a few minutes were some giggles. The couple had already begun focusing on mutual interests more suited to their preference for the rest of the evening.

It was time to leave. Bailey had found out what he'd suspected. The contents of the suitcases he'd transported into Italy were not to help the downtrodden LaCurso family. Knowing Willie LaCurso's antipathy for the Fascists and Benito Mussolini, how far was Willie and his family willing to go in causing the downfall of the Italian dictator?

There was a muffled laugh on the other side of the door and Sophia's voice coquettishly could be heard. "Luis, what are you doing? This is not the time to play."

Luis' voice was imperceptible in his response to her. Not wanting to hear more, Bailey hurried across the silent street staying in the night shadows along the front of two shops toward the tram tracks. He stood alongside a tree for further camouflage. A minute later the tram came down the mountain as if it had no brakes. The stop was only long enough for him to leap on board and be seated before it took off again. The same conductor saw him. His eyes narrowed as if he knew something evil about Bailey. Bailey was having none of the look. His stare back was just as piercing showing irritation and anger from what he'd overheard from Sophia and Luis. The tram operator finally blinked realizing his ornery nature was not going to win this staring contest.

Bailey would not sleep well at the Inn that night. He caught the 6:00 AM train to Geneva the next morning. During the long mountainous ride with his arm hugging his briefcase brimming with intelligence, he allowed himself to fall asleep.

It was Friday, December 1, when he boarded the Pan American World Airlines flight from Paris to New York. There was one stop in Dublin before heading west over the Atlantic Ocean. The flight was long but preferred to his former multi-day trip back to the U.S. via ocean liner.

All across the north Atlantic his thoughts wandered time and again to the war front developing in Europe and then to his mission for the State Department. His cover working for North American Distribution, Inc. was all but void. If his value to the State Department was based on that alias, he may as well talk to John Fena about planning business trips to South America.

When Bailey landed at LaGuardia late that Friday, there was no one to meet him. It was no disappointment. He worked very independently. Only he knew his schedule.

Bone tired as he hailed a cab to Grand Central Station, he hoped he'd awake when the train arrived in Washington D.C. Then it would be routine. O'Brien would likely still be at his State Department offices on Constitution Avenue. He'd be startled but relieved to see his 'observer'. Then as Bailey would dump his unprocessed rolls of film and his coded notes on top of the director's desk, the director of Western European affairs for the State Department would shake his head in wonderment. Starting Monday Bailey would be in the offices to further explain the photos and clarify his notes to O'Brien's staff. He hoped to learn that Andre Pizzorno was no longer being considered as a potential agent for the U.S.

His value to the State Department could now be limited. Others more experienced in the world of espionage would take over. It looked more and more like his life beginning in 1940 was more apt to find him representing North American Distribution, Inc. in Argentina and Chile. In some ways that wouldn't be so bad. He would be free of exchanging favors with Willie LaCurso.

By the end of the week, everything he expected while at the State Department offices came to pass. Not one time was he queried about Andre Pizzorno...nor did he bring up the name. Regarding Italy, O'Brien's staff members would not update their plans without his input. He was again brought into all meetings relating to Western Europe where he unhesitantly contributed.

By the next Friday, December 8, he was rushing to catch a plane to Minneapolis from Washington National Airport. Before he left the State Department offices, one unexpected exception did happen. O'Brien had leaned back in his chair and gazed at Bailey for a long moment. Sipping coffee from his omnipresent cup, he finally retorted, "Adam, this observer role you've been doing makes things uncomfortable for both John Fena and me. You work more independently than anyone I've ever seen because of your association with your company. And, your damned initiative is beyond anything imaginable. What concerns me is that you may be too independent. If anything had gone wrong while you were in Italy, my group and I wouldn't be there to help you. Or, when we did, it might be too late. You make your assignments with us more dangerous than intended...but I'll quickly add that your efforts have been greatly appreciated. What I'm getting at is this 'observer' status has to end. I need you full-time in this department."

Chapter 11

During a deathly cold blizzard after returning to Minneapolis during December, Adam Bailey was stuck in his apartment in Minnesota. It no longer seemed like home. He only kept the apartment in order to sustain the image that he was still employed at North American Distribution, Inc.

Things had changed. He'd undervalued his usefulness to the State Department and David O'Brien. When he was at the Constitution Avenue offices, it was just assumed he was part of O'Brien's staff with his specialty on U.S.-Italian affairs. His perspective and knowledge about geography, military capabilities, and political consequences of countries in Western Europe earned him respect.

Just four days into his rest back in Minnesota, O'Brien had started calling and reiterating his desire for Bailey to be working full-time job in D.C. beginning January 1, 1940. In the conversations there were no discussions about another mission to Italy...more that his immediate experience and knowledge of Italy were just too critical not to have Bailey as a permanent resource.

As he would repeat practically every day in different wording, "Adam, you're not yet thirty, but your perspective is missed when you're not here. Our country has to continue gearing up for war in Western Europe. So while you've become a needed player here in my office, we would need to discuss if you need a new identity next time you enter Italy."

In further telephone conversations before Christmas, Bailey would learn that O'Brien was inclined to engage Andre Pizzorno as a government agent. He planned to meet the man from Lugano, Switzerland in Paris to discuss how the Swiss entrepreneur and the State Department would collaborate.

That disclosure caused Bailey some concern. It could mean O'Brien would disclose Bailey was not just a young American businessman doing business around Europe, but he was also a valuable asset covering Italy as an American 'observer'. There was no telling how Pizzorno might react knowing of Bailey's apparent association with the LaCurso crime family in being a courier. With what had happened in Lugano in December two weeks before, Bailey had no trust for Andre Pizzorno.

In the end, that meeting turned out to have no consequence to Bailey. O'Brien was a professional in his field. He'd say nothing about anyone on his staff or in the field until a new agent had proved his value. It appeared Pizzorno had no reason to divulge anything about Bailey either. That information could be self-incriminating to Pizzorno since he also had a connection to the same crime family.

Upon his return from overseas, O'Brien did suggest Bailey should be able to consider the Swiss entrepreneur as a source of support. The best Bailey could respond was a non-committal mumble, "Yeh....maybe." The real voice in his head shouted out, "Absolutely not!"

By the last days of December, there had not been any official offer made or accepted by O'Brien or Bailey. There was just an assumption. In their last conversation two days after Christmas, O'Brien simply said, "We'll discuss your transition to D.C. after the first of the year."

Bailey's response was even simpler. He said, "Yes."

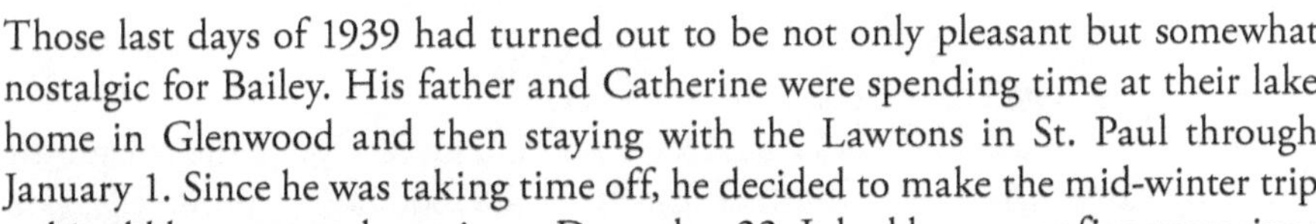

Those last days of 1939 had turned out to be not only pleasant but somewhat nostalgic for Bailey. His father and Catherine were spending time at their lake home in Glenwood and then staying with the Lawtons in St. Paul through January 1. Since he was taking time off, he decided to make the mid-winter trip to his old home town by train on December 22. It had been over five years since he'd last been in Glenwood.

When he arrived a fresh snow covered the community. Before calling his father to be picked up at the train station, he chose to stroll through the town. The buildings looked so much smaller than he remembered them and unfortunately more rundown. The 1930's indeed had been a tough decade for the lake community after the fall of Loni D'Annelli and Chippewa Lodge as well as the on-going effects of the Depression.

Glancing down the street at the Feed & Grain Mill, that business looked exactly as it had back in 1931. The business that had brought the former Henry Hanson to Glenwood had remained solvent. Ambling along Main Street, there were people out despite the cold. It was difficult to identify anyone. Each individual was bundled up with chin down to feet to ward off the frigid northwest wind.

As for him, no one recognized him. It made him feel old. Ten years since living in the town must have really changed his looks even though he was only twelve pounds over what he weighed in high school. A couple people almost stopped but only nodded and walked on. They were either too shy or too Midwestern to initiate a conversation with someone they perceived to be a stranger.

He felt some nostalgia as he looked at Big Bud's General Store and the Glenwood Café adjacent across the main town intersection from one another. He wondered if Big Bud's sons kept the back room of the store open as the social center in town. Now that Prohibition had been repealed, there was little reason. There were now two bars opened.

The short walk through the downtown surprised him for what the town lacked. It amazed him how an upbringing in such an insignificant part of the world could have provided a basis...together with his father's guidance... to make him capable of carrying out the work he'd been doing overseas and in Washington D.C.

Then again, it wasn't just the town or his father. It was the impact of other things that had happened in his life. He'd made older friends while he worked for six summers at the former Chippewa Lodge. Many of those friends happened to be hoodlums of all kinds. He didn't know it at the time, but they'd caused him to want to learn Italian. Those fellows had shown him respect not only for his competitive golfing skills but they seemed to enjoy being around someone innocent of their kind who felt a mutual kindness towards them. But the one man, besides his father, who supported him absolutely was Loni D'Annelli. He was the prideful uncle Bailey never had.

Still he wondered where his and his father's lives might have gone had they not met up with the Lawtons and Charlie Davis on that unbelievable weekend back in 1931. After the raid at the Lake Minnewaska resort, the two Bailey's futures had changed dramatically for the good.

Then he grimaced as a cold wind blew snow into his face along the downtown walkway. Of course his future had also been altered...not as positively...as a result of his having met Willie LaCurso at Chippewa Lodge and had that minor connection grow into a very disagreeable but cordial relationship over the years. He bit his lip thinking about Willie's daughter, Anna, now gone close to five years.

As for Glenwood, the luster and energy the town had enjoyed during the presence of Loni D'Annelli and that rowdy group who used the Lodge as a safehouse from 1926-1931 no longer existed. Even Chippewa Lodge was no longer...the golf course had long disintegrated into cow pastures and farm land.

Bailey sensed he'd been very lucky having all those people influence him... even the ones who lived on the wrong side of the law. And, since gaining his college degree, he couldn't imagine anyone in the town able to relate to his business efforts overseas and especially his covert work for the government...that is, except his father.

By the time Adam called and met his father and Catherine at the Glenwood Café, he'd pretty much seen the town. The three of them drove out to the new Bailey lake home on the east shoreline of Lake Minnewaska. The lake was frozen and looked like a vast wasteland of cold, hard Siberian tundra...a far cry from its more robust and beautiful times during the spring, summer, and fall.

Seeing his father laughing with Catherine in the front seat, Bailey appreciated the major impact that June weekend years had on John Bailey. He'd gone from a browbeaten farmer owning infertile land on the east bluff above the town to now being remarried and owning a summer home on the east side of grand Lake Minnewaska. Bailey was aware the two of them were busy working in support of an agriculturally based association, but it seemed as if they were doing more. They rarely were in Glenwood in the winter, choosing instead to be in remote coastal areas of Florida or Mississippi. Anyway, whatever else they were doing, their 1938 Series 80 Roadmaster indicated it was quite a step up from the days his father and him drove an old Plymouth around town.

The three of them would leave the town after only two days. Both Baileys had spent enough cold winters alone in Glenwood. Adam had seen a few people in Glenwood he'd known but not many. When asked, he just said he was working for a wine distributor in Minneapolis. That was all the locals needed to hear...that he was doing all right...and that his father was healthy and reasonably satisfied in his new life since leaving his Glenwood area farmstead.

The last days of 1939 the three Baileys stayed with the Lawtons at Lake Johanna in St. Paul. Charlie Davis fought heavy snows, quit driving at St. Cloud and then took the train the rest of the way. Once the group gathered, the main topic of discussion much to Adam's discomfort was his seemingly constant travels overseas. He focused his responses on business he still had in France and in Switzerland and tried to show enthusiasm about prospective revenue coming from Spain and Portugal and soon from South America.

It was Lindy Lawton and Catherine Bailey who pestered him more with questions about his social life. Lindy teased him about his constant mentions of weekend stops in Geneva, Switzerland when he did take a break. He hadn't realized he'd been so obvious about his preference for that city. Indeed he had met some attractive women in that city, but he'd also limited his time with them. The less familiarity anyone had with his life, he figured the better it was. Yet, he couldn't say that to the Lindy and Catherine. They'd find that response rather curious for a single male.

Putting up with their playful badgering was just part of having a secret life. The only time he got slightly concerned was when Lindy jokingly said, "Adam, you talk about Geneva as if it's your home away from home. You might as well tell us if you have a wife and family there. We'll find out soon enough."

Catherine continued the banter by saying. "Adam, obviously American, French, and Italian females don't interest you. What is so unique about the Swiss women?

He was able to divert their nosiness by quipping, "Ladies, I've never found any woman who I would compare to either of the two of you."

The flattery softened their lively interrogation but it was clear he had a real preference for the city of Geneva.

Returning to his North American Distribution, Inc. office on January 4, he was greeted by the familiar miserable north wind blowing across the parking lot.

By then John Fena was aware Adam Bailey was primarily in the office only to sustain his cover as a representative for the company. Fena, as president of the company, was the only one outside of the State Department who was aware of Bailey's increased work load with the government. Even he, however, didn't know the level of risk Bailey had been facing while in Italy.

They did chat about business plans if Bailey had the interest and the time to develop new clients. More importantly it was discussed solely so that Fena could make it clear Bailey's regular job was there if he became less interested in his assignments with O'Brien's group.

Mostly the two of them were attentive to limiting any suspicions amongst the other North American Distribution employees about Bailey. Fena let it be known Bailey's travels to Europe would be less considering the hostile environment. The word in the company was repeated that he'd be directing his attentions to domestic accounts in California...and imminently attempting more business development in Hawaii, Central America, Argentina, and Chile.

On that first business day of 1940, Kathy, the receptionist and mother superior of the company, greeted him as if he was returning from a long illness. "Adam, honey, I'm just so glad you aren't going to be going back to that hell hole in Europe."

She was already aware of his altered travel schedule. For a moment he wondered if she was the mole for Willie LaCurso, but cancelled that thought. She was just being friendly by showing concern for his safety.

He returned the welcome with a hug while thinking, 'if she only knew the real truth of his travels.'

The newspaper headlines that morning were all about the continued aggressive military movements by the Germans and to a much lesser degree similar activity by the Italians. He'd also gotten word the previous day from one of O'Brien's staff members about a hair-brained and unsuccessful scheme to assault Mussolini following a speech in early December. The would-be assassins had gotten away much to the chagrin of the Italian authorities.

Reports were that two young radicals, a young man and young woman, had been seen climbing up a church steeple across the street from where Il Duce was to speak. Direct shots could be fired from that location. Before Mussolini had even arrived at the hotel where he was to speak, the deafening sound of the steeple bells as Il Duce's vehicle drove up had rousted the two of them from their location. By then the military police had gotten word and were about to storm the cathedral. What they found was only a tripod for a rifle. It had mistakenly and stupidly been left.

As for the young couple, they were nowhere to be found. It appeared the two assassins' escape plan had been much more effective than the actual murder attempt.

It occurred to Bailey the failed attempt against Il Duce coincidently had occurred two days after he'd left Lugano. His mind streamed back to the woman,

Sophia, and the Italian man named Luis he had followed in Lugano. He kept telling himself, 'it wasn't possible' and then confirming that thought as he visualized the immature and seemingly inexperienced young couple. Then again, how much experience was needed? The deed only required fanaticism and reasonable skill as a marksman. Nonetheless, the two people he'd seen in Lugano were unimpressive enough that he disregarded any further thought about their possible involvement.

The first months of 1940 would become quite a unique start to a new decade. The moment he'd stepped back into O'Brien's office on Monday, January 11, it was evident he was no longer an 'observer'. There was more intense training at the marine training center in northern Virginia for three weeks then back in the department offices on Constitution Avenue for another week. By the start of February Bailey kiddingly asked O'Brien if the plan was for him to return to Italy as a foot soldier.

O'Brien was normally quick to laugh but seemed preoccupied. He motioned for Bailey to sit down. "Adam, I've definitely decided to bring Andre Pizzorno aboard as an agent for us. His contacts in Germany, Switzerland, and Italy are just too useful for us. I still wish you'd have met the man and was able to give me another perspective. I've met him twice...the last time a few months ago in Paris as you know. I have my doubts about him; however, he is undeniably anti-Fascist and definitely on our side. I'm concerned he has a lot of other things going on in his world. I find it hard to believe any of his businesses could be operating profitably with the problems over in Europe. My guess is he's somehow feeding supplies including guns and ammo to other countries opposed to Italy....countries like Greece and Egypt who he believes are vulnerable to attack. As long as he helps us, let him keep up his business connections.

During my second recent meeting Pizzorno told me it's not inconceivable that Italy will join Germany in an attack on France, possibly before summer. However, based on the intelligence you supplied to us from your recent mission in Italy, Pizzorno believes Mussolini simply doesn't have the trained manpower or the armaments to take on any kind of extended war. But, the dictator is such a God damned megalomaniac. He desperately wants to impress Nazi Germany and Hitler. He's liable to take on an offensive with any country that might offer any kind of worthwhile spoils of war.

Just because France is hopelessly unprepared for war and their leadership frankly quite inadequate, we believe also Germany will be taking on France in the foreseeable future. When they do, Italy will jump in and get as much as they can garner. The tragedy is that despite supplies not so secretly being shipped to France by the U.S., that country will fall....and I'm afraid rather quickly."

Pausing to collect his thoughts...something O'Brien rarely did....he leaned back in his chair and looked directly at Bailey. "Adam, Germany is determined to escalate the war in Europe. We want to impede Italy as much as we can in their so-called partnership with the Nazis. We have some plans to do just that and your knowledge of the manufacturing and shipping ports in Italy could expedite our efforts. What I wanted was to give you a couple months more of training, but we don't have time to prolong that need. Frankly, it's not as if the training was that essential anyway. You've been doing just fine in your role as an international businessman/observer. We now want you over in Italy for another assignment. We needed you there yesterday, but in the next couple days from now will due.

The bottom line is that Andre Pizzorno has some people who are explosive experts. We want to ruthlessly eliminate Italy's military productivity and put Mussolini even further behind efforts to make his country into a respected Axis power. We believe if we keep undermining Italy's training and military armament production, we can delay or interrupt their aggressive attempts against vulnerable countries like France, Greece, Egypt, and East Africa in the upcoming months.

What we need you to do is secretly enter northern Italy again and begin prioritizing which of the manufacturing plants or ammunition factories would be the wisest to hit first. We're not at war yet with Italy, but we can still choose to support guerrilla efforts to debilitate Italy's war machine before it can really gain any strength. We think with Pizzorno's contacts and your reconnaissance, the most important targets can go down systematically.

Adam, this means we need confirmation of the top shipping ports on the Adriatic Sea where Italy will likely first attack Greece and Egypt. Pizzorno has insurgents who can plant explosives at those ports. Air attacks can also be planned. We just have to be ready to make direct assaults on these seaports before or soon after Mussolini activates any aggressive plans. We think we can literally cripple Italy's war effort and keep it down for a long time. The damage we cause will be very costly to replace. Italy is not a rich country anyway, and with a leader with an unmeasurable ego and an insatiable need to impress Germany, he'll keep dumping money into maintaining the image of looking formidable until he bankrupts the country or is yanked from office one way or another.

I was hoping we had more time, but you have a flight scheduled to Marseilles, France on Saturday, February 3. From there we'll have a freighter available to sneak you into a port near Genova, Italy. As you know, so much of the military factory production is there in northern Italy. We want you into the center of that region as quickly as possible and then out of there in two weeks...three weeks if necessary. Time is crucial. When you're out of Italy, send me a coded message at our embassy in Paris. I'll be there the next day. We'll discuss your recommendations as to where to hit Italy first in your judgment."

He paused and then proceeded. "Adam, there is one question. Having your status as North American Distribution representative...can that still work as your cover?"

Bailey flinched. "David, that cover is questionable. I literally have no clients left in Italy. If I'm stopped, my reasons for traveling inside Italy's borders will be on shaky ground.

O'Brien nodded, "Yes...I was afraid that was the case. Still, I believe you're better off with that cover story than anything else we can muster in such a short time frame. If you're stopped anywhere in Italy, you can claim while your business has been curtailed, your company still expects you to maintain relationships with your former clients. I suggest you dress more casually, like a tourist. Carry a very visible camera and take pictures of historic sites or art. Play the 'innocent traveler' routine. You're certainly young enough in looks to get away with that game."

Bailey felt anything but young at that moment. This sudden jaunt overseas would be his most dangerous mission yet. However, that no longer mattered. The importance of his task was clear. He would have to accept the realities of war as Pizzorno's guerillas would initiate efforts to systematically blow up these locations.

He asked, "So...what's the exit plan from Italy? Do I catch that same freighter back to Marseilles, France?"

O'Brien looked uncomfortable. "Well, we haven't had time to work that part of the mission out yet. Right now we're inclined to seek help from Pizzorno for that piece of the puzzle. He has the contacts to help us. For now, though, until he proves his effectiveness, we won't be telling him who is making the recommendations for sabotage."

Everything seemed doable until Bailey heard the name Andre Pizzorno. His face paled.

O'Brien took notice. "Adam, why is it that anytime I mention Pizzorno's name, you show concern. This guy has been coming through for us. He's as anti-Fascist as one can be. Tell me, do you know something about him that raises a flag?"

Bailey chose to evade the question. "No...not exactly. It's only that I've worked under the relative anonymous safety of my business cover for over two years. I'm relieved you've so far only brought my name up to him as a family friend and an international businessman having no connection to the State Department. I'd like that story maintained until he's proven to be completely trustworthy. I don't want my identity compromised in anyway until we can both have confidence in the man."

Bailey had skirted around the issue and O'Brien seemed appeased. "O.K., Adam, I understand. Until you and I agree, the name Adam Bailey will not be mentioned at all to Andre Pizzorno. I'll keep working on a way to get you out of Italy once your surveillance and recommendations are completed. But, understand, I want you out of there in three weeks or less."

The two men shook hands with O'Brien repeating, "Travel with caution. Just because you're a full time player with my group, don't get sloppy. You're an innocent business and pleasure traveler. Keep that mentality."

Bailey only nodded. O'Brien's admonition wasn't needed. Being wary and playing the innocent traveler was the only role Bailey really knew.

On Friday Adam Bailey got a taste of his new life. He expected to be taking the Pan American flight introduced the summer before from LaGuardia to Marseilles, France. That flight now flew four times a week. Instead he was given a cot on a transport aircraft taking supplies supposedly in secret to Paris to aid that country. Despite the noise in the cavernous fuselage, he slept.

The flight underscored the urgency and secrecy of his mission. From Paris he was flown to Marseilles along with the Paris agent, Pierre Latif. Latif made certain there were no slip ups or delays regarding Bailey's passage on the Sunday freighter bound for Genova, Italy.

Before leaving the port at Marseille, Latif passed along a used looking passport and I.D. with Bailey's faded photo. He was impressed how real the fake identification looked. O'Brien had come through with a more acceptable idea of Bailey leaving Italy. If needed, his alias would be Salvatore Olaseni, a worker on the freighter.

Latif tried to convey confidence that the bogus passport likely wouldn't be needed. The Frenchman considered the Italian seaport police slovenly. He figured Bailey could walk off the boat, hail a taxi to the train station and begin his mission in northern Italy yet that day. True to Latif's conjecture, Bailey was on a train toward Torino within the hour with no one asking to see his passport. Once the boat had docked, he'd simply strolled down the gang plank as if an Italian citizen.

His journey across the heavy manufacturing area from Torino to Milan and then down to the Modena area before arriving at Rimini on the Italian east coast went flawlessly. It took him ten days to again examine and compare military production areas that he'd previously spied on. From his prior coded notes he was able to evaluate whether some plants showed increased levels of production compared to the previous November or December. Each night he compared his notes and began establishing the priority on which manufacturing locations should be on the hit first.

Once in Rimini about a third of the way down the eastern Italy coastline, Bailey's job became more challenging. Heavier numbers of troops guarded the ports. He took no photos as he walked along the shipping docks dressed as a dock worker. His American businessman cover had little credence if stopped by the marina police. For the first time he relinquished his name in favor of the Salvatore Olaseni identity Latif had given him. He'd become a worker on a freighter and could claim to be looking for work on the docks.

It was a good decision. He was stopped while loitering too long at the Pescara docks observing the large numbers of cargo ships and their consignment. A harbor sentinel was particularly doubtful about Bailey's explanation. The guard only let him pass when a ship's languorous whistle echoed across the dock area and Bailey became wide-eyed with angst. He told the patrolman his life would be over if he didn't get on board his boat to perform his duties. The sentry let him move on.

The incident brought up something Bailey had trained to do all during January. At the northern Virginia training center, his training focused on defending himself, how best to disable an attacker, and something that he'd found reprehensible...how to kill his victim fast with a pistol, knife or by hand. He was not at the stage in his short government agent career that he was willing to use that latter training exercise. He preferred his guile and language skills until heavier action was absolutely necessary. This time was a close call with the appearance of the menacing port guard. The question he pondered repeatedly from that day on was whether he would have acted more cold-bloodedly if his cunning had not been successful.

It took him another ten days to investigate the more important shipping docks and deciding which to systematically destroy. Even then he only covered the southeastern coast along the Adriatic Sea from Bali and then up to Venice. He still had to consider the ports on the west and southern seacoast of Italy. It hardly mattered. Wherever his recommendations would aim, it would trigger enough destruction to certainly cause havoc for the Italian navy and the port authorities.

By Monday, February 26, he'd been in Italy three weeks. He was overdue in his promise to O'Brien that he'd be out of Italy. His instructions were to send a telegram to Pierre Latif in Paris when he was about to leave Italy. The coded missive would say 'Italian wines are still the finest'. Knowing the message would be read by Italian authorities before it was sent, there was little doubt the respectful and innocuous phrase would be transmitted since it was a jibe at France and French wines.

The plan then would be for Bailey using his 'Salvatore Olaseni' passport to board a transport leaving for Marseilles where he would meet David O'Brien.

However, conditions had changed in the twenty-three days since he'd arrived in Genova, Italy. The guarantee of that telegram making it through the suddenly more strict Italian communication lines was hardly assured. The rumblings of war were more evident than ever. With his Italian passport he'd be questioned why he was on the freighter to France. Whatever his response, it would be feeble.

Realizing he had few other choices and his exodus out of Italy was urgent, Bailey faced his second and more trusting alternative. Marseilles would not be his destination. Crossing into France would be too difficult. Passing through Switzerland to France was better if he utilized the same method he'd used the previous December. If it worked, he'd have a guaranteed exodus from Italy into Switzerland with no questions from either Italian or Swiss border guards.

The contact number for Roberto LaCurso in Milan was still emblazoned in his mind. The LaCursos' fail-safe method of paying off border guards was unfortunately something that would continue his association with Willie LaCurso. It was the way things had to be.

Still, there was also the question whether Roberto or whatever LaCurso family member he would contact would be willing to help him and at what cost? Bailey had no bartering power. He'd not transported a suitcase into Italy; he'd smuggled his way into the country. With no 'favor' as a bargaining chip, the prospect of owing Willie LaCurso was disconcerting. However, given his desperate situation and the depth and importance of his intelligence, owing a favor to a crime member seemed trivial. At least, that was what he wanted to believe.

On that Monday afternoon when he arrived in Milan, he called the special telephone number for Roberto LaCurso hoping he was pursuing a viable option. He was ready to pay whatever the cost might be to get a guaranteed exit.

Bailey was nervous as he waited for the telephone to be answered. For a few moments he contemplated cutting off the line thinking his American I.D. might get him into Switzerland. But, would it...without him being searched?"

The phone was answered and it was déjà vu. The same gruff voice gave no welcome. He just said, "Yes."

Shaking his head in doubt while speaking, Bailey repeated what he'd said the last time he'd called in December. Back then he offered no explanation why he needed safe passage out of Italy. He offered no details either. And, this time there was no question asked in return.

The response was surprisingly stress-free said with no hesitation. "Adam Bailey....and you need help like last time. Yes, we can help you. Be at the border at 6:00 this evening. We will have someone there to accompany you past the border guards. Wait at the far left gate."

Bailey was amazed how convenient the gravelly-voiced Italian made the entire request seem so routine. Still, he was aware enough to ask, "Senore, can I pay for the inconvenience I am causing. This is very helpful what you are doing for me."

The voice paused before saying, "You have helped us in the past. If we can help you, we will do so. Favors require no money. Please be at the border promptly at 6:00."

Then the line was disconnected. He felt only relief. He knew he'd be safely on the overnight train in Switzerland to Geneva by 7:00 that night. He'd be in Paris later the next day where O'Brien could meet him instead of their original plan in Marseilles. They'd be discussing his findings and recommendations for insurgent bombing targets in Italy conceivably within thirty-six hours.

O'Brien would consider his decision to leave Italy via the Swiss border instead of the French border as brilliant. Bailey would simply claim his American I.D. along with his 'innocent traveler' look inspired by O'Brien helped him pass into Switzerland with no problem.

That evening crossing the Italian-Swiss border was again like clockwork. One very sinister looking Italian walked up to Bailey as he strolled to the left side of the barbed-wired gates. There was no greeting, just a rote statement of "Follow me."

This time there was no pretense of Bailey even seeing a customs guard. The baleful Italian connected to the LaCurso clan nodded at the customs guard and Bailey shot through the gate as if unnoticed.

Once on the Swiss side, this time the man accompanying him did not just disappear. He pointed to a taxi. "That car will take you to the train station, Senor Bailey."

Then, almost smiling, he said, "We will see you on your next visit into Italy."

Bailey had no response other than to nod passively acknowledging that the statement was likely going to be true. There was a wave from each of them as they strode off in opposite directions, the Italian marching back across the border into Italy as if he had the freedom of the Pope.

The night train across Switzerland was interrupted twice by guards checking all passenger passports. Bailey felt safe in showing his American I.D. to the guards in Bern and Lausanne. The looks from the guards were suspicious. When questioned, Bailey knew the game. He claimed to be on holiday readily showing his camera and some postcards. If they confiscated the film, the processing would only show pictures of historical sites and statues in Italy. Both times his passport was returned routinely with no further action. The neutral country, Switzerland, for the time being, offered no real difficulties.

Crossing into France from Geneva, he made it to Paris by Wednesday morning. O'Brien was already there having been informed of Bailey's change of itinerary out of Italy. Arriving at the American Embassy, O'Brien and three staff members were waiting in a private room around a large conference table. There were no questions how he made it out of Italy. The group was focused entirely on Bailey's overview and key recommendations as to where best to begin marginalizing the Italian military build-up.

By later that afternoon, Bailey knew his determined and intense effort over the previous couple weeks could pay great dividends. Andre Pizzorno would be instructed to follow the suggested priorities of destruction. If the Swiss entrepreneur's group of explosive experts did their job, the intent of Bailey's mission into Italy would be successful.

The plan materialized quickly with Pizzorno's contacts laying waste to twelve military factories in northern Italy over the following month. As for the shipping ports themselves, Bailey recommended not pursuing guerrilla bombing raids. He stated repeatedly there were just too many military police and soldiers congregated at the chief Italian cities along the Adriatic Sea for any mercenaries to plant enough bombs to cause serious harm. However, once France, Britain, and in all likelihood the U.S. forged war on Italy, these ports could be bombarded with great efficiency.

Bailey would leave the Embassy conference room late Wednesday night and catch the morning Pan American flight to LaGuardia Thursday, February 29. Taking the train down to Washington D.C., he checked into the Willard Hotel late that night.

It was unusually warm that first weekend in March. He chose to do some things he'd always wanted to do while in Washington D.C. For those next couple days he regained his energy by taking a passenger boat down the Potomac River to

Mt. Vernon to explore the home and acreage owned by George Washington. He took the elevator up to the top of the Washington Monument and took the stairs back down the tall obelisk. He visited the Smithsonian, the Lincoln Memorial, watched the construction going on of the Jefferson Memorial at the Tidal Basin. He was doing something he hadn't been able to do in Italy...to be a true tourist.

Monday, March 4, with O'Brien and his staff back in Washington D.C. Bailey found out there was no basking in self-satisfaction with the State Department. He was being asked to carry out the same kind of assignment he'd just completed but in the central and southern reaches of Italy as well. Factories were not as plentiful and more spread out. More time would be needed to garner the kind of information he'd just filed. But, a bombing strategy against Italy would still be the result whenever the decision would be made to proceed with bombing raids or guerrilla actions.

In preparation Bailey was required to undergo more training at the marine base in northern Virginia. O'Brien wanted him well-versed on all measures of subversive activities and to better recognize the best ways for attack. Those weeks in March he sensed he was receiving a crash course in war methodology and would be expected to accomplish more than his previous assignments. His last few days of instruction included parachute and basic flight training as well as continued grounding at the shooting range.

In the third week of March he took a few days off to return to Minnesota to be at the offices of North American Distribution, Inc. O'Brien still felt his international businessman cover should be retained. The concern was that he was too well known in that role. Changing his alias could become awkward as he moved freely around Italy.

The result was that John Fena had to be brought further into the world that Adam Bailey was now involved so as company president he could help maintain the facade that Bailey was doing work for the company.

Upon Bailey's return to the company headquarters in Minneapolis, he was greeted by fellow workers interested in the results of his travels. Mostly he had to lie about where he'd been including a fictitious tale of talking to potential clients in Argentina and Chile. Fena had to roll his eyes a few times but generally did well in sustaining the smokescreen of Bailey's supposed company efforts. Bailey's office, though dusty, was being maintained as well.

That first evening Bailey returned to his apartment, which also was being retained to continue his diversion as a North American Distribution employee, he felt truly the dwelling was no longer his home. He'd been mostly away from his apartment since the previous October. Knowing he'd be returning to Washington D.C. within a week, he ate all meals out and stayed mostly to himself.

It was the next morning while driving to the company headquarters that he felt that pall of someone following him. The mole in North American Distribution informing Willie LaCurso of Adam Bailey's return was earning his...or her...money.

He looked in his rear view mirror and his stomach turned. There it was.... the late-model Cadillac moving up close to his back fender. It was not the subtle movement of previous times when big Tony had gradually meandered his way into Bailey's presence. This time there was urgency.

Pulling to the side of the roadway, Tony's vehicle came up alongside Bailey's car. When their windows were down, the big man calmly said to the young man, "Hey kid, we thought we'd lost you. But then we figured, who'd want to kill an innocent guy like you?"

Bailey was used to Tony's jibes, but didn't really know how to respond. Given where he'd been during February in Italy, not only was he no longer innocent, but there were plenty of Italian war mongers who might wish him dead if they ever found out his purposes for having just recently been in Italy.

He waited for Tony to say something about his recent need for help getting across the Swiss-Italian border three weeks before. Having to use Roberto's phone number and asking for help in exiting Italy was already coming back to haunt him. But, the question never came up.

Ignoring the crack about being gone, Bailey smiled and kidded back. "Tony, I didn't think you liked early morning tasks. How's Willie?"

Tony chuckled, "You can find out for yourself. The boss wants to see you if you can spare some time in your busy day. You must have a lot to do before you go on your next jaunt overseas. We thought you'd moved out of the Twin Cities, but you're still on the payroll at your company, so we knew you'd be back sometime."

There was some sarcasm in his words. Again, Bailey ignored the slander. He also had to face facts. There was no doubt the gangster wanted payback from the extra favor his family had done. It would be unwise to ignore the man. It was better just to find out what the payment would be and then hopefully take care of the favor as soon as possible.

Bailey acted very friendly. "Certainly Tony, if Willie could meet me for lunch or dinner on one of the next few days, you can let me know what's convenient."

Tony seemed taken aback with how amiable Bailey always was with him. He never had to strong arm the kid. The young man kept his distance, but when called upon, he never felt compelled. Yet, Tony and his boss knew something had changed. Not only was Bailey rarely in Minnesota, but the fact he'd needed help in December and then again just weeks before to cross the Swiss-Italian border hinted that something else was happening in the kid's life.

Tony nodded. "I'll let the boss know. We'll be in touch."

Within an hour of arriving at the company headquarters, Bailey received a call. It was Tony. Typical of the big man, he was without social graces over the phone. All he said was, "Yeh kid, Willie wants to meet you for lunch today. Meet him at his club at 12:30."

The call ended without a "good-by." Tony just hung up. That was his way.

Bailey hated to think he was close enough to Willie LaCurso that he actually knew which club Tony meant. It was the exclusive Somerset Country Club over in St. Paul. Bailey could predict the cadence of the lunch. Starting out quite social, Willie would soon hone in on what was causing the changes in Bailey's life.

He spent the next hour before leaving for the Club practicing responses to Willie's anticipated inquiries...the most obvious being why Bailey needed surreptitious help in getting out of Italy. And, once explained, the gangster would certainly ask for the favor he desired in return.

Tuesday, March 19, in Minnesota felt as cold as a mid-winter day. While the temperature was above fifty degrees, the northwest wind and rain made the chilling air feel bitter. Arriving at Willie LaCurso's club a few minutes after his appointed 12:30 lunch, Bailey took his time entering the restaurant of the Somerset Country Club. It was a purposeful game he played. Being late showed the older man Bailey was not intimidated. Whether it had any effect on LaCurso didn't matter. It did make Bailey feel more in control.

The greeting in the club restaurant was not like two old friends meeting, but it was friendly and casual. They shook hands. Willie had ordered a bottle of Italian wine he knew Bailey preferred.

It took less than a minute for LaCurso to get down to the purpose of their lunch. His eyes were full of questions. "So, Adam, my friend, you've been traveling incessantly. Tony and I thought you moved from the area."

Bailey was already incorporating some lies along with some half-truths for his responses. "Yeh, Willie, I had to work in Spain and Portugal for clients since the European conflict has destroyed all my other business in Western Europe. It looks like South America is my next most obvious new market."

LaCurso digested that reply before more pointedly asking, "Well, obviously you were in Italy as well and had some problems getting out. Why else would you have called Roberto's number in Milan?"

Bailey grinned as he got ready to voice a blatant lie. "You'd better believe I had some troubles, but it wasn't exactly business related. As you might guess, I've got friends, not just clients in Italy. Both times I've asked Roberto to get me out of the country, I was doing a few favors for some vineyard owners. I had five different families ask me to smuggle some cold hard American cash out of Italy. Last month I had almost $100,000 in packets taped to my body and in a valise I was carrying. I could not be caught with that contraband. Once I made it to

Paris, most of the money was delivered to their family members or friends for safe keeping. For two business acquaintances they entrusted me to bring their money all the way to New York and deposit in bank accounts they had. So, I'm glad to be able to look you in the eye and give you a personal thank you for your family's help in sneaking me out of Italy and helping some other Italian families."

The complete lie flowed like a fine French wine and took Willie totally by surprise. He'd not been ready for that explanation. By his narrowed eyebrows, he wasn't buying Bailey's tall tale completely. "So, the only reasons you were in Italy these past few months were to do favors for these families?"

Bailey dove deeper into his fictionalized story. He was prepared for the doubts. Well, I did see some former clients, but only socially. Even then it was uncomfortable. It didn't want to cause them any problems if they were seen with an American."

Then he gave a melodramatic sigh. He leaned forward and in a low voice said to the gangster, "Willie, I was only in Italy for a short time, but I had some other more personal matters to handle. You can understand I haven't been a complete saint when I've been in your family's country. Italy does have more than its share of beautiful women and you should understand I've gotten to know some of them rather well in the past couple years. I had a casual but inspiring liaison with the daughter of a wine bottle manufacturer in Torino...and a slightly more than casual relationship with a gorgeous female, the daughter of a vineyard owner west of Livorno over on the coast. It had become....awkward...and I had to straighten out the potential mess. The war in Europe was secondary compared to the wrath I was facing if I didn't respectfully put an end to both....ah....friendships."

Bailey could tell by the glimmer in Willie's eyes that his fabricated love life story was breaking through the gangster's doubts. Willie began chuckling, "So you went back to see a couple girlfriends while making some contact with former clients as well. Wasn't that a bit chancy given the circumstances between our two countries?"

Bailey showed some exasperation. "Willie, it may not seem that important to you, but I still have my reputation at stake in Italy. I happened to like Italy and the people in it. When this damned war someday finishes, I want to be able to rekindle my business in Italy."

Willie finally showed some acceptance with a nod but then added curtly, "Yeh...your own business with the girls and the wine."

Bailey gave a weak smile and shrugged. He'd let the gangster's slight sarcasm trigger the end to that part of their conversation. Now it was his hope he could finish the lunch and move on.

It was a ridiculous dream, of course, for him to think that way. LaCurso hadn't gotten to his main reason for the luncheon. He finally did. "Well Adam, you seem to have created a very adventuresome life for yourself in the years you've been traveling back and forth across the Atlantic. Judging by what you just said, you'll be going back over to Europe to see your new clients in Spain and Portugal, but maybe to see some other females as well...maybe even those two gals in Italy. It does seem that you know how to get into Italy, but if you indeed are doing favors for some of your former clients slipping money out of the country, you no doubt will continue have concerns about exiting the country. If this is the case, I've got a proposition for you that should be mutually beneficial."

Bailey could see this request coming from a mile away. He sat back waiting to see what new mess he was about to get into with Willie LaCurso.

"Adam, my family continues to need my financial help. I need another suitcase delivered to my brother in Milan. To be upfront, the contents are entirely money. I was wondering when next you were traveling overseas?"

It was a simple, obvious question and one that Bailey had so hoped to avoid. Now it was not possible. He owed Willie LaCurso...and he might owe him again in vacating Italy after completing his upcoming mission in Italy.

Facing the reality, he nodded without hesitation. "Yeh, Willie, of course I'll help your family. However, I'll need that suitcase immediately. I'll be leaving Minneapolis in two days. Also, I may not be entering Italy until the end of the month. I first have to follow up with those new clients in Spain and Portugal. I'll not get to Milan until the last weekend in March. Once there, you can trust that I'll call Roberto so he can have someone pick the suitcase up at Hotel de Italiana."

LaCurso nodded agreement. In actual fact Bailey never planned on setting one foot in the two Iberian countries. While he'd told Willie he was leaving Minneapolis on Thursday, in truth he wouldn't be flying overseas for another ten days leaving Friday evening, March 29 on a military transport from Washington D.C. Willie would not know he'd be in Washington planning out his next assignment in central and southern Italy.

As for Willie, the timetable Bailey had just mentioned coincided well with the plans he was making with his brother. The young man said he wouldn't be in Milan until Sunday, the last day of March to deliver the suitcase. The timing was perfectly convenient for the two brothers.

Looking very relieved LaCurso added, "It would help, Adam, if you could cross at the French-Italian border. Roberto has more 'friendly relations' with border guards and customs officials at that site near Monaco. From there you can continue on the train to Milan. My family needs the contents of that suitcase as soon as possible."

While a waiter stopped by the table and filled the two wine goblets, Willie was momentarily silent. Bailey realized he had a problem. He was being asked to be in two places at once.

When he'd spoken to O'Brien the day before, it was determined Bailey should meet Andre Pizzorno in Lugano so the two had a chance to build some trust. The results Pizzorno's guerrillas had been accomplishing for O'Brien showed promise. In the previous week Pizzorno and his explosion expert contacts had already blown up a couple key military targets Bailey had recommended to take out first. Four of the twelve military factories had been crippled to the point of being non-functional. Two storage buildings near Torino had been fire bombed.

While Bailey appreciated the results of Pizzorno's group, he still had his doubts about the Swiss businessman. These bomb experts could be part of the LaCurso clan. While that might not be bad, Bailey was sensing Willie, Roberto, and Pizzorno were involved in other activities not under the scope of the U.S. State Department. What those plans were Bailey had no proof, but with the hatred those three men had for Mussolini and the money he'd be again sneaking into Italy, those 'other' activities could well be paying for a plot to go after Il Duce.

Without mentioning Bailey by name, O'Brien had already begun trusting Pizzorno to the point of requesting help for an American agent to be transported into Italy and later retrieved when the American's assignment was completed. Bailey was being given little choice but to put his reliance on the man from Lugano. Maybe it was time to bury his concerns about Pizzorno.

When the waiter finally stepped away from the table, LaCurso completed his thought. "I'll have Tony meet you at the Minneapolis airfield before your flight on Thursday. I'll let Roberto know you'll cross the French-Italian border and take the train to Milan on Sunday, March 31."

Bailey nodded. Already he was working out his travel to accommodate both O'Brien and Willie LaCurso. He'd simply stay on the train in Milan and continue to the Swiss border and onto Lugano on that Sunday. Going by rail across northern Italy was a much shorter trip than entering Switzerland via Geneva and traveling across the mountainous terrain to Lugano. And, having the advantage of using Roberto LaCurso's contacts to ensure no problems entering or exiting Italy that same day, the delivery of the suitcase in Milan would be reasonably convenient.

Bailey and Willie LaCurso had parted company on very friendly terms after their Somerset Country Club luncheon. Once the business was out of the way, the topic of golf dominated their conversation. Their different lives and diverse moral compasses were forgotten. They discussed the favorites for the upcoming Masters and U.S. Open golf tournaments as well as some of the latest golf equipment coming on the market. Willie was thinking of discarding his hickory shafted irons for the newer metal shafted clubs then being introduced. He repeated that the two of them had to get together for some golf at Somerset when the weather improved.

Bailey nodded blankly hoping that day would never come.

Two days later on Thursday, after meeting Big Tony at the Minneapolis airfield, Bailey had the suitcase for the LaCurso family along with his regular luggage on his flight to New York. LaCurso still was under the impression Bailey would then board an ocean liner to arrive at Le Havre, France approximately a week later. Instead, Bailey followed his more camouflaged route by taking a cab to Grand Central Station where he stored the LaCurso suitcase in a locker and then proceeded on the next train to Washington D.C. He had to make certain all his pretenses for still working for North American Distribution, Inc. were in order. He guarded his secret liaison with the State Department in utmost caution.

During that week before he was to fly to Marseilles, France from New York, Bailey had to finalize his itinerary with O'Brien and his staff. During his time in D.C., the Director insisted his mission central and southern Italy be completed in two weeks. Bailey would counter insisting on three weeks since his task in southern Italy would be delayed slightly with his having to meet Pizzorno in Lugano across the north border of Italy. O'Brien agreed.

A week later on Friday evening, March 29, Adam Bailey caught the LaGuardia Pan American flight to Marseilles with stops in Dublin, Paris, and then onto the southern border city. Exhausted from the flight he checked into a hotel near Monaco along the beach of the Mediterranean Sea. Before crashing for some needed sleep on Saturday evening, he called the number in Milan for Roberto LaCurso. The gravelly voice on the phone had become familiar. The answer on the other end curtly said, "Speak to me."

Bailey wasted no time. "This is Adam Bailey. I have a suitcase. I need to get across the border at Monaco tomorrow and then deliver the parcel in Milan."

The voice on the other end needed no further information. The voice softened while mumbling, "We've been expecting your call. Make your way to the border at 12:00 on Sunday. The entrance into Italy has become more difficult. Two men will meet you and drive you across the border. They will be driving a Fiat 522 C. Do whatever they say and you should be on the train to Milan within the hour."

Bailey confirmed the time saying, "12:00 midday on Sunday." It was superfluous as the man had already hung up the telephone.

He would sleep soundly that Saturday night and awaken very late on Sunday. He barely had time to eat and take a taxi to the French-Italian border. In thinking back he wished he would have taken more time to eat. Good food and uninterrupted sleep would be two things he had taken for granted. Very soon he would not only be eating bad food and hardly sleeping, but he would be living in conditions of the worst squalor he'd ever experienced....and it all happened after clearing customs in Italy and then being transported via the Fiat 522 C to the Ventimiglia, Italy train station.

The train ride through Torino went smoothly. He had his regular luggage stashed in the bin above his seat; the LaCurso suitcase remained beside him. He could only imagine how much money was inside the valise. He was looking forward to completing the favor quickly by dropping the suitcase at a pre-arranged locker at the Milan train terminal. Staying on the same train, he expected to be in Lugano that Sunday night where he would check into a hotel and call Andre Pizzorno. The man was expecting an American agent, but certainly not the same person who he knew as a courier for the LaCurso brothers. Pizzorno would share Bailey's wariness. But, they were both on the same team as agents for the U.S. State Department.

As the train approached Milan, Bailey grabbed the LaCurso suitcase and moved toward the door. The train was only making a ten-minute stop and then moving onward to the north for the three-hour ride to Lugano. The agreement was that he'd place the suitcase in a terminal locker and leave the key in the locker door knowing that someone connected to Roberto LaCurso would be watching his every step.

Once the delivery was completed, he would have that favor done. He'd be back on the Lugano bound train with time to spare.

Everything was going as planned as he hurriedly got off the train and strode resolutely toward the storage lockers in the main terminal. He was barely in the building when he was confronted by six Milan steely-eyed military police with guns drawn. One of them spoke in broken English. "Senore Bailey, we have orders to escort you to the city jail for questioning. You will be quiet and come with us."

It was an easy decision to go with them given the amount of artillery aimed at him. He was still shocked over the suddenness of what was transpiring. His surprise turned from nervousness to serious concern as one of the uniformed men took over the LaCurso suitcase. Bailey then was shoved into a waiting military truck and driven at break-neck speed through the winding streets of Milan. The vehicle jolted to a stop in front of a run-down, ominous looking city jailhouse where he was escorted forcibly to a basement cell without being checked in or charged.

Less than fifteen minutes since leaving the train to drop off the LaCurso suitcase at the Milan train station, Adam Bailey was confined to a jail cell not fit for animals. He'd barely had time to catch his breath, but he was alert enough to know something had gone very wrong. Worse yet, no one would know where he was.

Chapter 12

All night long in that dark, dingy cell, Bailey sat upright on his rock hard cement slab with fetid mattress. He wasn't certain but from his basement jail cell he sensed it was Monday morning, April 1. Life had become suddenly precarious. His mind skipped around to various reasons why he was sitting in that cell and being treated as the worst infidel known to mankind. Had he been found out? Was it known he worked for the U.S. State Department? Had he pressed his luck too far in masquerading as a viable businessman in a country where he had no more clients? Had he been watched during his recent assignment? Had the favors for the LaCurso family finally marked his doom?

Sometime during that Sunday night a tray with a warm broth and little taste, a hard roll, and some bland coffee was shoved under his cell door. While giving his hunger pangs little satisfaction, the liquid did supply him some warmth. More questions cycled through his mind. Why was he being jailed in such abject conditions? Only murderers or spies would be treated this badly. Had he been set up? Who would think so ill of him that they'd want him in such a hell hole?

For certain, he had to admit his preference for working alone had caught up with him. It would not be a great surprise to O'Brien that he didn't meet up with Pizzorno before entering Italy. The director knew if Bailey found a way into southern Italy, he'd take it and get on with his task. There would be no real concern from O'Brien for at least a week. Even then it was a two-week assignment. There was no telling where Bailey might be buried in the Italian prison system by then.

It was ten minutes...or maybe an hour or two hours later...when Bailey again was bolted awake after hearing a scream coming from far down the basement level corridor. He tried to recall why he'd felt some hope that allowed him to sleep. Nothing provided him any encouragement.

His despair turned to anger; his anger to fury as reality set in. He had to have been set up with the military police waiting for him like a welcoming committee.

He was tired but his senses were now on full alert. Whoever that person was, he knew Bailey would be crossing northern Italy with a stop in Milan. Someone from the LaCurso family was the obvious first thought, but he only knew Willie and Roberto. Why would either of them turn against him? The small favors he'd done for the LaCurso family had put him in elite company. In fact, Willie's brother, Roberto, might be in a position to help him when the transfer of the suitcase never materialized.

Adam Bailey was taken from his cell later that morning. He didn't know what time it was until he was paraded through the main lobby of the city jail on his way to the office of the commandant. It was almost 11:00 on the wall clock above the sergeant's desk as a long line of wide-eyed, frightened human beings waited to hear their fate from the overweight, arrogant uniformed man behind the main desk.

Bailey didn't know what to anticipate. That he was in a city jail and not a military prison left him also puzzled. Maybe his arrest was just a misunderstanding. That was the strategy he was going to employ when he was allowed to speak.

While he expected some unpleasantries, the time with the jail supervisor turned out to be more a visit than an interrogation. Surprisingly, the commandant seemed unaware why Bailey was being detained. He appeared to not want to admit his unfamiliarity.

Trying to show distain toward his prisoner, he queried in surprisingly fluent English, "So, why is a young man from America traveling in Italy? The relations between our two countries have not been exactly friendly? You must be a fool."

Bailey acquiesced. "Right now my family would agree with you."

The commandant snickered. Then more irritably he added, "So, why don't we go past all the lies and you just tell me what your true purposes are for being here in Italy. This is no time to play games. We'll find out eventually one way or another."

Bailey eyed the guard by the office door and rubbed his shoulder. This was his time to perform. He sat up straight and spoke respectfully. "Commandant, I have no intention of saying anything but the truth to you. You should know that I have been coming to your country repeatedly since 1936 working for a wine and specialty food distributor in the United States. I have personally helped many vineyard owners market their fine wines to America while increasing their revenues in the process. In the past year my clientele have diminished but I still come into your beautiful country to visit these former clients and make certain they know my company's interest in doing business with them when this whole political and military chaos eventually might ease."

The commandant creased his brow trying but failing to show doubt. Bailey continued, "I have never had a problem seeing my friends in Italy and this particular trip I was primarily going to see clients in Switzerland. I was only traveling across northern Italy so I could get to Lugano, Switzerland by last night. From Marseilles it is a much shorter trip than having to journey up to Geneva and take another train across the Swiss mountains. I was hoping to see one client this morning. I guess my plans are not working out and for no reason. Why on this particular trip after so many over the last four years was I met at the Milan train station and arrested? It makes no sense. I've never created a problem while traveling in your country...that I can think of anyway....that would cause me to be treated in such a discourteous and cruel way. I was not even given the opportunity to contact the American consulate whether in Rome or in Bern, Switzerland."

By the commandant nodding Bailey sensed he had played the game of innocence effectively. He'd lathered a mixture of irritation and puzzlement while still showing the jail supervisor some respect. Being young and not taking the enmity between the Italian government and the U.S. seriously enough seemed to be working.

The commandant lit a cigar and blew a ring of smoke in the air. He was having difficulty refuting Bailey's claims of blamelessness. Still the older man with his slight build and impeccably dressed in his uniform had to play his own tough-minded role.

Finally he responded, "I have not gotten the full dossier so what you are saying might be true...or it might be incomplete. We shall see."

He then inquired, "Tell me about your previous business travels in this country."

Bailey knew he had to be alert, but he displayed a casual countenance to show he had nothing to hide. "I have luckily been to many parts of your beautiful country, but mostly in the picturesque northern vineyards and the specialty food producers on both coasts of Italy."

He was hoping to be so complimentary about Italy that the commandant might relax and allow him to contact someone. He wasn't certain who he would call. He'd had second thoughts about calling Roberto LaCurso. The Milan jail was certainly not the kind of place any LaCurso family member would want to get near. He also discounted calling any of his former clients. In no way did he want to cause them any problems for helping an American. As for the American consulate office in Rome, that office had been evacuated a few months before at the end of 1939. Possibly his wisest contact would be Andre Pizzorno.

The meeting with the head of the Milan city jail lasted less than a half hour and never came close to being an interrogation. Bailey sensed the commandant saw no reason to keep the American in custody, but had orders to follow.

Bailey was paraded in cuffs through the main lobby of the jailhouse once again. It was a power play by the jailhouse guards who wanted all visitors seated in the large foyer hall to understand the elevated authority they had over all prisoners.

Back in his basement cell, Bailey sat back heavily on the hard slab. No situation he'd ever been in seemed so desperate. He stared up at the stained vertical window behind two crusty bars with glass so thick he could barely discern sunlight from overcast. He kept shaking his head in disbelief. He had to be patient. He still didn't know the charges against him.

Standing on the cement base of his bed, he stretched to see through the stained window at the top of his cell. He could make out one building in the distance. Not far away was the steeple of the famous chapel, the Duomo. He remembered more pleasant times in his recent past when he traveled through the city and stood in front of the majestic church. He couldn't see the ground, but he visualized families walking around the plaza enjoying the day. Children would be running. People would be photographing the impressive church front. Kiosks selling food and souvenirs would be everywhere. Pigeons would also dominate the scene eating seeds and scrapes of food, at times directly out of people's hands.

He now wondered if that picture was still the same. A lot of things had changed in Italy. There weren't as many smiles. People looked poorer, more demoralized. Military police vehicles raced through the streets. He could hear them even from the depth of his cell. He tried to find other familiar buildings or markings, but the dirtied glass made anything else blurry and unfamiliar.

A wail from another poor wretch echoed down the hall. Another prisoner was being hauled away for questioning. Bailey's first interrogation had been nonthreatening. He saw no reason why that should change as long as he maintained an innocent posture while trying to show his being as straight-forward as possible.

Some form of broth with occasional meat was served hours after he was brought back to his cell. His stomach hurt from lack of food, but when he saw what he was supposed to consume, the pain changed to nausea. He forced himself to eat what was served to keep up his strength.

It was later in the day when he was led out of the basement cell area and up the stairs. He was being allowed some time for exercise and fresher air in what was called the jail garden. There were some weeds on the ground. Otherwise it was just a dirt area for prisoners to shuffle around and think of better days.

The thirty minutes of daylight gave him a chance to watch the guards and observe their behaviors and actions. Already the word escape had entered his mind, but only if it became necessary. For now he would stay patient until he heard the charges against him. While shuffling around the dirt garden, his general impression of the city jail guards was that they were ill-trained and carried a pompous bearing. They were sloppy and enjoyed their superior position over terrified prisoners. There was no doubt in his mind he could overpower any one of them. It was figuring out where to go after he suppressed a guard.

Back in his cell for the remainder of that day and night was endless with only the interruption of a tray of broth, coffee, some unwashed carrots and a piece of bread that had to be soaked in the soup to be chewable.

The second interrogation on Tuesday was also devoid of cruelty or physical harm. Bailey maintained his claim as an innocent businessman completely dumbfounded as to why he'd been arrested...and constantly insisting he should be allowed to contact someone outside the prison so his family in America would know where he was.

Each time the warden gave him a laconic look and sighed, "Your request for outside contact will be handled soon enough. My orders are to keep you incarcerated until further notice."

Bailey's obvious retort was an exasperated, "For what?"

The commandant momentarily appeared frustrated and shot back, "Maybe if you would tell me why you are carrying out your unlawful activities in Italy, then maybe we could push this case along."

The statement had no real specific accusation. It was said only a basic attempt to get Bailey talking...something that might have worked on others. Bailey, on the other hand, found the question void of any real passion. He had to bite his lip not to chuckle.

Bailey's only response was to repeat his verifiable record of frequent travels in Italy, France, Switzerland, Spain, and Portugal on behalf of an American based food and wine distributor. He repeated three times he was only traveling through northern Italy from Marseilles to Lugano because of the time savings.

The jail supervisor nodded blandly each time. It was the same story from his captive as the day before only with different words. Bailey detected the commandant was befuddled as to what to do next. The only paper in the file apparently was the order to pick up Bailey at the train station and hold him at the city jail until further notice.

The commandant tried one more time to make sense out of the arrest. He reacted to Bailey's admission about taking the short cut to Lugano. "So, my young friend, with our respective countries having problems with each other, did you not think you might at least have been stopped and questioned?"

It was a logical question. Bailey responded easily. "Commandant, I'd gotten so used to traveling so freely around Italy in the last four years that I never presumed there would be a problem. Even as times worsened, I never figured seeing my friends and business clients in this country would cause that much turmoil. There has never been a delay or problem with me entering Italy....or exiting your country."

The explanation only made the jailhouse warden sigh once again. Bailey, though, had begun to sweat. He was playing a hunch that the inept system within the Milan city jail had not examined his passport. There was no entry stamp since he was accompanied through the gate by one of Roberto LaCurso's band and without so much as a nod from the customs official. The fact that the commandant didn't bring up that technicality meant that none of his people had bothered to look.

That Tuesday meeting lasted only twenty minutes and Bailey was transferred to a more civilized cell on the main floor. It gave him some hope that his incarceration might come to an end shortly.

While being led back to his new cell in handcuffs again he had to be routed through the congested lobby area of the jail. He observed everything around him even more closely. The city jail was definitely not set up to be a military prison. It was just a holding area for newly arrived detainees. They were all sitting hunched in submission on benches waiting their turn with the obese sergeant behaving as if royalty at the admissions desk. While that was going on, family members were arguing and screaming at the local police carrying the arrest warrant for their loved one. That day there were so many disgruntled people, even the sergeant looked harried. With two guards trying to push family members away from the admissions desk, the entire scene looked like an overcrowded waiting area at a theatre.

Observing this mayhem in the main lobby of the city jail brought the very real possibility of escape. Opportunities were everywhere. There was a loose coat on a chair. He could grab the coat and get lost in the crowded lobby. The handcuffs would offer a hurdle. Maybe he could overpower a slow thinking, inattentive guard and grab the keys. Revolvers dangling from overweight guards hips were like an invitation to create mayhem. A few wild shots in the air and everyone including the guards would dive to the floor.

Bailey still wasn't ready to take that action. He had to find out the charges. Maybe he had a reasonable chance of being released.

As he and his lackadaisical guard moved through the throngs in the entry way, Bailey advanced his thoughts of escape. He had to consider incapacitating the guard. Was he willing to kill the guard to make his escape? Then, once out on the street, where would he go? And, what were his chances of a continued escape? At least he could speak reasonable Italian and he knew the convoluted city. But, if he couldn't find a place to hide out while the authorities searched for him, his escape would be a wasted effort. It would also be a perceived admission of guilt.

The whole thought left him weary. Escape had to be the last card he would play.

As Tuesday evening got later and the horrible sounds within the walls of the Milan prison temporarily quieted, he drank the watery coffee and chewed some carrots after wiping off the dirt. The worst part of his incarceration was having so much time to think and not knowing what the next hour or day might hold. At times he'd find himself in a kind of trance as if he was reliving parts of his past life. Then his head would jolt and he'd see the drab, stained walls around him interrupted only by the vertical window with the dirtied glass and two bars.

For certain he had never contemplated having to deal with an experience like this one. The spring of 1940 was like no other. He hadn't yet been able to enjoy the fresh smell of grass and flowers in his native state on the golf courses. He pictured his friends walking down the green fairways. The patient face of his father would bounce through his brain repeatedly. The images of his mother and sister now gone for so many years were suddenly clearer. His stomach growled thinking about the tasty foods he so missed.

Gazing at the remaining jail food on the scratched up, filthy tray, he wondered how long his strength would last if he didn't eat. Escape repeatedly returned to his thoughts. He wondered what area of the city the jailhouse was located. Knowing the many serpentine streets in Milan, he rationalized that he'd have a better chance than many others. Maybe he could hide out in the attic of some unoccupied house or empty building. He knew some local citizens, but not well enough to trust them. They likely would be too scared to help him. Eventually for food he'd have to break into a shop or home and steal in order to survive.

Leaving the city would be his biggest challenge. If he somehow got to the Switzerland border to the north, traversing the border would be his ultimate test, especially without a passport or identification of any kind. The entire escapade sounded mercilessly daunting but less so with each passing hour in that lonely cell.

When thoughts of escape would wain, his mind would quickly return to why he'd been incarcerated in the first place. He was accepting that his arrest was not a mistake. He was being kept in seclusion for a reason. There was now no question he'd been set up. Why was still a mystery, but it had to be someone who knew his schedule.

That acceptance caused him to have a marked change in his thoughts about the LaCurso family. Somewhere there had to be a mole in the LaCurso organization who sought favor or money for turning in an American who was delivering money to an Italian mob family.

He gnashed his teeth. But why?! It had been forty-eight hours since he was brought into the city jail. He was as baffled that Tuesday night as he was the first minute he was thrown in a cell.

On Wednesday the commandant had no new information why Adam Bailey was being held in his jail. He nevertheless made another attempt at pulling apart his detainee's claims of innocence. His questions only provided repeated responses from Bailey. In Italian the jail supervisor mumbled to the guard at the office door that a mistake might have been made...that the American was too young and imbecilic to be a threat to the Italian government.

Then in English, he adjusted his statement to say, "Senore, I should be hearing from my superiors if not today then certainly by tomorrow. In the meantime you'll continue being our guest in our humble jailhouse."

Unsmiling, he then whisked his hand as if trying to sweep Bailey from his office. The evil guard grabbed Bailey roughly and ushered him out the office door. His manner was routine. The malevolent guard treated all detainees the same shabby way even though Bailey had been upgraded to a more livable cell. On the route back to the cell, Bailey did sense he felt weaker. He was shaky and his joints ached. Even if he had to choke down the scraps of food given him, it was essential he do so. He had to be strong enough in case escape did become his only alternative.

Trudging through an especially large group of assembled arrestees standing in line, Bailey saw their eyes gawking at him with revulsion. Bailey hadn't been beaten, but he certainly guessed he looked haggard. He was still wearing the same smelly clothing he'd been in for almost four days. His face was streaked with dirt and his growth of beard had to add to his gaunt look.

Their fearful gazes and the jaded jail staff did bring one possible idea. By creating chaos in that huge lobby, people would be running every direction. He could get lost in the hubbub. The guard might not even remember him. With a coat over his handcuffed wrists, he could appear as just another family member running out of the front entrance of the over-crowded city jail.

The notion seemed too easy, it was difficult not to be brash. Except for the commandant with his clean, well-pressed uniform, everyone else was slack. Every guard was overweight, dumb, bored, or all three. The smell of alcohol was secondary only to perspiration. Any impulsive, frightened prisoner could unholster a guard's weapon and take down every guard in that lobby starting with the haughty, obese sergeant sitting at his large desk. Again he fought the urge. He wasn't ready to take the gamble.

That afternoon he was allowed to walk in the exercise area of the jail property along with other detainees for over an hour...an extra half hour over those poor souls sequestered in the filthy and dismal basement cells. The exercise gave him renewed energy. The air was not completely fresh but it was decidedly better than the putrid environment inside the walls.

As he was being led back to his cell, he listened closely to the guards grousing about their work. They also smirked about where Bailey was probably going to be sent from Milan....something about a military prison in Rome...and what generally happened to a prisoner at that location. Pushed back into his cell, they laughed derisively and then plodded back down the hallway.

Given the cruelty of the guards, they might only be trying to make his jail time more miserable. Besides, how would the lowly guards know anything about his future? The overheard comments still discomfited him.

The rest of that afternoon, Bailey sat on the hard mattress, stared out the stained window, and exercised in his cell. When the food came, he ate the raw carrots with dirt still on them, softened the hard roll in the coffee, and finished the stew by holding his nose as he ate.

That evening the boredom and stress from being penned up made his mind wander. He could no longer labor over who had caused his arrest. Nothing made sense. However, when he was somehow released, there was nothing in his life more important than finding whoever was responsible for putting him in such hopeless and inhuman conditions. The anger he felt was beyond any emotion he'd ever felt. Revenge....retaliation...hatred were words barely describing the depth of his passion.

As the night slowly ticked by, his thoughts changed to visions of his life back in Minnesota. How far he'd come from his modest little farming community. He wondered what his mother and sister would look like in 1940. It had been almost fifteen years since their deaths. The picture of that horrible car accident dulled over the last fifteen years was amazingly unblemished including the ghastly sounds of twisted metal and broken glass.

His thoughts also roamed to likenesses of his father. After that accident Bailey recalled how it took many years to see his father laugh. Even then he never hooted or even smiled with the same looseness....that is, until his father met Catherine. That relationship had grown while he was in college. Bailey never got the full story how they met...just that Catherine was originally from Iowa and had been working in the Hoover administration as one of the press secretaries. She was back in Iowa tending to her father's estate and John Bailey was trekking south for the winter to Florida after selling the farm. It was early during that especially tough winter of 1931-32 not yet six months after the police raid at Chippewa Lodge that their paths crossed. Just weeks before Catherine had resigned her position on the Hoover staff realizing her boss' term of office was going to end with the election of 1932. Both his father and Catherine were facing a new life. That was it. There was no further explanation.

Over time until his father and Catherine got married at the end of Adam's sophomore year at the University of Minnesota, he'd gotten to appreciate how special she was. Noticing his father's changed mood and outlook, Bailey liked Catherine from the moment he'd met her.

Bailey was momentarily startled by a forlorn whine coming from another cell. That Wednesday evening was strangely quiet compared to the other nights. It helped being on the main level of the jailhouse. The basement level was the real hellhole. The commandant's whim to take him up to the more civil cells had been the only fortunate happening since he entered the jailhouse.

Returning to his wistful state of mind, Bailey recalled the aftermath of the marriage of his father and Catherine. With the farm sold on the bluff above Lake Minnewaska, the couple spent the summers restoring an older lake home they'd bought on the eastern shoreline. It was located only a mile down the lakeshore road from the former Chippewa Lodge. The rest of the year they were traveling while basing themselves either in Florida or Washington D.C.

He momentarily smiled thinking how Jamie Lawton and Charlie Davis had brought about the sale of the farm giving his father the freedom to do something else...and with some money in his pocket. Bailey was not entirely certain what his father and Catherine were doing for a living besides supporting a farmer's association. They were also involved with land investments with Charlie Davis and even running a fishing business during the winter months south of Tampa, Florida.

He closed his eyes now wishing he was closer to his father and Catherine.... and the Lawtons and Charlie Davis. If any of them knew where he was, he had every confidence they'd be doing everything to get him released.

He looked around his dank cell and wondered why he wasn't going crazy. The fear he should be feeling was translated more like a hungry lion's attentiveness. Bailey was focused on anything he might say or do to speed up his release.

Again his mind drifted...again returning to thoughts of his father. Not many people back in his hometown were aware that John Bailey had a superlative war record from World War I. He'd seen his father's medals up in the farmhouse attic. They were in a box with his mother's name on it; his father wouldn't have saved the decorations. Those Glenwood locals who did know about the older Bailey's exploits during the 'Big War' talked only among themselves respecting John Bailey's preference not to have bad memories regurgitated.

He recalled overhearing conversations among the older men in town talking about the silent hero, John Bailey. They knew he'd seen a lot of action, was injured, and performed secret missions behind enemy lines. They knew he had to kill and that his efforts saved a remarkable number of French lives as well as American soldiers. In confidence some had shared with Adam his father's preference for not being singled out for what he'd had to do in the Rhineland. He considered it only his duty...and that there were others who served just as fervently from many other towns around the country.

He never was aware of his father's injuries...at least the physical wounds. He had noticed how his father became restless during a loud thunderstorm. He'd also heard his father complaining about aches and pains in his joints prior to those same thunderstorms.

The true meaning of those many medals had never been made clear until he was sixteen. He was playing in his first Minnesota State Golf Amateur Championship. When the tournament had been completed, a gentleman claiming to be a war-time friend of his father had approached him. Scott Schneider was a small town newspaper reporter and just happened to be in Minneapolis visiting one of his professors at the University of Minnesota. He'd seen Adam's name in the newspaper and thought he'd come out to the golf course to watch him play.

The two eventually met, struck up a conversation, and had lunch at the clubhouse. Schneider had been a war correspondent in Europe when he met John Bailey at an army encampment near the Maginot Line. During that conversation Bailey learned more in five minutes about what his father had done to earn those medals than he'd ever heard previously.

Schneider ended the lunch by offering to send Adam many of the articles the reporter had saved talking about John Bailey's war career. As a result of reading those articles, it became more understandable how the war had affected his father. His mother before she died, had often mentioned to Adam how his father had changed from the free-wheeling young man she had married to the calmer man who rarely shouted or argued.

He remembered there were times his father would receive phone calls, letters or special invitations to attend military awards functions in both Minneapolis and

Washington D.C. He was asked to travel to the nation's capital in 1928 to be part of a Herbert Hoover inauguration parade. His travel, food, and hotel expenses would have been covered. All these invitations were dismissed with a shrug.

Adam recalled the only one his father was tempted to attend was a tenth anniversary commemoration in Paris, France. He'd received the highest military honor the French could offer at the end of World War I for the uncountable Parisians he'd saved. His expenses would also have been paid to make the transatlantic trip. His father considered the journey for only an instance before rationalizing to his son that there was too much work on the farm.

Adam had been crestfallen that his father wouldn't make the trip. It was one night soon thereafter that John admitted to his son how he'd carried out many behind the enemy lines tasks to wipe out cannons aimed at Paris and upset forward movements by the Germans. That was when he told his reasons for not wanting to attend any war anniversary celebrations. He didn't want to be reminded of those experiences on the French Rhineland. Secondly, he did not want people slobbering over the grisly and deadly deeds he had to perform while in uniform. He just wanted to leave the war and the unpleasant thoughts in his past behind him.

Bailey never again asked his father about his war experiences after he'd read the articles sent to him by Scott Schneider. But, there was a greater pride he felt. He also sensed whether it was bloodline or following the example of his father, while doing his intelligence work in Italy, he remained alert, calm, and determinedly never let fear steer his actions.

There was another shout and a scream again from down the hall of the jailhouse bringing him out of his trance. The jailhouse quieted again with only some soft moaning from that same direction. Bailey closed his mind and thought only of his father's courage and coolness during those times of high tension during World War I. He was eased with that example. He was certain he had the confidence to act swiftly and boldly if the situation arose.

Thursday morning started out better than the previous three mornings in the Milan jail house. One guard strutted up the hallway announcing that all inmates on that main level would be showering and given a change of clothing...either of which Bailey hadn't had since he'd arrived at the jail. When the guard came to his cell, however, the instructions had changed. He was to see the commandant immediately. The news he took as good. He truly expected to be released.

Unfortunately, the atmosphere in the commandant's office had changed dramatically. He could tell the moment he entered the office and saw the dark look from the frazzled supervisor. Even the officer's uniform seemed more starched to match his rigidity.

Bailey could feel the hair on the back of his neck stand up as the short, tense man gradually looked up and glared at him. There was not going to be any discussion about being released. The idea of when and how to escape became tantamount in Bailey's mind before the commandant said one word.

Expecting to be accused of being a spy, to his absolute surprise the commandant went off on a completely different track. With scorn blazing from his eyes, the jail superintendent yelled, "Senor Bailey, your claims of innocence don't seem to be consistent with the updated reports I'm reading in your dossier."

Bailey sat down without being offered a chair ready to refute the obvious claim against him.

"Senor Bailey, we have reason to believe you are part of a conspiracy working to assassinate our beloved head of state, Benito Mussolini."

Bailey was shocked beyond words. He couldn't readily come up with the right words to protest such a preposterous accusation.

As for the commandant, he'd had some experience in dealing with local criminals and enemies of the state. He'd witnessed the immediate fear and horror on the faces of individuals being accused. Looking into the eyes and observing the reaction by this young American left him mystified once again. There was no trepidation from the prisoner, only a disbelieving grin.

Bailey's first words reflected how stunned he was. "Commandant, you've got to be kidding."

His captor ignored the flippant remark and continued paging through a surprisingly thick file stopping at one page. He looked up over his reading glasses with the same cold stare trying to maintain his truculence. He shouted, "Who are the people you are conspiring with? What cities have you met these conspirators? Where are they now?"

Bailey pounded his handcuffed fists on the desk and bellowed, "I'm involved in no conspiracies. I know nothing about any assassination attempt."

The commandant was equally angry. He shrieked, "You lie!

A pin dropping on the floor would have been deafening compared to the absolute silence in that office as the two men stared resolutely at one another.

Bailey's jaw slacked and his head began to move unconsciously from side to side. The commandant just stared at Bailey as if he was lowest form of human. The guard in the room was at unbending attention...his eyes bulging having just witnessed something unbelievable. A real live assassin was in their city jail.

Bailey finally spoke. In disbelief he countered with his eyes piercing his questioner, "Commandant, why would I want anyone or anything to bring harm to the leader of your country? This country has given me opportunity to be successful in my wine and specialty food business. I travel in this country because it is my job to see my customers and clients. I have no desire to deal in politics or military matters."

The commandant shook his head not wanting to listen to the same diatribe from Bailey. He then continued paging through the file...more as a nervous gesture as he thought what next to say. He was over his head but he now had the opportunity to gain some respect from his superiors if he could get this notorious detainee to admit his guilt.

His questions were whimsical and poorly stated. "Are you denying that you are a conspirator against our leader?

"Yes."

"Are you really in this country to meet with your fellow conspirators?"

"No."

Where were you going to make the assassination attempt?

"I have no idea what you are asking?

"How long have you hated Il Duce?"

"I don't hate him. I just want to do business in Italy for my company."

Frustrated, the commandant had him repeat why Bailey had been coming to Italy since 1936. Bailey had explained it at least four times in previous question sessions, but did so again without hesitation.

More questions were shot at him...inquiries about politics and the war in Europe. He answered all the commandant's questions in English and made his answers superficial and ignorant. He misstated names. He displayed a complete lacking in knowledge of economics and recent military action. He kept repeating his only interests in Italy besides the geography and the arts were wines and specialty food items.

After forty-five minutes the commandant was drained. He had gained nothing from his attempts at interrogation. He finally sighed and spoke the first truly threatening statements of their entire session. My superiors, Senore Bailey, believe you are not being entirely candid, so we are not yet done with you. For one so young and apparently involved only in the business world, you seem to be attracting attention from our head of military police in Rome. I don't understand why but it is not for me to question. Tomorrow, you will be picked up by some of our Italian elite and transported to our capital city for further interviews. They will want to know all your contacts in our country...both in business and your friends. When they are finished with you, your fate will then be decided."

Just like that Bailey's future had turned very dim. Closing, then re-opening, then closing the file in an obvious nervous gesture, the commandant muttered almost painfully, "Well, Senore Bailey, in Rome they will find out the actual truth."

Then he motioned with a wave of his hand for the guard standing by the door to return the prisoner to his cell. As Bailey was being led out of the office, the Commandant offered one chilling final comment. "Young man, I pray what you say proves truthful. If not......" Then his voice trailed away to a deathly silence.

As the guard pushed him out the door, the prison chief mumbled not realizing Bailey could understand his every word in Italian, "Corporal, it is sad what will be happening to this young man. I sense he is speaking the truth, but that no longer matters. The military police will make him say whatever they want. If he survives their interrogation, one only wonders what prison he'll be sent. Certainly it will be someplace he'll be lucky to survive."

Bailey remained silent as he was led down the detention center hallway. Looking back at the commandant's office, the prison chief was standing at his office door staring at him. There was a saddened, disheartened look in the man's eyes. It was another moment in the commandant's life where he truly did not like the job he was being ordered to carry out. Then the jail supervisor shrugged and disappeared back into his office never expecting to see or hear of Adam Bailey ever again.

Bailey shuffled along in shock and bewilderment as he was led through the main floor corridor by the slovenly dressed guard. This time he was not going back to the cleaner cell on the main level. Though his mind was spinning, he marked once again the carelessness of the guards and the overworked sergeant at the front desk.

Escape was now central in his mind.

The guard prodded him toward the stairs. The commandant was angry and wanted to make certain his prize prisoner would be dirty, hungry, and exhausted when the military police arrived to transport him to Rome the next morning.

In the basement cells, the careless and unkempt guard slogged along the passageway to the end cell. He spat at some prisoners and yelled at others to shut their mouths as he pushed Bailey along. Seeing this particular guard caused immediate silence among those behind the bars. He'd proven to each of the detainees his preference for maltreatment. In that guard's mind, each of the prisoners jailed in the lower basement cells were despicable humans and already guilty. As far as he was concerned they should be led out on the jailhouse grounds and shot.

The cell door was locked with a loud clank echoing up and down the long musty, grimy corridor of the jailhouse. Bailey sat there in the dark cell not knowing if it was raining or the sun was shining...and not caring. He'd just been given what amounted to a death sentence. In Rome their only goal would be to elicit information about his apparent co-conspirators...whoever they might be. If he lived through that maltreatment his prognosis still would not be favorable. Further, his chances for escape in Rome would be nil. His identity and his location would continue to be held in secrecy. His only hope was that by the end of the following week, David O'Brien would likely begin a search for him. If that effort had any chance of finding him, he first had to live through the interrogations.

Thursday night would be the fifth night and the most difficult one. He'd played the card too long that he might be released. He was no longer at the main level where he could create some kind of disturbance and possibly walk out of the jailhouse amidst the disorder. The basement cells gave him little if any opportunity for escape. His one chance would be the next morning before the military police arrived from Rome. He'd be back on the main level...maybe taken to a holding cell.

Closing his eyes he imagined every second of those minutes he'd be up on the main level. There was no question he was going to make some play to escape, likely starting with one of the sloppy guard's revolvers being pulled from the holster. That would be the easy part. He would shoot any guard getting in his way. That was no longer a moral question. With luck there would be a crowd of new detainees and their families. He'd yell something to create a flood of people heading for the door. Along the way he'd take someone's coat to offer himself some camouflage. It was a loose plan, but what escape plan wasn't. The question would be where he would go once outside the building. That was the unknown; however, he expected to be running very fast.

The night grew longer. His predominant thoughts returned to whom the bastards were that caused this fight for his life. He found his outlook and attitude had changed from the first night he'd entered the city jail. His thoughts were darker. He'd gone from wanting to believe there'd been a huge mistake to not hesitating to kill anyone responsible for treating his life so callously. This more evil emotion now gave him an even stronger motivation to escape. Whoever it was who put him in these circumstances would have to face him sometime in the future. He swore that very hour would be the last time that individual would see the light of day.

Sometime in the middle of the night he awoke to the sounds of one of the detainees coughing loudly enough for other prisoners to yell at the man to stay quiet. Then he became truly awake. Suddenly, his focus was on Willie and Roberto LaCurso. No one else knew of his schedule once he crossed the border the previous weekend.

He contemplated the differences in this delivery compared to the other times he'd smuggled suitcases into Italy. This favor was asked at the last minute. Also, LaCurso was insistent Bailey cross at the French-Italian border near Monaco despite the poor relations between the two countries. That was curious since crossing the border between Italy and Switzerland would have been less potentially problematic. Lastly, Willie was adamant that the suitcase had to be in Roberto's hands by the last weekend of March. Sunday, March 31, became the only date that could satisfy the directive. He complied and curiously on that very day he was greeted by the local Milan police.

Bailey concentrated on that one factor. Only the two LaCurso brothers knew his travel plans. For the first time he wondered if there was any money in the valise at all. Either the suitcase could have just been a prop to bring him to Milan...or, there could have been some incriminating evidence inside the case that landed him in jail.

The commandant had accused him of being a collaborator on some kind of plot to murder Benito Mussolini. The LaCurso animosity towards the military leader certainly was passionate enough to qualify them as would be assassins. But, why would he be drawn into their conspiracy. He was an American. If he could be held responsible for such a plot, the repercussion would cause further furor between Italy and the U.S. and bring America into the war against Italy and Nazi Germany much sooner. Then again, that factor might have been the intention...for the U.S. to take the time and expense to defeat Mussolini and his Fascist government instead of the LaCurso family taking on the burden and risk themselves.

If there was such a dramatic plan by the LaCurso brothers, Bailey would be thought of as a mere pawn. However, that idea seemed far-fetched and long term. Bailey figured Willie LaCurso wasn't that patient. There likely was a conspiracy to kill Il Duce...and let anything that resulted be collateral misfortune. Nonetheless, the question that kept eating away at him was why Willie had decided to sacrifice Bailey's life. The shear coldness of such a decision when he had no right to make that kind of pronouncement left Bailey horrified and enraged.

His enmity would grow as each hour passed that long night. His furor was aimed unblinkingly at the two brothers. They had put him in an impossible situation. In so doing, they had also provided a motivation against them that would become so strong that he felt neither the weakness from little food nor the tiredness from lesser sleep. Nothing could block his desire to escape...and do so successfully. He wanted them to pay.

At some point Thursday night a tray of food was slipped under his cell door. It was the basement variety delicacy. The coffee was mostly hot water, the bread roll was rock hard, and the broth had one piece of some kind of meat in it. Bailey ate it. There were also three raw green beans on the tray from the prison garden. They still had soil on them. He ate them dirt and all in the filth and darkness of the cell. The surroundings no longer bothered him. He knew where he was going would be worse.

Later that night...at least he presumed it was night....a clanking noise outside his cell indicated a guard was approaching. Bailey didn't move and only opened his eyes slightly as a small window to his cell squeaked open. A pair of eyes looked in possibly hoping to see if the prisoner had admitted his guilt by committing suicide. Bailey moved his eyes toward the guard staring at him. Whatever fear he'd had of these guards had disappeared. He hoped his glare would agitate the guard enough that the slobbering fool would enter the cell for the purpose of striking a disrespectful prisoner. If so, it would be an escape opportunity. The self-defense training he had at the marine base two months before in northern Virginia would be put to use. He didn't think he'd be utilizing the training on how to disable a man. He'd likely break the man's neck. The result would be ownership of the jailhouse keys, a weapon, a guard jacket for camouflage, and a reasonable possibility for a late night escape.

To antagonize the guard even more, he lifted his coffee cup as if toasting the sentry. He then took a swig and immediately spat the liquid across the cell. It was the height of impudence. The action failed to get a reaction. The guard even laughed derisively as if he'd seen this behavior before when a prisoner's days were numbered.

The small window closed. The next sound was the guard waddling down the hallway, his keys jingling and his voice yelling at another prisoner.

Bailey was disgusted. He detested the guard even more for the man's callous reaction. He'd have to wait until morning and be primed like a boa constrictor coiled and ready to pounce the moment the next opportunity was presented.

He'd been dreaming again. A flight from reality was his only solace. Having not brushed his teeth for a week, his mouth had a taste he'd never experienced. His lips stuck together from little liquid. His unshaven face felt rough and hallow.

Suddenly he heard the unmistaken sound of some guards trudging down the hallway opening cells and shouting for the detainees to get ready for a shower and exercise. It was morning and just a short time before he would be picked up by the Rome military police. He'd seen Rome so often in the last four years...a beautiful, historic city...and now the last place he ever wanted to be.

The jailers wasted no time. They didn't like to be around the smelly arrestees. They entered Bailey's small tomb and threw a change of pants and long sleeved shirt at him yelling, "You will shower first."

Bailey's heart leaped. If there was any chance, it would be soon. Pushed out of his cell and standing in line with the other prisoners, he noticed everything... the carelessness of the two guards...the open holster carrying the pistol...even the keys hanging from both guards' belts.

As was routine, the basement captives were then herded up the stairs and through the main lobby to again strike dread to all visitors and new detainees. They were a ragged, disconsolate bunch with their heads down and shuffling along as if living their last day on earth. All, that is, except Adam Bailey. His face looked straight ahead; his eyes darting back and forth looking for any advantage.

With seven detainees hobbling in front of him, the guards were walking ahead as if guiding a flock of sheep. They pointed to the door to the outside exercise area at the end of the main hall and lazily tapped each prisoner with their stick as they hobbled along. The exercise area would be first...then the shower and change of prison garb.

One guard went first out into the courtyard leaving only one guard in an empty hallway watching the seven prisoners. With a shout from the first guard, the line proceeded through the door to the jail yard. Bailey was last and would be alone with the last guard before going through the outside door.

With the sentry scratching his belly and trying not to pay attention to the worthless humans, Bailey was quickly considering his choices. Overpowering the guard and stealing his gun seemed like the easiest and most obvious choice. It was what he was going to do once he had the revolver that he felt his odds would decline.

Instead, he urgently pointed toward the lavatory door. The guard was disgusted but nodded his head and led his prisoner toward the washroom only twenty feet down the hallway.

The sentry then pointed at the shirt and pants Bailey was carrying and said, "Change while you're in there. You don't need a shower where you're going."

The words were cruel but true. Bailey didn't need to be reminded. He didn't waste any time either. Nodding, he hurried into the washroom thinking the guard would follow. That would be the moment the guard would be subdued. Bailey's adrenalin was running so high, he had no doubt the unkempt sentry's neck would be broken in seconds. For the young American all morality had ceased. His life was in the balance and the guard was in the way.

Amazingly the guard didn't follow him into the putrid men's room. Bailey had another few seconds to consider his options. He took note of one window to the outside, but was momentarily interrupted by the mirror in front of him. He hardly recognized himself. His eyes looked sunken. His hair was matted and his whiskers were short but thick. He even saw some gray in the facial hair that stunned him. He still had some vanity. His clothing was so dirty that laundering it would be a waste of time. His smell was sickening.

He heard a noise and realized another person was using one of the closed stalls. His eyes flicked back over to the window. A faint smell of fresh air teased his nostrils. Without hesitation he scurried over to the window looking cautiously behind as he moved. And there it was...a horizontal crack in the bottom of the window...his first sight of freedom since he'd arrived at the jail.

He wondered if others had used this opportunity for escape. Then again maybe others simply didn't have the nerve. His decision was made. It wasn't so much daring as it was he had no other choice.

Quietly he pulled up the window. The fresh air greeted him like a cold Midwest winter breeze. The relative freshness of that air compared to the stale air in the jailhouse brought with it renewed energy. The sweat on his brow was immediately cooled. Leaning through the small opening, he sensed luck was momentarily on his side. There was only a thin walkway out to the street with the wall of another building less than five feet away.

The madness of that moment was something he'd never experienced. It was do or die. He couldn't be certain what was beyond the end of the walkway. It could be the main street. It could be a pathway to just another roadway leading to the front of the jailhouse. Even then if it was the main street, he might emerge next to the outside guards. They might shoot before even asking him to halt. Then again, with the notoriously poor training of the jailhouse guards, he wondered if any of the sentries could shoot accurately enough to put him out of his misery. But, none of that mattered. This was his chance....his last chance.

About to climb through the window, he noticed a brown overcoat slung over the side of the stall as he heard the man inside humming and grunting. Bailey slung the clean prison garb over the stall and in the same instance grabbed the overcoat. Ignoring the man's objections, Bailey squeezed his body through the window opening, put on the overcoat, and stole his way along the thin walkway. From making the decision to escape, barely ten seconds had passed. The insistent voice calling for the return of the overcoat became more muffled as he ran to the end of the pathway.

The brown overcoat reeked but not as badly as his smelly clothing underneath it. At least the long coat gave him a different look and the confidence to step out onto the street. Peering around the corner of the prison building, he observed two guards standing by the front door of the jailhouse not thirty yards to his left. There were some citizens walking by looking straight forward trying not to think what was happening on the other side of the walls. They were bent over slightly and bundled up trying to ward off a piercing spring wind against their faces.

He began sweating again not knowing how he could suddenly just appear and flow into the pattern of passers-by without drawing attention. He had but seconds before other jail guards would come streaming out onto the street ready to shoot anyone who looked like he was running.

His heart was in his throat as providence then played a role. A military truck was barreling down the street from the opposite direction. He could see the Fascist emblem on the side of the truck. That was likely to be his transportation to Rome. As the faces of the outside guards eyed the ominous looking truck, Bailey stepped out onto the sidewalk and began walking in the same rhythm as the other pedestrians. He hunched down trying desperately not to walk any faster than the pace of the pedestrians. His heart was pounding hard and felt like a lead weight in his chest. The sweat rolled down his back inside the warm, smelly heavy coat.

He forced himself not to look back until he came to the next corner. There he would turn either direction and disappear into the labyrinth of streets in the Italian city. That was another advantage he had. With the disorganized web of streets in Milan, getting oneself lost in the city was easy. It also made it difficult for pursuing sentries.

The walking pace was excruciatingly slow, but he finally reached the corner only to then hear a blaring horn from the prison. He glanced back and saw a number of guards running out of the jail entrance. They looked both ways but seemed exasperated not seeing anyone wearing the giveaway prison garb.

They split up and took off in opposite directions giving Bailey lesser jail staff to hunt him down. Once rounding the corner, he accelerated his walking speed causing some pedestrians to take notice. However, their faces showed the fear of involvement. They bent over even more and moved away from the man who seemed in a hurry.

Bailey now could be shot on sight. Remembering the dank cell he'd just left and his future accommodations in an Italian prison made him face the reality of his choice. Somehow being shot and killed didn't sound as scary as it should have. His mind raced. He knew he had to find a place to hide.

Trying not to call any more attention than was necessary, he began trotting casually as if trying to get out of the cold wind. He glanced back again. No guards had yet made it to the corner. Gambling, he streaked across the street toward a thin alley between two small shops.

This choice of direction left him even more stressed. His overcoat would camouflage him only for another few minutes. Surely by now the man in the stall had told the authorities that his brown overcoat had been taken by the escaped criminal.

Committing to the back alley between the two shops, Bailey's heart almost stopped when he saw it was a dead end. There were a couple garbage cans he could hide in, but that seemed hopeless. There were also two side doors that might open into either of the two shops. He checked the door on his right and naturally it was locked. There was no way he could jar it open without creating a scene to the pedestrians walking by the alley opening. He desperately went to the other door expecting it to be locked as well. It was....but the lock was loose. He frantically looked for a stick to pry open the door. Noticing the wood steps up to the door were worn, he wasted no time in ripping one off the base. His adrenalin was flowing at an amazing level. He tried to force the board between the door and the loosened lock, but the board was too thick.

With the sweat pouring off his brow, he could hear the non-stop wailing of the prison siren. There was no telling how many people would be looking for him He then saw a couple pedestrians walking by the alley quicken their pace as they glanced back most certainly in fear of some guards with guns running toward them.

Bailey was about to lay down under the stairwell as his final useless act of deception when he heard the door unlatch and slowly open to one inch. An eye appeared. It looked him over...and then miraculously the door opened wider.

The man's voice whispered urgently in Italian, "Quick! Come in! Don't say a word!"

Bailey asked no questions and slipped swiftly through the side door. The man closed and locked it quickly. Turning around to thank the shopkeeper for saving his life, he saw no one. The room was very dim with a small window on the far side of the room. He was in the back of a sewing shop. Clothes were hung all over in various stages of completion. There was also a box of what looked like remnants of old clothes. The place had an odor to it that Bailey hastily decided was to his advantage. He stunk of jail smell and knew his body odor had to be nauseating. The older man rubbed his nose as if realizing the pungent clothing could be a problem if a guard entered the tailor shop.

Bailey took a few steps forward and looked out into the main shop as the older man walked hurriedly toward his front door and then out onto the street. Bailey prayed the man was not going to turn him in. That prayer was answered immediately as the shopkeeper shouted to one of the guards running down the street what was wrong. Bailey's Italian was good enough to hear the muffled voice of the guard yell about a dangerous criminal wearing a brown overcoat had escaped the city jail.

The guard slowed asking the shopkeeper directly, "Did you see anyone run by your shop?"

The shopkeeper shook his head and shrugged his shoulders. The guard pressed on and Bailey realized he'd stumbled across a guardian angel.

Without being asked, he stripped off his filthy, smelly clothing and began stuffing them into the bottom of the box of remnants. Wearing only his shorts, he scanned the back of the shop hoping he could find some replacement rags. He finally grabbed a pair of pants and was about to put them on when he heard the voice of the shopkeeper. "No....no....those pants won't fit."

Bailey appreciated the keen eye of a man who could visually fit clothing to whatever size of man. The old tailor then glanced around the back of the shop until he seemed to randomly pull out a pair of pants and a shirt. In Italian he quickly ordered, "Put on these pants and shirt. They'll fit better. And, put on this cap. You'll look more like a worker. Those police guards will no doubt be back searching shop by shop. You'll need to be dressed and look busy around my shop when they return!"

The shopkeeper's voice was firm and gave Bailey the confidence that he was in good hands. Again his fluency in Italian was paying off. There was no lost time between the two of them wondering what was being said.

The clothes turned out to be warm, clean, and fit reasonably well. The older man then motioned for him to come to the front of the shop and begin operating a sewing machine by the cash register. He wanted Bailey out in the open instead of working in the back room.

He then gave Bailey a large needle with thread and showed him quickly how to stitch up the side of a pair of pants. It was a lesson in tailoring that lasted twenty seconds but his pupil was a fast learner by necessity.

Then as if summoned, two guards approached the front of the store, but dallied to have a smoke. The old man calmly said, "Sew as best you can and try not to say anything. I'll handle the guards. They're just a bunch of old women anyway."

Before the guards entered the shop, Bailey whispered loudly in Italian, "Senore, my clothing....they stink in the back room. The smell might give me away. It is the odor of the prison. I threw them including a brown coat in your remnants box!"

The shopkeeper simply nodded and walked to the back of the store. The odor had to be noticeable as Bailey saw him reach into the box and remove the rancid clothing. He looked with disgust at the dirtied prison garb. They were nothing but worthless rags to him. Then without hesitation he shoved the clothing into a container of liquid. He made certain every item was soaked even bringing the overcoat up to his nose to make certain the soapy liquid was eliminating the tell-tale odor. He then began spraying some kind of cleansing fluid with a sharp smell into his remnant's box as well as by the back door where Bailey had entered the shop.

There was still a lot of raucous action outside, but it was calming down. A guard walked closer to the front entrance and looked in before entering. Then the bell chimed as he strutted dutifully into the tailor shop and took notice of the shopkeeper and the apparent helper. Bailey nodded to him and went back to his sewing. He had no idea what he was doing, but the look on his face as he concentrated on sewing would make any individual believe he was doing something that was second nature.

The shopkeeper coming into the front of the shop carrying a suit he was working on appeared irritated, but not angered. He asked the guard only slightly sardonically, "Senore, are you here for a new suit of clothes?"

The overweight guard gave him a sideways glance as if to acknowledge the old man was making a joke. Self-importantly, the guard ignored the question and asked, "Have you seen a man running by your shop?"

The shopkeeper lamented. "No...people just walk by my shop. No one comes in. No one needs a new suit. No one will spend money. No one has any money."

Impatiently the guard began eyeing Bailey to see if the young man might offer some help. He was about to ask Bailey something when the tailor quickly inquired, "You are looking for someone...probably some murderer. Unfortunately, Eduardo and I have been here for the past couple hours trying to eke out a living and we've seen no one running by my shop. Too bad we cannot help you capture this terrible enemy of the state. We could use the reward."

With the shopkeeper now showing what seemed like proper concern, the guard realized he was wasting his time. Waddling toward the door, he responded almost civilly, "Nah, the man is just an American businessman wanted for more questioning. The American is stupid for running away. Now, he will be shot on sight as a suspected spy."

The shopkeeper acted bewildered and did a sign of the cross as he responded to the guard. "If this man is a spy, we want to get him off the streets so he won't be dangerous to our citizens. Bless Benito for getting rid of people like the American and for making our country safe again."

Reasonably satisfied, the sentry turned on his heels and marched out the door. The shopkeeper looked at Bailey with a finger to his lips indicating the young man should not talk or stop sewing. Then he strolled over to the front door of the shop and peered both ways up and down the street. Opening it, he stepped outside and remained there for a full minute greeting some passersby and seemingly just trying to get a breath of fresh air.

When he came back in he paused at the door to spit outside. It was probably his way of eliminating the rancid and obsequious words he'd just said to the sentry about Mussolini. It was already obvious the tailor's allegiance was not in Il Duce's corner.

Turning toward Bailey, he then said in heavily accented English, "It's clear, young man. You are safe for the moment. Your Italian is very good. I would not have thought you an American. But, I didn't want to chance the guard picking up on any type of accent you might have."

Then he paused and looked his young visitor over. "My friend, if you are in Italy at this time and indeed from America, you must be either very stupid or doing something very important."

Bailey put down the piece of clothing he'd been sewing and sat back in sheer relief looking skyward in appreciation. He didn't respond to the tailor until his heart rate calmed. Responding in Italian, he said, "Thank you, Senore. You have saved my life! I will simply never be able to pay you back for your boldness."

The shopkeeper was moved. Patting the young man on the shoulder, he walked to the back of his shop once again and returned with a bottle of red wine, two glasses, and some bread. Sitting down by his guest he poured some wine and talked as if the last couple minutes of excitement had never happened. "Well, my young friend, my name is Carlos Ferrendi. This is my shop and you are wearing some clothing I've repaired. Suppose we talk and figure out how to help you further."

Bailey almost choked on the wine given the kindnesses he was being given. When the bread was served, the young escapee gulped it down. It was the first decent looking food he'd seen since being arrested. He could see the old man felt badly for him.

Sipping a small goblet of wine, Carlos quietly asked, "First, my young friend, what is an American citizen doing running from the law in a country you should not have entered. You must have done some horrible things against the state, even though you seem so young to be such a violent criminal."

Bailey smiled at the shopkeeper's innocent and kidding observation. The man's complete lack of fear towards the armed guard who'd entered his shop or even towards a possible dangerous escapee now in his shop was refreshing but puzzling.

To the surprisingly brave tailor, Bailey tried to be as straight-forward as he could without destroying the man's feelings of generosity. "Senore Ferrendi, my name is Adam Bailey. I am an American businessman. I was being held at the jail since last weekend. I've been coming to Italy for my business interests with wineries and food producers for almost five years. This past year has been impossible to do any business at all in your country, but I decided to give it one last try. Obviously it was a huge mistake.

The authorities claim they found something about me they didn't like. I can't imagine what concerns them. The Italian people have been nothing but kind to me and appreciative over the business I've brought their way. Until this trip I've never had trouble with the Italian government. Now, after a week in your city jail, I still don't know what I'm being accused of doing. However, today I was to be transferred to Rome for more thorough interrogation. I understand they'll eventually want me to admit to whatever the charges they are bringing against me. For certain, once in Rome, I have the strong feeling my family would never hear or see me again. Even now, my compatriots and friends have no idea I'm here in Milan.

A half hour ago I decided to make an escape thanks to the slacker guards. Luckily I've made it this far, but it's been more luck than great planning. I believe my only chance to stay alive is to make it out of this city and then onto Switzerland. At least my odds of making it to free-France would be improved. My problem now is that I'll likely be shot on sight."

Carlos gravely nodded his head. "I believe you made a wise choice to leave that jail. Being transported to Rome does not sound favorable. However, you have only started your escape. You are still in a very difficult and dangerous situation. You are now a hunted man by every authority figure in Milano."

Then he glared at the young man. "So, tell me Senor Bailey, what do you think they found out about you that could possibly warrant you being such an important prisoner?"

Bailey had hoped his quick explanation would suffice, but the tailor seemed starved for conversation. Continuing to skate around the truth, he shrugged, "I just don't know. It has been my job since 1936 to travel into Italy, Switzerland, and France. I can see my travels could have caused your government some concern, but why not during my previous visits? I do believe someone has lied about my purposes and let the authorities know I was traveling on a train across northern Italy from Marseilles to Lugano, Switzerland. I haven't resolved as to whom that person might be, but now that I'm free I'll find him. He put me in a life and death situation. I will find out why.

The old tailor tried to ignore what sounded like youthful bluster. "Senore, you have other things more important right now that will require your attention. This is a different country even in the past year. You have certainly been noticed once you entered Italy. You may have even been followed by the military police. This crazy man Mussolini is trying to make our poor country into a world power. He befriended the German Nazis and Hitler rather than get smothered by them. He manages this country by fear and creates as much discomfort for neighboring countries as he can. But, we are not a wealthy country. War is very expensive. I guess he believes we can become wealthy by taking over other minor countries and reap what supplies they have. Those attacks on Ethiopia and Albania were shameful. What wealth do those countries have? The man is insane."

Scoffing over what he'd just said, the older man got up to stretch and gaze out the window once again at the quiet street. Bailey watched the tailor and tried to figure how much he should trust the old man. After a week in an Italian prison, trust was not a quality he would give out lightly. Still, it was stunning such a poor, oppressed shopkeeper would be so audacious as to provide a safe haven for a jail house escapee.

Bailey began exercising his neck trying to clear his thinking. The effect of the wine on a stomach that hadn't digested decent food in a week was making his mind dull. He didn't feel in control. His lethargy caused Carlos to take the hint that his young visitor had been under some extreme stress and needed some rest.

He responded humanely. "My young friend, you are in no condition to continue your escape for now. You are weak and need to build up your strength. You will be safer here in my shop. You can rest. Do not worry. They would never guess you are hiding out two blocks from the city jail. I will close my shop and let you sleep. I'll return later with some real food and then we can discuss your next steps in getting out of Milan."

Bailey only nodded. He moved from the chair at the sewing table to the back of the store eyeing a small cot with a pillow and blanket. The tailor brought him soap and a towel to wash himself. The smell of the jailhouse imbrued on his skin had to be removed. The warm water from the sink felt heavenly. Drying himself, the old man brought over some fresh clothing. As he dressed, his eye kept returning to the cot. Finally he just went over and fell onto the bedding. He would have no recall about the Senore putting a blanket over him, then putting on a coat, turning out the lights, walking out of the shop, and flipping a 'Closed' sign on the door's window.

When Carlos Ferrendi locked his shop door, Adam Bailey felt safer than at any time since entering Italy a week before. As if drugged, he slept through the rest of the day.

Chapter 13

Bailey awoke to the silence in the tailor shop and knew where he was immediately. The metamorphosis of trying to survive in a filthy jail cell versus the comfortable cot left no doubt. While lying in the semi-darkness he recalled a statement John Fena had made about the job with North American Distribution would open up his world and have untold impact on his life and career. Fena had been absolutely right, but likely not in the way the general manager had meant considering his overseas work had led him directly into another job spying for the U.S. government. Little did Fena or him ever contemplate he could face the undefined dangers and risks now part of every minute of his life.

He jerked up as the noise of a key opening the front door echoed through the darkness in the shop. Instinctively Bailey leaped off the cot and tiptoed over to a sewing machine to find any kind of weapon. He found a scissors and realized he was ready to use it. It finally dawned on him the tailor had returned.

The shadow of the man appeared and Senore Ferrendi whispered, "My young friend, it is me…Carlos. I have some food. You are still safe."

Bailey stood up only two feet behind the old man. Had it been anyone but the tailor, the scissors would have been at the intruder's throat.

Startled, Carlos turned around making certain his visitor knew it was him. Bailey's eased his grip on the scissors and went over to the cot and sat down. He looked up at the tailor and mumbled, "Senore, I am sorry if I scared you. I just can't be too careful."

The old tailor shrugged knowing Bailey's action was understandable. His guest now looked stronger and more alert than the desperate fellow who had crawled through the back door of the tailor shop only hours before. He walked over to the table without saying a word and pulled from a paper bag some bread, fruit, and chicken his wife had prepared. The young American gazed at the food like a crazed, carnivorous animal. Carlos simply said, "Please eat. This food is for you."

Watching Bailey devour the food brought sorrow to the old man's eyes. He just sat there quietly until his guest finished the banquet put in front of him.

Catching his breath, Bailey slowed for an instance. "Senore, there is no way I can repay your hospitality now. But, I promise you…someday…I will repay you… some way. You have been very brave and generous to a person you did not know.

It makes me wonder why you took such a chance on a man so popular with the local police."

Carlos chuckled. "It is my way of maintaining some sense of humanity. So many people are suffering. It seems to be contagious. My son unfortunately is deeply involved in the Mussolini regime. I've watched him change from a loving son to a fanatical follower of an ego-driven man. I do what I can to try to bring my son back to reality, but I am afraid he is lost."

Bailey showed some concern. "Senore, what does your son do for Mussolini?"

Carlos sadly shook his head. "He works only blocks from here. He is the commandant of the local jail. If you were in the jail, you may have talked to him or seen him."

Bailey almost lost the food he was chewing. He'd been playing cat and mouse for five days with the prison superintendent. The man had not been physically abusive, but he was doing the job his superior's expected even though he was struggling trying to justify why the young American had been arrested. Then he received information that Bailey was a probable conspirator in a Mussolini assassination plot and the commandant's entire tenor changed. He no longer trusted his captive. He likely was now sweating for allowing such a valuable prisoner to simply walk out of his jailhouse.

There was no question Bailey had to leave the tailor shop very soon if for no other reason than the commandant might casually saunter into the tailor shop to greet his elderly father. Bailey feeling a surge of vitality with the food, reached over to shake the hand of the tailor. "Senore, I don't want to put you in any more danger. It's time for me to leave. I will leave in the night. This timing will give me the best chance to escape the city."

The old tailor nodded blankly. He had no experience in such matters and realized Bailey was impatient and probably right. He got up to gather his coat saying, "It is your choice, my young friend. I can hide you in my shop or in the upstairs apartment for as long as you need. But, I can understand your purpose to leave this city. I will close the shop and take these last few hours of day to go home and listen to my wife lament about these difficult times. I will be back in the morning if nothing else just to escape her displeasure about life."

Bailey was almost emotional as the tailor ambled toward the door. He said to the tailor, "May each day be kind to you, Senore Ferrendi. You are a good man."

The old man waved hesitantly before opening and closing the door and locking it securely. Lest anyone was watching him, he took his time wiping off the front windows. Then he strolled off into the early evening.

Bailey finished every spec of food and crumbs from the food provided him. He then snuffed out the gaslight in the back of the shop and lay back on the cot once again. With the resurgence brought about by the food, his mind was sharper as well. Even the ache in his stomach had miraculously subsided. There was nothing else warranting favor in his mind as the next steps in his escape.

He had to wait until night to make his next move. He pulled the warm blanket around his shoulders. His body still craved sleep. With the food and wine settling him down, he allowed himself to fall back asleep. He'd wake fitfully soon enough.

It was dark when he awoke startled by the loud noise of another military truck speeding by the tailor's shop. Then the dead of silence returned with only a feint sound of a pedestrian shuffling by the shop. He looked through the dusty window pane at the side of the shop and saw some street lights. Looking at the wall clock, it was 11:00 Friday evening. He'd slept another four hours without so much as stretching his legs.

The realization of his plight now returned quickly. Groggily he sat up in the darkened back room feeling strangely jubilant for being free, yet desperate in his urge to move on. He'd faced some danger in the past but nothing like the previous five days in the Milan jailhouse...and now each minute coming forth. Death had driven right up to the front door of the city jail house that morning... and he'd defied it. He was nowhere close to being truly free, but now he had a fighting chance to survive. It felt as if he was beginning a new life, not just preserving an old one.

Another nerve-racking whine echoed in the quiet workshop as a second police vehicle sped by. He stood up stiffly feeling the discomfort of drenched cloth against his back. Though sleeping, he'd been sweating. His mind and body obviously still felt the strain of his predicament.

As it again got quiet, he crept around the darkened shop to locate some additional clothing for his continued escape. That he was actually stealing the clothing never entered his mind; survival trumped all other thoughts. As his eyes adjusted to the dark, he found the brown overcoat he'd taken from the man in the bathroom stall at the Milan jail. He palmed the pockets and felt a lump. It was a revolver. In fact it was a German Service Luger with a 45-caliber cartridge. It was loaded and there were extra shells in the same pocket.

In another pocket he found some identification and a badge. More luck was following him as he fingered some German marks and Swiss francs as well. The ID said the man's name was Ludwig Schmidt. The badge indicated the man was some German prison official visiting from Frankfurt, Germany. Bailey smiled. Herr Schmidt's loss was his gain giving him potentially a few more pluses in his quest to leave the city....but only for a limited time.

It was almost 11:30 with light rain outside when he was ready to leave the shop. He'd chosen another coat in the remnants box and left the brown one for the tailor in exchange. This one was a jacket, black in color and more suited to his needs. He had a week of stubble on his chin and looked not at all like the young American the authorities were searching for. As depicted on his passport, that picture would be copied and sent around to all border patrols and military stations. In the picture he was clean shaven; his scruffy look now served him well.

The chill hit his face as he slipped out the same side door of the Tailor's shop that he'd entered much earlier that day. He'd been in the tailor's shop fourteen hours. It seemed like two days. The rain and the overhanging mist in the air made the night even darker. But, the warmth of the black jacket over the clean smelling clothes from the tailor shop and his comfort with the twisting streets in Milan gave him the confidence to keep moving through the city.

Sneaking along the shops on the same street as the Milan jail, there was still movement of vehicles and guards in front of the hellish building now blocks behind him. Turning the corner away from the jail he began trotting feeling exalted with each step he took. When an occasional vehicle approached, he'd duck into a shadowy corner until it passed.

Feeling he was too vulnerable on the open roadways, he decided to head for the train station. It was the most obvious form of transportation out of the city. With Schmidt's coat and identification, Bailey thought the train would be worth the chance. It also might be the last place the authorities would take seriously since a normal escapee wouldn't make such a visible choice.

Only a mile from the train station, he slowed his walk. He still didn't feel at full strength, however, his eyes and ears were highly sensitized.

Another flash of headlights almost caught him unprepared, but he ducked into bushes as a speeding police vehicle careened down the street. He just had time to bow down behind the bush as the vehicle zoomed within yards of him. Then two more vehicles followed racing so close as to be touched. They were heading in the direction of the train station...at least that was what Bailey's paranoid mind was telling him.

Uncertainties crept into his mind as he pondered whether he was out in public too soon after his escape. Being only blocks from the Hotel de Italiana, he altered his plan and walked to that more familiar location. If he saw any of the staff that knew him from previous stays, he doubted they'd know he was now a fugitive.

In minutes he was across the street from the hotel. There was very little activity at that late hour. He knew places in the large hotel where he would be out of sight and he could rest and dry out from the incessant rain.

Striding briskly across the street and through the moving circular entry doors, his motions showed purpose. Bailey hiked the collar of the jacket up around his neck. He walked straight through the lobby toward the elevators with the air of a guest. The check-in clerk glanced up momentarily from adding receipts and said a routine, 'Good evening'. The lobby clock declared the time to be 12:15...not that late for a raunchy nighttime socialite heading for his suite. With a week's growth of beard, Bailey looked as if he could have been on a rampage that night. Grabbing a newspaper, he stopped at the elevators and turned around to make certain he wasn't being watched. Satisfied that no one was lurking in the foyer, he headed for the back patio door. The inattentive clerk gave him no notice as he slipped out onto the patio.

Then he strode to the rear of the patio where he could sit under the overhang until he was dry. Later, if still raining, he'd take a taxi the rest of the way to the train station. He'd be less apparent if he looked like just another late night traveler instead of a drenched vagabond seeking solace and comfort in the confines of the train station. It was a logical and easy strategy but certainly with no guarantees.

Feeling somewhat safe, he sat under the patio canopy and was about to congratulate himself making it this far in his escape when he saw another door open on the far end of the patio. Bailey got up hurriedly and stepped back into a darkened corner by a huge potted plant. His hope of sitting comfortably had vanished as he took in the sight of a uniformed man shuffling out onto the patio. He appeared drunk and not a fine representative of the hotel. He was the hotel night watchman...and he was feeling no pain. In one hand was a bottle of wine. In the other hand was another bottle of wine. The slovenly dressed security guard had obviously gotten his hands on some leftovers from a party at the hotel that evening.

The watchman staggered across the patio not twenty yards from where Bailey was hiding. Unfortunately, the drunken man sat down on the same chair Bailey had been sitting under the canopy. The swig the man then took should have emptied a full bottle.

Feeling raindrops falling on his jacket and running down his neck, Bailey cursed his poor luck. He now just had to remain quiet until the watchman either passed out or moved on.

For the next fifteen minutes Bailey remained crouched behind the patio plant at the corner of the garden area listening to the inebriated watchman hum one of his favorite classics while taking periodic sips of his one remaining bottle. The rain continued as Bailey gnashed his teeth trying to figure a way to end this comical but inconvenient interruption. His impatience was enough to consider strangling the life out of the security guard just to end this ridiculous predicament. In the past this thought might never have formed. However, something had changed him in the last week. Now the thought was anything but flippant.

Bailey finally decided he could sneak past the night guard now resting with his double chin on his chest. It was then the far door opened once again and another person came slogging out onto the hotel patio. This time it was a woman of similar proportions to the night watchman. She was dressed in a maid's uniform. Two regular-sized maids could have fit in her work dress. It appeared she was taking a break and going to join the inebriated hotel sentry. As she edged closer to the dozing guard, Bailey realized she was in much the same condition as her male friend.

She mumbled something incoherent in Italian that was definitely not complimentary and the besotted man began to shake noticeably with laughter. Taking her own bottle out of her pocket, she took a long enough swig to interrupt her breathing. Choking as quietly as she could, the guard reciprocated with some kind of derisive comment. She coughed some more while laughing. The two of them were obviously soul mates. Bailey didn't want to think they were anything else or he would have been sickened. There was no doubt the hotel's wine collection had been raided that night. With bottles in hand, the two of them chatted away amiably and drunkenly while Bailey was forced to remain in hiding.

He waited. That surprisingly serious thought about smothering the guard had passed. The couple continued talking...and laughing...reacting as if everything they said was hilarious.

Finally their bottles were exhausted. It had been almost an hour since they'd sat down together under that dimly lit patio canopy. Bailey hadn't moved because they seemed too conscious. His bigger concern was that one of them might recognize him from his previous stays at the hotel.

His muscles ached from standing in the same position behind the large plant only ten yards from the guard and the maid. Unfortunately, it didn't end there. Suddenly, a far door on the other side of the patio opened with a squeaking sound that could have woken the dead. The night watchman and the hotel maid sobered up for an instant and scurried off to their busy chores. Seven maintenance workers plowed out through the door and into the middle of the patio as more lights lit up the area. They had rakes, brooms, and shovels. It looked like they were beginning the nightly routine of cleaning the patio and the immediate grounds of the hotel.

With the new challenge Bailey could wait no longer as the half-asleep group began their work. His jacket had become drenched making him indeed look more like a vagrant than a guest. Strutting across the patio the maintenance workers began pointing toward him. The supervisor called out to him and Bailey just ignored him. It had been a mistake to find comfort in the hotel.

Realizing he was now making a scene and could be if not recognized then certainly described, he had to get their attention away from him. Seeing an empty wine bottle where the guard had sat, the idea came to him like a flash. He reached down and grabbed the bottle and held it in both hands away from his body. He then hissed loudly in Italian, "Gentlemen, I've discovered what could be a bomb. Please move back and away from the patio. Don't ask any questions. Just move now!!"

The workers didn't ask questions. They tripped over tables and chairs to get out of his way and back into the hotel. Bailey glanced nervously around in the semi-darkness and moved directly to the patio door that entered the lobby. His talk of a bomb in the patio had already caused commotion behind the front desk. The workers and two guests scurried toward the front entrance. Bailey saw the night clerk on the telephone likely contacting the police. Leaving the bottle in a garbage bin, he pulled off his jacket and put it over his arm. Then he calmly stood by the magazine rack and paged through a copy of *LIFE* magazine while appearing not to understand why there was a small rush of people leaving the hotel.

Trying to remain calm, the bell captain strutted over to Bailey and exclaimed, "Sir, could you move to the outside. We are concerned about a possible bomb being found in the patio."

Bailey showed proper shock and responded, "Of course...thank you for warning me."

Once outside he motioned for one of the bellmen to hail a taxi. In semi-panic the bellmen blew his whistle and a vehicle at the end of the parking lot moved toward the front entrance.

Bailey's small subterfuge had done the trick. Sometimes ruses work and sometimes they even work a little better. As he got in the back seat of the taxi, simultaneously police vehicles began arriving at the Hotel de Italiana.

As evenly as possible and looking straight ahead, he directed the taxi driver. "To the train station please."

The driver took off unhesitantly amidst some heavy action in front of the hotel. Bailey sat back and took a breath. He had a ten minute ride to decide how to discreetly get rid of the saturated black jacket that was certain to be the first thing the hotel workers would describe to the military police.

Perspiring though the late night was cool, he saw the cabbie eyeing him through the rear view mirror. Carrying and not wearing the jacket despite the coldness outside, looking disheveled with mussed hair and six days of beard growth, Bailey appeared anything but a model citizen.

Maintaining his stare, the cabbie asked, "So, Senore, you are visiting our city and now must leave at such an unkind hour?"

Bailey eyes grew dark. He didn't like nosiness. He didn't want any conversation with this man. The cabbie might detect an American accent. He also wasn't certain how public his escape from the city jailhouse had become. If it had been broadcast, it was likely he'd be described as dangerous and a foreigner intent on killing their beloved Italian leader.

Grabbing a handkerchief from the jacket, he faked a sneeze only responding to the question with a nod of the head.

The cabbie wouldn't stop probing. "Senore, so what business brought you to Milan?"

Again Bailey went into a coughing seizure holding up his hand indicating he was all right but not ready to talk. The cabbie finally took the hint seeing his customer rest back in the seat with his eyes closed.

As the taxi continued its circuitous route to the train station, Bailey felt the cabbie's steady eye on him. He touched the loaded revolver he'd acquired from Ludwig Schmidt's pocket. Anyone getting in his way was automatically vulnerable. He felt no compunctions for his macabre feelings. Someone had put him in this predicament and the Italian authorities had no mercy. He had to play the same game.

Finally arriving at the huge train station, the cabbie gave one more attempt to find out about Bailey. He said, "Senore, can I conveniently drop you closer to your intended train?"

In Italian Bailey gave him a loud one-word response, "Here". His accent would not be picked up from that one syllable.

Paying the cabbie more than what was expected in the fare with Schmidt's lira, the overpayment silenced the driver. He now seemed quite satisfied and no longer showed any curiosity. He drove off saying, "I hope you feel better, my quiet friend. Good travels to you."

It was now deep into the silence of the night. The train station was more like a morgue. The military police and terminal guards numbered more than the amount of travelers at that hour. Bailey felt suddenly naked. Ticketing a journey directly into France was a wish, but impossible given the circumstances. France and Italy were basically at war.

Switzerland was his only real choice. The trouble was that country's neutrality. The Swiss officials were obligated to return him to Italy if he was found...and that possibility would be most precarious at the border. Yet, if he could make it into Switzerland and continue onto Lugano he might have a wildcard by contacting Andre Pizzorno. If the Swiss businessman was sincere in his desire to work with the American government, Pizzorno's response to his request for help would be the test. It might reveal how closely tied Pizzorno was to the LaCurso brothers and possibly why Bailey had been so conveniently arrested in Milan.

He walked slowly through the train station reading the newspaper and trying to draw as little attention as possible. He still carried the black jacket. It was not as noticeable as long as he didn't wear it...and there was a chance he might need the jacket for warmth. Taking a deep breath he marched confidently up to the furthest ticket booth away from the many guards. With Ludwig Schmidt's money, he bought a round trip ticket since he had no luggage. The purchase made it look like he was only visiting Lugano for the day.

Whether the ticket agent was too tired or just didn't care, he took the lira and gave Bailey with no delay the change in cash and the ticket. Something had gone right. He turned and began walking away when the agent groggily yelled at him, "Wrong way....Track 8 is that way" as he pointed the opposite direction Bailey was walking.

Bailey said nothing but simply waved his appreciation. The ticket agent barely gave him a nod.

The train was not scheduled to leave until dawn. He had four hours of sharing space in the cavernous train station with what seemed like an entire Italian military brigade strolling around the complex. With nothing but a bogus I.D. showing him to be Ludwig Schmidt, he had to disappear until he boarded.

The constant stress was keeping him alert; under less pressure he had to fight to overcome exhaustion. If he sat down in one of the terminal benches, he could be asleep in moments.

It was almost four hours later when Bailey exited the men's room. He'd never slept while sitting on a toilet in a public rest room stall. It was another one of those times he'd remember if he was fortunate enough to have a future.

With dawn approaching, the number of travelers had picked up markedly. He no longer felt as if he was the only non-military official in the entire station. Nevertheless, there were soldiers at each entry gate to the various trains. Nothing was going to be easy.

He had a very short time before the train was schedule to leave. He considered trying to use his German badge from Ludwig Schmidt but thought better of it. He'd have to gain sixty quick pounds and shrink a couple inches in height before Schmidt's I.D. had even a remote chance of convincing one of those station guards. Finally discarding the jacket onto a luggage cart, he grabbed a suit bag from the cart practically in the same motion to change his look. The bag helped him camouflage the bulging firearm he was carrying in his suitcoat breast pocket along with Schmidt's I.D. and remaining money.

With no effective I.D. or passport, he passed by his Gate 8 entry point and proceeded to Gate 12. That train was just leaving and the police guards were walking away. One of the station ticket takers was completing his count and Bailey quickly approached him. Quickly flashing his badge at the man, he urgently asked, "Senore, which gate has the train to Rome?"

The civil servant was irritated over being interrupted and didn't look up but muttered, "Gate 6." Then he pointed down the rows of tracks without looking up.

Hoping for the ticket agent's inattentiveness, Bailey pretended to see a police officer friend at Gate 8. Again he flashed his fake badge at the agent and proceeded through the gate. The agent looked up quickly to protest.

Bailey waved again to a group of guards who weren't even looking at him and said to the agent, "One of the guards is a good friend. I have to talk to him before my train leaves"

Then he stuffed a couple thousand liras into the agent's coat pocket and shouted above the noise in the terminal, "Don't worry, Senore. My friend is in charge of all law enforcement officers. He'll vouch for me."

Before the puzzled agent could say another word in protest, Bailey was walking toward the group of guards now within the outside gates. Bailey was certain the ticket taker was watching every step to make certain he would greet one of the guards. When he was within twenty yards of the group of guards he turned around and waved back at the ticket-taker. The agent was still watching him while fingering the lira in his pocket.

Bailey then slowed his walk and stooped down to tie his shoe. The agent was losing his reason to care.

A tremendous gust of steam then shot out from below the Lugano bound train startling everyone. Bailey used that convenient distraction to walk right by the guards and proceed to the train on Track 10 instead of Track 8. It was leaving for Valencia, but not for a half hour. This would be his last effort of deception if any of the guards or the agent chose to follow him.

As he purposely boarded the wrong train, he looked back to make certain the agent had finally lost interest. Unfortunately, even with the lira stuffed in his pocket, the agent was sharp enough to know something wasn't right. He began racing toward Track 10 where he'd last seen Bailey.

As for Bailey, he swiftly moved from car to car towards the front of the train. He looked through the windows and saw that the Lugano train on Track 8 was beginning to move. Gazing back toward the entry gate, there was the agent wondering where the strange man who'd shoved some lira into his pocket had gone since the fellow had certainly not stopped to converse with any police guard friend.

Bailey saw the agent then approach a guard at the gate. When he was about to say something, he stopped as if it finally dawned on the man of the consequences if he admitted to letting a questionable character through his gate with what might prove to be a fake badge. The agent then seemed to shrug. He turned around and strolled back to his station at Gate 12.

It would be yet another poignant moment in Bailey's life. He was able to scamper down the stairwell of the Valencia bound train and immediately cross over to board the already moving Lugano train only a few steps away.

But the moment wasn't over.

A voice suddenly shouted out, "You there. Where are you going? It was a guard walking along between the two tracks. He had a rifle in hand and a stern look.

Without thinking Bailey held his ticket up and shouted back pointing to one train and then the other on Tracks 8 and 10. "Senore....quickly...I have my ticket. "Which one goes to Lugano?"

Bailey showed a confused and panicky look considering one of the trains was moving. The guard had to assume he'd been checked through and suddenly gave a look as if he was observing a complete imbecile. He impatiently pointed at the moving train and shouted, "Get on board, you idiot, or you'll miss it altogether."

Bailey happily complied and jumped onto the first step. As he looked back at the guard, he gave the man an appreciative wave. The guard did not acknowledge it. He just continued patrolling the platform.

As the train sped up and left the Milan terminal behind, Bailey had jumped another barrier. He'd deceived his way onto the one train that could help him on his next step to freedom. Relieved, he quickly climbed the remaining three footsteps, opened the door to one of the coaches and took the first vacant seat. It seemed it had been hours since he'd taken a complete deep breath. With the train gathering speed, he exhaled and sat back already anticipating the sight of the Alps far ahead.

His elation lasted but seconds before he began diagnosing his next obstacle. With no identification, he was like a bird without wings. In less than two hours he'd be at the Swiss-Italian border just past Como. Passengers would be herded off the train to go through customs. How he wished he would have had the advantage of calling Roberto LaCurso's number in Milan for another free ride across the border. That trust was gone. His only real hope for assistance was in Lugano and he wasn't certain whether Andre Pizzorno could be relied upon. Of course, first he had to get to Lugano.

He could feel his heart rate increase and perspiration already forming on his forehead as the train leveled off at full speed. His choices would be few. Leaping off a moving train was hazardous even as it slowed. The morning light was also not his friend. But, if he could jump without injuring himself or being seen, he might be able to continue his journey on foot and cross the border at night. That choice had a lot of perils but some favorable odds. No doubt there was a gaggle of soldiers and military police looking for him at the Swiss border. Hiding from them for the rest of the day lowered his odds.

He squeezed the remaining money in his suit pocket wondering if bribery was a possibility. There again it was long shot. What were the chances of him gambling on the right person to entice?

He then felt the other side pocket of his coat and squeezed the luger. His expression didn't change as he accepted that alternative. It was likely going to be his final choice. Using a revolver against another human caused him no hesitancy. His perspective had changed. The weapon could be the difference.

The train plowed along. While he took in the scenery, he would not remember anything about the outside landscape. Every avenue of further escape controlled his mind. No thoughts were too daunting or discarded. Occasionally he thought about his father behind enemy lines during the Big War. Though over twenty years before, Bailey was certain the two of them now shared the common emotion that death could be right around the next corner.

Placing his train ticket on the seat holder, Bailey leaned back pretending to doze. He wanted no conversation with the conductor or anyone who could guess he was American. He wouldn't let himself sleep. Nothing was going to catch him by surprise. Like his father he would have to react to each new challenge. The image of his father and him talking out on the porch during his high school years came to mind. A pained grimace came across his face. He was a long way from Glenwood, Minnesota.

A jolt from the fast moving train stopped his dreaming. He looked around. Every passenger was lost in his or her own thoughts. Seeing the outline of the Alps ahead, he found himself becoming more and more distrustful of Andre Pizzorno. There were too many questions. With his huge number of contacts, when the American agent never arrived in Lugano, did he really not make one move to find the missing man....whether he knew the individual was Adam Bailey or not? And, in five days had he not heard of an American being held in a Milan jail? Maybe not.... then again with any effort from him and his contacts rumors had a way of spreading.

Bailey's anger was rising, but he was well aware that his fury might be clouding his logic. Answers were needed to ease his wrath....even if the barrel of a revolver had to be pointed at the Swiss entrepreneur's head in order to get those responses.

Bailey's ears began to pop. The train was beginning to ascend the picturesque Alps. The border was just ahead. It was time to make his move.

His stomach was churning...like he was all alone in the world. Nobody in the west had any possible idea he was in so much trouble. O'Brien could easily understand Bailey was focused more on the assignment and bypassed meeting Andre Pizzorno...and therefore was already carrying out his clandestine activities along the southern coastline of the Tyrrhenian Sea on his way to Sicily. There was a point at which David O'Brien would become concerned after hearing nothing from his youngest agent. He'd made it clear to Bailey that though the young man was used to working alone, there was no reason to continue that way...not with the entire State Department behind him.

As the train groaned as it climbed to a higher elevation near the Swiss-Italian border, so did Adam Bailey. He had to be ready for his next test.

"Arrivederci", the porter said to a passenger gathering his bag from above the seats as the train was only minutes from Como, the last stop before the Italian-Switzerland border. Adam Bailey had seen this station often in his many business trips the previous four years. It was Saturday morning, April 6, just a week since he'd landed in Marseilles where his troubles had all begun. It seemed more like a month.

In the last hour he'd been juggling every feasible idea to continue his flight into Switzerland. He had considered getting off at Como, the last stop before the border. He could then make his way overland by whatever means possible if he could avoid being seen. It was his best hope until he saw the abundance of Italian military police swarming the station. He decided to remain seated.

He patted his luger in his breast pocket as if to regain some of his confidence. It was the strangest sense of hope; the only way the weapon would help him would be if he actually had to use it. While his anxiety was high, the actual danger he faced didn't really strike fear...as if he had no time to be scared. How his mind was working astonished him. He still felt like Adam Bailey, but there was a dark side to his brain. The extreme attentiveness and the ruthlessness that he felt was an emotion he'd never experienced.

Half the passengers exited the train at Como and then the train immediately pulled away having a schedule to meet. As the train gained speed toward the border station only a few miles ahead, he kept patting the German Lugar and the extra shells in his breast pocket. He fully expected to see bloodshed shortly and it was likely to be his own blood.

Gazing around the train car, he pictured each person's situation as if there might be a way of using them. Some were already pulling their luggage down from above the seats. Still others were in no hurry. They sat back in their seat nonchalantly reading a book or newspaper. He wondered if any of them were on the train undercover looking for a certain American businessman who would be straggly and jumpy. At least he was able to maintain calm and thanks to the Milan tailor he had chosen a suit that fit relatively well. Unfortunately it was cold outside and the suit was the only covering he had for warmth.

When the train was but five minutes from the final stop in Italy, Bailey got up and walked toward the rear of the train. As he began his move between railcars, he could see the Swiss Alps through the windows as if beckoning him to visit. During one switch to another railcar, he considered jumping off the train as it slowed. It was no better of an idea right then than it had been an hour before. The rocky land along the rail guaranteed injuries once he made the leap.

He reached the second to last railcar. It was set up differently with a thin hallway that passed by compartments. He eyed each passenger as he strolled by evaluating their height and weight as a possibility of stealing their passport. He was frantic. What he really needed was a place to hide.

The train was now moving very slowly as it approached the Swiss-Italian border station. Bailey felt the sweat rise on his brow and his heart beating faster. Nothing in his life could come close to the level of desperation that he felt. He moved on to his literal last hope. The caboose provided a private car where all the conductors and some train officials could make themselves comfortable. Gazing through the window he saw two men in railroad uniforms playing cards and another person dressed in a military coat seated away from them and seemingly trying to ignore them.

When the train finally stopped, Bailey had no choice but to enter into the caboose. When the man in the military coat then exited from the rear door of the caboose, Bailey stepped into the compartment. He had no real idea what he was going to say to the two conductors. At least with his tailored suit he had the appearance of some kind of businessman.

Initially he said nothing as the two railway employees looked at him strangely as he brushed himself off. One of them got up and came towards him as if to inquire what the visitor needed.

Bailey said the first thing that came to mind. He hoped his accent wouldn't give him away. Watching the German walk by the caboose window, he asked, "So, where's Fritz going? He's supposed to check in with me."

The man coming towards him stopped. Any acquaintance of the German was of no interest to the train steward. He seemed to no longer care about the intrusion and returned to his hand of cards at the small table.

The other conductor just shrugged and said, "Who knows...who cares. He's on some kind of mission for his country. I guess he wants to see how superior the Italian train schedules are compared to the great German trains."

The conductor's words were dripping in sarcasm and caused his comrade to break up laughing. The comment meant that both men didn't consider Bailey as any threat. His Italian had passed the test of authenticity.

As they laughed, Bailey chuckled along with them before adding, "I'm supposed to give old Fritz the train schedule through Switzerland. I hope the train moves on and we leave the son-of-a bitch behind."

The two railway men exploded in more effusive laughter even more relieved that the person in their caboose was likely a fellow employee of the government run railroad who didn't want much to do with the German officer on board either. It gave Bailey the assurance he could push his luck and stay in that caboose.

Sitting down away from the two men, he grabbed a newspaper and mumbled, "I'll wait for the bum to return. The sooner I give him his papers, the sooner my job is done for the day."

Then he opened the newspaper indicating he wasn't much interested in talking. They looked at each other and returned to the card game in front of them.

At that moment Bailey felt he had a chance thanks to the lackluster attitude of the two lazy conductors. He was within the length of a train of being in neutral territory in Switzerland. He did not want to allow them to begin questioning who he was...even if it was only small talk. He was not out to make friends. He had to take control.

With the gun feeling more valuable in his breast pocket, he began to bluster forth with a theatric performance that had little basis but his need to survive. Showing agitation, he got up and looked out the side windows. The platform was filled with military police and all the passengers who were required to get off the train and go through customs before getting back on the train.

He gruffly snorted, "Where the hell is that God-damned German?"

He looked at the two conductors who now realized they were likely in the presence of someone several ranks above them in the railroad administration. They began straightening their collars.

Seeing their discomfort he yipped at them, "So, what's going on with you two? Shouldn't you be helping out with the disembarking passengers at this stop? I'd say you better get off your asses before I feel the need to report you. We need every man we've got to help at this stop and keep this train running on time!"

The volume and intensity of his order was at a level he'd never used before. It was almost staccato in pitch reflecting great anger. It worked. The two men were immediately intimidated. They scrambled off their chairs while simultaneously putting their hats and coats on while tripping over each other trying to exit the caboose. They were out the door still buttoning their uniforms.

With the sudden quietness, Bailey was in a place the border guards were not going to check. He stared out a small window to consider any other maneuver that might be preferable to remaining right there in the caboose. He ducked away from the window as a military sentry shuffled along beside the train to the caboose. The soldier stopped between each car obviously looking for any vagrant trying to hide and then attempt to cross the border illegally. For a moment Bailey hoped there might be some others besides himself who might get caught. It would take the heat off him. Unfortunately, that was not to be. The guard turned and marched back toward the station platform.

Then in the next instant, a shadow crossed to his right between the caboose and the second to the last rail car. Someone else was approaching the caboose. Bailey put his hand to his breast pocket as the back door to the caboose opened. It was the same German military man returning to the relaxed atmosphere of the rear rail car. He appeared to be quite pleased to be done with his outside duties as he began unbuttoning his coat.

Upon entering Bailey sat down as the German official stared briefly at him and went for the coffee. As he poured his cup, a supercilious look etched his face.

Speaking brusquely with no pretense of respect, he barked in German, "Where are the conductors? Who are you and what are you doing here?"

Bailey understood the questions quite clearly despite lacking fluency in German. He now had a choice to make. There was no way around the haughty, impudent German sentinel. Next this man was going to ask him for his papers and passport; then all hell was going to break loose. Without identification, this official could shoot Bailey without the slightest provocation. He could also try to be a hero and make an arrest. Either way the German would be the winner after finding out he'd happened upon one of the most wanted men in Italy.

Bailey played dumb as if not understanding the German's words. Impatiently the sentry tried again, this time in broken Italian. He yelled, "Show me your passport and papers!"

That was it. Bailey was faced with the most pivotal judgment in his life. He would often think back how he nodded, got up from his chair, approached the arrogant guard as if to give him papers, and instead pulled out the luger placing it against the man's thick coat. He then unhesitantly shot twice with the coat muffling most of the noise created by the pistol.

The entire episode lasted just seconds as the startled German was thrown back against the door. During his last moments of life, he attempted to pull out his own gun from his chest holster. That was as far as the mortally wounded man got. He slid down the caboose door and landed on the floor with a deadening thud in a sitting position. There was no movement. His eyes had a death stare.

To Bailey it seemed abnormal to see a human being so still...not even displaying a twitch. He would recall how the lightning fast incident had caused him no remorse. There was no decision to make...no other choice to consider. Seconds later the circumstances would have been reversed if he hadn't acted so unwaveringly.

Then, as if he'd dealt with this situation multiple times in the past, Bailey rushed over to the small side window on the caboose to see if anyone outside was reacting to the subdued noise of his pistol. To his great relief there appeared to be no one who'd picked up on the sound. There were only soldiers and a few travelers down the track now re-boarding the train. There was no indication anyone had heard the shots. He could also have been helped by the continued clamor of the locomotive's engine camouflaging the crackling sound of the weapon. Whatever the case, he'd just killed a German official with apparent impunity...and the train was going to continue across the border with no further delay.

Bailey was surprised at the coldness he felt as he again looked at his victim. Approaching the German he was careful to keep observing if there were any signs of life. Truly there were none. He looked at the corpse as if he'd just eliminated one more obstacle to his survival. The only real emotion he had was the satisfaction that escape was still possible. Guilt did not exist. It had been a case of kill or be killed. He was in a personal war against countless people searching for him. If he was recognized, most would likely shoot first if they saw him. It was the way the cards were dealt at that point in his life. Anyone who appeared as a barrier to his continued existence would have to face the same consequences as the German official.

The dead German then caused a new problem. He was beginning to bleed quite heavily from the chest wounds. If anyone were to suddenly enter the caboose, a blood stained floor would be obvious.

Quickly he dragged the corpse away from the door and stuffed some convenient towels inside the dead man's shirt. Pulling off the man's coat before the blood could soak the cloth, Bailey made another split second decision to take the place of the sentry. Yanking away the German's cap he put the hat on and then the bulky coat.

Hearing the locomotive's whistle, Bailey slipped outside onto the small deck of the caboose to look up the train line. All the passengers and conductors were re-boarding as the train seemed imminently ready to proceed. Further ahead was the main platform. Two other men wearing similar coats to the one he was wearing were watching the Italian border control question the last of the travelers who were about to re-board the northbound train into Switzerland. Beyond that platform was his next step to freedom. His heart skipped a beat realizing he had a good chance of making it.

Stepping down onto the ground of the caboose staircase, he felt into the pockets of the German official's coat. In one pocket was a pack of cigarettes and some money. In the other he felt a weapon. He now owned two lugers, but this one had a silencer. That discovery made his heart leap. Any advantage could be crucial.

Strutting back and forth by the caboose as if patrolling the end of the train, he pulled out a cigarette. As he lit it, a wave by the station attendant to the engineer indicated that all was clear. Bailey could hardly believe his eyes.

The train jerked forward and he saw his counterparts jump up on the steps into the train compartments. He followed suit and leaped onto the stairs of the caboose. Looking ahead one of the men wearing a similar coat to his actually gave him a wave as if they were comrades. Bailey returned the distant wave and then remained on the steps like his cohort was doing.

The train began its forward motion slowly and was barely moving as the rear of the train passed by the station platform. A few more Italian military police had hopped onto the train as it moved along. Bailey had the German's luger with silencer in hand if any of the uniformed men had decided to jump onto the rear deck of the caboose. There was no doubt in his mind it would be that soldier's last act of his life.

Luckily no military personnel would make the leap to his death. Bailey just stood tall at the end of the train. Pulling the cap lower over his face as the caboose moved on past the platform, he simply nodded his head at the numerous militias looking hard-hearted as the train gained speed.

Gazing ahead he saw that the front of the train was already into the neutral zone before crossing the line that represented Switzerland. The caboose still had to pass by one additional small platform with six Italian border guards with weapons in hand. They would be his last challenge.

Holding his breath he took a long drag of his cigarette blowing a big cloud in front of his face as he passed by the stern Italian border guards. Seeing the recognizable coat and cap he was wearing, the six of them turned away showing as little interest and respect to the German overcoat and the man they thought was in it. It was an astounding final ten seconds of his time in Italy. The moments that should have been the toughest for him to cross the border had become the easiest.

The jubilation of passing into the neutral zone and then across the border into Switzerland was a feeling so spellbinding he felt an unavoidable tear running along his nose. He wasn't certain if it was from emotion or from the cold breeze. In no way was he in the clear, but he'd just scored a major victory in his quest to make it to France. The miles ahead would still be fraught with danger. He'd have to continue being deceitful and lucky as he moved through Switzerland. He would still have Italian military police searching for him in neutral Switzerland... many of them undercover. He'd also now have the Swiss authorities joining the search. After all, he was accused of being part of a Mussolini assassination plot. A neutral country walked a very loose tightrope.

With the train now at full speed, Bailey was already concentrating on his next maneuver. He'd been in Lugano several times in the past. He knew the train station but he figured the terminal would be busy with military and civil law enforcement. He had but a few stops before arriving. Mendrisio, Switzerland was a short distance away. He was tempted to disembark in that city. The longer he stayed on the train the more chance he would have of being found. Further, if the body of the German official was discovered, there would be police officials combing the train for the murderer.

Bearing down on that last thought, he hurried back into the caboose and glanced at the dead German lying in the corner where Bailey had left him. The man's shirt had become soaked but no blood had yet dripped onto the floor.

Sensing it was likely the two conductors would return to the caboose, he knew he had to get rid of the corpse. Bailey picked up the man's arms and dragged him out the back door onto the small caboose deck and closed the door. If it had been nighttime, he would have promptly thrown the body off the train. In the daylight he did not have that alternative as his action might be observed. Knowing the route, however, he recalled there were several tunnels on the way to Lugano. That would be when he'd dispose of the body.

He had no time to think further as he heard the two railway employees making their way through the connector from the last car to the caboose. As they looked through the caboose door window, Bailey turned away so they didn't get a full look at his face. They could only see a man they assumed was the same German official with whom they had such low regard. Bailey imagined they would be likely pleased if he remained out on the deck.

For the next twenty minutes as the train began climbing into the Alps, Bailey remained outside as if showing the two conductors the German didn't care much for their company either. As they continued their card game, Bailey could hear them chuckling...most likely about the stupid German standing out in the cold.

The small deck was slightly cramped for space. The dead guard's body lying by his feet didn't leave much room for Bailey to stand. As long as the two conductors did not come out to talk to him, they would not see the dead body..... and they would live.

Thinking about the train route up to Lugano Bailey knew there were no tunnels before Mendrisio. With no stop in that Swiss city, the train would then approach several tunnels thereafter.

A half hour later he was still standing over the body of the dead German. The coat kept him warm as long as he kept his hands stuffed in the pockets.

Finally, as he leaned around the corner of the caboose catching the full freezing wind and saw what he'd been hoping to see. The engine had already disappeared ahead into the first tunnel. He recalled it was a short one, so he'd have to move fast.

Readying himself, he began lowering his body to shove the corpse off the deck and down the steps of the caboose. Seconds later there was the familiar muffled sound of the speeding train inside the darkened passageway. Quickly he picked up the body to push him off the platform into the empty darkness. As he did the boot of the dead German got caught on the railing of the caboose's deck. The body was half off the steps yet being held back by the dead man's boot strap.

Not knowing how much tunnel was left, he couldn't fight with the buckle on the boot. He was forced to pull the body back onto the platform...inventing new words of profanity in the process. Working feverishly in the dark, smoke filled tunnel to unwrap the bootstrap of the dead guard from the railing, the boot was finally dislodged just as the end of the shaft was approaching. The sudden daylight blinded him for a moment. He also had inhaled enough bad air from the train's fumes to leave him choking. He was forced to stand up and cough violently until fresh air returned to his lungs.

Inside the two men were hooting themselves silly over the German's decision to stand out on the deck of the caboose while going through a smoke filled tunnel. Bailey's actions confirmed to them he had to be the dumbest German they'd ever met.

Bailey maintained his position on that platform and pulled out another cigarette continuing to show the two conductors he'd rather choke from train fumes than be in their company. The corpse was now awkwardly lying on the stairs; a slight corner could cause enough movement for the body to fall off onto the rocky ground from the fast moving train.

With another tunnel approaching, Bailey readied himself and made certain the bootstrap was free. Entering the next tunnel, the deed was done with no delay. Twenty seconds later as the train exited the short tunnel he was standing alone on the deck of the caboose huddled in the dead German's coat. With luck it would be some time before the German official's body would be found in the middle of that dark second tunnel.

Gasping for a clean breath once again, he glanced back inside the caboose and saw the spiteful conductors laughing convulsively. Most importantly they had not picked up on any of Bailey's hijinks. Seconds later they were ignoring Bailey and sitting back in their chairs continuing their card game.

His next challenge was his actual arrival at the Lugano train terminal. He expected there to be another assemblance of military guards. They probably wouldn't be as focused finding a fugitive wanted by the Italian authorities. Both the Swiss and Italian authorities had to believe the odds were poor that the American could escape into Switzerland.

A half hour later the train began slowing. Bailey had been standing on the caboose deck the entire trip since crossing the border. It was cold but he hardly noticed the weather as he intently looked ahead toward the Lugano station. When the railway employees stood up and exited the caboose through the opposite door towards the passenger cars, Bailey saw the time was near to jump down from the train as it crawled ahead.

Before the train had stopped one of the conductors returned to the caboose for his cap. He looked out the back of the caboose and no longer saw the strange German official in the bulky coat on the outside deck. He thought it odd the German official apparently stepped off the train while it was still moving. Then he looked out the side window and saw that strange man in the business suit... by his behavior some kind of railroad supervisor.

'So then,' wondered the conductor, 'where was that German idiot who had stood out on the caboose staircase since entering Switzerland? Now he was nowhere to be seen.'

As the conductor continued watching the man in the suit hastily making his way across some adjoining tracks to another landing, it was obvious something odd was happening. He scratched his head. It was an incident that should be reported.

In the next few seconds he regained his senses. He saw no reason to put his friend and himself in jeopardy. If the man in the suit was just doing his job, the conductor would appear to be lame-brained. If the man was someone wanted by the authorities, both he and his fellow employee could be accused of being lackadaisical and lose their jobs.

His decision was easy. He decided to forget he'd ever met the man in the suit. Life would be smoother if he remained silent. Grabbing his cap he went back to doing his job. Minutes later he would never think of the German official or the man in the suit ever again.

As for Bailey, he had thrown his cap and guard coat into a trash barrel as soon as he stepped off the barely moving train. He made his way quickly over a couple tracks and hoisted himself up on another landing. From there he quickly got lost in the movement of people walking to and fro on the platform to their respective trains.

His antics were hardly noticed. It was a cool and windy day and most of the trekkers were hunched over trying to protect themselves from the cold. Adam Bailey had a difficult time not jumping for joy as he strolled along toward the Lugano train terminal. He didn't smile, but he had a look of determined satisfaction. He'd done the impossible. He'd made it across the border of Italy into Lugano, Switzerland with no identification, no passport, and a fugitive from the Italian justice system.

When he'd taken his first step outside the Lugano train terminal, his self-congratulations had disappeared. He was still a long way from freeing himself in France, but his primary focus of escaping to the West was going to be delayed. He had to find out who'd set him up and his best chance for confirmation was living right there in Lugano...the home city of Andre Pizzorno. It was time to find out how extensive the Swiss man's dealings were with the LaCurso brothers... and if they included any knowledge of Bailey's previous week of incarceration and maltreatment.

Bailey planned not to leave the city until he was able to look Pizzorno straight in the eye. The man was either a legitimate U.S. agent who could be trusted to help a needy American jail escapee over the Swiss-French border....or, he was part of a frame-up treating Bailey's life as if an insignificant pawn on a chess board. Bailey sensed he already knew the answer and the bile of hate and revenge was building with every step into the city.

Finally calming himself long enough to flag down a taxi, he felt for the limited cash he still had in his pocket. He had but twenty German marks, one hundred lira, a pack of bad tasting cigarettes, the suit of clothes on his body, and two loaded revolvers...one with a silencer. He again needed to look for some help and he wanted to be careful in showing too much trust in Pizzorno. He doubted he'd find as generous of a man as the tailor in Milan. He'd likely have to steal to afford some kind of safety from the ever present police.

A taxi stopped and the driver yelled to him in Italian, "You have lira or Swiss francs?

Bailey shouted back, "Neither....only German marks."

The driver nodded, "O.K., get in. I don't like Italian lira. It's not worth the paper or the ink it's written on. German marks....that's all right. Just don't expect change."

Bailey jumped in the back seat, thankful to be out of the cold weather and the possibility of being recognized. As the taxi began the short trip to the center of town, he thought through his next step. He had to choose the time and the manner in which he would approach Pizzorno. Breaking into the man's home seemed extreme; taking a more tactful approach might be more preferred. Either way, he planned on getting what information he needed from Pizzorno.

He no longer felt how hardened he'd become. Every minute he was actively in the game of life and death. His reactions would be quick...his decisive maneuver against the German official was confirmation. The remainder of his flight to freedom would be easier if he found that the LaCursos or Pizzorno were not responsible for his Milan arrest. However, that was unlikely. He had a strong feeling that these men were now his enemies; they cared nothing about his life. He now shared the same evil feeling towards them.

While retribution was in his every thought, Bailey knew that emotion had to be contained. But, those three men would soon know he escaped and could cause them trouble if he successfully somehow found freedom in France. Even if captured, he knew too much. He would rail against the LaCursos and Andre Pizzorno. It would not just be Roberto but his entire Italian family who would then face the consequences from the Fascist government. Willie would only be saved because of his proximity in the States. As well, Italian undercover agents would certainly strike against Andre Pizzorno.

The only answer for Pizzorno and the LaCursos would be to silence Bailey. They would be after him as much as he was out to get them.

Chapter 14

Being in a city where he had some familiarity, Bailey directed the cabbie to drop him off at Ciani Park. The park was a beautiful flower and tree laden area next to Lake Lugano with hotels across the street and an assortment of mostly Italian based restaurants. This time he would not accept a meeting with Pizzorno at one of the local eating establishments. There would be no passing him off to a young female like during his last trip through Lugano.

Arriving at Ciani Park he was briefly dazed with the beauty of the scene. It reminded him of the vast Lake Minnewaska back in his hometown in Minnesota, except the bluffs over the town and lake were lower than the more dramatic surrounding mountains in the Lugano area. He sat down on a park bench to rest for a few precious moments. The constant stress of the previous twenty-four hours had taken a toll on his energy and concentration. He was starved once again. With his blood sugar low he could fall asleep on the park bench and be picked up for vagrancy. He chuckled how anticlimactic that would be after dodging multiple numbers of military police since escaping the Milan city jail.

Some low clouds began covering the city enough that it was difficult to see across the picturesque lake. Soon it would be raining and he'd have to seek cover. With now even less money, finding a secure place to hide was becoming imperative. He headed for the first hotel across the street from the park as the rain began to fall. Under the hotel canopy, he felt conspicuous. He had to move on. He ran to the next hotel and his soaked suitcoat began to emit a smoky smell from the tunnels he'd traveled through an hour before.

The rain came down harder. Feeling exposed, Bailey looked and felt like a bum. A policeman under the cover of an umbrella walked up and stood under the same hotel canopy. Bailey moved on to a restaurant three buildings down the street to stand under yet another awning.

In desperation he had to make a choice. Either he break into someone's apartment to find some dry clothes and shelter...or he make that telephone call to the residence of Andre Pizzorno. At least he would likely be received at the Pizzorno home. It didn't mean the man could be trusted; there was a chance the man could simply shoot him the moment Bailey stepped into the man's house. But, that seemed unlikely. Pizzorno would want to know what Bailey might have said while being interrogated at the Milan jail. Then he'd shoot his guest.

Having no trust in the man from Lugano but with few other choices, Bailey finally picked up the public telephone in the restaurant booth and asked the operator to connect him to the Pizzorno residence.

The operator responded blandly in Italian, "Would that be Otto or Andre?"

He responded, "Senore Andre Pizzorno, please."

He came close to saying 'Otto'. Whoever Otto was Bailey could be assured that Pizzorno would have nothing against him.

After a slight pause there was a ring and an immediate but almost inaudible response. Impatiently he said sharply, "Senore Pizzorno?"

The voice on the other end replied hesitantly but in a German accented Italian, "Senore Pizzorno is not home. Who's calling please or is there a message?"

Feeling as if he had nothing going in his favor, Bailey sighed, "Will the Senore be home before long? I very much need to talk with him."

Sounding perturbed the voice repeated, "No, the Senore is out of town. May I leave him a message?"

Not wanting to gamble talking further on the line, Bailey rejoined, "I'm the young family friend of an acquaintance of the Senore's. Mr. David O'Brien from the U.S. said I should try to make contact when I'm in Lugano. I happened to be in your city today and tomorrow. I'd like to schedule a lunch or dinner with him. Might he be returning by tomorrow?"

The voice picked up on Bailey's anxious and hesitant tone. It suddenly whispered in the line, "Senore Bailey, is that you?"

Bailey was shocked. He didn't know what to say but a desperate and quick, "Yes!"

The hushed voice shot back, "This is Ernst, Senore Pizzorno's house servant. We've talked in the past. Where are you? There has been concern as to your whereabouts. Senore Pizzorno and I are aware of your being jailed in Milan.... and of your escape. It is nothing short of a miracle that you've made it to Lugano. Senore Pizzorno truly is out of town but I know he would want me to help you in any way. I will come get you. Where are you now?"

The words, "help you in any way" were music to Bailey's ears, but he was still wary. His question about Pizzorno might have just been answered. The man and his houseman were aware of his being jailed in Milan...and they hadn't done anything about it. Making contact with David O'Brien through Pizzorno's own sources should not have been too great a task. But, it hadn't been done!

Feeling his fury building, Bailey was determined to stay calm. Ernst's offer of assistance whether sincere or not had to be accepted. He had few other choices if he was going to survive the night.

Whispering into the receiver he mumbled, "I'm across the street from Ciani Park in a small café down from the Hotel Lugano. Is that convenient?"

There was no delay in the response. Ernst took control. "That is fine. I'll come to you. Be at the front gate of 'Parko Ciani' in ten minutes. I will be driving a black 1937 BMW 315 Sport Roadster of the Senore's. If there are any police or military nearby, walk down the street and I'll pick you up as you are moving. Have some flowers from the park in your hands so I recognize you."

The phone then went silent. Bailey took off his suitcoat being careful to transfer the two weapons to his pants pocket. He then folded up the soaked coat and placed it on the floor of the telephone booth. As he exited the restaurant, he casually stopped at the coat rack and chose a garb that would fit him. An umbrella leaning against the wall also conveniently found his grasp. Without any further delay, he was outside walking across the street toward Ciani Park now looking for some flowers that would round out his ensemble.

A policeman was on the corner directing pedestrian and automobile traffic eyed him. Bailey tried to act casual as he huddled under the umbrella. The rain at that moment was beneficial. Everyone including the policeman seemed to be wishing they were elsewhere.

Bailey strolled along the park walkway toward the main entrance. Looking around and seeing no one he ripped some flowers out of a park vase along the fence and continued his stroll. The BMW couldn't arrive soon enough.

He walked by two more local police who gave him what Bailey thought was a curious look. Either that or it was his paranoia. It was the latter as the two uniformed officers marched onward under their umbrellas. Bailey rolled his eyes now realizing the two officers weren't looking at him but at the flowers. He might have broken an ordinance by stealing the flowers from a public flower pot. 'That would be the last straw,' thought Bailey, 'a supposed international criminal picked up for illegally snatching some flowers.'

At that moment a BMW Roadster drove along the street catching up to him as he passed another Ciani Park entrance. The rain began to lighten and the driver pulled down the top apparently to get a better view of any pedestrian strolling along the perimeter of the park...and carrying a bouquet of flowers.

Finally the driver drove right up alongside Bailey and motioned impatiently for him to jump in the car. Bailey wasted no time thinking. He strode over and jumped in the passenger side of the roadster. Neither man greeted each other; they were more intent on just moving along. Seconds later, they were on pace with the rest of the traffic.

Ernst glanced at him a couple times as if to confirm his intuition that the disheveled young man was indeed Adam Bailey. As much as anything for the noise from the wind blowing there were no words as they drove quickly along beautiful Lake Lugano. The driver was checking the rear view mirror every five seconds. His nervousness made Bailey discomfited until they finally turned off the main avenue and took a side road along the lake. That was when Ernst finally took a deep breath.

'Pizzorno's steward wasn't used to picking up a fugitive wanted in two countries, on a main street during the light of day,' thought Bailey.

Slowing the car, Ernst seemed genuinely pleased to meet Bailey. He grinned and offered his hand in welcome. "Mr. Adam Bailey...you look younger than I'd imagined despite your appearance, but you likely feel older than you actually are with what you likely lived through in the Milan jail."

Bailey wanted to ask the man how he was aware of the imprisonment in Milan, but he didn't want to create any rancor just yet. The idea that he might get warm, have some food and shelter, and be able to rest for the remainder of the day and night had greater appeal. He'd get that answer one way or the other soon enough as he felt the two loaded weapons in his trousers.

It was exactly sixteen minutes since he'd called the Pizzorno residence. Ernst sped through the gates to a beautiful lake mansion and dropped his passenger off within a few feet of the back entrance to the large dwelling. There was no one around. In the overcast he could see the mountain wall to the left of the lake and the dimmed city lights of Lugano in the distance on the other side of the water. It was without a doubt one of the most private, quiet, peaceful settings he'd ever seen.

Without hesitating he got out of the car while Ernst drove ahead to the open three stall garage. Bailey entered the home and just stared at the exquisite design of the three-story home. Andre Pizzorno was obviously a very wealthy man.

Walking through the kitchen, Bailey entered a large open living room with twenty foot ceilings and a series of windows displaying a stunning view of Lake Lugano. Again he was struck by the comparison to Lake Minnewaska back in Minnesota. Often he'd seen a low fog concealing much of the lake from his farmhouse home on the bluff.

Ernst soon entered the kitchen and noticed Bailey admiring the house. He exclaimed, "Senore Bailey, what can I offer you. Certainly a bath and some warm clothing would be in order. First, might I give you a small brandy to help you warm from the inside out."

Bailey was taken aback by the man's graciousness. He didn't expect it. Frankly he'd not known what to expect. However, given his desperate circumstances less than a half hour before, he was glad to have this small welcome be less challenging than it could have been. He'd take whatever hospitality he could until Pizzorno returned home. He responded modestly, "Ernst, thank you for being so kind. It's been a rough past week and I needed a break. Yes, I'll take that brandy and your offer of a bath and a change of clothing."

Ernst only nodded and went for the brandy and returned with two glasses. Bailey noted that Pizzorno's houseman needed something to take the edge off as well. 'Could the man be nervous...or just normally somewhat ill-at-ease?' thought Bailey.

Accepting a half-filled glass he slowly sipped the brandy so he wouldn't choke. The liquid felt medicinal as it flowed slowly down his throat.

As he continued appreciating the expensive relics in the study next to the living room, he asked, "Ernst, I realize I could be putting you and Senore Pizzorno in a very risky situation by seeking help from you. For that reason if the

Senore will not soon be home, I will take advantage of your hospitality for only a short time. I can soon be on my way so I don't create any trouble for either of you."

He looked carefully at Ernst to see the reaction. The response gave him no real clues. It was a natural look of astonishment from the steward. "Senore, please...you can relax. You are among friends. Take time to recover. The Senore and I will help you plan and take your next steps until you are in free France. You did the exact right thing to call this residence. He has been expecting your visit since last weekend. When you didn't show up in Lugano, he became concerned and guessed that you had probably ventured through northern Italy by rail instead of taking the longer route across Switzerland.

Then we heard yesterday that an American answering to the description supplied to us by your friend, David O'Brien had escaped from a Milan city jail. He had no idea where you would go and fully expected you to be recaptured. At least then he'd be aware where you were....more than likely right back there in the Milan city jail. That is where the Senore is right now. He's making contact with some acquaintances to work on your release.

When he finally calls me, I know he will be astounded that you made it this far into Switzerland. While he had some other business, he'll likely complete those responsibilities now that he knows you are safe and then take the express train back here to Lugano to meet you."

It was difficult for Bailey not to be cynical. Roberto LaCurso was located in Milan. Bailey's escape likely had caused some inconvenience. It was becoming even more of a certainty of collaboration between Pizzorno and the LaCurso brothers. He wondered if Ernst had any idea what all was transpiring. Bailey desperately wanted to understand why he was being framed. He was tempted to pull out one of his revolvers and find the answer quickly from the still rattled manservant.

He held back from his impulse. Instead, he chose confusion asking, "Ernst, how did Senore Pizzorno even know I was traveling to see him in Lugano last weekend? Not many people knew of my schedule."

The question created no discomfort. Ernst responded evenly, "Your friend, Mr. O'Brien, informed us that you would be coming again to Lugano and wanted the Senore to be certain to take time with you. He said you had an important matter to discuss with the Senore. We had no idea the subject, but simply awaited your contact. He didn't want to miss seeing you, so he had some contacts at both the Italian and French borders into our country to be on the lookout for you. He figured you'd enter Switzerland at Geneva given all the potential troubles for an American these days going into Italy. The Senore was perplexed when he learned you had decided to take the train across northern Italy. Your delay indicated you'd gone about whatever business you had in that country. We figured you'd pass through Lugano once you'd completed that business...maybe in a couple weeks. Then, like I said, we heard of your incarceration yesterday...and then a short time later of your escape. The Senore didn't know what to do but travel down to Milano to see what he could do once you were certain to be re-captured."

Bailey was impressed with Ernst's smoothness. There was a possibility he was speaking the truth as Pizzorno might not include his steward on all details of his life. Bailey asked one more revealing question just to hear Ernst's expedient response. "Ernst, so can I depend on not only the Senore's help in getting me into France, but he might have means to contact my family friend in the U.S. as well? I know David O'Brien would be able to let my family know I am safe."

Pouring even more brandy into Bailey's goblet...and then his own...Bailey noticed Ernst's hand shook slightly. The steward for the first time had become uneasy. His answer was abrupt and incomplete. "Yes, my good friend, contact will be made as soon as the Senore makes it back to Lugano. In the meantime please relax and consider this home as your place of safety."

Bailey nodded not believing a word. There should not have been any delay with Pizzorno contacting O'Brien promptly about Bailey's whereabouts. In one day's time that communication had not taken place.

Ernst seemed pleased that Bailey was accepting his hospitality to stay at the Pizzorno mansion. Then strangely instead of concentrating on making some food for his guest, Ernst followed Bailey into the study and became too familiar a bit too quickly. He asked, "So...Senore...it had to be a nightmare in that city prison. What were the charges against you? What did they ask of you?"

Bailey moved over and sat down on a huge leather sofa in the study without responding. Ernst's conversation had shifted rapidly from a concern about Bailey's health to what was discussed during his interrogations.

Speaking very carefully, Bailey did not want to divulge the charges. Instead, he skirted the question. "Ernst, it was a very dire situation in the Milan jail. People were being beaten hourly. I faced that threat constantly. The jailhouse commandant didn't have a firm idea what I was being charged with until Thursday, so I was not physically mistreated...just verbally abused and fed slop. When I found out that I was to be extradited to Rome for more questioning, I knew I'd better escape if I were to stay alive."

Bailey stopped to study Ernst's response. The man seemed genuinely shocked and showed actual sorrow for what Bailey had lived through. If Pizzorno's steward was part of Bailey's being arrested, hadn't he anticipated the American would be treated poorly in the city jail?

With the unexpected hospitality he was receiving, it was no effort to wait until the Senore returned. As he patted the luger in his breast pocket...an action becoming a habit...Bailey decided to end any further questioning. "Well, if you don't mind, I'd like to get cleaned up and take advantage of your offer of food."

The steward was stopped cold. His eyes got wide realizing he'd pressured his guest too far. He immediately became solicitous once again. "I'm so sorry, my young friend. I just feel badly for what you've dealt with this past week. Please go upstairs. Use what you need. You are about the same size as the Senore. In the second closet in the guest room, take anything that might fit. While you bathe, I'll prepare something healthy and more substantial for you to eat. I will likely be gone when you come back downstairs. There are a few local contacts I'll need to see to help you proceed in your escape. One man I know can provide you a passport possibly by tomorrow. In the meantime, I suggest you lay low. Switzerland may be a neutral country, but we have to show some support to our Italian and German neighbors. You may have more people looking for you than you think. So please, Senore, make yourself comfortable. While I'm gone, don't answer the door or telephone. Keep the lights low. The food will be waiting for you when you come back downstairs. If you are tired, the guest room is yours. Sleep would probably be welcome for you."

His attentiveness left Bailey uncertain what to believe. Were the two men... Pizzorno and Ernst...friend or foe? He had to observe the steward's reaction to one other incident.

Stopping at the staircase, Bailey turned and stared intently at Ernst. "You and the Senore should know one other thing. I am now truly a fugitive. Coming north on the train from Milan, I hid out in the caboose until I came face to face with a rather spiteful German official apparently monitoring aspects of Italy's train system. I had to have looked both ragged and probably on the run. When he arrogantly asked for my identification, I faced an uncompromising situation. You should know I shot him in cold blood before he started his next sentence. It happened while the train was stopped at the Swiss-Italian border. If I hadn't done it, I'd either be dead or back in an Italian prison right now. I dumped his body off the moving train as it passed through a tunnel down by Mendrisio. The body will no doubt be found and maybe already has. It will provide some very real evidence that the 'dangerous American assassin' is heading this way. Whoever you or the Senore contact to help me in my escape should be aware I am a high priority marked man. Undercover Italian military police will be asking a lot of questions in this city."

Ernst did appear to gulp but otherwise showed no signs of concern or fear. He only nodded understandingly. "Senore Bailey, you've had quite a time... already experiencing some of the consequences of war even though your country is not officially in it. There is a war going on right now in Europe. People are dying. You had no choice. The German official was a sacrifice you had to make in the name of survival. This episode will pass. Chances are they won't find the body for days or even weeks if the corpse is in the middle of a tunnel. By then you'll be safe and sound in France or back in the U.S."

Bailey couldn't help but feel some relief. Ernst's perspective of the German's death in such a straight-forward way indicated the man was not easily intimidated. It also hinted that Ernst...and likely Pizzorno...could have a similar attitude about their guest. Regardless, Bailey was not about to leave the Pizzorno mansion. He nodded toward the steward as he headed up the steps, "Ernst, thank you for your help. I will stay this night unless I feel uncomfortable for any reason. I will put my trust in you and the Senore."

"Senore Bailey, I understand your concerns and your urgency. I should be back within an hour. Now please relax upstairs in the bath. Your food will be warming on the stove."

Five minutes later Bailey heard the back door slam. Immediately the BMW roadster rumbled and pulled away from the estate. As he watched from a window, the vehicle sped along the lakeside roadway back towards Lugano.

'The man was wasting little time," thought Bailey.

Hungrier than wanting a bath, Bailey hurriedly stripped off his wet clothing and found the secondary bedroom where the extra clothing had been offered. He grabbed a long robe and some wool socks. The warmth of the robe along with the wool socks had him running down the steps to seek out the food being warmed on the stove. Inhaling a lukewarm broth with meat and vegetables, he'd not smelled anything so good for longer than a week....or maybe a month...or even a year. His insides literally ached as he accepted the constant mouthfuls.

Finally taking a breath, he held the pan and began touring the lakeside mansion. Pizzorno truly had a beautiful home. Bailey heeded Ernst's admonition and turned on no other lights save the one in the kitchen. It was better he not be seen ambling around the house by anyone driving by the property.

With the midday sun being blocked by the mountains surrounding the lake and the low lying clouds, the day seemed later than it actually was. The rain had picked up and danced on the roof giving the house an eerie and lonely feel. It was so quiet as to seem more like nighttime.

As he roamed and got used to the semi-light, he found it difficult not to turn on some lights and then turn them off as he left the room The house was a veritable castle beside the lake. The multistoried dwelling was built into the rock on the base of a high mountain. The ceilings on the main level were fifteen feet and even higher in a living room that boasted a floor to ceiling window providing a movie screen view of the lake. Because of the low lying fog, he could barely make out any of the buildings in the city far across the lake.

Continuing his tour on the second floor, he gazed upon the shoreline. From the master bedroom there was a wide deck overlooking a huge dock with a sizeable sailboat, a motor boat, and a small row boat tied to the moorings. 'Whatever the Senore did for a living, he did it very well,' thought Bailey.

Returning to the guest room with adjoining bathroom, he ran a bath...quite a contrast to his previous week. A minute later he lay back in the tub allowing his body to relax...but not completely...in the silent house. He realized this was just a minor solstice from what would likely become more dangerous in the days ahead.

He remained in the tub for less than ten minutes before putting the robe back on, going downstairs to grab the pan with some remaining broth and meat.

He ate while he headed back to the guest room closet. He picked through the clothing looking for items that would be warm. He did not expect to have his present accommodations on his way to the French border. In trying on some of the clothing, it was obvious he'd lost weight. Most of the apparel fit very loosely. The most important extra when it came to choosing some pants was a belt. Other than that problem, he found a dark sweater and a jacket with hood that fit much better.

After an hour since Ernst had left, Bailey began wondering what was keeping the steward. It was cool in the dark house but he thought better of starting a fire in the study fireplace. He sat down in the dimly lit study appreciating the high built-in shelves with the extraordinary collection of books. Except for the unusual quietness and the freshness of the air, the dark surroundings reminded him of the same environment in the Milan basement cells. The solitude of course was a huge difference.

The sheer comfort of the library sofa invited him to lie down. He allowed his exhaustion to prevail, at least until Ernst returned. Nodding off he went into a slumber that seemed only minutes, but indeed was a couple hours.

The wall clock showed 6:00 when he awoke. It was noticeably darker outside. Groggily he opened his eyes further. The rain had stopped pattering against the windows and roof, but he realized he'd been awakened by a sound....like the snap of a small tree branch. His mind went completely to thoughts of Pizzorno's steward. It had been now almost four hours since the man had left the house in haste.

He stood for a moment and looked out the library window across the foggy lake toward the city. He could see some subdued lighting from the street lights in Lugano. It was so tranquil as if a painting.

He sat back down on the sofa. With the extra layers of clothing he was warm and comfortable yet bothered that Ernst had not returned. What could have kept him?

No one left a guest...especially someone not really known...in such an exquisite house alone. Bailey's feelings of trust were thin anyway. The delay only accentuated his wariness.

With only the kitchen light on, he moved around in the darkened house from the study to the living room with the large picture window...the one with the best view of the lake and the road. He strained to see if there were any cars approaching. He saw no movement on the lakeside roadway. In fact, the solitude was a bit unsettling. The house and outside were so serene that except for the slight tapping of drips of rain off the drain spouts there were no other sounds at all...not of any wind, no moving leaves, and no cries of nocturnal animals. It was just too quiet. Something wasn't right.

It was that moment he heard a twig break...and then another. There was definitely someone outside. It couldn't be Ernst. Why would he be trudging about in the dark? Besides, no vehicle had approached the estate.

Bailey moved slowly along the wall of the darkened dining room until he could see through the lighted kitchen to the back entrance to the house. Again he heard what sounded like a branch falling on the ground...only there was no wind to cause the branch to fall. He stayed in the dark and focused through the kitchen windows. There was only the foggy din of the back lawn and parking area. He began to get a bit disgusted. His paranoia was getting the better of him. Of course any noise would be pronounced in the stillness outside.

Still, he remained cautious...the relative protection of Pizzorno's home didn't guarantee safety. If there was a prowler, he'd likely already looked into the kitchen and determined no one was home. Even the car was gone to confirm the intruder's thoughts.

Then Bailey detected what he feared. There was movement of a shadow from an outside light by the non-attached garage. It was just a flicker as if the electricity had been temporarily lost...or a branch blew against the light. But, there still was no wind...not even a breeze.

Then, there it was again...some kind of movement beyond the garage by the storage barn beside it. Bailey got low and crept across the kitchen until he reached a window away from the lighted area. He was now better able view the back landscape. This time he saw the movement very clearly. There was a person and it wasn't Ernst. The man was carrying something metal and it reflected against the light on the garage. He then disappeared around the corner of the house toward the front of the huge dwelling.

Then he saw another stalker...this one carrying a rifle. That man hurried across the driveway toward the front entrance. Something was about to happen and it didn't appear to be a simple break-in. Otherwise the two men would already have broken down the back door and been in the house.

Bailey began silently swearing to himself. How long had the house been under surveillance? His presence might be known. Then again, it was hours ago he'd furtively been delivered to the Pizzorno home. He'd been dropped off and outside only seconds before entering the house. The culprits probably saw Ernst leave or assumed so with the BMW roadster gone from the open garage. There'd be no reason anyone else would be in the house with no lights turned on.

A break-in seemed imminent. He needed to hide or leave the house without being seen. If he was caught, his life could end as the result of a petty robbery. He pondered momentarily how absurd that result would be considering all that he'd done to escape death in the last day".

He crawled back across the kitchen floor below the window and ran upstairs to the guest bedroom. Interested only in the luger with silencer, he grabbed it from the soaked pants he'd discarded earlier. Now with dry shoes, socks, pants, a hooded sweater and jacket from Pizzorno's guest closet, he hastily crept down the second floor hallway to the master bedroom. There was a door there onto a balcony facing the lake.

Hearing nothing outside, he gently opened the balcony door and snuck out to the railing. Still he detected no movement below. With a large tree right next to the railing, he opted to scale down the tree if the way was clear. Seeing no one below he hugged the tree as he descended while simultaneously hearing a more obvious noise on the opposite side of the house. The perpetrators had just somehow made it into the house.

Running across the back lawn to the dock, he chose the small rowboat to hide. It was wet inside but there was some canvas so he wouldn't be lying in water on the bottom of the boat. Under the canvas were some still dry small rugs. While soaking up the water with those rugs, he looked over the boat's side. There were shadows of the invaders swiftly moving throughout the house. He wasn't certain if the two stalkers were aware of his presence in the house, but something had set them off to be so urgently running around checking every room in the house. Maybe it was the empty pan on the floor by the sofa in the study....or the wet clothing on the floor of the guest room closet. If so, he fully expected one of them to eventually trek down to the dock to see if anyone was hiding there.

Without a second thought, Bailey released the rope from the dock and silently let the small rowboat float by itself away from the dock. There was a fishing pole and one oar in the boat, but he chose to wrap himself in the canvas and let whatever breeze there might be drift the boat away from the dock. With the darkness and fogginess, it would soon be very difficult to see his small vessel from the end of dock.

Keeping his head low, he glanced once again over the side of the rowboat and followed the movement inside the house. Flashlights were shining within the walls like specs of lightning. He could see there were possibly more than two people inside that house...and they were not burglars. As they didn't respectfully knock on the front door, they also weren't the law. The dark-clothed plunderers were looking for someone or something. Their focus could have been on him. It was difficult to calculate. They also could have been seeking out Andre Pizzorno... or even Ernst. The question only added to his bewilderment.

Then he saw one of the housebreakers standing out on the balcony of the master bedroom and shouting in Italian to another man on the ground to check out the two boats tied to the dock. By the time the vague figure of the man could be seen standing over the sailboat and motorboat, Bailey could barely see the Pizzorno home through the dense fog. The man in turn appeared not to be able to make out his little dinghy in the thick mist.

Bailey had dodged another obstacle. It did not get by him that Ernst could have summoned someone to break into the house and eliminate him. He certainly hadn't contacted the local authorities. Otherwise, there'd be enough military police vehicles and well-armed law enforcement people to start a small war surrounding the house.

With nothing else to do, but remain puzzled, he lay back and let the rowboat continue float out to the middle of serene Lake Lugano. He intended to do nothing until the fog lifted. Then he'd be able to see if the aftermath of the break-in had changed anything. It was a long shot, but maybe the Pizzorno BMW would be back in the garage and Ernst will have returned. If so, Bailey could somehow sneak back to the house. This time he'd not be mellowed by Ernst's convenient and soothing words...not with a revolver pressed against the steward's head.

It would be hours into the early night that Bailey would maintain his vigil in that small rowboat. The thick clothing was keeping him warm and the canvas was giving him some cover from the intermittent rain. The slight breeze had drifted his boat so that it was almost equidistant between the Pizzorno mansion and the downtown area of Lugano. That got his attention. He couldn't let himself be seen from the city shore and possibly face any well-meaning water patrols offering to assist him.

He grabbed the lone oar and silently began steering the small boat back toward the house yet closer to the shoreline of the nearby mountain wall next to the lake. Twenty minutes later the fog had lightened but the darkness allowed him only to see a few lights around the property.

Wanting to see if the intruders had finally left the house, he moved along the mountain side shore line only to hear a vehicle pulling away from the Pizzorno house. Seeing just the headlights, he followed them along the lakeshore roadway. It was too dark to make out the type of vehicle but the engine noise indicated it was not the same car Ernst had picked him up in that afternoon.

With the car disappearing into the haze as it traveled back toward the city, the Pizzorno mansion was only a black mass barely distinguishable in the mist. Not trusting anyone or anything Bailey decided not to go near the mansion that night....that it was safer just to remain where he was. Unfortunately that would mean the small rowboat would be his bed for the night.

Securing the rowboat under an overhanging tree branch protruding from the mountain wall next to the lake, he felt hidden enough to feel safe. He was able to be comfortable by shaping the canvas into a kind of mattress still having some left over to cover his body. After a week in an Italian jail cell, being warm and covered by a water repellent canvas, he had no complaints.

Chapter 15

Within two hours of getting a startling call from the American who escaped from a Milan jail to Lugano, Ernst Lund arrived at the Monte San Salvatore Mountain flat of two of the main accomplices involved in carrying out a plot to assassinate Benito Mussolini. Luis Macarti and Sophia Bochi, both Italian mercenaries from Valencia had been hired by Roberto LaCurso and Andre Pizzorno the previous fall to be part of the conspiracy. Along with Lund and Pizzorno and two other older conspirators, the group had seen nothing but failure over five months in their quest to kill the Italian leader. As a result Luis and Sophia had been using the Lugano mountain retreat owned by Pizzorno in between the various failed attempts.

Seeing Ernst looking quite frenetic as he entered the mountain cottage, Luis and Sophia were ready to share their own frustration. Failure had become expected and the Italian couple was contemplating leaving the Pizzorno team after their latest fiasco if the next attempt in Torino didn't happen. They were ready to talk out their complaint with Ernst except he told them first he had to make a telephone call. As he disappeared into a private room, Luis and Sophia looked at each other in exasperation. Pizzorno's steward was not the type of man who generated optimism.

There'd been five planned attacks on the Italian leader since they joined Pizzorno's troop the previous November; four of them had been scratched because the Italian leader's plans had changed at the last minute. The other opportunity had gotten within rifle range when the would-be assassin, no longer with the team, changed his mind and didn't fire his weapon. The former member of the group later claimed shooting Mussolini at that church square in the seaside city of Genova would have been suicidal as his escape had been plugged by military vehicles. It was an exasperating and feeble excuse and it cost that assassin his life by one of his fellow comrades.

Luis and Sophia had just gotten as close to taking out Mussolini as anyone on their team the previous day, Friday, April 5. Their other two accomplices, the older couple, known only as Angelino and Dominique were in the audience near the podium where the Italian leader was to speak. They were to give a hand signal if the assassination was to be stopped for any reason from their close position.

Giving no signal they were waiting for the shots from Luis as Mussolini began strutting up the steps to the speaking podium. When no shots were fired, the two abettors realized something again had gone wrong. They were even more agitated since they could not leave their position only ten meters from the speaker's platform. It would appear a slight to Italy's fearless leader and draw attention to them. Everyone was of course supposed to show rapt attention during the arrogant dictator's rant on stage.

Il Duce was famous for his interminable discourses. The young couple would hear from Angelino and Dominique the next day how they had to sit through the man's two-hour tirade. By then Luis and Sophia had taken the well-planned escape route and were already across the Swiss-Italian border.

The opportunity to kill Mussolini in the plaza in front of the Duomo had taken almost a month finding where he was going to be speaking in Milan that day. When Angelino and Dominique later met Andre Pizzorno at a nearby Milan bar, they were expecting some kind of valid reason why the shots weren't fired. They silently stared at their glasses of wine when Pizzorno explained his decision. They found the reason difficult to accept.

As Pizzorno explained it, the American named Adam Bailey who they all knew had been set up to take the blame and become the top suspect in the shooting death of the Italian dictator had unbelievably escaped from a Milan jailhouse.

But, at the last minute, on that very Friday morning, there had been miscommunication and Bailey was still being held in the city jail. He was to have been helped to escape on Wednesday and that hadn't happened. Now, hours before he had eluded the city jail guards. He was on the run with no doubt little interest in assassinating anyone other than the military police already chasing him.

Pizzorno didn't get into any other detail other than showing extreme disappointment and understandable anger. He appeased his more experienced conspirators by reminding Dominique and Angelino of another scheduled attempt on Mussolini's life the following week if this one failed. He repeated to them that they should be at his estate in Lugano at their normal hour on Sunday. There they would finalize that murder scheme.

Dominique and Angelino were almost baffled by Pizzorno's incredible sense of purpose. Nothing seemed to deter his determination. He showed certainty that along with Luis, Sophia, and Ernst, their next attempt would absolutely end the Mussolini era. The Sunday late afternoon rendezvous had unfortunately become so repetitive and enjoyable that they all had been commenting how they would miss those afternoon meetings once Il Duce was finally taken out.

Andre Pizzorno had never intended to be the leader of any assassination team. He fell into the plan as it was developing by the highly emotional LaCurso brothers. He'd met Willie LaCurso from the U.S., when the American was visiting his overseas family. That was in 1938 when Pizzorno and Roberto LaCurso were collaborating on a number of illegal shipments into and out of Italy. Their large business operations depended on moving products that included food, clothing, and eventually stolen armaments to other countries in the Mediterranean Sea opposed to the Fascist government in Italy. However, with the Italian government clamping down even harder on export businesses from their ports, the LaCurso family was struggling to remain profitable with their shipments.

That brewed the relationship with Andre Pizzorno whose businesses were primarily based in neutral Switzerland. The LaCurso family would soon work in partnership with Pizzorno's shipping company. Italian authorities could not stop or confiscate any shipments on land or sea with a Swiss manifest.

The association was working adequately but the LaCursos didn't like the delays or the extra cost of merchandising through Switzerland caused by the Fascist regime. It was Willie LaCurso who reminded his brother that in America he typically expunged any obstacles in the way of full profits. The inference was that getting rid of Mussolini would rid the LaCurso family operation of its greatest foe. Roberto in turn prompted his older brother of the unique risk in Italy. Any hired people in Italy caught in a LaCurso funded plot against the Italian leader would result in fatal repercussions to many in the LaCurso family.

That conversation led to the LaCursos discussing their idea with Andre Pizzorno who certainly had his own problems with Fascist government restrictions. They discussed the sensitivity of keeping the LaCurso family name out of any attempts on Mussolini's life. The agreement was if Pizzorno planned out the assassination plan, the LaCursos would finance the action anonymously. Their secret cabal was formulated in the spring of 1939 with the agreement that a team of assassins would be hired secretly by Roberto LaCurso, but trained and sheltered in Switzerland by Pizzorno.

The collaboration was more ideal than effective. What had become clear after those first months of their alliance was that Andre Pizzorno was no genius at planning any kind of hit. He was more concerned about any of his team being captured...and then being forced to talk inculpating the remaining team including Pizzorno himself. The anonymous LaCursos wouldn't have to face those kinds of consequences.

The first two attempts on Mussolini's life seemed more for the purpose of testing Pizzorno's escape plans for the members of his team. Shots were not even fired. Information was inaccurate. Il Duce had cancelled both engagements in Rome and Valencia the day before. Obviously, the two would-be assassins made it out of both cities with no problem. As the furious Roberto LaCurso said to his brother in a coded cable to the States, "Their escape from the assassination site was successful. Why not....they hadn't broken any laws but loitering in the hotel where Il Duce was to speak."

The third attempt came after Roberto and Pizzorno had a heart to heart talk about the risks involved in killing someone. It was what Roberto described to his brother as one of the more insane talks he'd ever had with a man who dealt just as strongly in illegal contraband as the LaCurso family. The difference was plain. Andre Pizzorno never directly killed or resorted to violence to get ahead. His mantra in business was simply to underprice or sabotage his competition.... or allow them to join his own conglomerate with of course Pizzorno at the helm. Those alternatives had always worked for the Swiss entrepreneur.

Pizzorno promised the LaCursos the third attempt on Il Duce's life would have the best chance of all the plots to date. The location was to be at the port city of Pescara along the Adriatic Sea. It was to be an anniversary celebration of Italy's victory over Albania showing the superiority of Italy's air force and navy. The event was just another opportunity for Mussolini to deliver an ego filled address to thousands of enlisted military underlings for the purpose ostensibly of building morale.

Three of Pizzorno's team would be dressed in Italian uniforms with silencers on their pistols. When one of the assassins could get a clean shot, he would shoot the Italian leader and then disappear into the mayhem of similar uniforms. It indeed was one of the better plans devised by Pizzorno. Even Roberto was impressed.

By this time, however, the LaCursos had added their own insurance policy by hiring two gunmen to kill each member of Pizzorno's assassination team. Roberto had become troubled that the LaCurso silent role in the assassination attempts had been breached. If the killers were captured, there was no assurance that the LaCurso name would not be brought up as the money behind the crime.

In the end the scheduled event was cancelled. Italian military police had reports of various assassination attempts being planned in Pescara or further up the coast in the city of Ravenna. Again Pizzorno's three-man team left the seaport with nothing but souvenir banners claiming 'Victory over Albania'.

The fourth attempt was scheduled in January, 1940. By this time the two LaCursos were livid with the lack of successes and delays. Pizzorno continued to speak with confidence of upcoming opportunities to put Il Duce away for good and downplay, as he termed it, the bad luck his team was having.

Meeting with Roberto in Milan, he outlined a plan including his two Italian boarders at his Lugano mountain cottage as well as two others to support the conspiracy. These two people Angelino and Dominique had acquired counterfeit invitations for themselves and the young couple, Luis Macarti and Sophia Bochi to attend a gala for Mussolini in Rome. The details included another cautiously orchestrated escape plan.

Again the LaCursos worked behind the scenes with hired gunmen to silence the four conspirators if their attempt was successful. The LaCursos had become as paranoid of being discovered in the plot as Pizzorno. Silencing Pizzorno's team of assassins following their murdering Mussolini had become an absolute priority.

Unfortunately, the LaCurso hired guns were part of the Italian military police. They lived in fear for their own lives if the murder of the Italian leader actually happened and they hadn't divulged what they knew. They decided to spread a rumor that a younger couple and an older couple were going to be in attendance with the expressed purpose of killing Il Duce. Days before the gala, a dragnet covering the city was imposed to find the male and female culprits. The assassination plot was immediately shut down.

That was when Willie and Roberto knew they needed to be in charge of any future assassination plans. They were no longer confident leaving their family name in the hands of Andre Pizzorno.

Pizzorno readily accepted the LaCursos' insistence that they be more in charge. He was in fact quite relieved. However, the change did create another delay in the preparation as the LaCursos had to plan the follow-up multiple killings to keep the assassins from talking. It was the young couple, Luis and Sophia, who the LaCursos were most concerned about eliminating. Angelino and Dominique took on secondary roles and were less likely to be arrested. If they were, they could be taken out by Roberto's hired guns.

It was during the two brother's discussions about the next planned attempt that Roberto and Willie concocted a further idea to assure the blame for the assassination would never be aligned to them and their family. It was Willie's brainchild to use Adam Bailey as a decoy to further ensure the assassination team from being detected. The suitcase Bailey would be carrying to Milan would include a small amount of money and plans in English implying the take down of Mussolini and his entire government.

On Wednesday, April 3, Roberto arranged to have his hired men dressed in military police uniforms handle the transfer of Bailey to the Rome central military headquarters in a military truck. Those men were to report that Bailey escaped, though he was to be held by them until Friday when he would be set free near Milan. Once the assassination took place, Bailey already at large would become the number one suspect

With no knowledge of Il Duce's murder, Bailey would be given a train ticket to Switzerland and false passport where he'd be easily corralled by the Italian military police and possibly killed on the spot in the clamor around Milan following the killing of Mussolini. To ensure that ending, Roberto had enough paid off military police to make certain Bailey would not live long enough to be interrogated.

To the LaCursos, Bailey's unwitting sacrifice would preserve the family name and reputation. There would be appreciation but no remorse for his death.

The details of this plan were shared with Pizzorno in late March, 1940, just prior to Adam Bailey's planned trip overseas. This addition to the overall plot was supposed to relieve him. His assassination team then would have even more assistance as they made their undetected withdrawal from the crime scene. Pizzorno's job at that point was only to pay off his accomplices and send them to pre-planned destinations away from the European continent.

Pizzorno was still apprehensive. He'd become even more worried in recent months as he thought through the aftermath of the assassination. The LaCursos seemed confident Luis and Sophia along with Angelino and Dominique would make their escape after Luis made the kill on Il Duce. Pizzorno kept thinking, 'What if they didn't? The older couple helping out with the escape plans was not as much a concern. It was Luis and Sophia. If they somehow were captured, they'd eventually give in and disclose the real leader of the assassination team. Pizzorno sensed he'd be hunted down like a dog. Mercifully he might be killed before he was captured.

There was yet another adverse possibility he'd considered as well. He knew the shear brutality of the LaCurso brothers. They could want him silenced as well since he was the only one who knew they were the money behind the assassination efforts. It was not something he liked to contemplate, but he had to be aware his partnership with the LaCursos could be quite fragile.

As all these possibilities set it, Pizzorno came to the conclusion he had to preserve his own name and reputation if any of his team were captured or in the future if they began to speak loosely over their involvement in the historic death of Benito Mussolini. While he'd gotten to know and like the two couples, they had to be expendable. A week before the planned assassin on Friday, April 5, he'd begun putting his own extra plan in place.

The LaCurso plan was working like magic for the first couple days of April. Adam Bailey was to be transferred to central headquarters in Rome on Wednesday, April 3, according to one of his moles in the city jail, a sergeant at the front desk. The overworked jailhouse monitor wasn't paid enough to deal with the constant and oppressive uproar in the main lobby of the jail house. The extra money he was compensated by the LaCurso family to do them various favors made the job almost bearable. He had the power to process a detainee to whatever wing of the jail the desk sergeant preferred. His control included burying a detainee into the confines of the basement cells notorious for causing ill-health and even death. Initially Adam Bailey had been given one of those cells until the commandant ordered the American to be held in more civil quarters. For the sergeant he had to still generally follow the orders of the real man in charge.

The sergeant had the understanding that the American was to be extradited to Rome by Wednesday. When that didn't happen, he figured there simply was a delay. He was too busy at his front desk job to check with his contact in the LaCurso family. On Thursday Bailey was still in the city jail, but word was out among the guards that the American would be transferred to Rome on Friday. The sergeant assumed the LaCurso family was in control.

In fact, the assumption of extradition to Rome by Wednesday had somehow broken down. The paid off informants inside the military police in Rome had not had it stressed enough to them that the American sitting in a local Milan jail was such a treacherous threat to the beloved leader of Italy. So, Bailey sat in the low-grade city jail for an extra two days before the papers arrived to have him relocated.

During those two days Roberto LaCurso and his first-line subordinates never got word about the delay. Roberto...and Pizzorno...simply assumed Bailey had been picked up by the transport truck Wednesday. Once that had been done, Bailey would go missing after being hijacked from the transport truck taking him to Rome. He'd be held by other LaCurso family associates on the outskirts of Milan until Friday's successful attack on Mussolini.

Roberto would not hear Bailey was not in the hands of his hired men until Friday morning when reports came to him that the American had vacated the Milan city jail. It was not possible...but it was true. Roberto's first thought was that Pizzorno could not be told. The assassination team had to move ahead with their plan to take out the Italian leader at the Duomo plaza that afternoon. The venue for the assassination had been planned out for two weeks and was the best chance yet to take out the dictator. Roberto had secured a room at a hotel across from the church plaza. Luis would have ample time and a workable location to covertly fire the killing shots. Sophia would provide the escape for the couple in her Fiat parked only two blocks from the hotel.

The only obstacle to the plan would be if Andre Pizzorno would hear of Adam Bailey's escape. He'd call off the attempt just as sure as the Pope would be eating fish that very day. Roberto did everything to keep Pizzorno from hearing the news including asking his ill-fated business partner to a long celebratory lunch in anticipation of finally finishing off the hated dictator of Italy.

Roberto also wanted to be with Pizzorno when further reports of the deaths of the suspected killers....a young man and young woman...were made public. On the morning of the planned shooting, Roberto had hired a bomb expert to attach a timed explosive device to the undercarriage of Sophia's vehicle. Following his killing shots, Luis would dash down the back stairs of the hotel and walk briskly to Sophia waiting in her Fiat. Once inside the vehicle it was Roberto's orders to blow the young couple to bits.

Watching from his own cubicle from a building across the street from where Sophia was parked, the hitman would press the button that would stop the assassins before the Fiat moved from its parking spot. No longer would there be any worries about Luis or Sophia being forced to talk if captured by the authorities.

By being with Pizzorno when the car bomb was discharged, Roberto would have the chance to rationalize and explain to his partner why ending the two heroic young martyr's lives were for the good of the LaCurso family and Pizzorno's future as well. What Roberto wouldn't know was that Pizzorno would be highly relieved himself that the young couple had been silenced.

It was one of Pizzorno's own moles at the city jail that got a hold of him just before he was to taxi over to Roberto LaCurso's office to have lunch that Friday. He and Roberto were to be together anticipating a call from either Angelino or Dominique that the deed had been done. Pizzorno's infiltrator, a lowly guard at the jail, only learned that morning of the American's delay in being transferred to Rome...and then his escape from the city jail. As of mid-day Bailey was still at large.

Pizzorno was livid with the guard's delay in not contacting him sooner. The lunch with Roberto LaCurso was no longer important. He was immediately going to call off that day's assassination attempt and deal with what Bailey might say to the military police once recaptured.

Because of the crowds, his walk to the hotel was full of interferences. He was breathless as he hurried through the hotel foyer to the elevators. At the sixth floor he gave the assassin's door an urgent rap with two quicks knocks followed by one more. He was relieved to see Luis still only ready and waiting to take out Mussolini once the dictator climbed the steps of the temporary stage to deliver his speech. The scene in the hotel suite was such a contradiction. Luis had a priest's collar around his neck with a big-powered rifle in his hands; Sophia was dressed in a nun's habit with binoculars focused on the Duomo plaza.

He said forcefully to the young would-be assassins, "The two of you need to leave this hotel immediately and return to Lugano. This mission has been scrapped due to a tightening of security. You will have little chance of making a clean escape."

Luis was livid for only seconds. He was so close to making history. But, he also knew in the many months of failed attempts, he'd again better trust Pizzorno. If the older man didn't feel good about the opportunity for success, the assassination would be postponed. There would be another time. He was being paid to not only kill but to respect his leader's judgement. Luis and Sophia had to accept that something had gone wrong and Pizzorno reacted in order to save their lives.

As the Swiss businessman observed the young would-be assassin disassemble his rifle and remove his priest's collar and Sophia remove her habit, the two glumly and wordlessly left the hotel suite. Pizzorno would remain seated by the window to watch Il Duce finally arrive and spryly take the steps up to the podium as he waved condescendingly to the crowd.

At that moment if Luis had been sitting there, history certainly could have been made. Now it was only another missed opportunity. The unexpected antics of Adam Bailey had ruined the best plot his group had concocted to date.

Fifteen minutes later Pizzorno shuffled down the hallway hearing Mussolini's overbearing voice echoing through the walls pontificating about the greatness to come for the homeland. He would make his way back to his hotel and call Roberto LaCurso with the bad news. He was in no rush to face the wrath of Roberto for calling off the mission.

Pizzorno was more patient than the hot-tempered younger LaCurso brother. He would appease Roberto by reminding him of the next opportunity to murder Il Duce the very next week at a Fascist rally in Torino. He thought about Bailey and the inevitability of the young man being recaptured. The ideal would be for the American to be shot by any overanxious military policeman bent on taking out a man planning to assassinate Italy's leader. That policeman would be a hero in the eyes of the public.

Above all when Bailey was finally found and not killed, it would be imperative to have him eliminated before he balked about having been framed and then saying any number of things that could be damaging to the LaCursos and possibly even Pizzorno himself. He had to depend on Roberto's inside contacts in the military police to snuff out Bailey.

In the meantime Luis and Sophia would make the four-hour drive north through the border to Lugano by evening. They talked with Pizzorno in the past month of being frustrated that their missions were constantly being cancelled. But, it hardly mattered. It was not difficult to take the disappointment when they could relax and enjoy the easy life at Pizzorno's mountainside flat overlooking splendid Lake Lugano and spend time in the city's downtown area. Food was provided and they found themselves living in partial luxury compared to the previous months and years as downtrodden Italian citizens squeaking out a living on the streets of Valencia.

Their upgraded lives would simply continue for at least another week at the mountain side retreat. They had an allowance given them until the assassination task was completed. Then they'd be paid a large sum of money and then they'd disappear to some other part of the world. Until then, they had money and time to relax, shop in the city, walk in Ciani Park, and eat at any of the good restaurants along the lake and the main boulevard. Their only obligation was to attend the upcoming Sunday afternoon meeting to finalize the Torino assassination attempt.

The following day, Saturday, April 6, the two of them were barely dressed when Ernst Lund banged softly but determinedly on their door during the mid-afternoon. They'd gotten used to this diminutive man, who worked for Pizzorno, arriving at various times twice a week with some cash in an envelope. Luis joked with Sophia that the small man was trying to catch Sophia with no clothes on as a reason for his random visits.

That Saturday afternoon, he'd almost succeeded. She'd barely got her robe on when Luis let the Pizzorno's steward into the flat. Ernst seemed not to care whether Sophia was in a state of undress or not. He was preoccupied. In fact he hardly greeted the young couple as he went to telephone in a private room in the back of the chalet and closed the door. Sophia shrugged and went back to the bathroom to finish dressing. Luis went across the street to a tiny café for some coffee.

Asking the operator to connect him to a pre-arranged number in Milan, it took time to make the connection. On the fifth ring a groggy and slightly intoxicated Andre Pizzorno simply answered the telephone by saying, "Speak."

Recognizing Pizzorno's terse greeting, Ernst tried to hold back the excitement in his voice. "Senore, please guess who we have as an evening guest at the Lake Lugano house?"

Pizzorno was in no mood for guessing games given the failure of the assassination the day before and the conversation he'd had with Roberto LaCurso. Nonetheless, since his steward's voice seemed strangely upbeat, he sarcastically played along. "Let me see, Ernst, how about both Hitler and Mussolini are at the house drinking some of my brandy and discussing their next moves against the world….and someone just shot them. Please tell me I'm right."

Ernst chuckled but wasted no more time. "Senore, we have none other than yesterday's escapee in the mansion. Adam Bailey literally delivered himself to us this afternoon after somehow getting on the train and crossing the border and making it to Lugano. He looked in desperate shape and is seeking help getting to Geneva and then across into France."

There was only a small delay before first Pizzorno then Ernst broke up in unfamiliar laughter. Even Ernst had never heard his boss laugh so uncontrollably.

When the hilarity had finally abated, Ernst continued with his staccato delivery. "Senore, this young man shows great nerve. Not only did he escape yesterday from the Milan jail, but he snuck onto a train to Lugano and made it into the city with no passport. He seems to know nothing about why he was arrested in Milan. Since he was never transferred to Rome, apparently he was never really interrogated. I believe he said very little to the Milan jail commandant, because he had very little to tell. Still, he showed very little relief or happiness that he'd made it this far. His escape is not complete until he gets to France. He was very soiled and looked as if he'd had a very bad experience in the Milan jail. It was no wonder he took advantage when he had the opportunity to escape."

There was a pause on the telephone before Ernst added in a lowered voice, "Oh yes, he admitted to me that he had to kill a German official on the train to Lugano in order to complete his escape. So, not only is he being sought for his role in a possible assassination attempt, but once the body is found, he'll be sought for murder as well."

Both men pondered what just got said. To Pizzorno the young man was nothing more than a minor acquaintance of Roberto and Willie LaCurso who had done the brothers a few favors. Coincidentally, Bailey also happened to be a family friend to a key government contact of Pizzorno's named David O'Brien. It had turned out to be that O'Brien was head of the U.S. State Department's office in charge of espionage in Western Europe. Pizzorno had been talked to about being a quasi-agent for the Americans; he was considering the work based primarily on the business advantages he might gain. Up to the day before, Pizzorno considered the young American a gadfly...nothing more than a frivolous traveler looking for enjoyment from his work experiences in Europe. Bailey had been a perfect patsy to take the blame as the leader of a Mussolini assassination team.

But, in just twenty-four hours Pizzorno's impression of Bailey had been altered considerably. Not only had he escaped a city jail, he'd dodged all attempts to find him and he'd amazingly crossed into Switzerland with no identification. Then, this last bit of news from Ernst...that the young man had not hesitated to kill a German official who was undoubtedly going to arrest him...made Pizzorno wake up to the realization that Bailey had more grit and unwavering resolve than thought possible.

Pizzorno suddenly lost his laughter. "Ernst, I believe there's something more to this story. If you say he's relaxing at the house and he knows I'm returning tomorrow, I believe he may want to see me for more than just my help to get him to France. He'll stay put until I arrive. For now I want you to stay at the flat with Luis and Sophia. We have the Sunday afternoon meeting with our team at the regular time. I should be back in Lugano by suppertime on Sunday. Have all of them stay the night if I'm delayed too long. We can meet over Monday breakfast as well as a Sunday dinner.

By the time I get back to Lugano I'll have a plan as to what to do with our young American hero. It's important I see the mental state of this fellow. Something doesn't add up. He knows he was set up and would likely not leave Italy alive. I believe he's a volcano ready to blow. I would suspect he has no doubts Willie and Roberto set him up. He sounds like he's perfectly capable and motivated to seek revenge on those two gentlemen. What I want to observe is whether his wrath extends in my direction. That will determine what we do with Mr. Adam Bailey."

Ernst understood his orders. He responded obsequiously, "I'll accompany Luis and Sophia over to the house tomorrow afternoon. We'll keep the young Senore entertained until you arrive."

The two of them then cut the line. They knew each other well enough that no words of farewell were required.

As Pizzorno stared at his telephone, he recalled something else about Adam Bailey. Months before Pizzorno had arranged for Sophia to meet Bailey for dinner in Lugano. He'd hoped the fletching young Italian female might seduce some more intimate information out of the American. As it turned out the ruse never materialized. Bailey disappeared when Sophia showed up instead of Pizzorno. For a supposed international playboy that response made no sense. The question why Bailey didn't take advantage of the situation remained in Pizzorno's mind after than incident....and now after many months, the same thought had returned. There was definitely more to Adam Bailey than what met the eye.

Chapter 16

When the slight glow of the sun began working through the Sunday morning haze, Adam Bailey sat motionless in the rowboat. He wasn't chilled, but his body was stiff and his joints ached. The fog resting closely to the surface of the lake remained, but the rain had subsided to just a bothersome mist. Looking across the lake's surface towards the city, he could see a few other small boats with fishermen already trying their luck. He imagined springtime on Lake Lugano for many promoted feelings of a new beginning and well-being. His temperament was quite the opposite. His mind had gone very dark, especially regarding Ernst. The man had whipped up some food and then disappeared out the back door. Now, nothing the man had said could be taken as truth. Help to get a fake passport was a lie. Even the statement that Pizzorno would arrive later that Sunday could hardly be believed. If Bailey was to make it across Switzerland to France, he'd have to be dependent solely upon himself.

When the sun finally burned away the smog, he decided to move the rowboat closer to the Pizzorno mansion to get a better view if anyone was at the house. With other small vessels on the lake with fishing lines in the water, he threw out a baitless line trying to look less conspicuous. Moving the boat out from under the tree branches along the shoreline, he rowed with the single oar out onto the lake and positioned his rowboat some one hundred fifty yards from the Pizzorno property.

If Ernst had returned to the house sometime after the night marauders had left, it was also possible Pizzorno's manservant had stayed away after turning Bailey into the local authorities. Those men could have been the authorities searching for Bailey. On the other hand, that option seemed improbable. Pizzorno's steward showed every indication he was pleased Bailey was trying to contact the Senore. And, if the raiders had been the local police, there would likely be more police visiting the estate that morning to investigate further. In fact, the entire property looked unoccupied. What he really sensed was that the previous night's invaders were up to no good and carried out their work...whatever it was....with stealth and purpose. Robbery didn't seem a priority.

As the mist above the water completely cleared, he had a full view of the Pizzorno estate. The mansion truly was one of the most beautiful homes along the entire shoreline of Lake Lugano. The entire scene looked like a painting. The BMW was nowhere to be seen indicating Ernst had still chosen to stay away.

For the next two hours Bailey remained in the rowboat with a canvas covering his hunched shoulders and occasionally casting that baitless line out into the large lake. He was not going to do anything until he saw some action at the estate.

As he sat there, the boat hardly made a ripple. The horns and drone from the early morning church bound traffic on the other side of the lake was muffled but could be heard.

And then suddenly something finally happened. An automobile drove up and parked by the home. It was not the Pizzorno BMW. Bailey could see the driver get out of a small Fiat and stand for a minute looking out at the lake. He was taller than Ernst and stood with a stooped posture. The other person...a lady...remained in the car. She was panning the property as well as the lake with some binoculars. He felt himself being watched. The thought make him hunch down under the canvas while still holding his fishing pole and making it impossible for her to see his face.

The man then disappeared for a moment before showing up down by the dock. He paused to examine the boats out on the lake. Appearing not to suspect anything untoward, he casually strolled back to the car.

Bailey couldn't understand their purpose. It was as if they were visitors and had arrived too early since no one was home. The man got back in the sedan. A minute later Bailey followed the vehicle as it drove along the lakeside road back toward the city. If he ever met up with Pizzorno, he would suggest the Senore needed a security guard more than a steward.

There were now several more fishing boats out on the lake making him less conspicuous. It was warming slightly, enough that he removed the canvas from his shoulders and pulled down the hood of the sweater he was wearing. It gave him some satisfaction that all the military police and undercover agents looking for him were wasting their time. One of the last places they'd consider finding him was sitting in a small fishing boat on Lake Lugano. He smugly felt like a ghost. It had to be frustrating and even embarrassing to the Italian and now the Swiss military police how someone could evade them with such apparent ease.

It was late-morning Sunday after too many hours hiding in the rowboat when Bailey decided to end his 'fishing' expedition on Lake Lugano. He was not gaining anything by just sitting there. His hunger and discomfort only added to his edginess. Besides, the other vessels on the large body of water tended to remain closer to the docking area in the downtown. He was feeling too exposed. It was time to move towards the shore.

Unfortunately the only way to make any progress with the one oar was to awkwardly paddle as if the small skiff was a canoe. That gawky maneuver made him feel especially noticeable.

As he finally neared the shoreline with the mountain wall of shrubs and trees, he detected for the first time a small cottage around a corner that couldn't be seen from the Pizzorno mansion. It was stuffed in the woods and appeared as a more normal lake home. It was one level with a thatched roof. A small dock protruded out onto the lake almost imperceptibly with a basic twelve-foot motorboat tied to the dock and a rowboat pulled up onto the shore. The cottage looked vacated with no individuals in view, the curtains all closed in each window, and no vehicle parked near the dwelling.

Thinking that there might be a path along the mountain edge toward the Pizzorno property, he decided to moor his boat temporarily onto that dock. It would be less than a quarter mile to walk along the shoreline and he had tree and branch cover so as not to be easily seen.

With the day warming, he finally pulled off his hooded sweater and left it in his small craft. Spotting the owner's rowboat, he noted two oars. Upon his return one of those oars would be commandeered.

Scurrying up the dock to the little house, he was reminded of a little gingerbread cottage from a child's fairy tale. It was complete with white picket fence. Life being that simple seemed far, far back in time.

Approaching the back door of the house, he knocked. There was no noise inside the house. Indeed, no one was home. It was just as well. He'd be forced to tell some kind of story. Having to be deceptive was always a challenge when trying to remember the details of the lie later.

Being hungry he contemplated breaking a small pane of glass for entry. His desire for food made that idea sound more and more appealing.

Gathering his sweater he was about to put his elbow through the glass on the backdoor when he was surprised by a voice echoing from the woods. It was a female voice completely devoid of concern or fear. She spoke Italian, but with an accent he couldn't pinpoint.

She walked toward him with a smile. The closer she got the more attractive she appeared.

Chuckling, she said, "Senore, I wondered how long you were going to sit out on the lake. You looked to be in such deep thought. I was surprised to see you come to this side of the lake. I thought you'd return to the city marina until I saw you struggling with the one oar."

Bailey was momentarily speechless. He'd been watched by more than just the lady with the binoculars. The nice-looking female was dressed in hiking clothes. She had long light auburn hair hanging down her back below a stocking cap casually placed on her head. Carrying a camera and tripod, it occurred to him the fogginess may have provided some spectacular backgrounds for her photographs...and hopefully partially obstructing her view of him floating in the rowboat.

He was both dazzled and surprised how she unhesitantly approached him. Like a typical Minnesota lake dweller, she behaved as if anyone living around the lake was simply a neighbor. She seemed so out of place relative to the types of people he'd been associating with during the past week. He almost wished she was a bit more cautious given the dangers going on in the world in the spring of 1940.

Bailey could see she was startled by his looks as she moved closer. He'd likely appeared like a bumbling old man out on the lake with one oar.

Seeing him now as a much younger person, she did slow up and became more wary. Discomfited she chose to continue talking. The pace of her voice indicated her slight nervousness. "I saw you coming to shore towards this cabin. I'm a photographer and have been taking a lot of nature photos in the Lugano area. A favorite spot is a rock ledge along the lake about fifty yards up from the water level. I was out of your view with all the haze and fog. It took me a couple hours but I finally got some spectacular early morning photos of this picturesque body of water. I think this lake is so stunningly beautiful."

Bailey was tongue-tied. It had been so long since he'd talked to someone who just seemed friendly and normal....and good-looking. When he finally spoke, his words came out in English, even though she'd chosen Italian to speak to him. By her accent he guessed she'd be far more comfortable speaking in English.

"Yes, Miss.....ah...Ma'am, I found myself too far out in the lake. I lost one of my oars and it was hard enough just maneuvering my rowboat over to your dock. I hope that was all right. I certainly didn't mean to scare you."

He couldn't tell by her response if she believed him, but she readily changed to speaking English. "Well, I will be happy to loan you another oar so you can row your way back to your home. You're a visitor. You sound American."

Bailey nodded having no interest in having a conversation on that topic. He quickly responded to her offer. "Thank you. That would be very kind of you. I'll bring the oar back later. I'm staying for a short time at the big house around the corner. Even with the fog you couldn't have missed it. My friend has a rather impressive home."

She nodded without saying anything as she pulled off the stocking cap and unfurled her long hair. She looked very fit. Her confident air added to her attractiveness. A lot of Swiss girls had attractive red hair, yet she didn't seem local with her particular European accent.

As she put down her tripod and camera, she held out her hand. "My name is Greta Mendosa. My uncle who owns this cabin is a banker in town."

He was surprised how trusting she was. He had given her no information, but seemed to expect her friendliness to be reciprocated.

In a flash he realized he had to share his name...or at least a name with her. He gave the first thought that came to mind other than his own. He somewhat weakly retorted, "Yes....ah...my name is Charles....Charles Davis." He hoped his friend back in the U.S. would not mind the pirating of his I.D.

Then, wanting her to remain comfortable, he meekly added with a twinkle in his eye, "With your preference for the outdoors, you don't look like you have much interest in the indoors....like banking."

She seemed to take the kidding remark in the right way and laughed.

He continued, "I lost my way in the hazy conditions....and then one of my oars...well, it kind of disappeared. I feel kind of stupid. With my friend, Andre, not home, I couldn't even depend on him to help me out."

Greta seemed to accept his story. "Well, Mr. ......Davis. Would you like some hot chocolate to warm up before you paddle your way back to your host's home with my uncle's oars?"

They both snickered. Comfort had been established. He nodded pleasantly and accepted her offer.

Out of practice with small talk, he tried to recover. "So, Greta.......I didn't mean to insinuate you didn't have an aptitude for banking, but you seem more suited to the outdoors. Is photography what you do for a living?"

Using her key, they entered the house as she spontaneously replied, "Yes, Mr. Davis, I do have quite an interest in photography when I don't have to be too busy with my print advertising work. I work for a firm in Lugano. We create promotional advertising for local and regional businesses."

She gazed at Bailey to see if her brief deception satisfied him. She then added with a wry grin, "We do have some Swiss 'banks' who are clients."

Her eyes were playful. He appreciated her humor.

As she heated some milk, he sat down at the kitchen table. From that angle he could see a Mercedes parked in a small garage that wasn't visible from the lake. Her only way into town was to pass by the Pizzorno mansion. He wondered if she'd met the man...or maybe had reason to chat with Ernst.

As she placed a cup of hot chocolate in front of him, he poured the warm drink a bit too urgently into his mouth. The sweet warmness literally made his taste buds twinge. He had to breathe slowly to keep from choking.

Trying to maintain some composure, he sat back and commented, "Greta, I should be more in control of my thoughts. For all I know you could be president of your own bank. At times my mouth says things I regret later."

Her accepting grin kept their brief meeting on track. "Oh, think nothing of it. People aren't used to a woman who prefers to be out in the field taking photographs instead of contained in an office all day. I do prefer the independent life."

Their mutual nods fueled more animated conversation that lasted for an extended time. They were especially interested when they found traveling around Europe was a commonality. She admitted nothing about her familiarity in the U.S., in particular her schooling at the University of Chicago.

It didn't take long for their discussion to move onto the subject of war in Europe. Her fervor against the Nazis and what she termed the egomaniac in Italy came across strongly. Bailey kept his emotions to himself, but nodded his head in agreement with her tirade. He only admitted that he represented an American company that was trying to partner with Andre Pizzorno.

It was the first comfortable social time he'd had for a long time. At another time or place, he would not have hesitated reciprocating her kindness by asking her to share dinner with him that evening. That being impossible, he knew it was best he simply take the offer of the borrowed oar and leave. He didn't want to risk having her getting involved in his troubles.

Standing up he politely offered his hand. "Thank you, Greta. How fortunate it has been that I could meet you. It's been a bit lonely over at Andre's empty house."

He caught himself. He'd just said he was alone. Here he was a desperate, on-the-run criminal and he was saying what was natural in trying to strike a chord with an attractive female. It was a habit even in his situation that was hard to break.

Greta and he strolled down to the dock with Bailey cautiously glancing in every direction while she spoke. Being out of his little world of paranoia for the past hour had left him feeling vulnerable.

As she gave him the extra oar, she commented, "So....Charles...as family friends of our neighbor, Senore Pizzorno, have you met his brother, Otto, who's putting so much effort into beautifying Ciani Park? My uncle says Andre travels so much and has so few local friends that no one really knows what he does. Whatever it is, though, he seems to do it very well. More recently he and I have noticed he's had a lot more visitors. You're a testament to that fact."

Then her voice trailed off as if hoping he'd latch onto the openness of her comment. Bailey found her statement rather odd. From her uncle's little home along the shore and around a slight corner of the base of the mountain, there was no straight vision towards the Pizzorno mansion. How would she or her uncle know if the Senore had visitors or not?

He couldn't help himself. What he was thinking spilled out. "Your cottage is quite isolated. Whether he has visitors or not, how would you know?"

As soon as he made the remark, he bit his tongue. He'd overstepped his bounds. He hadn't meant to put her on the spot.

She appeared untroubled. Her answer was very straight-forward. "You can imagine that beautiful estate owned by Mr. Pizzorno has to be a subject for any budding photographer. "I've photographed that house numerous times at different hours from various angles. My favorite position, though, is that perch I just mentioned. My photos of his estate are like a painting with the remarkable surrounding scenery."

Bailey found himself intrigued for a number of reasons. He took a chance and asked, "Hey...I'm in no hurry. I'd love to see some of your work...especially photos of Andre's property. If his house is as social as you claim, there must be some evening shots showing all the lights glimmering from the two story windows in his living room. "

Greta was complimented but hesitant. Then her professional pride changed her mind. "I guess I could show you a few. Artistically, some of the photos are quite spectacular if I do say so myself."

Bailey sat in the outdoor patio overlooking the now sunny lake while she went into the cottage soon to return with a surprisingly thick file of photographs. Spreading a few she thought were her best out on the picnic table, Bailey studied each one noticing what vehicles were in the driveway and whether any people could be seen.

Seeing there were other photos still in the file, he continued being complimentary. "Greta, these are very professional. You've caught the lighting very imaginatively. Please....let me see some of your other prints."

Nervously she handed Bailey another stack of pictures. He gave the appearance he was studying them for their creative quality. In fact he was examining them very closely for any people on the dock or in the sailboat out on the lake. Unfortunately, he recognized no one except Ernst until he got to a picture of a young couple. They were wearing clothing not up to the standards of what visitors might wear when visiting the celebrated mansion of Andre Pizzorno. Upon seeing some closer pictures of the couple, he was certain the young lady was the one who'd tried to seduce him in the restaurant. The young man was also somewhat familiar looking. He tried to remember their names. The girl was a beauty. He recalled her name was...Sophia. When he'd followed them to a Lugano mountain flat, he'd heard her speak his name...but now that reference drew a blank. It didn't matter. He'd pegged the couple. They were more than just visitors to Pizzorno's home. They apparently lived in that mountain cottage.

The memory became even clearer as he recalled overhearing the couple talk. They'd referred to the contents of the suitcases he'd brought over to Italy containing money and needed supplies. They'd known who he was.

Bailey continued to piece together the puzzle. Seeing the young couple with Ernst Lund and Pizzorno and yet another middle-aged male and female in another photograph gave him the confirmation he needed. Pizzorno and the LaCursos were working together. Whether the others in the photos knew that fact wasn't important. They were likely as much puppets in whatever Pizzorno and the LaCurso brothers were planning as Bailey was.

Hoping for more information, Bailey inquired, "Greta, the Senore...I actually have not met him personally yet. That pleasure will come when he arrives home this afternoon."

Greta showed surprised. Bailey had to quickly recall what he'd said to her about his familiarity with his supposed host. Dealing in a series of lies required a good memory. He hoped he hadn't crossed the line of deceit. "Do you have some close ups of him?"

A bit sheepish, Greta nodded. "I don't want you to think I'm spying on them, but the people do add some interest to the photos. I got some close-ups. I wanted to see how clear I could make out their faces with my new long lens on my camera. I did the same thing with you this morning to see how clear my photos of you fishing might be in the haze. I bet I took ten shots of you. Every time you cast your line, there would be a singular ripple in the water that would eventually disappear as it flowed out into the larger body of water. I believe I made some very imaginative shots.

For a moment Bailey's heart skipped a beat. Those pictures could prove his whereabouts. Then again, did it matter? By the time she processed her film, he hoped to be long gone from Lugano.

Rifling through her photos of the Pizzorno property, she finally found one with six people standing on the dock. She pointed to a taller man with grayish black hair and a slight paunch indicating he liked his food and wine. "That's Senore Pizzorno. I wish I'd get a chance to meet him, but the opportunity just hasn't happened."

Bailey peered closely at the picture. There was something sinister about the eyes of each subject. None of them were smiling which was odd since they appeared to be going out on an afternoon lake excursion. Most people would show some excitement or anticipated happiness. The six people looked like they were going to a funeral.

He had no doubt he was seeing something macabre. Three of the six people he knew in the photo were involved in some kind of scheme...likely all six were part of the conspiracy. Puzzle pieces were coming together.

The accusation by the Italian commandant against Bailey being part of an assassination group now was becoming clearer. Whether he liked it or not, the allegation was probably irrefutable if the favors he'd done of transporting the suitcases overseas to end up with a group of assassins. In fact, it was probably safe to assume he'd been involved with some developing plans against Mussolini since the first time he'd delivered a suitcase to Roberto LaCurso in Milan the previous year. His notion of simply doing a favor for Willie's Italian family showed his ignorance. The most disturbing part...his life meant nothing to Willie, Roberto, or Pizzorno. His being framed, incarcerated and interrogated while the group took care of their business was diabolical. It also fueled his drive for revenge... an impulse he'd never felt so deeply. His motivation was selfish; his animosity all-consuming. It even superseded his desire to escape to France. With Pizzorno and Roberto LaCurso being so close, he might never have them so conveniently within his grasp. He wanted them to pay for their disrespect and his misery. Then, he would find some way to cross the border and eventually concentrate his vengeance on Willie LaCurso.

One other factor did occur to him. As he fingered through the photos, he paused to count the number of times he'd transported a suitcase over the Italian border and made it accessible to Roberto. Three times counting the previous weekend! Had they really bungled that many attempts on the life of Il Duce? The man was still alive. Bailey considered he might be studying some photos of one of the more inept assassination teams ever assembled.

Greta noticed his face changing color. "Charles, are you all right? You look pale. Maybe you should rest before taking the rowboat out. You were obviously up early this morning and out in the elements...maybe you caught a slight fever. Would more hot chocolate help?"

He caught his breath. "No, I just realized that I've seen some of these people on this photo before."

Then he gazed in the direction where he'd first seen her walking towards him and had pointed a quarter the way up the sheer mountain wall. "Greta...is that the direction of the elevated area where you took your photos?

Glancing up the path, she nodded.

He suddenly showed an extreme interest in her photography. With a rush of energy he said, "You know, I'd like to climb up to that place...that is, to see the beauty of the lake from that perspective. I'll not bother you to show me. I can go by myself and find the trail."

Finding his behavior puzzling if not a bit strange, she felt for something in her coat pocket and then shrugged, "No...I'll be glad to go with you and show you the way. There are places where the climb can be a bit precarious. I hope you're in shape."

Bailey was off before she'd finished her sentence. Following a path along the water, the route became as hazardous as Greta had warned. In places they had to climb straight up using some jagged rocks as steps. With her leading the way, he had to work to stay up with her. Her feet were agile, her legs were long and strong, and she climbed the cliff as if it was a slight hill. He gained even more respect for her strength knowing she typically dragged her photographic equipment up the rock face as well.

It was plain the week Bailey rotted in the Milan jail, the lack of good food, sleep, and exercise had robbed him of some strength. He was noticeably weaker. If Greta ever became uncomfortable around him, all she had to do was run. Keeping up with her would be impossible.

He'd fallen back but finally arrived at the flat rock area overlooking the lake. She was already seated just enjoying the spectacular view. The two of them were roughly fifty yards above the water. The city of Lugano was on their left; on their right the Pizzorno property was directly below. They were close enough to the house that he could practically see furniture inside the study through the floor to ceiling lakeside windows.

Forcing himself to look more toward the city, he let his enthusiasm abound. 'Wow...what a wonderful location. You must come up here daily."

She didn't respond only moving over and hanging her legs over the ledge showing no fear of the height. He went over and sat beside her, but held back from slipping his own legs over the steep cliff. He'd been dodging death enough. Testing his courage in that way was unnecessary.

As she pointed to some buildings in the city, he kept switching his head back toward the Pizzorno mansion. Looking for any changes since last he'd seen the estate, nothing appeared to have been altered from the day before when he arrived...that is, until the lakeside door opened onto the patio and two men stepped out. One was definitely Ernst with his short stature and slow movement. The other man was younger and dressed casually. Bailey guessed the man was that boyfriend of Sophia's.

Simultaneously a smaller Fiat then drove up and parked by the unattached garage. A middle-aged man and woman then joined the two men on the patio. Without being too obvious about staring at the Pizzorno estate, he guessed they were the same couple he'd seen in her photos who he'd seen visit the house earlier that morning.

While Greta talked on about the refurbishing of Ciani Park, Bailey looked beyond her and watched as the four never greeted each other with handshakes. They just flowed into very animated conversation. Then all of them got into Pizzorno's BMW in the garage and drove off leaving the Fiat.

Bailey brightened for a moment. That Fiat represented a way he might transport himself to Geneva. It might also be a trap. They might hope he was hiding close by and take the bait. He wouldn't make it out of the Lugano city limits before being stopped by the local police.

From his elevated vantage point Bailey followed the BMW all along the lakeshore back toward the city. He was high enough that he could trace the vehicle until it stopped at a parking lot near the tram station for Monte San Salvatore. Minutes later he saw the tram begin its slow journey up upward. Bailey had a good idea where the four people were going.

Greta had been staring at him the entire time he was watching the vehicle driving into town. She knew he had something more important going on the way the way his eyes barely blinked and turned dark. His artistic interest in her perch on the mountain had dissipated. It was as if she wasn't even there.

Finally interrupting, she said, "So, Charles, are you going to be in Lugano long...."

Unconsciously, he looked strangely at her and said, "You mean Adam..."

The moment he corrected her he knew he'd blundered. Instantly he tried to recover with another lie. "Ah...I'm sorry...I mean actually Charles is my father's name. Adam is my middle name. Those who know me, call me Adam Bai..... rather Davis."

Any trust she had of the young American was dissolving very fast. Suddenly his being out in a rowboat so early in the morning fishing half-heartedly and covered with a canvas to ward off the light rain seemed more questionable than ever, especially if he had the comfort of the mansion at his disposal.

Her uneasiness caused her to stand up and begin moving toward the path back to the cottage as she nervously joked, "Well, when you figure out what your name is for certain, let me know so I can call you by your preferred name. I guess I've got some errands in town. I think I'll take off. You can certainly stay up here and admire the view if you'd like.........Adam."

His laugh was as factitious as hers. However, he no longer cared. He didn't have time to be concerned about the name mix-up...not when he'd likely never see her again. There was something going on with Pizzorno and his visitors. He now had a hunch he was seeing a group of people working together to do exactly what the commandant in Milan had finally accused his American detainee of planning...of doing away with Benito Mussolini. His only question at that moment was how deeply his name had been dragged into their quest.

Shaking his head, he behaved as if the slip-up hadn't occurred. "No...I'll climb down with you. I should get over to the house so I don't miss Andre when he finally gets home."

They returned to her uncle's cottage in half the time. The pace had been hurried and their silence spoke volumes....her for her distrust...him for his preoccupation with Pizzorno and his companions.

When they approached the cottage and then the dock, Bailey grabbed the spare oar and was about to jump into the rowboat, offer his thanks and be on his way. What he didn't expect then happened. As he turned back toward her, he found himself gazing right into the barrel of a small derringer she'd had in her hip pocket. That explained immediately to him why she'd not been daunted by his presence. With his coat pocket containing his own luger lying in the rowboat, she had him cold.

This time Greta's voice had a sharp edge. "O.K....Adam....Charles....or whatever your name is, I believe you'd better show me some identification or answer some questions before I call the local police. I saw you staring with an evil eye at the Senore's BMW when it drove into town. It was not a friendly look. Also, it makes no sense that you were fishing in the lake near the mansion considering you had no bait on your fish line. Like I told you, my new long lens picks up great detail. So, based on your rather strange behavior, I question whether you're a guest of the Senore...or, you have some other more dreadful deed planned. How do I know you're not going to row over to the Senore's mansion and murder the man and his steward? From what I'm noticing about you, it wouldn't be a surprise."

Bailey sat down on the dock and just wheezed out a long breath saying nothing. His mind flashed to a number of things he could say or do including nonchalantly grabbing his coat, taking out the luger in the pocket and shooting the young woman point blank before she knew what hit her. If she actually planned to contact the authorities, he'd have to neutralize her someway. He prayed she wouldn't go to that extreme.

Continuing to say nothing, he pulled out a cigarette, lit it, and leaned back on his elbows while he stared out at the lake. All the while the barrel of her pistol did not move from its aim. Her eyes were very determined. She looked like she would shoot if she was provoked.

He didn't like trusting anyone, but in this instance and what he knew about her, he had to make a choice. If he could cool her down, she might just allow herself to listen and even believe the predicament he was in. He didn't have to tell her everything...just enough to win her over. Then it would be her choice. If she could legitimately help him, the rest of her day would be happier. If she wasn't willing, he didn't want to consider that consequence.

Bailey then sat up and calmly said to her, "Greta, you may as well sit down on the dock, because I'm going to tell you a story that you may find far-fetched, but it'll be the truth.

She hesitated.

He repeated more sharply, "Sit...for God's sake...and I'll tell you the rather desperate situation I'm in. When I'm done, I am going to get into this rowboat and head toward the Pizzorno mansion. If you believe I'm actually here to kill or maim the Senore, then I'd suggest you shoot me or run to your telephone to call the authorities. If you can believe me, I'm likely going to have to ask for a little help. You should also know that if you wait until I get out of sight around the corner on the lake and then call the Lugano police, I will not be at the mansion. I will be long gone...including dead if you decide to shoot me."

Greta offered a slight grin. He could tell she wanted to believe whatever he was going to tell her. She then sat down on the dock about fifteen feet from where he was sitting. While still pointing the gun directly at him, she mumbled, "Try me."

He began by introducing himself. "My name is in fact Adam Bailey. Charlie Davis is a name I briefly stole from a friend of mine, since my name may be in news reports. I am an American businessman. I've been in an Italian jail for about a week on suspicion of plotting to murder a high government official in Italy. I was arrested at the Milan train station last Sunday and given some questionable quarters and seriously bad food at the Milan city jail.

I found out I was to be extradited to Rome for what they called 'in-depth' questioning. You should know, Greta, based on what I finally learned from the commandant of the jailhouse, you are looking at a fugitive in charge of a maniacal international plot bent on assassinating Benito Mussolini."

The young lady's eyes widened for a moment. Bailey raised both his hands and then lowered them slowly. "Now calm down. There's not a bit of truth to the charge. I have been framed very thoroughly and professionally. From the Italian authorities' standpoint, I am guilty. By Friday morning, two days ago, I had no reason to believe I'd ever leave the interrogation in Rome alive. My good fortune, if you want to call it that, was that I was being held in a low-grade city jail. It was overrun with unimportant and frightened detainees and too few overworked, unprofessional guards. The bottom line was that I escaped before I was to be taken to Rome. I crawled out through the city jail's lavatory window and I've been on the run for the last forty-eight hours. It wasn't easy but I was able to take the train up here to Lugano in the hope that Senore Pizzorno might help in my further escape to France. He's supposedly a friend of someone I know in the U.S. I have no passport and little money. Furthermore, I have no way of communicating with people who could help me. The Senore is my last hope for assistance or I have to continue my flight to France on my own."

His story regarding Andre Pizzorno had just turned into a lie. He stopped talking figuring he'd said enough to create some sympathy.

Greta's eyes showed genuine shock. Collecting her breath she gasped, "You don't exactly come across as an international crime figure, but then again I've never met one. I can't compare you to anybody."

Her small jest gave him some hope she was buying into his story. Her small pistol still pointed at his chest instead of his head indicating he was winning.... but only gradually.

Bailey slowly grabbed an oar from her uncle's rowboat and then stepped into his rowboat hoping he wouldn't hear a shot. As he sat down feeling for his luger in the coat pocket, he added, "Greta, that's it. I was doing business with clients in this country and Italy until I was painted into a corner by this false charge."

He stared directly at her eyes to gauge what level she was buying into his understandably bizarre explanation. Moving his hand slowly he finally grasped the cold metal of the luger inside his coat while continuing to talk evenly. "Greta, if you don't believe me, I guess you are going to have to seriously consider shooting me. I will not go back to any city jail or allow any military police to arrest me. That would be certain death for me."

Her face gradually relaxed and the gun finally lowered. Releasing his own hidden weapon, his relief was all-consuming. While her response was encouraging, he sensed she didn't completely trust him.

"Adam, you seem to be operating without a plan. I hope the Senore can help you."

Whether she made that mollifying statement just to reduce her own fear didn't matter to Bailey. She'd saved herself.

Trying to ease the tension even more, he chuckled, "Greta, I definitely have a plan...only it seems to change with each hour depending on what new struggle I'm facing. Geneva is my destination if I have any hope of completing this escape. I have a better chance in that city of making contact with someone who can help me over the border. Even then, my passage into France won't be easy. That border will be heavily guarded on the Swiss side and every man with a uniform likely has a copy of my picture."

Greta seemed lost in her thoughts. Finally she talked and actually sounded reassuring. "Look, I sense something strange is going on with those people connected to Andre Pizzorno in the photos I showed you. Also, you should know I have no loyalty for the Fascists or certainly not those rancid Nazis. I can promise you I will not turn you in unless you prove me an idiot for believing in you. I have to meet a friend for lunch in the plaza and it'll seem odd to him if I just stand him up. I'll finish the lunch and be back this afternoon. I'll bring back some food. You can stay here or go over and meet up with Pizzorno...whatever makes you more comfortable. It sounds like you want to leave Lugano as soon as possible. If the Senore seems hesitant to assist you, come back here. I'll try and help you if I can."

Bailey nodded. He had no choice but to believe her. Her expression of hatred against Nazism and Fascism carried legitimate emotion. He had a growing feeling she did want to assist him. If he was wrong, he'd be the idiot.

He raised his right hand...the same one that had been grasping his luger in his coat pocket just minutes before...and waved to her as he began rowing away from the dock. He said to her, "Greta, thank you. If I don't meet up with the Senore later this afternoon, I will make my way back here and stay the night before moving on if that is all right."

She nodded but not enthusiastically. "I'll leave the backdoor open if you return before I do. But, be aware. My uncle is returning either tonight or tomorrow from his business trip. If his return is this evening, he'll be glad to put you up for the night if you explain you're a friend of mine."

Her final words were not a glowing statement of support, but they would have to do. He watched as she marched back to her cottage. She stopped once to turn and gaze at him as if questioning what she'd just offered. Then she turned back and disappeared into the cottage.

Within minutes he'd rowed the small boat close to shore and around the corner of the rock cliff within full view of the Pizzorno estate. Fifteen minutes later he'd guided the rowboat to Pizzorno's dock and tied it to a mooring. Looking along the shoreline back toward the city, he kept his eyes peeled for any vehicle approaching the estate. The Fiat left in the driveway was enticing, but he wouldn't let himself fall for that potential trap.

Scampering from the dock across the large lawn, he entered the mansion the same way he had exited the day before when fleeing the intruders. He climbed the tree to the second floor patio off the master bedroom. It was an easy climb on a wide tree. In less than a minute he was through the unlocked patio door and felt the warmth of the large home.

Now familiar with the layout of the house, he moved quickly to the guest room to replace the generally soaked clothes he'd borrowed from Pizzorno's extras. In the closet he replaced his clothing with slacks, a shirt and sweater, a sport coat and thick socks for added warmth. He had to be prepared. His continued escape across the country could ignite at any time.

Racing down the steps to the kitchen in the darkened home, he raided the icebox and began gorging himself on some fruit and leftover roast. Taking some long swigs of wine to wash down the cold food, he sighed. Though pleased with how far he'd come, every minute still seemed a challenge.

As if on cue, a feint sound could be heard of an approaching car. Swearing under his breath he placed the remaining food and wine back in the icebox and retreated up the stairs. What next? Maybe it was Pizzorno finally returning. Maybe Greta had contacted the local police. They were now coming to get him.

He cautiously peeked out a second floor window. There were no police vehicles. What he did see was the BMW. It had returned and four occupants got out and headed for the back kitchen door. He recognized the four individuals from Greta's photos. Pizzorno was not one of them. Ernst had been driving. The older couple followed him into the house. The other fellow was bringing in what appeared to be some weapons. It was that boyfriend of Sophia. He finally remembered the young man's name. It was Luis...and he looked adolescent compared to his older three accomplices.

Concealing himself behind the guest room door, Bailey heard the four burst into the kitchen talking loudly and irritably. Because of the echo in the empty home, he couldn't make out what was being said...only that they were highly agitated.

As they moved below him into the large library, he could finally make some sense of their conversation. The older male was the most vociferous. He ranted, "Where the hell could that American be? Ernst, with what you told me, everything was working while he was imprisoned in Milan; then he escapes and disappears. Then he comes back into our lives yesterday here in Lugano....and then...poof....he's gone again. How does he just vanish...especially when he's wanted all over southern Switzerland and northern Italy? Unless his brain is dead, by now he has to have figured he's been framed...and that Andre probably had something to do with the set up. It's been a day since he again disappeared. I'd be surprised if he wasn't still here in Lugano. And, if he's been able to sidestep the authorities this many days, he's probably watching this very house for when Andre finally comes home. Frankly, I don't want Dominique and me to get caught in the cross fire. I have to question whether we should go ahead with the next assassination attempt...not with that God damned American having Andre and possibly the rest of us in his aim. If I were him, I'd be seeking revenge."

Bailey then heard the woman, Dominique, exclaim, "Angelino, you might be right, but the American doesn't have the time or resources to go after Andre or any of us right now. He's on the run. His chances of making it out of Switzerland are small. Ernst has told us he has nothing...no passport....no money.....no weapon..... just the clothes on his back. How he made it to Lugano is beyond belief. He's tired and most likely weak and confused from his ordeal in Milan. He'll get caught. He should not be an obstacle to our mission on Wednesday."

The unmistakable voice of Ernst then echoed. The man's tone was more assertive than the weak, servile sycophant Bailey had talked with the previous day. "Angelino, we can't be bothered by the young man's disappearance. We have the schedule of Mussolini for this Wednesday evening. We will all be in Torino; he will certainly not follow us back into Italy. We'll deal with young Bailey after the assassination."

There was a pause and the pop of a wine bottle cork could be heard as the older man, Angelino, blurted out, "My friends, this is the best plan we've had so far. We still have our American patsy as long as he's not captured between now and Wednesday. All we need is Il Duce to remain on schedule and be at the armament factory as is his plan."

With the wine the atmosphere warmed somewhat with laughter and general good cheer. Bailey was not impressed with this group of so-called assassins. With the possible exception of the younger man named Luis, the other three sounded irresolute and weak. 'Maybe their strength was in their planning,' he thought, 'because it appeared their execution had been pathetic.

The echo of Ernst's voice could then be heard again. "Let's drink to our coming success. We've had some bad luck. That will end by Wednesday night. Andre is certain things will be in turmoil following Mussolini's death, but Italy will soon be better for the change. We pray a people's revolt will be spurred to end the reign of the Fascists."

There was a clicking of wine goblets and forced laughter followed by an uncomfortable silence. Bailey couldn't believe the group's lack of forethought. They were obsessed with Il Duce being eliminated. What happened from there was only the hope that things would get better for Italy. And, with their further expectation that an American named Adam Bailey would be their scapegoat, they were already celebrating how their deed would be free of consequences for them.

The female chimed in once again. "Well, gentlemen, we're set for Wednesday. I have a ticket on the 9:45 morning train to Torino. Mussolini's lieutenant is expecting to take me out that night after Mussolini's speech. There will be a convocation dinner. The lieutenant and I will be having drinks in Il Duce's suite with fifteen other dignitaries before going onto the banquet. I will make certain one of the windows is ajar before I leave. Luis has rented a room two floors below Mussolini's suite. From that room he can go out on the window ledge, use the fire escape stairs to climb up the two flights and enter Mussolini's suite through that unlocked window. Andre will have things set up with a pistol with silencer for Luis taped to the underside of the chest in Mussolini's suite. He will hide under that bed until Il Duce returns. If the paramour accompanies him, she will be shot as well. Once the task has been completed, he'll make his exit back through the window to the room two stories below. From there he'll depart the hotel. We have the fake evidence including train ticket stubs and the suitcase Adam Bailey brought over from America. Every detail of the crime will be conveniently pointed at the American while Luis will simply drive out of Milan and head toward Florence where Sophia will meet him."

There was general cheer shared among the four conspirators while Bailey remained motionless in the second level of the home. There appeared to be no way out at that moment. Whether captured by the authorities or by this group of killers, neither alternative looked healthy. His discomfort, though, was giving way to increasing rage. The assassins' complete lack of humanity towards him brought back the more prevailing dark thoughts he'd been carrying in his mind since breaking out of the Milan jailhouse. At that moment he considered taking the luger in his breast pocket and finish off the four people downstairs before they could take their next drink of wine. But, his better sense stopped him. He'd have no chance. He couldn't fire fast enough to take them all down. A gun battle would ensue in the large mansion. He had a silencer, but noise from their weapons would echo across the lake.

The laughter amongst the smug four assassins kept echoing throughout the house. Hearing the cocky merriment downstairs, he decided it was time to leave. He could not let himself be caught by these people. Moving quietly to the master suite patio door, he slipped through the unlocked door to the balcony. Shimmying down the tree as he'd done the day before, he now felt raindrops. He welcomed the inclement weather and cloud cover to camouflage his scurrying into the woods.

Sneaking along the side of the house, he stopped at the windows to the study where the four gloating collaborators were pouring more wine. It was odd seeing four people whose entire existence was aimed at murdering Benito Mussolini. They were about to initiate their shining moment in history; celebrating too early made no sense.

Bailey studied each person. As he had guessed, the female called Dominique was no Sophia. She was lanky with a slight stoop and likely twenty years older than either Luis or Sophia. With short shapeless hair, black glasses, and a face tight and severe as to appear paralyzed, she looked like she could cool molten lava with her icy stare.

The man named Angelino was almost as tall as the woman but with a large girth causing him to also stand with a slouch. His gray hair was waxed against his head and his constantly shifting eyes looked as if he expected to be surprised at any moment. Standing by the drink table was Luis holding a large cocktail and a cigarette lodged on one side of his mouth. His clothing looked tattered and his manner plebian. Except for his apparent ability to kill, he appeared to have nothing in common with the others in the study except their plan.

Then there was Ernst who was stunted compared to his compatriots. He looked no more an assassin than Calvin Coolidge looked presidential. But, he carried with him a confidence the others didn't have.

Over all, it was their manner that struck Bailey. There was no warmth in their eyes or any sense of friendship or loyalty. To him they all looked guilty of something heinous and ready to add to their list of crimes. Bailey felt fortunate he hadn't fallen into their hands.

Continuing around the house to the driveway, he stopped for a moment to let the air out of the rear tires of both the BMW and the Fiat...anything to cause them a delay. The coincidence of both cars having flat tires might make them nervous that he was onto them. It was a small prank to make them edgy and provided him some elemental satisfaction.

Retreating back through the woods towards Greta's cottage, the afternoon already looked as if darkness was looming with the overcast sky and it was only past 4:00. Hesitant about what he might find at the cottage, he slowed. If Greta Mendosa had called the local police, they might be waiting for his arrival. He figured he'd better approach the cottage with cautiousness.

Striding along the shoreline, he found himself just below the high perch along the cliff where he and the young lady photographer had sat earlier in the day conversing and appreciating the view. He chose not to return to the cottage just yet. He'd wait until it was darker. Then he could better see if Greta's uncle had returned home or the local police were surrounding the house. Eyeing the perch he also thought he might witness the Senore finally returning home.

Climbing up the uneven rock wall and walking cautiously along the precarious pathway to the perch, his mind was as muddled as the trail was muddy. He was somehow going to come face-to-face with Andre Pizzorno, but the man's compatriots staying at the house made his effort more difficult.

When he finally reached the small cliff where Greta and he had sat, he slumped to the ground with his back resting against a large stone. From his location he could see the light on in the study at the mansion and the figures of the four people moving around. They seemed to be enjoying their temporary life of luxury while waiting for the owner of the house to return. The only other person missing was Sophia. She seemed the least significant person amongst the group, so her absence seemed not to matter.

He sat there for a long time just glaring at the lights glimmering in the mansion. No cars approached the property. It was 4:30 on that cloudy and gloomy Sunday afternoon. Everything was so quiet. He swore he could hear the murmur of their voices resonating from the large house. From the opposite direction across the lake towards Ciani Park and the downtown area of Lugano, cars could be seen moving but no hum of traffic could be heard.

He kept wondering, 'Where was Pizzorno? What was keeping him?'

Finally, with the late afternoon getting darker and a chill in the air, he was ready to climb back down the cliff and hike his way through the woods to Greta's cottage. He hoped she'd kept her mouth shut and there'd be no local police to welcome him. He would take refuge in the small cabin overnight. Maybe she actually brought some food; there might even be a chance to have some pleasurable conversation with the young lady.

There was no libido in that thought...until that moment. Ever since survival became his hourly chore, he'd not had one sensual thought. But, things had slowed with his escape. It felt like he had a safe place to hide. She was attractive. He wondered if she was intrigued by him at all. With luck he hoped to find out yet that evening.

As he rose to finally leave his convenient lookout, he hadn't even taken a step forward when something powerful knocked him off his feet. It was so quick, even unnatural...as if God himself had picked Bailey up and threw him to the ground for having such philandering thoughts. Simultaneously, a huge flash lit the sky with an accompanying resounding explosion that left him planted to the ground.

Quickly twisting around to see what caused the bizarre occurrence, his mouth dropped open at the spectacle before his eyes. There was a ball of flame encompassing the entire Pizzorno house. The structure momentarily rose off its foundation before splitting apart in thousands of pieces...like a 4th of July fireworks display but with the realization it was much more horrific. That thunderous cloud of fire and smoke would remain etched in his skull forever.

Though the explosion happened fast, the entire spectacle seemed like slow motion as he witnessed every mille-second of the disaster. Upon blowing apart like an enormous grenade, in just those few seconds the entire structure simply did not exist anymore. Wood, mortar, and brick blasted into the sky as if shot from a cannon. Large pieces of the burning house landed well out onto the lake. The BMW was even launched in the air to land upside down on what was left of the unattached garage. The Fiat just disappeared in flames. Bizarrely, one of his many thoughts in those seconds was how taking the air out of the rear tires of both vehicles had been a complete waste of time.

Bailey tried to define his emotion. One was a prayer he'd never see anything so horrible and stunning again. Secondly, he couldn't understand how anyone could be so inhumane to carry out such a horror.

As he watched the conflagration, it wasn't until the pungent smoke from the blast gradually drifted under the cloud cover over to his location that he smelled the overpowering odor. It was then he finally considered the consequences of the explosion. Four people no longer existed. It no longer mattered if they were killers and flawed in any number of ways; their existence was no more. One moment they were holding a wine goblet and looking forward to their quest; a second later, the goblet, their minds and bodies and their plans had disintegrated. Just like that, there would be no attempt on Mussolini's life the coming Wednesday evening in Milan...at least not by Andre Pizzorno's team of killers.

Ten minutes later he was still sitting spellbound on the ledge of the cliff. In awe of the devastation and the crackling of the various fires blazing around the property, he finally heard the sirens approaching. From the city he followed the flashing lights of the parade of emergency vehicles speeding along the lake shore roadway. When they arrived, the firemen and emergency workers jumped out of their vehicles and began running toward the disaster to do what they were trained. Then they all seemed to just stop as if they didn't know how to proceed. There was just utter destruction. Small fires were not going to spread. Whatever was combustible was mostly completed. Nothing seemed salvageable including any people who'd been in the dwelling.

Bailey remained on that ledge for another hour oblivious to the light rain that had started to fall. He was transfixed on the emergency workers and firemen as they carefully tip-toed around the decimated property as if afraid they were going to step on something valuable...or worse yet...a body part. They of course had no idea yet that four people had been in the dwelling.

He imagined the investigators were concerned one of Lugano's richest and most prominent residents and owner of the estate, Andre Pizzorno, was one of the victims. There was nothing any of them could do, but hope he hadn't been home...or anyone for that matter. Not hearing from or seeing Pizzorno's steward, Ernst Lund, would also create great concern since he was typically at the house. Any living being would be unrecognizable; dental records would assist, but that might only identify Andre Pizzorno and Ernst Lund. If there were others at the house, they might never be identified.

Bailey shook his head contemplating the macabre thought that some of those workers already were sifting through the rubble for teeth. He presumed the initial talk of the tragedy would be an accidental gas explosion. However, the authorities would soon deduce the blast had been planned.

Shaking his head he thought back to the plunderers from the previous evening. The house hadn't been ransacked. They were there to set the timed explosives at various places around the base of the mansion. He wondered if they had any idea of the magnitude of those bombs they planted. How soon would they discover their probable main target was still alive? They would have the same question that had been troubling Bailey. Where was Andre Pizzorno?

And something else....there'd been surveillance on the Senore. The stakeout had to have been in operation for a couple weeks in order to have established some kind of routine. The timing had been set for when he'd typically been at his house. Pizzorno had picked a good time to not be entirely predictable, although his visitors had obviously followed the repetition of previous Sunday afternoon meetings.

Someone was out to destroy the entire group of assassins....and they'd almost done it. The planned bombing was done professionally and showed no mercy. Bailey's couldn't help but believe the LaCursos were somehow involved. Given the lack of success in eliminating Mussolini, there could easily have been a falling out.

Seeing this complete catastrophe in front of him, Bailey's mind was no longer jumbled. He was seeing how far a mobster would go to rid what was perceived to be a problem.

Everything he did from that minute forward had better be done with the idea of overcoming Willie and Roberto. The alternative...constantly looking over his shoulders...would be unacceptable. He'd take down the two brothers anyway possible. He had no other choice but to be the hunter while also being the hunted.

It occurred to him that Pizzorno was now in a similar situation. Once he found out his estate was in shambles and his compatriots all dead, his future would be dim. He could disappear or show his own assertiveness.

Making his way down the cliff, Bailey had his path somewhat lighted by the disaster. He cautiously retraced his steps made more difficult with his eyes constantly glancing sideways toward what was once a beautiful estate. How circumstances had changed. Just a short time before he was in the Pizzorno house ready to blow away the would-be assassins for their part in setting him up. Then... in the next minute...the job had been done for him.

Once in the woods back to Greta's lake home, the dark made it difficult to follow the path. Coming to a slight clearing, he could see the cottage. There were no lights on. He felt disappointment. Greta Mendosa had chosen not to return. It was understandable. Why get involved with his problems. At least there was no sign she'd contacted the authorities. He'd have a roof over his head for the night and some remaining food.

He strode cautiously to the back door. She'd left it open for him. Prematurely dark with the overcast and drizzle, Bailey walked through the house turning on no lights. He took care of his immediate needs lighting the gas stove and preparing some food from the icebox. Eating gave him no pleasure. He was only aware of nourishing his body to stay healthy.

When his repast was completed, he cleaned the kitchen leaving no trace that he'd been in the house. Plopping down on an easy chair in the small living room, sleep was coming surprisingly easy. Before he closed his eyes his thoughts bounced from the whereabouts of Pizzorno to the now only one other remaining member of the assassin team, the young lady named Sophia. She could well be huddled up in the mountain flat too scared to leave. Making a visit to her seemed like the next logical step to find Pizzorno, but not while the entire city was swarming with every law enforcement person available after the devastating explosion.

Bailey had a safe place to stay that night. He couldn't think of a reason to leave the safety of his small cocoon. In seconds he was fully asleep.

Hours later Bailey awoke with no idea where he was. With the black of night, he couldn't see across the room. For a moment he thought he was in the Milan jail cell. Then a branch scratched against a window and he was both relieved yet feeling the stress of what lay ahead of him. He got up quickly disturbed that he'd allowed himself to sleep so soundly.

Seeking the time, the small clock above the fireplace indicated half past midnight. He was still tired....and starved....like a bear waking up from hibernation. Again he invaded the ice box. There was little food remaining. Greta had definitely never returned with any additional supplies. Grabbing a roll of bread and the remainder of the wine, he strolled back to the living room and stared at the vast nothing through the trees out onto the lake. It was hard to imagine right around the corner and down the shoreline were pieces of house, furniture and body parts strewn over the land and water.

It was barely Monday, April 8. The previous week was one he'd never want to repeat. Death seemed to be surrounding him. It actually heartened him to be starting a new day, one that had to be better than the previous eight days.

Lying down on the sofa, he hoped by now there might be some anxiety brewing among the people who cared about him. David O'Brien would be the first person who might suspect something was wrong. This was the longest Bailey had been out of communication with the head of the European Division of the State Department. His habit from previous assignments was to send an innocent but coded telegram to O'Brien through the State Department's office at the American Embassy in Paris. Having received no such message, O'Brien might already have begun contacting a few sources to be on the lookout for his youngest agent. Then again he was used to Bailey working independently and this mission required that capability. Unfortunately, that understanding was now operating against Bailey.

Chapter 17

Andre Pizzorno was planning to spend a long weekend in Milan following his judgement to scratch Friday's assassination attempt against Il Duce. He had to repair some damage caused by his decision. It had not gone down well with his financiers...Willie and Roberto LaCurso. He had to ease Roberto whose temper was notorious. Then he had some other business to handle regarding the very next attempt on the Italian leader's life the following Wednesday in Torino.

He also was waiting for a call from Ernst Lund that Luis and Sophia had safely returned to Pizzorno's mountain villa near downtown Lugano. Luis had been highly agitated when the assassination had been called off. Pizzorno was worried his most emotional yet capable assassin would bolt the group leaving the Wednesday attempt in jeopardy.

The instrument of doom for yet the fifth attempt against Il Duce was news that the group's scapegoat, Adam Bailey, had escaped the Italian authorities that Friday morning right there in Milan. Pizzorno had assumed with the serious trumped up charges against Bailey, the military police would already have the young man under interrogation in Rome. It was the last time Pizzorno imagined he'd hear of the American again. No one survived the treatment by the Italians when they wanted information from someone. Since Bailey had no idea he had been set up as an assassination master mind, he would deny everything only exacerbating the poor treatment he'd already be receiving.

With Bailey's escape things were in turmoil. The American would have a good idea who was framing him. If recaptured he would be repeatedly excoriating the LaCursos to the Italian authorities. If Mussolini was attacked, it would be only a matter of time before Roberto and other family members would face their own interrogations.

Pizzorno's thoughts were not entirely benevolent toward the LaCursos. If Roberto went down, Pizzorno and his many businesses would follow. The Friday assassination attempt had to be postponed. With no attempt on Mussolini's life, once Bailey was recaptured....and that would certainly be very soon...Bailey's torrid words against a respected Italian family would likely and hopefully fall on deaf ears. If questioned, Roberto could scoff at the accusations by professing the American had a vendetta against the LaCurso family. The question would eventually become who were the Italian authorities more likely to believe.....a long standing high ranking member of an albeit, loyal but criminal family in Italy.... or a desperate, wild-eyed American angry that his business contacts in Italy had all forsaken him because of the Fascist government.

That was Pizzorno's immediate thoughts after hearing of Bailey's escape. By Saturday things had changed. He'd heard from Ernst that the American was in Lugano looking for help and unbelievably resting comfortably at Pizzorno's own home. He hadn't figured this American to be as tough and resolute as to actually make it out of Italy. However, with him now under Ernst's watchful eye, there was a chance to still use Bailey as a fall guy for the Wednesday attempt on Mussolini.

Saturday morning Pizzorno and Roberto had met. Pizzorno was surprised the Italian was not as inflamed as expected. Roberto didn't even seem worried about what Bailey might say to the authorities once inevitably recaptured. When the two men departed Pizzorno had the strong feeling that everything was all right between them and they could rise above yet another failure. Roberto had even given his blessing once again to the Wednesday attempt in Torino. Pizzorno had assured Roberto that following his team's strategy meeting Sunday afternoon at his home in Lugano, Wednesday's attempt would be the best laid out plan they'd ever formulated to take down Mussolini.

Roberto had only smiled patiently about the group going over the details Sunday afternoon. He knew it was Pizzorno's custom for the group to be together each Sunday, especially before traveling to the next assassination site.

What Pizzorno had not read in the emotionless conversation between the two of them was that Friday's failure had been the last straw for Roberto and Willie LaCurso. The two brothers finally resolved that their business partner from Switzerland was simply not competent and therefore a liability. If either of the two LaCursos had been in charge of killing Il Duce, the military leader would already be cold in his grave for months.

Also, of late, Roberto had become concerned that Pizzorno may have mentioned how the assassination team had the financial backing of the well-known LaCurso family in Italy. If any of the assassins were ever caught or chose to talk, Roberto was convinced the LaCurso family would witness a blood bath on their family name.

For those reasons Willie and Roberto agreed they needed to eliminate the entire assassination team...including Andre Pizzorno...to insure silence. It was Roberto who would take charge of this task and he planned on completing the job quickly and in one motion.

Aware of Pizzorno's meeting the past few months on those Sundays before each attack on Mussolini, he had only to secure the time when the group routinely were together at the Lugano lake mansion. Tricking Greta Vespucci into becoming Greta Mendosa and doing photographic surveillance on the property during the two previous Sundays, Roberto had a lock on the 4:00 Sunday time period. Ernst Lund, the young couple Luis Macarti and Sophia Bochi, the two experienced killers who went by their first names only, Dominique and Angelino, and finally Andre Pizzorno himself would all be taken out Sunday afternoon, April 7, by three hitmen prominent in the use of explosives. They would set a series of time bombs the night before in the stealth of darkness.

Those explosive experts were already on their way to Lugano when Pizzorno met with Roberto Saturday morning. They were instructed to place enough self-made bombs around the mansion to destroy everything on the estate.

That one act of butchery would end the LaCurso brothers' concerns about being named in any assassination conspiracy. Furthermore, following the mass murder, Roberto had already covered his tracks with the paid-killers. They had no idea of their employer...only that they had half their money in their pocket while planning and actually placing the explosives. The second half payment would be released to a private Swiss bank account made available to the killers when the killings were completed. That was the way a contract kill should be negotiated. To Roberto he was only angry at himself for not having taken charge of the Il Duce assassination from the beginning. He had no idea his Swiss partner, so successful in business, would fail so miserably in the game of life and death.

That Saturday afternoon after Ernst's call about Adam Bailey seeking help to get to free-France, Andre Pizzorno called Roberto LaCurso with the good news. The Italian seemed pleased but still strangely quiet and almost distant. His mild response was unusual. "Yes, Andre, that is good to hear. By the grace of God we can only hope young Mr. Bailey will not get apprehended and have the chance to spread ill-will about the LaCurso family name or your name with the Italian authorities."

Pizzorno made another attempt, which had become almost ritual, to reassure Roberto that the Wednesday plot against Mussolini had a high success probability. But, younger LaCurso brother had his mind elsewhere. What Pizzorno of course didn't know was that Roberto was more concerned that the hitmen he'd hired were already in Lugano and only hours away from setting the explosives on Pizzorno's property that evening.

He mumbled, "Andre...of course we don't know whether this American has incriminated us or not. The fact that both of us have not been visited by the military police does indicate Bailey has not mentioned our names to the military police in Milan. But, let there be no doubt...by now he's figured we've framed him. He's running free and a danger to us. I don't give a damn about making him a scapegoat anymore. We need to silence him immediately. Now that you have him literally at your house, might I suggest something? Andre, do you think you or one of your people could possibly complete the minor task of putting a bullet in his head as he sits in your dining room eating your food or while he's sleeping in your guest room?"

The sarcasm didn't get by the Senore. He ignored it saying, "Roberto, it would be a waste. We will leave plenty of false evidence that will point to him as the lone assassin after Wednesday's success. We have people we know at the Geneva crossing into France. We can arrange for him to be shot before he's even arrested."

There was silence at the other end of the phone. Roberto sighed realizing Pizzorno was just not made out of the same stuff as members of the LaCurso blood line. He should have never agreed with Willie and Pizzorno to make Bailey the scapegoat. It all sounded so easy back then; now the American was a major concern. No one had perceived the young man as having the grit and resourcefulness that allowed him to escape and make it all the way across the border to Lugano. But, he'd done it. His motivation to escape had been fueled by certainly an obsession to retaliate against those who framed him.

When Roberto finally responded, his voice was almost a groan. His hitmen would not be called off. The sooner they placed the explosives at the Pizzorno estate the better.

Like his brother, Roberto was at his best when he was saying the opposite of what he was truly thinking. "Sure....Andre.... you go ahead with your plans and your meeting with your group on Sunday afternoon. You'll need everything to go right for this final assassination plan. And, if you want to place the responsibility on the American, you have my support. Let's make this attempt work. Death to fascism!"

Pizzorno was greatly uplifted by Roberto's final words. The Italian seemed to finally appreciate the Wednesday assassination attempt was going to succeed. The spark in the Italian's voice gave Pizzorno the feeling that the call could be ended in a more upbeat manner. He said, "Roberto, this should be it. I can feel it. Luis has the heart and courage of a lion. He'll take care of Il Duce. The authorities will take care of Bailey."

Roberto only shook his head at the other end of the telephone line, but still equivocated by saying, "That is my belief as well, my friend. Take charge in the meeting at your home tomorrow afternoon and we'll share a special bottle of wine when the deed is done."

The phone line then went dead. Roberto just stared at the phone knowing it would be the last time he'd be talking to his Swiss business partner. The would-be assassins would all be dead, their mouths permanently closed. Roberto would take over and get the job done. He'd deal with the threat of Adam Bailey as well.

Then he smiled. While admiring the young man's efforts so far, they were all bravado; Bailey's luck was about to run out. He could only hope Pizzorno might order Bailey to be shot even before the bombing of the estate since the American was staying right there at Pizzorno's house. But, it had to be done before the next afternoon when Pizzorno and his bumbling team of killers would be wiped out in a single explosion. Otherwise, if Bailey had left the mansion to continue his escape, Roberto would have to assign other hitmen to hunt down Bailey and shoot him on sight. The young man simply could not be allowed to be re-captured.

Andre Pizzorno stayed in Milan that Saturday night with the confidence that Adam Bailey would not leave his house. According to Ernst, young Bailey appeared to have the utmost hope and assurance he'd be helped once Pizzorno returned. He would likely follow any direction given him...even to lay low until he could secretly be transported to Geneva. By the coming Thursday, the day after the anticipated assassination, Pizzorno could get a fake I.D., a train ticket to Geneva, and an unintended promise to Bailey that he'd be in France by the following Friday evening. Instead, the young man would be dead by then. That would be assured once Pizzorno anonymously called the Geneva police and informing them the ruthless assassin, Adam Bailey, would be on that train. If Bailey was arrested instead of killed outright, a couple policemen owing a debt to Pizzorno would make certain Bailey would die before he made it to the city jail in Geneva.

Pizzorno had to remain in Milan anyway until Sunday. There was some other business regarding the Wednesday assassination plot he had to finalize. In the past few weeks, he'd been fretting about his visibility as the leader of the assassination team. If captured by the authorities there was no telling what any of his team might say. They'd become frustrated with the many failed attempts. Recently he detected at times they'd showed some aversion toward him. They'd been together over six months with five failed attempts on Mussolini's life. His concern for their escape mechanism after doing the assassination was appreciated by each of his team. His care didn't ensure loyalty. None of them would stand for being a martyr and be executed alone. They'd take the entire team down with them.

For that reason he'd unilaterally and privately laid an additional piece to the over-all assassination plan. A sacrifice would have to be made. The primary members of the team involved in the upcoming Wednesday plan...Dominique, Angelino, and Luis were to be summarily eliminated by another killer Pizzorno had hired. The innocent one, Sophia, would be spared since she had little to do with any of the previous plans. That could change if she ever threatened to talk. The other team member, Ernst Lund, had unquestionable loyalty toward the Senore. He would be in no danger.

The gunman had instructions only to kill the three if Il Duce was finally shot and pronounced dead. The added details to the plan still had to be discussed. Pizzorno was to meet his Swiss National contact Sunday morning before taking the Sunday noon train back to Lugano to meet with his assassination team later that afternoon.

Pizzorno was agitated when he awoke Sunday morning. He'd eaten and drunk too much the night before. There were a lot of particulars that had to happen in the days ahead; he was having difficulty remaining calm. With only intermittent sleep, he finally found his deepest slumber as dawn approached. He was groggy when the telephone in his Milan hotel suite rang at 8:00.

Stubbing his toe while rushing over to the credenza to pick up the receiver, things got a lot worse. It was Ernst.... a far different Ernst compared to the day before.

Ernst was mortified as he yelped into the phone line, "Senore, the American is gone. I can't believe it. I left the house yesterday to call you. You advised not to return until you made it back to Lugano. I had no concerns. The lad looked exhausted enough to sleep for two days. I stayed away from the house as you ordered, but I had Angelino and Dominique go over to the house this morning with more food and to check on the American. They looked all over. He was nowhere to be seen. They said it didn't even look like he'd slept in the guest room. The food I'd prepared was only half-eaten. That made no sense for a man who was starved."

Pizzorno could see his next assassination plan gradually slipping away for the sixth time. Adam Bailey was on the run...either heading for France or still in Lugano looking for retribution. What did the American know....that was the question? He had to figure the LaCurso brothers had framed him. But, did he know Pizzorno was part of that conspiracy? If so, the young man could remain in Lugano to settle his score with him. Would he then go after Roberto LaCurso? If the American was adept enough to dodge the Italian and Swiss military police in escaping Milan and crossing the border to Lugano, all of that was possible.

Pizzorno was enraged. This next attempt on the Italian leader's life could not be halted. His team had to go through with the plan. Fuming, he spoke as calmly as he could to his steward. "Ernst, with or without Bailey as our fall-guy, we will continue with our plans for a hit on Mussolini this Wednesday. I expect Luis, Dominique, Sophia, Angelino and you to be ready for our final meeting to work out the details this afternoon. I should be back in Lugano by 4:00. If I'm delayed, have our group stay the night at the house as they have in the past. We can then meet Monday morning. Adam Bailey's disappearance might still work in our favor if he can remain hidden and on the run until our Wednesday deed is done. We'll have time to create the evidence that will be found to assure his guilt."

Ernst meekly responded, "Yes sir...yes sir...we will be at your disposal this afternoon, this evening, or tomorrow morning for whenever you arrive home."

The steward tried to apologize once again to his boss for Bailey being missing, but the phone line had already gone dead.

Pizzorno filled his goblet again with his favorite burgundy and slumped into a chair in his Milan hotel suite. He thought again how he wished he'd never joined the LaCursos. Killing Benito Mussolini had seemed so logical given their mutual hatred for the Italian leader. The alliance had started out so positively, since they'd already had proof of their loyalty through their business ties. But, their partnership in crime taking Il Duce down had depreciated their friendship. He could sense it. Wednesday's plot had to work; it would repair his damaged relationship with the LaCursos.

Pizzorno had gone back to sleep after the discouraging call from Ernst while trying with difficulty to erase from his mind the many ways Bailey could be a problem in the days ahead. When the telephone rang again later that Sunday morning, he would learn his 11:00 meeting with his hired gunman had to be delayed until Sunday evening. The man would not arrive in Milan until 6:00. Only then could the two of them detail when and where the slayings of Dominique, Angelino, and Luis would occur as soon after the Torino assassination as possible. Pizzorno would have to take the later Sunday night train to Lugano. The Sunday afternoon meeting at his estate would simply have to be postponed until Monday morning. The inconvenience was not a problem. None of them would mind staying the night at his plush mansion.

That Sunday evening following his meeting with his hired gun, Pizzorno returned to his hotel room to find an urgent message. It said, 'Call Sophia...an emergency...telephone the villa!'

Pizzorno couldn't imagine why the youngest and least important member of his assassination team would be calling him. She was supposed to be at his home with the rest of the group. What possibly could have happened causing her to be spending Sunday evening at his mountain flat in Lugano? Maybe she was having a love spat with her boyfriend, Luis.

Not expecting anything dramatic, he poured a generous amount of brandy into a large goblet before sitting down in his hotel suite to return her call. He would find nothing good from the moment she picked up the receiver.

Her voice was hushed as she choked out, "Senore Pizzorno...is that really you? Please tell me I have the right person. This is Sophia."

He was annoyed, but he spoke patiently. "Sophia, why are you calling me from the villa?"

His alarm began to rise as she tried to speak and failed. She was overcome with emotion. His voice rose with more impatience and exasperation. "Sophia... speak...for the love of God. What is wrong?"

Her tone was almost inaudible as she wept, "Senore, they are all gone...
Angelino.....Dominique....Luis....Ernst...your house...........all gone!"

Her voice was but a choked whisper. "Your entire home was blown up a few
hours ago....and they were all in it. One minute they were with us; the next they
no longer existed."

Obviously in shock, she regained her breath and gasped, "They had arrived
early for the 4:00 meeting at your home. I was going to come later with more
food and drink if your schedule changed. When I got the call that you would
be delayed and we would all be staying at your home for the night, I took my
time. I was just leaving the villa when what felt like a small earthquake shook
the ground. I ran to the tram stop where I could see most of the lake and looked
in the direction of your estate."

She was unable to continue and Pizzorno was no longer impatient. He just sat
numbed by what he was hearing. She would recover and continue soon enough.

When her voice came back, she was almost inaudible. "Senore.....do you
hear me? They were all there....Ernst...Angelino...Dominique...and my Luis. The
house simply blew apart...our friends...they blew up in pieces. They are all gone!"

Her voice weakened to the point she could talk no longer. Pizzorno sat there
on the leather chair of his Milan hotel suite with his head down. He'd not even
taken a sip of his brandy. He'd never considered any of the dead as friends, except
for possibly his manservant Ernst. That was a relationship bred by longevity and
having a common cause.

His own thoughts were so puzzling and flawed. He felt despair yet he
couldn't understand why he was so stunned and broken up. He'd just authorized
three of them to be shot the coming Wednesday after carrying out the Il Duce
murder. Angelino, Dominique, and Luis were supposed to live until that day,
not taken away so violently four days before by some unknown explosive experts.
They were owed at least the courtesy of the extra four days for completing the
mission. Now that sixth assassination attempt had failed...just like the previous
ones...only for an entirely different reason. He had no one to carry out the
assignment.

Pizzorno grabbed the goblet of brandy and downed three healthy swallows
before coughing and fighting to gain his breath. The reality of the bombing
finally hit him. It was premeditated. The explosion had been set to go off during
his group's regular Sunday meeting at his estate. He was supposed to be part of
the rubble. It was only by chance he was delayed...waiting for his hired gunman
contracted to kill Angelino, Dominique and Luis on Wednesday to meet him
in a few hours.

For a brief moment he thought of calling the hired gun to inform him
the assignment was cancelled as the intended targets were already dead. But,
a wave of futility covered him. Contacting the hitman neither mattered nor
did he care. All the work he'd done to find the people, develop a trust in them,

involve them in the many plans to kill the Italian leader, and make them proud their actions would effect a new future for Italy....all that had been a waste of time with one well-timed explosion.

Hearing the still sobbing Sophia on the line, he took another swig of brandy and collected himself. Someone was pursuing him...someone who knew what his group was planning on doing. He had to think and remain calm.

It then dawned on him; he had one advantage. It would be assumed he was part of the debris. He was being given a chance...as if a ghost...to remain 'dead', yet being among the living. He would have the relative freedom to pursue incognito whoever was after him, discover why and generate his own revenge. The pure horror of the incident, though, indicated his pursuers were ruthless and heartless. He wondered if he had the fortitude for payback.

Maintaining his composure, he stated firmly to Sophia still sobbing on the telephone line, "My dear, you need to stay in the villa until I get to Lugano. I'll be there as soon as I can. I'll take the late train tonight or sometime tomorrow night so I'll have less chance of being recognized. It's best if the killers think I'm dead."

Then less confidently, he wheezed, "I need time to think. Don't worry. I will help you get out of this trouble. You have been loyal. You can depend on me."

The voice on the other end of the line sounded like a wounded mouse. "All right, Senore, I'll do what you say. Please don't make me wait too long."

Then she added the oddest thing. "Senore, I guess this means we will not be going ahead with our plans."

Pizzorno looked at his receiver as if the words he heard were coming from a child. Sophia was unstable and now just babbling. He had to get to Lugano quickly and decide if he could allow her to live. There was no telling what she might say or do.

Again he spoke softly. "Sophia, listen to me. Stay calm. I will see you during the wee hours of the night. Yes, our plans are cancelled for now. You have nothing to worry about because we have done nothing that warrants arrest. So, drink some wine. Try to sleep. I'll see you no later than late Monday night."

There was no response. The line simply went dead.

Then he realized he'd just said something brainless. Something big had happened. There was plenty to be worried about. When would those people who set the explosives learn they had eliminated only four of the six on Pizzorno's team? He didn't know where to start in finding who was responsible.

He sat for the next few hours ordering more brandy from the downstairs desk clerk and remaining in his suite staring at the walls. His fear had gradually turned to furor. He'd been spied upon. He was likely the key target of the blast. That realization trumped anything else floating in his mind.

It took well into the second bottle of brandy before he could relax enough to contemplate who his attackers might be. The coincidence of Adam Bailey being at large and in Lugano loomed large if the young man had reasoned Pizzorno was behind the Milan arrest. But, it was improbable. Bailey was just trying to survive and escape to France. He didn't have the contacts or the means to carry out such a devastating plan. It was more apt to be somebody who'd studied the group's habits and then had the know-how to rig a closely calculated bombing device to detonate at a specific time.

Roberto LaCurso's name came to mind but Pizzorno found that possibility unlikely. The head of his Italian family had shown no dislike to him...even admitting months before his preference for not being directly involved in the conspiracy to kill Mussolini. The two of them had talked Saturday after the cancelled attempt against Il Duce the afternoon before. He'd expected Roberto to be irate. Instead, the man seemed to accept the reasoning....even resigned that it was but more bad luck that had thwarted their effort. When Pizzorno had spoken assuredly of the coming Wednesday's attempt, Roberto had exhibited great patience. His voice was not that of someone planning to eliminate the entire assassination team.

Then his mind rested on Willie LaCurso. He'd only met the U.S. mobster once. The man was intense and laughed as if the very act was painful. But, the American mobster had been impressed enough with the relationship Roberto had with Pizzorno to invest an exorbitant cash outlay into wiping out Benito Mussolini. However, with all the misfortune and continued failures, financing the efforts had to have become burdensome. As a prominent American gangster, Willie could well have reached the end of the line and wanted no witnesses making accusations against the LaCurso family.

Firing an assassination team would not be easy. Disillusioned assassins could act on their own displeasure for being sacked. Whether blackmailing the LaCurso family or secretly communicating with the Italian authorities, the LaCurso name could be endangered. Willie could easily have acted alone gone around his brother and hire a couple explosive experts to destroy Pizzorno and his entire assemblage in one giant blast, thereby ending any threat of some disheartened assassins blurting out anything to the authorities.

That was the final thought Pizzorno's inebriated mind carried as he passed out that Sunday night in his Milan hotel suite. He would awake at dawn glad that he hadn't caught the late train to Lugano. Despite a headache he was sharp enough to remember he'd survived a bombing attack on his house. He would be thought dead; now his anonymity was his advantage. He wanted no one to know he was still alive. Still he was tempted to call Roberto for advice on how he should go forward.

Deciding not to trust anyone, he waited until dusk that Monday before entering the Milan train station. Pulling his hat low over his forehead, he caught the 8:08 scheduled to arrive in Lugano after midnight. There was a scheduled stop at the Swiss-Italian border. He would have a compartment all to himself.

Most importantly, he would utilize one of his own alternate passports so as to have an even better chance not to be recognized by anyone.

As the train pulled out of the station, Pizzorno's head was aching and his eyes were tired and dry from little sleep. He opened the latest addition of the Milan newspaper while the train gained speed. The sketchy article about the bomb blast at his estate was on the front page but had little detail. It read:

Lugano Bomb Kills Businessman/Others

"The home of local businessman Andre Pizzorno was totally destroyed by a large blast Sunday afternoon. Identification has not been secured, but so far three bodies have been found in the rubble. The owner of the magnificent mansion is feared dead. A gas leak is being blamed for the catastrophe.

It was odd to read about his own death in the national newspaper. Pizzorno showed no emotion as he rolled up the newspaper and let it fall to the floor. He gazed at the periodic lights of homes in what looked like the peaceful piedmont and flowing fields of the northern Italian wishing his life could be that simple once again.

Chapter 18

Adam Bailey laid low the rest of that Sunday night and Monday in the aftermath of the disastrous explosion at the Pizzorno estate. Relative safety was found in the cottage owned by the uncle of Greta Mendosa.... if indeed that was her actual name. She had said she would return after leaving him Sunday afternoon, but had chosen to stay away. He could hardly blame her. At least she'd kept her word and not contacted the authorities. He'd be in a jail cell at that very moment if she had.

Now after the horrible disaster, he was guessing she had to have major doubts about him. In her mind he could easily have been the culprit who placed the explosives around the mansion. It was upsetting for Bailey to think someone might believe him capable of such a ghastly deed.

Throughout that night and into the early overcast Monday morning, he'd kept the lights off so no one investigating the area near the bombing site might stop by the small cottage. He was jumpy and only slept in short periods. Any sound outside...a squirrel jumping from branch to branch or an intermittent breeze causing the crackling of brushwood and twigs caused him to hold his breath and instinctively reach for his revolver.

In no hurry to display his face in public during the day, instead he took one more hike up the trail to Greta's photographic perch and peer down on the ravaged Pizzorno estate. He knew whatever challenges he faced would seem miniscule after taking in a few minutes of the unsightly scene.

Knowing the path and more confident climbing up the sheer cliff brought him a stunning mid-day view of the destruction. Civil servants were like ants crawling over the debris. Heavy equipment had been brought in for clean-up. His interest to remain waned after just ten minutes.

Walking back to Greta's cottage, the skies opened up with heavy rain. If ever his escape seemed hopeless, it was that morning.

Trudging against the rain he came to the small meadow that marked a clearing to the small cottage, he abruptly stopped. He ducked down behind a nearby tree as a small Ferrari came driving slowly into the driveway with windshield wipers on full speed. If not for the rain, the driver might have seen him.

He watched as the driver stepped from the car and waddled toward his front door. He was a large man and carrying a suitcase in hand as if he was returning from a trip. Fighting to find the right key, he finally opened the front door and rushed in closing the door with a bang. Bailey guessed the man had to be Greta's uncle. With the cloudiness and cover of the trees, the owner of the cottage began turning on some lights. He seemed familiar with the place as he lit the stove and put a kettle on the burner.

With the downpour, Bailey now had another predicament. He was drenched and getting chilled. Hypothermia could be a concern. He had to find shelter and get some dry clothing. Eyeing the Ferrari he now had a way of getting into town. The man would have identification, some money and dry clothing. Mendosa looked stouter than Bailey, but style and fit were not high priorities at that moment. Raiding the house was his only wise choice.

Feeling the luger in his pocket, he hoped harming the man wouldn't be necessary. As he snuck up to the window of the living room, he saw Mendosa reading his newspaper. Then he got up, poured himself some tea, and returned to his warm chair. Bailey was about to blow through the kitchen door when he noticed the man taking off his reading glasses; the newspaper was lowered to his chest. He seemed on the verge of falling asleep.

Bailey remained patient, but his body was shaking from his severe chill. At the kitchen door he looked through the window and saw the man's head slumped down. His prayer had been answered.

As he quietly opened the kitchen door, he could hear the snores from the living room. Tip-toeing over to the man's coat hanging over a chair, Bailey rustled through the pockets. He pulled out every item to consider its possible value. Within a minute he had the man's wallet, car keys, and passport. Making out the print on the Swiss driver's license, he found the man's name to be Gephardt Mendosa. The address indicated he was the owner of the cottage.

Bailey noticed on the identification that the man was thirty-eight years old, rather young to be Greta's uncle, but not impossible. He certainly didn't seem too concerned with the whereabouts of his niece.

In Mendosa's other coat pocket was some loose cash in Swiss francs and German marks. The passport indicated he'd been in Germany the past two weeks. For a moment Bailey considered using the vehicle for the journey through the Swiss Alps to the Swiss-French border, but promptly shot down that idea. Once Mendosa realized his car had been stolen, the authorities would have an alert out for the missing car. He wouldn't make it up the road to Lucerne much less to Geneva. He stuck with his first thought to only use the car to get into town making it a minor stolen car incident.

With Mendosa continuing to snore in the background, Bailey pilfered some dry clothes from the man's closet. The clothing was baggy but functional. Exiting silently out the back door, the rain was still falling hard. It would muffle much of the sound of the car being started up. Still the noise from the ignition was loud enough to wake the dead. He expected the semi-conscious Mendosa to come running out of the house at any moment.

Luck was on his side. Mendosa's exhaustion was Bailey's good fortune. He slowly made his way out the circle driveway and onto the mountain road. Making his way carefully along the serpentine road, he was aware he'd have to drive by the smoldering remains of the Pizzorno mansion. Rounding the next corner, there it was...the smoking cinders and the sickening sight of the debris being plowed together by a road grater. The thought of the four people's remains being part of the rubble made his stomach turn.

He was about to turn onto the lakeside roadway when a guard suddenly appeared with a machine gun in one hand and a stop sign in the other. For both reasons, Bailey chose to stop.

Coming up to the window, the guard inquired in Italian, "Where are you going, Senore?"

Bailey showed the guard Mendosa's driving permit while keeping his head shaking back and forth and his face lowered as if not wanting to see the wreckage. He murmured, "I live up the road. I'm a neighbor. I just got back from traveling. I'm going into town to eat. I have very little food in my ice box. Could I move on? What has happened here is difficult for me to see."

The guard saw the neighbor was repulsed by the scene. He gave the license a cursory look and motioned for Bailey to drive on.

As he slowly maneuvered the Ferrari onto the paved road into town, he was able to see the complete destruction of the estate. Whoever planted the bomb under or around the house knew what they were doing. Workers had stacked barely salvageable pieces of furniture, bathtubs and sinks alongside the edge of the property. Truly there weren't many other things that could be recognized.

Driving into town, he thought more about the attractive Greta Mendosa. There had to be more to her story. There was no suitcase with her belongings in the cottage. She was using the cottage, but staying elsewhere...possibly in town where there was more activity. But, there was no question she'd come to the cottage often given her huge number of photographs. So many pictures had been taken from the cliff overhang. She claimed to be testing her new long lens; it didn't take much imagination to believe she was taking surveillance shots as well. Adding to the puzzle was her virtual disappearance just hours before the bombing. The oddity was that she could have played a role in the bombing just as she could believe the same thing about him. He wondered what their responses would be to one another if they ran into each other again.

Approaching the city with Ciani Park on his left, he headed for the train terminal. Once at the station he would use Mendosa's identification and Swiss francs to buy a ticket to Geneva. It sounded too easy...and it was.

Passing the Lugano train station, the numbers of military police were staggering. The previous evening's bombing had brought out everyone who wore a badge. His chances of making it through that quagmire of military and local police looked improbable. He had no chance passing himself off as Gephardt Mendosa. An alternative plan had to be considered.

That was when he thought of the tram station a few blocks away...the same one he'd taken up the mountain when he'd followed Sophia and Luis months before. He knew that Pizzorno's villa was on Monte San Salvatore but he couldn't recall the stop on the incline. That led to some further logic. For whatever reason, the girl, Sophia, had not been in the house when it blew up. Why she wasn't there didn't matter. It had saved her life. Now, in all likelihood she could well be at the mountain villa wondering what to do next with her compatriots all dead. There was also the chance Andre Pizzorno might be using his own mountain flat for the same reason. Under these macabre conditions, there might be an opportunity to actually meet the Senore.

Parking the stolen car a few blocks away from the tram station, he left the keys in the ignition to further make it look like a local crime. At the tram ticket counter he asked the ticket agent for a round trip ticket to the observation deck at the top of the mountain. Along the way he had to recognize where to exit to find the Pizzorno villa.

Waiting for the tram to begin its incline, Bailey remained in the shadows of the boarding platform. When the bell sounded, he boarded the tram. As it crawled up the tracks, it moved within yards of homes built surprisingly close to the rails. He hunched down pretending to sleep but staring closely at each street as the tram stopped and then continued on.

Finally he heard the tram operator call out 'Strausser Street' in a muffled tone and something clicked in Bailey's head. It was a roll of the dice, but he sensed the next stop was it. Pizzorno's mountain villa would be just down the one-lane street. It would not take long to find out.

Pulling the rope to ring the bell for Strausser Street, the tram stopped only long enough for Bailey to get two feet on the ground. Then it shot forward up the mountain as if that stop was an inconvenience.

Once the last rail car was out of sight, the atmosphere became noiseless as death. The small area of villas was like a tomb. He cautiously walked away from the tracks; each step echoed in the stillness. With the late Monday afternoon sun doused by the heavy cloud cover and wisps of fog floating above the roofs, occasional street lamps provided only some light. He strolled slowly along the one lane street trying to recall his last visit when he'd followed Luis and Sophia. They were hiding out in a villa on his right. At 'Number 3 Strausser' he saw movement and stopped at a bench pretending to tie his shoe.

Looking peripherally into the bungalow he saw a person...a woman....sitting on a sofa in a robe with her legs stretched out on an ataman. She was combing her long locks. From that short distance, he became convinced he'd found Sophia. Now he only had to discover if Pizzorno was also at the villa. Cautiously moving toward the front door, he looked around making certain he wasn't being watched by neighbors.

At the front door entrance it was dark and through the small glass window he followed her as she'd moved to the kitchen, poured herself some coffee, and returned to her chair in the small living room. He wasn't getting a full view other than she was definitely eye catching. Finally seeing her face, he decided she had to be Sophia. Her actions also gave a hint. Trying to read a magazine, she got up again and began pacing. She seemed unnerved an understandable emotion with the loss of her boyfriend. It was entirely possible she was both unstable and in shock.

Seeing she was alone, Bailey knew he had to make a move or risk being seen. Hearing some Tommy Dorsey music on her radio, he made a quick decision. Knocking on the door, he whispered urgently, "Sophia....Sophia....open the door!"

He saw her rush to the door. Hearing her name she didn't bother to look. It had to be someone who knew she was there. She whispered loudly in return, "Is that you, Andre?"

His only response was a muffled, "Yes....yes....open up!"

Unbelievably the door was unlocked and Bailey slipped through the opening pushing her back against the wall before she could utter a sound. He hurriedly placed his hand over her mouth and stuck his revolver with silencer under her chin. If she had any inclination to scream, she held it in check knowing full well the probable consequence. In the mild scuffle her robe had come open. Bailey was actually relieved she was wearing undergarments. He didn't want to lose his focus; gaining control was his only purpose.

In his coldest voice he spoke sharply into her ear. "I am not here to hurt you. Settle down or I will."

He felt her body surrender. He wondered if she'd already fainted. In a steady voice, he told her exactly what was going to happen. "Sophia....we're going to turn out the lights and pull the drapes. Then we're going to talk. Nod your head if you understand."

Her eyes were saucers, but she nodded.

Holding the gun to her neck they moved together and completed the task until only a small lamp lit up the living room. He then pushed her down on the sofa. Her body was rigid with fear. For a moment he felt sorry for her....first, the loss of her boyfriend...then the rest of her colleagues...and now to be attacked in her only safe haven by someone knowing her name. Her life had to be in a complete mess.

Bailey calmed his voice. "Sophia, I will take my hand away from your mouth and the gun away from your neck providing you stay quiet. If you make one peep, I will kill you. If you stay silent, you won't be hurt. Please don't doubt me. Do you understand me?

There was another nod and a hoarse whisper. "I understand. I won't move."

There was silence in that room as he took his revolver away from her throat and sat on the ataman in front of her. Her robe remained open. She showed complete unawareness. Preserving some sense of modesty had no importance.

As Bailey stared at her, whatever sympathy he'd momentarily had was gone. She'd been part of a conspiracy that would have left him to be tortured and likely dead in an Italian prison. He spoke loathingly to her. "You can pull the robe over your legs if you're getting cold. I have no interest in you."

She snapped back to reality and hastily covered herself. Her eyes gave her away. Not only did she not know who her assailant was, but it was a rare male who showed no interest in her physically.

He had no reason to keep her in suspense. Still aiming the gun at her, he bluntly announced, "I'm Adam Bailey. Does that name mean something to you?"

Her eyes got bigger. She was scared before; now she showed abject fear. He doubted he'd ever seen a person look at him with such absolute trepidation. She held her arms close to her body and actually began to shake as if awaiting her last second of life.

Bailey still had no compassion. His words came out biting and echoing the malevolent look in his eyes. "Why are you here? Why aren't you with your friends? You should be dead."

She didn't know how to respond as if it didn't matter if she was blown to bits the day before...or now. Returning the barrel of the revolver to her forehead, he showed no patience. "Start talking, Miss. I need to hear the right things or your body will not move from that chair alive."

He needed to say no more. "Senore Bailey, please don't shoot," she begged. "I am only part of Andre's group because of my boyfriend, Luis. My job was to keep this flat clean and ready to house my friends after we finished our task.

Gritting his teeth, he exclaimed, "And that task was to kill Mussolini...is that right?"

She nodded. "But, we have had many slipups, so Luis and I have been staying here for many months as each attempt is planned out...and then called off for whatever reason. We failed again last Friday. We had one more opportunity this Wednesday in Milan. We were to meet at Andre's big house and detail our strike. And then...." Her eyes got big again...this time with hatred.

She scoffed while sobbing into her hands, "It was you. You set the bombs. You killed Luis....and the others. You are the murderer!"

Bailey only shook his head and let the young lady cry. She was obviously still bewildered and grief-stricken over the deaths of her acquaintances. Offering her solace was the last thing on his mind. What was chilling was her sudden reaction against him....and she was part of a group of assassins bent on killing a major political and military leader in Italy. Her emotional outburst made little sense.

He let her think what she wanted. He didn't care.

Then he sighed, "So...what about me. Why was I chosen to be the fall-guy for the assassination?"

She didn't hesitate responding as she fiercely hissed, "You were only being used because it was convenient. Your previous travels around Italy and you being an American made you the perfect........"

".......patsy," he said simmering in his own anger.

Her hesitation showed his word was accurate. She gasped, "But, we didn't think of you as naïve...just someone who could help us. You were to be used as a decoy killer until we could find our way out of Italy after assassinating Mussolini. Angelino and Dominique would be bound for Norway; Luis and I would eventually get there via ship. As for you, we figured your innocence would soon be obvious to the authorities."

Bailey knew better. She was not completely unbalanced if she was attempting to soften his hatred towards her. He shot her another question. "So...who has been providing your group financial support besides Andre Pizzorno?"

Sophia seemed to relax slightly until he put his glaring eyes two inches from hers and pressed the gun firmly against her head.

Her eyes teared knowing she was giving out crucial information Luis had confidentially told her. "There are two brothers. I don't know them. Andre speaks of them generally as a leader of a family in Milan....and a brother from the U.S."

She didn't need to say more. He had his confirmation. It wasn't necessary to force her to say the name. It was just so ugly hearing verification of his ignorance and how it had been used against him. Willie and Roberto LaCurso had played him like a puppet helping him enter and exit Italy in exchange for transporting the suitcases full of money and likely firearms as well.

He wondered if he always was deemed expendable...like so much trash. Was that really the mentality Willie and Roberto lived by....that others could be used so cheaply? His answer could be seen by the unfortunate young lady in front of him. Sophia was supposed to have been cast off just like the others.

Bailey now had the satisfaction that they'd miscalculated. He'd become a different person over the last couple years. He could imagine being described erroneously by Willie LaCurso to his brother and Pizzorno as an innocent, rather green international business traveler and gullible to however they wanted to use him. If that description was ever accurate, it was no longer.

Sophia eyed her attacker in his moment of silent thought. His gaze at her was equally as intense. She was evaluating her circumstances and contemplating whether she had any chance to survive. His anger had no rest. She was in the clutches of a maniacal killer...someone completely the opposite of the insignificant American Andre had described. She'd not seen this level of madness in her cohorts...and they were joined to carry out a killing for the benefit of millions of Italians. This American was like a powder keg. His emotions were more personal and impulsive.

Bailey leaned back on the ataman his glaring eyes and revolver staring at her. More explicitly he queried, "I need to know about this man you call Andre. Where does he fit in on this plan to kill Mussolini and to use me as a decoy?"

There was no reason not to talk. It was her one hope of staying alive. She sniveled, "He was our leader. He hired Angelino and Luis as key members of our group. They have killed before. Andre and Ernst had worked together for many years as had Dominique with Angelino. As for Luis he is...was...an acquaintance of a man in Milan...someone he didn't name but let slip to me a couple times. The man's name was Roberto. I don't know his last name. I joined the group because of Luis; he and I have gotten close in the last year. Both our families have been seriously crushed by the dictatorship of Il Duce. Luis knew I would have no hesitation to help out when he told me of his part in this assassination team.

Our first couple attempts to kill Mussolini failed. I found out quickly Luis and Andre respected each other but always seemed at odds. He had a fear of being named if anyone of us were captured after an attempt on Il Duce's life. The entire team appreciated his determination to help us all escape after the murder. Too often he was too conscientious. Too many of our attempts were called off.

Last week something new was told to us. The time and place of our next attempt would coincide with your next travel plans into Italy....something Andre said would be soon.

We were delayed but finally got word you'd be entering Italy during the first week of April. We already had Mussolini's schedule. All we had to do was plug the two timetables together. Last Friday in Milan became our next planned attempt. We didn't know what exactly was happening but you were to be set up as the assassin giving us the chance to escape out of Italy within hours after the murder.

Then just moments before Luis was to take the shot at Mussolini, the attempt was cancelled because you had upset the plans. We were all highly frustrated but Andre kept reminding us we had another opportunity only days away when Il Duce was going to speak in Torino. Yesterday afternoon we all were to meet at Andre's beautiful home to discuss the details of our next attempt. It's the same thing we've done so often on Sunday afternoons in the past."

Sophia's voice then got very soft. "Earlier yesterday afternoon, Luis took off from this villa to pick up Angelino and Dominique from the train station. I was to take the tram down to the city and buy food for our dinner at Andre's home. Luis would pick me up. Then he called and said Andre would be delayed. The meeting would not be until Monday morning but we were all invited to stay at the mansion Sunday night for convenience sake. I was just about to leave this villa and buy the food yesterday afternoon when.....when I heard this tremendous explosion."

Then her eyes looked down and tears appeared on her cheeks. "The next thing I hear is a report that the Pizzorno house had been blown off its foundation... and they were looking for survivors."

Bailey found her story plausible but incomplete. Keeping the gun barrel pointed at her head, he showed no mercy. "So, why are you still here? Wouldn't it be better if you boarded the next train out of Lugano and get on with life?"

The question came out harsh given her boyfriend had just been blown into oblivion the previous day. She nonetheless responded. "Andre called and told me to stay here. He said for now it was too dangerous for me to go anywhere. He believes someone will be after him and also me when they find out we were not killed in the explosion. He's supposed to come into the city within hours. His advantage right now is that the people who planted the explosives have to assume he's dead. I'm uncertain what his next steps will be once he arrives here at the villa. I can only hope he has a plan for where I should go as well."

Bailey reacted quickly. "So, why hasn't he come sooner?"

She shrugged, "He said he had to be careful not to be seen...that he might be delayed until later tonight.

Then her eyes went trance-like as she blankly said, "He has to find the people who tried to kill us."

Bailey took a second look at her. He'd never seen someone so overcome. Her mind wasn't functioning normally. The daze she showed indicated she was still in shock. He sensed she could start screaming at any moment. For the present she was putting her complete faith in Andre Pizzorno. That was keeping her quiet.

Putting her odd behavior aside, there was no question he would remain right there in the villa until the Senore arrived. He was conscious his own mental state was a bit unsteady as well. He hoped he'd be able to control himself from outright shooting the man the moment he walked in the door. Those thoughts dismayed him. He'd become hardened and more imprudent. He wondered if he'd ever return to the more familiar Adam Bailey.

He got up and paced looking at Sophia holding her legs in her arms as she sat on the couch. He couldn't let her become so catatonic. He sat down on the chair in front of her and brought his face inches from hers. "Sophia, the only way I'm going to relax is to tie you up. There's no need for you to get upset. If I don't secure you with rope, then I'll just shoot you. You better understand right now... your life means nothing to me."

His words scared him as much as they did her. In his frame of mind he had no problem being spiteful.

He mumbled to her, "I need some rope."

She was back in the present. She pointed down the hallway. "There's rope in the closet."

That job completed, he went over to the sofa and fell fitfully to sleep.

There was barely daylight remaining on that Monday afternoon when Bailey bolted awake hearing the tram continue up the mountain from the Strausser stop less than thirty yards away. So many trams had gone by since he'd fallen asleep. Why this particular one distracted him he had no answer.

Sophia hadn't moved...couldn't move...and was sleeping restlessly on the chair. She looked so innocent. Once she awoke, her nightmare would continue. Fear would return to her eyes and the furrow on her brow would be etched.

Bailey let her sleep. Looking out the window at the corner of the drapes, the incessant fog and rain caused him to wonder if the sun ever shined for more than a day in Lugano. Gazing down the short, hazy street with some small shops closing for the day, he contemplated Pizzorno's dilemma. 'Someone wanted him and his associates dead,' he thought, 'since the Senore had likely acquired a number of enemies along the way through his many business ventures. It still bothered Bailey the U.S. State Department was inclined to trust this enigmatic man from Lugano. David O'Brien and his staff had to take a risk on people to work with them. Finding eventually certain new agents to be treacherous and double-crossing like Pizzorno maybe didn't matter.

Waiting around for Pizzorno required patience Bailey didn't have. He looked again at Sophia as she slept on the chair still tied like a package. Bailey wished he had some kind of appreciation for her beauty, but his senses had been dulled. He felt only hatred and distrust towards her.

To break the monotony, he forced himself to eat. There was no joy or satisfaction. It was only necessary to keep his health and strength.

With eggs, some meat, and bread available, he prepared a meal large enough to include his hostage. Sophia awoke as the food was cooking. At first she tried to stretch until she realized she was hindered by the rope. Then her eyes regained that same dreadful look of fear as she stared at the man she still thought may have set the explosives at Pizzorno's mansion.

Bailey remained intense and spoke coldly to her. "I'll give you some food. We'll wait right here until Pizzorno shows up no matter when that might be. If he calls, I'll hold the telephone while you respond. You'll say nothing about my presence. You know the result if you do."

She nodded.

Bailey ate some of the food he'd prepared and then brought some to Sophia. With her hands tied in front of her, she looked at him expecting the ropes to be loosened. He turned away letting her awkwardly take bites with a fork held by her two hands bound together.

For the next few hours there was only the sound of the rain tapping on the roof and the occasional tram moving up or down the nearby rail. Bailey stood staring out the window. Sophia remained silent deciding it was best to keep the madman from talking.

Monday's daylight, what there was of it, was finally coming to a close when Bailey heard the noise. It was so slight as to be a wonder the human ear could pick up the vibration. The tram had just stopped slightly longer than normal and then moved on. Not a minute later, the footsteps could be heard clomping on the paved street with an occasional splash when a foot landed in a puddle. Sophia didn't even react to the insignificant noise, but Bailey was alert and stealthily moved across the living room.

The faint footsteps suddenly stopped at the front door of the flat. A key was inserted into the door lock and turned. Sophia's eyes grew wide knowing the next minute could have a great influence on her own life.

Bailey was at the door waiting to pounce. His luger was ready. His eyes penetrated Sophia's indicating any sound from her could be her last.

As the front door opened, a voice whispered into the darkened living room, "Sophia….Sophia…are you here?"

The man stepped in closing the door. Two things then happened simultaneously. He saw Sophia wide-eyed tied to a chair...and the sensation of cold metal of a gun barrel pressed against his neck. The voice ordering him to remain still was chilling. He could only think of one person who would have such antipathy for him at that moment.

Pizzorno tried to be light as he allowed himself to be prodded by Bailey's gun to the middle of the living room. Staying calm he tried to speak with some confidence. "I'm guessing I have the good fortune to finally meet the precocious and I might say highly resourceful Adam Bailey. Welcome to Lugano. I am so relieved you are all right."

Bailey wanted nothing to do with the fakery. His manner was foreboding as he mumbled, "Senore Pizzorno....I cannot say I'm happy to be meeting you under these circumstances. Sit down. We do have a few things to discuss before your life as you know it might continue."

He pushed the older man down to the couch. Pizzorno turned and stared up at an intimidating barrel of a revolver pointed directly at his forehead. The weapon was being held by a person who didn't match any of the descriptions Roberto LaCurso had given him of the man holding the gun. Adam Bailey's facial cheeks were sunken and the skin under his eyes was unnaturally dark. His hair was unkempt and he had an uneven growth of whiskers on his face. There was no doubt the young man had been living under constant stress with no end in sight. Given he likely hadn't been sleeping or eating well and wearing ill-fitting clothes, he bore a look as fierce, angry, and potentially impulsive as any man Pizzorno had ever seen.

For a moment both men stared at each other saying nothing. Pizzorno showed the most obvious discomfort not expecting anyone but Sophia in the house. His focus on what to do with her eventual dead body by his own hand had ended abruptly with Bailey's presence.

As for Bailey, he examined his adversary. Pizzorno was taller and thinner man than Bailey had imagined, yet with a paunch indicating he'd enjoyed the good life with food and drink. It was his eyes that told the real story. They were intelligent but cold and calculating. Pizzorno's gray hair also made him look older but Bailey had no doubt the man could defend himself if challenged.

Finally Pizzorno recovered some of his dignity and attempted to ease the prickly air between them. "Adam, might I reach into my coat pocket and grab my cigarettes? I assure you I have no desire to harm you. You may not believe it but we are on the same side."

Bailey sneered. "If I see anything but a pack of cigarettes being removed very slowly from your pocket, the last thing you'll feel is a bullet entering your brain."

The pack of cigarettes was pulled slowly from his coat pocket. He took one cigarette from the pack and lit it. Then he extended his hand offering one to Bailey. The magnanimous gesture was met with no movement or reply. Being rebuffed, Pizzorno returned the cigarettes to his coat pocket staring at Bailey every second.

Then Bailey gave the man a thorough frisking with his free hand before tying the older man's hands and feet with the excess rope. Finding no weapons he brought the ataman over in front of Pizzorno. His gun pointed a foot from Pizzorno's nose while saying, "You might as well start talking. Whenever I think you're lying, I'm going to simply shoot you...first in the legs...then in the arms. It will be painful for you.

Sophia's eyes again grew large.

Pizzorno looked straight into Bailey's eyes deciding if the threat was real. He tried again to soften the American's posture. "Adam, you've been through a lot. You need to let me explain. You were not going to be left in any Italian prison. It was the LaCurso brothers. They had plans to break you out and get you back to France."

Bailey raised his gun, took aim, and fired one shot just missing Pizzorno's ear and hitting a lamp at the other end of the room. The silencer made but a 'poof' sound; the lamp exploding when it landed on the floor was more attention getting.

Sophia gasped. Pizzorno pulled back in shock not believing what Bailey had just done.

Bailey stared menacingly at him and enunciated very clearly, "I guess I missed. The next shot will be your knee. I want to know the entire story and how Willie LaCurso got involved with you. I want to know how I got pulled into this plot. And, I want to know where Roberto LaCurso is now located. You might as well start talking. We'll take what time we need before your injuries make you faint and unable to walk or talk. What gets said dictates what condition both of you will be in when I decide it's time to leave. Right now your chances of leaving this villa alive don't look good."

Bailey's stare was evil. Pizzorno was slow in responding and a second shot was fired at his right leg. The slug went into the cushion on the couch. The older man jolted upward like he'd been struck by lightning. Seeing no blood he was relieved but mortified in fear. The shot had missed again....just barely.

Bailey stated again. "Start talking. One of these times my aim will be true."

With sweat now dripping from his forehead, the frightened Swiss businessman wondered what the LaCursos had been drinking when they chose Adam Bailey as the pawn for the assassination plot.

His throat was dry but Pizzorno began talking.

It was very late that Monday night, April 8, in the mountain villa and Adam Bailey was still questioning what he should do with his two hostages. Andre Pizzorno would be of no help in getting him to France. The only thing gained was that under duress the older man had filled him in on all the details regarding Bailey being chosen as a scapegoat in a Mussolini assassination. Pizzorno's explanation had been s so casual as if Bailey was nothing more than a puzzle piece to Willie and Roberto LaCurso.

When Pizzorno was done, the disgust and hatred in Bailey's eyes was intense. The downtroddened Senore kept trying to separate himself from the LaCursos. His eyes were low as he muttered, "You were supposed to be moved to Rome last Wednesday or Thursday. It was then arranged to have you escape while you were being transported. You'd be at large on Friday when my people would gun down Mussolini. There would be a military dragnet out to find you giving my people a possible easier chance to escape. Roberto LaCurso was to have some of his people in Rome help you after being re-captured. Once in that city, he was to arrange for your release based on mistaken identity by the military police. You'd be out of Italy the next day. "

Pizzorno eyed Bailey hoping the American was buying some of his explanation before quickly adding, "Of course the delay of your transfer to Rome and your escape from the Milan jail put that plan in disarray."

Bailey seethed at Pizzorno's fabrication. Receiving help from Roberto after escaping the military transport truck to Rome was a blatant lie. The LaCursos would use him until he'd fulfilled their purpose. He'd then be cast aside for the authorities to re-capture and probably be shot on sight. He aimed his pistol at Pizzorno's leg and barely kept from taking the shot. A moment of reconsideration and he hesitantly removed his finger from the trigger. He might need the Senore to be mobile. Crippling him eliminated that option.

Pizzorno's shirt was soaked with perspiration. Staring at nothing, the older man sat on the couch tied tightly as if encased in a bubble of doom. Whether death by gunshot from the irate American pacing the floor....or, eventual death by those hired to kill him in the explosion made his options seem hopeless. Sophia, tied up and gagged seemed equally resigned.

As much as he hated them, Bailey realized the moment he'd simply murder them had passed. Killing two people hogtied and defenseless was beyond even his darkest thoughts. The hell they were living in at that moment gave him some satisfaction.

Pizzorno watched Bailey head toward the kitchen, prepare some food and then eat alone as if no one else existed in that mountain villa. When finished Bailey brought scraps to his hostages and fed them. When thirsty he poured water into their mouths. As the night went on and they needed the facilities he loosened the rope around their wrists, but not around their legs. Both had to hop with Bailey's assistance to the bathroom. The door remained opened with the young man holding a gun on them as they answered the call to nature. It left no doubt in either Sophia's or Pizzorno's mind the level of his antipathy. He would not give them one chance of escape. His manner showed no sympathy... only indecision as to his next step.

After midnight, the weather outside deteriorated, if that was possible. With the rain and a blustery wind, branches from trees scratched at the windows as if prodding Bailey to make a decision. Pizzorno figured the odds still favored the young man taking Pizzorno's money and passport leaving two dead bodies in the villa. The two corpses might not be discovered until they began to decay. He kept contemplating an alternative but his ideas were feeble. Bailey would have to trust him; that alone was not likely.

As for Bailey he found contentment in his lack of urgency. He had food and shelter. The more time that passed, the stronger he felt. He hoped even life in the city might calm with each passing day since the bombing. It might aid his movement out of the city.

That Monday night continued as if time stood still. The three were reconciled to sleeping as best they could. Bailey stoked the fire, at times slept intermittently, and constantly looked through a crack in the drapes at the outside to inspect the weather.

While making some more food from the remaining rations, his voice suddenly rang out for no reason from the kitchen. His statement was meant to provoke Pizzorno. "So, Senore Pizzorno...you have failed yet again on killing Il Duce with Wednesday's opportunity now gone. And, you have lost four of your people. Now, you and Sophia are tied up like dogs facing your own mortality. In addition, what has to be heavy on your minds is if I don't kill you, someone out there in the darkness is looking for you...or they will be when the authorities find that your body is not part of the debris. Efforts to find you will be renewed. You'll be pursued until they succeed in killing you. I'd say Sophia's days are numbered as well just being associated with you."

His words were pitiless and brutal. Sophia's eyes widened. It was another reminder that she was no more than a piece of dust in the entire picture. She looked at Pizzorno with glazed eyes. His response was silence. Countering the truth was a waste of time.

Bailey returned to the small living room with a cup of coffee. He offered none to the two of them and only stared at the traumatized Pizzorno. Leaning down he whispered, "You're more of an idiot than even I was. You failed too many times. You became expendable. Your people have always been expendable."

Pizzorno gave him a puzzled look.

Bailey shot back, "Senore, think about it. How many times were the LaCursos supposed to support you and risk having their names found out in another bumbled attempt on Mussolini's life? You and your team were scheduled Sunday to be completely taken out in order to keep your mouths shut. That's as obvious as the rope around your wrists and legs. Last Friday had been your last attempt to end Mussolini's life. Whether your people succeeded or not, that explosion was going to happen. Willie and Roberto LaCurso had to eliminate all of you."

He paused and got up to fill his coffee cup and added, "If you can't see the writing on the wall then you're more of a waste of time than I thought."

Pizzorno reacted furiously to Bailey's comment, but said nothing. He couldn't disagree with Bailey's assessment. Sophia even caught on. Her eyes were heated. If she'd had a gun, Pizzorno would be dead. She and her associates had been duped. Her loyalty to Pizzorno had disappeared in an instant. Thoughts of murdering Benito Mussolini no longer stained her mind. Her immediate aim was to see the next day's sun.

The dreary Monday night ended as did the rain. In the pre-dawn hours on Tuesday the conditions had improved. It was dry with low hanging clouds. Food was low and all three knew a decision would be made that day. Bailey had tried to sleep on the chair with ataman, but had no real success. He'd awakened to the eyes of Pizzorno glaring at him.

Bailey sensed his reactions were not quite as sharp as Pizzorno's at that moment. He was the captor with all the advantages and power; the Senore was the captured evaluating every moment and noticing every move his dulled, yet stressed, captor was making. Realizing this, Bailey showed extra caution and kept checking the tightness of the ropes.

Bailey had hoped an answer would come to him during the night and that he might even gain some sympathy for his two hostages. That didn't happen. He could muster no remorse and it was upsetting to him. He'd killed a German guard on the train. He kept rationalizing if he was going to burn in hell for that act then killing these two people wouldn't make any difference. He'd always thought of himself as a forgiving and moral person. It was clear these attributes had limits.

It was 5:00 on that Tuesday morning when he opened his eyes. Bailey had fallen into another of his short, fitful sleeps across from his two captives. Pizzorno was trying to stay warm under the blanket. He was having difficulty with his hands tied behind him and his legs tied to the table. Bailey unconsciously went over and finally showed some humanity by helping the man with his covering.

Pizzorno expressed appreciation. "Thank you, young man...but I do wish we could reach some agreement, so I could get these shackles off my arms and legs."

Bailey nodded and adjusted the blanket on Sophia as well. She hardly moved. He looked back at the tired looking older man. "Senore, what do you know about your neighbor, Senore Mendosa?"

Pizzorno was surprised at the question and the pleasant change of Bailey's voice...as if the young man had regained his senses.

The Senore asked in return, "How do you know him? He has been my neighbor for over five years. We don't know or see much of one another since we both travel heavily each month...and our houses are around the corner and unseen by one another. But, we've had our times where we've talked...as neighbors. He markets medical equipment and is divorced with no compelling wish to remarry. I find him a loner...but a very decent man. Why do you ask?"

Bailey ignored the question. "So then, do you know much about the girl named Greta Mendosa...apparently his niece...who has been staying with him these past couple weeks? Certainly she has visited him before. She'd have to drive right by your home when going into the city. You've had to have noticed her. She's quite beautiful."

Pizzorno gave him a curious look. "I don't know any Greta. In fact I've never seen or been aware of him with a woman whether at his house or having dinner in the city. He guards his privacy."

Bailey said no more. There was something that continued to be odd about the young lady's purpose at the cottage with all her photographic equipment. Yet, she could have turned him into the Lugano police and she did not. Sighing, he wished he had someone like her to help him. But, it was just an empty wish. By now she could have left the city, especially in light of the horrific scene at Pizzorno's estate. Still, he found it peculiar that a person so interested in photography would not have remained to document in pictures one of the worst disasters in the history of the city. Photographers had a nose for dramatic pictures. Why not her?

With dawn approaching, he'd made up his mind. Whispering loudly to both captives to wake up, their eyes opened as if hearing an expected alarm. Both looked pensive.

He mumbled to them in the darkness of the living room, "This may be your lucky day, that is, if you prefer to live. As I see it, your lives won't be worth two bits when your pursuers find out both of you are still alive. I believe you need as much help as I do in escaping from this city and probably from this country. You have a choice. It all comes down to you helping me get into France. I have no travel papers and my picture is plastered on every train station wall in Switzerland and in Italy thanks to the predicament I've been put in by you, Senore, and the two LaCursos. You and Sophia are actually more fortunate than I. While authorities in two countries are hunting me down, you only have some hitmen pursuing you...and of course me....who cares very little about either of you.

Then he stared at each hostage for a moment before mumbling, "Here's the deal...my life for yours. You help me get across the border into France, I'll let you go. I'll consider our scores even."

Pizzorno and Sophia looked at each other....she with some hope; he with extreme doubt.

Bailey added, "I know you wish me dead right now. Then the two of you could disappear into the mountains and possibly out-wit the hired killers...at least for a while. I frankly don't believe either of you has the experience or the imagination to ward them off for long. You'll be found...probably within days. They won't pause. You'll perish in the very spot they find you.

So, you have a choice. You can trust me that I'll let you go once I'm in France or you can plan on not being alive by this time next week. The LaCursos cannot afford to let either of you ever talk to the authorities. In fact, I'm giving you more of a chance to live than I was being given while rotting in that Milan jail cell.

Pizzorno and Sophia came around fast. They suddenly were nodding their heads. What else could they say? They were being given a chance to live... something entirely unexpected. In addition, if Bailey was caught in the upcoming hours and days while they moved together through Switzerland, the two of them had a rock solid story of being kidnapped by the mad American.

Not trusting the sincerity of their response for a minute, he clarified his position. "Do understand this gun will be aimed in your direction at all times until we're safely in France. If I sense either of you is setting me up for capture, I will not hesitate to shoot both of you in the next second or leave your worthless bodies tied up somewhere in the Alps. Waiting for the elements to end your lives sounds unpleasant. Have I made myself clear?"

Both were attentive and nodded briskly. Bailey then untied each of them and allowed them to change clothes...in front of him...for their upcoming journey. There was no conversation. They knew they were trusted about as far as their captor could see in the early morning dark. They had individually decided they were not going to do anything unwise...at least just yet.

Sophia was given permission to cook some food. Pizzorno sat at the kitchen table and listened to Bailey's plan to get to Geneva with all the commitment of an agnostic at a church picnic. Bailey knew the man would be looking for any way to free himself at his first opportunity.

Outlining the travel by automobile through the Alps and onto the Swiss-French border by Geneva, Pizzorno gave only a nod to his captor. Sophia's eyes were more hopeful. "I know the route," she said. "I've driven it several times."

The three of them quietly exited the small mountain villa while it was still dark that Tuesday morning. Hearing the tram bell ring, they hurried to the stop three houses away with Bailey's powerful revolver with silencer aimed at their backs.

The tram appeared as if by magic coming out of the early morning fog. It rumbled to a stop and seconds later it moved down the line with the three additional passengers. Ahead and below, the feint lights of Lugano and the vast darkness of Lake Lugano could be seen under the ceiling of the haze. Bailey noticed nothing of the beauty. His eyes were locked on his two captives.

With the car he'd hijacked from Mendosa's home parked two blocks from the tram station, the plan was for the three of them to drive north a couple hours to Locarno and then push on to Brig, Switzerland. Sophia and Pizzorno would be up front; Bailey would keep his luger trained on them from the back seat. From Brig they would finish the journey driving through to Lausanne and then onto Geneva. The mountain driving would not be fast with some winter snow still not melted, but speed was not the priority.

Arriving at street level the three of them headed for the parking lot. It was only then Bailey considered his new problem. He'd stolen Mendosa's vehicle. The authorities might already be on the lookout for the car.

For the first time Pizzorno showed what his personality might have been like in better times. Seeing the absolute frustration in his captor's eyes, he cracked, "Are we going to walk to Geneva?"

It was then Sophia dug in her purse and produced some keys. Her own unsteady mind was only focused on her their plight. She'd live if Bailey could get to Geneva. She blandly pointed to a nearby vehicle...a 1936 Mercedes Benz 770k Cabriolet owned by Pizzorno himself. She and Luis had been using this vehicle since being given access to Pizzorno's Monte San Salvatore mountain retreat through all the months of delays to assassinate Mussolini.

She mindlessly mumbled, "We'll use that car."

Pizzorno looked as if he wanted to strangle her. The bland look she gave the former leader of the assassination team indicated she cared little for his thoughts. Survival was now her only spearhead.

Suddenly there was no problem. Bailey even looked rather stunned at Sophia. It was as if she was in another world. Her eyes were glazed showing no emotion. Under the circumstances he had to let her drive.

In the vehicle Bailey unfeelingly gave them another reminder from the back seat. "If I sense something is wrong I fire the first shot into the head of the Senore. Seconds later there will be two dead bodies. Then I will have to make my sojourn to Geneva by myself. Somewhere during my passage I will dump your bodies off the edge of a mountain overhang. Maybe sometime later this spring or early summer, someone might find unidentifiable parts of your decomposed bodies washed up along the shore of some river far below the cliffs."

Pizzorno's shoulder's slouched slightly. Bailey had painted another gruesome picture of their deaths; fear was still his best tool to maintain their compliance.

Sophia displayed no response only starting the vehicle and staring at the street ahead.

As the Mercedes Benz moved ahead, Bailey comfortably aimed his weapon at Pizzorno and thought about what he'd just said. Even he was surprised. Gruesome descriptions flowed from him so naturally. Two weeks before he would never have used such grisly detail. He was a different person...and he didn't exactly like what he'd become.

There was only silence in the vehicle as they advanced through the empty early morning streets of Lugano at a steady pace. While Sophia showed she'd blindly follow orders, Pizzorno displayed tension. He was facing not just possible death from the American, but his entire life had been turned upside down. It had become quite clear the LaCursos were behind the complete decimation of his house and colleagues.

Already as the Mercedes Benz left the city, Pizzorno periodically began glancing back at Bailey. The American had been pacing during the night and not sleeping. It was a long way to Geneva. It was highly likely Bailey would have a hard time staying awake. Then he would pounce.

<h1 style="text-align:center">Chapter 19</h1>

Greta Vespucci was born in Chicago and named after her mother's only sister who still lived in the old country. Her father and mother made their home in Chicago for many years until they decided to move back to his family's winery and vineyard sixty kilometers west of Venice, Italy. During the 1920's Greta traveled back and forth from Italy to Chicago in order to get the kind of schooling the family wanted for her. Since they could afford it, she was primarily educated in a private girl's school on the near north side of Chicago along Lake Shore Drive.

During the summer months she returned to her family and worked in the vineyards. Highly intelligent she was accepted at the University of Chicago in 1933 where she majored in business. There she also acquired an interest in photography. Her summers continued the same during her college years. Back home from her schooling, she concentrated on the financial and operational side of running a large vineyard. With no brothers and three younger sisters, her father, Armani, took a special pride in her precocious business acumen.

The Vespucci family had a respected second generation wine business shipping their product to various European and Mideast markets. During her last year of college, her father mentioned to her in a letter about a handsome American only a few years older than her who had been stopping by and enticing Armani to distribute his family wine into the United States market. In a follow-up letter he told her that he succumbed willingly to the persuasiveness of the young American and set up channels for distribution up and down the U.S. seaboard through a Minnesota-based distribution company. It took but a couple months and the Vespucci family wine business was enjoying a new source of revenue from the U.S.

Greta's father even suggested she meet this American wine and food representative since on his map Minneapolis, Minnesota was just 'up' the road from Chicago. She wrote back that she'd prefer a proper introduction when she returned to the vineyard the next summer. Unfortunately, the introduction would not happen even after she moved back to Italy upon graduation. Not ready to immerse herself completely in the family business, she took weeks off at a time to travel and concentrate on her interest in photography. By 1938 she was displaying some of her photos in a few art shops in Venice.

Armani wasn't shy about suggesting to his American representative, Adam Bailey, that he meet his daughter. Bailey never warmed to invitations of this type from his Italian clients. He knew he was marriage bait. He was single, fluent in Italian, loved the country, and proved himself a competent businessman. His concern was actually becoming smitten with a client's daughter or niece. How would that be received from his other wine clients making offers to meet their daughter or niece? Winning business clients was challenging enough without making the pavement more difficult.

Before completing his first business trip in 1936, Bailey had figured his best defense was claiming to be engaged to a nice Italian girl back in the States. That took the pressure off most of his Italian clients who wanted him as a son-in-law.... except for Armani Vespucci. Vespucci kept hinting to Bailey that he should travel down to Chicago to meet his daughter when back in the States.

As for the new revenue from the U.S. for the Vespucci family business, that valve had hardly been flowing when it was turned off abruptly like a faucet. It happened in late 1938. The Italian government was nationalizing many businesses. Converting certain food or wine processing plants into war supply factories were taking Italian business owners by surprise and giving them no alternative. Armani got caught up in this internal fight with the Fascist regime to keep his very livelihood from being completely swallowed up by the government. By June, 1939, the Vespucci vineyard had lost almost two-thirds of its land to the government and the winery was now making medical supplies. Needless to say, the Vespucci exportation of their wine products to the U.S. evaporated...as did one of Bailey's last true clients in Italy.

Greta watched this declining process of the family wine business and had decided to go back to America in the fall of 1938. Through a University contact she found a job with a family owned travel and distribution company. Her job was to arrange transportation for individuals to national and international locations as well as to compare shipping costs for clients who exported. The company she worked for was owned by a man named, Louie LaCurso. He was purported to be part of a major crime family, but Greta never saw any signs that this accusation was fair or true. Louie worked hard, was a good husband and father, and from her perspective, he seemed to be running a very straight-forward, law-abiding, profitable business operation.

When she visited back in the old country in the spring of 1939 she witnessed a heart wrenching sight. The spirit and motivation was being squeezed right out of her father and other family members. They were in charge of running the medical supply factory but they were mostly just going through the motions. They hated everything about what they were being forced to do for the Mussolini regime.

Those two weeks in Italy had an unquestionable impact on the young lady. Her hatred toward the Italian premier had become deep-seeded. She hoped daily

Il Duce would trip over his ego and soon be cast aside by the citizens of Italy. However, he'd been in power for so long that wish seemed improbable.

Back in the U.S. she found her life and new job more satisfying. The work she was doing with Louie LaCurso's business was met with praise from that entire family. Mr. LaCurso, as she referred to him, and his wife and family had been nothing but kind and generous, especially knowing of her family's hardships back in Italy. When she needed that extra time in the spring to travel back to see her family, there were no questions asked. Her tickets were paid for by Louie LaCurso and she took what time she needed.

It was during the summer of 1939, Louie and his wife, Maria, introduced Greta at a LaCurso family gathering in Chicago to Louie's older brother, Willie, from Minnesota. She was awed by the differences between the two men. Willie was so intense; he made her uncomfortable. He had cold eyes and an untrusting nature, the exact opposite of Louie.

It took another meeting with Willie before she found him more tolerable. He seemed to recognize her discomfort and took time to converse with her socially. His manner was that of an uncle; she never felt he had any other purpose than to show his respect knowing she was a favorite of Louie and his family.

He insisted she call him 'Willie' as everyone in the family did except his children. He liked the young lady a lot. At one point he commented that if his daughter, Anna, was still alive, he hoped she'd be as sweet, resourceful, energetic, and smart as Greta Vespucci. That bit of flattery won over Greta.

Their rapport would build in the remainder of 1939. Even from his home in the Twin Cities, he directed business to Louie's travel and distribution company always having the referral work done through Greta. There was nothing Willie wouldn't do to help Greta be successful in Louie's business.

It was in February, 1940, that she told both Louie and Willie that her family was suffering far more than she had realized. Her father had suffered a minor stroke and she felt obligated to return to Italy to help salvage the family business. She hoped to return to Chicago if she could be assured the rest of her family would take on more of the family business responsibilities. Her situation only fueled more fire in Willie's blood against Mussolini.

In early March 1940, Willie and his family journeyed to Chicago to be part of Louie's youngest daughter's confirmation. With Greta's photographic skills, she was asked by Louie if she would handle that need for their special occasion. When Louie went to pay her for her effort, she refused insisting her intention was always to do the job gratis since she owed the LaCurso family so much more for all their kindnesses. The gesture warmed the hearts of Louie and his wife...as well as Willie...beyond anything else she could have said or done.

Willie had other reasons to attend his niece's confirmation. Knowing Greta was about to return to Italy, an idea developed to use her photographic skills for another job. This one was in Switzerland in the weeks before her planned arrival at her family's vineyard in northern Italy.

This thought germinated from the continual failures of Andre Pizzorno and his assassination team in taking down the Italian leader, Benito Mussolini. The bumbling attempts at disposing of Mussolini alarmed Willie and his brother in Milan, Roberto. The anxiety had become serious enough that Willie and Roberto had already been working on a scheme to simply eradicate the group so none of them would remain who could find it personally profitable or life-saving to incriminate the LaCurso family.

On the pretense of supporting Pizzorno, both brothers spoke in favor of the next two probable dates for a Mussolini assassination. The Italian leader had speaking engagements Friday, April 5 in Milan and Wednesday, April 10, a short distance away in Torino if the first date didn't work out. Both Willie and Roberto surmised in those weeks leading up to the next assassination attempt, there might be a pattern when all six of the team would be together at the Pizzorno estate....a place the group had typically met, often on Sunday afternoons to further discuss or finalize the details of their next mission.

Willie's brainstorm was to bring Greta Vespucci into the picture. She could be the trusted confidante to make a photographic record of when various people visited Pizzorno's home. The hope was that she would confirm the Sunday afternoon meeting time. Willie put on quite a performance Sunday, March 17, at Louie's home when he pulled her aside and introduced the temporary job he wanted her to do in Lugano, Switzerland prior to her visit with her family in Italy.

It was the end of Louie's and Maria's party that Greta and Willie sat across from each other by the crackling fireplace in Louie's study. In his most avuncular manner he lamented, "Greta, my dear, I hurt so for your family. As you know Louie and I are also in pain for our family ties in Italy as well. The Mussolini regime has brought misery to our homeland at the expense of so many people. If you had nothing to begin with, then IL Duce does you no harm. He might even give the poor folks in our home country the feeling that he is doing something good. As you can attest from your father's business...or what's left of it...many loyal Italians are having difficulty discerning what good he is doing."

Her nods spurred him on. "Greta, I am trying to help my family recover some of their business losses by finding other acceptable markets in the Middle Eastern countries. A key contact who might help us is a man who lives in Lugano, Switzerland. His name is Andre Pizzorno. His own personal businesses do well in several countries including in northern Italy. I have met the man only once, but I am inclined to believe my younger brother, Roberto that we should consider collaborating with this international entrepreneur. However, we have to be certain of his affiliations before I invest time and money with this man. He potentially could help yours and my families given his business activity that includes exporting wines.

What I want you to do...and I would pay you handsomely as well as cover the cost of your round trip over and back from Europe...is to leave this country as soon as possible and make your way to Lugano. Roberto and I would like you to stay in Lugano for at least two weeks and more or less be our eyes and ears on this man. More specifically, we'd like you to use your photographic skills to record pictures of the people who come and go from his rather stately lakeside mansion off Lake Lugano. Your surveillance photos and notes when people are typically frequenting his home could be critical in our decision making whether to join forces with Senore Pizzorno or not. Times are difficult in Europe. We can't be too careful who we decide to partner with in our business dealings."

Willie liked the way Greta was hanging on his every word, but she did have some concerns. Her questions reflected her innocence. "Willie, this is most generous of you. I would want to do a good job for you, but what you are suggesting isn't exactly my line of work. And, I have my responsibilities with Louie's firm and I don't want to disappoint him. He and his wife have been very kind to me."

Willie smiled patiently. "Be not concerned, my dear Greta, I have asked my brother Louie already if I could borrow you for those extra weeks before you see your family in Italy. Of course he doesn't like you being gone. You are a very effective and loyal worker and friend to his family. But, he also wants to help our family in Italy as well. He realizes your assistance on this Andre Pizzorno matter could be the beginnings of some better times for all of our folks back in the old country.

We'll make things as comfortable for you as possible in Lugano. Roberto has a friend who owns a lake cottage near Pizzorno's home. He will arrange for his friend to have other business dealings away from Lugano during your stay. With all the mountains surrounding the lake, I leave it to you to find some secluded locations where you can take the kind of photos Roberto and I need. My brother will travel to Lugano a couple times while you are there to pick up any photos and notes you have taken about Senore Pizzorno.

Just so you know, the man who lives in the cottage you'll be staying is named Gephardt Mendosa. I might suggest if you are questioned at any time, you can just say you are his niece and you're visiting him. As far as your photographic activities, your story should be that you are completing a series of photos for a national magazine. So, make certain you are taking other pictures around Lugano besides your focus on the goings-on at Pizzorno's home."

Greta was nodding in full appreciation for what seemed like a helpful and innocent job for the LaCurso family. Willie was relieved and pleased. He always felt he was at his best when deceitful.

Leaning toward her, he whispered, "Greta, I should remind you that your work for me...the information you find out on Pizzorno and the pictures you will be taking...all this must be held in absolute secrecy. Roberto is even arranging some fake identification for you to use while in Lugano. If you're going to be temporarily the niece of Gephardt Mendosa, it would be appropriate to have a passport and visa made out in that name."

She nodded once more showing her youthful exuberance over the secret task she was carrying out. Greta's innocence was endearing.

She smiled and said, "My goodness, Willie, you would think this Senore Pizzorno was an international criminal."

Willie coughed into his wine goblet, but recovered quickly. "Well, we don't want him to be anything of the kind. That is why we check out potential partners as well as the people who do business with them or socialize with them. Your efforts should give us a good overview and confirm that he doesn't have that kind of hidden agenda."

Greta, overcome with appreciation, reached over and gave Willie a daughterly hug. "Willie, I will be glad to carry out this favor to you and Roberto, especially since Louie is all right with losing me for a month. Besides, the task will be challenging. I can give some good time to my love of photography.

They parted that evening with Willie giving her $500 to arrange her flight to Marseilles, France where she'd then take a train to Lugano. He told her Roberto would have another envelope with the money she would be paid once he met her in Lugano. She seemed ecstatic as she floated out of the library that Sunday night.

As Willie took the train back to the Twin Cities from Chicago, he sat staring out at the cold, dark, still snowy countryside of Wisconsin. He had used his charm to persuade Greta Vespucci to virtually spy on Andre Pizzorno. Through her observations the two brothers could decipher typical times Pizzorno's people met together...even other times than Sunday afternoons. If that could be determined in the upcoming two weeks, the failed team would meet their destiny and the LaCurso family would eliminate any hints of collaboration with this failure laden assassination team.

⚊⚊⚊

When Greta Vespucci two days later on March 19 took the transatlantic Pan American World Airlines passenger flight over to Marseilles, France from New York, she was excited about soon seeing her family, but additionally enthused by her secret assignment. Willie's needs for photographs and observations on a future LaCurso business partner seemed excessive, even strange, but she wasn't going to question his methods. In her mind all the LaCurso brothers were successful businessman. They knew what they were doing.

Greta had some additional responsibilities upon departing Chicago. A large trunk from Willie became part of her luggage. Securely locked it was explained to her that it contained gifts and clothing to make life a bit more pleasant for the LaCurso family struggling in Italy. She would be met by a friend of Roberto's at the Marseilles airfield who would take the trunk from her when she arrived.

When Greta arrived in Marseilles, there was the man who claimed to be part of the LaCurso family. He took charge of the trunk and then helped her to the train station for her land journey up through France to the Swiss border. The international situation had made any train travel very difficult crossing the border between France and Italy. Taking the alternate route through the neutral country of Switzerland made the trip longer but less problematic considering she was carrying her photographic equipment.

Before boarding the train, the man gave her an envelope with some Swiss francs and a note ostensibly from Roberto. The man then disappeared. The note read:

Greta:

Enclosed is a Swiss driver's license with the name Greta Mendosa. The personal information should match your physical description. It would be helpful if you use this alias through the duration of your assignment. The Mendosa cottage on Lake Lugano is now available to you. The key will be under the welcome mat. In one of the kitchen drawers you will find some extra money for your living expenses and photographic supplies. Also, a key for a car in the garage will be found in the drawer as well.

Willie and I thank you for your assistance. We have every confidence Senore Pizzorno who you will be observing will be a good business partner. We just want to be certain. Your surveillance will help us discover if he has certain people we wish not to be involved. In the days ahead I'll contact you to see your photos and discuss any observations you might have.

R.

The terse, secretive note made her feel the importance of her task. Roberto hadn't even signed his full name. She found the 'Mendosa' alias he'd given her almost playful.

Arriving in Lugano on Thursday night, March 21, a taxi took her out to the vacated Mendosa cottage on Lake Lugano. The mountains hovered over the city and the vast lake like a stadium. For a photographic artist the setting was especially pleasing.

The very next morning Greta went hiking along the lake front hoping to recognize the big house that was described to her. Surveillance had to begin promptly.

Climbing the rocky wall of the mountain she came upon a perfect platform half way up a jagged cliff. Before she sat down to enjoy the view and ready her camera for some landscape shots, the impressive lakeside mansion simply appeared. There was no doubt. The description did not do the lake home justice. The gated estate with the huge two story brick frame boasted a separate three-car garage and a long lawn leading down to a sizeable dock where a large sailboat, a motorboat, and a small rowboat were moored. It was obvious the Swiss entrepreneur was a very well-to-do businessman.

The moderately concealed spot she was sitting offered her a generous view of not only the entire Pizzorno property, but a gorgeous view of the lake and the city of Lugano on the opposite side of the water. She figured this assignment was going to be a snap.

Willie had told her Pizzorno had a house servant named Ernst Lund, a slight man who used a 1937 BMW 315 Sport Roadster to go in and out of the city. Before she went back to the cottage, she'd singled him out. He was alone at the house, carrying in groceries and then sweeping the short sidewalk between the parking lot and the back door.

Pictures of him were unnecessary, but she took them anyway just to experiment how the overcast conditions might cloud her pictures. She set up a dark room in one of the Mendosa closets in order to gain prints right away.

Beginning the following day she climbed up the rock incline to the perch along the cliff three times daily in between going into town for supplies. She passed the mansion each time along the way and rarely saw any movement in or around the house. At night she stayed close to her small bungalow. The last thing she needed was some male noticing her when in town and trying to make her acquaintance.

It was not until the next Monday, March 25, that she met Roberto at a restaurant in downtown Lugano. That first weekend had been very active at the Pizzorno mansion. She had several photos of a young couple fishing off the dock on Saturday and another slightly older couple drinking wine on the patio with Ernst and a taller more distinguished dressed gentleman she presumed was Andre Pizzorno. Through her long lens she could see the woman was extremely tall and her male counterpart seemed a foot shorter. She chuckled imagining something a young woman like her was not supposed to picture in her mind.

She noted on Sunday all six were gathered in the spacious study of the mansion in the late afternoon. The large gothic shaped windows gave her amazing photographic access into the house from her cliff side perch.

She picked the best of her photos and presented them to Willie's brother. While pleased with her work, he was more interested in the times the various visitors were at the Pizzorno home. She recorded the dates and times on the back of each photo from then on.

Roberto was all business. As the youngest LaCurso brother, she wondered if he'd make a play for her. She was almost disappointed that he showed no interest. The job was more significant than she had realized.

Before exiting the restaurant, he plopped some money on the table to more than cover the bill and then arranged another meeting with her three days later at a different restaurant down the street. As he put on his coat to leave, he said to her, "Your work is helpful. In appreciation there is more than enough money to pay for the lunch. Please use the extra and buy yourself something nice this afternoon."

With that short, very kind farewell, he left hurrying to catch the 1:50 express train back to Milan. Indeed, she had double the amount needed to cover the lunch bill. The bonus from Roberto spurred her to want to do even better. That afternoon she chose between a better tripod for her camera and a warmer, more stylish coat for the cool evenings at the Mendosa cottage. She chose the new clothing. Photography equipment didn't win over fashion.

Their next meeting ended up being postponed until Monday, April 1. Again Roberto was more interested in the weekend pictures and notes. As previous, he left her with extra money for her efforts. She bought the tripod while wearing her new coat.

After two weeks of carrying out her assignment, she was finding the task repetitive and a bit dull. In the final meeting with Roberto on Thursday, April 4, he indicated that her job was likely done. He asked that she remain through Sunday morning. No more pictures would be needed, but he asked that she maintain her surveillance and call him if she spotted anything out of the ordinary occurring at the mansion. He also reminded her that Gephardt Mendosa was scheduled to be back at his cottage on Monday, so she'd need to vacate the cottage before that time anyway. He then left her some extra money to buy some gifts for her Italian family before scurrying back to the Lugano train terminal.

With her assignment essentially done, she was sorry she hadn't socialized more in town as Greta Mendosa. It might have added some spark to her two-and-a-half weeks in Lugano. In those following days she climbed the cliff to view the Pizzorno mansion for two hours in the morning and a similar time period just before dusk. Her plan was to leave the cottage Sunday and stay at the Hotel Lugano that night. She'd then leave for Venice by train Monday morning. She would find, however, those last three days, Friday, April 5 through Sunday, April 7 that not all plans go the way they were intended.

That Thursday night she watched with interest from Mendosa's boat out on Lake Lugano Ernst and the two couples she'd photographed so often the previous two weeks having an extended dinner without Andre Pizzorno anywhere to be seen. Then, instead of staying overnight, the four left the mansion that evening carrying small bags. Although Ernst stayed at the mansion, the actions of the other four people were very much unique. She considered calling Roberto, but eventually decided it was unimportant.

Instead, Greta spurned the lonely cottage and dressed up for an evening of fun...hoping to mix it up with a few local fellows over some drinks. She could make her alias into anyone she wanted herself to be. If a guy sparked her interest, she had the choice to go as far as she chose only to drop him like an inexpensive gigolo when she left town on Monday.

She took the Fiat Roberto had arranged for the past couple weeks into town. Driving past the Pizzorno home, she saw Ernst in the window of the kitchen. Other than him, the mansion was dark. The other four individuals were traveling someplace that evening, but Greta no longer cared. Her mind was more on playing the game with some fellows hoping to get lucky with her while she had some free drinks at a few bars across from Ciani Park.

Unfortunately, that Thursday night turned out to be a dud. The few guys who approached her were similar to the drips who tried to buy her a drink back in Chicago. While she understood their intentions, they were dull-witted and not particular good-looking.

As she sat alone over a glass of Chardonnay in the bar at the Hotel Lugano, she felt the wad of cash in her purse and took the time to contemplate what she'd been doing the previous weeks for the LaCurso brothers. Though Roberto seemed to appreciate her photos and observations, she felt somehow unclean for the work she was doing. She was spying on a man who appeared to be a fine, respectful citizen. It made such little sense why Willie and Roberto were apparently so interested in the people Pizzorno maintained as friends or business associates? The man was generous enough to allow four people to stay at his house whenever they were in the city. Then again she did question why these same people were so often overnight guests when the Senore had been rarely home. Only Saturdays and Sundays had he been at the house to host his guests.

That brought another question regarding the four people languishing at his mansion. They were not impressive and did not appear to be of Pizzorno's stature and international social standing. She had plenty of photos showing the younger couple dressed like drifters. The other peculiar older couple mostly drank his booze and sat in the large study playing cards with Ernst. As for Pizzorno's steward, Ernst seemed the perfect, well-mannered host when his boss was not in Lugano.

Over a third glass of wine, she centered on the bottom line of her unease. She didn't understand why the Pizzorno-LaCurso relationship wasn't more trusting? Why was it necessary to have this man scrutinized for such an extended period of time? If there were that many questions about Pizzorno's acquaintances or his character, why didn't the two LaCurso brothers simply look for a different partner?

She'd kept those thoughts to herself whenever she met Roberto. Now after receiving her final pay, she'd become disillusioned. Never again would she use her photographic skills in such an unsavory and unfulfilling way. In fact the entire experience had left her so dissatisfied that she was tempted to pack up that night and leave Lugano Friday morning. But, she'd given her word. She decided to stay and climb to the perch twice daily through Saturday.

That next morning she was again on the ledge with no camera just reading a book and enjoying the beautiful scenery around her. Other than watching Ernst drive into the city once on Friday, the estate appeared more like a photograph than real life. She lasted until lunch and then boredom caused her to go into town to shop and have lunch. She went back for only an hour to the perch on the cliff later that Friday afternoon.

Friday night she decided not to cavort at any Lugano bars. One more day at the cottage and then she'd stay Saturday night at the Hotel Lugano. Her questionable LaCurso assignment would then be done and she could catch a later train on Sunday or an early train on Monday to Venice.

It was cool Saturday morning when she rose from her bed in the Mendosa cottage. She had no interest climbing up the cliff. She drove into town and perused a small art gallery. Her lunch overlooking the picturesque Lake Lugano was pleasant; being alone her enjoyment was limited. Early that afternoon she took Mendosa's small row boat out onto the lake to take some photos of the mountains surrounding the city. With so many fishermen out on the water and the beautiful spectacle of the water brought her around to taking more photos. While doing so, she hardly noticed the Pizzorno mansion until a movement at the estate caught her eye. There was Ernst running out of the house and jumping into one of Pizzorno' vehicles. After two weeks of watching Ernst Lund live in the Pizzorno mansion, she could recognize the man's movements and style of clothing even from out on the lake. That he was running was inconsistent. The man never hurried anywhere.

Only a hundred yards from the shoreline of the Pizzorno property, she watched him take off in Pizzorno's 1937 BMW 315 Sports Roadster. He sped along the lakeshore and barely slowed as he approached Ciani Park. Then she lost sight of him as he disappeared into the city traffic. Not knowing what to make of his behavior, she began rowing back toward the cottage. Not five minutes later his vehicle was retracing the same route at the same elevated speed. As the car got closer, she noticed he had a passenger. Something was amiss. She rowed closer to the house and used her camera's long lens to sneak a peek at the visitor.

The guest was someone she'd never photographed. He looked haggard wearing clothes that looked as if he'd slept in them. He looked as bad as the young couple...even scruffier. She couldn't tell his age as he walked swiftly into the house via the back kitchen entrance. Hoping to see him walking around in the study with the large windows, she remained out on the water in the rowboat for another half hour before she began to feel somewhat conspicuous.

As the clouds moved in and droplets of rain began to fall, she began rowing back toward her cottage. Just before turning around the corner of the high rock shoreline where she'd lose sight of the mansion, she observed Ernst taking off in the roadster once again. This time, though, he drove at a more sensible speed. The guest was now alone at the house apparently taking time to clean up and rest.

Hurriedly she tied her rowboat at the Mendosa dock and slung her camera bag over her shoulder. She sensed something was abnormal and marched along her worn path leading to her familiar perch along the cliff. With the visitor left alone, she was hoping to take a few shots of him in the house before it became too dark to take any photos at all.

With her legs hanging over the edge of the cliff, she waited...and waited... for some kind of movement in the house. Surely Ernst would be returning. But, her patience went unrequited. Ernst had not returned and it had been almost an hour. She figured the guest must be sleeping.

With darkness approaching, she retraced her steps very carefully down the cliff. She'd stayed too long on the cliff. It had become difficult to see the path back to the cottage. Moving toward the shoreline where there might be more light, she gave one more last look before disappearing into the woods.

It was then she stopped. There was something she saw...some movement around the outside of the mansion. She grabbed her camera and with the long lens she confirmed there was definite movement...strange shadowy figures. She wondered if the shadows could be deer or maybe the visitor enjoying a relaxed view of the lake.

She remained still; her eyes having gotten used to the semi-dark were sensitized and she counted not one but two figures. One was on the side of the house; another was doing something on the opposite end of the house.

As her eyes strained to see anything definable, she then saw a third person. This one was running down to the dock. He then jumped into one of the boats moored at the dock.

Within seconds one of the other two individuals could be seen moving across the broad lawn toward the dock. The man stood on the dock looking around for only a short time before returning to the house. From that point on, she could not make out anything but shadowy movements. At times their voices echoed across the lake but nothing discernable could be heard.

She remained motionless peering as hard as she could to decipher what those shadows were doing. Within fifteen minutes all was quiet again. The shadows had disappeared. Whoever they were, they had apparently given up.... or finished whatever they were doing... and left the Pizzorno property. She stayed for five more minutes to see if the person hiding in one of Pizzorno's boats would reappear. But, it had gotten too dark. She couldn't see the boats much less a human being leaving the dock.

She perceived the entire episode significant enough that she tried to telephone Roberto the moment she arrived at the cottage. There was no answer. She tried once more a half hour later with a similar result. Given her uncomfortable feelings about her entire assignment, she found herself less interested in trying to contact him. Nonetheless, she couldn't help mulling over what she'd just witnessed. There was no doubt one of the shadowy figures was running from the other two and he'd successfully found refuge in one of Pizzorno's boats. Could it have been the visitor? It was the first time she sensed something more was going on at the Pizzorno mansion than for the purpose of which she'd been told. That last night at the cottage, she processed her pictures and tried to put the weird Saturday happenings at the estate out of her mind.

On Sunday morning she was bothered and curious enough that she made what she expected to be her last jaunt through the woods and up the trail to her mountain perch. If for no other reason, she wanted to observe that everything appeared normal on the Pizzorno property. At 9:00 she moved through the haze and light rain with her camera bag over her shoulder. The poor weather didn't bother her; she moved with much greater urgency than normal. Panting and perspiring as she arrived at the flat spot on the cliff, she stood without moving as she looked down at the mansion. Everything looked the same. There were no lights on in the house. She figured the house guest might still be sleeping.

Then she noticed there was something different after all. The small row boat had been dislodged from the Pizzorno dock. Casting her eyes through the light mist over the lake, she finally saw it below her. At first she thought the boat had simply gotten loose from the dock and drifted out onto the lake. Then she saw some movement under a tarp covering most of the boat. The man tried to make himself look as if he was fishing, but mostly he was trying to stay dry. He didn't even have a bobber on his line. She couldn't imagine anyone out fishing on such a miserable morning unless they were dressed properly. This man was not. Furthermore, there was only one oar visible.

As she began taking some photos of the odd spectacle, the man began using his one oar to maneuver his boat toward shore in the direction of the Mendosa cottage. It looked like the man was going to seek some help. She quickly collected her equipment and left the cliff. She wanted to be at the cottage when he arrived. As she hurried through the woods, she became more wary. She opened her camera bag made certain her small derringer was easily accessible. She decided to transfer it to her pocket for even more convenience.

She would arrive back at the cottage about the same time as the mysterious fisherman was about to knock on the cottage door. Feeling the derringer in her pocket, she put on a smile and decided to greet the man and help him if she could.

That was when she met Adam Bailey.

Chapter 20

A lot had happened by that Sunday, April 7, before Greta Vespucci, alias Greta Mendosa, called Roberto LaCurso at 3:00 only an hour before the devastating bomb blast that would level the Pizzorno estate. Her assignment for all intents and purposes had been completed by Thursday; she had done what Roberto had asked and remained on lookout at the Pizzorno mansion right up through that very morning. He'd wanted a report if she'd observed anything occurring out of the ordinary. Neither of them expected to talk again.

She'd held off calling despite seeing the visitor arrive Saturday afternoon and observing the shadowy figures creeping around the mansion that evening. But, it was the extraordinary meeting Sunday morning with an unkempt American at the cottage that made her feel compelled to call.

Although saying to Adam Bailey she'd be returning to the cottage after her fictitious meeting with someone that Sunday noon, she had no intention of doing so. She intended on staying at the Hotel Lugano that night before taking the train out of the city early the next morning. Besides, she didn't totally trust the American and his story anyway.

After checking into the hotel, she made one more attempt at calling Roberto LaCurso in Milan. This time there was an answer. When he came on the line, he seemed at first bothered by her call, as if he hadn't really wanted her to check in with him. His voice was terse like Willie's the first time she'd met him. Annoyed he said, "Greta, you should be gone from Lugano. Why are you still there?"

She thought, 'Had he forgotten he'd asked her to stay? Here she was, doing him a last favor.'

Confused by his irritation, she showed little patience. "Roberto, you need to listen to me. You said to call if anything happened at the mansion. I am now doing so. You should be aware of a number of things that I've seen since last we talked."

His voice suddenly changed in tone showing some appreciation and restraint. "Go ahead, my dear. Tell me what you saw."

The words came out like a flood. "Roberto, Saturday in the early afternoon I saw Pizzorno's servant drive very fast into town and only minutes later return to the estate with a very worn-out younger man. Not twenty minutes later that servant left the house alone...and never returned. He left his houseguest alone for the rest of the day. I thought that kind of strange. I decided to remain at my lookout and stayed for two hours and saw no movement until dusk. Just at the point I was ready to leave, I saw in the feint darkness two or possibly three figures moving quickly around the house. There was a flashlight in the house as if it was going to be ransacked. Then I observed yet another shadowy figure running from the back of the house down toward the dock. It was so difficult to see, but I did follow him as he slithered into one of the Senore's boats. I'm not certain, but it would not have surprised me that it was that visitor Pizzorno's servant had picked up earlier in the day.

While that man hid in one of the boats, those other people were doing something on the outside as well as inside the house. What was peculiar was their purpose. They weren't there to burglarize the house. They were performing some other task and they completed it very quickly. Suddenly they were gone and the entire estate was dark and quiet. I no longer could see if that visitor had gotten out of the boat or not. I finally gave up and returned to the cottage."

She stopped for a moment waiting for his response. All she could hear was his sighing on the other end of the line.

As for Roberto, he'd been listening intently to Greta's every word and holding his breath that she hadn't seen too much. When he assigned his men to plant explosives around the Pizzorno mansion that Saturday evening, he hadn't figured there'd be a houseguest or that Greta would be observing their actions. She had been conscientious to a fault. At least she seemed not to have any idea what the men were doing.

Trying to stay calm, Roberto commented hesitantly, "Greta, it does sound more like an attempted burglary. With that visitor at the house alone, his presence might have caused the intruders to leave. It doesn't sound like anything more needs to be done, but I'm glad you called."

Roberto was ready to end the phone conversation, but Greta was not. She quickly interrupted. "Roberto, there's more. There's a lot more. This morning I was up at dawn to make my way back for one last observation of the mansion. Everything appeared to be unchanged. I noted there was no car. Pizzorno's servant had not returned to host his visitor. Then I noticed something else. I had seen three boats tied up along the dock. Sunday morning the two larger boats were there but the rowboat was gone. Immediately my attention panned across the lake until I saw the rowboat. It was right below me in a cove. I presumed that same man who'd run down to the dock was still hiding in the boat. He was hunched over with some canvas as a cover to keep him warm. He had one oar. I was certain he'd spent the night in that small boat. For being a guest of Andre Pizzorno, it didn't seem this guest was being treated as kindly as he might have hoped.

The flash of humor evaded Roberto. Impatiently, he snapped, "Who was he?"

Greta immediately noted Roberto's change in interest. She talked on. "I began snapping photos of the man. It was difficult to see his face from my elevated angle. I noticed he kept glancing toward the mansion. I stayed out on the perch for another hour just watching the man until he began maneuvering the rowboat with that one oar toward the cabin I was staying in....you know, Mendosa's cottage. I moved down the cliff hoping to see who he was and if he needed some help.

We arrived at the Mendosa cottage about the same time. He really looked quite a sight...like he hadn't had a good night's sleep in a month. He stood over six feet tall and had a patch of wild blondish brown hair on his head and shabby looking facial hair. I had a pistol in my camera case for safety, but he didn't seem interested in hurting me. We talked for a while. Indeed he only wanted to borrow an oar, so he could paddle back to the Pizzorno estate.

What I noticed was his constant discomfort. He kept glancing around while we conversed as if he was ready to run if he saw anyone else approaching. As tired as he looked, we talked for quite a spell. I didn't want to lose the possibility of finding more information for you, Roberto, so I eventually invited him into the cottage to warm up. I made him some coffee. I never did feel endangered. He seemed just too desperately exhausted to cause me any fear.

Our exchange was general at first. He asked me about my photographic equipment. I said nothing about what I had been doing, but did show him some of my personal photos of the lake and the city. He brightened up seeing those shots as if truly appreciating the artistic quality of the pictures. Then he just happened to grab another group of pictures showing Pizzorno's home and a picture of his servant and the young couple who often came to the house. He took great interest in those photos."

Roberto grew edgy. "Greta, this story must be going somewhere. Who was the fellow and I hope you used your assumed name?

"I certainly did, but I didn't want him to leave until I found out why he was at Pizzorno's home the night before...and maybe who those other looters were who had been sneaking around the house. Once he'd had the coffee and some food, he recovered and talked a bit more. He claimed to have gone fishing that morning using the Senore's rowboat and lost an oar. He of course had no idea I'd seen him run down to the dock the previous evening and that he was lying.

That was when he stuck out his hand and introduced himself. He was a perfect gentleman...totally non-threatening. I couldn't believe he was the same exhausted man I'd seen practically crawl into the Pizzorno house the day before.

Transfixed and afraid how she might respond to his next questions, Roberto lamely repeated, "So....did you help him so he could be on his way?"

"Yes...although curiously he falsely identified himself at first. As we talked and he got more comfortable, he told me some of his predicament and admitted his real name. He said some people were looking for him for something he hadn't done. He was heading for Geneva to cross into France. It was so obvious he was hoping for some kind of offer from me to help him.

When he said his actual name, it sounded surprisingly familiar, but I couldn't place him. Anyway, his name was Adam........ Adam Bailey. I didn't really learn anything more about him. I loaned him the oar he needed and he rowed back towards the mansion. That was the last time I saw him. I invited him back to the cottage if he had any further problems once he returned to the Pizzorno home. I further told him I'd ride into town and get some food for later. I couldn't believe it, but he actually trusted me. I had no intention of returning...his story was just too bizarre to believe. I had intended all along to leave the cottage anyway with Senore Mendosa returning. I was intending to check into the Hotel Lugano this night and catch the first morning train to Italy to see my family.

When Roberto heard Greta say the name 'Adam Bailey', it was like a bad dream. He was unable to speak for a moment. He'd heard from Pizzorno that Bailey had escaped the Milan city jail on Friday. The escape hardly mattered to Roberto until Pizzorno made it clear how much a threat the American could be if recaptured. Who else but the LaCursos could Bailey believe was behind him being framed and incarcerated? It was obvious Bailey was not the innocent, inexperienced international traveler his brother had described. The American had now proved his ferocity and resourcefulness by not only sidestepping the Milan jail house guards, but evading the Italian military police dragnet when he somehow crossed the border and made it to Lugano. It was madness. It was not possible. But, according to Greta, it had actually happened.

Roberto tried to remain calm as the talkative Greta seemed to be nearing the end of her story about meeting Adam Bailey. He finally calmed himself and responded, "My dear, you have done well getting in touch with me. This man you met...this Adam Bailey...he could be the type of person Willie and I don't want to be associated. If he's a friend of the Senore, then this could scuttle our plans to work with Pizzorno. I plan on being in Lugano this coming week to meet with Andre. I'll need to ask him about his relationship with this....this American."

Then looking at his watch, he knew there'd be something happening at the Pizzorno mansion in another hour. He had wished Greta would not be in the city to experience what promised to be a terrifying event. In turn, he hoped that Pizzorno had already taken the Sunday train back to Lugano and was meeting with his people at his mansion that afternoon as planned.

Roberto made one last stab at getting her out of the city. He pleaded, "Greta, my dear, you have gone overboard to help Willie and me. Please...you are free to go. Take the express train that leaves Lugano this afternoon. Willie and I don't want you to miss any more time with your family than you have already. Check out of the hotel and leave now. We'll pay your hotel bill."

His urgency sounded so manufactured to Greta. He'd gone from impatient to absorbed once she mentioned Adam Bailey. It was as if the American was some kind of threat.

She had no reason to hurry. She had the hotel room for the night. She appeased Roberto by replying, "Your offer is very kind. I'll consider making that express train. Again, I must thank you for putting so much trust in me in completing this assignment."

There was nothing more to be said. They bid each other farewell and hung up the line.

Greta then left the hotel. She had no intention of leaving Lugano that afternoon. She wanted to spend some of that wad of cash she'd earned. Her assignment had been nothing more than a lonely but paid for vacation in a heavily Italian influenced Swiss city. She wished she'd taken more time to get to know Lugano, especially now that she wasn't particularly proud of what she'd done to earn her money. Something odd was going on and she was inquisitive enough to wait around to see if she might be right.

She crossed the street seeking a relaxing walk along Lake Lugano. The cloudy conditions were making it difficult to see across the lake towards the Pizzorno mansion, but her artistic eye wanted to take some final photos from the park looking out over the picturesque lake.

Looking at her watch there was just time to walk back to the hotel and gather her photographic equipment. As she strode down the street, her mind wandered to thoughts of Adam Bailey. The fellow had so many troubles. She felt sorry for him in his situation, but glad she hadn't gotten further involved with his predicament.

It was just after 4:00 that Sunday afternoon that she climbed the staircase to the front entrance of the hotel. She stopped occasionally to observe the beauty of Ciani Park and take pleasure in the view of the lake over the tops of the trees. Through the slight fog she could just barely make out the outline of Andre Pizzorno's beautiful home. She had a moment of nostalgia knowing she'd likely not see the stunning estate along the lake again. She would leave Lugano with very positive thoughts about the Swiss businessman and his classy tastes in home design.

Stopping at the top of the hotel staircase, she turned to take in one more view of the lake. Turning her eyes in the direction of the Pizzorno estate, she momentarily saw a unique glimmer that seemed to frame the house, as if a lighted border in a painting. In the next instance that flicker turned into a massive fireball that momentarily shook the very earth beneath her. Causing her to clutch the rail to maintain her balance, she witnessed a sight inconceivable followed by an accompanying muffled explosive sound. The flash lit up the lake and the mountain slope beside the mansion. It was a flash of such magnitude that the sky stayed lit unnaturally for too long a period of time before a bright fire settled on the land. At that point the entire estate just looked like a broad brush fire remaining underneath the ceiling of smoke and fog.

Greta stood there as if in a trance. She wondered who might have been in that house. Likely Ernst was there, but had Andre Pizzorno made it home yet? How about the American she'd met...Adam Bailey...he'd paddled the row boat that morning back to the house. Had he still been in the mansion?

Then the real shocker hit her. It was Sunday afternoon. Previous Sunday afternoons the mansion had the four visitors enjoying the pleasures of the estate. She'd seen them. She'd recorded their presence in photographs. If they were in the house, they all could have been blown to bits...their body parts scattered indiscriminately with pieces of the large house. It was a travesty beyond imagination. Only days later after body fragments and teeth would be found in the rubble might the true shocking result be told.

The image of those men with the flashlights poking around the base of the mansion the previous evening then rushed through her mind. Who else would have set the explosive charges? It had to be them...whoever they were. And, they likely knew the six people were going to be together precisely at that hour on Sunday afternoon.

Realizing the probable depth of the tragedy, she became faint and had to sit down on the steps. She watched emergency vehicles and fire trucks racing down the avenues towards the lake side estate. Everywhere she looked people wore stunned faces. Up to that moment her prevalent thoughts about Lake Lugano had always been that it was a 'little bit of heaven'. That fantasy had now disappeared. Her head was scrambled with the panoply of different people who could be involved in the disaster....both those who might have caused it as well as those who likely were killed in the explosion.

She sat on the stairs for another half hour just watching the blaze on the other side of the lake. She wouldn't remember when it finally hit her, but the moment arrived when she wondered if she could have had something to do with the catastrophe. It left her numb, but she never could take the depressing thought seriously. She'd only shared her surveillance with Roberto LaCurso. He couldn't have had anything to do with the explosion. Pizzorno was practically a business partner.

Greta wouldn't remember eating or even walking up to her fourth floor hotel suite. About midnight she awoke from a sleepy daze sitting outside on her hotel room patio. She'd never even gotten into her night clothes; she'd just sat down and got lost thinking of the horrible nightmare she'd witnessed.

She slept poorly the remainder of that Sunday night. Three more times she shuffled out to the small patio. By then, there were floodlights glaring at the damaged property. The reflection on the water made the scene look even bigger.

Greta awoke Monday morning as if she had a hang-over. Stepping out once again to her patio, it was a clear day. The lights at the Pizzorno property were no longer lit. She could see plainly the smoke off in the distance still rising from the debris. She could even make out some investigators and firemen clawing like ants around the rubble.

She made one decision for certain that morning. She was not going to leave Lugano. Somehow she felt strangely involved...not that she was about to go the local police. How would anyone possibly explain one was taking pictures of a house right up to the very day it ceased to exist? Even to Greta it sounded more than coincidence.

Her guilt was magnified only because she'd seen the previous evening shadowy figures hanging around the outside of the house. Could they have had such a grudge against Senore Pizzorno that potentially seven people could have perished by their possible actions? The only thing that would soften her feelings of guilt for not going to the local police was if investigators found evidence leading to who the murderers were. Her mind also wandered to the mysterious Adam Bailey...if that was indeed his name. He could have planted the bombs on Saturday. Then again the killers who set the explosives could have been any of those people she'd taken pictures of at the mansion.

The only thing mollifying her exasperation was that she was fulfilling her promise to Willie and Roberto. She assured them she'd never speak of her photographic surveillance of the Pizzorno estate. Nonetheless, Greta wanted to stay in the city and hear what progress the investigators were making. She wanted no pangs of guilt that her work had provided any help to those people who had caused the disaster. That possibility seemed so far-fetched.

All day Monday Greta stationed herself near the police station and twice traveled out to the disaster scene by taxi. With her photographic equipment...and her good looks...she walked under the roped off areas and took pictures of the smoldering mess of wood, tar, and blackened bricks. There were three sheets covering the partial remains of bodies. She heard a couple firemen mumble that the remains were inconsequential.

She kept her ears open to any rumors. A couple reporters remarked that the job was obviously a professional one. Bombs had been positioned at six different locations around the base of the house. Damaged timers were found. It was assumed by every investigator and emergency worker that Andre Pizzorno was part of the rubble. If the bomb was meant for the Senore, why would the bombs have been ignited if he wasn't home.

As Greta was about to leave the devastated area, one of the reporters even offered her a ride back home. She found quickly he wanted to continue their one-hour relationship as photographer and reporter in a more intimate way. Besides him being unattractive and smelly, it sickened her that anyone would have sex on their mind after covering such a devastating death scene. She wondered if the man had any sense of civility at all. Then again, as a reporter covering many ugly things that had been transpiring in recent months in Germany and Italy, she allowed him some slack. Nevertheless, she told him to 'go to hell' when he finally dropped her off at the Hotel Lugano.

Her words hardly bothered him. The reporter only shrugged lamenting what might have been as he watched her strut into the hotel. He'd been turned down often in the past. The wound was superficial.

As for Greta, she settled on Wednesday as her day to leave Lugano. If by then the authorities were still fumbling over the evidence and no new information was forthcoming, she had no reason to remain. She could be at her home near Venice by Wednesday afternoon. She hated to think her final days in the quaint Swiss city were destined to leave such a bad taste in her mouth.

Chapter 21

It was going to be a long automobile ride that Monday morning through the mountains to Geneva despite the use of Pizzorno's more comfortable Mercedes Benz Cabriolet. Adam Bailey was seated forwarded in the back seat with his hand on his luger pointing it directly at Pizzorno's head. The discomfited Swiss businessman sat glumly in the front passenger seat. Sophia was in another zone hardly blinking as she navigated the mountain roadway. She was driving too fast considering the early morning darkness and traces of ice and snow still on the mountain highway. Her death grip on the steering wheel only made this initial leg of the journey to Geneva that much more nerve-racking for both Pizzorno and Bailey.

Pizzorno wished he could trust the man from Lugano to drive, but nothing favored that thought. He'd been bound once again at the wrists and feet making the ride that much more unpleasant. The American had promised to release him upon gaining freedom into France. He sensed the young man was simply too unstable to live up to that offer. Logically, Pizzorno had to be alert to any chance of escaping the dilemma he now found himself.

The angst on Pizzorno's face as he watched the young woman struggle with the roadway brought Bailey further satisfaction. Both men, though, could not help dart their eyes from Sophia to the passenger windows on the right side of the vehicle. The right tires were only a couple meters from the deep chasms on the other side of the guard rails.

They were but ten kilometers out of Lugano when Bailey had to admit the young lady was not up to the task of being the driver. Pizzorno might have to drive after all. It meant that the older man's hands and feet would no longer be bound. He'd be free to try something sudden.

Bailey shouted at her to slow down. She did...and then she gradually speeded up again having gained more control of the vehicle.

Having not slept well the previous night and constantly watching his hostages, Bailey was fighting his own exhaustion. His eyes would close as the car weaved from side to side with Sophia's erratic driving...something Pizzorno was sure to take notice. Bailey knew if his guard relaxed enough, Pizzorno would likely use that opening to pounce on him and try to gain control of the revolver. The older man really had nothing to lose.

It took but the next slippery corner for Pizzorno to act. He was like a snake having patiently waited until the time was just right to strike at a passing mouse. Although his hands were still bound in front of him, Pizzorno turned and grabbed at Bailey's hand holding the gun while diving toward the backseat to wrestle with the American. With his body and arms he tried to immobilize his captor. In turn Bailey fought determinedly to keep the barrel of the gun pointed away from his body and that of Sophia who was fighting her own battle keeping the swerving vehicle on the road.

Pizzorno was stronger than Bailey anticipated. He began pounding on the Pizzorno's head with his curled up left fist as he held onto the revolver with a vice grip. The scuffle was not progressing with any real winner and it wasn't being helped by Sophia's screaming. Why she didn't just stop the car would always be a question in Bailey's mind. She just kept on driving and even speeding up as if she was helping Pizzorno gain the upper hand.

The acceleration only added to the frantic scene as the car banged against a guard rail and continued on along the snowy roadway. As each tried to gain the upper hand, the grunts from both desperate men got louder.

Then the inevitable happened. The luger suddenly went off. Both of them seemed to ease their wrathful fighting for a moment to examine which of them might have been hit.

In seconds they realized the shot had missed both of them. The continuation of their brawl should have begun promptly except for a piercing scream echoing within the car. It was the earsplitting shriek from the driver. Sophia had been hit, but both men could not tell if her wound was serious. They were also not willing to stop their battle. While they fought, both had an eye on the driver since the car was now lurching from one lane to the next. Sophia no longer seemed to be fighting the road...she only maintained a penetrating stare out the front windshield.

Bailey shouted, "Stop the car for God's sake!"

Pizzorno said nothing only using the momentary lapse to grab for the revolver one more time. The gun went off again and smashed the windshield. Pizzorno seemed not to care. Bailey wasn't certain if he was winning or losing, but as long as he had the pistol in hand, he felt he had the advantage. His real concern was the condition of Sophia. She was no longer screaming.

He yelled again, "Sophia, stop the car! You're hurt. Stop the car!

Getting no response from the driver, Bailey tried a different maneuver. He began kicking Pizzorno violently on the shoulders and head. These blows began to take a toll on the older man. He began to weaken. As he did, the car began to slow. Still, the continued fight kept either from paying any heed to the wounded driver.

There was a moment Bailey thought the car had already gone over the cliff as he looked out the side window and could only see the pre-dawn mist down into a deep chasm from the right passenger window. He could even make out a mountain stream far below the cliff. The thought of that being his final resting place propelled him to initiate one more violent kick to the head and Pizzorno's grip on the pistol finally slackened as he fell back into the front seat laboring to catch his breath. That was when both he and Bailey noticed the severity of the wound to Sophia. Blood was streaming down the side of her head and she began to lean forward against the steering wheel.

The car began picking up speed once again. Without a second thought, Bailey dove toward the back left door. He opened and slipped through it just as he felt the automobile smashing through the guardrail. The back door closed onto his leg as he was dragged along the pavement. The pain from the door pinching his leg never ceased as he somehow finally got his leg free from the automobile. Then he felt pain from a new source...the gravel on the edge of the road as his body rolled. He stopped only when he was able to grab a broken post from the guardrail. He laid there at the very edge of the precipice.

Though groggy he looked ahead and was conscious enough to follow the swerving car still speeding ahead and bouncing off the guard rails. That was when he was given a never forgotten sight. The fast-moving car never slowed as it took flight. It was as if on film in slow motion. He followed the back of the vehicle as the heavier front of the car began to point downward. As it descended down along the mountain wall, it flipped only once while in the air. He saw Pizzorno's right arm flail out the side of a window. There were no screams heard...only the vehicle's blaring engine. The driver, Sophia, was motionless behind the steering wheel possibly already dead as her foot had lodged on the accelerator.

His eyes glanced quickly down to the mountain stream far below, then back to the car fast approaching. The river could just as well have been a brick wall as he watched the vehicle smash against some rocks. Pieces of the Mercedes Benz Cabriolet then began to float wildly down the swollen stream as the car continued to break up as if being torn apart by an uncontrolled group of feeding wolves.

The pain in his left leg was excruciating, but the spectacle of the horrible crash had his eyes riveted. He blinked and turned away for a few seconds when he thought he saw a body being carried away by the stream. It didn't seem big enough to be a complete body. His stomach turned over for a moment. He thought the reaction odd considering he'd shot and killed a German officer only a few days before and then witnessed four people being snuffed out of existence Sunday evening in the explosion.

He yelled madly at the horrific scene. The two people didn't have to die if they'd just taken him to Geneva. Fate had taken Pizzorno and Sophia. He hadn't killed them. If anything he was trying not to injure either of them even as Pizzorno and he were fighting to get control of the luger. The result was two deaths and very nearly a third....all because of Pizzorno feeling like his own life required him to take a risk at that moment.

The rationalization that the entire ghastly incident was Pizzorno's fault didn't ease the severe pain in his left leg. It didn't feel broken; he could move it. But, there was blood showing on his pant leg. He struggled to sit up but felt himself blacking out with the pain. As he went in and out of consciousness, at one point he thought he was sitting up and leaning again the bent guard rail post. Then he realized he was still lying on the gravel. His head ached. He touched some blood oozing from his scalp.

Fighting his way up to a sitting position, he stared down the steep cliff where he could still see remnants of the vehicle. His mind visualized the young lady, Sophia. He'd threatened her and scared her unmercifully even though he never believed she was vicious enough to be a killer. Somehow she'd gotten caught up in a momentous scheme of which she had little to contribute. If not innocent she was certainly ignorant. He hoped she'd been unconscious from her serious head wound as the car plummeted into the deep chasm.

He pulled himself over to the damaged guard rail post and comforted himself as best he could. There were no other vehicles on the road. He wondered if he was destined to just sit at the edge of a precipice and slowly have his blood and his life seep away. He leaned back and this time his thoughts were more macabre. His hatred toward Pizzorno was unceasing. He found himself hoping Pizzorno had been totally conscious during the entire flight to his death. He didn't like thinking that way, but there was no denying it. He wondered if he'd become as cold as Pizzorno and his group of assassins...or as emotionless and cruel as Roberto and Willie LaCurso.

He blacked out again....and then abruptly woke up. Still no vehicles could be seen or heard coming along the mountain road. If there was, he might not even be seen. Who would expect to see an injured man with one of his legs flopping over the crest of the cliff leaning again a broken guard rail post?

With his pant leg and the flesh of his left leg having been ripped open, he looked for something to tie around the leg above the wound. He had nothing except the arm of his coat. Taking off one arm of the coat seemed as painful as the cause. Eventually he was able to tie the arm of the coat tightly around his upper thigh leaving half his upper torso with only half the coat covering him. He smirked to himself. Nothing was easy.

As he huddled against the bent guard rail, he took inventory of any other wounds. His head seemed to have stopped bleeding, but he couldn't be sure. He didn't know how serious the injury, but it was contributing to his feeling woozy.

Noticing the luger lying beside him, he quickly grabbed it and stuffed it into his coat pocket. It gave him a shot of energy knowing that he still had some fight left in him. He looked again at the wreckage far below. While anything was better than the fates of his two travel companions, he had to face his reality. He was seriously wounded and incapacitated. If he was found and then brought to a clinic, he'd likely be recognized eventually. When he recovered enough to be moved, he'd be back behind bars. This time he'd not have the physical capability to escape.

He blacked out once again as he felt the chill on the part of his body that wasn't covered by the coat. There were moments he felt as if his situation was hopeless, but his spirit disallowed him from admitting it. Though sapped of energy and immobile, he still had the use of his brain. That was enough to spur him to use every resource he had to live.

At that moment the sun began to appear over the far snow-covered mountain peak. It provided some warmth and helped him feel thankful to be alive. He chuckled sardonically for a moment. He had no change of clothes, a fake passport, little money, and he was wanted by any number of police and military authorities. His continued escape that morning to France from Lugano had lasted about twenty minutes.

His momentary bravado was waning. He knew he was at the lowest point of his life. As bad as jail had been in Milan at least he had his entire mind and body functioning in order that he could escape. He sat there wondering what the next five minutes in his life would have in store for him. Sitting motionless gave him some respite from the pain in his thigh, shoulder and head. Mostly, though, he just felt drowsy.

He rested his head back against the post and breathed in the cool mountain air. He sensed he'd reached the limit of his endurance. His eyes closed and he again fell peacefully into semi-consciousness.

It may have been a minute or fifteen minutes later when he became aware of a vehicle's engine as it was moving down the mountain road. It was a curvy road and he could see it was a truck. Though bleary eyed, he prayed it wasn't a military vehicle.

Deciding quickly he knew he had to take a chance on the compassion of the passing driver. Struggling to stand up, the pain in his thigh shot through his body like high voltage electricity. He could stand but it was obvious he was not going far with the leg injury.

The vehicle rounded one last corner where the headlights streamed directly at the scene of the accident. Bailey knew he had to be quite a sight with his rumpled and ripped up clothing. Slowing, the truck drove by him thirty yards before yanking on the brakes and backing up. The driver looked at him as if Bailey was some kind of ghost. He gave the driver a weak wave as he sensed himself ready to pass back into unconsciousness. Figuring between the injuries and the low mountain temperature, maybe his last minutes on earth would come to a cold but calm ending.

Then he heard a voice shouting at him in German. The man cried out, "Hey there, are you all right? What are you doing out here alone?

Bailey couldn't answer. He just dragged his left leg toward the driver until he felt the man's supportive arm around him. The driver helped him around to the passenger side, opened the door, and carefully lifted him up to the seat. The leg had become very stiff. The deep gash on his bloodied thigh had soaked his pants. Between his head and his leg, he had lost a fair amount of blood, but he had to try to respond. He finally did so in Italian.

He mumbled, "I was beaten up and robbed and then left by the side of the road."

The German looked at the smashed guardrail and took a fearful look over the cliff and kind of gulped. He read something more into Bailey's response than a simple assault and battery. Then gazing at the serious leg wound, he had no more questions. The compassionate German truck driver quickly got into the driver's side and spoke with some urgency. "Young man, whatever happened, you are definitely hurt. I'll take you into the city. You need to see a doctor in Lugano."

Bailey moaned and felt the side of his head where the blood had begun to crust along the hairline above his right ear. He nodded knowing there was no other choice.

As the driver moved on with more earnestness, he seemed to want to keep Bailey conscious. "Senore...tell me your name...or where you live. Can you do that?"

Bailey couldn't think of a quick reply other than the truth, so he ignored the question. He replied, "My head hurts a bit...thanks for your help."

The German trucker could recognize his passenger likely had a concussion the way he couldn't respond. He then stayed quiet except to say, "I know where there's an infirmary. We're only ten minutes away. Please relax. You will be all right."

The man's attempt at placating his injured passenger was appreciated. Bailey hadn't had much of any legitimate acts of kindness thrown his way for what seemed like a long time. He welcomed the thought of ten minutes in the safety of a person who cared about his condition. He laid his head back and closed his eyes.

It seemed like only a minute later that he felt the truck slowing as it entered back into the city. Bailey forced himself to stay more attentive. He'd hoped he wouldn't be seeing Lugano again for a long, long time but circumstances had changed all of that.

With the sun rising there was some activity on the streets. The truck turned sharply left causing more pain to shoot through Bailey's leg. He winced but the driver seemed more interested in getting him to immediate medical assistance.

They drove by the train station where Bailey had arrived only days before thinking there was a good chance a man named Andre Pizzorno could help him. How things had changed.

The truck slowed for some pedestrians crossing to the train terminal entrance. The truck driver hit the horn as if to prod the people to walk faster. They only looked back at the truck in disgust over his impatience.

It was in that momentary stop something unbelievable happened. It was the kind of serendipity that a person could never forget. There passing right in front of the truck carrying a travel bag was none other than the young lady living at the cottage. He strained to remember her name. Was it Erika? He strained...no, it was....it was...he just wasn't thinking clearly enough to remember. She'd been so friendly, even offering him some food. Then she'd left the cottage claiming she'd be back with more food. That was the last time he'd seen her on Sunday. A while later the explosion wiped Andre Pizzorno's mansion off the face of the earth and the inhabitants with it.

He watched her walk and couldn't react. He thought for a moment he was hallucinating, but as another adrenalin rush spurred him, he sat up. In those passing seconds he suddenly realized she represented hope. If he was brought to a hospital by the driver, his chances of being identified would be almost assured. He'd be patched up, arrested, and in jail possibly by the end of that very day. His escape would end.

The driver was intent on the pedestrians and ready to step on the accelerator. He rolled down his driver's side window and put out his arm to halt any more foot traffic. When a walker finally stopped to let him pass through the intersection, he looked back at his wounded passenger. The only thing he saw was the passenger side door closing. His injured passenger had decided to depart. The driver yelled at Bailey to get back in the truck, but the young man seemed in a trance as he trudged toward the train station dragging what seemed like a dead left leg. With other traffic behind him, the driver finally threw up his hands. He couldn't just stop and chase down his passenger...especially one who no longer wished his assistance.

A traffic controller angrily motioned for the driver to get moving. All the driver could do was shrug and mutter, 'So much for trying to help someone.'

When Bailey dragged himself out of the truck and let his left foot hit the pavement, it was like a cannon shot to the brain. But, the adrenalin firing through his veins was giving him the fuel to head in the direction of the young lady he'd met two days before.

Limping and dragging his injured leg, he tried to yell her name but the word came out as only an inaudible gasp. His only chance of survival was catching up to her before she entered that train station. Inside the terminal there would be an array of military police. He'd be noticed...and then recognized.

He was aware people along the sidewalk were staring at his blood soaked pant leg and likely the injury to his head, but he just kept moving. His entire focus was to get the attention of the young woman who was walking ahead so unaware of the desperate person trying to catch up to her.

As if reading from a script, he saw her suddenly pause outside the train terminal entrance to look at her train ticket one more time. Instinctively Bailey slowed to try and call less attention. He was having difficulty speaking. He couldn't formulate her name, but he was adamant that something had to be done to gain her attention before she strolled through the train terminal doors.

A man held the door for her. She slowed, nodded and smiled, but she never looked behind at her pursuer. Bailey was but twelve seconds behind her when she passed through the door. He wouldn't give up. He had to keep trying. He didn't feel any pain as he hurried to catch the closing door. Once through he saw her continuing to walk. He again tried to shout her name. He was breathless. A noise came out like a loud whisper.

He looked quickly around for any military police. He felt for his luger. He knew he wasn't thinking clearly, but he was not going to go down without some kind of fight. Whether he died in the next few minutes didn't really matter. It was preferred to dying in an Italian prison.

He slogged on ignoring the looks of passers-by. He couldn't be bothered with their astonished looks when they saw his torn pants and wound. As he got closer to her, it occurred to him that she might not even recognize him. She might tell him to please leave her alone.

He felt for his pistol once again. He was of course not going to shoot her, but he couldn't let her take any time to decide whether she was going to help him or not. He would hold the gun against her side and order her to assist him. It wasn't ideal, but it was the chance he had to take.

His eyes were only on her as she finally stopped by a locker and inserted the key. At that moment Bailey finally caught up to her. Her auburn hair was covering the left side of her face so she did not see him approach. A couple people walked by looking doubtfully at Bailey as he reached for her arm. He could think of nothing more to do. He shouted, "Erica, my darling!"...and then he threw his arms around her and hugged her for all his worth. He hoped he'd accurately said her name.

She was of course shocked, but she felt completely safe being in plain public view. Certainly no one would let her be assaulted. Thinking it was some kind of joke or huge mistake, she played along.

Knowing she had not a clue who was hugging her, Bailey continued in a now softer and raspy voice, "It is so good to see you!"

Greta 'Mendosa' Vespucci tried to pull away to see who was accosting her and that was when Bailey spoke directly into her ear. "Erika...listen carefully...put your arms around me and hug me. It is Adam Bailey. I'm injured and in serious trouble...and not of my own doing. You are my last hope. If you scream, my life is over. If you can put a smile on your face and help me over to that bench and pretend like we're old friends, I have a small chance of survival. I need to get out of view of that station master and any military police. I can't let them see me in this condition for very long."

Greta pulled her head away and looked square into Bailey's eyes. Immediately she saw a disheveled, severely weakened Adam Bailey with an injury on the side of his head. She looked down at his pants and saw the shredded pant leg and the drying bloodstain. Her eyes got wide; she didn't know how to react.

He gasped again, "Erika...or whatever your real name is...the wound on my head is nothing. It's the wound on my leg that's killing me. I've lost a lot of blood. I'm not going to be able to walk very far."

Years down the road he would think often of her reaction that day...and still not believe what she did. Her response was immediate. She relaxed and put her arm under his arm and balanced Bailey as they walked slowly over to a bench at the side of the terminal. She helped him sit and then sat closely next to him.

Then with a false smile on her face she whispered, "Adam...it's Greta. For God's sakes...what has happened to you? For that matter, who are you...really?"

Semi-conscious, he forced himself to respond. "You have the truth. When we said our farewells, the bombing occurred a couple hours later. You can believe what you want, but I had nothing to do with that blast. The people I was hiding from when you saw me in that row boat obviously planted the bombs. I had no regard for Andre Pizzorno. He and a couple other friends of his framed me. I'm being sought by the police for supposedly planning an assassination on Mussolini. You have to believe me. I'm innocent."

Then he paused as they both looked at his lame leg. "As you can see, I've run into some difficulty trying to pass through 'neutral Switzerland'. I'm wanted by almost anybody wearing a uniform or a badge. No one from the West has any idea I'm in this kind of trouble. With no identification...no money...and on the run, I've had no chance to seek help. I came to Lugano thinking Andre Pizzorno would be someone I could rely on. I found out in the last couple days how wrong I was. In fact, thanks to him, I'm in even worse condition than I was when I arrived in Lugano last Saturday."

His eyes kept slipping up into his head. He'd remained conscious as long as he could. He mumbled his last words, "I've got to get out off the street and out of the public eye."

Then he passed out.

Greta was looking directly into his eyes and listened closely to every word he'd said. Whether she believed his entire story or not, she understood his greatest fear was being picked up by the military police. She also wondered if he'd been thinking she had anything to do with the Pizzorno estate explosion. After all, she admitted going daily up to the perch along the cliff ostensibly for artist photos. And, he'd seen enough of her pictures of the people at the mansion to understand she could easily have been a spy for those hitmen who'd planted the bombs. 'In fact,' she thought, 'how could anyone not believe I was involved if my photos were seen?

She hesitated no further. This Adam Bailey was hardly in a position to lie very creatively. She had to help the man.

As his eyes opened and closed with equal difficulty, there was a longing...as if he was willing her to believe him. The last thing Bailey remembered was talking with the female he knew as Erika....or Greta...or something like that. There were a lot of voices in his dream, but soon it was quiet.

His eyes opened unwillingly. He had no idea where he was, but Adam Bailey knew two things for certain. He was alive and he was not in any jail cell. In fact, he was in a better place than he could believe. It was some kind of hotel room... and a very spacious one at that. There was a crisp smell to the air coming through the opened hotel room French doors. As he stretched, he felt some bandages on the side of his head as well as on his right leg. He took a full breath and began putting the pieces of his life together since the last time he was conscious.

Hearing the traffic below the hotel room patio made him assume he was still in Lugano. Looking under the sheet that was covering him, he noticed he was wearing only a gown...the hospital type...and nothing else. He'd evidently had some professional medical attention on his head and leg. He was about to move the left leg until he saw the large wrapped bandage about fifteen inches in width around his thigh. Remembering the pain he'd suffered after the car mishap, he reconsidered moving the leg at all. He then felt the wrapped bandage around his head. He felt like a mummy. Still, with each breath of crisp air filling his lungs, his vision was clearer and he had no lingering headache. If not for his leg, he'd be ready to trek onto Geneva. He was energized just knowing that possibility still existed.

Then he did try to move his leg. It was a bad decision. The pain shot up through his body to his brain in a flash...so much for trekking onto Geneva. Time that he didn't have would be required for his leg to fully heal. But, he knew he couldn't wait too long. Mobility was his only next hope. The leg would just have to be a lingering inconvenience.

Sitting up to get his equilibrium, he realized immediately the medical attention and the hotel room had to have been because of Greta. He then remembered calling her 'Erika' and felt badly. He didn't even know a female by that name. Somehow, though, she'd gone far beyond bigheartedness and kindness. She was also risking her own freedom and life by assisting him. He owed her more than he owned, yet he wondered why her generosity had gone this far?

A knock was heard followed by a key to unlock the hotel room. A man Bailey didn't recognize stuck his head in. He was wearing a hotel uniform and likely had been given permission by Greta to check on the injured, unconscious man lying in her hotel suite. The staff person looked pleasantly surprised seeing Bailey sitting up in bed.

"Ah....Senore Mendosa, it is so good to see you awake. My name is Miguel. Your wife told me to bring you up some breakfast. She said she would be back shortly."

Bailey didn't know why Miguel was referring to him by Greta's last name, but he wasn't about to correct the hotel employee. Bailey waved the man into the room and felt his hunger pangs explode with the smell of food on the tray.

Miguel seemed very willing to help. "Senore, I hope your pains have subsided. Your wife told us that you were hit by a car and very lucky to be alive. Until she gets back to the room, I'll take care of whatever you need."

Bailey finally spoke. At first his voice came out in a whisper. He wondered when the last time it was that he'd talked...or had some liquid. Hoarsely he said, "No, but thank you. I believe I can handle a fork. I need to take things slowly. Thank you for the food. I'll be all right until my......ah....wife returns."

Miguel said no more. Nodding he retreated to the door and before closing it added, "Senore, you need only to call down to the desk and ask for Miguel."

Grabbing a piece of sausage without the use of the fork, Bailey ate it ravenously. He stuffed a croissant into his mouth and moistened his throat with some orange juice. He would never forget the taste of that food.

While taking another bite of the roll, he took a chance and positioned himself to stand. There was some initial pain, but not as serious as it was when he was chasing down Greta at the train station.

He stood for a moment and got his balance. Though very stiff, he was heartened that the leg was not broken.

He then moved slowly around the room bending his knee and looking for a newspaper or something that might give him a hint as to what day it was. Another breeze came through the patio doors and he got a direct smell of the lake. He'd been on and around Lake Lugano enough that the aroma was imbedded in his senses. He also got a minor whiff of the exhaust from the car traffic below.

Moving over to the French doors, he stepped out onto the patio. The breeze was invigorating. He could see part of the lake only a couple blocks away and the park right below. He was staying at one of the nicer hotels in the city.

Back in the room he continued to walk around putting more and more weight on the injured leg. There were some pills on the dresser. Figuring they were pain pills, he promised himself not to touch the bottle unless absolutely necessary. For the foreseeable future he had to be especially conscious.

It was about an hour later and still Greta had not returned. Instead there was another knock on the door. It was the attentive Miguel. He entered as if he'd done so a few times in the recent past. Bailey was standing and the hotel staff person seemed to be pleased with his rapid recovery.

Smiling, he said, "Senore Mendosa, I have a message for you. It was left in your mailbox this morning and I didn't see it until fifteen minutes ago."

Miguel gave him the envelope and again asked if there was anything Bailey needed.

Shaking his head, he held out his hand in appreciation to Miguel. Embarrassed that he had no money for a tip, all he could say was, "Miguel, you have been very helpful. Thank you."

The door had not been closed for two seconds when Bailey gingerly sat down at the desk and tore open the envelope. He expected it was a note from the young lady. He had an inclination she was about to disappear again. He read the note with full attention oblivious to any pain in his body. It read:

Adam:

I do hope you are feeling better. I checked you into this hotel
yesterday. A doctor gave you some pain medication which has
likely kept you sleeping. It is Wednesday morning and I have
had to leave Lugano upon advice from the person who has been
employing me.

You should be safe. I registered the room for an extra night
under my name. By tomorrow morning, that same person will
be stopping by the hotel to give you whatever help you need. I
told him confidentially of your situation. He understood and
advised me to leave Lugano today. With his connections he told
me he would arrange your safe passage to France.

The doctor said your head injury was not serious, but that your
leg will take time to heal. It will be stiff and sore for a while, so
I am happy my contact is so willing to assist you. It makes me
feel that I've done the right thing.

For your information, my contact's name is Roberto LaCurso.
He showed great interest in wanting to help you. You should
expect him later today to arrive at the hotel.

Safe travels and maybe our paths will cross again someday.

Greta

Roberto LaCurso!!!!!....the name hit Bailey like a sledgehammer to the side of
the head. Questions reverberated through his mind. How had she ever gotten
connected to Roberto LaCurso...or to the LaCurso family? And, she was working
for them...actually spying on the Pizzorno mansion. That was why all the pictures.
She had a record of when the people who worked for the Senore were most often
in the house. Her note confirmed in Bailey's mind that she was supplying crucial
information to Roberto LaCurso, yet. She seemed so guiltless when he'd talked
with her. She had to know what her purpose was....and, if so, she was as much
the murderer as the men who set the explosives.
     Yet, here she was coming to his aid. That was not the habit of a killer. He
hadn't known her long, but she simply was not cold-hearted enough to turn him
into the local police. He resolved to only believe she was unknowingly involved
in a LaCurso plot....just as he had been.

He felt badly for her. As the third person he'd put some faith since coming to Lugano, her future didn't look bright. He wondered what mayhem was going to strike her just for helping him.

As much as he was concerned about her whereabouts and safety, there now was a more pressing matter. Greta had unwittingly divulged his exact whereabouts to the one man Bailey had to fear even beyond the military police. Roberto LaCurso would be coming to Lugano with the specific purpose to silence him. The LaCurso brothers could not allow him if recaptured to disclose any connection to a plot to put away Benito Mussolini. Roberto and Willie would be incriminated; the entire family would be killed or persecuted.

Knowing that Roberto was already on his way to Lugano, Bailey made himself move toward the terrace to again get some fresh air. Maybe the resurgence of oxygen could somehow help him create an idea how he might escape his next calamity.

Looking down on the traffic four stories below, there was a steady stream of military vehicles and police vehicles driving along the avenue. Dealing with the younger brother of Willie was not his only concern; however, for the present he had to concentrate only on Roberto LaCurso. The man could literally be in the lobby of the hotel waiting for him...or even walking down the hallway to his suite. The next knock at the door could be fatal.

His heart rate doubling, he moved slowly back inside the hotel suite to the closet. He hoped Greta wouldn't leave him with torn, blood-stained clothing to replace what amounted to a bed gown. Like an answer to a prayer, in the closet were a sweater, shirt, shoes and pants. She'd come through once again. He now owed her money besides his life. He again couldn't imagine why she'd been so thoughtful, but he appreciated very much she was on his side.

He carefully pulled the pants on over the thick leg bandage. He conjectured who stripped his clothes off and pulled the dressing gown on him. He decided to let that thought pass.

Now focused on his immediate problem, he figured Roberto would assume he'd have little problem simply entering the hotel suite and promptly ending the American's life. Bailey had an advantage. The surprise would be that Roberto's victim would be waiting with a hidden weapon with silencer. It would only be a matter of who shot first would be the winner. Bailey had to adjust his thinking that he should not wait for any small talk or pretended kindness. He had to shoot to kill from the moment he saw Roberto. To anyone not knowing the situation, it would look like a cold-blooded killing. But, that was the way it had to be. Otherwise, Bailey was defenseless.

His leg began to throb and he eyed the pain pills on the stand beside the bed. He again fought taking one. He could not let himself be dulled by any drug.

Sitting down by the bathroom mirror to rest his leg, Bailey carefully unwound the cloth bandage around his head and examined the stitches above his ear. His growth of hair generally made the wound unnoticeable. With fresh clothes and no outward appearance of being seriously wounded, it boosted his confidence that he might be able to walk very slowly down the street without showing obvious injury. He could not draw attention to himself. Outrunning anyone in his condition was not possible.

It was Wednesday afternoon, April 10. He'd need a couple more days of recuperation before he could seriously continue his escape. As far as the imminent threat, if he could keep his wits, his best shot at overcoming Roberto LaCurso was to sit patiently and wait.

Chapter 22

David O'Brien sat in his office on a beautiful spring morning in Washington D.C. taking in the spectacle of the Washington Monument just blocks from his office. It was Monday, April 8. His window was open and faced out onto to Constitution Avenue. Shortly he'd have to close the same window. Pollen so prevalent in the District at that time of year made him sneeze and his eyes water. The coming weekend he and his wife were going to attend a ceremony for the seventy-fifth year since the shooting death of Abraham Lincoln on April 14, 1865. He didn't especially like observances of this kind. It only reminded him of the potential loss of his own people doing their government service.

The entire morning he'd been particularly agitated with thoughts of the wherewithal of his newest agent. Adam Bailey had been out of the loop for ten days...something Bailey promised would not happen if his travels into Italy had become a bit more precarious. Nevertheless, Bailey had become inaccessible and O'Brien was kicking himself for allowing his protégé, so new to the espionage game, to have such free rein. But, it had been easy to let it happen. Bailey had been working independently for the previous four years in Western Europe.

The young man had been a real find. His reconnaissance work was without precedent. Furthermore, his cover as an international wine and specialty food representative had been a workable shelter right up through his prior journey into Italy in the last month of 1939. O'Brien now had to wonder if that international businessman smokescreen had somehow become flawed.

The original intention was to bring Bailey along slowly in his scouting of Italian military facilities and manufacturing locations. It became unnecessary; he'd adapted quickly to his assigned tasks and shown amazing creativity when even the least problem surfaced. After just two missions he'd proven himself indispensable. The data, maps, and photographs he brought back were astonishing in their completeness. On his last mission in 1939, he'd traced military supplies and stored armaments from shipment centers along the coast back to the very factories where they were produced. He'd located two secret training centers that were only recently set up. When the U.S. inevitably would be drawn into the European conflict against Germany and Italy, O'Brien was confident the information Bailey had supplied the State Department would allow the Allies to cripple Italy with strategic air strikes. Time and many Allied lives would be saved.

Now his most recent mission had barely begun and Bailey was missing. The two of them had agreed to continue using his international businessman cover adding a further angle...that of being a wine connoisseur and writer. If questioned anywhere in Italy, he would express his intentions of documenting various Italian wine specialties in a series of books that would be sold in ten different languages...all the intentions of showing benevolence towards the Italian culture and economy.

O'Brien had insisted Bailey travel first to Lugano to meet Andre Pizzorno, even if Bailey felt uncomfortable identifying himself as an American agent to the Swiss businessman. Bailey's knack for probing and uncovering information was what O'Brien hoped to gain from those two meeting. What he'd learned in the past week was that get-together never happened

By Wednesday morning, April 10, circumstances as well as the weather had changed. There was a light but dreary spring rain bouncing against David O'Brien's office window screen as he stood staring out onto Constitution Avenue while he held two coded messages from Pierre Latif, his chief operative at the American Embassy in Paris. He had hoped the information would give him some indication his newest agent was actively embarked on his vital reconnaissance work along the southern coast of Italy.

The news was a bit more grim. The first message mentioned the rumor that Bailey had been detained in Milan only hours after crossing the French-Italian border. That occurrence was eleven days before! O'Brien was puzzled. He'd wanted Bailey to travel first to Lugano, Switzerland to see Andre Pizzorno, but why Bailey had chosen to go immediately into Italy was a mystery.

The second message was more horrifying. That very Swiss entrepreneur Bailey was to have met in Lugano was feared dead after his palatial home in Lugano had been incinerated by a frightening explosion four days before on Sunday evening. It was assumed he died in the blast along with a number of house guests.

The destruction of Pizzorno's lavish estate brought with it not only sadness but the realization that the man had some skeletons from his past. Only recently O'Brien had again represented himself to Pizzorno as a vice counsel at the American Embassy in Paris until Pizzorno finally learned that O'Brien was actually head of European reconnaissance for the U.S. State Department.

Crumbling the coded messages and discarding them in his waste basket, O'Brien was upset. He should have been more on top of Bailey's travels with so much at stake in this latest assignment. But, he'd gotten used to Bailey working so autonomously and then suddenly showing up with a gathering of intelligence that left him and his staff awed by the quality.

But, he knew there were other factors affecting his time. He'd been preoccupied with a few other 'minor' matters. Germany had just invaded

Denmark and Norway. Denmark had accepted a "protective" truce offered by the Germans, but Norway's response was to declare war on Germany with Britain's support. Unfortunately, Britain's backing looked woefully inadequate. Countries were dropping like flies to the aggressive Nazi imperialism. It appeared only a question of time before the Germans would occupy Belgium, the Netherlands and Luxemburg. Once this occurred there would be numerous open roads for German forces to enter France....and that country was less prepared to defend itself than most of the world was aware. France's economic difficulties, poor leadership and the inadequate military build-up made them highly vulnerable to German attack. U.S. responses had to be discussed and decided upon regarding all these developments.

And then there was Italy. That country had been dragging its feet on joining Germany in its war efforts but was now being pushed by Adolph Hitler to take a stronger stand with the Nazis. Hitler would most certainly expect Mussolini to live up to his country's obligations as set down in their Axis Agreement.

Bailey's espionage efforts regarding Italy's war assets and locations had given the State Department a very accurate picture on how serious a factor Italy might be in support of Nazi Germany....and how to depreciate or destroy those assets at the right time. O'Brien only needed Bailey's priority reconnaissance on the southern regions of Italy to complete the overall strategy to neutralize that country.

After those two discouraging messages that Wednesday morning, O'Brien was ready to move heaven and earth to find Bailey. Being detained could mean anything. Bailey could have been detected as a possible spy by the Italian military police. The best hope was that he was only held until his story about being an international businessman could be corroborated. Knowing Bailey, the young man would doubtlessly still find some way to travel down to southern Italy to complete his mission.

Then there was the worst...he was being interrogated or already shot as a spy. Or, maybe Adam Bailey had only recently made it to Lugano to fulfill O'Brien's request that he make contact with Andre Pizzorno. His young protégé could have been one of the victims in the professional hit at the Pizzorno estate.

O'Brien would not let himself focus on the worst case scenarios. He had to believe even after eleven days Bailey was still alive. He ordered that morning a coded message to his entire European spy network to be on the lookout especially in Switzerland and Italy for Adam Bailey.

By the afternoon, O'Brien received another coded message from Pierre Latif. This one was even more mindboggling. Bailey had been arrested in Milan and held in the city jail for a number of days until escaping only the past Friday. It meant that the young agent, if he was still alive, had been on the run for five days.

Despite that anxiety O'Brien carried hope. He was always being amazed at the young man's ingenuity. Bailey seemed to have been born with the instincts to survive...and likely was hiding out at that moment seeking ways to get out of Italy.

Despite his contacts in and around Milan, Bailey would have to be careful. With the fear engendered by the Mussolini regime, how far could he trust anyone?

At 3:00 he felt obliged to contact some key people in Minnesota who were closest to Adam Bailey. That did not include John and Catherine Bailey. He was not going to cause them any undue stress until he had more information. O'Brien was aware of the older Bailey's World War I record. While Adam's father was a quieter man, his nature was to not hesitate when action was needed. He'd insist on O'Brien sending him overseas to help find Adam....and he'd want to leave that evening!

He thought about the first time he'd met John and Catherine Bailey. O'Brien knew Catherine from her Washington days working on the hill for President Herbert Hoover. Since her marriage to John a few years before, he'd seen them periodically in Washington D.C. The three of them had gone out to dinner a few times, but one dinner conversation had stood out. It was two years before at an Italian restaurant on Pennsylvania Avenue. John and Catherine were not the only ones at the eating establishment that night. Also invited and introduced to O'Brien was John Bailey's personal friend, a well-known hotel tycoon who made his home in Charleston, South Carolina. It never came up how a former Minnesota farmer and this southern business magnate had become such close friends. Both men held their cards very close to their chests on anything personal.

In the dinnertime conversation O'Brien found out among other things that Granville, besides owning a plethora of hotels along the Atlantic ocean sea board, was as well the silent owner of an international distribution company in Minneapolis where Bailey's son, Adam, was employed. As any proud father, John couldn't help but talk of his son's extensive travels in Western Europe during the past few years. The 'small world' aphorism then clicked in with O'Brien, a Minnesotan as well. He realized he knew John Fena, the General Manager of North American Distribution, Inc. owned by Granville. That spearheaded the conversation along even more.

When John talked of Adam's business accomplishments in France, the Netherlands, Switzerland and Italy, O'Brien perked up. He had critical needs for intelligence coming out of Italy. When he learned Adam was fluent in Italian and knew the geography of Italy as well if not better than the map of his own home state, O'Brien asked John for an introduction the next time Adam was back in Minneapolis. Without divulging he was in charge of intelligence in Europe, O'Brien suggested it would be good for Adam to have another contact in Paris where O'Brien was known to work for the U.S. Embassy.

That had been how the whole things started. Within a week O'Brien and Adam Bailey had lunch at a quiet restarant in downtown Minneapolis. O'Brien chuckled how Adam had grabbed onto the concept of being an 'observer' in Italy while carrying out his North American Distribution responsibilities. It was after than meeting with Adam that O'Brien confidentially talked separately with Fena and with Granville and leveled with them about his true work. Fena had expressed concern about the risks Adam would have to take; Granville knowing the father of Adam showed no surprise that Adam had agreed to 'observe' for the State Department. Granville sensed the 'minor' assignments given young Bailey by O'Brien would eventually grow into something likely more important...and dangerous. Both Granville and O'Brien agreed to not mention this government job to John and Catherine Bailey until the young man gained some experience and showed his true interest in possibly working for the State Department.

O'Brien shook his head thinking how natural Adam Bailey was in carrying out the extra task for the government. The initiative and wits Adam showed bordered on remarkable. The aim had been not to put Bailey in any danger while gathering intelligence in Italy. The problem was that the 'part-time spy' worked at an entirely faster and more aggressive pace with each assignment.

By the end of 1939, Bailey was carrying out acts of espionage far beyond what O'Brien had generally discussed with Fena or Granville. As an observer, Bailey had instincts for survival and pushing for more complete reconnaissance that many of his other agents didn't have the drive or disposition to try.

Bailey would receive the offer from O'Brien to become a full-fledged employee of the State Department just months before. O'Brien smiled recalling Bailey's reaction as if befuddled what took the State Department Director of Western European Intelligence so long to make the decision.

Now, with Bailey missing and likely facing peril at every turn, O'Brien felt responsible for the mess Bailey was obviously in. Now he had to pull out all the stops to find the young man...and that included seeking private help, in particular from the wealthy silent owner of North American Distribution, Inc.

O'Brien's call to Henry Granville came yet that day. In their previous conversations, O'Brien had detected about Granville a more personal interest in the career and undertakings by Adam Bailey. It was as if Bailey was family to Henry Granville.

As O'Brien's call went through to Gransville's headquarter office in Charleston that Wednesday afternoon, his stomach was grinding. Granville would be highly upset not realizing Bailey had been taking on even higher risk reconnaissance.

The phone call turned out not to be as difficult as O'Brien guessed. The hotel mogul showed restraint and didn't question O'Brien's need to use Adam in more precarious assignments. It was as if Granville knew Bailey would draw himself deeper and deeper into various agent responsibilities.

After explaining how long Adam had been missing...and that he was ostensibly on the run since escaping a Milan city jail five days before...Granville responded in his strange drawl, "David, 1940 brings on some more hard times. I know you have to utilize people in the best way you know how for the good of our country. I'll check in with John Fena in Minneapolis as to any other planned business travels and call you back."

O'Brien replied, "Henry, you should be aware Adam had another special assignment from me to meet a potential colleague in Lugano, Switzerland. He was to call on a man named Pizzorno on matters not important right now. Long story short...this man had his house were blown up in what appears to be a professional hit judging by the pieces being strewn all over Switzerland. We're not certain, but Pizzorno was likely killed in the blast. Therefore, he'll obviously be of limited assistance in finding the whereabouts of Adam."

He paused for a moment after making his darkly humorous statement and then added, "Henry, there is something else....and it might have gone wrong. I'm aware he had some kind of assistance getting into and out of Italy apparently something he'd worked out with someone as a North American Distribution representative. As you can imagine with the world in the shape it's in right now, crossing Italian borders by an American is not easy. I believe he's secretly been giving aid to one of his close Italian clients in exchange for entry in and exit out of Italy. I can't be certain of that factor, but everything points to my hypothesis being true. If we can find out who this business client might be, that might provide a clue."

Granville suddenly seemed to want to get off the telephone saying, "David, I appreciate the call. So you know I have a couple confidants who happen to be as close as brothers to Adam. I'll be involving them in this matter. Please call me if you get anything else regarding Adam's whereabouts.

The call ended with both men now focused on finding Adam Bailey. For O'Brien he could only wait for any further word about Bailey from his operatives in Western Europe. He wished there was more he could do, but felt relieved he had Henry Granville intensely interested in helping. Granville seemed to have the connections and spontaneity to take effective actions. With that additional hope, O'Brien and his wife attended a ceremony that Wednesday evening at Arlington National Cemetery commemorating another anniversary....this one for the end of the Civil War. As the speeches spoke solemnly about the war dead of that four-year struggle within America's borders, it somehow seemed like a simpler time back in 1865 compared to the world situation in the spring of 1940.

As for Henry Granville, in the next minute after hanging up the telephone line with David O'Brien in Washington D.C., Granville placed a call to Charlie Davis in Alexandria, Minnesota, Granville's corporate counsel for his holding company, Triple H Development, Inc. Davis' secretary directed Henry to find Charlie at Jamie and Lindy Lawton's Lake Johanna lake home north of St. Paul.

Granville didn't ask for the phone number. He simply asked how the weather was that day in Minnesota. Davis' secretary dutifully responded, "Mr. Granville, it is just another beautiful spring day in our lovely state."

On that April day 'beautiful' meant the snow was gone, trees and bushes were barely budding, and the temperature was at best fifty degrees. That was a good weather day in central Minnesota at that time of year.

Granville shook his head and smiled. A Minnesotan's description of a fine spring day and the definition from a South Carolinian were quite different. Nonetheless he knew where to find Davis and Lawton if the weather was good on a Wednesday afternoon.

In another minute he was dialing Midland Hills Country Club pro shop in St. Paul. The golf professional Wally Mund answered the phone. Without so much as a greeting, Granville exclaimed, "Wally, no time to talk. I need Jamie or Charlie on the line as soon as possible. When did they tee-off?"

Mund was used to calls from the southern businessman for his two members and could tell there was greater than normal urgency. "Henry, they teed-off about two hours ago. They should be stopping by the club between nines very shortly. I'll have them call promptly."

Again, no number was exchanged. Midland Hills Country Club seemed like an office at times for either Lawton or Davis....especially on the weekends....and always on Wednesday afternoons.

The return call to Granville came within fifteen minutes. After ten minutes on the telephone, Charlie Davis and Jamie Lawton asked Wally Mund to put their golf clubs in the locker room. Golf had become secondary. They were on their way home.

That evening Lawton and Davis drove out to Wold-Chamberlain Airfield south of Minneapolis to pick up their friend. Henry Granville was flying in from the east coast on a private plane. As he always did when visiting, the Lawton lake home was the place he always stayed. It was understood the three of them plus Lawton's wife, Lindy, would remain together or in close communication until Adam Bailey was found. And, they would not sit quietly waiting for further word from David O'Brien. Action had to be taken about Adam's situation.

On the short trip home from the airfield, the three of them were already surmising where Adam might be. Having escaped from a Milan jail, they were certain he'd head toward neutral Switzerland in an effort to enter France. They also knew about Adam's travel habits including his strange on-going and unwanted relationship with a local Twin Cities gangster, Willie LaCurso.

Even Adam would forget how much they knew...in particular the brief liaison he had with LaCurso's daughter five years before. Adam never talked much about the night she was gunned down while sitting beside him on a joy ride along the River Road bluff overlooking the Mississippi River. Lawton, Davis, and Granville knew he was lucky to have lived through that ordeal.

As the months and years followed, Bailey refused to talk about the tragedy. They could tell he was even more wounded emotionally with his treatment by Willie LaCurso. The St. Paul gangster never forgave the young man for outrunning the security car that drove behind the couple. LaCurso had said he never wanted to see Adam Bailey again. While the two Lawtons, Davis, and Granville considered that a blessing, the avowal did not hold.

The three of them hadn't said anything to Adam, but they were aware LaCurso had learned a few years later how Bailey had become a highly seasoned international traveler with a lot of time spent in Italy. Adam had even been invited....unwillingly...back into the good graces of Willie LaCurso.

It was Lindy Lawton who would learn in her own private talks with Adam that he was fulfilling a favor for the gangster by carrying overseas a suitcase full of gifts and some cash to help out Willie's extended family in the old country. He intimated to Lindy he'd taken on the task a couple times out of shear empathy for the LaCurso family. He said he'd witnessed a lot of hardship in Italy under the egomaniacal Benito Mussolini and his regime. Helping out Willie and his overseas family seemed like a small kindness and was of little inconvenience.

Logically, Lindy figured there had to be a quid pro quo for Adam to be obliging the gangster. They never got that far in their conversation...or Adam would change the subject if the question was broached.

As the three men arrived at the Lawton home along Lake Johanna and filled Lindy in on the reported travails of Adam, all four of them immediately became alerted that the young man's days as a courier for Willie LaCurso may just have caught up to him.

Chapter 23

Roberto LaCurso was annoyed that Greta Vespucci was still in Lugano when he received a second telephone call on that Wednesday, April 10. He'd hoped she followed his strong suggestion that her job was done and she'd taken the previous Sunday afternoon train out of Lugano to Venice. He didn't want her in the city when the Pizzorno mansion and its inhabitants were blown into the sky later that Sunday afternoon. He was already astounded she'd not put the details of her previous two weeks of surveillance into any thoughts that her work had provided valuable information in setting the time for the explosives to go off. But, there she was...still in Lugano on that Wednesday... for reasons understandable and even laudable. Greta had thought her additional reconnaissance work after the blast might benefit Roberto and Willie.

What she had to say made Roberto grip the telephone so tightly he thought he'd crush the receiver. Her voice was soft and showed a different kind of distress as she said, "Roberto, I met that same young man...that visitor to the Pizzorno mansion named Adam Bailey. He was seriously injured. I decided to help him and I now need a favor."

Roberto tried to speak calmly but his voice gave away his impatience. "Greta, what about the young man....was he injured in the blast?

"I thought he might have been until yesterday when I intended to catch the Tuesday train to Italy. The same young man somehow saw me and flagged me down as I was entering the train depot. The physical change since I'd last seen him only two days before was dreadful. He had been seriously injured in some kind of car accident north of Lugano. Again, I couldn't just leave this fellow wobbling there in the huge train station. He had nowhere to go and was barely able to walk with a serious leg injury. He pleaded for some help; I gave it to him.

I got him a room at the same hotel where I'd stayed the previous two nights in downtown Lugano. I asked a very helpful hotel steward to find a doctor. I claimed the man was my fiancé and needed medical attention immediately after being hit by a car. Thankfully, he asked no more questions nor did the doctor when he arrived. No broken bones were found, but the fellow had two severe wounds...one to the head and another...a deep gash on his left thigh. The doctor bandaged him up. I went and got some medicine to further help the man's recovery.

At that point I recalled your words of concern, Roberto. I'd helped the man as much as I could without getting more involved. I decided right then not to delay my exit from Lugano any longer. I was concerned I could get mixed up in something that suddenly could make me quite visible. That was something Willie specifically asked me to not let happen.

I stayed an extra day to help him and switching my train ticket to today. When he began to gain consciousness, I paid for the hotel room for both tonight and Thursday night in advance to give him more recovery time. Hopefully by then he might be more mobile. I felt badly for leaving, but I have my obligation to you and Willie to remain unseen.

I'm now at the train station ready to catch the train to Milan. Roberto, I'm hoping I did the right thing. I think this young man is innocent but he's in a bad way. The favor I'm asking is whether you might help this American get to France through your connections in Switzerland?"

Roberto LaCurso's throat was so dry he could barely speak. One of the two people he wanted dead was laid up in a Lugano hotel room just waiting to be finished off. His entire outlook changed in those few seconds. He was barely able to hold back his exhilaration as he then pandered her efforts. "Greta...my dear... that was a very brave and generous act you did for this Senore Bailey. I'm proud of you and I will get in contact with this young man right away. I'm certain there is a way I can help him find his freedom no matter where he wants to go."

His response greatly reassured her.

He continued to soothe her. "Greta, you now should leave Lugano. You've done what you can. You really don't know what he's done, so it's better to separate yourself from this man. If he's on the run, I'll find out why and where he needs to go. It's best you not be seen as an accessory anymore in this man's plight. I can take it from here. I'll take the short train ride up to Lugano this afternoon and see what I can do for this unfortunate soul. I'll see that he won't have any more problems."

Greta was taken aback how caring Roberto sounded. With Roberto arriving later that day, she felt it was practically a guarantee Bailey would reach the French border as soon as he could travel. She gave him the details of the hotel and room number where Bailey was recovering.

Roberto responded urgently, "Now, Greta, don't delay. Be on that next train to Milan and then onto your parent's place towards Venice. Willie and I will be worried about you until we get word that you are with your family."

Upon hanging up the line, Roberto was on his way to Lugano within the hour. Having all the information he needed to find Bailey, he'd packed his revolver and silencer visualizing the death of the American within minutes after he entered the hotel suite. He felt less pressure to find Pizzorno. The latest report was that the remains of Pizzorno had not been found in the rubble left by the blast. If the Swiss entrepreneur was still alive, he would be in hiding knowing the bombing was meant for him above everyone else. Once done with Bailey, he would personally not rest until Pizzorno was eliminated as well.

It was later that Wednesday afternoon as Roberto LaCurso was making his way to Lugano that he mulled over his simple plan to kill Adam Bailey. With but six blocks to the Lugano Hotel, he'd go directly to the hotel suite, complete his business with a bullet to the head of the injured Bailey while the American lay defenseless in his suite, and then shortly thereafter be on the 7:10 train back to Milan. His intentions to kill Bailey seemed fool proof....like ending the life of an injured animal.

The train ride was uninterrupted arriving on time at the Lugano station under relative clear skies around 5:00. Never had a victim been presented to him so conveniently. Striding confidently down the street feeling his luger with silencer in his pocket, he even pondered taking a later train so he could dine at his favorite Lugano restaurant.

When Roberto arrived at the stylish hotel, he took the elevator to the fourth floor. Peering up and down the hallway and seeing no one he went directly to Room #411. He figured to knock and just say 'room service'. When young Bailey opened the door, it would be the last thing the American would ever experience.

Unfortunately, that convenient plan did not materialize. When he knocked there was no sound in the room....no voice....no movement. He pounded the door once more with the same statement and got the same silent response. Greta had mentioned she'd bought Bailey some pain medication. Maybe he was fast asleep....or in the bathroom. Roberto was about to use his revolver with silencer to blow open the door when he saw a hotel steward cleaning an ashtray at the end of the hall. Roberto held back from causing a scene and blowing the lock off the door.

Keeping his revolver in his pocket, he decided to just wait until the steward shuffled up the hallway to finish his clean-up task. The last few hours had gone smoothly. There was no reason not to be patient. He pulled out a cigarette impatiently waiting for the slow moving worker to walk by him. Looking irritably at his watch, he thought Greta Vespucci had described Adam Bailey as being seriously injured and practically immobile. If he wasn't in the room, where could he be? This inconsistency troubled him.

As he pondered what else might have happened, he got edgy. He'd most assuredly gained some respect for the American for his survival instincts. The young man had broken out of a Milan jail house...an extraordinary and bold act in itself. If not for his being crippled in a car mishap, Bailey might already be in France. And, what were Greta's standards as someone being disabled. The young man may have already ignored his seriously damaged leg and left the hotel to continue his journey to freedom. If that was so, Roberto had to admit the American could be one of the slipperiest people he'd ever known.

But, he had to be certain and check out if Bailey was in the suite.

Looking down the hall, the hotel worker was cleaning yet another hallway ashtray. Roberto realized he'd begin to look too conspicuous to the steward if he didn't say or do something.

He angrily called out, "You there...please help me. I've forgotten my key in my suite. Do you have a master key to let me in?"

The maintenance man seemed to hesitate, but then waved and began moving toward Roberto.

That Wednesday the hours sitting in that hotel suite had moved along as if stuck in sand. Adam Bailey was a sitting duck for Roberto LaCurso. But, he was still one step ahead of his pursuer. Bailey was aware of Roberto's imminent arrival, something unknown to the would-be killer. One of his strengths used liberally in the last few days was his willingness to lie, steal, and deceive with impunity in order to survive. Gone was any sense of morality or remorse for anything he'd done since his imprisonment. He intended to win against Roberto LaCurso in any way that was required. Fairness and sportsmanship learned in his previous life had little to do in this game of life and death. For him to have a future, Roberto would have to die. It was that simple. No one else could be accountable. No doubt Roberto had a similar kind of weapon with silencer that Bailey had in his pocket. It was whoever got the first open shot when the hotel suite door opened.

That very thought caused him to reconsider his position. He wanted a further advantage over his foe, so he could be more guaranteed to pull off the first shot.

Bailey's thoughts went to the very loyal hotel services man Greta had obviously tipped handsomely. Miguel had been looking in on him as if he was a close relative. Bailey now needed a different type of support from the hotel employee.

Calling down to the front desk, he asked Miguel for some room service food and drink. Five minutes later Miguel entered the room and showed immediate satisfaction with Bailey up and sitting by the desk, dressed casually, and showing little of his serious injuries.

The steward said something about returning from the dead, but Bailey disregarded the kind retort and got right to his point. "Miguel, you met my fiancé and I've now ordered her away from the city because the accident was actually an attempted murder. I obviously survived, but the killers are not about to give up."

Miguel's eyes got as wide as saucers. With the steward's abiding attention, Bailey continued, "I need to ask you for a few favors. You won't be in danger, but you could be of great help to me. I believe the people trying to kill me may have learned I'm at this hotel. I need to dodge them somehow. I'm thinking that a disguise...like the very uniform you are wearing...would give me the cover I need to be a less obvious target. I need to create whatever advantages I can craft until I'm healed. With a hotel staff uniform I might be able to walk away from this hotel unnoticed.

Pausing, he looked straight into the hotel staff person's eyes. "What do you think, Miguel? Can you help me?

Amazingly, Miguel showed no hesitation. He seemed caught up in the intrigue not truly understanding the life and death nature of the help he was being asked to provide.

He nodded and left the room without further words. Bailey couldn't imagine what Greta had tipped the man for him to be so willing to assist. Within two minutes Miguel returned with a hotel maintenance uniform complete with hotel logo on the lapel. The uniform was slightly large but useable.

Miguel noticed the look on Bailey's face and assured him. "Senore, with your leg injury, better some pants too loose than too tight.

Bailey couldn't help but smile. The steward was thinking of everything. Acts of extreme generosity by certain people like the tailor back in Milan, by Greta Vespucci and now by Miguel would never be forgotten. He thanked Miguel repeatedly giving him every Swiss Franc and Italian lira Greta had left for Bailey. He figured if the evening ended successfully, he'd be using Roberto's money to get out of town. If the result was the opposite, he'd need no money.

Changing into the uniform with help from the steward, he then asked one more favor. "Miguel, this is imperative. As much help as you've been, I have to insist that you never admit you've ever seen me. I want you to be safe. So that you know, there might be some kind of incident happening in this very suite in the next few hours. Don't be alarmed if the police ask you about the Mendosa couple staying in Suite #411. Just say you saw them leaving the hotel with their bags earlier this afternoon around lunchtime."

Miguel looked shaken.

Bailey tried to appease his concern. "Miguel, you no longer need to check on me. I'll be leaving shortly. While you don't know my real name, it's best that we leave it that way. But, do know that I'll always remember your kindnesses."

Miguel nodded solemnly.

Bailey added with a smile, "And, if you ever do learn of my real identity, just don't believe everything you hear or read.

Miguel nodded again this time with a small grin.

Bailey then said urgently, "Now, it's important that you leave. There is a very dangerous man who will be sneaking into this hotel. There's a good chance only one of us will be leaving alive. Promise me you'll stay quiet and stay as far away from this room for the rest of the afternoon."

The color in Miguel's face had returned...only concern now showed. As he headed for the door and opened it to leave, he looked back and murmured, "Senore, whoever you are, I wish you well. I'll follow your instructions but I will be there for you at any time today if further assistance is required. You have only to call."

Bailey smiled hoping that would not be the case. As a further gratuity, he offered the services manager the clothing Greta had purchased. Miguel raised his hands as if to say nothing more was needed. Bailey had no time to argue. "Miguel, I'll be wearing the uniform. I won't need these clothes and I don't want them found in this room.

Miguel nodded and accepted the new clothing on that basis and left. Again Bailey had to trust someone he didn't really know to follow his instructions. His instincts told him Miguel would do so.

Alone in the suite, Bailey stood to check the status of his leg. While he wanted to exercise it, the stiffness made movement quite painful if he moved it too quickly or for an extended time. He looked at the bottle of pain pills longingly but shook off the temptation. If the day was to be his last, he wanted to be thinking as straight as he could. He figured adrenalin would supply an extra sharpness when the critical time arrived.

Now every moment became crucial. He sensed Roberto could burst through the door and simply shoot whoever was in the suite. Vacating the room was now necessary.

Sticking his fully loaded revolver in the coat pocket, he caught a glance of himself in the mirror. He hardly recognized his reflection...and it wasn't the uniform. He was bent over as if a much older man. But, there was something else. He looked closer in the mirror and could see a different look in his eyes. Gone was the mirthful, quick to smile image of his youth. He'd aged ten years in the last ten days. He'd killed. He'd held two people hostage until he led them to their accidental death in the Swiss mountains. He'd barely escaped death himself a number of times. He hoped he could live with himself if he ever made it to freedom....but he wanted a chance to find out.

Bailey straightened up while still staring at himself in the mirror. Putting the uniform cap on his head, he didn't take his eyes off the figure in the mirror until he finally staggered slowly out of the suite and closed the door. He had some matters to attend before Roberto LaCurso made his presence.

Going down the hall he tried not to hobble, but lifting the injured left leg was difficult. At the floor exit he shuffled down the back stair case. He was perspiring liberally from the pain when he finally reached the main floor.

Removing the cap, he took a side door to the street and began moving better as he walked. The limp was noticeable and the pain unrelenting, but he did feel less of a target with the uniform.

Seeing a small boarding house, he entered and asked for a room. If what he had planned would occur, he'd need a room to hide out and rest that night.

Nothing was easy. The proprietor seeing the uniform asked directly why he needed a room since he obviously worked at the Hotel Lugano. It was just another question that made every action seem a challenge. Bailey rolled his eyes knowing he had to lie and deceive yet again.

Flashing a strained smile, he winked at the boarding house owner. "I'm getting the room for a relative. I can't afford the Hotel Lugano."

The proprietor laughed and turned the registry around for Bailey to sign in. Bailey's mind went blank for what name to write down. The man gave him a curious look. "So, you don't know the name of your relative?

He smiled at the proprietor and then quickly wrote down a name...someone from his past...someone he recalled would have been quicker at the draw when the chips were down. He then backed away slowly from the desk saying, "No Senore, I can remember my uncle's name quite well."

Then he nodded at the proprietor and calmly walked out of the small rooming house with a room key in his hand. He felt good using the name of a former friend...a man who had been so kind to him in his youth.

The owner of the small hotel turned the registry around and looked at the name. The name meant nothing to him...Loni D'Annelli...just another Italian name. Unfortunately, the proprietor would never meet the actual Senore D'Annelli since the special man to Adam Bailey had been dead for almost nine years.

Bailey strode carefully back to the plaza thinking of the name he'd signed. It seemed like a lifetime had transpired since he last saw the man who had treated him like a favorite nephew. If Loni D'Annelli were alive that day, Bailey was certain no matter how mixed up in corruption the Chicago conman was, he'd do everything in his power to help out the naïve and trusting kid he'd known from those many summers back at Chippewa Lodge near Bailey's hometown in Minnesota.

The nostalgic moment brought a slight tear to his eye...or was it more the pronounced pain shooting through his leg as he passed across the plaza opposite the Hotel Lugano? Needing to sit down, he plopped down on an outside chair at a café. Concealed by a large plant, he had a bird's eye view of everyone entering or exiting the front of the hotel. Ordering some wine he sat at the table his eyes riveted to every person who might be Roberto LaCurso. He'd met a few of LaCurso's family, but had never laid his eyes on the actual brother of Willie, even when delivering the suitcases with money intended to help the LaCurso family.

Getting impatient looks from the restaurant staff, he finally ordered that day's special and mindlessly ate the food. While the rest helped his leg, he also realized he was sitting there with no money in his pocket. Every moment seemed to be a predicament. He wanted to be unnoticed, but now he was down to stiffing the café owner. Nothing seemed to work smoothly.

The sun had gone behind the mountains and clouds and still no Roberto LaCurso. Bailey began to doubt whether he should have ever left the hotel. Whether it was the wine or the pain in his leg, he was getting too fidgety to remain at the table any longer.

Suddenly a hand touched him lightly on the shoulder. His hand automatically reached inside his coat for his revolver before he realized it was Miguel.

The loyal hotel steward leaned over quietly and whispered, "Senore, there is a man in the hotel who just asked if the 'Mendosa' room number was #411. I have observed you sitting across the street since shortly after you left the hotel. I know it is important that you see this gentleman. He is having a drink in the hotel bar. He is wearing a very nice dark overcoat and hat."

Bailey patted Miguel on the shoulder in appreciation. Then he pulled the man closer and said, "You just screwed yourself out of some of that tip you earned. I have no money. Please pay my bill and by the grace of God, someday I'll repay you."

Miguel smiled and took the bill. He strolled away saying in a more serious than joking tone, "Senore, I'll hold you to that. I want you alive so you can pay me back."

Then he looked straight ahead never placing his eyes on Bailey again as he paid the ticket and ambled back across the street to the hotel.

The time had come. Bailey had to make his move. With Roberto LaCurso in the bar, it was just a matter of time before he would make his way to the fourth floor.

Marching with but a slight limp across the plaza to the back stairs of the hotel, he gingerly climbed the four flights of stairs. It was painful, but the discomfort was secondary. He was already into a kind of fog; his senses acutely aware of everything around him.

He opened the stairway door at the end of the hall just as the elevator door at the other end of the hall began to open. A well-dressed man in a dark coat and hat slipped out of the elevator and began making his way slowly down the hall examining each room number as he moved along.

Sharply dressed as Miguel had described, the man was heavier than his brother, Willie, but they had the same gait the way they walked. There was no doubt the fellow was Roberto LaCurso.

Bailey, dressed in the hotel staff uniform, began cleaning a hallway ashtray as he moseyed along. He kept his back toward LaCurso. Out of the corner of his eye he saw Roberto halt at Suite #411. It was a strange sight watching the antics and behavior of a man who in seconds intended to kill him.

He watched Roberto reach into his pocket while knocking on the door and mumble something incoherent. With no response he knocked again, this time harder. There was of course again no reply.

Then he glanced up and took more notice of the uniformed hotel maintenance man. He shouted down the hall demonstratively, "You there...please help me. I've forgotten my key inside my suite"

Bailey answered in his own low-voiced Italian, "Yes Senore, I'll be there momentarily."

As the maintenance man moved closer, Roberto impatiently exhorted, "I am Senore Mendosa. I have forgotten my room key. Could you open the door with your master key? I need to retrieve my room key and some papers I've forgotten."

Bailey appreciated the deception. When two adversaries meet, they had to be of quick mind and ready to say or do anything in order to win.

He pulled his cap lower over his eyes and continued shuffling along the hall only slightly faster. He knew he must appear as a much older and broken down man to the younger LaCurso brother.

The voice of Roberto reminded Bailey of Willie. Both brothers requested things in the same way. It was voiced in a question, but it was meant as an order. In other words, "get over here and open this damn door!"

Moving closer to the man who intended to kill him inside that suite, Bailey was now standing but five feet from Roberto with his face down, shoulders slumped, and seeming to be searching for the master keys. LaCurso's hand was in his own overcoat pocket no doubt wrapped around his revolver.

The would-be killer was anticipating action the moment he stepped into the hotel suite. It was also likely Roberto would waste the maintenance man as well so no recognizance could ever take place. That thought maddened Bailey even more. Neither Willie nor his brother, considering the life style they followed, cared little about the preciousness of life.

That day Roberto's plan to kill Adam Bailey would not come to pass. As Bailey moved closer to the door, Roberto was tapping his shoe in impatient anticipation.

Bailey knew it was now or never. He had no keys...just his sweaty palm on his own revolver with silencer in his pocket. His heart was beating like a flashing bar sign...his mind as cold as the winter wind.

He did not hesitate. He pulled out his luger, aimed it at his would-be murderer's heart and pulled the trigger. He shot the man as easily as snapping his fingers...and with no remorse. With the silencer the noise from the gun sounded like a man spitting a wad of tobacco at a spittoon ten feet away. As the well-dressed man fell in the thin hallway, Bailey grabbed the man's right arm to make certain he didn't have enough life in him to fire a return shot from his own weapon in his coat pocket.

Crumpling to the floor, Bailey put his face exactly in front of the dying Roberto. He wanted the worthless hood to know who had bested him. The look of shock on Roberto LaCurso's face was something Bailey would never forget. And, when he did think about killing that man years later, he never felt regret...

only satisfaction that a high-powered mobster didn't get away with another murder....and never would again.

Bailey felt an odd haze passing over him as his victim lay breathless by the unopened door to the suite. The realization he had another chance to live and another chance at escape gave him renewed energy. Like a robot he quickly reached in the dead man's coat and pulled out Roberto's pistol with silencer. He also pilfered LaCurso's wallet and passport...and train ticket. He had money again...and a passport he might be able to use for a short time until the dead body was identified.

With his injured leg, he had neither the leverage nor the time to drag LaCurso's body into the suite. The body would be found as soon as someone arrived at the fourth floor.

He hurriedly limped down to the end of the hall where he had to navigate the back stairs once again. The trip down seemed easier with his adrenalin rush, but it still took more time than he had.

At the first floor he was perspiring as if he'd just run a mile. He caught his breath and then walked as casually as his leg would allow out the exit door onto the hotel's patio. He pretended to clean some ashtrays and then showed surprise at the sudden commotion. People were already rushing out various exits. He couldn't believe LaCurso's body had already been discovered.

Playing ignorant he asked one patron racing away from the hotel, "Why all the panic? What is going on?"

The man was wide-eyed and didn't answer. He just kept moving along as if his own life was in danger.

Finally another bystander striding along with his eyes continuing to look back at the hotel said to some onlookers excitedly, "They found a dead man in one of the hallways. The police are on their way, but the gunman has still not been apprehended. He's somewhere in that hotel."

With those words seeming to strike even more fear, the wide-eyed bystander quickened his pace and disappeared down the street.

Suddenly a number of police vehicles began arriving. With his uniform giving him an effective disguise, Bailey showed no hurry. It was better to sit and watch the turmoil he'd caused. Walking away from the hotel at that moment might look suspicious.

Someone else walked through the courtyard and shouted to concerned hotel guests lounging on the patio, "They found a body. He was found shot and dead on the fourth floor. The police are about to comb the hotel looking for the shooter."

Bailey felt the still warm gun barrel in his coat pocket. He now felt an urgency to leave the hotel area. He did not want to face any questions as to where he'd been in the last fifteen minutes.

Hearing that bit of news, the bystanders in the patio began to disperse. In their case they were more concerned about unexpectedly coming face to face with the gunman escaping down the back stairs and running out onto the patio...as the limping maintenance man had done minutes before.

When the patio area was bare of people, Bailey stealthily transferred LaCurso's wallet and revolver to his pants pocket as well as his own pistol. Removing his hotel staff coat, he slowly began treading down the street amongst the panic around him. At the corner he stuffed the coat into a trash barrel, tore the train ticket into shreds before depositing the strips into the same container and continued on his way to the rooming house where he'd rented a room for the night. He now had cash to pay for the room and two weapons that provided him some sense of protection.

Limping by the front desk with his pants pockets bulging with his acquisitions, the proprietor was arguing with his wife in the back room. Bailey slipped by the quarreling couple and climbed one flight of stairs. This time the leg really throbbed. The adrenalin kick was no longer supplying him the extra vitality. Entering the small room he wanted to collapse on the single bed but he thought better of it. Instead he removed the two revolvers and placed them under the mattress. Then he eased down on the bed and picked his leg up with both hands before dropping it slowly on the bed. He'd given the injured leg quite a work out and he was now paying the price.

Laying his head back against the pillow, he noticed he was not shaking or sickened that he'd just killed a man not twenty minutes before. His lack of compunction bothered him momentarily, but he'd come more to accept the terms of his circumstances. He had to make a choice...and he had unhesitantly made it. Two weeks before he might not have acted so swiftly and found himself the one collapsing to the floor mortally wounded.

His mind eased. All he wanted was rest. What better place to be at that moment than a small out of the way Lugano rooming house.

He moved his leg and a shock wave of pain flashed up through his body to his brain. The leg desperately needed time to heal. He'd give it the night and see what his limitations were in the morning.

Slowly his moaning stopped and he fell into a deep sleep.

It was 11:00 later that Wednesday night when Bailey awoke from his deep slumber. His body was stiff. He hadn't moved his sleeping position for hours. His encounter with Roberto LaCurso came immediately to mind. Any shame he might have had about dispatching Willie's younger brother simply never materialized. More on his mind was his mobility.

Rising and then sitting on the edge of the bed, he slowly rubbed his left leg to stimulate more blood flow. Minutes later he stood bending and straightening his leg to test the motion and strength. He wanted it to feel better, but it didn't. Any reduction in pain meant the sooner he might continue his quest for freedom in France. Right then that country seemed like a million miles away.

Rubbing his face he thought about what might be happening at the hotel crime scene. The LaCurso body had neither his revolver nor any identification. The local police had a corpse they couldn't identify and a killer still at large. Eventually Roberto would be identified. Even when that happened, there would be no reason to connect the death with the escaped prisoner from Milan.

The authorities had to be somewhat dumbfounded. Why would an unarmed man be shot in the hallway and then left there? Also it would be normal for the murderer to drag the body to the stairwell or leave him in a suite just to delay having the corpse being found. Why had that not been done?

The incident would be deemed a robbery that went bad as the dead body had nothing remaining in his pockets. There were no signs of a scuffle; it was just a quick, clean shooting from extremely close range instantly killing the victim. The authorities would have little to go on in finding the murderer.

Bailey took inventory of the things he'd poached from Roberto LaCurso's coat. The wallet contained a stack of cash in both liras and Swiss francs. While he now had two weapons with silencer, having an extra weapon seemed potentially helpful. Having the passport gave him rise to his chances for moving onward to Geneva.

As he examined the extra pistol and silencer....the actual weapon whose purpose was to end Bailey's life...the thought flashed in his mind that the Swiss might want to escort him to the French border just so he'd quit shooting people. That bit of jest hardly raised a smile and only caused a wave of coldness toward Willie LaCurso back in the States. Bailey had never felt such hatred towards another human being. Willie had known him for years, had entrusted him with suitcases full of cash for his Italian relatives, and the two of them had even met socially for lunch or drinks. Bailey tolerated the older LaCurso not to gain a friendship, but truly believing he was helping a demoralized family suffering under the Fascist regime.

While his efforts had to have been appreciated, in the end he was only someone who could be manipulated. It was a pattern of behavior Bailey simply could not understand. He was being used...like an animal pulling a wagon. The disrespect shown towards him was far beyond disappointing; it caused an animosity that was seared into his brain. One of the LaCurso brothers had just paid for that indifference. Now, only hours later, Bailey was already thinking of similar vengeance on the older LaCurso brother.

It would be the same hunt. Once Willie learned of his brother's death...and soon come to the realization that it was Adam Bailey who pulled the trigger, the young man would become the number one target in the hoodlum's life. Willie would not rest until his brother's death was avenged. For that reason alone Bailey knew he'd kill again if given the chance...and with no qualms.

The dark cloud in his mind dulled the pain in his leg. He had to move on. With Roberto's money, he could be in Geneva in a day by train. The more he altered his looks, the better chance he had of actually making his destination. Some hindrances could be seen, but there would be other surprises. That brought him no real concern. Confidence in his ability to react had brought him this far.

His eyes turned to LaCurso's passport and picture. The man was stockier but the photo was just dark enough that Bailey thought it useable. With a hat over his lighter hair coupled with his dark beard, he did look older. He just might pass for Roberto.

Figuring the authorities would have the deceased's name within a day, it was best he try to utilize the I.D. while it was still possible. Once Roberto LaCurso's body was identified, his name would be spread out all over Italy and Switzerland as a murder victim. The stolen passport would be useless.

He forced himself to think logically. Taking a midnight train would be best. A nighttime guard might more cursorily gaze at the passport, especially if Bailey interrupted the man's attention with conversation. If the guard questioned the validity, he would die. The revolver with silencer would complete the task quietly. There could be no hesitation.

Anticipating he wouldn't have to face that decision gave him hope he still had some humanity left in his otherwise compassionless soul. For now, his tactics had to be decisively harsh, callous, and merciless.

Concerned about his being recognized in public, he also perceived a better disguise was needed...even if it was just stealing another coat at a restaurant. That idea was still percolating as he left the rooming house before midnight to find a taxi.

Walking slowly into the same plaza where the Lugano Hotel was located, he observed people leaving a theatre. The idea came to him immediately. Hobbling down a side alley to the back door of the theatre, Bailey was ready to bribe the guard for entry. It was unneeded as he strode by the sleeping guard. Inside the back stage were actors and actresses scurrying around having just finished that night's performance.

He hardly noticed the scantily clad females. His objective was something else. Finally he saw what he needed....a closet full of various types of costumes used by the players. Slipping into the moth ball smelling room, he quickly sought out the kind of clothing that might work to his advantage. Three minutes later he slipped out the back door in a well-used suit of clothes with matching fedora. In his pocket he also stuffed a fake moustache and beard. The clear-lensed spectacles gave him a more studious, conservative look.

As he'd left the theatre via the back door, the guard at the bottom of the outside steps abruptly woke up and tipped his cap to yet another actor done for the night. The guard watched the young man's gait and sadly shook his head. The old man could see the persistent limp was not an act.

Catching a taxi, Bailey was at the train station in five minutes. Another day he would have just walked the short distance. At the ticket master's desk he found there were plenty of overnight tickets to Geneva available. The ticket master didn't even ask to see the passport since the travel was within the country.

The 12:35 train took off on time and Bailey thought for the first time since arriving in Marseilles twelve days before that something was going right. Lying down in a sleeping berth, he slept deeply at times and fitfully at other times during the long train ride. The change in elevation in the Alps as well as the long tunnels caused varying pressures in his ears. It was a welcome inconvenience.

By the time the train approached Geneva on Thursday morning, Bailey had secured his next plan. Crossing the border from Geneva into France was his only objective...and it would not be easy. He was still the wanted American would-be assassin who escaped from a Milan prison. There were undercover Italian agents at all Swiss border cities. As for the Swiss authorities, they still had to perform the obligatory search for him as part of being a neutral nation. It was a requirement of their political stand.

Worse yet Bailey felt as if he was leaving a trail wherever he went. Escaping through Switzerland to Geneva was so predictable. The dead German railway official he'd thrown off the train had likely been found. Then a highly respected Swiss businessman had his house blown up. While he wasn't part of the debris, he was still missing. Then two days later a major crime figure was found shot at a Lugano hotel.

To the paranoid Bailey the mounting deaths were pointing at him as if he was in a spotlight. He was ready to go underground in Geneva for a few days just to ease his paranoia.

As the train slowed entering the Geneva station, Bailey took note of all the police and military officers patrolling the gates. It helped in the early morning that there were so many people scurrying around the terminal. Nonetheless, he knew he'd be scrutinized by each guard, military policeman, and train official as he exited the terminal.

Placing the wide moustache and beard he'd acquired at the Lugano theater on his already whiskered face, he adjusted the spectacles and fedora as he waited for all other passengers to depart before he took the few steps down to the station platform. Nodding to the conductor he walked more confidently behind the other departing passengers. He allowed his limp to be more pronounced as he slowly strode by two military policemen. He touched the brim of his hat and they disinterestedly did the same. His heart leaped. He felt like a rabbit walking through a den of foxes, but his disguise was working.

At the street exit of the Geneva train terminal, there appeared an army of police and guards routinely checking everyone's identity. Not wanting to put Roberto's identification to the test, he had to react and try something else.

At that moment he noticed a hunched over man pushing a cart selling food to passengers. Following his instincts Bailey directed his attention in that direction.

Patiently waiting his turn to buy something, the old gentleman looked up at Bailey curiously and then commented in French, "Mousier, I hope your toupee sticks better to your head than your moustache does."

Bailey immediately drew his hand to his mouth and felt the phony moustache hanging from his upper lip. He tried to re-position it but the glue had hardened. With his heart rate having just doubled, he finally pulled the false moustache and beard off. His actual twelve day grow of facial hair would have to suffice to continue his masquerade. The food seller had probably saved his life.

Looking sheepishly at the old man, Bailey felt as if he was on stage and an ad lib had to be contrived. With but a couple seconds of delay, he whispered to the old man, "Sh...sh...my girlfriend and my wife are both here to meet me. My friend, you can imagine this could be quite awkward. I'm trying to make myself unrecognizable to both of them."

In empathy the eyes of the man behind the cart widened. He whispered back, "Ah, my good man, you are in trouble. I've had the same problem...granted many years ago...and it ended badly. You I will save."

Bailey almost laughed. He'd stumbled upon a man who was swallowing his made-up story with the credulity of a schoolboy. After selling an apple to a passer-by, he motioned for Bailey to get behind the cart. "Mousier, put on the extra apron hanging on my cart. You now work for me."

And, that's what Bailey did for the next half hour helping the man sell most of the food remaining on the cart. A couple of the train station patrols came by to purchase some fruit. They paid no attention to the old man or to Bailey. His confidence in his disguise was growing by the minute. He even thanked a military policeman and told him to return if he got hungry.

The old man was delighted with the support. When the passengers finally began to clear out, he leaned over to Bailey and murmured, "Senore, you are helping me more than I can maybe help you. Have you seen either of the two ladies yet?"

Bailey had almost forgotten his spurious story, but recovered quickly enough to act out his anxiety. He nodded vigorously and didn't say a word as if one of the ladies was close by.

The old man began pushing his almost bare cart towards the street exit nodding for Bailey to keep up with him. "My good man," he murmured, "I have a feeling you need to get out of the train terminal and on your way. Please just push the cart toward the exit while I get my license stamped by those God damned soldiers. Don't stop. They'll likely just ignore you. I'll join you out on the sidewalk. "

Bailey began to sweat. Was this impetuous move linking himself with the food merchant going to be his undoing? Was the old guy about to turn him into the military police?

Bailey placed his hand in his coat pocket to locate his revolver. After all the close calls he couldn't believe he was going to go down in one weak impulsive moment by trusting an old fart pushing a food cart.

At the door two guards looked at the remainder of the food still in the cart. At that moment the old man returned, grabbed two apples and gave them to the two guards saying, "Gentlemen, let this be for my gratitude in keeping this hallowed terminal so safe from danger. Arriva derche. I'll see you tomorrow."

The two guards smiled and bit into their apples not noticing that the cart man had an associate wearing a very nice suit under the long green apron he wore.

In the next minute, the cart was outside and the old man noticed his new friend was pushing the cart very fast despite a very palpable limp. The cart man shouted out, "Young man, slow down. It looks like you have a flat tire the way you are walking. You're fine. Your lady friend and your wife are not going to notice you anymore. You have Guido to thank and you can do so by stopping by that shop across the street and buying your new best friend a bottle of wine....maybe two bottles since I plan not to sell any goods this afternoon. Guido's cart needs a rest and so does Guido."

Bailey re-directed the cart towards the shop and sat down on a bench waiting for the lame old man to complete his journey across the avenue. The cart proprietor sat down heavily on the bench seeming to be quite satisfied how the day had gone so far. Bailey reached into his pocket and pulled out some of the money he'd pilfered from Roberto's pockets. He pushed a hundred Swiss francs into the shirt pocket of the old man and said, "My friend, you have been a life saver. Go in and buy what port you desire. Make it three...even four bottles...if that's your pleasure. I'll guard your cart while you fuel up."

The cart man laughed easily now seriously believing he'd just been blessed with the kind of day people only dream could happen. Five minutes later he returned to the bench as Bailey calmly sat there resting his leg and watching the pedestrians.

Already swigging one wine bottle from the five bottles he'd purchased, the old guy sat back and offered some quick advice to his new friend. "Mousier, never have your wife and your girlfriend live in the same town. Guido speaks from experience."

Bailey laughed out loud. It was the first time he'd experienced true humor in what seemed like an eternity. He slapped the cart man on the back and took a drink from the open bottle offered by the old fellow.

Guido didn't realize what he'd said was so funny. He'd given the advice in all seriousness. But, it didn't matter. If it brought some pleasure to a young man who'd just repaid a favor with a hundred marks, then Guido was going to let his new friend enjoy his counsel anyway he chose.

Bailey slowly got up from the bench and extended his hand. The old man had already downed the first bottle. He wiped his hand and grabbed Bailey's open mitt. He was accepting thanks from a true gentleman. He'd saved this man from a fate worse than death...the wrath of two women finding out they'd been two-timed. Guido had stood tall for the male population and succeeded. It wasn't often he felt success. In fact, he couldn't remember if he ever had.

Bailey took off the green apron and placed it neatly on the cart. He waved back at the old guy as he hobbled down the street. Guido would enjoy one more bottle of his celebratory wine before he staggered down the street to his old shanty. That afternoon he would sleep off his private festivity after downing a third bottle for lunch. He still had plenty of money for dinner...or booze...from the leftover Swiss francs he'd received.

As for Bailey, his momentary joviality disappeared very quickly when a police vehicle screamed by him. The piercing noise brought him back to reality. He had to hide out while he devised some possibilities to get over the border into France. It frustrated him he was so close to freedom yet so far from actually being free.

As he continued down the street, he decided his best chance to cross into France was in the municipality just north of Geneva called Le Grand-Saconnex. Located along the southern tip of the lake, it was one of a limited number of border crossings into France. In the past while on business, he'd stayed at some lakeside hotels. Close by was a plaza contiguous to the border gates with shops, street side vendors and kiosks. If he was to have any chance at all of finding a way into France that area might be his best bet.

He counted the money he had remaining from Roberto LaCurso's wallet. There was more Italian lira than Swiss francs. He no longer had enough money to stay in one of the higher quality hotels he'd stayed in the past. With the cooler weather it became necessary to buy a coat for warmth if he couldn't find nighttime cover.

Within minutes of arriving at the plaza, he'd purchased a European style coat from a street vendor. Heading toward a small plaza bar, he observed his reflection off a shop window. With his unshaven face, the glasses, the fedora, the frumpy used theatre suit, and his newly purchased used coat, he hardly recognized himself.

Seated at a table outside the bar, he ordered a beer and looked longingly across the wide circular plaza and the Le Grand-Saconnex border entry into France. There seemed to be twice the border guards milling along the barbed wire barricade. He saw another change. There was fifty yards of no man's land between the wires of Switzerland and similar barbed wired wall entering France. The conditions in Western Europe had become so much more nerve-racking. Even though, Switzerland had declared its neutral position, there was obvious insistence by Italy...and especially Germany...that the Swiss-French border no longer be the easy walkway into or out of either of the two countries.

The built-up border with barbed wire and the towers with soldiers manning them made the crossing seem intimidating. He took a swig of his beer as he rested his throbbing leg on a chair. He sat there for the next hour just staring at his challenge. The task of crossing into France looked more unlikely with his bum leg.

Two Swiss military police walked by his table. Bailey pulled up the collar of his coat and drew the fedora down lower over his eyes. He had no idea what his next step was going to be, but that was of little consequence if he didn't keep a low profile everywhere he went. He took a deep breath wondering where he was going to look for his next good break. There was no question luck was going to have to be on his side.

Chapter 24

Sitting in the Lake Johanna home of Jamie and Lindy Lawton on Thursday evening, April 11, their guest, Henry Granville was watching the sun disappear behind a western cloud bank. Rumbling from an approaching storm seemed to be the ultimate metaphor for the atmosphere within the household. The ice had only been off the lake for two weeks. With the humidity unusually high for so early in April, the lake seemed as inviting to dive into as it did during the summer months. But, he knew better. The cold water would be numbing.

Lindy was playing with her newest addition, a one-year old youngster named Marion. Her husband, Jamie, was playing cribbage with his fellow attorney friend, Charlie Davis. Normally there would be a lot of banter at the card table, but that evening all four of them were preoccupied. Adam Bailey had been missing in Europe since arriving in Marseilles, France on Sunday, March 31. It was almost two weeks with little hint as to where he could be.

They were discussing possible places Adam could be hiding out while waiting for another update from Granville's friend, David O'Brien, at the State Department in Washington D.C. That Adam had escaped a Milan jail the previous Friday was now impressive but old and useless information.

Lawton and Davis had hardly said a word since pulling out the deck of cards. They simply dealt, laid down each card, moved the pegs and counted their points in silence. Granville, who rarely showed his face in the Twin Cities, had flown to Minneapolis to give whatever support he could to the distressing situation.

The four of them had not yet included John Bailey and his wife, Catherine, in the news about Adam being missing. Henry was following David O'Brien's suggestion to let things play out a bit longer in hopes of gaining new information about Adam. In previous trips to Western Europe and Italy, O'Brien reminded Henry how Adam had often been out of reach for a period of time...unfortunately never for this length of time.

Everyone in that room had been unaware that Adam was so heavily involved in carrying out some assignments for the government while in Italy...that is, everyone but Henry Granville. Granville had known of the growing risks Adam had been taking since O'Brien needed Bailey to remain on the payroll for North American Distribution as a cover. John Fena, the general manager of the company, also knew of the observation tasks being asked of Bailey, but not the advancing risks his employee was taking on.

It wasn't as if O'Brien was not being straight-forward; it was more that Bailey was creating the angst. Since agreeing to help the State Department, he'd gone far beyond the lighter observation tasks asked of him. Even David O'Brien had become more concerned how Bailey was at times being too reckless.

Back in the Twin Cities when he wasn't overseas or in Washington D.C., the Lawtons and Davis had noticed some changes in their young friend. He was not as jovial and he didn't stop over for dinner as often. They didn't suspect anything right up to Adam's latest flight overseas. When Granville suddenly flew up to the Twin Cities to bring them up to date with the predicament young Bailey was in, he also relayed to the Lawtons and Davis the full picture of Adam's secret life for the last two years.

The phone rang about 7:00 Friday morning at the Lawton residence. It was an overdue call Granville was expecting from O'Brien. The greeting was minimal. Granville remained silent for the next two minutes. When he finally hung up the line, he was surrounded by impatient looking eyes.

He seemed only slightly relieved. "Well, O'Brien confirmed the latest report of Adam being jailed in Milan and then escaping after a couple days. But, he added since Adam's disappearance there have been some strange happenings in a southern Swiss border city named Lugano directly north of Milan. This included a dead railroad official found lying by the tracks at the border one day after Adam's escape. O'Brien said it made sense that Adam would head north into Switzerland giving him a better chance of escaping into France from a neutral country. In Lugano Adam apparently knew a man and might have sought help from some fellow named Andre Pizzorno."

Granville paused to scratch his graying beard. "That possibility has faded because of two rather unfortunate occurrences in the last couple days. Apparently Pizzorno, a rather wealthy gentleman, had his lakeside mansion obliterated in an explosion in what O'Brien described as a 'professional' job this past Sunday. Secondly, this man, while not killed in that murder attempt, was found by some hikers dead along a mountain stream fifteen kilometers north of Lugano. Supposedly it was an accident. A car under his name had plunged down a mountain cliff. Pieces of the automobile were actually imbedded in his body. He had been dead for only a day when his body was found yesterday.

To add to all of this horror, yet another man was gunned down in a hallway of a Lugano hotel on Wednesday. It turns out he's the kingpin of a large Italian mob family. The coincidence is he's a relation to a rather sordid local gangster living here in the Twin Cities who we all know quite well. The dead man's brother is Willie LaCurso."

The Lawtons and Davis looked at Granville like he was joking.

Granville held up his hand. "I'm not done. The dead man was from Milan and was stripped of everything on his person...his identification, money, and likely a firearm. O'Brien seemed not to be as well versed as we are in Adam's unwanted and uncomfortable relationship with Willie LaCurso."

The nods around the Lawton living room showed agreement.

Jamie Lawton was the first to react. "I believe there's enough evidence to suggest Adam is not only alive, but we can guess his route. He's heading across Switzerland as sure as you can bet he had a run-in with Willie's brother.

Charlie Davis nodded. "And, he's got half of Switzerland and no doubt some undercover Italian agents and police looking for him after his escape. It's likely forced him to go underground while he tries to move on toward France.

Granville while lighting an oddly shaped porcelain pipe nodded. "I don't know about the other deaths, but the demise of Willie's brother and Adam likely being in Lugano at the same time...that's a connection. Something further tells me the LaCursos had something to do with Adam being arrested and jailed... especially since the brother obviously didn't come to Adam's aid when he was jailed in Milan.

If I'm reading this situation correctly, I can't imagine what Adam was going through in that jailhouse, but once he figured the LaCursos had something to do with him being imprisoned, he has revenge as much on his mind as seeking freedom in France. I believe we should be aware with Adam having settled the score with Willie LaCurso's brother, our young friend might be an entirely different Adam Bailey than the one we picture over the many years we've known him."

Lawton nodded. "If that's the case, it would appear Adam made it somehow to Lugano and Willie's brother found out he was there. He might have gone to Lugano to finish off Adam....and it ended up badly for Roberto LaCurso. How Adam could have won that fight is difficult to envision, but he did. It's now been two days since Roberto's death. Adam likely absconded with the guy's money and identification and is long gone from Lugano. Now the question is where would he have the best chance for crossing into France while dodging every authority figure in Switzerland?"

Lindy had been sitting idly listening to the back and forth amongst the three men. She finally reacted. "Gentlemen, you have to be exaggerating. I can't picture Adam killing an animal much less a person."

Granville, Lawton, and Davis only looked at each other while she talked. Lindy was thinking of the young man from Glenwood, Minnesota...the same one who lived with them during his first three college years at the University. While they appreciated her loyalty to the younger Adam Bailey image, they weren't affected by her words. They were all visualizing the nightmare he'd been living for the past two weeks...and he was still at large and fleeing the authorities. If he was recaptured, he'd be in the hands of the Italian militia in no time. Whatever they were holding him for, it had to be very serious. It was likely he'd not be heard from again.

Lindy forced the three men to hear her out. "Let's not jump to conclusions about what he might or might not have done to get into Switzerland. Regardless whether he had anything to do with any of those deaths, he's definitely in Switzerland and desperately looking for passage to France."

She then sat forward riveting her eyes on each person in that room. "This may be a long shot, but I believe I have an idea where he might try to cross into France. He talks constantly about his fondness for the city of Geneva, Switzerland. He's mentioned spending weekends there when taking breaks from his business trips. He speaks of staying near the border crossing in a section of the city in the section of the city called Le Grand-Saconnex. I'm suggesting he's either somehow traveling to that city or he's already there. Although he likely has some acquaintances in that city, in his predicament I doubt he'd put their lives in jeopardy to help him. He's on his own and no telling what shape he's in considering living in what had to be inhuman conditions in that Milan jail."

Granville, Lawton, and Davis slowly looked at each other. Jamie smiled at his wife. "She's right. I don't know of another city he talks about more than Geneva. He's often mentioned if he lived in Europe he'd live in the northern part of the city. That's where 'Le Grand-Saconnex' is located alongside Lake Geneva. That's where he stays at various hotels. He describes the background of the mountains reflecting on the waters of Lake Geneva as if God himself has a summer home nearby. He talks fondly of the busy plaza with shops and cafes right next to the border gates to catch visitors coming and going."

Davis agreed but showed some doubt. "I repeat....our young friend has enough law enforcement people looking for him to fill a small stadium. He's gotten this far with apparently little help. He can't trust anyone...not in the fix he's in....except us."

Davis looked at each person in that living room. There were nods and momentary silence.

Granville replied, "O.K., we all want to help him. Hell, I wish we were in Geneva right now. But, let's think this through. His ingenuity in escaping from Milan was remarkable. He has to be so well disguised any one of us could be standing next to him and not recognize him."

Lindy offered a further concern. "Gentlemen...that dead man...shot at the hotel in Lugano...if he is the brother of Willie LaCurso, Adam has another problem. By now Willie knows about his brother's death and of Roberto's intention of getting rid of Adam. Willie might not want to believe it, but Adam and Roberto clashed and Adam somehow came out the winner."

As the three men nodded in further agreement, she added, "Let's be absolute on this matter. We know the way Willie LaCurso and the mob operate. A situation this serious regarding a family member would suggest Willie's already on the trail seeking restitution. There's also a good chance Adam knows too much about the LaCurso family's actions in Italy. Willie's family could be facing some real trouble from the Mussolini regime if someone like Adam were captured and started spouting off what he might know about the LaCurso clan."

She paused to look into the eyes of her husband. "Jamie, I suggest Willie LaCurso is doing the same guessing game we are doing right now with maybe even better information and arriving at the same conclusion. Adam Bailey has to be heading across Switzerland to Geneva. Our young friend is going to have more to contend with than the border patrol, military police and Italian undercover agents. I believe Willie LaCurso will be seeking him out in the hope he can finish off what his brother failed to do. Adam Bailey is a dangerous man to the LaCurso family for what he might say to the authorities. And, when Willie finds Adam... and he'll not stop until he does... there will be no questions asked...only shots."

The three men grimaced into their respective drinks. Lindy had proven again why she'd been in charge of the U.S. Attorney's branch office in Minneapolis until the previous year. Her decision to become a professor at the University of Minnesota law school better fit her days with a husband and young family, but that investigative unit was certainly missing a very key component when she resigned.

Charlie broke the silence. "Lindy, I believe I want to marry you. Leave this weak minded man you've been married to for seven years. Escape with me to Alexandria, Minnesota, a hot bed of international crime, where we can enjoy solving crimes to our dying day."

Lindy laughed. "I'll keep that in mind."

Lawton chuckled. He was used to Davis' jokes no matter how serious the situation. But, his grin didn't last long. "O.K., Lindy's overview sounds very solid. Adam has a more difficult road to follow than he can imagine. We're at least in a position to possibly slow down or even stop Willie LaCurso if we act promptly. I say we get the St. Paul police involved. They should be able to pick up Willie on some kind of trumped up charge. Whatever delay can be created gives us more time to find Adam."

Granville rarely used profanity, but he was obviously comfortable in the Lawton home. "God damn it!" he said, "I never figured this work Adam did for the State Department would put him in such dire straits. He's obviously become valuable enough that David O'Brien counted more and more on him for intelligence gathering in Italy.

John Fena, my general manager at North American Distribution, has kept close tabs on Adam, but even he has no idea the risk Adam has been facing. O'Brien did intimate to me in confidence during a recent telephone call that Adam Bailey had incredible mentality for intelligence work. He was confident, quick thinking, and had the ability to remember everything in detail. But, what O'Brien didn't say and we all know to be true, our young friend does not have the mindset of a killer. However, what Adam has likely gone through in the last two weeks makes me look at things differently. If he was subject to cruelty and maltreatment, that type of experience can change a man's disposition. Survival could have altered his normal behavior and made him do whatever he had to do to escape his captors."

Granville turned silent too lost in his personal thoughts. Lawton and Davis caught each other's eyes. Some things they'd had to mastermind and instigate in their past defined what Henry had just said. They said nothing to console Henry since nothing could be said. He'd spoken the truth.

The phone rang in the study once again. This time Lawton answered it. It was David O'Brien. The phone was handed to Granville. He only said, "This is Henry."

Staying quiet throughout the call, he finally laid down the receiver after thanking O'Brien.

Charlie was impatient. He huffed, "For Christ's sake, Henry, talk!"

Granville gave a small grin to Davis' outburst. "O'Brien confirmed the shooting victim in Lugano was definitely the brother of our local huckster, Willie LaCurso. Swiss authorities are looking for someone who somewhat matches Adam. Bystanders told police they'd spoken with a scruffy looking young man wearing a Hotel Lugano staff uniform. Not only did he look out of place...like the uniform wasn't really his...but he was remembered because he spoke 'American English' to them in the hotel's patio just after the shooting and walked with a noticeable limp.

O'Brien doesn't have as complete a picture why Roberto LaCurso and Adam could have been at odds with one another. I think we have a pretty good idea Willie LaCurso's brother ventured to Lugano to snuff out our young friend...but failed in his mission. It's a pretty good bet as well that Adam was the reason for the failure. How he might have gotten the leg injury is anybody's guess...maybe during his altercation with Roberto."

The Lawton living room was silent for just a moment when Davis finally bolted upright. "O.K. folks, we have Adam with no passport, little money, dirtier than a coal miner, and moving through Switzerland by train or automobile on what could be a seriously injured leg. He's a sinking boat with no life jacket. I ask you, what the hell are we waiting for?"

In the next minute Lindy was on the phone to the airport while Jamie and Charlie were packing. Henry arranged passports and visas to France for Lawton and Davis through O'Brien's office. By that Friday afternoon the two men were on a flight to New York's LaGuardia where they would pick up the personal identification supplied from O'Brien. Later that evening they were on an overnight transatlantic flight to Paris on Pan American.

Arriving in Paris on Saturday, April 13, the bleary-eyed Lawton and Davis took the late afternoon train to the French border town of Vernier. They arrived with enough daylight to survey the chain fence borders and the heavily guarded gates both on the Vernier side and across a short piece of no man's land to the similar type of gates at the border city of Geneva, Switzerland. It was the one main border entry into the Le Grand-Saconnex section just north of the main city that Adam had always preferred. With the mountains and the large lake looming to the northeast, both men, despite their exhaustion, could see why Adam was so entranced.

Having slept intermittently at best on the train to Vernier, they decided to cross the Franco-Swiss border on their tourist visa yet that Saturday evening and stroll around the plaza area with the many shops and cafes. They were operating on a host of hunches, but they all made sense...as long as Adam Bailey was still alive. Even if they'd found he was in the hands of Swiss authorities, they were in a position to raise hell legally with the Swiss consulate to delay Adam being transported back to Italy. For the time being they only wanted to believe there'd be no other place to find Adam but at that Geneva border crossing.

Late into that Saturday evening the two men strolled around the Le Grand-Saconnex plaza bouncing from bar to bar, café to café hoping they might be seen by him It was a long shot, but everything they were doing was a gamble.

By midnight they were cross-eyed from exhaustion. Staying on the Swiss side of the border that night at a small hotel near the plaza, they both flopped on their respective beds without changing into night clothes.

By mid-morning they were awakened to the sounds of church bells. They had forgotten it was Easter Sunday. It would be an especially busy day with families shopping and wandering about in the plaza and otherwise trying to take their minds off the omnipresent stress of wartime Europe.

Returning to the plaza, church services were still in session so the marketplace was not yet packed with people. In the afternoon it would be more difficult to find someone they knew trying to disguise his looks completely. Davis remained at an outside table at a cafe while Lawton sought some way of sending a telegram back to America. With it being Sunday, offices were closed. He was finally directed to a local police station where he was eventually able to send a telegram. He claimed to just want to let his wife back in the States know he had arrived for his pleasure trip to Lake Geneva.

There was truth to his claim, but the message was intended to relieve both Lindy and Henry Granville back in the Twin Cities in a more purposeful way. The coded telegram read:

Lake Geneva is beautiful. Still shopping.

Throughout that Sunday morning, Charlie and Jamie spelled each other every hour sitting at a small outside plaza café while the other caught a catnap or strolled close to the border watching every maneuver by the patrols. There seemed to be an inordinate number of guards making any clandestine crossing seem implausible.

When Lawton had the vigil at the outside café table, Davis did what he did best. He went from shop to shop around the plaza talking with anyone who spoke English. It didn't matter the subject. His main purpose was to remain visible.

Around lunch time Lawton crossed back through the border just to observe any glitch that might allow someone to sneak across the border without being instantly shot. He sent another telegram to Lindy from a Vernier telegraph office asking if she had any new information. He waited for a reply. It came within a half hour. She had nothing new to report.

Returning across the border to the plaza at Le Grand Saconnex, he was eyed by some curious officials since he'd passed through the gates only an hour before. An officious French guard approached him and asked again for all his identification. Then he stared at Lawton saying in a strong French accent, "Your back and forth travel to the Swiss side is irregular. What is your purpose?"

Lawton stared at the French official and responded with a slight smile, "Mossier, I am deciding between my French girlfriend and my Swiss wife. With luck when I get over to Geneva, I will soon be passing back into France for good... if you understand my preference?"

The Frenchman's face relaxed and a slight grin appeared. Maintaining his stiff, snooty posture, he gave Lawton a nod and returned the visa without further examining it. He touched the brim of his hat with two fingers and walked away allowing Lawton to return into Switzerland.

Back at the plaza Davis was intently staring at the increasing number of people ambling about the marketplace. With Lawton ready to spell him, Davis remained and let his eyes close. Periodically he'd open them to reach for his beer mug. Since 9:00 that morning there had not been one minute when one of them didn't have his eyes peeled on the activities surrounding them. Though both knew Adam Bailey's gait, posture, and mannerisms, they also looked for a younger disguised man with a noticeable limp. They were convinced they could see past whatever masquerade Adam might employ. Nonetheless, it was a wearisome chore doubled by the frustration that there were no guarantees he would be in the plaza area.

It was a half hour later when Davis snapped awake from his catnap at the table. A pigeon was eating some food scraps he had dropped on the ground. He looked at his friend and noticed Lawton staring even more intently at an area of the plaza near the border gates. Without saying anything, Lawton suddenly got up from the table and began moving with seemingly no real purpose along the edge of the plaza. Occasionally he'd stop to look at a kiosk but Davis noticed his friend's movements and eyes were honing in on something or someone.

It was fifteen minutes later and Lawton had moved to the opposite side of the plaza...his eyes always returning to that one place in the corner of the plaza. Davis kept looking in that same direction but could not decipher what was catching his friend's attention.

When Lawton sat down on a plaza bench, Davis thought his friend just needed a rest. He figured Lawton's eyes were closed behind the sunglasses he wore. It was when Lawton abruptly sat bolt upright that Davis threw some Swiss francs on the table and moved over toward that same bench.

Lawton didn't even acknowledge him as Davis sat down. He just continued to stare at something about a third of the way around the square.

Finally he hissed, "Chas... I want you to take notice of something and then tell me if I'm nuts."

Davis nodded and sat back casually on the bench waiting to confirm that fact and pleased he was being given a chance to jibe his friend.

In a whisper, Lawton hardly moved. "I've been noticing a man selling chocolate candy from that rickety cart over there on the corner of the plaza close to the border patrol and the gates. His clothes don't fit him very well. I think he's wearing a wig and a fake moustache as his facial hair doesn't quite match. He seems kind of bored with his current stature in life. While all that isn't important, do take notice how he constantly turns his gaze toward the people talking with the border patrol...and then watching who was being allowed or not allowed through the gates to France. He doesn't walk much but when he moves around that old cart he does so very slowly...like something's wrong with his leg. He also doesn't seem to care whether he sells any candy or not. People walk by and he doesn't say a thing to possibly peak their interest."

A mother pushing her baby in a stroller momentarily stopped by the bench and Lawton drew silent. When she finally walked on, Lawton continued in the same low volume. "Charlie, I want you to visually remove that vender's droopy moustache, disregard the lengthy, uncombed hair, and then watch how he gazes at the border guards. Does it remind you of someone who stares that same way as he appreciates one of his well-played shots on the golf course?"

Davis focused hard at the man selling chocolates. The fellow looked much older with the ill-fitting clothes. Sure enough, there was some natural colored hair on his face yet his head of hair showed a lot of gray. Typically the beard is the first hair on a man's head that shows gray. As for the clothing, it was almost comical. The pants barely came down to the top of his socks. The floppy hat on top of the wig looked older than the person wearing it. The vender was slouched but when someone asked for a chocolate, his body movements were of a much younger man.

Finally responding, Davis said in a hush, "I'll be damned. He needs a shave and some new treads, but it looks like our young businessman has gone into candy sales. Jamie, how long has he been there?"

Lawton shook his head. "I've been observing him occasionally all morning, especially when he moves around with that limp. I had to get closer to see through his masquerade."

Reenergized, Davis reverted to his normal joking ways. "Jamie, do you suppose we should go buy some candy. He looks like he could use the money."

Lawton hurriedly whispered, "I think we'd better wait. We've made ourselves too noticeable all day. If we're being watched, we shouldn't go over there and just start talking to him. I think we'd create problems for him. We've got to let him know we're here, but meet somewhere else."

Smiling at each other like two kids, both men had to fight the urge to sprint across the plaza. Enjoying the moment, they suddenly held their breath as two military police strolled by the mustached vender. The vender suddenly dropped something as if to prevent the two military police from looking directly into his face.

When they moved on, the vender straightened up, took a deep breath, and adjusted his clothing and moustache. Deciding to move his cart, the man hobbled along with his head down seemingly more interested in leaving the plaza than selling any more chocolates.

Lawton whispered again, "He doesn't look in the best of shape. He may not be mobile enough to carry out too strenuous of an escape. Let me go alone over to check out his condition and let him know the cavalry has arrived. You're likely to get to damned emotional and start hugging him.

Davis snickered, "You're probably right. You go. I'll stay here just to observe if there are any other players in this little scene. There could be some other eyes on him as well."

They split up with Lawton slowly sauntering the general direction of the cart. He got closer and then whimsically appeared interested in buying a chocolate. The older man's head was down seemingly uninterested in dealing with any potential customers. His face was turned more toward the border patrol at the gates.

At that point Lawton was standing by the cart waiting to be served. The older man without looking at his patron robotically said in Italian, "Can I sell you some candy for your children, Senore?"

Lawton pointed to a box of chocolates with cherry centers and promptly responded, "No, but we've got a tee time this weekend back in the States. I was wondering if you'd be interested in losing some money."

The proprietor suddenly glanced up. In seconds tears appeared on the corner of both his eyes. While the candy salesman didn't change his facial expression, he was moved to the point that he had to lean on his cart for support.

Reaching for a box of chocolates a very emotional and scruffy Adam Bailey chokingly gasped, "I can't believe you found me. In fact it scares me that you have. It means I'm recognizable. But, I'll admit you are a sight for sore eyes."

A person walked by and Adam changed back into his role saying in Italian to Lawton, "Senore, try some of our chocolate covered pecans. They are delightful. Your children will adore the treat."

When the pedestrian got out of earshot, he returned to a hoarse whisper. "Jamie, as I guess you figured out, I'm in some serious trouble. I've got more people looking for me than I care to think about. You can bet we could be watched right now, so for Christ's sake, buy some chocolates so our conversation looks legitimate. It'll be some of my first sales of the day. As you can imagine, my mind hasn't been on the chocolate business."

Lawton noticed immediately Bailey's obvious weakened condition with loss of weight and hallowed, bloodshot eyes. And, in those eyes, there was no longer the fun-loving, teasing eyes of a youthful Adam Bailey. Instead, his eyes darted about as if constantly on the lookout for potential trouble. His face was ruddier and his hands shook as if he'd been on a three-day drinking binge with no food.

Lawton took the bag of candy and handed over some Swiss francs while whispering, "Adam, meet us at the Lake Geneva Hotel down the street as soon as possible. We're in room #512. Give us three knocks, wait, and then give three more quick knocks. We're here until we get you out of here."

Adam seemed momentarily surprised. "Who's we?"

Lawton pretended to count his change. "Look past my right shoulder and you'll see a large lush trying desperately not to run across the street and give you a bear hug."

Bailey quickly wiped another tear from his eye and stayed in character as he put another chocolate sample in Lawton's hand. Then he said brightly in self-styled broken English, "Thank you kindly, Senore. Take this special chocolate to your friend. It has some rum in it. He'll like it."

Then he turned away from Lawton, got behind the cart, and began pushing it up a hill. Under his facial hair while moving on, he said quietly, "I will hope to see you at the hotel.........very soon!"

Lawton turned away and continued in the direction of the hotel. He knew Davis would stay behind to observe if the conversation at the chocolate kiosk had created any other onlookers. He would not leave until both Lawton and the old man pushing the cart were out of sight.

With no one following either person, Davis would be satisfied. He then would take a circuitous route back to the small hotel knowing it would be very soon that the three of them would be together.

Chapter 25

It was Thursday, April 11, when Adam Bailey had caught his first glimpse of France across the barbed wire border from the plaza around Le Grand-Saconnex. It was both energizing and frustrating knowing the difficulty in passing over to French soil. So far his costuming and slower gait had kept him from being detected. He looked nothing like a youthful escapee or dangerous murderer. With his slovenly appearance he looked more like a drifter as he limped around the plaza from shop to shop. Still, his paranoia got especially high seeing all the military police paying close attention at the plaza to every pedestrian that got near the border gate.

While resting his stiffening leg, he observed all the activity around the plaza as if someone or something might spearhead an idea how to continue his escape. People were selling produce, houses wares, or clothing from kiosks and moveable carts. The plaza itself was crowded as locals and visitors just strolled leisurely seeming to enjoy the view of the surrounding mountains and trying to ignore the problems of the world at that time.

Keeping his head down so his face couldn't be as readily seen whenever any law enforcement official or border guard walked by his café table, he had time to face a new and immediate threat. Once Willie LaCurso would learn of the circumstances of his brother's murder, he would have a good idea who the assailant was since he knew Roberto was there to eliminate Adam Bailey.

Willie LaCurso would be relentless in his pursuit. He also had an advantage having some familiarity with Bailey's life and preferences. The two of them had met often enough over lunch or shared wine at Willie's St. Paul home so the hoodlum actually knew of Bailey's partiality for staying in Geneva, Switzerland, in particular at the hotels on the south end of Lake Geneva near the Swiss-French border. It would be logical that location would be Bailey's escape route and cross over point into France. There was good reason to believe Willie and even the LaCurso family might already be after him. They'd certainly not stop their hunt even if he made it to France. Bailey closed his eyes and visualized being greeted by a volley of bullets delivered by members of the LaCurso family with his first step into freedom.

Thursday night, Bailey found a rooming house a few blocks from the Le Grand-Saconnex marina on Lake Geneva. Since the lake was entirely within the confines of Switzerland, there was no water route to France. He did, however, watch a seaplane land and take off from the lake. He had to be aware of every manner possible to complete his escape.

Friday, April 12, was especially stressful. His leg was very stiff indicating the wound might not be healing properly. It required him to remain immobile most of the day. That evening he did venture out to buy some food at the plaza. He found another rooming house closer to the plaza figuring he shouldn't stay in any one place too long. He spent a restless and discouraging night in a windowless room. Every hour he was immobile, he was letting his pursuers get closer.

By Saturday morning, his leg had improved. It was not broken but there was obvious ligament and nerve damage on the lower part of his thigh. He knew the pain would return if he moved around too much.

That morning he put aside the throbbing leg to limp over to the marketplace to keep studying possibilities for crossing the border. Remaining out in public too long, however, could be his undoing. He didn't feel comfortable remaining visible in the plaza.

Running out of money had also become a concern. By Monday he would be out of Swiss francs and have only a few Italian liras which most proprietors in Geneva preferred not to recognize. No longer being able to cover the cost of a rooming house meant no guaranteed roof over his head. Something had to develop Saturday or Sunday or he might have to resort to robbery. How successful he might be in that endeavor with a bum leg didn't look promising.

Saturday morning the plaza was especially busy. The street vendors seemed to be part of the scenery and were busily trying to make what money they could. Sitting down to rest his leg, his expectation was simply to notice one thing...one quirk... that might give him a chance to be in France yet that day. One observation he did make, the border guards and military police paid little to no attention to the street merchants. Maybe that realization caused him to pay attention to one particular street vendor who had parked his cart near the bench where Bailey was sitting.

The man seemed to be struggling and hardly paying attention to potential customers who flowed by. The man looked and behaved older than he really was and Bailey quickly saw the reason. The guy kept taking some nips from a small bottle he'd hidden in his cart. He was selling chocolates but seemed more interested in becoming inebriated. If the man was more sober and a bit more enterprising, he would locate his cart closer to the border gates to catch the incoming and outgoing pedestrian traffic.

An idea began to germinate. Bailey rose and stood next to the cart perusing the man's array of chocolates. The small business proprietor hardly noticed his new customer.

Starting the conversation in Italian, he was fortunate to get a favorable eye from the intoxicated chocolate salesman. Bailey said, "Senore, how's your business? Are you going to be out on the plaza all day until you sell out all your chocolates?"

The semi-conscious proprietor bounced out of his stupor suddenly realizing he actually had a customer. Jaded with boredom and a thick tongue, he tried to be friendly but was out of practice. He lamented, "Ah yes, my friend, business has been slow and I am tired. I do not look forward to pushing this cart around all day. But, that is the life God has given me. Maybe you might want some of my tasty chocolates?"

Bailey didn't waste any time. "Actually Senore, I want to buy all your chocolates….and your cart….and your coat and hat. I have to make some money and I am looking for a small business. Since you are tired and I am not, there might be a reason for you to consider selling your business to me."

The proprietor just stared at Bailey as if the words didn't make sense. Bailey sat down next to the man and just stared at him awaiting an answer.

The flushed looking fellow hesitantly came toward Bailey with his hand outstretched. Suddenly he showed some vigor. "Senore, you have come to the right place. Your timing is exquisite. For the right price we can make this transaction right now."

Bailey countered, "Of course, Senore, I don't know if I'd like to sell chocolates. I might get tired of it like you are. Then, I might start taking a few nips of wine to pass the day. The next thing you know I would be sitting in this plaza feeling as miserable as you do right now. I would be taking a big risk just to buy your business outright."

The drunken businessman's grin began losing its spark realizing this dream was not yet one minute old and it was already losing steam. His shoulders began to slouch.

Not wanting this gift from the heavens to go away, he took a generous swig from his bottle, wiped his mouth and slobbered, "Well, my young friend, you could give me a down payment on my business and try the business out for a while. If you like it, you pay me the remainder of the purchase price. If not, you forfeit your down payment and pay me half of what you have sold. Does that sound fair, Senore?

The fact that they hadn't even exchanged names and were already bartering gave Bailey the strong sense that the down payment would be quite affordable.

He nodded. I like your idea, Senore. I have one other need. I have to find a place to stay while I try out the new business. Might you be able to help me on that need?"

The proprietor was all smiles knowing the request was easily answered. "Absolutely, Senore, you can have a room at my humble home just a few blocks from this very plaza. My 'esposa' has moved out...rather she's visiting her sister so there is plenty of room. I will give you the coat off my back and the hat off my head while you work my business...and all for a small cost of eighty Swiss francs…….per day....a bargain by anyone's standards."

Bailey had what he wanted for the weekend. Not to appear too easy he countered at sixty Swiss francs…..per day.

The older man almost choked with glee. He hadn't expected more than twenty Swiss francs. It was as if he was experiencing the second coming with only a slight difference. It was Easter weekend and he was being given the opportunity to rise from the dead.

Bailey knew he was supplying his new friend with some good drinking money. Drunkenness to the point of unconsciousness would likely be the rule for this fellow over the remainder of the religious weekend. It was doubtful the jubilant drunk would even remember their business arrangement later that day.

Pushing the cart towards the proprietor's flat, Bailey had to listen to the worst hard luck story known to man. There was noticeable hyperbole and obvious inconsistencies. Two blocks away from the plaza, the old man pointed to where Bailey should park the cart. Then the drunken man threw a dirty canvas over the wheeled kiosk motioning Bailey to enter his home.

The door didn't open as much as it fell open with only one of the hinges able to hold the door in place. The quaint quarters made Bailey's Milan jail cell look like a medium quality hotel room. Everything was filthy. The old man practically crawled over to his bed and sat down. He took another huge swig of his drink.

Before lying down, the old man pushed an old cat off his blanket. He muttered, "Now, my strong and good young partner, go to work while I take a break. You can pay me later when I'm more rested."

With that the inebriated chocolate salesman lay down and disappeared into a deep alcohol induced sleep. He hadn't asked for one dime of the down payment. Bailey looked at the poor man and felt pity, but he had to concentrate on his own challenge.

Examining the ramshackled one room cubicle, he spotted another change of clothes owned by the old man. It was another drab baggy coat and pants that had never seen a crease. It was as if he was back at the theatre in Lugano. That clothing would be quite satisfactory for him to carry out his new role as a street vendor.

Five minutes later he looked almost as ragtag as his business partner. The fit was short and roomy, but only added to the disguise he needed.

Grabbing the comatose man's hat, Bailey attached his droopy fake moustache and fitted his gray wig he'd absconded from the Lugano theatre under the hat. There was no mirror, but Bailey felt very authentic and unrecognizable.

Rolling the cart back down the street, he ate some of his product, a dividend he hadn't considered. He hadn't tasted something that good for so long his taste buds actually hurt.

Heartened by the chocolate and his ability to make something happen, he pushed his cart into a position close to a couple other vendors who were selling non-edible items. They seemed to appreciate that the additional kiosk might attract more people.

With no intention of selling any chocolates, he was so close to the border gates he could watch the procedures as people showed their passports and were allowed to take the walk through the gates and cross 'no-man's land" for twenty yards to the French side.

Unfortunately there were still enough uniforms to start a war. The whole process seemed so easy. All he had to do was find a fake passport expert.

Suddenly there was a border guard standing in front of him. The man looked sternly at him. Bailey thought his escape had finally been stopped.

The guard asked, "So, how much for a box of your chocolates with nuts?"

Bailey almost fainted with relief, although he was facing a problem he hadn't considered. He had no idea what to charge. He made up a number and held a box of that type of chocolate in front of the guard. He didn't want to carry on a conversation in case the man detected an accent. "Three Swiss francs," he finally replied.

The guard looked at him coldly. "That's too much...how much for half a box?"

Bailey gritted his teeth and repeated, "Same price."

The guard chuckled and gave him the three Swiss francs grabbing the box with chocolates and strolling back to his assigned area. Five minutes later Bailey noticed that same guard munching away on his purchase. He seemed more content than his colleagues.

When one of the officers began handing out pictures to each guard, Bailey got especially paranoid. The photo could be a copy of the image on his passport he had to leave at the Milan city jail house. He patted his fake moustache and slouched down even lower. He opened another small box of chocolates and began munching on some cream-filled delights as if they might be his last meal.

As Saturday came to a close, Bailey was particularly dispirited. He pushed the cart back to the drunken proprietor's home. He felt his pockets and was surprised how much money he'd pulled in from his chocolate sales. He'd find out shortly if he underpriced his stock.

Throwing the dirty canvas over the cart, he carefully opened the door expecting to see the old man still sleeping. Instead the drunk was gone. The drunk could have gone to the police complaining of his business being stolen. More probable he was out buying more wine.

Bailey felt sorry for the guy and decided to look for him. The man was in no condition to go far.

Making his way slowly along the lake back toward the plaza, Bailey wondered if he could even recognize the wayfaring inebriant without his hat or pushing his cart. As traumatic of a situation Bailey was in, there seemed to be another level of misery as he looked for his partner among other intoxicated men sitting in a stupor on some park benches.

Finally he recognized the guy. He was standing in a fountain relieving himself while taking a swig of his favorite drink. It was not the drunk's finest moment nor did it endear him to some local police yelling at him to get out of the fountain....and themselves not wanting to retrieve him from the fetid waters.

The old fellow then began climbing up the stone statue in the middle of the fountain yelling some inebriated blasphemies against Hitler, Mussolini, and his mother-in-law. The man seemed satisfied. He was relieving his mind as well as his bladder.

The incident was getting silly until the drunken man slipped and fell down into the fountain. There was some derisive laughter till everyone noticed him lying face first in the fountain and not moving. He would have drowned if one of the policemen hadn't leaped into the water and saved him.

Another policeman felt for the drunken man's pulse. He shrugged as if to say he couldn't find one. Bleeding from the forehead, the two policemen were trying to decide if an ambulance or a hearse should be called. A medical vehicle was finally summoned.

The last thing Bailey saw was his 'partner' being lifted on a stretcher into an ambulance...and a hand reaching over and successfully feeling for his bottle of wine in his pocket. The guy was a trooper and obviously playing the odds for a comfortable sleep and a free meal at some hospital that night.

It was a pathetic sight with a silver lining. It also meant Bailey had a place where no one was apt to find him that night. Thinking about the squalor of the well-oiled chocolate salesman and his rancid shelter, he didn't expect to overstay his welcome. A second night in that rubble might induce some kind of disease.

He also had to consider moving on. Geneva was not the magic for escape that he'd hoped. He had to consider moving further up Lake Geneva towards Lausanne and seeing if crossing into France via some smaller border towns might be more possible.

Bailey slept better that night despite the filth. Sunday morning he awoke to church bells. It was Easter. How his life had changed. He recalled Easter Sundays of his past...in church as a kid, on the golf course in later years, and just three years before enjoying Geneva as a businessman/tourist. Of course then he'd had the proper identification and money. Laying on a cot still in his street vendor clothing thinking about food...he hoped never again to have a worse Easter day.

He had enough Swiss francs to last a few more days thanks to his take from the previous day's chocolate sales. He found more inventories of chocolates in the old man's living quarters and restocked the cart. He decided to spend one more day...a busy Sunday... selling chocolates and giving the plaza one more chance to stimulate an idea how to cross the border. At the least his prospective chocolate sales would give him more money for food if he was going to leave Geneva that night. After one more night in the old man's filthy quarters, he hoped to find a fisherman the next morning willing to drop him off further up Lake Geneva at

Coppet or Gland for a price. He'd still be in Switzerland, but he would be better placed to explore escape possibilities in the more rural areas. Somehow, being a stowaway on a boat felt more progressive than sitting around the plaza.

Staying out of the busiest area of the plaza but still near the border gate, he managed to sell two-thirds of his chocolates through the middle of the afternoon despite having to sit and rest his leg each hour. He'd gotten so confident in his fool proof garb that he hardly paid attention to the swarm of military police. Many even bought chocolates from him.

With his stock down to just a few remaining boxes, Bailey decided to make one more pass along the edge of the plaza, make what money he could, then head back toward the marina to find a more suitable place to sleep. He didn't look forward to one more night in the drunken man's shanty.

Positioning his cart near a park bench, he mostly sat. His leg was aching and his interest in selling more chocolates had all but stopped. He even opened a box and ate some of his product just to gain some pleasure in the day. A pedestrian edged up to the cart and bought two boxes. Bailey took in three Swiss francs for each box and then watched the buyer walk away happy. Happiness seemed a long way off as he slouched over his cart watching visitors file through the gate back toward France. The day would soon be ending as the sun's light began to disappear behind a mountain top.

He sighed realizing the last couple days in Geneva had been a waste except that he'd earned some money. As he prepared to leave the plaza, he lifted his head only high enough to see there was another patron waiting to buy some chocolate. Languidly and without meeting the eyes of his customer, Bailey asked whether the man might like some extra boxes of chocolate for his children.

The response shocked him beyond description. It was an invitation to play golf back in the States. It was a voice from so far back in his mind it was as if an echo from oblivion. He didn't even have to look up to know it was Jamie Lawton. In that moment his life had changed once again. The words were a simple assurance that everything was going to be all right.

Adam Bailey choked with emotion. After a few breathes he was able to maintain his composure and his street vendor masquerade. And when Lawton quietly directed him to cast his eyes across the plaza to see Charlie Davis slightly raising a mug of beer as a further supportive gesture, Bailey's eyes welled up.

Lawton retained his interest in buying chocolate, gave Adam some directions where to meet them, and then casually sauntered away eating the chocolate he'd just purchased in great delight and satisfaction.

For the next half hour Bailey was in a dream. If he could get to the hotel room of Lawton and Davis, he was going to make it.

He had a renewed gait to his still halting walk as he pushed the cart away from the plaza. The short partnership with the sad drunken chocolate salesman was done. Arriving at the fellow's one-room pad, Bailey put the dirty canvas over the cart and entered the shelter. The cart man had still not returned. In Bailey's mind, he wondered if the man ever would. He gathered his regular clothing and decided not to change. It would be a tragedy if he were recognized before he met up with his two friends. He left twenty Swiss francs under the man's pillow hoping the money would be used for better sustenance than alcohol. He didn't feel confident that would happen.

It was now dusk. He was to meet his friends at a local hotel in ten minutes. He felt like skipping but his injured leg wouldn't allow it. He'd always remember two things that flowed through his mind on that little journey to the hotel. First was the emotion of knowing true friendship. Somehow what Lawton and Davis were doing went beyond the normal definition. He recalled how from the moment his father and he had met those two men as well as Lindy, they'd been like extended family. He'd been a recipient of their loyalty and generosity from that very first summer he'd met them almost ten years ago when he still lived at his father's farm near Glenwood, Minnesota. Unbelievably, they'd put everything aside and flown overseas to find him once they'd heard his plight. It was only due to their close friendship and association with him that they had a fairly good idea the route he would probably take to freedom in France.

The second thing he would recall was the difficulty in keeping the floppy fake moustache in place as patrons at the hotel looked at him disapprovingly. Tears from his eyes were washing away the stickiness of the glue on his upper lip. By the time he was taking the elevator to the fifth floor of the Lake Geneva Hotel, he had to hold the prop in place.

Each step he took down the hallway seemed too long. Never had he imagined freedom would be such a fight. As directed by Lawton, he knocked three times, paused, and as he began knocking three more times the door burst open to loud laughter and hugs. When the emotion of those moments was completed, his stage moustache was stuck to his collar.

In the next minute a sandwich was thrown to him by Davis and a beer given him by Lawton. Bailey had barely sat down and taken a few bites when his two friends began peppering him with questions about his previous two weeks. It was as if he was semi-conscious from shock and relief. And, even though their queries were only meant to gather information while figuring a way to sneak him over the border into France, he just didn't know how far he wanted to bring them into his life. He was astonished and stirred by their efforts to find him, but he'd changed. He had become more restrained. The alteration had been gradual as he took on the secret assignments for the State Department. The more dramatic change in his manner and his personality, though, had only happened since being arrested in Milan.

He looked at Lawton and Davis now smiling and throwing kidding remarks at each other like always. Bailey wondered if they'd still want to save a guy named Adam Bailey who'd changed so radically from the image he had over the last decade. He no longer felt like that same person. They considered him still the quick thinking jokester and little brother. Now he couldn't remember the last time he'd laughed uncontrollably. He was now more cautious, even edgy. He gazed into people's eyes more deeply. He evaluated their words more thoroughly to decide how far they could be trusted. His brain seemed always on full alert.

Now he also wondered if the friendship he had with Lawton and Davis would be altered if they knew some actions he'd had to take since they'd last seen him. By them being in Geneva and actually finding him, it did appear they'd been drawn in by someone into his double life as an agent for the State Department. It could only be David O'Brien. The director of Western Europe Intelligence had to have been desperate in his concern for his newest agent if Lawton and Davis were brought into the search.

But, none of them, including O'Brien would have any knowledge of his shooting and killing two men during his escape. They wouldn't know the drastic measures he'd taken....and the unhesitant manner in which he'd carried out those actions. He'd reacted unwaveringly in the first slaying on the train against the German. The second time...the shooting of Roberto LaCurso...that was premeditated. It was kill or be killed. There had been no choice. The firmness with which he'd acted would have been unthinkable two weeks before...and something Lawton and Davis....and Lindy....and his father would not believe possible from the Adam Bailey they knew.

Though safely lying on a couch in the Lake Geneva Hotel suite he found himself holding back certain factors about his previous two weeks because he didn't want to disappoint them. What he had come to realize in his shooting of Roberto LaCurso, that it had been more than just survival. Retaliation had been fueled by his extreme hatred towards the man. And, the result was that his spite had not been satisfied. He had the same dark feeling toward the man who thought of him as a pawn and whose life was dispensable. Bailey's antipathy towards Willie LaCurso was unrelenting. He didn't feel right sharing his deep-seeded deathly thoughts with Lawton and Davis. It was his vendetta...his fixation. That was the Adam Bailey his friends didn't know and the character he didn't want them to see.

Chapter 26

Willie LaCurso had been waiting two days on Friday, April 12, for the telegram from his brother Roberto indicating the mission in Lugano had been accomplished. How could it not be? Adam Bailey was a sitting duck in some hotel room apparently too injured to even walk. It was just a case of Roberto taking a train up to Lugano from Milan, taking a taxi to the hotel, finishing the job in the hotel suite, and catching the evening train back to Milan. It was about as clean and neat as a hit could be.

As the hours had drifted by on Thursday with no message, he felt something had gone wrong. Bailey could have checked out of the Lugano Hotel and Roberto was searching for him. Maybe Bailey had been captured.

When the messenger finally knocked at his St. Paul home with the telegram, the short script was the last thing he expected to read. The message was not from Roberto but from another family member living in Como, Italy...a nephew named Pablo. The telegram read simply:

> Uncle Roberto is dead. Found shot in hotel in Lugano. Passport
> and cash missing. Will wait for any instructions.

Willie slowly crumbled up the telegram and flung it into the blazing fireplace in his library. He gazed out the window and visualized the smile on the face of his younger brother. They had grown apart through the 1920's but only because of living on two different continents. In recent years they'd come together after Roberto repeatedly told his older brother of the hardships the LaCurso family was dealing with under the Mussolini Fascist regime. The family businesses, especially the one distributing firearms and ammunition had been seriously crippled. Smuggling goods in and out of Italy had become more difficult with the increasing numbers of military police and border controls.

By 1939 the two brothers decided they had to do something. By carrying out what they believed to be the crime of the century...assassinating Benito Mussolini...the disorder would almost immediately spearhead the return of profits from their illegal businesses.

Now that dream was over. An inept assassination team including their leader had spelled doom for the operation. Even offering Adam Bailey as a scapegoat to the team to give them a better chance of escaping unscathed after assassinating Il Duce had not materialized. Bailey had upset the entire plan with his escape prior to the most recent assassination attempt. The young man showed moxie far beyond what Willie could have imagined.

By mid-day of that same Friday, Willie was twisting a second telegram from Pablo telling of the mysterious death of Andre Pizzorno...the apparent victim of a horrible mountain car accident only days after the man's estate had been demolished by a bomb. The coincidence of the two deaths was hard to believe... and Bailey following his escape from the Milan jail, could well have been in the vicinity of Lugano. Still, Willie scoffed at the possibility that Bailey could have learned Pizzorno and the LaCursos were working together and had framed him? But, in the small chance that he'd figured it out, it was understandable revenge would be on his mind. Carrying out that retaliation was another matter. But, just maybe, it had actually happened.

As Willie changed his drink to brandy, he had to admit Adam Bailey was someone he might not really know any more. He was no longer a kid or even a credulous foreign businessman. Willie sat there grinding his teeth in disbelief. How could this highly decent young man in such a short period of time become a bona fide killer? Vengeance was one thing; many people could feel that way against someone who had wronged them. The difference was that Bailey was apparently doing something most people would not dare to do. He was going after the individuals who were responsible for victimizing him. He was taking action. He was actually pulling the trigger without hesitation when coming face-to-face with his adversary. That was not normal for a small town Minnesota kid.

Willie downed his brandy and sat there just shaking his head. There was a good chance young Bailey was now visualizing him as his next target. The thought wasn't daunting....just difficult to grasp.

It was within fifteen minutes of finishing that glass of brandy that Willie LaCurso made some decisions important to his overseas family and himself. Revenge for the blood of his brother was the main motivator, but there was that constant secondary concern. The young man held the lives of Willie's entire old country LaCurso family in his hands. If recaptured and he decided to inform the authorities what he knew regarding the LaCurso family and their involvement in plots to kill Benito Mussolini, the freefall of damage and death to his relatives could be widespread...Willie could do little about it.

Bailey was alive somewhere in Switzerland and moving toward France. In his various meetings with Bailey, the kid had often mentioned his interest in Geneva,

Switzerland, a convenient border city to France. It was an easy conjecture for Willie to presume Bailey was heading for not only that city, but the very lakeside area he usually took lodging...a place called Le Grand-Saconnex right on the border. Even if he was wrong, he'd be close...and Willie wouldn't rest easy until he'd caught up and ended the life of someone who'd become a dangerous nemesis.

He called in his trusted right hand man, Big Tony Bando, and filled him in on the bad news about Roberto....and who the probable killer was. Tony had to ask twice to make certain the boss was talking about the same Adam Bailey he'd known over the same years as Willie had. But, it was Tony's primary role to take orders and not to understand nor question them.

To raise the big man's ire even more, Willie fabricated a story that the last time Bailey had taking a suitcase with Willie's currency over to Milan for Roberto and the family, the young man had gotten greedy and taken some of the cash.

He completed the lie by saying, "Tony, he murdered Roberto and now holds some cards he could use against the family with the authorities if he chose. His false accusations would bring scorn and even worse from those God-damned Fascists in Italy. We need to stop him."

Tony still couldn't imagine Bailey being that heartless and evil, but he'd learned a long time ago not to doubt the boss' words. His only retort was, "So, where do we go to find him, boss?"

Willie always liked Tony's fiery, dependable loyalty. He replied, "The law in at least two countries is after him for killing Roberto. He's heading for France and I have a good hunch I know his route. The kid and I have had enough drinks together that I know his love for Geneva, Switzerland...a convenient spot to find passage into France. We need to start there. He's likely desperate... no passport, probably not much money, and in the most recent telegram from Pablo, apparently slowed by some kind of serious leg injury. Even if he makes it across the border into France, he would still be dangerous to the family for what he knows. Our pursuit has to be continuous until we can shut him down for good. Besides, I have a personal need to fire the weapon that kills Bailey in tribute to my brother."

For Tony, Willie's story had so many holes, but it didn't matter. Maybe the man wanted to see his family. Maybe he wanted to attend Roberto's funeral. For certain, though, he wanted Adam Bailey to pay for shooting Roberto.

Without being asked, Tony booked the next flight from Wold-Chamberlain Airfield southwest of St. Paul for the flight to LaGuardia. From there they would catch the overnight 'Yankee Clipper' flight to Paris. Then it would be a train to Vernier, France. With luck they would be in Geneva by Saturday night.

The itinerary went even better than could have been expected. By shear happenstance Tony recognized two individuals sprawled in the back of the 'Yankee Clipper' flight to Paris. The flight was not full so the two men were using three seats to lie down and sleep as normally as they could.

Both Tony and Willie had recognized the two men from the past including the the last golf tournament nine years before at Chippewa Lodge near Glenwood, Minnesota....and then more recently at Adam Bailey's college graduation five years before. Figuring there'd be little reason for the two men to be on that same flight unless they were enroute to help out Bailey. There was even the possibility they had an idea where the young man was hiding out. Suddenly, remaining unseen and following the two friends of Bailey became the main plan for Willie and Tony.

When the long flight to Paris was completed, Tony and Willie sitting in the front seats were the first ones off the plane. Both men hid by the baggage truck until they saw the two Americans groggily exit the plane five minutes later completely devoid of any thoughts they were about to be followed.

On the train to Vernier the two gangsters split up and were seated in different cars so as not to be seen or recognized if they were together. Off the train Lawton and Davis went through customs in Switzerland later that Saturday afternoon. Tony stayed out of their vision and was able to follow them all the way to Le Grand-Saconnex while Willie crossed the border fifteen minutes later.

Tony was able to shadow the two Americans right up to them checking into the Lake Geneva Hotel. They seemed to have the same idea...that Bailey would at some point be casing the possibilities for crossing into France at Le Grand-Saconnex. As Lawton and Davis stayed late into the evening at the plaza near the border crossing, Tony studied every movement they made until they returned to the hotel.

Meeting up with Willie, the two mobsters took a suite at the same hotel as Bailey's two friends. By Saturday evening all four men were sleeping soundly in their suites at the Lake Geneva Hotel only blocks from the plaza. Willie and Tony were on the 3rd floor; the other two Americans were two floors above them.

The less recognizable Tony had the job of maintaining surveillance on Davis and Lawton the next day on Easter Sunday while Willie LaCurso stayed back unseen at the hotel. To Tony's disappointment it appeared Bailey's two friends were unsure of Bailey's whereabouts as well. Both were very attentive to everyone walking around the plaza near the border gates. While one sat at an outside café table, the other one mindlessly walked into small shops but transfixed on every movement or person in that marketplace.

Sipping on a few beers from under an umbrella on the second floor of a bar, Willie's right hand man had been on plenty of stakeouts waiting for the right man to appear. When it happened...when patience paid off...Tony knew what to do. His persistence and ability to take action were legendary in the gangster community. However, by late that Sunday afternoon even his endurance was wearing thin.

As the crush of people hanging around the Easter day activity of the marketplace began to diminish, Tony repositioned himself to gain an even better view of the two frustrated Americans. It was as if that change of position triggered something. The thinner man, the one Tony knew as the Minneapolis lawyer named Lawton appeared to lean over toward his cohort and say something very intensely. Then he got up from a bench where they were sitting and sauntered toward some kiosks near the border gates. Abruptly he stopped at one of the mobile carts and began talking to a shabby looking street vendor who was selling chocolates.

Tony scoffed thinking the American was only satisfying a quick lust for something sweet. What became curious, though, was the other American sitting back at the café table. He seemed entranced with his friend talking to the vender. Tony's eyes moved back to the slender American as he talked to the disheveled kiosk owner. Moving closer to the conversation, he saw the discussion had become emotionally charged. The street vendor seemed shaken. Though frumpily dressed with a hat drooping over his forehead, Tony noticed something else. The floppy moustache was crooked and there were tears in the man's eyes. Even the clothing being worn didn't fit.

The impossible had happened. Tony realized he had found the man Willie and he were pursuing. Immediately he toyed with taking out Bailey with one shot from eighty feet away, but quickly reconsidered. With the crowd dispersing it seemed there were more military police in the plaza than pedestrians.

He'd follow the disguised Bailey when he left the plaza...to find out where he was residing. He'd get Willie and the entire episode would be a quick hit. He and Willie could cross back into France and be on the evening train from Vernier to Paris. They would be back in the States in less than two days.

At that point everything seemed to work like clockwork. The nattily dressed friend of Bailey purchased some chocolate and then ambled down the street away from the plaza. His friend, the larger man, still seated in the plaza remained apparently to see if his friend was being followed. Once satisfied, the friend downed the last of his beer, threw some francs on the table and followed the same pathway away from the plaza as his friend.

Within five minutes, the chocolate candy vendor began pushing his cart up the street. Tony stayed in the shadows looking for a clean shot. Twice he had a shot but good fortune seemed to follow the slow moving Bailey that Easter evening. Four military police just happened to be following close behind the street vendor. Tony had to stay patient.

Then Bailey suddenly disappeared between two ramshackled buildings of dilapidated flats. People were hanging out drinking and smoking. Partially cleaned sheets and clothes hung from the railings. Tony decided to wait not believing Bailey would be staying the night in such a rundown location.

Five minutes later the young man reappeared. He'd ditched the cart, but still wore the same disguise. He limped so badly Tony paused to make certain the slovenly dressed man was indeed Adam Bailey. Maybe the fellow was just a contact for the two Americans to meet up with Bailey. Then he saw the moustache slip to the side of the man's face. It was a fake. The quick movement by Bailey to recover the falling facial hair showed again that a younger man was underneath the masquerade.

Tony had his man. He was only thirty yards away with an open shot. But, something wasn't right. An unfamiliar wave of sympathy for the kid hung over the big man. He'd known the young man since the 'kid' was just a caddy out at Chippewa Lodge golf course near Glenwood, Minnesota. The image of Bailey as a favorite of Willie's friend, Loni D'Annelli just wouldn't go away. Then even after D'Annelli was gone and the years passed on, Tony had enjoyed watching Willie's daughter and the college student Bailey begin a cute but tragically short kind of courtship. Her death was not Bailey's fault. Tony knew that. Willie eventually allowed the same conclusion and seemed to take the same kind of liking toward the kid as he grew into adulthood. And, whenever Willie wanted to see Adam Bailey, it was Tony who was sent. Young Bailey responded to Tony with nothing but smiles, politeness and kidding remarks. That went a long way with Tony. He'd always liked the kid; then as a young adult, he liked Adam Bailey even more.

Now for the first time in his long career in crime, he found himself clutching. In the past he would have just pulled the trigger. Things didn't make sense why Willie truly wanted Adam Bailey dead. Willie had said Bailey had become greedy; that he killed Roberto for the money in the suitcase on his latest trip overseas. Tony was having a hard time buying into the story. It was inconsistent with the very character of Adam Bailey.

Now he watched the young man move along with a pathetic limp...the result quite likely caused by breaking free from one of Willie's schemes. Tony had seen it all before. Willie used people; if he thought they might talk, they were eliminated.

For the first time he just wanted more assurance that Adam Bailey deserved to die. It would be such a waste if Bailey's death was truly unwarranted. The hesitation caused Tony to miss out on multiple opportunities for a clean shot. Instead he stayed in the shadows shaking his head caringly as the kid he liked dragged his bum leg slowly up the street. Never before had Willie's right hand man doubted his boss and now was caught with indecision.

What then astonished him was seeing the young man hobble up to the entry of the Lake Geneva Hotel...the same hotel Willie and Tony had followed the two Americans. Bailey was obviously going to meet his friends there. Watching Bailey slowly climb the short stairwell, Tony considered not even telling Willie he'd found Adam Bailey. Let the young man enjoy the evening with his friends. It would delay Bailey's death at least for a while.

Tony waited outside the entry of the hotel for ten minutes before entering. His chin was resting on his large chest. He knew when Willie LaCurso wanted somebody dead, it was a foregone conclusion.

Adam Bailey had eaten three sandwiches and drained two beers given him by Charlie Davis and Jamie Lawton as he rested in their Lake Geneva hotel suite. The level of relief he felt was without definition even if his freedom wasn't yet assured. He wasn't yet out of Switzerland. The slightest mistake could put him back behind bars. But, on that Easter Sunday night he was in the hands of two people he trusted implicitly. Just the fact that his two friends found him was an example of their logic, tenacity, and willingness to play the odds.

He lay comfortably on a bed in their hotel suite resting his still damaged leg while the two of them debated various possibilities of getting him across the well-guarded Swiss border into France. He'd given them an overview of his previous two weeks...in particular his escape and his venture over the Swiss-Italian border to Lugano. They nodded their heads routinely, but in truth were amazed at his boldness and ingenuity. Already knowing some of the horrible story, they didn't ask for details...and Bailey offered them none. They just were pleased he'd made it to Geneva...and relieved their assumption had been correct.

To Bailey their lack of inquiries regarding his escape was unlike them. It left him wondering what they knew about his recent challenges. Now they didn't seem to care. Their focus was only on getting him into France and then home. But later they'd have questions. His father would have questions. He still wasn't certain how much he'd divulge to them in order that they would still hold him the same esteem they always had.

The entire atmosphere in that hotel room was so energized and so amusing with Lawton and Davis in the room. There was a lot of reminiscing and laughing about past stories...even recalling their experiences during that June 1931 weekend back in Glenwood when the three of them had first met. Bailey knew the conversation was solely meant to relax him. Sometimes he laughed because it felt so good...once or twice he did so more to make them feel their story-telling efforts were working. A few times his mind trailed off to the faces of his two victims as well as Sophia and Andre Pizzorno just before the vehicle catapulted over the mountain cliff. At other times his thoughts went dark thinking about his unconditional and unmitigated quest to get Willie LaCurso. Whether it was his training as an agent, his blind confidence in his instincts and abilities, or his shear hatred against the man, he would never give up balancing the slate against this major crime figure. While it might not be soon, Bailey was determined his face would be the last face the gangster would ever see. He wondered how many people would personally thank him if they ever found out he'd eliminated Willie LaCurso. This top level gangster had affected so many peoples' lives in such a negative way. However, Bailey wanted no acclaim. His action would never be known....not by Willie's personal guards, not the police, not his friends and associates....only by Willie. That was the way Bailey wanted it.

Davis interrupted Bailey's hateful thoughts. "Adam, Jamie and I tomorrow morning will pursue some ideas we have about getting you across the border. The fake I.D. and passport is probably our best bet. We'll see about asking the right people where this little shenanigan could be completed while you stay secluded in this hotel suite. Sleep....eat....drink...do whatever you want, but don't leave this hotel room. We'll be back with some lunch and maybe something we can act upon.

Bailey had no doubt they'd succeed. They seemed to know how to find the right people no matter where they were in the world. He gave them an appreciative nod and fell asleep a few minutes later while Lawton and Davis played a boisterous game of gin.

Bailey's sleep was intermittent. He got up before midnight later that Sunday evening. Lawton and Davis were asleep looking as if a detonated bomb wouldn't wake them.

Being chilled, he grabbed the shabby coat he'd worn into the room and placed it over his shoulders as he stepped out onto the small balcony of the fifth floor suite. The sky was mostly clear and he took a deep breath of mountain air. His entire body felt invigorated...except for his left leg. There was numbness and stiffness from not having moved it for a couple hours.

Though late, he looked down on the street. There were still some people walking along the street despite the late hour. Otherwise there was no movement and no breeze.

Leaning over the railing he gazed below at the front entrance of the hotel. He noticed a stocky man talking to a Swiss officer. Just seeing the policeman created some restlessness, but there was something about the larger man that made Bailey feel even more disquieted. It was the big man's movements, his slightly hunched shoulders, but mostly it was his size. He'd seen that man before.

The large man then went back into the hotel as the police officer went to his car and proceeded to make a call into his station. Now an alarm went off in Bailey's head.

Bailey remained on the patio five floors up just to see if his worst thoughts were about to be shown. Within five minutes they were. Two patrol cars arrived with two local policia in each car. The five uniforms then marched directly into the front entrance of the hotel.

Not waiting another minute, he closed the balcony door into the suite and remained outside. With some difficulty he climbed up onto a cement shelf that circumvented the hotel. The protruding ledge allowed him to tread on a width of about ten inches along the side of the building. Normally that would be plenty of space to walk easily, but with five stories between him and the ground, he felt like he was balancing on a tightrope.

Stepping cautiously away from the small balcony, he could hear the loud knock at the door of Jamie's and Charlie's room. There was commotion as the suite door was opened. Davis became loud and indignant...a performance typical of his friend when something wasn't going quite right.

Shuffling by a roof dormer, he squeezed by an open window of the adjoining suite. He contemplated stepping in, but the consequences seemed ill-advised. He'd been so careful. This was not a time to create a disturbance.

Then the balcony doors of the Lawton and Davis suite swung open not twenty yards behind him causing Bailey to simultaneously dive onto the roof on the other side of the dormer. Raising his head slightly he looked back and saw two police officers with guns drawn examining the outside including the roof in all directions. They did so hastily seeming to believe no one would have had the time or the inclination to take that escape route just because of the sudden knock at the suite door.

Not seeing anything suspicious, the officers went back in the suite. With the patio door left slightly open, Bailey could hear Lawton and Davis demanding the reason for the interruption. The words weren't entirely clear except when Davis spoke. Bailey chuckled hearing Davis threaten a declaration of war against Switzerland and how Davis' Swiss ancestors were turning over in their graves seeing such maltreatment being done by the local Geneva police. Davis' antics were as much designed to give Lawton and him time to best figure a way to handle the disturbance.

What had become abundantly clear...someone had discovered Bailey's location and had called in the law. He figured Lawton and Davis had to be thinking the very same thing. So much for his effective disguise!

The clamor in the suite eased. The picture was clear. There was someone on Bailey's trail. With Lawton's nod, Davis' fake rage had ended as fast as it had begun.

Lawton spoke clearly to the officers. "Gentlemen, you obviously have the wrong room and are accusing us of something we know nothing. My friend and I are simply visiting your beautiful city on a spring holiday...and on a religious weekend at that. We were hoping to be alone with our spiritual thoughts, but your interruption has ended that sense of peace. How can we celebrate our sacred beliefs after being accused of sheltering a fugitive?"

Bailey snickered as he heard a couple police officers clearing their throats in embarrassment. They began retreating out the door apologetically. However, one of the officers, still unconvinced, warned Lawton and Davis in no uncertain terms. "Gentlemen, enjoy the rest of your visit but we'll be watching to make certain your claims of innocence are the truth. We're looking for someone and word has it that the two of you were giving him aid."

Lawton said no more. Bailey was certain Davis was having a difficult time keeping a straight face after Lawton's holier than thou complaint to the local police.

The suite door finally closed and Bailey continued lying on the roof feeling quite vulnerable. He didn't feel safe going back into the suite. One of the officers could be listening from outside the door.

He watched the officers file out of the hotel. Two of them walked across the street and stationed themselves to keep watch....one behind a pillar, the other behind some bushes in a park. Lawton and Davis were now under surveillance reducing the effectiveness of any further efforts they might make on Bailey's behalf.

Back in survival mode, he had a burst of energy. Suddenly the roof didn't seem as steep nor did the ground seem as far down. His leg ached but it was not as disabling. He shuffled along the concrete shelf until he found the fire exit stairs. He had another place to hide by simply making it back to the grungy shack where the alcoholic chocolate salesman spent his nights. Bailey had hoped to never see that place again; now it was fortunate he had an alternative place to stay. He figured to hook up again with his two friends somehow later...and with an improved disguise.

As he quietly descended the outside fire escape staircase, he kept his eye peeled for any other officers assigned to keep watch. As for his thoughts, the only thing he could contemplate was who'd turned him in to the authorities?

The answer was not hard to consider. It had to be someone connected to Willie LaCurso. Then the image of the big man flashed in his mind he'd seen on the street only minutes before. It was LaCurso's right hand man, Tony Bando! It made too much sense. LaCurso had figured out whose Roberto's shooter was. The gangster had to have been both amazed and infuriated....and then vengeful. The telling factor, though, was Willie's familiarity. The two of them had a past. They'd shared a few lunches; they'd had wine at Willie's St. Paul home. The gangster knew of Bailey's preference for staying at Lake Geneva...and even favoring the Le Grand-Saconnex section.

It was not unthinkable to accept that Willie had zeroed in on Bailey's escape route and the location he'd seek in crossing into France. LaCurso only needed some good luck....and they'd found that luck likely through the inadvertent sighting of Lawton and Davis during the overseas travel. LaCurso and Big Tony only needed to follow them.

Bailey's mind turned very dark once again. LaCurso had delivered himself into Bailey's presence. If he wanted cold-hearted revenge on this gangster, he'd never have another better chance. Only Big Tony stood in the way and as formidable as that man was, Bailey couldn't let that body guard lessen his resolve. The plain hard fact was that as long as Willie was alive, Bailey would be the hunted. Whether LaCurso could believe it or not, the reverse was true as well.

There was only one question that made no sense. Why would Big Tony have informed the local police to have Bailey found in the hotel suite and arrested? A mob killer like Tony would avoid law enforcement as if they were diseased. Why hadn't Tony taken him out already if he knew the target was right there in Lawton and Davis' fifth floor suite?

That paradox would hound Bailey for the rest of the night.

When the police had left the hotel room, Charlie Davis had turned off his phony theatrics and calmly sat down. Pointing to the door of the suite knowing there might be a policeman's ears on the other side, he whispered "Adam must have a sixth sense to know those cops were coming down the hallway. Let's face it, Jamie, we got followed and led someone straight here like two idiots."

Lawton shrugged while opening the suite door to see if someone was listening. The coast was clear. He went over to the patio and looked outside and then at the thin protruding shelf Adam had to have traversed in order to have made his escape. He then looked down the five stories and watched as two of the policemen stationed themselves across the street. He and Davis were going to be followed wherever they went.

Coming back in the suite, he was rubbing his two-day growth of beard. "Chas, there's something going on here much deeper with Adam than simply slipping him over the border into France. You're right. The only thing that makes some sense is that we've been in someone's vision since we left the Twin Cities....maybe even since we left the house. Think about it....Willie LaCurso is no dummy. He knows you, Lindy and I are very close to Adam. He got the news about his brother about the same time we did. I believe he knows a hell of a lot more about Adam's situation than we could possibly know. If he thinks Adam is responsible for besting his brother, he's got blood in his eyes and motivation to follow us like a starving lion. I wouldn't be surprised if he's in this city right now."

Davis nodded. "But if he is, Adam has got to be thinking the same thing we are. Why would LaCurso get the law involved? That's not his style. In his business he would prefer supplying his own brand of justice.

That question stumped them both.

Davis reached for a half-filled bottle of scotch and poured two glasses. Handing one to Lawton, he eyed his friend. "O.K., counselor, you've got that look in your eye. I've seen it more than a few times. What have you got in mind?"

Lawton grinned, "Charlie, we've done enough deception in our lives that we shouldn't let the law enforcement in this neutral country or the likes of some hoodlums cramp our style. Let's not be concerned about Adam for now. He's been hiding out for a couple days someplace. He'll be O.K. for now...and then he'll find us when the time is right. We've got a couple hoods who have us in their sights. We've become targets as much as Adam, but they aren't going to do anything to us until we hopefully lead them to their real target. I'd like to roost them out and see who's been following us."

Davis stared at his friend and shook his head. "Counselor, in all the years I've known you, it completely befuddles me how you consider us in the driver's seat while we have our heads in rifle sites of a major crime figure. I admire your attitude. I also think your mother dropped you on your head as a child."

He looked at Davis and smiled ignoring his friend's aside. "Charlie, it's time we find out who tipped off the police about Adam? I'm going to go out and make myself visible. There're some cops across the street. They're waiting for one of us to make a move. They'll follow me. My guess is that Adam will be lurking in the shadows. I'll find some way to communicate with him. I'll meet you back here in a couple hours."

Both left the room together with Lawton taking the back staircase to a side exit door. Davis ventured straight down to the lobby. He sat down by two obvious undercover police and offered them a drink from his omnipresent flask. They kind of laughed realizing Davis knew what they were doing. He showed them some respect and in turn they lowered their apprehension about him. Both of them spoke good enough English and one of them eventually intimated to Davis he was tired of always being on the night shift. Charlie nodded shaking his head in sympathy.

Offering the same officer another nip from his flask, Davis shared a humorous story about a cop he knew back in the States who had been caught sleeping right through a robbery while in his squad car across the street from where the burglary took place. When he woke, the robbers were long gone, but sought forgiveness from his sergeant claiming that at least he was the first officer on the scene when the bank alarm went off.

The Swiss officers enjoyed the laugh. In the next minute the night clerk presented the three men with a bottle or wine and three glasses.

The two policemen saw nothing wrong with what they were doing. Their assignment was to keep one of the two Americans under surveillance. They were doing so. When Davis poured them a generous amount of wine and then toasted to their health, they were not only appreciative but they were completely won over by Davis' unique friendliness.

When the officers declined a second glass of wine, Davis showed concern. He said to them, "Gentlemen, if you're not supposed to sleep tonight because you have to watch me, then I feel personally responsible for causing you this kind of discomfort. Well, I'm going to sit right here the rest of the night so you can watch me just because I feel guilty keeping you up for the rest of the night. We can drink and talk……or we can just drink. But, I'll not be responsible for ruining your evening." He raised a glass to them repeating, "To your health."

While they sat in the lobby of the Lake Geneva Hotel, anyone walking by would have guessed they were all long-time friends. At the right time, Davis figured to inquire to his new friends about the person who called the police about a fugitive being sheltered in his fifth floor suite.

While Davis was entertaining the two officers in the hotel lobby, Lawton was already out on the side street walking visibly along the sidewalk right in front of the hotel. The two undercover officers standing outside and across the street from the hotel at first didn't recognize him.

Lawton then stopped, put two fingers to his mouth and gave out a piercing whistle that got two policemen's attention...and woke up five dogs in the neighborhood. He yelled, "Officers, you're supposed to be following me. Tell you what...don't be concerned. I'm just getting some fresh air. I'm going down by the water for some exercise and admire the lake. You'll see me on the dock from where you're standing. I'll be back shortly."

The two policemen looked at each other a bit sheepishly...so much for keeping an eye on the two Americans. They were supposed to be upset that they were being watched by the local police. Instead, one was having drinks in the hotel lobby with two of their colleagues while the other had been out walking and had to whistle to get their attention. The two Americans certainly didn't seem like desperate criminals helping a nationally wanted man. Instead, they were friendly and quite cooperative, even helping the officers with their duties. They were in Switzerland for a good time and obviously their body clocks had not yet adjusted to the time difference. They seemed pleased to have the company.

True to his word, they watched Lawton light a cigarette and stroll down to the docks along the lake. He seemed to find pleasure in looking at the moon shining on the lake so late at night.

The more nattily dressed American had been standing on the dock hardly moving for fifteen minutes when the two officers took note of a chauffeur driven wagon pulled by two horses go trotting slowly by the docks. The horseman wearing an old coat and crumpled hat was hunched over in his seat like he wished he was sleeping in his own bed. The wagon then stopped about thirty feet from where Lawton was standing. The policemen watched the driver get down off his seat. The American paid no attention and just continued staring out at the lake. The driver seemed equally as oblivious as he checked a wheel on his wagon. When that was done, he took a pail of water and stuck it into the snouts of first the left horse, then the right.

While the two Swiss policemen were watching him down at the dock, Lawton waited right there believing Bailey would see him and make some effort to make contact. When the horseman and his steeds suddenly stopped within earshot, he soon heard a throaty whisper from the waggoneer. It was barely audible, but Lawton knew immediately he'd re-connected with Adam Bailey right in front of the two listless officers standing up the street.

Without looking toward Lawton, the voice said, "I think I know who's onto me. There was a fat guy talking to a police officer just minutes before the police arrived. I've just seen him again...and with a thin fellow. They're now just sitting on their third floor patio having some wine and watching you admire the lake from this dock. You don't know the fat one, but I do. The thin one....well, that's Willie LaCurso. Somehow he must have followed you guys here."

Grabbing another bucket containing some oats, Bailey under his rumbled hat began feeding each horse while Lawton continued to look straight out onto Lake Geneva. His voice barely audible, he continued, "Jamie, I've never told you or Charlie this, but that bastard has been a headache for me for years. I've learned Willie and his brother, Roberto, have been financing some assassination attempts against Mussolini. I've also discovered the two of them decided I was expendable. They framed me and got me arrested for being a suspected assassin. I was supposed to be some kind of patsy for them while the actual assassins did their dirty work. That's the whole reason why I'm in this international mess."

There was a pause as Bailey pretended to check the hoofs of the two horses. In a final very raspy whisper with a cold, bitter tone, Bailey mumbled vengefully, "And Jamie, I'm going to get Willie LaCurso for what he did to me."

Lawton had never heard Adam utter such belligerent words. Without turning toward the wagon, Lawton continued staring out onto the darkened lake and finally replied, "We'll catch up with each other later."

The wagon driver then slowly guided his horses down the street away from the two patrols standing by the front entrance of the hotel. He touched the brim of his cap at them from a distance and they gave him a perfunctory nod in return.

As Lawton retraced his steps up the street toward the hotel with the new information Bailey had passed onto him, his eyes narrowed. Knowing Willie LaCurso and his body guard were at the hotel on the third floor possibly staring down at him, it was apparent the gangster had not assigned the killing of Adam Bailey to anyone else. The death of his brother made it a personal vendetta. He was hunting down Bailey and wasting no time in doing so.

But, there was now a new problem...Adam's own vendetta against LaCurso. It superseded any other need including escaping to France. Charlie Davis and he had jumped into a situation far deeper than they could have imagined. The deep pit of animosity between Bailey and LaCurso indicated a clash was inevitable. With a body guard and Adam having a bum leg, the advantage was entirely on the side of LaCurso. Saving Bailey's life had become more than dodging military police and crossing a barbed wire fence into France. With Adam's obsession against LaCurso, Davis and he were going to have to save the young man from himself. Bailey's determination and grit were now his weaknesses. He was blind to his frailties.

The new challenge was clear. Davis and he had to consider other ways to take care of Adam's nemesis because in truth Willie LaCurso had now become a problem for all three of them. The gangster would likely never give up until he'd wasted Bailey...and his two friends who Willie now knew quite well.

As Lawton approached the hotel he could feel LaCurso and his body guard staring down at him from their third floor suite. He almost paused to look up at them in a gesture of defiance, but then thought better of the impulse. It was better they think they had the upper hand....for now.

Lawton doffed his hat to the two patrolmen assigned to keep watch on him. He paused to offer them a cigarette saying, "Gentlemen, I'll be sleeping in my room for the rest of the evening. I'll be down for breakfast about 8:00. Join my friend and me if you'd like. It would be our treat."

The two local cops were dumbfounded. They'd never conducted surveillance on such agreeable and obliging people. Lawton continued inside and strode by three semi-inebriated souls in the lobby who seemed to be enjoying each other's company. The fun loving group included Charlie Davis.

Seeing Lawton return, Davis bid his two tipsy law enforcement friends a good night. He gave a magnanimous wave to the two officers outside as he swaggered towards the elevator. He appeared drunk and ready to sleep well into the next morning.

The moment the elevator doors closed, Davis was mentally as sharp as a knife blade. He'd had only one glass of wine and had gotten the answer to his question from his drinking mates.

At that same time Willie LaCurso and Tony were drinking their own bottle of wine while talking on their third floor veranda. It overlooked the front entrance of the hotel and across the street to the marina on Lake Geneva. Tony was privately lamenting what could have gone wrong with the police raid at the Lawton suite on the fifth floor.

He'd purposely tipped the local police off that the American renegade who'd killed the man in Lugano was being sheltered by two Americans in suite 512. Tony had done it for his own piece of mind. For the first time in his life he didn't feel right recklessly following an order by the boss, Willie LaCurso. He liked Adam Bailey. The kid had been framed and placed in a desperate situation. Tony wanted to give the kid a chance to explain himself to the authorities, be exonerated based on self-defense, and have the chance to live a few more days. If Willie wanted to find Bailey later and waste him for killing Roberto... then so be it. But, Tony was not going to be the one who pulled the trigger.

He now listened to the wrath of Willie LaCurso swearing about how the cops had missed how Bailey was being sheltered in the suite of the two Americans. It would never occur to him that his absolute loyal right-hand man, Tony Bando, for once not only unilaterally countermanded Willie's order to kill someone but he actually was trying to save or at least prolong Bailey's life.

Willie growled in his tobacco laced voice, "Tony, there must have been someone on the hotel staff that recognized Bailey and tipped off the cops. He's got more people looking for him than a politician on the take."

Tony shrugged complacently. "Well, boss, they didn't find him. The kid is still on the loose. That attorney, Lawton, and his friend somehow got Bailey out of the suite before the cops knocked on the door. So, he's out there still looking for a way to avoid being captured while trying to find a way of crossing into France. And, we still have the advantage. Bailey's two friends have no idea we've been following them. They know where Bailey is. We'll just keep following them until they lead us to the kid."

LaCurso was still storming. "What in the name of God do we have to do to get to Bailey? He's always disappearing on us. He's got to be the luckiest God-damned human being I've ever known. He's as slippery as an eel."

Tony blew a steam of smoke contentedly from his cigar. He'd seen Willie quite often in this state of confusion and rage. It went away. He smiled to himself knowing that he was going to misdirect LaCurso away from finding Bailey as much as possible.

At his tender age of forty-eight after thirty-five years of crime, Tony had found some sympathy for someone. Tony had seen the development of Bailey from a kid to a man back in Chippewa Lodge in Minnesota. The thought of ever having a son was so far out of his imagination he'd never contemplated the idea, but Tony would have wanted his kid to be like Adam Bailey. Wasting young Bailey would be destroying one of the few positive images in Tony's mind.

The two men sat their distressed in their own different thoughts on that balcony as they suddenly watched Lawton saunter by the front entrance of the hotel, talk briefly with two patrolmen, and then continue on across the street to the marina. It appeared he was having trouble sleeping. At the dock he stood there smoking a couple cigarettes in relative solitude and seemingly enjoying the view of Lake Geneva in the late hours.

Willie had calmed down...as he normally did...and pointed at Lawton. "You recall, Tony, the first time we met up with that guy. He'd been invited to play in Loni D'Annelli's annual charity tournament at the Chippewa Lodge golf course. We never did learn how those two got to know one another. But, that same weekend was when that Lawton fellow and his large friend apparently got to know Loni's caddy, Adam Bailey. And, while the kid caddied for Loni, it was a foursome competition. That damned kid knew every blade of grass on that golf course and every subtle break on every green. He helped Lawton with club selection and reading the roll of the greens. The kid was as responsible for D'Annelli's foursome winning that God-damned golf tournament as Lawton with all his spectacular shots that day. As I remember, you and I both lost a good deal of money that tournament.

Tony chuckled. "Yeah Willie, those were good days back then. We had some great summer golf and enjoyed playing cards at night with the other fellas staying at the resort." He sighed and repeated, "Yeh...some really good times."

Willie nodded with a wistful look. Both men were living now in much tougher times...in many ways made more difficult as a result of their life styles, choice of vocation and their illicit, underhanded dealings.

They then noticed a chauffeur driven milk wagon pulled by two horses was clunking by the marina with apparently no destination in mind. They watched as the driver stopped the wagon near the dock apparently concerned about a bad wheel. He kicked at it and then gave both horses some water out of a pail and some food before continuing his late night journey to nowhere.

Moments later Lawton returned to the hotel and seemed to hesitate at the entrance for a moment before conversing once again with the outside patrolmen. When he re-entered the hotel, LaCurso and Tony decided to get some sleep. They had to be ready the next day to follow the two Americans. To LaCurso the day might mean his vendetta against Bailey could finally be fulfilled. To Tony he had to be alert to supporting Willie while misdirecting the boss away from Adam Bailey.

Chapter 27

Lawton and Davis were having breakfast in the hotel patio Monday morning after Easter in full view of the two patrolmen monitoring the entrance to the hotel. The two bleary-eyed officers from their overnight duty had half a mind to join the two Americans since they knew the invitation from Lawton the night before for breakfast was sincere. But, they knew the appearance would look curious to their replacements. Nonetheless, when they were finally relieved by two other patrolmen, they gave Lawton and Davis a hearty but tired wave as they completed their shift.

As for the two hung over policemen in the lobby, they looked as if death might be preferable. When released from their overnight assignment, the two of them staggered to their patrol car and thought better of driving. They ended up taking a taxi to their respective residences to sleep off what had been a very pleasant and eventless evening drinking session with Charlie Davis in the hotel lobby. They'd kept a good eye on their subject until he went up to his room to sleep. They'd done their job exactly as assigned.

Following breakfast, Lawton and Davis behaved as if they were nothing but tourists caught up in a case of mistaken identity. Lawton went up to the two fresh patrolmen who'd been informed how cooperative the two American's had been and said, "Good morning, gentlemen. My friend and I are going over to the marina and arrange a travel tour before we leave Geneva. Would you like us to arrange tickets for you as well, so you can keep us under surveillance?"

One of the patrolmen sensing that keeping the two Americans under watch was approaching nonsensicality. He shook his head. "Thank you but we'll just remain here. You can check in with us when you return. We hope you have a pleasant cruise on the lake."

The four men shook hands and Lawton and Davis strode across the street to the marina ticket agent. By the time they reached the ticket station only one of the two was there. Lawton had peeled off and found a taxi to the small airfield of Geneva. Davis remained at the marina as much as anything to give Bailey ample time to see him.

As for the local police, they had become doubtful the tip off from the fat man to find Adam Bailey had any validity. With the openness of the two Americans and their absolute cooperation with the local authorities, it had been deemed a waste of time to track them further.

At lunchtime Lawton had returned from his trip to the airfield. He and Davis met at the marina and both strolled back to the hotel in full view of one officer left to spy on them.

Lawton strolled up in his disarmingly amiable manner and said to the policeman, "Officer, you might report to your office that my friend and I are planning to check out of our hotel this afternoon. We haven't decided whether we'll return to France or take a boat up to Lausanne for some sightseeing. If you'd like to join us for the excursion to Lausanne, you are most welcome to do so. We dislike seeing you wasting your time overseeing us. You may as well get some enjoyment out of your tedious assignment."

The patrolman just shook his head. "Gentlemen, I just heard from my sergeant. We obviously received some very inaccurate information accusing you of hiding an American fugitive just because you are U.S. citizens. Let me apologize on behalf of the department. You both have been very patient and cordial."

The officer then gave Lawton and Davis a respectful salute, wished them a good day, and marched down the street.

Davis smirked, "Well, that was easier than I thought it would be. If they truly knew you, they'd keep a double guard on us at all times."

Lawton chuckled as the two men headed toward the hotel entry. Just before opening the doorway, an elderly gentleman in a city worker uniform leaning down and cleaning scraps of paper from the street lightly stabbed Davis on the toe of his shoe.

Davis was startled and showed momentary irritation until a much younger voice sprang from behind the city worker's moustache. The worker whispered, "The huge guy with Willie LaCurso is his bodyguard named Tony Bando. I've known this enormous fellow since I was a kid working at the Chippewa Lodge golf course. The guy's got a heart of gold for the right people; he's ruthless to everyone else. I'm out to take care of that bastard Willie LaCurso. With Tony protecting him, I can't do what I need to do alone. I need your help. I'll make my way to your suite in ten minutes."

The hotel worker then busied himself with his clean up job as Lawton and Davis looked away as if involved in their own conversation. Davis offered his friend a cigarette and lit it as Lawton replied quietly, "Adam, that's a smart decision. You're in no condition to do anything alone right now. See you in a few minutes."

The two Americans then strolled through the front entrance never once looking at the maintenance worker. Three pairs of eyes had been watching Lawton and Davis as they paused and then entered the hotel. The policeman who said he was done with his surveillance of them....and Willie LaCurso and Big Tony who were staring at them from their third floor balcony.

None of the three suspected anything.

Ten minutes later Adam Bailey in his stolen city maintenance uniform was sitting once again in Lawton and Davis' hotel suite. He'd already helped himself to Davis' liquor supply and sitting on the couch lost in his thoughts. He looked in pain and it wasn't all from his leg injury.

He finally exclaimed, "Jamie.....Charlie.....you know you both mean a lot to me. Coming here and finding me...and now trying to get me across the border. But, just by you being here, I've now got you in trouble. You can't imagine how deep the pit is that you've stuck your feet. You need to understand I'm being stalked by Willie LaCurso...and he's not going to stop until he hunts me down and kills me. You have an idea what he did to me and I know this is my best chance of not just getting even with him...but eliminating the threat he represents not just to me, but to you guys, to Lindy, my father, and to Henry. He's like a disease and I want him gone."

The coldness of those words was chilling and unlike anything they'd ever heard Adam Bailey say. Both Lawton and Davis got themselves a drink before responding. Lawton was first. Shaking his head he stated very directly, "Adam, we're not going anywhere. You might believe you have a fifty-fifty chance to wipe out one or both of those two hoodlums, but I'd like to think Charlie and I could improve those odds. And, you're right. We're both up to our ears in this ordeal, but we're both glad we are. Willie LaCurso is going to be a threat to us...all of us... including family and friends if we don't do something about it. LaCurso has been operating too long in his bubble of illegal contentment. He's almost untouchable in the States. But, he's now taken himself out of his safety zone. I think it's time to do whatever it takes to cut this guy off at the knees."

Davis chimed in. "Adam, you know Jamie and me. We aren't the type who normally subscribe to vigilantism, but we're in a different country with war all around us. Let's just say Jamie and I have been hashing out a few ideas to permanently get this jackass out of your hair....and our hair.

Bailey perked up. He did not expect the response. Mystified he clarified, "I respect your thoughts, but what you guys are implying brings with it a lot of risk."

For once Lawton reacted irritably. "Hey! Life is a risk. At times it can be riskier when you're dealing with mugs like LaCurso. Nothing is guaranteed. You might as well know, Charlie and I have a plan and we've already started it. It's going to require getting LaCurso and his pal out of this city where we won't be so noticeable."

Surprised, Bailey chuckled, "So, how do you expect them to follow us? Are we leaving by boat with LaCurso and Tony in hot pursuit?"

Lawton's retort had a touch of his unique humor. "No, we plan to make it look like we're sneaking you over the border into France. We've rented a seaplane right down here at the marina."

Bailey glanced over at Davis seeing him roll his eyes. Charlie's discomfort with flying...especially small planes...was always a joke amongst themselves.

He whined, "Counselor, if I miss the flight, I'll see you back in the States."

There was some question whether Davis was joking.

Willie LaCurso was sitting concealed behind two large plants on his third floor balcony when Tony returned Monday afternoon from following Lawton and Davis. He looked more tired than normal. In fact, LaCurso had noticed his bodyguard and confidant of twenty years lately had seemed older than his years.

Breathing heavily and sweating, Big Tony sat down and poured himself some of Willie's scotch. It was a freedom he took when Willie seemed to be more depending on him. This was one of those times. Wiping his head with his handkerchief, the big man sighed, "They're up to something, Willie. I followed the thin guy Lawton. He took a taxi out to an airfield. He was there for an hour. Then he came straight back to the hotel and met his friend down at the marina. I don't know what the hell's going to be happening. They never made one attempt at meeting up with the kid so they must know where he is. They might be trying to fly the kid out of here.

Next time they leave the hotel, I say we split up and follow each one until we figure out their plan."

LaCurso sat there simmering. It didn't feel right. He and Tony were supposed to be in control and it didn't seem like it. He nodded his head without thinking. "Yeh Tony, let's do what you say."

It was almost dusk when the two American mobsters again left the hotel. Tony was in the corner of the lobby staking out the front entrance; Willie remained in the third floor suite so as not to be recognized.

Big Tony watched closely as Lawton and his friend strolled slowly through the lobby. Lawton wore a tweed overcoat and matching hat. He was hunched over a bit as if he'd drunk too much or eaten some bad food. His friend carrying a small piece of luggage helped him into a waiting taxi. It appeared that Lawton was sick and might be going to the infirmary.

Willie had observed the same scene at the taxi and came promptly down to the lobby. As the first cab took off, LaCurso and Tony were right behind in another taxi. Instantly they noticed two police vehicles were also following the first cab as well.

Willie gritted his teeth and bellowed, "Those God-damned cops are still doing surveillance on Lawton and his friend. They think the same thing we are...that those two guys are going to be meeting up somewhere with Bailey. Something smells, Tony, something smells awfully bad."

Expecting the taxi to make a run to a hospital, instead it was moving at breakneck speed as it passed one infirmary and then another. In fact the taxi appeared to be heading toward the train station. Willie felt for his revolver knowing this could be the chance to gun down the kid.

Tony sat back hoping the cops might get control of this incident and take young Bailey into custody so Willie wouldn't get his opportunity for revenge.

The first cab screeched to a halt in front of the station. Lawton's friend got out of the taxi and hurried into the train station alone. The two cop cars and the second taxi slowed and parked a short distance behind. No one....not Tony or Willie or the patrolmen intended to leave their vehicles until both Americans were in the terminal.

The wait became five minutes.....then ten minutes. Willie and Tony looked over at the frustrated officers in the two police cars. They undoubtedly had the same questions. Was the American in a long line to buy some tickets? Was he there to meet up with Adam Bailey? Finally the Lawton's taxi driver got out of his vehicle and slowly shuffled to the front door of the train terminal apparently to see what the delay was. He stood outside looking through the doors and then appeared to be waving for the American to return to the cab. Then, impatiently he strutted into the terminal with his hands up in the air displaying a high degree of frustration. While this scene went on, there was Lawton in the tweed coat and hat still appearing miserable and hunched over in the back seat of the taxi.

Another five minutes went by and a lieutenant finally decided to investigate the odd circumstances. He nervously got out of his police vehicle and slowly proceeded toward the taxi while motioning for two of his officers to go into the train station and find out what was causing the delay by Lawton's friend and the taxi driver. The officers were in the station less than twenty seconds when they came running out with their arms in the air indicating Davis and the taxi driver were no where to be seen.

The lieutenant's swear words were either German or Italian, but they were definitely loud. He ran over to the taxi and quickly opened the back door. There in the back seat was the taxi driver tied up with a big tweed overcoat covering his t-shirt and a matching hat plopped on his head. The two Americans had managed a switch sometime during the taxi ride to the train station. They were now on their way to someplace undetermined.

Willie watching this scene play out was irate. Tony sat there enjoying the ruse. It looked like Bailey's friends had more on the ball than he thought. The kid was in good hands.

Returning to the hotel, Willie was cussing every minute of the ride. He was certain Bailey had slipped through their fingers. Tony sat their coolly hoping that was the case.

Charlie Davis had casually stridden into the train station from the taxi as it waited for him to return. With Lawton still in the cab, they wanted to give the impression to the two police cars and the second taxi with Willie and his bodyguard that Davis was just buying some train tickets.

Inside the terminal he headed for the men's lavatory careful to notice if anyone was following him. He barely slowed as he passed the men's room door and proceeded to the west side of the huge terminal and out the door. Hailing a taxi he got in and told the cabbie, "Start your meter running. I've got a friend who will be slightly delayed. He should be here shortly."

The cabbie nodded appreciatively and started the meter. Two minutes later another man jumped in the taxi. The cabbie didn't even notice this second man was dressed as a taxi driver as well.

Davis thundered, "O.K....let's roll. We need the east marina...and hurry!" The taxi was at high speed within ten seconds.

Lawton looked out the back window and smiled, "Nobody's following us yet."

He stripped off the tight fitting taxi cab uniform and put on his more comfortable flight jacket and cap from the small bag Charlie had been carrying.

Within eight minutes the taxi was pulling up to the east side of the marina. Davis shoved a twenty dollar bill in the man's pocket and glared deep into the cabbie's eyes. "Now, my friend, go find a café and buy yourself a few drinks. Forget you ever saw us."

The taxi driver's eyebrows went up on his forehead until they almost touched his hairline. A twenty-dollar bill was more than he made in a day by a long shot. He smiled and waved. He knew just the café.

At the marina Lawton and Davis marched hurriedly over to a rather bizarre looking biplane. It had no wheels, just pontoons. There was a marine worker getting the plane ready. Upon seeing the two Americans approach, he got into the cockpit and began warming up the engine. Down the shoreline about a half mile the worker could see a couple police vehicles arriving at the main marina just down from the Lake Geneva Hotel. They were scurrying around the dock area looking for someone.

With nothing but a tourist boat still boarding its passengers, the cops had to take time to watch each of the sixteen people who wanted to view city from out on Lake Geneva at night. None were American and only two were men.... both from Holland.

Wavering not a moment, Lawton and Davis climbed up into the biplane. The worker untied the rope and gingerly stepped onto one of the pontoons while Lawton revved up the motor.

Davis was trying to make himself comfortable in the front seat of the two-seated biplane as Lawton looked over the controls waiting for the propeller to warm up to full speed.

It was then almost fully dark as Lawton put on his goggles and yelled, "O.K....let's go.

With that the marine worker climbed very awkwardly into the front cockpit hole that Davis was already occupying. Davis wailed above the noise from the propeller, "For Christ sakes, Adam, will you let me get the God-damned seat belt on before you sit on top of me!"

Bailey turned back toward Lawton with a big smile and roared. "Does this flight include lunch?"

Lawton was now busy trying to figure out how to fly a plane with pontoons that he'd never seen before. He maneuvered the biplane away from the dock and drove it out into the relative calm of the darkened lake.

Without further delay Lawton shouted, "You guys better be tied in, cause we're going!"

With that he accelerated the biplane. Davis sat back and held Bailey tight with his arms. The wind was whipping into their faces and the first spray of ice cold water hit the two in the front cockpit like a high-powered hose. Bailey and Davis lowered their heads not interested in experiencing that thrill again.

Lawton turned his head and saw the main marina dock area with the flashing lights of the two police cars. The plane sped by them not two hundred yards away. As hard as the city police had tried to follow them, Lawton and Davis had their fugitive in the plane and were about to escape their grasp. There was some doubt; however, as it seemed improbable the biplane was going to lift off the lake anyway.

But it finally did. Lawton inched the pontoons above the water until the engine sputtered slightly and the biplane went back into the lake. The ensuing wave of cold water swept over Bailey and Davis drenching them with another breath-taking shower.

Davis groaned and shouted at the top of his lungs, "Lawton, you son of a bitch, you did that on purpose. Get this hog in the air!"

Bailey looked back at Lawton with his eyes narrowed to the task at hand. He had that determined smile on his face as if he couldn't think of a better place to be at that moment.

Pulling back on the throttle once again, Lawton had the heavy biplane above the water...this time for good. The buildings and the lights of the city appeared on the right as the plane rose. As it leveled off no more than a thousand feet above Lake Geneva, Bailey was exhilarated. Hating to fly, Davis was simply putting up with the distress of sharing a single seat. He later would describe the experience as being womb-like but with less comfort.

Bailey leaned back and shouted above the din of the propeller, "Charlie, where we headed?"

Typical of Davis, his response was short and didn't help. He yelled, "Some water.......I hope!"

The plane's engine cut out again as Lawton steered the plane in a westerly direction. Their heading took them over French land. All three were aware the one challenge to this method of escape was finding some water to land the contraption. In the dark that could prove to be challenging.

Lawton was aware, though, of a long lake in France by the name of Lac d' Annecy on the other side of the town of Annecy in France. The lights of the small city would help them locate the lake. He turned the sputtering plane to a more southerly course.

As they continued the bumpy ride, there was mostly blackness with only occasional lights under some lower clouds. Disconcerting to the two passengers was Lawton dodging the mountains as he guided the biplane through a serpentine, low level route in the southern French Alps.

As the biplane's motor began to cough, the machine descended rather dramatically. Lawton didn't seem bothered but Davis and Bailey were aging considerably. He shouted to them, "It's about time we should be coming up on Lac d'Annecy. Look for the lights of Annecy."

Davis and Bailey looked at each other like Lawton was crazy. To both of them, Lac d'Annecy could just as well be the Mediterranean Sea or a pond in back of a farmhouse.

Davis shouted into Bailey's ear, "If we ever land this machine and we live to talk about it, I likely won't have a solid bowel movement for about a week."

Within five minutes of Lawton's yell, all three of them finally saw the lights of a city. They could only hope it was the city of Annecy, France…and then further pray that the pitch black emptiness next to the lights of the city was indeed the large lake where Lawton intended to land.

As the sputtering biplane continued to descend, Davis could be heard by Bailey either talking to God or using His name in vein in reference to the pilot. The noise made it difficult to discern the difference.

Given he had no seat belt, Bailey readied himself to be shot out of the front cockpit and into the lake the moment the pontoons hit the water.

Lawton showed every confidence the huge black area was his landing target. The biplane passed through some more low level clouds and finally there was the city and the outline of Lac d'Annecy. As Lawton adjusted the flaps and turned the plane, it descended like a rock amidst the moans of the two passengers.

Suddenly the biplane straightened up and it seemed the plane was hardly making headway in the breezy conditions. Twenty yards above the water, the machine kept jumping up and down. At times it seemed the waves on the lake were higher than the biplane. When the pontoons finally touched the water, it bounced causing a huge wave to flood the front cockpit.

That brought out Davis' ire once again. He screamed out, "God damn you, Lawton. You did it again…..on purpose!"

The second plunge by the pontoons was smoother…and just like that the ride of a lifetime was over. Lawton cut the engine and the biplane slowed down as if caught in molasses. Davis, a twice-a-year Presbyterian, did a sign of the cross and then turned around cussing at Lawton for getting the cigars in his breast pocket soaked. Bailey sat there relieved as if he'd been re-born…and baptized.

They were now in the safety of France…but their job was not over. The three of them were now about to become bonded in silence for the second time in their lives. It was a matter they'd agreed to take into their own hands and never share with anyone else including Lindy Lawton, Henry Granville, and John Bailey.

Their ears still rang from the loud noise engine and their clothing drenched as Lawton directed the biplane toward the quiet Annecy city dock. The only sound heard besides the biplane motor was Davis. He was elated he was going to see another sunrise. He pushed Bailey off his lap yelling, "God damn it, Adam, get the hell off my legs. I haven't felt the flow of blood for the last half hour. For a while I didn't think the numbness mattered since we were going to crash anyway."

Lawton drove the rickety biplane slowly towards the end of the dock. While they had a plan, the three had no idea how they might be greeted having flown illegally into France. They could be arrested. There might already been a communiqué from the Swiss military police admonishing the French law enforcement that a rogue aircraft had penetrated their airspace. What they were counting on was that Willie LaCurso would not let a border get in the way of his vengeful objective. It was expected the gangster and his right hand hit man would not be too far behind.

Luck appeared to be with them as they parked the biplane at an empty mooring at the city harbor dock. There was no gendarme welcoming committee, only a man sitting in the main office at the harbor with a light on. That he didn't move when the blaring sound of a biplane landed close by indicated the man was either asleep or dead.

As they stole past the harbor master office without being detected, the three made their way in the now quiet evening to a nearby plaza along Lac d'Annecy. There was virtually no activity going on given it was the first weekday night after a busy Easter weekend. They checked into an inviting French hotel that seemed empty of occupants. The desk clerk signed them in. Seeing only the one small piece of luggage carried by Davis and the soaked clothing of the three travelers, he commented sardonically, "For three Americans, you travel very light."

Lawton responded quickly, "The rest of our luggage is behind." It was a true statement.

In the suite only Davis and Bailey had to strip to their skivvies and hung them up to dry. Lawton's flight jacket had kept him dry.

There were no clothes in the small suitcase, just two bottles of wine. A toast was made to 'better times ahead'...and then they waited for things to unfurl. It was as predictable as rain.

Only Bailey didn't know the specifics of the plan. He asked, "So Jamie, how do we know LaCurso and Big Tony will find us?"

Except for sipping his wine, Lawton replied with no qualms. "That's easy. Charlie and I left them enough tipoffs that a dog with a cold could find us. LaCurso and his large friend will figure by the timing that we helped you escape by flying that contraption on pontoons out of Geneva and into France. In the biplane's condition it would be logical to assume we landed on the first body of water across the border. Lac d' Annecy is one of at least three lake destinations that answer that description. We had to be careful not to make the hints too obvious. They'll have to call three marinas and find out if a dilapidated biplane with pontoons had landed and was now tied to the city harbor dock.

My guess is those two hoodlums could be traipsing around this marina and plaza very soon and certainly no later than tomorrow morning. We just have to be ready for them.

When Willie and Tony watched the biplane cough and sputter its way off the water into the twilight of the Lake Geneva evening, Willie was livid. He was watching yet another escape by young Bailey. Between his onslaught of profanities, Tony was already looking at a map of the area inside the marina main office.

He called over to the boss, "Willie, listen to that motor. That machine will be lucky to stay airborne much less make it into France. It won't go far. And in the darkness, they're looking for the first lake they can find in France to set it down. If they're in the air more than twenty minutes, I'd be surprised."

The aerial map showed three lakes that seemed suitable for a landing....a small body of water by Bonneville...a large lake called Lac d'Annecy...and yet another lake further south called Lak du Bourge.

Tony tapped the furthest choice at Lak du Bourge. Willie disagreed. "Tony, it ain't going to go that far. The most convenient landing spot is Annecy. It's the only city big enough to be recognized at night by its lights. Let's give them a chance to land. Shortly we can call that marina. Somebody should be aware if a piece of junk with pontoons just landed on their lake."

A half hour later, Tony placed a call to the Lac D'Annecy marina. After a number of rings, a sleepy voiced Frenchman answered the phone. In broken French Tony asked, "Did a noisy pontoon biplane just land at your marina?"

The marina night watchman was slightly irritated over the interruption to his evening. First, there had been the ungodly sound of the biplane edging up to the dock with three men inside a two-seater. Then the phone rang when he'd been trying to enjoy some wine and a book in the corner of his office. The American caller speaking the worst French known to mankind wanted to know if the damned biplane had landed at his marina.

The irritated watchmen responded cynically in his own broken English, "Ya, what of it?"

The line then went dead. The night watchman swore under his breath and went back to his wine and book.

Within a half hour Tony and Willie had checked out of their Geneva hotel and taxied across the border into France. They were at the train station waiting for the next train to Annecy, France just forty minutes away. It was 10:30 Monday evening when the train finally pulled out of Vernier, France for the short journey to Annecy.

Davis got the bed in the marina hotel since he claimed he lost the most minutes off his life expectancy after the twenty minute ghastly air trip from Geneva to Annecy.

Grinning, Lawton scoffed, "I thought the flight was kind of picturesque."

Davis was sound asleep within fifteen seconds of his head touching one of the pillows. Lawton lying on the couch was asleep almost as fast.

Bailey just looked at them shaking his head. They were opposites in so many ways but as a twosome one of a kind. He wasn't at their level of being able to relax when danger loomed.

He lay down on the other bed trying to get some shut eye before their adversaries Lawton and Davis practically guaranteed would be arriving. He heard the lingering sound of a train as it approached Annecy a few miles away. It reminded him of the yawning train whistle he'd hear nightly as a kid at the farmhouse near Glenwood, Minnesota. The remembrance helped ease his mind enough for him to fall into a light but fitful sleep.

When the night train arrived in Annecy that Monday night, Willie and Tony took a taxi straight to the marina at Lac d' Annecy. They were looking for a seaplane. When they arrived, they found three of them tied up to the moorings of a dock. Tony walked forward on the dock. He awkwardly jumped onto the pontoon of the first plane and felt the engine. It was as cold as the water on Lake

Superior. Back on the dock he moved to the next biplane and repeated the same measure. The engine was still slightly warm. He pointed his thumb up toward Willie.

Striding by the marina office they saw the night watchman fast asleep with his reading light on and his book peacefully resting on his chest. They walked across the plaza to the first of many hotels and lodging houses convenient to the marina. LaCurso patiently asked the night clerk if some friends of theirs had registered. The night clerk was groggy but asked, "And their names?"

Tony and Willie looked at each other. Sleep deprived, Tony's tolerance had declined. He pulled out his revolver and attached the barrel to the tip of the night clerk's nose. In his gravelly voice, he growled, "Show me the register. I'll let you know if we see their names."

There were very few people registered. He then gruffly asked, "You remember three American's walking into this hotel within the past few hours?"

The night clerk's eyes were crossed looking at the barrel of the gun. His legs were crossed as well to keep him from soiling the floor. His voice was high-pitched, but he managed to respond. "No......there has been no one registering in the last two hours."

That's the way it went at the next two hotels and an inn. No night clerk had remembered anyone registering. The fifth hotel, the Inn D'Annecy, was a smaller five-story hotel. The night clerk was reading at the front desk.

Willie went in alone and asked, "Has anyone registered at your hotel in the last couple hours. The clerk hesitated and then nodded his head. "Yes, a young couple registered about an hour ago. That's been about it."

Willie looked squarely into the clerk's eyes and decided he was telling the truth. Willie then went out the front door and met Tony. "They have to be in this city. There are no more night trains out of Annecy. Let's get some rest. We have to be close to them. We'll find them in the morning."

They got a room at the Inn on the second floor courtesy of the night clerk. He gave one look at the heavy set, exhausted Tony and showed pity on the man despite his being Italian. The large man looked as if he'd need medical attention if he had to take too many flights of stairs.

When the late registrants were up the stairs to their room, the night clerk felt the American $20 bill in his lapel pocket. He called room #315. It rang twice before a sleepy voice answered.

The night clerk whispered into the receiver, "Just now there were two gentlemen inquiring if three Americans checked into the Inn. I did not tell them anything."

The sleepy voice responded, "Thank you for the call. You earned your tip."

The night clerk then added, "The man and his large Italian friend registered and took a room about five minutes ago. They are in room #202."

The groggy voice became even sharper. "Thank you," he said.

Putting the receiver down, Jamie Lawton whispered loudly to his bunkmates, "Charlie......Adam.......they're already in Annecy and right here at the marina. In fact they're staying the night on the floor below us!"

The three of them bolted up. They had been sleeping for almost two hours. Bailey watched as Lawton and Davis calmly went about their preparation. They had guns of their own and the limited sleep they'd had seemed to be satisfactory.

As planned Davis split and went down the back staircase to carry out his part of the task. Lawton and Bailey silently went down the stairs to the second floor. Room #202 was at the end of the hall. A house phone was on the wall by the stairs. Bailey picked up the receiver and asked for room #202. The night clerk obliged.

The voice of Tony was unmistakable. He was testy and untrusting. He said one word. It came out as an order. "Talk!"

In his best obsequious French accent, Bailey inquired, "Mosier, I just had an American gentleman register at our Inn. He is staying on the fourth floor, room #411. You were inquiring earlier and I thought you'd like to know."

Then Bailey disconnected the line.

Lawton was already down the hall listening through the door of suite #202. There was no question the two hoodlums were up and preparing to exit the room. They were about to sneak up the back stairs and pay a visit to the newly registered American whoever he might be. Unfortunately for them, there would be an interruption.

Motioning for Bailey to hurry down the hallway, the two of them got prepared to catch LaCurso and Tony off guard before they could reach for their weapons. Shooting them in the hotel room was not the plan. Disbelief was their ultimate aim.

The tension was unbearable, but finally the two of them heard Tony's muffled voice inside the room say to LaCurso, "You ready?"

The next thirty seconds seemed like slow motion. The door opened slightly and that was all that was required. Bailey hit the door hard as it opened. Tony was pushed backwards against Willie. They both lost their balance and ended up on the floor in a completely undignified fall. LaCurso made a groaning sound as if something huge had just kicked him in the stomach. He began gasping for air until Tony finally rolled off him. The large man automatically reached in his coat pocket for his pistol until he felt the cold iron of a pistol suddenly get thrust into his left ear. He immediately and unconsciously held his arms straight out in surrender. Lawton pulled the revolver from Big Tony's suitcoat pocket.

LaCurso was still writhing on the floor trying to catch his breath. While Lawton held his revolver in the ear of Tony, Bailey quickly rushed over to LaCurso. As the man began to recover from having his lungs temporarily crushed, Bailey relieved the man of at least one of his weapons in his breast pocket.

Lawton then kicked the door closed and turned on the light. What Bailey and Lawton saw would have been comical if the circumstances hadn't been so grave. As Tony slowly struggled to his feet with Lawton's gun barrel still in his ear, the big man helped his boss up. Willie was suffering but Tony showed no pain or concern. He just stared at Lawton and then at Bailey...back and forth. His eyes were cold as ice. Big Tony was in his element and not intimidated in the least. His mind was already thinking of a way to win this predicament.

As LaCurso finally caught his breath, he too didn't say a word. His loathing, piercing eyes said it all.

It struck Bailey how intimidated he'd have felt even a month before. Now he was emotionless.

Lawton broke the silence with specific orders. As he pulled his gun barrel away from Tony's ear, his voice was harsh. "Big man, take your coat off and throw it across the room. And if you try anything at all, Willie gets it in the head."

Without blinking, Tony slowly did as he was told.

Lawton wasn't done. "Now, turn around so we can see the other weapon in the back of your belt."

Sure enough, Tony had a pistol in a back holster as well. "Now, lift up both pant legs and get rid of your other weapons. Tony lifted up one pant leg displaying a holster with yet another pistol. The other leg had a holster for a six-inch knife. The weapons were dropped on the floor and kicked over to the feet of Lawton.

LaCurso was then ordered to do the same. He only had another pistol in a holster on his right leg.

With the two hoodlums now weaponless, Bailey broke a cord off one of the lamps and tied Tony's arms together behind him.

He didn't like it and growled, "You're making a huge mistake, kid."

His voice was as daunting as he could make it. Bailey only made the cord tighter. Tony reacted with a groan. He didn't get the reaction from the kid he'd expected.

Bailey then took his own pistol with the silencer and pointed it into the mouth of LaCurso. His voice was evil. Even Lawton looked at him in wonder as Bailey hissed to the crime lord, "After what you've put me through these last weeks, I'm glad my friend is here or you'd be dead."

Continuing to stare into the eyes of LaCurso, he added coldly, "This is the weapon your brother was supposed to use on me. I guess it didn't work out the way you and he wanted."

For the first time both Tony and LaCurso blinked. Bailey had just admitted besting Roberto.

Lawton then cut another lamp cord and securely tied Willie's hands and arms behind his back. The extreme hatred in both gangsters' eyes no longer mattered; it was very evident the cards were stacked against them.

The discomfort of being bound caused LaCurso to blurt out, "So, we either make a deal or you shoot us and get it over with. You have a silencer on that gun."

Lawton looked over at Bailey as if to humorously nod his head in agreement; Bailey just stared at LaCurso. His preference didn't have to be stated.

Tony remained calm. He'd played this game of threats before. Willie had as well, but normally from the safety of his home or office as the game was being played by those who worked for him.

LaCurso began voicing ideas for a deal but Bailey and Lawton just sat at a table on the other side of the room mostly ignoring their two quarries. Finally, Lawton exclaimed, "Gentlemen, if you prefer a cloth in your mouth to keep quiet, we'll do that. Otherwise, stay still. We'll be moving on shortly."

Somehow that didn't sit well with LaCurso. He didn't like not being in control. But, he remained quiet.

It was another hour...about 1:30 in the morning...before a slight tap could be heard on the door. A muffled voice said, "It's me."

Lawton opened the door to a hurrying Charlie Davis. He hardly glanced at the two characters tied up and sitting on the floor. It was as if they didn't exist as human beings anymore. His only attention was to offer some food and wine he'd picked up for Bailey and Lawton. Pouring some wine into three glasses, they gave a somber toast to each other. There was work yet to do. The food and wine was not for celebration; it was more to help them remain attentive.

Being ignored the unruffled Tony began to show some unease. LaCurso began to appeal to his captures once again. Lawton unceremoniously walked over and shoved a handkerchief in the gangster's mouth. LaCurso immediately spit it out, but he said no more.

Lawton looked placidly at the conman and said, "Talk once more and I'll put tape over your mouth." Bailey and Davis hardly paid attention. The three finished up the food and showed themselves to be ready to move out.

LaCurso and Tony continually eyed each other wondering what was going to happen. They'd never been in a situation where individuals were not traumatized about what might become of them if they weren't straight with Willie LaCurso.

Then it was Charlie's time to take over....as part of the scheme. He spoke only to Lawton and Bailey. "Well, it's set. I've contacted the local French police and told them we've got the two Italians leaders of the group planning to assassinate Benito Mussolini. I told them how these two meatheads tried to pin the responsibility on an American businessman named Adam Bailey. I told them both men are seeking safe haven in France."

Davis paused to sip his wine and then added, "You know, it makes for a sticky situation since France doesn't want to have any part of these two would-be assassins. It could turn into a confusing international incident. I'm certain the authorities in France would like nothing more than having these two killers brought back to Italy with no incident. The relation between Italy and France is bad enough the way it is."

LaCurso scoffed, "You don't think the French authorities are going to buy this story. Tony and I are Americans. You can't prove we had anything to do with any assassination plot against Mussolini. I don't know what you three are trying to pull, but it won't work."

Davis ignored LaCurso. He continued, "Yes, when these two gentlemen are given over to the Italian authorities, they'll have a chance to plead their case. But, like the man just said, the two of them are just Americans. What do they have to do with any scheme to kill Mussolini?"

Then Davis answered his own question. "Oh yes....what's wrong with me... there's the question of your two associates now dead. I'm speaking of Andre Pizzorno and Roberto. Isn't Roberto a brother of yours, Willie? That could be a problem."

Lawton then added, "Willie, your brother's and your name and that of your large accomplice beside you will be publicized all over Italy and back into the States. We're going to make the LaCurso name known by everyone in your family's country. Gosh, I guess that type of publicity could cause problems for your relatives in Italy. You know Mussolini. He holds grudges."

LaCurso shifted uncomfortably and his voice sounded shaken. "You can't do that. You'll put my family name in Italy to shame and all my relatives will face immediate hardship if not death by Mussolini's henchmen. You would be causing many useless murders.

Bailey finally spoke up showing not an ounce of sympathy. "That's a damn shame. I'm certain you took family consequences of those you've killed or ruined under consideration in your dealings over the years."

Willie LaCurso was purple with fury. He began calling his three captors every disparaging name he could think of until the handkerchief was again stuffed in his mouth and tied their securely with one of his socks. The room became quiet again.

With Willie's voice silenced, the calmer voice of reason came from Tony. His voice still exuded confidence, but he was in a difficult bargaining position tied up on the floor. His words were conciliatory. "O.K. boys, you've got us. Let's start talking what it's going to take to end this game. We don't want you turning us over to anyone or talking to the newspapers. And, I would expect the three of you want a guarantee not ever to be followed again. The answer seems obvious."

Bailey began to chuckle. Lawton and Bailey joined in. Tony realized his appeasing tone was being mocked. It was Bailey who made the situation as clear to both Tony and LaCurso as possible.

He looked directly at the two conmen while barely holding his wrath. "Gentlemen, there will be no negotiations. You've both put me through hell... and countless other people as well. The difference is that I've made it back and I'm not afraid of you. I may go through hell again, but it'll not be as the result of your actions. You two have to be shut down...forever. I'd like to think the Italian authorities will do just that."

Tony's jowl began to move somewhat uncontrollably. He looked at each of his captors and saw there was no weakness to their resolve. They were impassive.

Now his face showed true concern. LaCurso with his mouth stuffed could only glower in what he'd just heard.

Tony tried one more time. "Let's get reasonable boys. Willie has plenty of money. If that's what you want, I know he'll pay you. Tell us what you want."

The level of desperation from Tony's voice was what the Lawton, Davis, and Bailey were waiting for. Lawton took over from there.

"Yes....there is a way out but both of you will have a lot to do. To save your skins and those of the LaCurso family in Italy, we're offering to still take you to the French authorities in Marseilles. You'll have a letter stating that Adam Bailey had nothing to do with a plot against Mussolini. Instead the letter will explain that your unstable brother, Roberto, was plotting to kill Il Duce and you hired Andre Pizzorno to kill your brother in order to keep your family in Italy from being blamed. You'll end your letter explaining that the deed had been done... Roberto was dead... and you were saddened to hear that Pizzorno was killed in some mountain accident north of Lugano."

Tony was trying to keep from being overjoyed. Astonished, he replied, "Is that all?"

Lawton continued, "No......there's a bit more. You will also never be in contact with us or any of our family or friends again. If you do, it will cause a letter to be sent to the offices of Mussolini, our state department, the Prime Minister's office in Paris and some other people we can't think of right now that will implicate both of you and the LaCurso family in a grand plot to kill Mussolini as well as his key Fascist henchmen."

This still did not worry Tony. He seemed pleased with the easy out.

Willie, on the other hand, was sitting there like a defeated dog looking very undignified with the sock tying a piece of cloth over his mouth. He didn't like the deal, but he shook his head in agreement. To the three captors, they expected his insincere promise.

In the next half hour Davis penned the letter. The sock was undone and LaCurso could breathe from his mouth once again. To show his disgust, he didn't read the letter. He just scribbled his name at the salutation and threw it aside.

Lawton read the letter again and put it in an envelope. Then with a smile on his face, he declared, "Well, I'm happy all of us could come to such a fair agreement. Charlie, if you'll arrange for our flight down to Marsailles, I'll get our passengers ready."

LaCurso was rubbing his arms where the cord had bound him so tightly. He questioned the next move. "What do you mean......flight down to Marseilles? Why don't we take a train?"

Lawton almost dismissed the question but finally responded. "We want to make certain there are no interruptions or attempts to escape. By flying both of you to Marseilles and handing you over to the French police, we'll have more of a guarantee the letters will be delivered. In fact, I'll fly the two of you myself while my two friends contact the French authorities and let them know what they can expect. I'll land the plane on Lake Martigues near Marseilles and we'll wait for the police to arrive."

The whole plan sounded peculiar but the two hoodlums had little choice. And, to Tony and LaCurso, anything away from being tied up in the hotel suite sounded more hopeful.

It was almost 5:00 in the morning when the five of them walked down the stairs together. The night clerk gave the five a precarious glance seeing that two of the men looked rather glum and the other three men had their hands in their coat pockets as if pointing something. He knew something was up, but chose not to say a word, especially when Lawton paid the bill for both rooms with an added tip from LaCurso's wallet.

The five then left the hotel and walked across the plaza to the marina. The morning was still dark and quite cool. There was no chatter among the group.

Walking by the biplane with pontoons that Lawton, Davis, and Bailey had flown into Annecy the night before, they continued strolling toward another slightly larger biplane moored at another dock. This three-seater didn't have pontoons, but skis. It didn't look that much more reliable. Davis was relieved he didn't have to fly in it. LaCurso and Tony were still trying to figure out what was going on.

With the three places to sit, two of the cockpit openings had controls for flying the plane. Lawton got in the rear seat and began revving up the engine. Bailey and Davis nudged the two culprits into the other two seats. Willie took the middle with controls in front of him. His hands were untied. Tony took the front seat but his arms remained bound.

Willie and Tony, rightly so, looked very uncomfortable as Lawton continued warming the engine of the biplane. The other two captors were not saying a word other than helping the two gangsters fasten their seat belts. With that action done, Bailey and Davis no longer held the men by gunpoint.

As Lawton began pulling away from the dock, Bailey and Davis just stared at the two hucksters for a long moment before giving the pilot a thumbs up signal. To Willie and Tony it was a blank stare devoid of emotion.

The sun had not risen as the plane gathered speed on Lac d'Annecy. It gradually took off above the water in a southeasterly direction rising up against the mountains that were becoming visible in the morning light.

Bailey called for a taxi from a marina pay phone while Davis went in the marina office to settle up on some additional costs on the biplane....in particular the insurance. A minute later Davis and Bailey watched as the seaplane disappeared in the cool morning fog. Shortly, the taxi then took them to the train station.

Davis still had some cash in his hand as the taxi squealed to a stop a few minutes later. Bailey noticed all the money and asked, "Where'd you get all the money?"

Matter-of-factly he responded, "Where they're going they won't need the cash. Besides, I thought it only right those two hucksters kick in for some of the costs for their transportation. "

As the biplane rose over Lac d' Annecy and continued in a southeasterly direction, Lawton yelled up to LaCurso sitting hunched in the middle seat, "Hey..... there seems to be something wrong with one of the attachments on the lower wing. You'll have to help me fly this contraption, so I can fix whatever the problem is."

Willie looked behind at Lawton as if he was crazy. He shook his head and raised his hands giving an absolute negative reply.

Lawton called out again. "Put your feet on the pedals and use the stick in front of you to maintain this level. I'll watch you for a minute to make certain you have the feel."

LaCurso again looked back at Lawton...his eyes wide with fear. Finally he grabbed the stick and put his feet on the pedals. Then Lawton gave the gangster temporary control to see if the man could keep the biplane level.

Immediately, the plane lurched downward but then recovered dramatically upward. The movement was so violent Tony sitting up front lost his lunch. Lawton took control again and brought the aircraft back to normal level.

Then he patiently yelled, "Come on. You'll get it. Try again."

LaCurso could not believe what he was being asked to do for the second time. He hadn't ever even been in the cockpit of a plane. All the gauges and dials looked intimidating. The noise from the open air only added to his feeling of being in hell.

LaCurso took the stick in front of him and placed his feet on the pedals and made another effort. The plane wavered but this time he was able to maintain some control.

Lawton again shouted above the engine noise, "You fly it for a while until I know you have some control. Then I'll go to work on the mechanical problem."

To Lawton LaCurso's hair seemed grayer since they had gotten on board the plane just minutes before. True to his word Lawton let LaCurso handle the controls for another ten minutes until they left the presumed safety of the water below and were mostly flying over land.

Lawton gave LaCurso some guidance in keeping the nose of the plane level as they flew into some higher mountain elevations. By the light of the morning sun, Tony and LaCurso began to realize their pilot was directing the plane in a more easterly than southerly direction...actually away from Marseilles on the French border. They didn't know why, but they weren't in a position to ask too many questions. It was about a half hour later when Lawton pointed down to some mountain lakes.

He hollered, "We're at the French-Italian border. Let's bring this plane down and try to land on one of those lakes. LaCurso still operating the biplane only nodded not understanding why but looking forward to ending the flight.

Lawton took the controls for only a moment as he lowered the plane to an altitude of two thousand feet. Leveling off and heading for one of the larger lakes in Italy, Lawton again yelled for LaCurso to take the controls so he could tackle the mechanical problem.

LaCurso was exasperated why he was expected to fly a plane while the pilot fixed something that seemingly had no impact on the ability of the air machine to remain airborne. Above all, it wasn't as if the actual pilot was going to leave the landing on water to anyone but himself.

As instructed LaCurso made the plane gradually lose altitude as the engine decreased in revolutions. He could see the morning lights of a small city by the lake just ahead. Still the water was far below. He waited for the pilot to retake the controls.

The novice pilot LaCurso hit another wind shear and the plane dipped down and then back up. He was fighting with the heavy machine trying to keep it somewhat level.

Tony was of no help sitting in front seat with his hands tied. His head was down, almost as if he was asleep. For a moment LaCurso thought the man was actually praying.

LaCurso continued to gradually lower the plane against the inconsistent winds. He was shouting as loud as he could to the pilot to take over the controls. Losing whatever resolve he had, he finally turned around to scream something at the pilot. It would be the most horrific moment in the gangster's long life. To his horror he saw no one in the rear pilot's seat. He kept stretching backwards while trying to keep control of the plane, but the pilot was simply....gone.

The primeval yell that echoed above the engine noise finally sparked some attention from Tony. His hands still tied, he turned around as best he could. To his own shock and revulsion, he saw his boss struggling alone trying to keep the plane aloft.

They both looked over the edge of the fuselage simultaneously and saw the worst sight imaginable. Below and behind them a parachute had just opened. The pilot had chosen another method to reach land. LaCurso was now on the controls after a casual, stress-filled half hour of flying lessons. The fear engulfing the two Italian mobsters was beyond anything they'd ever experienced. The biplane began to lurch to and fro and LaCurso fought keeping the plane level. Despite the cold temperatures in the air, sweat was pouring off his face as if he were standing under a waterfall.

The biplane continued to chop through the air downward toward the lake by the small Italian city of Susa less than fifty kilometers from the major industrial city of Torino in western Italy. The down drafts were throwing the plane all over. The novice pilot was doing everything his limited experience would allow to keep control of both the plane and his frantic emotions.

Approximately one thousand feet above the lake, LaCurso couldn't believe it but the strong winds had subsided making it easier to keep the wings more level.

Tony was holding onto one side of the fuselage with his bound hands dealing with the reality he was already traveling toward Hell. It was just a matter of time before he'd become a permanent resident. Flashes of the way he lived his life burst through his brain. Somehow getting what was coming to him kept him from screaming.

From his descending parachute, Lawton watched the plane continue its descent toward Susa, Italy. He knew the terrain from a road trip in previous years. He watched coldly thinking that the flying lessons he'd given Willie LaCurso gave the two gangsters some chance for landing and surviving. That was more than LaCurso likely gave to his victims. If the two hoodlums somehow did survive what at best would be a crash landing on water, they would be picked up by the Italian police. When the letter signed by Willie LaCurso would be found in the gangster's pocket, there would be major controversy of the two LaCursos involvement in not one but many assassination schemes against Mussolini. Willie would be as dead as his brother. Tony would be guilty by association and would meet the same end.

Realistically, however, Lawton knew the fate of the two men was not good with Willie LaCurso barely able to keep the biplane steady. There was a very low chance of survival. If the plane came down at too steep of an angle, the fuselage would explode on the water as if it was hitting a brick wall. From his unique perspective under the parachute, he watched as the biplane descended further toward the lake near Susa, Italy. The angle did not look favorable for the two gangsters.

He thought about the conversation he, Bailey and Davis had the night before when they knew Willie LaCurso and his right hand man, Tony, were at their disposal only a floor below at the Annecy hotel. Adam had no sympathy but Lawton and Davis decided they'd give the two hucksters a fighting chance to live. Bailey remained compassionless. He strongly voiced how so many others impacted by the two mobsters would share his merciless feelings.

Lawton eventually reasoned with him stating, "Adam, it'll do you no good to be arrested here in France if you're found responsible for those two hoodlums' murders. Reprisals from the mob back in the States could be waiting for you. Charlie and I are willing to give them as much of a chance to survive....maybe more....than they've given others tenfold. We want them to be responsible for their own deaths...one way or the other."

As Lawton descended in the parachute over the Franco-Italian border, he was depending on the mountain winds to drive his chute as far back into France as possible. He had a certain French border outpost he had to find by the name of Madane, France. He'd traveled over the mountain roads a few years before and recalled a small restaurant in that community.

At less than a thousand feet he steered his parachute toward the French town he saw in the distance. Before concentrating on his landing, he gazed off to the east and saw the wings of the rented seaplane. It appeared to be lurching back and forth as it moved speedily toward the lake just north of Susa, Italy. Then the fast approaching ground caused him to lose sight of the plane.

Lawton had parachuted a couple times before but only for fun. This was a different circumstance. He had to have a reasonably soft landing with the parachute so he'd be able to walk down the mountain side to the small town. This would not be a good time to break an ankle.

There was just enough morning light for him to see a small meadow next to a roadway. The morning winds were gentle. His landing was soft enough to allow him to roll over twice to minimize the jolt. He could feel some rocks grinding into his back and legs, but he'd rolled up like a ball and cushioned himself. The brief pain was a small price to pay to eliminate two gangsters who'd done untold damage to so many people's lives and no doubt their families as well.

But, there were some more personal factors. Lawton and Davis had long been aware how Willie LaCurso had stayed too close to the real story surrounding the Loni D'Annelli incident back in Glenwood, Minnesota now almost ten years before. LaCurso and D'Annelli had been friends for years. Something was forcing LaCurso to remain vigilant on finding who the culprits were who brought down his friend, D'Annelli.

Adam Bailey was a link to that past time. To Lawton and Davis that was why LaCurso maintained a relationship with Adam, D'Annelli's former caddy. He wanted to believe Adam might open the door to some new information that would find those who brought down D'Annelli. But, that hadn't worked out. When LaCurso realized he was getting no good out of his relationship with Bailey, the young man became expendable.

Lawton stood in the meadow wiggling his body to confirm he'd survived the parachute landing with no major injuries. He gathered the parachute and stuffed it into a bag. Pulling the bag's strap over his shoulder he hiked up the slope of the flowered grass field to the mountain road. Lifting his legs over the guard rail, he began strolling down the road to Madane. He guessed it was ten kilometers to the small town. If he was picked up by some generous driver or local farmer, he'd get to village sooner. If not, Lawton was perfectly willing to enjoy his stroll into the mountain town on such a beautiful day along the French/Italian border.

For a moment he thought he heard the biplane's engine still roaring in the sky as it headed toward Susa, Italy, but the soft mountain breeze prevented any other sound but the din of the wind. He picked up his pace looking forward to meeting up with Charlie Davis and Adam Bailey. It would take them a few hours to make it to Madane by train. The memory of the café in the border town brought back the taste of that special French white wine indigenous to the area. He planned on enjoying some of that port before his two friends showed up and then more after they arrived.

Chapter 28

Relaxing in a conference room at the American Embassy in Paris just a day and a half later after returning from Madane, France, Jamie Lawton, Charlie Davis and Adam Bailey were drinking coffee and waiting for a duplicate passport so Bailey could feel whole again and take the 'Yankee Clipper' flight back to the States.

An aide came in pointing to the conference room telephone. "Mr. Bailey, the call is for you."

The voice he heard sounded distant with the echo reverberating in the telephone line. It was a very exhilarated David O'Brien. "So, welcome back to the western world, Adam. I heard you had some trouble on your sight-seeing trip through Switzerland."

Bailey chuckled over the frivolous quip. "You're a real comedian, David. I did wonder if anything was going to go my way. As a murder suspect hiding from seemingly everyone, it can get a bit lonely. At least I was found by the right people. I have a few good friends who simply will not let me die."

O'Brien didn't let that comment go unrecognized. "You're right. You are very lucky. I have recently been made aware that a certain Italian-American businessman from your home city back in Minnesota has been hounding you for a long time and you've had trouble getting him off your back."

Bailey stayed quiet as he'd been trained to do when something was said that could cause him problems.

O'Brien continued, "Anyway, it has been reported that this man and his gangster colleague were looking for you this past weekend in Geneva for reasons relating to the shooting death of his brother, Roberto LaCurso, in Lugano, Switzerland. Why this 'Mr. LaCurso' and his associate were blaming you must be quite a story. Someday when we both have the time, maybe you might share this rumor over a drink. For now, though, it's not important. I'm just glad you're back with us.

I will tell you some news you and your two friends should know. I believe what I have to tell you might relieve all three of you. Apparently these two men in pursuit of you were trying to fly into Italy for reasons that may never be explained. They were flying one of those open cockpit biplanes along the French-Italian border to a mountain lake just west of Torino, Italy. Word has it that they ran into some engine problems. Witnesses said they made an attempt to water land...and it was less than sterling. In fact those same witnesses agreed it was as if the pilot had never landed a plane on water before. The biplane hit the water at such an extreme angle, the fuselage basically disintegrated as if made of balsa wood. The two men didn't fare much better. Let's just say they didn't survive the landing. Those same witnesses reported the passenger in the front cockpit flew out into the open air like a cannon shot. They found him in not very good condition with a piece of the wing imbedded in his body.

The pilot was in worse shape if that was possible. The parts of him recovered so far...well, you get the idea. The report is kind of grim."

As O'Brien spoke, Bailey found himself not sickened as the normal person might be about the deaths of the two Minnesota mobsters. He'd become hardened. He tried to feel some remorse thinking about the periodic lunches with LaCurso or sharing some wine in the gangster's library. He'd accepted those invitations mostly under duress knowing LaCurso wanted something from him. Bailey just could not find any sadness for two men who were responsible for countless illegalities and cruelties...and who always had been able to dodge prosecution.

The previous two weeks had proven the true coldness of the man to Bailey. As long as the older man could use him, Bailey stayed alive. Once LaCurso felt Bailey was just so much baggage, getting rid of him was done with a mere shrug. What Willie LaCurso hadn't calculated was Adam Bailey's training as a government agent...and his motivation to stay alive.

LaCurso was a skillful player in the game of life and death, but he learned quickly Bailey and his two friends were just as adroit. And as Willie piloted that biplane lower and lower to his and Tony's deaths, he had a long enough time to realize he'd been bested before the biplane crashed decisively into the mountain lake.

Bailey tuned back into O'Brien's report. The head of the State Department on European affairs was gently trying to probe when Bailey might be able return to Washington where he was needed. Bailey appreciated how O'Brien was talking to him as equals, that he would no longer ever be considered too young or referred as an agent-in-training. The respect Bailey had gained for his missions in Italy and his escape effort from Milan could never be diminished.

O'Brien was aware that Bailey had not come through his ordeal unscathed. In his mind the leg was only a physical injury that would mend. O'Brien was not conscious of some of the deep-seeded mental stresses that were hounding Bailey each night.

O'Brien tried to be empathic but he had his own responsibilities and pressures. He finally made what was supposed to be a responsive suggestion. "So, Adam, take some time off. Let your leg heal completely and then call me when you're ready. The pot is overflowing in Europe. It's just a question of time before Germany attacks France. Great Britain is vulnerable. Italy will soon declare even more loyalty to Germany hoping they'll gain more from the Axis side of the growing conflict than what they gained from the winning side after World War I. Bottom line, we could use you as soon as you are ready."

Bailey thanked the man who'd become as much a friend as a boss. "David, I'll be in touch. I'll need to check my work status with John Fena's company. I'd like a fall back job in case you change your mind about my value."

O'Brien hardly chuckled, "Well, I wouldn't be too concerned. I should also tell you from a reliable source that your business paychecks are in your office in Minneapolis waiting for you to cash them. Fena has a boss who will never let you go without a paycheck. In fact, you should meet the man sometime. He's a hell of a guy."

Then O'Brien snickered, "Hey...I'll be out in Minneapolis next week. I'll call you. We'll have dinner. Until then, get well."

When O'Brien hung up, Bailey looked over at Lawton and Davis. They had their feet up on the conference table lost in their own conversation of which only they were privy. He marveled how the two guys had been so crucial in his life from the very first day of meeting them. Both men were always conscious of protecting the team of five who brought down the mob operation back at Chippewa Lodge as well as Henry Granville who had soon become a sixth member of their conspiracy from back in 1931.

Bailey sat there wondering how much the Lawtons and Davis...even his father and Henry Granville knew about his double life. Yet, it was only these two guys who understood his uncompromising attitude toward Willie LaCurso... that Bailey's aim was beyond just making it to freedom. And, like two capable attorneys, after taking everything under account about the Twin Cities hood, they shared Bailey's view that LaCurso was an extreme and perpetual danger to all of them. They didn't have a choice. Something had to be done to stop this high level mobster. The difference was that they conspired to do it their way... giving the two gangsters a chance for survival. And, if the two gangsters had lived through the predictable plane crash, in many ways their survival would be a worse penalty than death in the hands of the Italian military police. LaCurso's Italian family would pay the price as well.

There was something else very cunning that Bailey respected about Lawton's and Davis' plan to eliminate the two hoods. They had made certain the deaths would appear accidental so the mob world would not seek obligatory revenge.

Bailey went over to his two friends at the conference table and sat down staring at them. He said to Lawton, "O.K., I know something else has been going on under my nose. How did that three-seat open air sea plane happened to be waiting for us at the Lac d' Annecy marina?"

Davis looked at Lawton and smirked. "So, you finally thought of that part of the deal, did you? Well, yes, our plan against those two bastards didn't just materialize overnight. Henry Granville, Jamie and I have been musing over how to deal with Willie LaCurso once and for all. We've tried a number of times to assist in getting him imprisoned by the legal system, but that hadn't worked. When we realized that bum had set you up, that was it. We knew he would never stop stalking you even if you lived through your nightmare in Italian custody and made it to France.

Frankly, when we heard about your escape and the death of LaCurso's brother in Lugano, it didn't take much to figure out you had realized the same thing about Willie LaCurso. We knew he'd be on your case immediately and that we'd better find you before some of his hired thugs did. When we discovered LaCurso himself along with his big body guard were on the prowl for you personally, that was an opportunity we never thought would materialize. There he was, right under our noses in a foreign country. We had a chance to take him out, but do so without getting our hands too dirty.

We communicated through one of Henry's business contacts here in Switzerland. Within hours, Henry had a Paris hotel financier friend of his fly the three-seater plane down to the Lac d'Annecy marina. All the three of us had to do was get there while leaving LaCurso and his body guard plenty of bread crumbs leading to where we flew that rickety two-seater from Geneva.

Once in that three-seater biplane, the beauty of our plan was that none of our names were ever connected to the rental of that wobbly old air machine. Once LaCurso and his bodyguard were in the biplane by themselves, they were responsible for their lives. We were absolved other than the moral issue....which I might add, given the circumstances, Charlie and I will lose no sleep."

Lawton nodded and then added, "The mob back in the States won't know what to think other than believing Willie LaCurso was a bad pilot. The incident will not cause any mob backlash or retaliation against anyone."

Bailey was impressed. It really was a masterful plan. Still his brow was furled. "So, you talked with Henry. He's been a part of this? Does he know much about my background? He's a man I don't get a chance to see since he rarely makes it to Minnesota and I just as rarely make it to Charleston, South Carolina."

Lawton and Davis didn't respond.

Adam's eyes held a squint before commenting. "Why is it I'm getting a strong sense Henry knows something about my involvement with David O'Brien and the State Department? I don't quite understand how those two men connected."

Davis grinned. "Adam, it's not that difficult. John Fena works for and North American Distribution, Inc. is owned by Henry. That company among many other things has been shipping military supplies to England on behalf of the government for three years. As for Henry, he's kept an eye on you...and really all of us...since our days back at Chippewa Lodge. You've been working for our friend, Henry, since you started there in late 1935. He met David O'Brien through a friendship with Catherine and your father. When O'Brien heard of your business exploits in Italy he talked with your Dad and Henry about whether he could use you in some minor observation actions while on business in Italy. When you showed not only interest but value, Henry's been fully aware of your exploits through his friendship with O'Brien. He's insisted with Fena that everything possible should be done to show that you're still working for the company so your cover could be maintained.

Lawton then added, "Lindy, Charlie and I didn't really know about your State Department work until the past year when we began wondering about the length of your travels overseas while your clients were dying on the vine with the conflict growing in Europe. One other thing, nothing has been said to your father or Catherine about your recent Milan problem or the status of your escape to France. Everything was being done to find you. Better you tell him about your recent challenges when and if you want. O'Brien, Henry, Charlie, Lindy, and I won't be saying a word to him."

Bailey sank back in his chair. He had a third person to thank for helping save his life...as well as providing him the job at North American Distribution, Inc.

Friday, May 17, 1940, was Greta Vespucci's last day of work at the travel and shipping business owned by Louie LaCurso in Chicago. It had been only a month since she'd returned to the States after visiting her family near Venice, Italy. It took but a few days to realize she would always be a sad reminder to Louie and his family of the deaths of his two brothers.

She had been disconsolate since hearing that first Roberto had been shot shortly after she'd left Switzerland and then learning that Willie had died in a plane accident a few days later along the French-Italian border. Adding to her befuddlement were two other incidents that occurred as she was about to leave Lugano, Switzerland after completing a two week photographic reconnaissance of the Andre Pizzorno estate. The first instance was the entire estate being blown to bits that wiped out the lives of four people in the dwelling.

The second curious incident was meeting an American named Adam Bailey. She'd found it difficult to trust what he had to say the first time she'd met him just hours before the Pizzorno disaster. She still wondered if he'd had anything to do with that explosion. The second time she met him was a few days later after the bombing. He was seriously injured and she took pity on the man. She'd even called Roberto just hours away in Milan to help the crippled Bailey somehow get to freedom in France.

She still found it amazing how willing Roberto was to travel up to Lugano to help the injured American. Two days later she read in the Venice newspaper that an Italian businessman, Roberto LaCurso, had been found shot in a Lugano hotel hallway. Days later the same newspapers reported of the horrible death of the Swiss entrepreneur, Andre Pizzorno, in a mountainside car accident. It occurred to her Bailey had been injured in a car mishap in the mountains as well....and on the same day. Not only was the twist of fate so unbelievably coincidental, but Bailey seemed to be in the middle of every one of those tragedies.

The final straw came less than a week later while she was enjoying her time at her parent's home in Italy. It was all over the press about the strange circumstances of the prominent American, Willie LaCurso, whose brother was killed the week before. The older LaCurso brother was killed with a colleague in a plane crash along the French-Italian border. Nothing was explained in the reports why Willie was flying toward Italy in an open-air three-seater sea plane. For that matter she hadn't even known he was going to be in Europe. He hadn't mentioned such a trip the last time they'd seen each other in March. Most of all, she had no idea he was a pilot! She would find out later upon returning to Chicago that Willie being a pilot was a surprise to his brother, Louie, as well.

At that point she didn't know what to think. Too many people she'd become acquainted with were losing their lives, that is, with the possible exception of Adam Bailey. She had no idea if he ever made it to France or not....and no way of finding out either.

Back in Chicago she had explained to Louie LaCurso and his family the task Willie and Roberto had asked her to do. When she mentioned the name....Andre Pizzorno...none of the remaining LaCursos in Chicago had ever heard his name. In her final comments about her assignment she had decided not to mention meeting Adam Bailey...only that she was paid generously by Roberto and then she took the train down to Venice to be with her family. That was the last time she saw him. She did not mention it was her phone call to him about Bailey that precipitated his traveling to Lugano.

Her explanation had been accepted and she went on with her job. Unfortunately, in the weeks that followed, she found herself drifting from the close-knit Chicago LaCurso family. When there was another baptism in the family, she was not asked to be the photographer. She wasn't even invited to the event.

The tipping point in deciding to find another job was the day two Federal investigators stopped by her workplace. They wanted to question her with regards to the strange coincidence of the three mobster deaths and a horrible bombing that killed four people in Lugano...all within approximately a week's time. Records showed that a Greta Vespucci had arrived in Lugano in late March and then left the city by train a couple weeks later after the bomb blast and the same day Roberto was found dead at the Lugano hotel. Her using the alias, Greta Mendosa, as suggested by Roberto was possibly going to haunt her.

Louie offered one of his lawyers to sit with her while she was being questioned. She decided it would look better if she simply declared she had nothing to hide and a lawyer was not needed.

She made her explanation very succinct. She admitted to knowing nothing else beyond taking a vacation in Switzerland, a country she'd always wanted to visit and then journeying onto Italy to see her family. In no way did she reveal her photographic assignment on the Pizzorno mansion or her meeting up with Adam Bailey. She could not allow herself to be tied to the two brothers regarding her travels. It could well be guilt by association if the Pizzorno bombing was ever tied to either or both LaCursos.

Greta admitted nothing only stating that she'd met Willie in Chicago and that he suggested she meet Roberto for lunch since she worked for the third brother, Louie. The Feds left her office seemingly satisfied. Greta, though, found it increasingly difficult to sleep for many nights after meeting with them. She knew if the investigation went too deep, they might eventually uncover that she had lunches three different times with Roberto in downtown Lugano. Not giving all the facts would point very directly that she knew more than she was admitting. Further, if Adam Bailey turned up alive, what would keep him from telling the story of his ordeal and identifying a young lady named Greta in Lugano who'd been photographing the Pizzorno mansion in the days before the bombing. Then she could be in big trouble. Her only hope was that Bailey likely wanted to keep his own mouth shut. He would not want to admit being in Lugano during the time of Roberto's death or the Pizzorno mansion explosion. In addition, he would not want to talk of his injury from a car mishap in the mountains the same day that Andre Pizzorno was killed in a similar type of accident.

By the middle of May she was looking for peace of mind in finding a new job in Chicago. Keeping a low profile was her primary aim. Daily, however, the image of Adam Bailey and those brief times they'd been together showed up very clearly in her mind. She kept wondering if he'd made it to freedom. Had his wounds healed? Where did he live in the U.S? Maybe more importantly, was he the man who killed Roberto? Had he been connected to the Pizzorno bombing? Was he in the same car mishap that took the life of Pizzorno?

The more she thought about those questions through the summer of 1940, the more she found it impossible that he could have killed anyone. He was so battered and bruised the last time she'd seen him. She couldn't see him besting anyone in the condition he was in.

But, it no longer mattered. Though she had found him likeable, she figured their paths were destined never to cross again. Besides, with his injuries it was hard to believe he hadn't been re-captured. It would be a miracle if he was still alive and had actually found his way to freedom in France. She hoped for his sake he was safe, healthy and back in the U.S.

By the middle of June she'd found employment with a Chicago law firm as a secretary. She had qualifications far beyond her pay grade and responsibilities, but she liked the invisibility. She even preferred not to be recognized by anyone she'd known including the Chicago LaCurso family if they happened to pass her on the busy streets of the city. She wore glasses she didn't need; her hair was styled with no emphasis on being attractive. Her own family would have had difficulty recognizing her altered look.

As for the law firm where she was employed, they soon realized they'd gotten a steal for the money she was being paid. She was fluent in Italian, was willing to take on any responsibility thrown at her, would work all hours if needed, and her photographic skills were very professional. She was often asked to go with the firm's attorneys to photographically document evidence.

By the fall of 1940 she had earned two raises and felt she needed no further precautions. The German blitz on London had begun. The war in Europe had escalated with the U.S. continually looking for ways to supply England and other allied countries while still trying to stay directly out of the conflict. There were far more important things going on in the world than investigators taking time to track down clues about the peculiar deaths of Willie and Roberto LaCurso, the car mishap causing the demise of Andre Pizzorno, and the equally macabre killings of those four people in Lugano. The fact that all the deaths happened in a span of little more than a week would always be a curiosity...just no longer a priority in the news

From September on, Greta Vespucci had mostly put her work and her relationships with the LaCurso family behind her. Thoughts of Adam Bailey would surface occasionally but mostly in ways of what might have been. Mostly she enjoyed her new job and a new hairstyle. She slept very soundly in her north side Michigan Avenue apartment.

By Monday, May 2, 1940, while Greta Vespucci was making her decision to leave her employ with Louie LaCurso in Chicago, it had been just two weeks since Adam Bailey returned from his nightmare of being jailed in Italy and escaping across Switzerland into France. His recovery had been slow. He still walked with a noticeable limp, didn't sleep or eat very well, and his normal spirited, outgoing nature no longer seemed to exist. He was convalescing in the Twin Cities at times alone at his apartment in Minneapolis, but more often staying at the Lawton's home on Lake Johanna in St. Paul. He was uncomfortable being alone, yet at times he needed the solace.

The days that had followed Bailey's immediate return to Minnesota, the doctors at the University of Minnesota hospital did find he had some torn ligaments in his leg that would require more time to heal. They didn't necessarily diagnose the need for his mind to recover as well from his unrelenting two week battle to survive. Rest and mild exercise was the word from the doctor for his leg; Bailey hoped the same might help his head.

Within days of starting his convalescence, Bailey met David O'Brien in downtown Minneapolis for dinner as they had discussed. Right away O'Brien noticed the hitch in Bailey's stride. While that could heal he was more concerned about the young man's lack of vigor. He'd seen it before in some agents and government officials he'd known who'd been on the doorstep of death and survived. Most regained their spark and their confidence, but there was a change. He could see it in their eyes. They showed more caution; others more impatience. Common to most was an appreciation for being alive.

Following what was defined as 'recovery', many never again had the same behavior and attitude to continue working effectively in the field. Still others seemed to chalk the experience up as something that was part of the job. They were able to move on and continue their valuable work almost immediately as an American agent.

He couldn't be certain where Adam Bailey fit in; it was just necessary to allow the complete recovery process to heal to whatever degree that it could. Then it would be up to Bailey whether he was cut out to continue with the State Department. Upon leaving that dinner, O'Brien sensed he hadn't lost a valuable man. Something told him Bailey would be calling him...when the time was right.

As for Adam Bailey, he could feel he wasn't right mentally as well as physically at that dinner. He didn't kibitz as he normally did with O'Brien. And, he wasn't about to admit he was still seeing the Milan prison walls in his sleep, the German official's body hanging from the steps of the fast moving train, the Pizzorno mansion being blown off its foundation with pieces flying into the sky, or the Mercedes Benz diving off the cliff on the mountain highway north of Lugano with two bodies inside plunging to their deaths in a fast moving stream far below.

To his great relief the images of the two LaCurso brothers were less or a bother and rarely in his mind. It helped that Lawton, Davis, and he had spared little time debating whether or not to take down Willie LaCurso and Big Tony while the opportunity existed. The chance was there to end this crime boss' reign as a freewheeling mobster impacting so many people's lives...including theirs... and they'd taken it. They'd been vicious and unfeeling criminals who'd always be able to dodge prosecution and incarceration. The very action Willie took in using Bailey proved how treacherous the man could be.

When Bailey told Lawton and Davis of the gangster's obsession with who was to blame for the Loni D'Annelli downfall back in 1931, it showed further how the gangster's vengeance had no end. The three of them had decided right there in Geneva that the threat from LaCurso and his body guard had to end....and they were in a place where the playing field to bring those two hoodlums down was more equal. It had been a hastily secured plan, but it centered on LaCurso and Big Tony following their own path to Hell...one way or another. But, Lawton, Davis, and Bailey had no false pretenses. They had little doubt the two gangsters would perish in the inevitable crash of the biplane....and they were satisfied to live with their decision. In their minds there was little other choice to make.

Within days of his dinner in late April with O'Brien, Bailey found himself taking the Lawton's offer to use their membership at Midland Hills Country Club for his recovery. With his leg injury and his lack of focus he wondered if he was wasting his time. But, it had become a daily ritual starting on that foggy Monday morning in May.

At first his leg hurt too much for him to finish a golf swing. He mostly walked slowly to the practice range and hit some balls with half a swing...and then returned to the clubhouse for lunch alone unless Lindy or Jamie Lawton stopped by to join him. Only them and Charlie Davis, when he was in town, were part of his social scene at that time.

While on that practice range it turned out to be the place for the solace and the revitalization he needed. He was able to clear his mind of some of those nightmares. He also allowed a more pleasant recollection...about the young lady, Greta, he'd met in Lugano. He'd stand there on the range and allow her face to burst forth into his mind. He thought it odd considering he didn't really know who she was, where she lived, and what she actually did for a living. But, she'd helped him and she'd trusted him at a crucial time in his life.

There were moments he wondered if he might see her again...just to thank her. The opportunity wasn't completely incomprehensible. But, then again he'd counter that thought knowing that she'd been doing some work for Roberto LaCurso for reasons he couldn't understand. He was bothered by her possible involvement in the bombing of the Pizzorno mansion. Then again, she was likely thinking the same of him. But, there was no denying she'd saved him when he'd been seriously injured. Why she'd done so much for him...putting him up at the Lugano Hotel and finding a doctor...was beyond what he could comprehend.

Then she'd disappeared. It left him puzzled...and still left him bewildered why she had such faith in his innocence. Occasionally while hitting practice shots on the range, his thoughts would also return to the beautiful Anna LaCurso now gone for five years. She'd been someone special and he'd lost her. But, over the years he'd come to accept that any relationship with her had been doomed from the outset given who her father was. Still he wondered how long and how far that connection might have gone.

He compared that ill-fated romance to anything that might have developed with Greta Mendosa...or whatever her last name really was...had she stayed with him in Lugano. Her association with the LaCurso family would have to be explained. Likely, for that reason alone, their relationship would have had no future. Anything having to do with the LaCurso name always seemed to be poisoned. He wanted nothing any more to remind him of the LaCursos if that was possible. He just wished he could eliminate Greta from his thoughts.

During those May days when he began first venturing out to the golf course, he also was reunited with an old friend, the caddie master at Midland Hills, the ageless Nelly Robinson. Nelly had known Bailey since he'd first showed up as a college student and family friend of club member Jamie Lawton nine years before. He'd liked the young man from the beginning...very respectful and polite with a quick wit and a strong golf swing. After graduating, Bailey hadn't played as much at the club and apparently gone onto other interests, but he still played on many weekends with Jamie Lawton and Charlie Davis. However, in the last two years, Robinson had even more rarely seen Bailey's smiling face. He learned from Lawton the kid was doing quite well in a job that required constant travel in Europe.

Robinson at first didn't recognize Bailey with his leather golf bag strewn over his shoulder as he limped out to the practice range...just another golfer trying to re-discover his golf game after a long winter. However, the second day Robinson did make the connection, but it hadn't been easy with Bailey's hat pulled so purposely low covering his face.

Bailey was far different than the college student Robinson had first met. He was still tall and lean but he moved more slowly with the limp. The shuffling manner of his walk seemed to be copied in his behavior and countenance as well.

When the two finally met up after Bailey's second day on the range, the young man was polite and greeted Nelly with a smile. But, it was a short conversation...almost awkward. Bailey didn't have much to say and Nelly didn't want to make him uncomfortable.

The young man continued to hobble out to the practice range each morning. Nelly would greet him and Bailey would nod, call him by name with a similar short retort. He wanted to be alone; no one had to tell Robinson that Bailey was recovering from something mental as well as physical.

Later that first week, Nelly asked Lawton what was wrong with the lad. The usual talkative member only shook his head and said, "Adam had some problems during his last trip overseas. He's working something out in his head while his leg heals."

That was all it took for Robinson to get involved. The next day he accompanied Bailey out to the practice range just walking with him and not saying anything. Bailey looked at him a couple times and finally asked, "What's up, Nell? You lost?"

Robinson shook his head. "Nah...I'm just enjoying the day and waiting for my friend, Adam Bailey, to talk with me."

Bailey gave him a slight smile but tried to end the effort by saying, "I haven't got much to say these days."

Robinson was undeterred. "That's fine, son.....but you and me go back a few years. It's just a matter of time before you tell old Nelly how you hurt your leg? I can see that you're already walking a bit better each day and that you're transferring your weight better to your left side on your golf swing. But, I've got some strengthening exercises that might help you heal faster."

Bailey was still quiet as he hit a few practice shots with a half swing. Robinson just sat on the bench watching. Finally the response came. It was short and terse as if he didn't really want to talk about his injury. "My leg got hurt when I was overseas."

Nelly understood the inference of the short answer and just nodded. Then with a brighter tone he patted Bailey on the shoulder and said, "Well, laddie, then let's get that leg healed so you can get that swing back you had a few years ago. Practicing is fine, but let's go a few holes so you can appreciate the progress you're making. I'll carry your bag for as many holes as you can make. If I need to carry you and the bag back to the clubhouse after a couple holes, then so be it."

Bailey couldn't help but chuckle. The man obviously cared and was throwing a challenge out to him. Bailey quipped, "I'll think about it. Thanks." Then he hit a few more balls and called it quits for the day. But, the test came the very next day and every day thereafter when Bailey ventured to the golf course. Nelly was there to grab the young man's golf clubs as he hobbled by the clubhouse to the practice range.

There was ten minutes of warming up and then the two of them went out on the golf course. The two of them went three holes the first day before heading back to the clubhouse. They made five holes a few days later but then only three holes when Nelly wrapped some three pound weights to Bailey's ankles. Not once did Nelly have to carry Bailey and the golf bag back to the clubhouse.

During those first two weeks of being together on the golf course, Robinson came to understand that Adam Bailey had been doing something more important than just representing a wine and specialty food company overseas. While he didn't get into anything specific, he did say there were times his business efforts put him into some more difficult situations. Also, he talked less of business and more about the war going on in Europe and some of the things he was seeing. He slipped up a couple times and mentioned traveling in Italy. Nelly knew at that time most Americans no longer traveled in Italy unless they wanted trouble.

It was the young man's eyes that mostly caught Robinson's attention when the conversation at times switched over to Bailey's work overseas. Nelly had been in the Big War over twenty years before. He saw the same look in the eyes of many soldiers who'd seen action. While he never fired a shot, he'd witnessed the horrors of war. As a colored person he was in the medical corps taking the wounded to field hospitals or giving immediate aid to them when needed.

Now there was that same look in Adam Bailey's eyes. While the U.S. was currently not yet officially in the growing struggle in Europe, the young man showed too many signs of having faced death in a war. Physically he was getting stronger; he still lacked the energy and spontaneity of his former self. And, the limp became more pronounced whenever their conversation covered his travels in Europe. Altering their discussions back to golf and the golf swing and if by magic Bailey would perk up. Even his limp became less noticeable.

And that was the way it was for those many warm spring weeks in May. Bailey played six holes, then nine holes, then twelve holes up to the last days of the month. He had no interest in playing golf with anyone, even with his friends Lawton and Davis, because he didn't think he could walk eighteen holes. But, he never missed a day with Nelly or doing the exercises the caddie master recommended.

For Robinson there was satisfaction...even joy...watching Bailey recover. He was regaining his confidence and his golf swing and began to exhibit some of his spark and personality. Nelly didn't know when Bailey would no longer need help, but Robinson figured to keep pushing Bailey until finally the young man simply did things for himself with no help carrying his golf bag.

That time did occur. Nelly would always remember the day. It was a Saturday morning, May 31. The club was busier on the weekend. Bailey usually didn't come out until later on those days when most players were done playing.

But, there he was carrying his leather golf bag and shaking hands with a member he hadn't seen for a long time. While talking he waved a greeting over to Robinson busy with setting up caddies for some other players.

Nelly then noticed Bailey looking over at the practice range. There was Lawton warming up and hitting shot after shot while talking with Charlie Davis. Davis was warming up by drinking a Bloody Mary and telling another member, John Fena, and their caddies a joke. They all waved when they saw Adam and motioned for the young man to join them. Bailey didn't hesitate. The limp never showed up as he strolled over to his friends. He was smiling as he approached them.

In that instance Nelly knew Bailey was going to find the energy to play eighteen holes that day. For years he'd seen Lawton and Davis enjoy a round of golf together. Nelly had been around the club since the 1920's when James Lawton and Charlie Davis were still in law school and playing at the club. Now they were close to forty years of age, respected lawyers, and rumored to be business partners on a number of exploits. They no doubt had changed over the years, but at the golf club and out on the links, they were still the same.... competitive and throwing barbs at one another. Then he'd witnessed them taking Adam Bailey under their wing during his college days. Through those years Bailey attained the same allegiance and esteem from Lawton and Davis.

Bailey called over to the caddie master, "Hey Nelly, can you tote my bag. I'm not sure how far I can go, but I'd sure like the opportunity to empty the pockets of these two sand baggers for as long as I can walk today."

The caddie master laughed as did Lawton and Davis. It was more the typical, droll comment Bailey was known for saying in past years. There was no doubt in Nellie's mind that Bailey would make the eighteen holes. His friends would take over pushing him to a full recovery.

Nellie handed off his caddie master duties to his assistant and joined the group on the first tee box. As he handed the driver to Bailey, he chuckled listening to the four golfers whine and complain while negotiating for the best wager they could get from their fellow competitors...a ritual played out hundreds of times by these same four characters.

Bailey was first to tee off as Lawton and Davis were still comically arguing over their individual bet that day. They only quieted when Bailey addressed his golf ball and swung. As Bailey's ball sailed high down the right center of the fairway, Lawton and Davis continued their playful scrapping about the stroke differential on their bet. When the strokes were finally decided with Davis getting three shots per nine holes, they both turned toward Bailey. Lawton said, "Same game as always?"

Bailey nodded.

Davis, however, wasn't done solidifying his wager with Bailey. Still admiring the man's opening drive he mumbled, "Nice drive, hotshot. That'll cost you. I want four shots a side."

Bailey reacted immediately. "You are so full of crap. I can barely walk. I'll give you two shots a nine and Fena and I will take on the two of you in a Nassau match for the lunch tab.

Davis winced and shouted, "You're nuts. You're walking just fine. Who do you think you're talking to...some idiot off the farm? I'll take three shots per nine holes and one mulligan on the hole of my choice."

Lawton, Davis, and Fena hit their drives and the four golfers began walking down the fairway with Bailey and Davis still arguing about their wager. They would agree before they hit their second shots but they'd be playfully quarrelling right up to that moment.

While Bailey stepped up to hit his approach shot to the first green, Nellie looked over at Lawton and Davis. They were smiling.

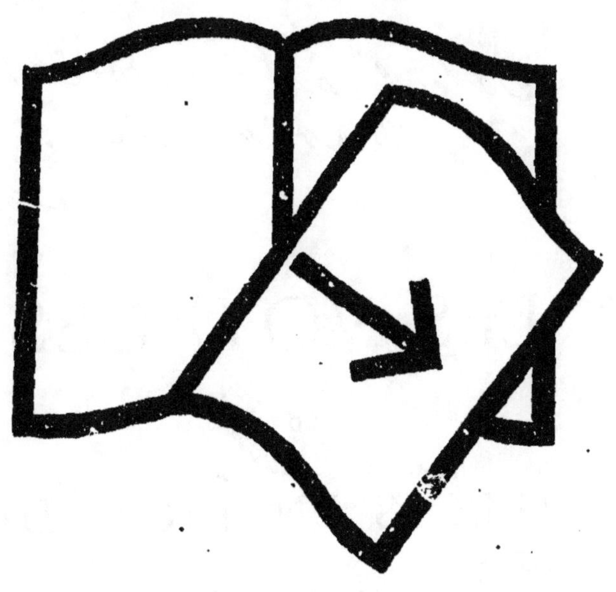

Couvertures supérieure et inférieure
manquantes.

LES VOYAGES

D'UN

Jacobs d'Hailly

LILLOIS EN PICARDIE

(1692-1697)

———

Extraits suivis de Notes sur quelques Voyages dans cette Province au XVIIᵉ siècle,

PAR LE COMTE DE MARSY

AMIENS

IMPRIMERIE YVERT & TELLIER

Rue des Trois-Cailloux, 64, & Galerie du Commerce, 10

—

1881